The Brennen Siding Trilogy

The BRENNEN SIDING
Trilogy

THE AMERICANS ARE COMING

THE LAST TASMANIAN

THE LONE ANGLER

HERB CURTIS

GOOSE LANE

Published by Goose Lane Editions with the assistance of the Canada Council, the Department of Canadian Heritage, and the New Brunswick Department of Municipalities, Culture and Housing, 1997.

Edited by Rhona Sawlor.
Cover photograph of Jason Curtis by Helen Burke.
Cover design by Julie Scriver.
Book design by Ryan Astle.
Printed in Canada by Transcontinental Printing.
10 9 8 7 6 5 4 3 2

Canadian Cataloguing in Publication Data

Curtis, Herb, 1949-
    The Brennen Siding Trilogy

ISBN 0-86492-193-4
1. Title.

PS8555.U842B74 1997   C813'.54   C97-950156-3
PR919.3.C94B74 1997

Goose Lane Editions
469 King Street
Fredericton New Brunswick
CANADA E3B 1E5

for Iris

Contents

The Americans Are Coming

Silas Gordon sold everything he had, boarded a heavily masted sailing ship and went to Saint John. In the inside pocket of his jacket he carried a royal blessing — a deed to a hundred acres of land in a place called Dungarvon.

In the year 1821, Silas Gordon built a house, store and a mill, fourteen miles west of a place called Blackville, and promptly named the three buildings "Gordon." The wagon trail that led from Blackville to Gordon was named "The Gordon Road." Gordon was three miles upstream from what was later called Brennen Siding.

Silas Gordon did not have it easy. There was an unlimited amount of massive pine needed for the building of ships, but his location was bad. He not only had to pay men to cut and yard the lumber to what was called "Silas Landing," but also had to pay men for the drive.

The prop was pulled, the large logs tumbled into the spring waters of the Gordon Brook, floated two to five miles to the Dungarvon, another fifteen miles downstream to the Renous, ten miles down the Renous to the Miramichi, and then on to Newcastle fifteen more miles away. He was barely breaking even.

The sawmill was losing money. It was too small. He needed a pond and more settlers to buy his plank and shingles. Silas Gordon didn't have it easy, but he was optimistic. His optimism crumbled, however, in October 1825, when a fire lit in Juniper swept a hundred miles of Miramichi forest out of existence. It burned down everything from shipmasts to fenceposts, houses to sawmills. It burned down everything from Juniper to Silas Landing. It burned the store, the mill and every house, barn and outhouse in Gordon.

In 1827, Silas Gordon froze to death trying to find his way

cross-country from Gordon to Renous. Because of the frozen ground and the lack of digging implements, they buried him in the soft clay of the spring.

Silas Gordon did not whoop.

one

Buck Ramsey got his name from the fact that he only showed up once a year, like a buck deer in mating season, made love to his wife Shirley, then headed back to Fredericton to his full-time woman. Buck Ramsey sired eleven children that way.

"He's just like an old buck . . . ," said Lindon Tucker, remembering that someone had said it many years before.

"An old buck, yeah. An old buck, yeah, yep. Buck the buck. Yes, sir."

"Every time he comes home, he adds a point to his antlers," said Bert Todder. "Tee, hee, hee; ha, ha, ha; sob, snort, sniff."

When Bert Todder laughed, he sounded, at times, like he was crying. Bert's mother, Maud, had had the philosophy that it was not good to laugh too much. She believed that for every time you laughed, you cried; so she always laughed and cried simultaneously. The only time that Bert was ever seen to cry in his adult life was when Maud died. At the gravesite he went, "Tee, hee, hee; ha, ha, ha; sob, snort, sniff," and everyone thought he was laughing.

"Boys, I went into Shirley's to get the mail and she stunk some bad," said Dan Brennen.

"Poor bugger Shad sets beside some o' them young lads in school and, and, and, and I guess they're pretty coarse. He said that at times he kin hardly stand the smell o' that Dryfly and that, that, that Palidin," said Bob Nash.

"Well, they never took a bath in their life!" said Dan.

"They jist smell like a jeezless rag barrel," said Bert Todder and laughed . . . or cried.

"That Shirley don't look after them, ya know," said Dan.

"They claim that Buck's makin' all kindso' money in Fredericton," lied Stan Tuney.

"Boys, if he is, he ain't spending it on her!" said John Kaston.

"No, no, no. He ain't spendin' it on her, is he, John old boy," commented Lindon Tucker. "No, sir. He ain't spendin' it on her, that's fer sure."

The post mistress, Shirley Ramsey, and her family, were always a favourite topic of conversation at Bernie Hanley's store. The only time that the men didn't talk about Shirley, was when one of the Ramseys was there. The Ramsey boys seldom frequented Bernie Hanley's store; they couldn't afford to.

"That Shirley Ramsey'd be a good woman for you, Lindon," said Bert Todder. This was a way that Bert had of making fun of Lindon and Shirley at the same time.

"I, I, I, I, I, I don't want want nothin' to do with the likes o' that old bag, so I don't. Kin git meself a better woman than that if I want, so I kin."

"Tee, hee, hee, ha, ha, ha . . ."

"Ya don't think she'd look too good in the mornin', do ya, Lindon?"

"Couldn't stand the smell o' her!"

And so went the conversation. When they exhausted Shirley Ramsey, the conversation drifted to the price of pulp, gold in the Yukon, cars, and whether or not they had enough potatoes in their bins to last them until digging time. Then, one by one, they reluctantly (the most reluctant of all was Bert Todder) sauntered off home.

Dryfly lay crying on the mattress amidst the coats and rags. They could not make him go to school. He would not go today, tomorrow or any other day. He would never go to school again.

For the tenth time Shirley yelled, "Git out here, Dryfly! Git out here 'n' eat yer breakfast before it gits cold."

"Who ever heard of bread and molasses gittin' cold!" yelled Dryfly in a fit of temper, caught himself and moaned, "besides, I'm too sick to eat. I'm poisoned, so I am!"

"Sick, me arse! A little bit o' rabbit shit never hurt nobody! If ya don't git out here and go to school, I'll give you to old Nutbeam and you kin live in the woods and be a hermit jist like him. Is that what you wanna be? Ya wanna be a hermit fer the rest of your life?"

"Bein' a hermit wouldn't be so bad," thought Dryfly. "It would be kind of nice to live alone in a snug camp in the woods and not be tormented with thoughts of school. And being alone would mean not having to face Shad Nash ever again. What's more, I'd never have to contend wit' the Protestants."

"Is that why Nutbeam lives in the woods?" wondered Dryfly. "Could the giant Nutbeam be living in the woods alone because he'd been picked on by the Protestants?" Dryfly went through the events of the previous day.

*

Everything went well until noon hour when the sixteen children who made up the Brennen Siding school were set free by Hilda Porter to eat their lunch.

The March sun had weakened the crusty snow so that it gave way periodically beneath the feet of the four boys who wandered into the woods fringing the little school yard.

On the sunny side of a clump of jackpine the snow had receded several feet, and it was here, sheltered from the wind, on the dried pine needles (pine and spruce needles were locally referred to as sprills) the boys sat to eat.

Max Kaston and George Hanley were both in grade six. Shadrack Nash was in grade five and Dryfly Ramsey was in grade four. They were all the same age.

Max Kaston was fat with tiny shifty eyes that peeked over puffed and shiny cheeks. The style of his hair had obviously been simplified with a pisspot. He wore a blue-checked hunting jacket, heavy green woollen pants and black rubber boots that came to just below his knees.

Max was the son of John Kaston, and perhaps because he was constantly being preached to, he was obsessed with and plagued by mistrust and fear. John knew that he, himself, would never become a preacher, but he was determined to make one out of Max.

Max had been told to respect and fear God; that Satan was forever present; that God was everything that was good and Satan was everything that was evil. Fearing both God and Satan meant that Max feared everything.

George Hanley's ears, hands and feet all seemed too big for the rest of his body. The size of his ears, indeed, seemed exaggerated, because of the brush-cut style of his black hair. George played with the girls a lot, but because his father ran the store, he was never teased as being a sissy. He was too valuable a friend — he could steal things for you from the store.

Stealing was the only way George could get anything from the store, because Bernie gave him nothing.

Shad Nash had fiery red hair, cut by Dan Brennen for the price of a package of tobacco and a book of papers. He was slightly smaller than the rest and his tiny body was clothed neatly in a black windbreaker, blue jeans and leather-topped gumshoes. He had pale ivy eyes and a cluster of freckles that contrasted with his white skin. Shad was a fast talker and seemed forever in control. These were traits he'd developed coping with his father's frustrations and moodiness. Unlike the others, he'd been to the village, Renous and even Newcastle. He came from the first family in Brennen Siding to own an indoor toilet.

Dryfly was the mystery boy — not weird like his brother Palidin, but still mysterious. Perhaps his mystery came from the fact he was a Catholic and God only knew what God they prayed to. Dryfly was thin, had broken teeth, a long snotty nose and a peaked chin. His clothing never fit him right — hand-me-downs from whoever took pity on him — and he smelled . . . like a rag barrel.

There, on the pine needles — the sprills — a rabbit had taken a meal the previous night, nibbling at the grass and blueberry bushes that yesterday's sun had uncovered. Shad eyed the tiny dung balls the rabbit had left. He bit into a large, round, hard molasses cookie. All the boys, except Shad, drank tea from pickle jars. Shadrack had a thermos with the picture of a cowboy twirling a rope on it. He ate from a square lunchbox that matched his thermos. Max and George ate from Ganong's hard tack candy buckets. The Ganong's candy bucket had a picture of a Ganong's candy bucket on it, which had the same picture on it, etc. . . into infinity. Dryfly ate from a chocolate box that had seen better days. The chocolate box with the barely distinguishable rainbow across the top had one soggy piece of bread and molasses in it.

A crow cawed, prophesying spring.

The four boys were saving hockey cards from the five-cent bags of Hatfield potato chips. Shad had found a second Bobby Hull card in last night's treat and knew that Max had two Andy Bathgates. With Andy Bathgate added to his collection, Shad would have the whole New York Rangers team. Shadrack endeavored to trade with Max.

"You wouldn't want to trade your Andy Bathgate for a Bobby Hull, would you Max, old buddy?"

"Can't. I already have Hull and I gave me other Bathgate to Dryfly."

"You gave your Andy Bathgate to Dry? What for?"

"I dunno. Thought he'd like it, I guess."

"I'll give you a Bobby Hull for it, Dry."

"I'm lookin' for a Boom Boom Geoffrion," said Dryfly. "Wanna play cowboy after school?"

"I'll throw in a Moose Vasgo," said Shadrack, "that's a Bobby Hull and a Moose Vasgo for one old Andy Bathgate."

"Nope. I might consider a Gordie Howe, though. Got a Gordie Howe?"

"Just the one," sighed Shad, wondering how he'd go about swinging a deal.

"Sounds like a pretty good deal to me, Dry. I'd trade with him, if I was you," said George.

"Ya wanna play cowboy after school, Shad?" asked Dryfly.

"I dunno. Maybe."

"I'll play," said Max.

"Me too," said George.

"Maybe," said Shad.

"I'll tell ya what," said Dryfly, "you gimme yer Bobby Hull and Moose Vasgo and let me play wit' yer cap gun after school, and I'll give you me Andy Bathgate."

Dryfly wasn't very concerned about hockey cards anyway. His family could rarely afford to buy potato chips, which made it practically impossible to collect any amount of cards. Nor did he know one hockey player from another. With no radio, he never got to hear a hockey game.

Shad gave the deal some thought. He needed that Andy Bathgate, but Dryfly was striking a hard deal. Moose Vasgo wasn't that easy to come by either, and giving up the cap gun would mean that Dryfly would get to be the "Good Lad." Dryfly would be Roy Rogers on Trigger, or the Lone Ranger. The best Shadrack could hope for, under the circumstances, was being Pat Brady, or Tonto. Shad hated using a stick for a gun.

"What if you broke my cap gun?" he asked.

"I won't break it," promised Dry.

"But you might."

"I won't."

"What would you do if you did?"

"I'd buy you another one."

"What with? What would you use for money, beer caps?"

"I won't break yer gun, 'pon me soul I won't."

"Well, I might let you use it for one short game, if you're careful."

"Nope. All evening. I never get to be the good lad."

"Me nuther," put in George Hanley, slurping his tea.

"I'm always the bad lad," said Max Kaston, "and it's always our barn that we play in."

"We kin play in our barn, if you want," said George with a glitter of hope in his eyes. It was true, perhaps because of his ears, or God only knows for what reason, he was never selected to be the good lad.

"You lads don't have a cap gun," snapped Shadrack, "like I told you a thousand times, you can't expect Roy Rogers or the Lone Ranger to go ridin' around with a stick for a gun!"

"Well, it ain't fair," grumbled George.

"Well, that's me deal. Take it or leave it," said Dryfly.

Shad couldn't handle the trading any longer. He wanted the Andy Bathgate too much. And he'd be ahead of the others anyway, with his full set of New York Rangers. It would be weeks before any of the others collected that many, and by the time they did, he'd probably have a set of the Toronto Maple Leafs or even the Montreal Canadiens.

"Okay," said Shad, "ya gotta deal, but if ya break me cap gun, you're dead!"

"I ain't gonna break it. I wanna be the Lone Ranger the first game and Roy Rogers the second. If there's a third, I wanna be Matt Dillon. And you must cross yer heart and hope to die that you'll show up with the cap gun."

"Cross me heart," said Shad, "now give me the card."

The boys traded cards, all knowing that Dryfly, for the present, was the winner.

Shad was not about to be bettered by an Irish Catholic, however. Shadrack Nash had a new scheme. Shadrack Nash had thought up his new scheme while he was eating his first molasses cookie.

When he felt the time was right, Shad said, "Let's play a game, boys."

"Sure, what game?" asked Max.

"Let's see who can open his mouth the farthest," said Shadrack. "I bet I can."

"How much ya wanna bet?" asked Dryfly, feeling confident.

"I bet ya this marble," said Shad.

"Let me see the marble," said Dry.

"Nope. You have to take me word fer it. I'll give this marble to the one with the biggest mouth."

A marble was a rare thing in Brennen Siding, but the boys all knew that Shadrack Nash was the most likely one to have one, and he definitely seemed to be hiding something in his hand.

"Okay," said Max, "I'll give it a go."

"Me too," said George.

"Count me in," said Dryfly, "I could do with a marble."

"Okay," said Shad, "we'll judge each other. I'll count to three, then everyone gape as wide as they can. Ready? One, two, three."

Max, George and Dryfly all opened wide, revealing their cookie-coated tongues and teeth. Shad started to do likewise, but instead, he took careful aim and tossed the marble into Dryfly's mouth.

The marble was not a marble, however, but one of the dungballs the rabbit had left behind.

When he saw that his aim had been perfect, Shad snorted with laughter, spraying tea and cookie crumbs all over the blue-checked hunting jacket of Max Kaston.

The first thing Dryfly did was swallow.

Secondly, he gagged.

Thirdly, he ran home crying.

Dryfly could still hear the boys laughing when he crossed the railroad tracks. He felt he would never be able to face his friends again.

In his bed of old coats and rags, Dryfly could still hear them laughing. "I'll hear them laughing," he thought, "for the rest of my life." Dryfly sighed. "I'm a hermit already."

"If you don't git out here and go to school, I'm gonna go out and cut a switch!" yelled Shirley from the kitchen.

Dry relaxed a bit. Shirley's threat was idle, had lost its spark. "Her tail's probably waggin'," thought Dryfly and began to plan his day of freedom.

*

Dryfly was right about the spark. Shirley had lost it, but her tail was not wagging. Shirley had lost her spark the last time that Buck came home. In a manner of speaking, Buck's last visit was the last time she had wagged her tail to any degree.

"It's been" — Shirley counted — "five, six. Dryfly's eleven. Must be twelve years since Buck was here. No letters, no money. What's become of him, I wonder?"

Although Shirley was not aware of the anniversary, Buck had landed twelve years ago to the very day. Palidin was the baby, Junior was twelve . . . Bonzie was still alive.

Buck had taken her to the Legion in his old Ford. She drank three beers and Buck had a half dozen or more. They danced. She remembered he smelled of aftershave and his hair had been slicked back with that fancy grease stuff. When the Legion closed, they went to Bob Nash's and drank rye until four in the morning. Bob played the banjo and Buck played the guitar and sang Hank Snow and Doc Williams songs. Buck had been the hit of the night and Shirley had never been happier in her life.

Later they drove around to the pit and parked. Buck put his hand on her knee and told her how pretty she was; then he said he loved her and then he got serious.

"I suppose you're wonderin' why I never send you any money?" he asked.

"No, Buck, I know you ain't got any."

"Had me a job as a janitor for awhile. Good job, too. Only had to clean the ground floor."

"What happened, Buck?"

"Got caught stealin'. Took some old jeezer's pipe and it fell right out of me pocket in front of the boss. Fired me on the spot. Livin' in Fredericton now. Workin' at the bottle exchange and junk yard. Breakin' batteries mostly. No money in it though. How you gittin' long?"

"Gladys sent me a bag o' clothes and Dad sent me a bag o' potatoes. Know what I'm thinkin' bout doin'?"

"Gettin' in the back seat?" Buck slid his hand up her thigh.

"Don't be foolish! No, I'm thinkin' 'bout takin' over old Maud's post office."

"Kin you do that?"

"Sure kin. All you have to do is collect the mailbag at the Siding, bring it home and give it out, stamp a few letters — anyone kin do it and Bert said he'd like me to do it. Thirty dollars a month."

"Why don't Bert do it?"

"Can't read. Maud did it all. I'm gonna set it up in the livin' room."

"I'd ask you to come to Fredericton with me, but there'd be no room for the kids."

"I know, Buck. I know you mean well. What d'ya think o' me runnin' the post office?"

"You'll have to do it, I guess. It'll be good for ya."

"You could come home and help me, Buck. I'd run the post office and you could go to work."

"Who for?"

"You could talk to Frank Layton. He might give you a job at the club."

"I ain't workin' for Frank Layton!"

"Why? Frank's a fair man!"

"I'd rather break batteries."

"You got another woman in Fredericton, Buck?"

"You know I ain't got no other woman, Shirley. You know I ain't that kind of man!"

"Then why won't you come home?"

"Let's not talk about that now. Let's get in the back seat."

"You're crazy, Buck."

"If I do come home, I'll have to go back and get me clothes and me radio."

"You got a radio?"

"Yep. Heard the last Joe Louis fight, settin' right back in Fredericton. Ever hear of Hank Williams?"

The conversation continued. Shirley fell in love again and Buck negotiated seduction with promises and lies. Shirley was never happier. Buck was leaving and hadn't asked for her family allowance check.

They climbed into the back seat and Shirley wagged her tail to Buck's delight. Nine months later Shirley added another point to Buck's antlers and called it Dryfly.

*

Dryfly figured the time was getting on to nine o'clock. The rest of the children had already left for school and Dryfly was left to himself to enjoy the little room.

Dryfly shared his bed with Palidin and Bean. Jug and Oogan slept in the bed across the room. Naggie slept in Shirley's room and Neeny and Bossy slept in the room next door. Junior was married to Mary Stuart and lived with Mary's father, Silas. Digger, as usual, was tramping the road somewhere. Skippy, the oldest girl, wasn't married, but was shacked up with Joe Moon in Quarryville. Joe Moon had a dog that occupied more of his time than Skippy. Skippy was the homeliest one of the family and considered herself lucky to be living with a bootlegger. Bonzie, of course, was dead.

It happened on a Sunday. The family was having a picnic back of the big hollow. Some of them were fishing in the nearby

brook, others sat in the shade discussing members of the opposite sex and some picked flowers. Palidin, Bonzie and Dryfly
were pretending they were moose.

"I need to have a dump," said Bonzie and hurried into the
woods in search of a roost.

Bonzie Ramsey found his roost, a broken down birch tree,
and dropped his pants, sat and found relief. He was just pulling up his suspenders when he heard the sound of rustling
leaves and the crackle of a dead alder bush giving way to a
passerby.

The sound was nearby, but it was only a sound; he could
see nothing but the trees and underbrush of the forest.

"Who's there?" he called.

No answer. Bonzie waited and listened.

"Who's there?" he called again.

"It would be just like Palidin and Dryfly to be watchin' a lad
havin' a dump," he thought. "They're prob'ly tryin' to scare me."

"All right boys, come out! I know you're there!"

He heard the sound again, but this time it had moved — it
was more to the left.

Without giving what he thought was Palidin and Dryfly
any chance to flee, he dashed into the bush, thinking he would
take them by surprise.

There was nobody there.

He listened once more. "Palidin? Dryfly?"

The song of a bird came up from the brook. He could not
identify it.

"When I get my hands on you lads, I'm gonna introduce
you to the rough and tumble!" he shouted. He hoped he
sounded like the Lone Ranger.

There was a bit of a clearing ahead of him, where the sun
had nourished the ferns to waist height. He thought he saw
an unusual movement in their midst. He went to check it out.

Nothing.

"Must've been a bird," he thought.

"The hell with yas!" he yelled, turned and headed back to
where he thought the family would be.

He walked for half an hour, realized they couldn't be that

far away, turned and walked for an hour, came to a barren and realized he was very lost.

He zigzagged back and forth for several more hours, calling, "Mom! Palidin! Dryfly! Naggie!"

Occasionally he got an echo, but that was all.

He grew warm and panicky; his pace quickened; he scratched his arms and legs on dead limbs and brush. The flies found him.

At dusk, he found himself at the barren's edge once again. He didn't know if he was on the near or the homeward side of it.

When you step into a barren, your foot sinks ankle-deep into a wet, moss-like vegetation. When you wander into a barren, you'd better mark your point of entry, for once you get in a few hundred yards, everything starts to look the same — look down, look up and you're lost.

Bonzie thought he saw something on the barren. Bonzie was already lost and had nothing to lose — he headed towards the something.

It took him a half hour to get to what he was looking at, and it turned out to be a huge boulder. Exhausted, he sat on the boulder to watch the stars as, one by one, they appeared. He cried for a long while, slept for a little while, then cried some more.

He heard something walking, splush, splush, splush, off to his right. He held his breath, for better hearing. He prayed a silent Hail Mary.

Splush . . . splush . . . splush — whatever it was, was passing him by.

At first he thought it might be a bear, or a moose, but he wasn't sure.

"It could be a man. It could be a man looking for me. I got nothin' to lose," he thought.

"Whoop! Over here!"

A game warden found the fly-bitten, crow-pecked body of Bonzie a month later, back of the barren.

As a result of Bonzie getting lost, Dryfly feared getting lost more than anything else in the world. The thought of being alone in the woods to battle the flies horrified him. He even had nightmares about it. The flies — the more you battled, the more you attracted — would be the worst thing of all. And to die and have your body exposed to the woods . . .

Years later when Dryfly was asked the whereabouts of Bonzie by an elderly, absent-minded teacher, he replied, "He went for a shit and the crows got him."

*

Dryfly was giving way to slumber when Shirley passed through the curtain that served as the bedroom door to stand before him at the foot of the bed.

"I've made up your lunch, Dry," said Shirley, "and wrote an excuse to the teacher fer ya. I'm gonna need you home tomorrow, Dry, so's I want ya to go to school today. I got yer lunch all packed."

The emotional cloud over Shirley was thick and black and it spread over Dryfly as if instructed by a magic wand. His heart quickened, his stomach fluttered and tears of defeat commenced to flow.

"But I can't, Mom!" he sobbed.

"You might have to stay home tomorrow, Dry. We've run out of grub, so's I want you to go today."

"But I'm sick, Mom!" Tears, tears, tears.

"I'm gonna write yer father askin' him to send me enough money for that cap gun you like in the catalogue. C'mon, Dry darlin', be a good boy and go to school. I'm not gettin' any younger, you know. One day I won't be around to look after you and you'll need lotsa schoolin' so's you kin git a job."

"Ah, Mom!" Still more tears. "You kin stay home tomorrow, Dry, cause I ain't got the heart to send you to school on an empty stomach, but you have to go today. C'mon Dryfly darlin', git dressed, ya still have time."

"But I don't want to go!"

"Poor Ninnie didn't take nothin' to eat wit' her. Said you could have it, Dry. Poor little thing was thinking of you and how you'd like a good sandwich. So, c'mon, Dry."

Dryfly knew he was defeated, and to make sure that Shirley's victory would be a difficult one, he cried all the time he was getting dressed. He cried in the kitchen and refused to eat his biscuit and molasses. He was still crying when he crossed the tracks.

When Hilda Porter opened Shirley Ramsey's excuse note for Dryfly's absence on the previous afternoon, it read:

Deer Mrs. Porter.
Dryfly stayed home in the afternoon yesterday, for he was sick from rabbit dung poisoning.
> *Yours truly,*
> *Shirley*

Hilda Porter already knew.

Shadrack Nash was not laughing as he watched Dryfly Ramsey enter the school, deposit his excuse on the teacher's desk and make his way to his seat; the memory of Hilda's two-inch-wide, foot-long piece of woodcutter strap on his stinging hands took care of that little pleasure.

Nothing was ever kept secret in Brennen Siding.

two

Shirley watched Dryfly until she was sure he would not run off into the woods.

"Poor little lad, he's different from Palidin. Pal's only a year older, but he's a lot wiser. Palidin's smart, wants to be a somebody. Kinda fruity, I'll admit, but he wants to be somebody. Kin read and write and do 'rithmetic better 'n me. It's more important to keep Pal in school than Dryfly."

Shirley figured that Palidin would eventually get a job as a timekeeper or a store clerk in Newcastle or Chatham. To Shirley, being a timekeeper or a store clerk was having the ultimate good job. Anything more intellectual than these two occupations was beyond comprehension.

That's the way it was all over Brennen Siding.

When Jack Allen went off to Hartford with Dr. MacDowell and eventually became a dentist himself, everybody in the settlement disowned him — disowned him not so much because they didn't like him, but because Jack had become a different creature — looked different, spoke different, walked different and even smelled different.

When he came to Brennen Siding and put the word out that he needed a guide to go fishing, none of the local men would guide him. When Stan Tuney took the job out of financial desperation, he found Jack as alien as any other American Sportsman. Jack Allen could have been Nelson Rockefeller sitting in the front of the canoe as far as Stan Tuney was concerned.

The people of Brennen Siding couldn't understand foreign places, wealth and formal education, and thought it pretentious to even try.

When the Connecticut lawyer asked Dan Brennen if the

boys fishing across the river were natives, he replied, "No, sir, jist some of us lads."

To Dan, a native was a black man from Africa.

When the locals got together with the American sportsmen they were guiding, the common denominator was humour. Bert Todder did not know that all the food a salmon eats originates in photosynthesis. Bert Todder did not have a hunch that the life and death of algae depended on chlorophyll and its reactions to various colours of the spectrum.

When the American sport asked Bert why the salmon would not bite while there were bubbles on the river, Bert did not think of oxygen and carbon dioxide. Had he known the existence of such words, he might have had a better answer to the American's question . . . but probably not.

"Why don't the salmon bite while those bubbles are on the river?" asked the American.

"They're on the toilet," said Bert. "Them bubbles are fish farts."

Stan Tuney had grown up with Jack Allen and had recognized the difference in him immediately. Stan couldn't understand how money could change a man so much.

"How's she goin', Jack?" asked Stan.

"Great. What's happening with you, Stan?"

"Not too much. What are you doin' these days?"

Stan knew that Jack was a dentist. He didn't know that Jack was earning a hundred thousand dollars a year, but he could tell that Jack seemed rich. Like all the people of Brennen Siding, Stan was pessimistic and egotistical. When asked, "How's she goin'?" it was a rare occasion that one answered "Great." "Not too good" was the expected answer. Stan Tuney, like all the Brennen Siding dwellers, lived in isolation from the rest of the world. In Brennen Siding, life was difficult; being a timekeeper or a scaler was the ultimate success. Jack Allen was a Brennen Siding boy, but he had become a dentist. Stan couldn't understand how anyone could "become" a dentist. To Stan, dentists were born in foreign places like Fredericton, Saint John and the United States. Dentists did not come from Brennen Siding. "Great" was not the way a man from Brennen Siding should be.

"I'm still pulling teeth," said Jack.

"Doin' pretty good, are ya?"

Jack Allen had worked hard and was on a badly needed and well-deserved vacation. He did not see a difference in Stan Tuney. Stan would never change. Jack wanted to fish, drink scotch and relax. He had worked hard to become a dentist and was proud of his accomplishment. Confronted with Stan Tuney, Jack couldn't understand why he was reluctant to admit he was a dentist. For some reason, he felt he might offend Stan by such an admission.

"Oh, not too good," Jack Allen, the dentist from Hartford, lied. "Just makin' ends meet." The lie eased the tension between them, but Jack could never call Brennen Siding home again.

*

Shirley hoped that Palidin would not become a lumberjack. She also hoped he would not become a dentist or a lawyer. A timekeeper at the mill in Blackville would be just right.

Although Shirley was somewhat puzzled about the future of Palidin, she had no doubts about Dryfly.

Dryfly hated school, hated books and teachers. Thoughts of the future went no further than this afternoon or tomorrow.

"I hope," thought Shirley, "he will not be afraid of hard work."

When Dryfly disappeared from her view, Shirley sighed and went to the cupboard. She knew there was nothing in it to eat, but she wanted to take inventory anyway. She pulled back the curtains and scanned the shelves.

No bread and no flour to make any.

No molasses.

No potatoes.

No brown sugar.

No milk.

No beans.

No tobacco.

Shirley Ramsey sighed as she picked up the empty yellow and red Vogue tobacco package. She shook the package over the palm of her hand and a few dried, almost sand-like grains of tobacco fell from it. She tore the package apart and in the folds of the foil liner, she came up with a few more grains. She spied a butt lying on the rim of a dish. The butt was only a half-inch long, but there was tobacco in it. Shirley tore the butt apart and added the contents to the grains she'd collected from the package. She closed her fist around the tobacco and blew gently into it to moisten it. She then rolled a cigarette the size of a wooden match into a Vogue cigarette paper. She sighed again as she went to the stove for a light. She lifted the cover and added a stick of alder to the fire. "Alder burns too quick," she thought. "Should have maple, or beech." She broke off a splinter from a second piece of alder and set it afire. With this she lit her tiny cigarette.

She pulled up a rickety, backless chair and sat by the table to smoke and to think.

"No money, no food, no credit left at Hanley's store . . ." She could charge a few things to her father's bill, but that was doubtful. The fact of the matter was, her father hadn't any money either.

"If it was a month later, the ice in the river'd be out and the boys could ketch a salmon, or maybe some trout . . . even chubs would be better than nothin'."

She contemplated setting a snare for a rabbit, but quickly brushed the thought aside.

"That could take days."

"I'll go to the store and lie," she thought. "I'll tell Bernie Hanley that me cheque's comin' tomorrow and that I'll be right up to pay 'im as soon's it comes. Surely the Blessed Virgin wouldn' mind such a little lie."

She arose and went to the bedroom and grabbed her coat from Dry's bed. The coat was green and old and smelled; it had a frayed collar and cuffs, the pockets were torn and it had but one button. It wasn't much, but it was all she had for protection against the cold March wind. She put it on and went back to the kitchen to size herself up in the piece of mirror that hung on the wall above the water bucket. She removed what was left of the tiny cigarette from her mouth and dropped it in the slop pail and smiled into the mirror. Most of her teeth were missing, the remaining few decayed and dirty. "They won't matter. I've got no reason to smile anyway." She washed her face in the same dirty, soapy water the children had used earlier, ran a piece of comb through her greasy, straight brown hair and sized up the finished product. "I'm a hard lookin' ticket," she muttered.

*

Ten minutes later, Shirley Ramsey was at the store pleading her case.

"I git me cheque tomorrow, Bernie, and me allowance cheque should be here in a week or two, so's I kin pay ya more. I thought maybe you . . ."

"Shirley, I know as good as you do, your cheque don't come till the end of the month! This is only the eighteenth. You owe me over a hundred dollars already and you didn' pay me nothin' last month. Everybody in the settlement owes me! Who ya think I am, Santa Claus? I can't afford to pay me own bills anymore! I'm gonna have to close down, if somebody don't soon pay up."

Bernie was a big, good-looking Baptist with good teeth and wire-rimmed glasses. He wore leather-topped gumshoes, heavy woollen pants, a plaid shirt and a hat. Bernie was never without his hat.

Shirley hadn't wanted to say it and she had no intention of saying it, but she found herself confused and lost for words. "Then, how's about chargin' a package o' tobacco and a book of papers to Daddy?" she blurted.

"Tobacco and papers? Tobacco and papers!"

"And a box o' asberns! Dryfly's sick!" she quickly added. She was frightened and humiliated. She recognized her mistake. She should never have given tobacco priority to a Baptist. Tobacco had been the last thing on her list.

Bernie, too, was lost for words. He was amazed at the request. "Her kids are prob'ly starvin' to death, she hasn't got a stitch o' clothes worth puttin' on, and she asks for

tobacco!" he thought. He grabbed a package of Players tobacco (not even her brand) and practically threw it at her. The
papers and aspirins followed in much the same way.

"There!" he snapped. "That's the last thing yer gettin' till I
git me pay! Don't come back till ya got some cash!"

Shirley was about to cry and she knew it. To save perhaps a
shred of dignity, she grabbed the items and left. "Thanks
Bernie," she said.

Through the window, Bernie could see her walking, too
fast for a woman, too masculine, towards the road.

"She smells like a rag barrel," mumbled Bernie. "God only
knows why I'm so generous."

Bernie Hanley popped a peppermint into his mouth, sighed
and added tobacco, papers and aspirins to Daddy's bill.

*

Shirley cried, but not for long. It was not the time for crying. It was the time for action. She wiped the tears from her
eyes with the back of her hand. She wiped her nose on the
green, tattered cuff of her coat.

"Includin' me, there's one, two . . . nine mouths to feed
and there's nothin' to eat," she thought. She would not get a
cheque for as long as two weeks. She could not starve her
children for two weeks.

The north wind sweeping up Gordon Road was so strong
that at times Shirley had to turn away from it and walk backwards in order to breathe.

A pair of men's long underwear hanging on Bernie Hanley's
clothesline danced and flapped as if the spirit of their owner
remained in them. The trees, too, bent and sighed in the howling
wind as if possessed by some forbidding and tormented spirit.

With some difficulty — she was walking backwards —
Shirley quickened her pace. She was determined to win the
struggle against this devilish wind so set on holding her back,
its cold breath its greatest persuasion.

"The line gales," she thought, "they come every spring, just
like Buck use to. The whole world is gettin' screwed. What's

the sense in having young lads, if they all gotta suffer and die?"

She turned and faced the wind once again and suddenly, eerily, she had the strange feeling the underwear was following her. She quickened her pace again and found herself nearly running towards the safety of her home.

"The whole damned country's full o' ghosts," she thought. "It's like that strange bird that keeps singin', but ya kin never see; and what do the dogs bark at at night?"

It had taken her ten minutes to go to the store; it took her five minutes to return home. Home — the grey, weathered shingles, the tarpaper patches, the stovepipe with its wafts of smoke so quickly consumed by the wind. On a warmer day, the March sun had melted and deformed the dirty snowbanks lining the path to the door; today the pools, some foot-sized, some larger, were frozen so that Shirley half ran, half skated to the door.

Before entering the house, she glanced over her shoulder. "I must be going crazy," she thought, but was thankful the underwear hadn't followed her.

Back in her kitchen, she went to the stove and placed a couple of sticks on the fire. The wind was rising with the sun and it slapped the plastic, threatening to tear it from the kitchen window. She sat by the table and opened the new package of tobacco, wondering who she might turn to for help.

She thought of the priest twelve miles away. It was very cold, the wind too strong.

"Perhaps tomorrow, though."

She thought of the neighbors. "Damn near as poor as me."

She thought of prostitution, but dropped the thought with the recollection of the morning's portrait in the mirror.

She thought of Nutbeam, the mystery man who lived in the woods, seen so seldom, always hidden behind his collar, or hood. Nobody in Brennen Siding could say for sure what he looked like.

Everyone had a different opinion of Nutbeam. Dan Brennen thought he might be the mad trapper from the Yukon, "Albert Johnson, or whatever his name is." Dan Brennen did not know that Albert Johnson had laid his last Mountie low and had been resting in the Yukon permafrost for many years.

Lindon Tucker thought Nutbeam might be a ghost, "or even the devil, yeah, yeah, yeah. The devil, yeah. Oh, yeah."

Stan Tuney claimed to know Nutbeam. Said he was a fine gentleman with lots of money. "Money to burn, so he does!" Nobody ever believed a word Stan Tuney said.

Whoever Nutbeam was, Shirley Ramsey knew she could not turn to him. Besides, she didn't even know where he lived. Nutbeam, to Shirley, was all of the above.

Then, Shirley thought of the post office. There was maybe as much as ten dollars in the post office float. She could borrow the ten dollars and manage until her cheque came and then pay the money back. But the stamps were due to arrive and she needed the stamps to keep the post office operating. If she took the money, she would not be able to pay for the stamps. Her supply would run out and people would want to know why they couldn't mail a letter. They'd report her. The head post master from Blackville would pay her a visit and there'd be nothing for Shirley to do but tell the truth.

"Something came over me. I don't know what it was. I stole the money."

She'd be taken off to jail and maybe fined, the children trotted off to orphanages.

But the money was there. Handy. Accessible. Twelve dollars maybe, if she took the change, too. And nobody would know unless she ran out of stamps. If nobody mailed any parcels or letters for a couple of weeks, until she got her cheque, nobody would ever know. She fought back the temptation. "What's happenin' to me?" she asked herself. "Why am I settin' here thinkin' of stealin', when I should be on my knees prayin'?"

Then, as if to answer her questions, she heard the lonesome, distant whistle of the train. It was not the train they called the Whooper. The Whooper had been replaced by a diesel years before. This was only the Express, the train that brought the mail every morning; the train that picked up and dropped off a few passengers going to and from villages and towns; the train whose whistle now seemed like a mournful cry from the forest, causing a chill to course its way down Shirley's back. The whistle seemed too timely, as if it had heard her, as if it was showing its approval or disapproval of her thoughts of stealing, its voice enhanced and amplified by the wind.

Shirley stood. "It's no time to be settin' around," she thought. "An idle brain is the devil's workshop, Daddy use to say." She went to the post office, retrieved the mailbag with the two letters locked inside, donned her coat once again and headed· for the siding, the weight of poverty heavy on her shoulders, the winds no less haunting, no less cold.

When she arrived at the kempt little red building with the veranda that stood no more than a couple of feet from the tracks, she found she was right on time. The Express — a diesel engine, one passenger car and a caboose — pulled to a squeaking, grinding ten-second halt.

There were several people aboard, some of whom gazed down at her as though with pity; sad, unsmiling eyes, staring at her as if she was an animal in a zoo.

Shirley drew back her shoulders a bit, feigning dignity. But the attempt was feeble; she was too aware of herself; her ragged old coat; her fear. She looked away.

"Ya'd think they never saw a poor woman before in their lives," she thought. "Am I the only one? Why am I the only poor woman in the world?"

A tall, thin man dismounted from the train.

Shirley experienced a twinge of fear at the sight of him. She couldn't believe that so many things could be haunting her on the same morning. "What's goin' on here?" she thought, and "speak of the devil." The man was wearing a parka with an oversized hood. The hood was furry and hung low enough to hide his face, but she knew it was Nutbeam. She had never seen him before, but she knew.

"Lovely day," she said.

Nutbeam did not speak to her, did not nod his hooded head, did not even look at her. He strode swiftly away, carrying a black case under his arm.

Shirley traded mailbags with the porter and the train moved on toward its destination, Boiestown.

When she got back to the house, Bert Todder, John Kaston,

Lindon Tucker and Dan Brennen were waiting for her. They stood in the sun, on the south side of the house away from the wind.

Shirley led them inside and unlocked the mailbag. The men waited. Dan Brennen eyed the untidiness of Shirley's house with disgust.

John Kaston got a copy of *Decision Magazine*, Bert Todder a letter from Linda who lived in Fredericton. Lindon Tucker, as usual, got no mail at all. "Yeah, yeah, yeah, oh yeah, no mail's good mail, yeah, yes sir, yeah, yeah, yeah." Dan Brennen got a bill from Lounsbury's in Newcastle. Dan Brennen owed for the battery radio he listened to every night.

The men left and when they were a step further than an earshot away, Dan Brennen said, "Boy, she's a hard lookin' ticket, ain't she?"

"Hard lookin' ticket, yeah. Oh yeah, that's right, Dan old boy, old chummy pard, yeah, hard lookin' ticket, yeah." Lindon Tucker agreed with everything anybody said.

Back in the post office, Shirley sorted the rest of the mail: a letter for Helen MacDonald, a bill for Bob Nash, the *Family Herald* for Bernie Hanley and a bill for Lester Burns. She placed the mail in their rightful compartments, then opened the cash box and commenced counting the money inside. Twelve dollars and sixty cents.

Then, she counted her stamp supply. Eight ten-centers, six five-centers and nineteen two-centers.

She went into the kitchen, knelt before the only wall adornment in the house, the crucifix, and prayed. "Hail Mary, full of grace, blessed art thou among women . . ."

That night the family ate baloney and potatoes for supper. No one questioned where the food had fallen from, and only Shirley knew for sure.

*

Thursday night, the twentieth of March, Bert Todder was watering his horse, Queen, by the light of a kerosene lantern, when he heard the strange cry from the forest. It was a lonesome call that resembled nothing he had ever heard. It sounded neither human nor animal and it couldn't have been a train whistle; the railroad was in the opposite direction.

He was about to shrug it off as a car horn, when it came again . . . again . . . and again.

"It's comin' from back on Todder Brook," he said to Queen. "No cars back on Todder Brook. It's not a car horn anyway."

Queen didn't answer, sighed contentedly and continued to drink.

Lindon Tucker was seeing a man about a horse, which was his term for having a piss behind the shed, when he also heard the eerie call.

Both Lindon and Bert, as well as John Kaston and Dan Brennen, heard it on Friday night. On Saturday night, because nothing is ever kept secret in Brennen Siding, everyone in the settlement was out beneath the stars listening to the still uni- dentified scream from the distant forest.

Saturday night was the first night in Brennen Siding's his- tory that every door was locked.

It was heard again on Sunday night, but only for a few moments.

On Monday evening, fifteen men and boys stood around in Bernie Hanley's store, eating oranges and drinking Sussex gingerale.

On Monday evening in Bernie Hanley's store, the conver- sation was not about Joe Louis, the Saturday night jamboree, or the price of pulp wood. On Monday evening in Bernie Hanley's store, the conversation was not about Shirley Ramsey and Ford cars; nor did the men dwell on gold in the Yukon, or horses. Monday evening, the conversation rambled around everything from rabbits crying to the eerie screams of the east- ern cougar; from the strange and numerous variations in the fox's bark, to ghosts and the devil.

"I wouldn't take a million dollars for goin' into that woods over there tonight," said Bob Nash. "Not even with me .303."

"No, sir! A panther kin climb and he'd git ya from a tree. Ya'd not know he was there till 'e was on top o' ya," put in Bert Todder. The panther was the cat that everyone decided upon. It somehow sounded better than cougar.

"Me? I don't think we're dealin' wit' a pant'er at all," began Stan Tuney. Stan Tuney always ate his oranges with the peel still on them. That's how they ate them in the Yukon, he'd been told. "I was back Todder Brook last Tuesday and I must've seen a thousand moose tracks. The biggest moose tracks I ever seen!"

"Are you sayin' we got us a moose runnin' round through the woods blattin' his head off, Stan?" asked Bert.

"I'd say t'was a panther, meself. Me father always said that the Dungarvon whooper was a panther!"

"There ain't been a panther in this woods for a hundred years!" said Dan Brennen with authority. "They never were panthers anyway. They were what you call eastern cougars."

"I ain't sayin' we're hearin' moose, or panthers," said Stan. "What I'm sayin' is, I saw tracks that I thought was made by a moose. Cloven hooves is what I saw, so I did, if ya know what I mean, like, see?"

"What would the devil want back Todder Brook?" laughed Dan Brennen, as if the whole idea was stupid and nobody could possibly know anything about this except himself.

But John Kaston was the true authority here. John had read the Bible, and only the Bible would have the answers to such a mystery. He demanded attention by thumping his fist on the counter in the way that Reverend Mather might thump the pulpit.

"Don't you know that the wilderness is the playground of Satan?" yelled John, as if frustrated with their stupidity. "Did he not tempt the Savior in the woods? Wasn't it in the woods where he tried to get the good Lord to turn the rocks into bread, and Jesus said that man can't live on bread alone? I tell ya, that he walks the Dungarvon jist the same as he walked . . . the Jordan. It's right there in the Bible! All ya gotta do is read yer Bible!"

Later, walking home, Dryfly was thankful he had his gun-shaped stick in his pocket. Somehow, its presence made him feel more secure. He was also thankful Palidin was with him. Palidin did not seem to be afraid at all.

*

38

The next morning when Constable Bastarache pulled up in front of Shirley Ramsey's house in his RCMP cruiser, Shirley experienced a twinge of fear like none other she had ever experienced before. The constable was the handsomest and most fearsome man she'd ever seen. He was six feet tall and muscular, wore a gun and big brown boots, and perhaps the most fearsome thing of all, the Royal Canadian Mounted Police uniform. The yellow stripes down the outside of his breeches screamed, "We Mounties always get our man . . . or woman!"

Her first thought was that she'd have to kill him and run off with his car. The thought dissipated quickly, however, for Shirley Ramsey knew she couldn't kill a fly and not feel guilt. She also knew she didn't know how to drive a car.

"How did he find out so soon?" she asked herself. "Who could've know'd I took the money from the post office? The kids must've guessed and told it at school."

Shirley had visions of bars and chains, of the kids being taken to orphanages all over the country, never to see her, or each other again. She grew so terrified that her legs began to tremble and weaken. She sat by the table and began to cry. When the constable knocked authoritatively on the door, she had already finished her second Hail Mary.

"Come in!" she sobbed openly. There was no sense in trying to hide the tears.

The door opened and there he stood like God himself. Three clunks of his big boots and he was in the kitchen looming over her.

She could smell his aftershave and thought she could even feel the warmth of his breath.

"Are you Mrs. James Ramsey?" he asked.

In the emotional condition she was in, she did not hear the gentleness in his voice.

She nodded. "I'm so very poor," she whimpered. "I needed food for poor little Dry and Pal . . . and everyone."

"My name is Constable Bastarache of the RCMP and . . . and, well, it seems you already know. Anyway, I was to inform you . . . I'm sorry."

"You're sorry. It was me that did it."

"You shouldn't blame yourself, ma'am, I'm sure you must have loved him very much."

"Him . . . who?"

"Your husband, ma'am. I'm sure you will miss him terribly. I lost a loved one myself recently. We just have to be strong."

"My husband? Buck? Has something happened to Buck?"

"Ah, then you don't know, ma'am?"

"Know? Know what?"

"Ah, Mr. Ramsey has been found, ah, dead, ma'am."

Shirley uttered something incoherent. What she was trying to say was, "My God, my God, my God!"

"I'm terribly sorry," said the Mountie. "Can I get you a glass of water, a cup of tea, perhaps?"

"No, no, I'll be all right How did it happen? When? How did he die?"

"He was found on a wharf in Saint John on the ninth of February. Exposure. He may have frozen to death."

"The ninth of February? That's six weeks ago."

"Yes. He wasn't carrying any identification. It took the Saint John police until yesterday to track things down."

"Is he buried yet?"

"I'm afraid so, ma'am. You could have him exhumed and brought back here, if you wished."

"No, no. I wouldn't do that. I suppose he should've been buried in Gordon. Buck's Catholic. But he never liked it around here much. He's prob'ly happy where he is."

"He was buried in a public cemetery, ma'am, but we could arrange for a priest to sanctify the grave, if you wished."

"Yes, yes. Could you? And I'll see the priest in Blackville about a Mass."

"Of course, ma'am."

"Thank you."

"There's one more thing, ma'am."

"Yes?"

"His belongings."

"Yes?"

"Mr. Ramsey had a room at 371 Collier Street in Saint John.

There's this envelope" — the constable handed Shirley an envelope — "and I've several items in the car."

"Yes, thank you very much."

Buck's worldly possessions consisted of a guitar, a radio, a pocket watch that didn't work and a hundred and sixty-three dollars and eighty-two cents in cash. The cash was in the envelope.

After Constable Bastarache left, Shirley Ramsey cried a few solemn tears, but the twinge of fear she had felt was replaced with a flood of relief.

*

A week later Shirley Ramsey's bill at Bernie Hanley's store was paid in full. There was ten dollars worth of new stamps in the post office and Dryfly was being the Lone Ranger more often than not, with his shiny, new cap gun.

Shirley's family allowance and post office cheque had arrived and she found herself sitting, for the moment, on the proverbial pig's back.

three

Shirley Ramsey, in a peculiar sort of way, was becoming famous. She was becoming a symbol of poverty, ugliness and untidiness for Brennen Siding, for all the Gordon Road area, and even mothers as far away as Blackville and Renous were telling their children, "You'd better get to school and learn, or you'll grow up to be poorer than Shirley Ramsey!" Because of her few yellow teeth and straight unkempt hair, her neglected figure and ragged clothing, she was literally becoming a household word in the community.

When Helen MacDonald was washing out the barrels she used for salting gaspereaux, she remarked, "Smells worse than Shirley Ramsey!"

Bert Todder got drunk on rum one night and told Helen MacDonald that she was the prettiest woman in Brennen Siding. Helen promptly replied, "Git out with ya, ya drunken fool! I'm homelier than Shirley Ramsey!"

Bert once described the antlers of a buck he'd shot. "'Pon me soul to God, they had sixteen points and were wider than . . . than . . . than Shirley Ramsey's arse! Tee, hee, hee, sob, sniff, snort!"

Dan Brennen drove all the way to Newcastle for a pair of boots for his son Charlie. When he entered the boot store, he realized he hadn't asked Charlie his boot size. Dan muttered, "Bejesus, I'm getting stupider than Shirley Ramsey!"

Shirley's name was used in other ways as well. For instance, if Shirley had a tool shed (which she didn't), it would have but two things in it, an axe and a dull rusty bucksaw.

Besides the chopping and sawing of whatever stove wood the Ramseys could collect, the saw and the axe were also used for the execution of whatever repair jobs were needed to be done. The outdoor toilet was built, for instance, with the saw and the axe. The porch over the door was also built with the saw and the axe, and so was the lean-to shed erected every November for a wood shelter.

These constructions did not go unnoticed. Most of the cuts were crooked, and many of the nails, driven with the back of the axe, were bent over.

John Kaston started the Shirley Ramsey-the-bad-carpenter ball rolling when he made a bad cut while making his kitchen cupboards. "Darn!" he swore, "I Shirley Ramsied it!"

While Buck was living, nobody in Brennen Siding would lift a finger to assist Shirley in any way. Buck was supposed to be responsible. If the Ramsey family starved to death, the inhabitants of Brennen Siding would not have felt the slightest twinge of remorse or guilt. After all, if a man can't look out for his family, he can't expect someone else to. "Buck went away and let that whole family starve to death," Dan Brennen might say, while cutting into a roast of beef.

When the people of Brennen Siding learned of Buck's death, however, Shirley Ramsey took on a different status, "the widow." Shirley Ramsey, the estranged wife, deserved nothing. Shirley Ramsey, the widow, needed help. Stan Tuney gave Shirley a bucket of potatoes and a bucket of carrots. "You kin keep the buckets," Stan told her. Dan Brennen gave Shirley a bucket of corned beef. "The bucket kin be used for carrying water from the brook," said Dan. "Water is good for bathin' in." Dan Brennen said this as though it was a great new revelation. He said a lot of things that way. Brennen Siding was named after his grandfather. He felt that made him special, that he was perhaps smarter and better than everyone else.

John and Max Kaston were cleaning out the summer kitchen. Max was gazing into a keg of brine.

"What'll I do with these old gaspereaux?" he asked. "They ain't no good for anything."

"Might as well throw them out. The gaspereaux will soon be runnin' anyway."

"Maybe we should give them to Shirley Ramsey."

"Good idea, Max. I'll take them down to her later."

John Kaston was religious; he wanted to be a preacher. When he got up to Shirley Ramsey's with a bucket full of gaspereaux, he said, "When the fish are gone, you can use the bucket for carryin' water. Cleanliness is Godliness, you know."

Shirley Ramsey was a Catholic and John Kaston was a Baptist forever trying to convert her. He had one reservation though; he wasn't sure if he wanted the likes of her associated with the church. Who'd want to sit beside her?

Lindon Tucker, who was never previously known to give anything away, gave Shirley an old galvanized tub he'd found in the barn.

"No, no, no, I want you to have it, Shirley old girl. Want ya to have it, yeah, yeah, yeah. Good tub, that. Yep. Oh yeah, yep, good tub, yep."

"Thanks, Lindon. It's awful good o' ya."

"Don't, don't, don't mention it, Shirley old girl. Glad, glad, glad to do it, don't, don't, don't mention it."

Bert Todder showed up, too, with a black salmon. Bert Todder was short and fat; he had a single tooth in the front of his mouth that you saw whenever he laughed. He'd show his tooth, squint his eyes and commence to jiggle and shake; the sound coming from within, more like sobs than laughter. Everyone liked him and he visited everyone in Brennen Siding once a week. He was the reporter. When he visited, he'd mean only to stay for five or ten minutes. When ten minutes was up, he'd stand and say, "Well, I gotta go." Then, he'd talk for five or ten more minutes and say, "Boys, I should be off." Before he got through the door, though, he'd remember that he hadn't told you about Lester Burns falling in the river and narrowly escaping drowning, the story taking ten minutes to tell. He might sit down again to tell it, at the end of which he'd say, "It's time to leave, I gotta go home."

Bert Todder usually stayed all evening.

Bert Todder even paid weekly visits to Shirley Ramsey. She made good news.

Because of Bert Todder, there were no secrets in Brennen Siding.

Todder Brook was named after Bert's grandfather and ran

through Bert's property. Bert lived the nearest of all to the Todder Brook Whooper.

*

Shadrack Nash wanted to investigate the Todder Brook Whooper, but didn't want to do it alone.

He went to Max Kaston and was laughed at. Max snorted, said, "You're crazier than Shirley Ramsey.

"There ain't nothin' to be scared of," said Shad.

"Then go alone." Max eyed Shad over his chubby cheeks.

"You're just too lazy to go," said Shad and left.

Shad found George Hanley and Palidin Ramsey, smoking cigarettes, out behind BernieHanley's barn.

George Hanley's ears were too big, as were his hands and feet; but his teeth were white and even, he had long eyelashes and was almost pretty in the face.

"I wouldn't take a million dollars to step one foot into that woods!" said George.

The fair-skinned, brown-eyed, mysterious Palidin Ramsey (all the Ramseys were mysterious) said nothing. Palidin knew he was not being invited on the adventure. Shadrack Nash did not know that Palidin Ramsey had no fear.

Out of desperation, Shad went to Shirley Ramsey's. He found Dryfly sitting on the doorstep, strumming a G chord over and over again on Buck's guitar. Shad had learned a few chords from his father and had passed his knowledge along to Dryfly. He had traded the G chord for a Glenn Hall. By mid-June, he was on the verge of completing his hockey card collection. He was only missing Johnny Bower of the Toronto Maple Leafs. A Lou Fontenato and a Johnny Bucyk and he'd have the whole NHL. He was holding on to a C chord, just in case Dryfly might get lucky enough to get one of the cards he needed.

"What're ya doin'?" asked Shad, as if he didn't already know.

"Playin' me guiddar."

"Soundin' pretty good."

Dryfly shrugged. He was thin and needed a haircut.

"Don't know any more chords yet, eh?"

"No," said Dryfly.

"Gonna listen to the jamboree tonight?"

"Might."

Shad was referring to the Saturday Night Jamboree that was broadcast from CFNB Fredericton every week — Earl Mitton on the fiddle, Bud Brown the emcee, Kid and Ada Baker the guests more often than not.

"I am," said Shadrack. "Wanna come over and listen to it with me?"

"What for? I can hear it on me own radio."

"I got something I want us to do afterwards."

"Gonna be awful close to dark by the time the jamboree's over."

"I know," shrugged Shadrack. "I want it to be dark."

"What're ya gonna be doin' in the dark?"

"I'm goin' back to see what's makin' that noise."

"The Todder Brook Whooper?"

"Yep."

"What if it's a ghost?"

"I don't care."

"What if it's a panther?"

"Takin' Dad's .303."

"Yeah? How'd ya git that?"

"I know where it is. I'll just sneak it out. Know where the bullets are, too. Wanna come with me?"

"Nope. Ya'll never catch me in that woods!"

"Why not?"

"Cause."

"Cause why?"

"Cause, ya wouldn'."

"Scared?"

"No, but I ain't goin'."

"Why?"

"I just told ya!"

"Yer scared!"

"I'm not!"

46

"I'm taken the .303."

"You'd be a pretty lad, shootin' a ghost with a big rifle like that! Knock ya arse over kettles!"

"Don't kick hardly at all. I'll let ya try it, if ya want."

"You fire it first."

"I'll fire it. It don't kick. Fire it all the time, so I do!"

"What if ya get lost?"

"All we'll do is follow the trail back and then follow it home again."

"The flies will eat us up, back there in the woods at night."

"No flies hardly at all. Work up a sweat and they never touch ya."

It was approaching the middle of June and Dryfly doubted very much that he could work up enough sweat to combat the forty-two thousand and one flies that would be attacking him back in the Dungarvon woods. "Come with me and I'll tell ya how to put a C chord on."

"C chord?"

"Yep. Dad says if ya know C and G chords ya kin play any song at all."

"How far back ya goin'?"

"Not far."

"What if it's a ghost?"

"It's a panther."

"How do ya know?"

"Dad says."

"How ya gonna shoot a panther in the dark?"

"Takin' Dad's flashlight, too."

"Yeah?"

"Yep. You kin carry the flashlight and I'll carry the rifle. We'll jack 'im. You hold the light on his eyes and I'll down the bugger."

Dryfly thought of the rifle, the flashlight and the two of them gunning down a panther. Dryfly wasn't sure what a panther was, but he reckoned it was a throaty creature, by the sounds that came from it every night. He thought of the C chord and himself being able to play every song ever sung. He thought of the adventure and the stories that they'd tell everyone. He thought of being Shadrack Nash's friend; of being closer to Shad than George Hanley or Max Kaston were.

"I'll come over after supper," said Dryfly. "Wanna come in and have some supper with us?"

"What're ya havin'?"

"Salmon."

"No thanks. Never cared much for salmon."

Shad left thinking that he wouldn't take a million dollars for eating Shirley Ramsey's cooking.

*

Sneaking the rifle and the flashlight out was almost too easy for any kind of interesting adventure. Bob Nash had gone fishing and Shadrack's mother was sewing in the kitchen. The rifle stood behind a chair in the livingroom. Shad hid the flashlight under his belt. To get the rifle, all Shad had to do was pick it up and go with it.

Outside, Shad gave Dryfly the flashlight. They reckoned they had an hour before it would be dark enough to use it.

The trail that led to Todder Brook country was an old, neglected trucking road, originally used for hauling out pulp, logs and boxwood, but it was evident that the road hadn't been used for years. The tire ruts were still there, but blueberry bushes and even the odd alder bush flourished in the center. Shadrack walked in one rut and Dryfly in the other. Neither boy felt like talking. Both boys were scared. Neither would admit it. Shad cocked the rifle the moment they entered the forest.

There was the odd bird singing and insect buzzing, the setting sun sat like a golden bonnet on the tops of the taller trees.

"How much further we goin'?" asked Dryfly after a while.

"I don't know. Maybe a mile. I don't know."

"Seems to me we've come a long way already. Do you think it's that far away?"

"I don't know."

They continued to walk until they heard the rushing sounds of Todder Brook. Here, they noticed that the ground was speckled with numerous hoof prints — some deer and some bigger prints they hoped were those of moose.

"I don't smell anythin'," commented Dryfly, staring at the hoof prints.

"What odds if ya smell anything?" asked Shad. "I doubt if a human could smell a panther, anyway, unless he had his nose right up against 'im."

"Mom told me that the devil's s'pose to smell like shit."

"How's she know that?"

"Don't know. That's what she told me."

"That's foolish," said Shadrack, but he sniffed the air anyway.

Dryfly noticed that the sun had left the treetops and the twilight had replaced it. The anticipation of the approaching night and the inevitable darkness of the forest was not what Dryfly considered to be a good time.

"I think we should go home, Shad. I have to cross the footbridge tonight. It's tricky in the dark."

"You kin have the flashlight."

Dryfly sighed.

Shadrack and Dryfly found a big pine tree and after eyeing it to make sure there were no cougars in its midst, they sat close together with their backs against its trunk. They could not be attacked from behind.

Time ticked on and darkness fell.

There in the night, every sound — the snapping of a twig, the hooting of an owl, a breeze whispering in the boughs above them — quickened their imaginative young hearts. Every shadow, every form, seemed a potential threat, and sometimes what they knew was only a tree or shrub seemed to actually move. Dryfly checked out his surroundings with the flashlight about every ten seconds. Shadrack didn't complain.

"What's that?"

"Where?"

"There!"

"I don't see anything."

"There. I heard a thump."

"Where?"

"Listen!"

Dryfly couldn't hear anything, except his heart beating, but he wasn't sure. There might have been something. He might have missed something . . . he wasn't sure. "I think we should go home," he whispered.

"Why?"

"It's gettin' awful late."

"Shh!"

"Mom'll kill me."

"Wait a few more minutes."

Another deep sigh escaped from Dryfly.

A bird sang, its song piercing the silence, crisp and clear. Dryfly could not identify it — he hadn't heard it before. "Indians," he thought.

Palidin had read a book about cowboys and Indians in which the Indians had used the songs of birds as a form of communication. Dryfly remembered Palidin's reference to the tale.

"I hope they're dead Indians," he thought.

The bird sang again and somehow sounded mournful and forsaken. "No," thought Dryfly, "I hope they are alive."

A Gander-bound plane rumbled far up amidst the stars, its flicker somehow reassuring as it crossed the Dipper.

A mosquito hummed by his ear. The bird sang once more.

"What bird is that?" whispered Dryfly.

"What bird?"

"That one."

"Don't hear it."

A few minutes passed and Shad decided he'd had enough.

"Let's go," he whispered. The words "let's go" came like poetry to Dryfly's ears.

They followed the flashlight beam out on the trail, their feet thumping the ground and swishing the bushes as they hurried along.

Dryfly counted to himself, "One less step, two less, three, four, five, six . . ."

When a rabbit has lost the chase and finds himself cornered by a hungry fox, a strange phenomenon occurs. The rabbit gives up, goes into a trance-like state, a fear-induced state of paralysis, and sometimes even dies, robbing the fox of the thrill of the kill.

When Shadrack and Dryfly heard the honk from no more than a hundred yards off to their right, they stopped in a trance just short of death. The flashlight dropped from Dryfly's hand to smash the ground and go out at his feet. Darkness reigned supreme.

Thump, thump, thump, went a heartbeat.

Dryfly wasn't sure if it was his own heart or Shadrack's.

Shadrack wasn't sure either.

BEEP-BARMP-BARMP! went the noise in the forest. The brief silence that followed was disrupted by a fart. Both boys knew that it had been Dryfly's release. For a moment it was impossible to say if, or if not, they were smelling the devil.

Shadrack gripped the .303 so tight that he might have been attempting to leave finger dents in the wood.

"What do we do now?" asked Dryfly in a tiny voice that seemed not to be his own.

Shadrack didn't know. He couldn't think. To run seemed to be the logical move, but in his confusion he prayed instead, silently. "Now I lay me down to sleep, I pray to God my soul to keep . . ."

Thump, thump, thump, went a heartbeat Dryfly identified as his own. "Hail Mary, full of grace, blessed art thou amongst women . . ."

BARMP! BARMP-BARMP, BEEP-BEEP! went the noise that sounded like a sick car horn, an elephant, perhaps the scream of an eastern cougar, or all three.

"Got the gun, Shad?" asked Dryfly, his voice still very tiny in the great dark forest.

"Right here!" said Shadrack. "Want it?"

"You know how to use it?"

"Just pull the trigger, I think."

BARMP, TWEEP, BLEEP!

"You scared?"

"What'd you say?"

"You scared?"

"No. I don't think so."

BARMP-BARMP HONK! BEEP-BEEP, BARMP-BARMP!
As their eyes adjusted to the darkness, they were able to make out the trail before them — a navy line in a black-forested field, a mere reflection of the azure. Dew drops imprisoned the azure.

"The noise is coming from down by the brook," whispered Shadrack.

"Fire the gun! You might scare it off, if it's a cougar." Dryfly whispered back, spying for the first time since he dropped it, the flashlight. He knelt and picked it up. He pushed the button. The bulb was blown.

"Won't it work?" asked Shad, musing over Dryfly's suggestion to shoot the gun.

"The bulb's blowed," said Dryfly.

"Do you think a shot would do it?"

BARMP-BARMP! BEEP-BEEP! BARMP! continued the noise in the forest.

"It can't hurt!" said Dryfly.

Shad pointed the rifle at the sky. "I hope it's a cougar! I hope it's a cougar, I hope it's a cougar . . ." he chanted to himself. "I hope it runs away when I shoot, runs when I shoot, runs when I shoot . . ." He could have been memorizing a poem. "Oh God, make it run. I'll be good and go to church and everything," he prayed.

BARMP-BARMP-BARMP! BAR-AR-AR-ARMP!

POW! went the rifle. Silence and the smell of gunsmoke.

*

Lindon Tucker never installed electricity in his house, but he had a battery radio. Lindon Tucker lived with his mother and an old tomcat called Cat. When Lindon called Cat in at night, he called, "Kitty, kitty, kitty."

"Kitty, kitty, kitty," called Lindon.

"Meow," went Cat and zipped through the kitchen door into the dimly lit room, meowed as it scanned the dark corners for mice, then jumped onto the cot behind the kitchen range.

Lindon closed the door and went back to his rocking chair.

Everyone in Brennen Siding figured that Lindon kept his lamps turned low to save on kerosene. He may have kept the volume of his battery radio equally as low to save on batteries. Lindon Tucker wasted nothing. When he shopped at Bernie Hanley's store, Lindon saved every inch of twine from the parcels; he also saved the brown paper. He saved the aluminum foil from the inside of tobacco packages and the remains of used wooden matches.

Lindon Tucker picked his teeth with the remains of used wooden matches.

Lindon Tucker's mother sat with her ear not more than six inches from the radio speaker.

From the CKMR station in Newcastle, Brother Duffy was busily condemning sinners. CKMR, the community voice of the Miramichi.

Hayshaker's Hoedown at 7:00 p.m. News, sports and weather followed by the marine weather forecast with its Brown's, LeHavres and Fundy Coasts, came on at 7:30. The exotic names mentioned in the marine forecast, the sound effects — ships bells and fog horns — were soothing, like poetry to Lindon. At 8:30 some heathen Catholic thing came on, which Lindon always turned off. He'd turn the radio back on at 9:00, set the dial at 550 and listen to the Saturday night jamboree on CFNB.

"The jamboree was better than usual tonight," thought Lindon. "Freddy McKenna, Freddy McKenna, that blind lad, Freddy McKenna was on it tonight. They claim he plays his giddar turned up on his lap."

At 10:00 p.m., Lindon had to oblige his mother and shift the dial back to CKMR for a Bible-thumping half hour of Oral Roberts.

Lindon didn't mind the preaching. At least it kept his mother from complaining for a half hour.

Clara, Lindon's mother, was eighty years old and hadn't been sick for forty years. The gift of health didn't keep her from complaining, however. Lindon was subjected to her complaining day in and day out, her voice whining and whimpering even when she was talking about it being a nice day.

"Bless us and save us," she whined. "Yes, yes, Lord. Dear Jesus!"

When Oral Roberts said "Hallelujah!" for the last time and went off the air, Clara leaned back in her chair and squinted her eyes to see Lindon. Her eyesight was good, but the lamp was turned down to a mere glow.

"My toe's botherin' me, Lindon. You think a person could git cancer in a toe? Some claim ya kin, some claim ya can't. You kin git gangrene in yer toe. Old Billy Todder died of gangrene in the toe. I've heard of people dying of cancer of the bowels and the stomach, but I don't know about the toe. I don't know about gangrene of the stomach either. Do you think a corn could turn to cancer, Lindon?"

"Oh yeah, yeah, yeah. Yeah. Cancer, yeah," said Lindon, reaching for the dial.

Lindon stopped turning the dial when he heard the rich and mellow voice of Doc Williams talking about a picture Bible. "Just write 'Picture Bible,' WWVA, Wheeling, West Virginia," Doc was saying. "And now I'd like to do y'all a song I very much enjoy and I hope y'all at home will enjoy too."

The guitar was strummed. It sounded deep and rich. Doc Williams was the best guitar player in the world —

> *Hannah! Hannah!*
> *Hannah won't you open the door.*
> *Hannah, Hannah, Hannah,*
> *Won't you change you manna'*
> *This is old Doc Williams,*
> *Don't you love me no more?*

— and Lindon thought that Doc Williams was the best singer in the world, too . . . with the exception of, maybe, Lee Moore.

When Doc Williams ended his show by picking "Wildwood Flower" and had gone the way of Brother Duffy and Oral Roberts, Lindon stood, yawned and headed for the door. He needed to have a leak before going to bed.

"Where ya goin'?" asked Clara.

"To see a man about a horse," said Lindon.

The night was moonless, the deep blue sky spangled with a million stars, the milky way straight up. The air was warm and scented with lilacs and grass. The songs of a million night creatures (peepers, Lindon called them) betrayed the presence of a swamp. The air buzzed and hummed with midges, black-flies and mosquitoes. A bird sang . . . like a robin . . . but not a robin; a swamp robin, perhaps.

Off in the east, back on Todder Brook, came the now familiar screams of what Lindon figured was the devil.

Then suddenly a rifle shot sounded from the same direction and the devil fell silent.

"Hmm, a shot in the dark," muttered Lindon.

Somebody standing behind him might have thought that Lindon was directing his comment at his penis.

four

Nutbeam lived in a tiny camp in the forest back on Todder Brook. He'd built the camp five years ago on somebody's land — he didn't know that it was the lumber section of the old abandoned Graig Allen farm — and none of the locals, as of yet, had located him. A couple of hunters came close a couple of times, but that was all.

Although Nutbeam could not read or write, he was not uneducated. He knew all there was to know about living in the woods. He was an expert trapper, hunter, fisherman and axeman. He knew every shrub, weed, wildflower, fern, berry, cherry, mushroom and nut; which ones were edible and which ones were not. He was an expert in a canoe and on a pair of snowshoes. He had gathered his knowledge from experience, mostly in the last five years.

Nutbeam was six feet six inches tall and had a thirty-two-inch waist. With a nose four inches long, big negroid lips and ears the size of dessert plates, Nutbeam was, indeed, homelier than Shirley Ramsey.

Although Nutbeam was independent, he was completely without confidence.

His appearance was the reason for it — his appearance and the fact that nobody normal could face him without laughing. His appearance was also the reason he had never gone to school, never liked people and had left his home in Smyrna Mills, Maine, to journey into Canada's Dungarvon country.

Although Nutbeam didn't like people, he wasn't necessarily uninterested in them. He liked to look at people, but he didn't want people to look at him. Nutbeam kept his distance from people, ran into the woods when he saw someone coming, hid behind his hood, or collar, when it was absolutely necessary to pass near someone.

Nutbeam sat in front of his camp, eyeing the treetops adorned by the setting sun. He watched a mosquito feasting off the back of his hand.

"Gorge yourself and then you die," said he to the mosquito.

"That's about all there is to life," he thought. "A man ain't no different than a mosquiter. Yer born, ya eat and drink, ya dump it out again and then you die. If you're born ugly, or not too smart, ya might as well have your dump right away, die and get it over with."

"You, little mosquiter, are prob'ly pretty for a mosquiter," said Nutbeam and commenced to hold his breath. In a few seconds the capillary the mosquito was tapping tightened around its tiny proboscus, trapping it so that Nutbeam could reach out at his leisure, slap, pick off, or set it free. The mosquito's fate depended on Nutbeam's decision. Nutbeam's decision came with a sigh. He took a breath (the sigh), the mosquito filled his tank and flew off. It'll die soon enough Nutbeam thought and scratched the itch.

Nutbeam's first year on Todder Brook had been a difficult one. He nearly froze to death. Without the few rabbits he managed to snare, he would have starved. On several occasions he came very close to seeking help from the Brennen Siding dwellers.

"I'm sure glad I didn't have to do that," he thought. "I'm all right now. I don't need nobody now."

He remembered that he had frozen his massive ears so many times and to such an extent that they flopped over and stayed that way. The experience turned out to be a beneficial one, however.

"Ya kin hear better with big floppy ears," mumbled Nutbeam.

Nutbeam could hear a bird singing for a country mile. Nutbeam could hear a deer walking a hundred yards away. He could hear the mosquitoes humming outside his camp at night.

Nutbeam had no difficulty hearing Lindon Tucker's radio

and frequently stood outside Lindon Tucker's house on Saturday nights, listening to Kid Baker singing.

Nutbeam recalled the night Lindon had taken an early break to see a man about a horse. Nutbeam had been standing in the shadows of a shed listening to Lee Moore sing "The Cat Came Back."

"Lindon didn't see me there in the dark, but he pissed all over me boot," thought Nutbeam.

As he learned and practised the art of survival, life grew continually easier. He began taking the train into Newcastle once a month (at the risk of being seen) to trade his furs. At first, he traded for traps and snares; later, he traded for food and ammunition, fishing tackle, aspirins and candy. Later still, he traded for boots and the wonderful parka with the big hood that protected his ears and hid his face whenever he looked down. Last winter, Nutbeam lived very comfortably trading mostly for vegetables, Forest and Stream tobacco and money.

"I spent a bunch of money on that trumpet," he thought, "and I doubt if I ever learn to play it."

Nutbeam had been trying to play the trumpet for nearly three months and still couldn't blow a recognizable melody. At first, he couldn't even get a noise out of it, but now, after three months practice, he was making more noise than he realized. He was making enough noise to send chills down the backs of everyone in Brennen Siding.

Nutbeam always waited until nightfall to practice his trumpet playing. Somehow, playing in the dark seemed easier. He didn't know why. Perhaps it was his fear of being caught. He didn't know why, but he knew he would die of embarrassment if anyone ever saw him playing an instrument. Nutbeam was very shy.

"I'm nearly a mile into the woods. Surely nobody kin hear me playing this far away. I might hear it, but I've got these big floppy ears. Nobody in Brennen Siding got big floppy ears." After three months, Nutbeam was convinced that nobody could hear the trumpet. Nutbeam underestimated the ears of Brennen Siding.

When he felt it dark enough, Nutbeam went into his camp and fetched his trumpet.

"Tonight, I'll practice that Earl Mitton tune," he thought. "What's it called? 'Mouth of the Tobique'?"

When fishermen waded down Todder Brook, they could not see Nutbeam's tiny camp embedded in the forested hillside twenty yards away, nor could the camp be seen from the bushy old truck road, a hundred yards to the south. If you were to stand thirty feet from the camp, looking directly up at it, you might not see it, unless you knew it was there. Nutbeam had built three quarters of the structure under ground, with the slant of the roof parallel with the hill. He built it down and into the hill like a mine shaft, so that he had to actually tunnel out a path to the door. All that could be seen from the front was a small door and two grey logs. Once a deer had actually walked on the roof. The tiny seven-by-ten-foot square camp contained a table, two chairs, a cot to sleep on, a barrel stove and three tiny kegs. In one keg he kept salty salmon; in another, he kept salty gaspereaux and in the third, flour. There was a shelf on the eastern wall, on which sat a can of tea, a can of Forest and Stream tobacco, a can of baking powder, two pipes and a can of molasses. On another wall hung two rifles and a wrinkled, frameless picture of the Virgin Mary. On a nail beside the picture hung Nutbeam's rosary beads. On a wall beside the stove were some more shelves occupied by pots, tin plates, cups, a frying pan, a box of matches, knives, forks, spoons and a tin can full of odds and ends — a pencil, a small magnifying glass, a ball of string, some fish hooks, one of a set of dice which Nutbeam called a "douse," a spool of thread, buttons and a red squirrel's tail. Clothing hung haphazardly on all four walls.

In a box in the corner he kept his traps, a revolver, ammunition and his trumpet.

There was no window in the camp, so that when he entered he either had to leave the door open so he could see, or light the lamp that sat on the table. Lit, the lamp was usually turned as low as Lindon Tucker's.

By the light of one tiny star, which shone through the open door, Nutbeam found his trumpet.

He took the trumpet outside, put it to his lips, pointed the horn at the star-spangled sky and blew.

HONK, HONK, BEEP, BEEP, BARMP-BARMP!

The sound of the trumpet echoed from hill to hill, crossed brooks and rivers and shot through windows and doors all over Brennen Siding. Nutbeam played what he hoped sounded like "There's a Mansion in the Blue" for several minutes.

Then the rifle shot went off, the retort slamming against his big floppy ear, startling him into a sudden, silent trance just a hair short of death.

Darkness reigned supreme.

*

Shadrack and Dryfly stood on the steps that scaled the east end abutment of the bridge, panting heavily from running all the way from the forest to the river. Shadrack was particularly tired from carrying the heavy .303 rifle. Both boys were very happy to see the lit windows of the little settlement. The sight of the river, calm, reflecting the starlit sky, restored their courage. The river, a symbol of home, strength and identity, would give them courage for the rest of their lives. At the age of eleven, they already loved it.

During their lives, Shadrack and Dryfly would travel to Vancouver and New York, Toronto and Nashville, England and Italy, but their hearts would always remain on the Dungarvon, the Renous and the Miramichi. At the age of seventy, they would still at times speak a little too fast and at other times a little too slow and would repeat the word "and" too much. At the age of seventy, they would still speak with a Miramichi accent, softly, as the river people do, and refer to themselves as "Dungarvon boys."

"You gonna be able to go home by yourself, Dry?" asked Shadrack.

"Yeah, I'll be all right."

"I have to sneak the rifle and flashlight back in. If I git caught doin' it, I'll be killed."

"What d'ya s'pose happened to the whooper thing?"

"Must've scared 'im, that's all."

"Me and you scared the whooper, Shad!"

"Yeah, I know. Can't be nothin' too dangerous if me and you scared it."

"We gonna tell what we did?"

"What d'ya think?"

"I don't know. Maybe."

"What d'ya think it was, Dry?"

"I don't know. Panther, I guess."

"Well, we kin talk about it tomorrow. I gotta git home and try and git this rifle in the house without getting caught."

"Okay. See ya later, Shad."

"Yeah. Night."

The boys separated.

Dryfly's fear might have climaxed back in the woods, but its memory still shook him from within. What was more, he was still out in the dark night and now he was alone. The boardwalk of the footbridge ribboned before him; the river swept below, another ribbon with its reflections of forest and sky.

Reasoning told him not to be afraid of the bridge. "It'll hold the devil," everyone always said, and he was accustomed to its bounce and squeaks; he'd walked it many times. But in the daylight . . . always in the daylight.

When he reached the middle abutment, it loomed dark and menacing beneath. He quickened his pace and hurried by.

"I wished I was more like Palidin," thought Dryfly. "Pal's always out in the night. Ain't scared a bit."

"How can Palidin do it? How kin he not be scared?"

"Scared?"

"Of what?"

"The dark?"

"A ghost?"

Dryfly didn't know why he, himself, was afraid. "Other people crossed the bridge and nothin' happened to them," he reasoned. "Why should anything happen to me?"

When he reached the west end abutment, he realized he was confronted with a decision. "Cross the fields to the road, or go down along the shore to Stan Tuney's brook and go up through the woods." He knew the path along the brook better, but the thought of walking through the woods did not appeal to him. He dismounted the abutment and headed across Dan Brennen's field, passed the house, barn and sheds. He came to the road. "I made it to the road," he whispered, and headed north toward home. He passed Billy Campbell's farm and Bernie Hanley's store. He was nearing the railroad crossing when the bird sang — the same bird he'd heard in the woods.

Dryfly's heart leaped and began to drum in his chest. The hairs on his neck and back lifted, feeling like a chill. "I'm gettin' outta here!" he gasped and ran as fast as he could all the way home.

It would be many years before he'd be man enough to admit that he'd been so afraid of a bird.

*

Shadrack climbed the hill toward home. His shoulder was sore from shooting the rifle, but he was not afraid of the devil himself. Shadrack had the rifle.

Outside the house, he peeked in through the window. His father sat in the kitchen, reading the *Family Herald*. That was a good place for him.

His mother was reading the Bible. Good enough, too.

"I'll sneak through the front door," thought Shadrack. "I'll have to be quiet, though."

Shadrack was just putting the rifle behind the chair, when his father yelled, "Where you been with that rifle?"

Bob Nash was standing in the livingroom door, slapping the palm of his hand with a tightly-rolled *Family Herald*.

Shad turned to face his father, knowing there was no escape, that a severe application of the tightly rolled *Family Herald* was about to occur.

"I shot the Todder Brook Whooper," said Shad, quickly.

"You what?"

"I shot the Todder Brook Whooper!"

"WHAT! What did I hear you say?"

Bob Nash had already decided upon his course of action

and hit Shadrack, hard as he could, on the butt, with the tightly rolled *Family Herald*.

"Don't, Dad!" yelled Shadrack.

"Don't 'don't' me!"

Whack! went the *Family Herald*.

"Take my rifle, will ya!" Whack! "Young lad like you!" Whack!

"OUCH! That hurts! Ouch! Stop!"

Bob Nash had a terrible temper. Bob Nash had fire in his eyes. Bob Nash's fiery eyes could almost see the *Family Herald*'s John Deere Tractor ad imprinted on Shadrack's behind.

WHACK! went the *Family Herald*. WHACK, WHACK, WHACK . . .

Monday night in Bernie Hanley's store, Bob Nash took a drink of his Sussex Ginger Ale and said, "Yes sir, that boy of mine and that young Ramsey lad, Dryfly, took my rifle and went back in that woods alone, just the two of them, and scared that devil off. I haven't heard it since, have you?"

"No," said Bert Todder, "didn't make a peep last night, far's I know."

"Heard the shot, so I did, yeah. Not a peep last night, no. Heard the shot, so I did," said Lindon Tucker.

"I wouldn't even have the nerve to do that meself!" said Bob Nash, proudly.

"Them boys got good stuff in them, I can say that," said John Kaston.

"Did they see it, Bob?" asked Bernie Hanley, from behind the counter.

"Sure, they saw it! How would they fire at it if they didn't see it! Shad said it was as big as a moose and had horns like a cow. Said he saw his eyes shining and they were as big around as saucers!"

"I heard the shot, so I did. Yeah, yeah, yeah, I did, yeah," commented Lindon Tucker.

"Gimme a new flashlight bulb, would ya, Bernie? And a bag of them peppermints fer me young lad."

five

From the fifteenth of April to the fifteenth of October, Helen MacDonald cooked for the Cabbage Island Salmon Club. The job paid well. Helen was a good cook. She worked fourteen hours a day, seven days a week for thirty dollars. Occasionally, one of the club guests would tip her five or ten dollars. Helen MacDonald's financial goal was to be able to afford an indoor toilet.

In order to have breakfast ready for the early-rising anglers, Helen had to leave home at five o'clock in the morning. Rex, her old brown dog, always followed her to work. Rex was fed very well on the scraps left over from the Cabbage Island Salmon Club dinners.

One hot July day in 1962, Helen MacDonald found herself in a bad mood. She had baked a blueberry pie and had left it in front of an open window to cool. An hour later she looked to see how the pie was doing, and to her amazement and great displeasure, the pie had vanished. She had paid little Joey Brennen fifty cents of her own hard-earned money for those berries, hoping to impress a tip from the Americans with a pie.

It wasn't the first time she had lost food from that window but it hadn't happened since the previous year. Helen thought that maybe the thief had grown up and had developed some conscience. "It's plain to see that Dryfly Ramsey ain't ever growing up."

Dryfly Ramsey naturally got the blame. Dryfly Ramsey was a Catholic and, therefore, bad enough to do it. Besides, earlier, Helen had seen Dryfly snooping about the place. She should have known enough then to remove the pie from the window sill.

That night, Helen related her frustration to Bert Todder.

"I don't know what I'm ever going to do! That tramp! If a poor woman can't make a livin' without the likes o' that tramp botherin' her, what's the world comin' to!"

"Are you sure it was him?" asked Bert.

Bert Todder was making his rounds. Whenever Bert made his rounds, he always made sure to visit Helen MacDonald. Helen MacDonald was an old maid, Bert was a bachelor. Although Helen liked Bert, sexually she wouldn't touch him with a ten-foot pole. However, Bert thought there was always a chance. After all, he was male and she was female.

"Course, I'm sure! Who else would do it?"

"Did you ask anybody about it?"

"I saw 'im snoopin' around!"

"Ya can't leave stuff layin' around where he is."

"If ya can't leave a pie on a window sill without some no good tramp takin' it right out from underneath your eyes, it's gettin' pretty damn bad, I'd say! If I get my hands on that . . . that tramp, I'm gonna strangle 'im! I'll put him in his place, I tell ya!"

"You need a good man, Helen dear."

"There ain't no such thing as a good man, you old coot!"

Bert squinted up his eyes and laughed. Helen eyed Bert's lone tooth. "He sounds like he's cryin'," she thought.

"Ya know what I'd do, Helen darlin'?"

"What?"

"Well, I gotta go, but I'll tell ya. Must be gettin' late, ain't it? Anyway, what I'd do is, I'd make another pie and put Ex-Lax in it. Put it on the window sill just like ya did before. Let 'im eat that and see how he likes it. That'll fix 'im!"

"Ex-Lax," thought Helen. "It'll cost me fifty cents, but it would be worth it."

Helen was glad she had thought of it. She liked the idea very much. It would teach Dryfly Ramsey a lesson.

*

William Wallace tied on a Black Bear Hair with yellow hackle and green butt and picked up his eight-foot Orvis. The bamboo Orvis was the ultimate in fishing rods as far as William (Bill) Wallace was concerned. The Orvis had been a parting gift from the vice-president (Jimmy), the bastard who was after the presidency. Bill Wallace was the president of the company and had no intentions of stepping down.

"Here's a fishing rod for you," Jimmy had said. "Why don't you go fishing, get away for a while. I'll look after things."

Bill Wallace didn't know what Jimmy was up to, but Bill figured something was being schemed. Bill Wallace didn't trust the vice-president as far as he could throw him.

Bill accepted the rod and went fishing. He knew that something negative could happen, but he was not overly concerned. Bill Wallace had a fifty-million-dollar concept for Phase One of the new regional hospital that would leave Jimmy, the vice-president, gaping in awe. Bill Wallace was the president of a construction company, with a contract with the government of Massachusetts to build a hundred-and-fifty-million-dollar hospital in Pittsfield.

Bill Wallace waded ankle-deep into the Dungarvon River and stopped to look around.

"You have a beautiful rivah here, Lindon, ghosts or no ghosts. You say it was never heard after?"

Lindon Tucker, the guide, was lying amidst the shore hay, fighting flies.

"'Pon me soul, yeah," said Lindon. "No one around here's heard a peep since."

Bill looked at the river flowing peacefully by. He looked downstream to where the river bent and vanished behind a forested wall. He could see the hills, the fields, even the reflection of some houses on the mirror-like expanse before him. A swallow dipped and dashed, a salmon parr jumped, an unfamiliar bird could be heard scolding something, perhaps its mate, in a nearby spruce.

"Are we going to catch a salmon today, Linny? Is there anything in heah'?"

"Ya might, ya might, ya might. There ain't no amount o' fish, though."

"Well, I'll give it a try. Christ, there's got to be somethin' in heah'."

Bill Wallace waded in to his knees, released ten feet of his pink air cel line and made a cast. He pulled another four feet from his Saint John Hardy and cast again. He could feel the pressure of the current against his legs, dry in the canvas-topped Hodgemen waders. He lengthened out a few more feet and made another cast. The Black Bear Hair with yellow hackle and green butt drifted past what Bill thought was a potential hotspot. Nothing. He moved downstream a few more steps and cast again.

"I hope Lillian likes it up here," he thought. "She's been wanting to come with me ever since she wrote that essay on the Dungarvon Whooper." Bill chuckled to himself, "The Dungarvon Whopper!"

Bill kept stepping and casting, stepping and casting until he had covered the whole rocky area the locals referred to as a pool, reeled in his line and waded back to where Lindon lay. Lindon was nearly asleep in the morning sun.

"Did the boys actually see the . . . the whooper?"

"Oh, yeah. Yep. Yeah, oh yeah, they seen it all right. Looked like a cow, yeah. Big as a moose, so it was, yeah. Took a shot at it, so they did. Heard the shot meself, so I did, yeah. Oh yeah, yeah, yeah, heard it meself. .303. Never even slowed 'im down. Stopped him from screaming, though. Yes sir, never saw 'im after. Never peeped since!"

"Where's this young . . . what did you say his name was?"

"Shad? Peelin' pulp, I think. Back with John. Workin' with John Kaston, yeah."

"And the other one?"

"You'd prob'ly find Dryfly home. Home, yeah. Playin' guiddar. All he does is play guiddar. Good at it, too, yeah. Another Hank Snow, that lad, yeah. Gonna give it another try?"

"I think I'll give it one more try, then head back to the club. What do you think, Linny?"

Lindon yawned. He wanted a break from sleeping on the shore. The sun was too hot and the flies were bothering him. Lindon knew that there were very few, if any, salmon in the river and that Bill Wallace's chances of catching one were close to nil.

"Can't ketch 'im wit a dry line," said Lindon.

Bill Wallace started the procedure again in much the same fashion. Bill knew that his chances were very poor, too. The weather was too hot for good, productive fishing. But Bill Wallace was standing in the cool water away from the flies. Bill Wallace liked being on the river and liked the scenery and the fresh air. He changed flies, went to the Squirrel Tail with yellow hackle he'd purchased from Bert Todder.

"Bert Todder ties the best damn salmon fly in the world," thought Bill. "So delicate, yet so strong and durable."

Bill took his eyes off the colorful little flyhook and scanned the scenery again. "So scenic and peaceful," he thought.

Across the river stood a massive log cabin, with two stone fireplaces, a breezeway between the kitchen and the living quarters, a full length veranda, shaded in a grove of pines.

"Nice little place," thought Bill. "Belongs to Sam Little. Sam's a Yale man, I think. Out of Hartford. Made his money in the hotel business. He's got the best salmon pool on the Dungarvon and I'm casting directly into it from Lindon Tucker's shore. I wonder why he never bought Lindon Tucker out?"

"Does Sam Little spend much time at his lodge?" asked Bill.

"Too much, too much, too much. Like the, like the, like the feller says, too much."

"Did you ever guide for him?"

"Yeah. Oh yeah. I guided the old sonuvawhore, so I did. Yeah, I guided him, all right. Guided him too much."

Bill Wallace waded deeper in the river, smiling to himself.

"Lindon Tucker wouldn't sell Sam Little anything," thought Bill.

*

A freshly peeled stick of pulpwood is as slippery as a greased eel, or, in the words of Bert Todder, "slipperier than Shirley Ramsey's slop pail dump." Shirley Ramsey dumped her slop pail on the grass, ten feet east of the house, and on more than just a few occasions, while waiting for the mail, a man would go around the house to "see a man about a horse" and slip and fall on the accumulated grease. The only way to identify a slop pail dump is the longer grass that grows from its constantly enriched situation.

The pulpwood stick slipped from Shadrack's hands, taking a fair amount of the skin with it. Shadrack didn't swear. He was too hot and sweaty and fly-bitten to swear. He was beyond swearing. He was speechless. He was fourteen and his mind was on more interesting things. If he'd been in a state to speak his mind, he'd have yelled "That American girl at the Cabbage Island Salmon Club is the prettiest thing on Earth! I hate this jeezless job," and "There's gotta be a better way to make a livin' than this."

"Hurt yer hand?" asked John Kaston. John Kaston was but a few feet away, trimming the limbs from a fir he'd just felled.

Shad analyzed the scratch amidst the dirt and pitch on his palm. "Just a scratch," he thought.

"I cut it damn near off!" he said. "I'd better go home! See ya later!"

That was how Shadrack Nash quit his first job.

John Kaston shook his head in dismay.

"The lazy bugger only lasted three days," muttered John to his axe.

*

Dryfly Ramsey sat in the shade behind the house, playing his guitar and singing Hank Snow's "Sentimental." It was a pretty song. It had nice chords in it. Dryfly liked it.

Dryfly felt somewhat embarrassed when Shadrack rounded the corner. Although Dryfly had played and sung a thousand times to the accompaniment of Shad and his banjo, he still didn't want Shad to think he played alone. Dryfly was shy. He stopped immediately.

"How's she goin' today?" asked Dryfly.

"The very best," greeted Shad.

"Not workin' today?"

"Naw. Quit. Got ugly."

"Yeah?"

"Told old John Kaston to shove his spud up his arse!"

"Ya didn't, did ya? Wha'?"

"Got any makin's? I'm dyin' for a smoke. Never had a cigarette all day."

"Yeah. Awful dry though," said Dryfly, handing Shadrack the package of Vogue tobacco and papers they referred to as "makin's."

"See that little lady at the club?" asked Shad.

"Hasn't everybody?"

"Let's go down."

"Now?"

"Why not?"

"Liable to get shot."

"What for? We never did nothin'."

"You didn't, maybe, but I did."

"What ya do?"

"Stole a blueberry pie."

"Where from, the kitchen?"

"Off the window sill."

"Was it good?"

"The very best."

"Ya git caught?"

"No, but ya never know who might've seen a lad. They'll blame me anyway. They always do."

"That's because it's you that always does it."

"You do it, too."

Shad shrugged and grinned. "There might be another one today," he said. "Let's go down."

"You ain't scared of gittin' caught?"

"Naw. What're they gonna do, put us in jail for stealin' a blueberry pie?"

Dryfly sighed. "Guess it won't hurt to go down," he said, leaning his guitar against the house. He rose from the grass, leaving a bum print where he had been sitting.

The two boys crossed the tracks and Stan Tuney's field. They came to Tuney's brook and took the shaded path that followed the brook to the river. The large spruce and elms that grew beside the brook sighed in the dry summer wind.

Just before they got to the river, they crossed the brook on a footbridge Stan built and went up the hill to where the six log cabins that made up the Cabbage Island Salmon Club sat. Like Sam Little's lodge, the Cabbage Island Salmon Club camps sat in a grove of gigantic pines. From the front of each camp, one had a view of a mile of river in either direction.

In the shade, outside the dining camp, sat Bert Todder, Dan Brennen and Stan Tuney. They were waiting for the Club owners to finish lunch. The guides might have as much as three hours before they would be obliged to go back into the glaring sun of the river. The guides all were thankful that the Americans took a long time to eat their lunch. Lindon Tucker still hadn't returned with Bill Wallace. Bert Todder, Dan Brennen and Stan Tuney all were thankful that they weren't guiding the "fish hog," the name they called Bill Wallace.

Lillian Wallace sat in a snug bathing suit, on the lounge veranda, reading *Gone with the Wind*. High up in a pine tree, a red squirrel chattered. The good-time voices of the Americans came in bursts of shouts and laughter from the dining camp. A jeep, a Ford station wagon and a Cadillac sat in the driveway.

When they neared the kitchen, Dryfly was delighted to see another blueberry pie on the window sill.

The boys, hidden behind a nearby tree, eyed the pie.

"Looks kinda suspicious to me," said Shad.

"Why's that?"

"Well, if you had a pie stolen from you yesterday, would you put another one out in the very same place today?"

"No, I wouldn't, but there's a pie there. Same kinda pie, too, by the looks of it. Blueberry."

"It's blueberry, all right, and maybe a little poison mixed in with it."

"They wouldn't poison a man, would they?"

"Damn right they would."

"So we just leave it there?"

"Damn right. I ain't eatin' no poisoned pie. I'm gonna go up and striker up a say with that little darlin'. You wait here."

"Why can't I go, too?"

"She can't be with the both of us, kin she?!"

"Why not?"

"Damn, you're stupid! I wanna maybe pass the hand. Can't do that with you watchin' us, can I?"

"Well, don't be all day, then."

"I won't be no time. Jist gonna feel things out."

"Okay, I'll wait."

Shad walked from behind the tree and rounded the camp to where Lillian Wallace sat reading. He was unsure of what his approach should be, but he feared he'd mess it up if he got too near her. He moved to within ten feet of where she sat, and with hands in his pocket and shoulders back, he pretended to be eyeing the river for something or other. From the corner of his eye, he could see her watching him. He knew he would have to acknowledge her sooner or later, but was hoping she would make the first move.

Luck was with him.

"Is something wrong?" asked Lillian.

"Naw, jist lookin'. Nice day, eh?"

"Yes, it is." Lillian had the strong, confident, arrogant voice of an American. Shad was thrilled with the sound of it.

"You from around here?" asked Shad.

"No," smiled Lillian, "I'm from Massachusetts."

"Heard of it. Big place?"

"Yes, it's quite big. Where do you live?"

"See that house down there on the bend, the one with the blue bottom and the pink top?"

"Yes."

"That's where I live. It's got an indoor toilet."

"Really?"

"Yep. Only one around here."

"Well! How wonderful."

"You stayin' here long?"

"We can only stay a week, I'm afraid."

"Doin' any fishin'?"

"No. I'm not a fisherwoman, I'm afraid. I'm leaving the fish for my father."

"Is yer father gettin' any?"

"Not yet."

"Must be usin' the wrong fly."

"Perhaps you could point him out something more productive."

"Is he around?"

"He's still out, but he should be back any minute."

"Like to meet 'im. Hear he's a nice lad. Got a big salmon this morning on a fly he might be wantin' to know about."

"Really? You caught a salmon this morning?"

"Oh yeah, I kin ketch 'em any time at all."

"Well! You should, indeed, talk to my father. He's not very productive when it comes to salmon, I'm afraid."

"Usin' the wrong fly. Gonna be here tonight?"

"I imagine so."

"I'll come up."

"Well . . . all right. He likes to fish in the evening, but he'll be back about dusk."

"Good. That a Gene Autry book you reading?"

"No, it's called *Gone with the Wind*. Have you heard of it?"

"No, read a lotta Gene Autry, though. Any good?"

"It's not bad. Not as good as Gene Autry, perhaps, but it's not bad." Lillian smiled so beautifully that it quickened Shad's heart.

"Well, I gotta go. I'll come up later and talk to yer father."

"Good. I'm sure he'll be delighted."

"Yeah, well okay then, see ya later."

"Bye."

Shad went around the camp to where Dryfly was waiting behind the tree. The first thing he noticed was Dryfly petting Helen MacDonald's dog. The second thing he noticed was that the blueberry pie was gone from the kitchen window.

"What happened to the pie?" asked Shad.

"Fed it to the dog. Hope it don't hurt 'im," said Dryfly.

*

That night when Shadrack went to the Cabbage Island Salmon Club, he did not take Dryfly with him. He would meet Dryfly later. Shad had no intentions of going to work in the morning and that meant that he and Dryfly could play on the river for as late as they wanted. Shadrack and Dryfly's favourite pastime was playing on the river at night. Dryfly would be somewhere on the river (he always was), and all Shad would have to do was whistle and wait for an answer. Dryfly would eventually answer and they would swim or just canoe about until the wee hours of the morning.

"Good evening, my boy! Come in! Have some lemonade. You're just the man I've been wanting to see. I hear you have a fly to show me."

Shad didn't have a fly to show Bill Wallace, but he had prepared himself.

"Yeah, but I kin only tell you of it," said Shad. "I lost it in a big salmon earlier this evening."

"Really! Christ, I've been whipping the rivah all day and never had as much as a rise."

Shad sat on the sofa beside Bill Wallace. Lillian sat at the table eyeing her father and the strange boy with the greased red hair. The boy had cleaned up since the afternoon and had changed his awful clothes for a plaid shirt with the collar turned up, blue jeans and sneakers. Lillian saw in Shadrack's icy blue eyes a certain zest for life . . . and naughtiness perhaps. She thought she kind of liked him.

"It's what you call a Green-arsed Hornet," said Shad. "Jist looks like a hornet, 'cept it's got a green arse 'stead o' yellow."

"Well, I'll have Bert tie me up a few. A Green-assed Hornet, huh?"

"Yep. Best fly on the river!"

"Lillian, I don't know if you've heard, but young Shadrack here is somewhat familiar with the Dungarvon Whooper."

"Really!"

Shadrack leaned back on the sofa, put his arm on the back, crossed his legs and made ready for whatever lies he might have to conjure up. He wished he had brought Dryfly, after all. Dryfly was good at lying and stuff.

"Lindon Tucker told me about it this morning," continued Bill Wallace. "Young Shadrack here is quite a hero in these parts."

"Tell me about you being a hero, Shadrack," said Lillian in the same way Shadrack reckoned she would talk to a child. Shadrack was losing confidence. These people were very different from the people he was used to. He couldn't read their faces. He couldn't decide whether they were making fun of him or not.

"What did Lindon tell them?" was the question on Shadrack's mind. He tried to remember all the stories. Shad decided he would go into the story in a roundabout way. That way, he'd have time to remember things.

"Well," breathed Shad, "this thing was screamin' in the woods, see, and . . ."

"What did the whooper sound like, Shad?' asked Lillian.

"Well, sorta like a . . . a . . . a train whistle, a panther hollerin' . . . and the . . . the devil screamin', all in one . . . only louder. Everyone was scared to death of it. So one night when the moon was full and the thing was makin' more noise than usual, me and Dryfly thought we'd better be doin' somethin' about it. So, by God, I grabbed the old .303, and, and, and Dad's flashlight and struck 'er for the woods."

Both Lillian and Bill were smiling friendly smiles. Shad thought that they might be swallowing his yarn and it gave him a bit more confidence.

"So, anyway, we didn't get no more than a mile or two in the woods when we smelt this awful smell. 'Pon me soul, it just smelt like . . . like Shirley Ramsey's arse and, and I had to swing and throw up right then and there. And, and, and then this awfullest scream struck 'er up and Dryfly turned as white as a ghost. I said, 'By God, Dryfly, we're done for.'"

"So, what did you do?" asked Lillian.

"Well, I said the only way we'll be able to git rid of it is to go down to the brook where the thing seemed to be, so we went down. Well, sir, you never heard anything like it in all your life!"

Lillian and Bill exchanged glances.

"Anyway," continued Shad, "I saw this big black thing down through the woods and I said to Dryfly, I said, I said Dryfly, I think I see it. Dryfly never said aye, yes or no. I didn't know what it was, but I could tell that it had horns like a cow and was about the size of a, of a bull elephant."

"Dryfly said ya'd better shoot the sonuvawhore before it sees us, or we're as good as dead. So I pulled up the old .303 and let 'er drift. Well, anyway, the noise stopped right up and that thing swung and took a look at us, I could see its eyes shinin' in the flashlight beam and, and, and they were about as big around as that ashtray. I thought we were dead men but it didn't do a thing, just swung and trotted off down through the woods. I wanted to go after it, but Dryfly said, he said, he said, we'd better not. We might get lost, so we swung and come home. We never heard it after, but you could smell it for three days."

"Did anybody else ever see it?" asked Bill.

"Not that I know of," said Shad.

"Did anybody else ever go back to look for it?"

"I don't think so. Not that I know of, anyway."

"Do you think it was a ghost?" asked Lillian.

"I dunno, maybe."

"Or, maybe Satan?"

"I don't know. Could've been."

"Did you go back after to look for its tracks or anything?" said Bill.

"No, no, I never went back."

Shadrack was beginning to feel uncomfortable with all the smiling questions. "They're makin' fun o' me," he thought. "They think I'm lyin'. Course lyin's what I'm doin', so I might as well stick with it."

Bill Wallace got up from the sofa and went to the bar, poured himself a double scotch and tossed it back, grunted the hot liquid along to his stomach, then poured himself another. He was moving away from the kids. He was not interested in the Dungarvon Whopper, as he called it. The Dungarvon Whooper was Lillian's thing. Bill Wallace commenced to think about salmon pools and a place of his very own, private, away from this club of cabbage heads.

Between the chair where Lillian sat and the sofa where Shadrack sat, it commenced to rain electricity.

Shadrack was unprepared. He wanted to get outside with Lillian so that he might get a chance to pass the hand.

Lillian, on the other hand, experienced a feeling of bewilderment as she eyed the thin, red-haired boy. "He's lying about the whooper," she thought. "He's a liar, just like every other boy. Except . . . he's not the same. I'd hate to see this one in an Elvis Presley haircut."

"Ever hear of Elvis Presley?" she asked.

"Yeah," said Shad, thankful for the fact the topic had changed. "I heard 'im on the radio."

"Have you ever seen him?"

"No."

"I have a picture of him in the bedroom. I'll get it."

Lillian went off to get the centerfold from the *Teen* magazine she'd brought from home. Shad removed his wallet from his hip pocket and slid it between the cushions of the sofa. "An excuse to come back, in case I don't get invited," he thought.

Bill Wallace stood at the window, eyeing the river. "I should fish for an hour before dark," he thought, "but I can't leave Lillian alone with this hick . . . or would it matter? Lillian's not about to get involved with the likes of him . . . she's only fourteen . . . I could talk with Lindon . . ." Bill Wallace was still thinking about his very own salmon pool.

Lillian returned with the picture. She placed it on the coffee table in front of Shadrack.

"That's Elvis," she said.

Shad looked at the greased black hair, the black leather jacket with the turned up collar, the tight black pants and the jet boots. Shad looked at the smooth tanned skin with not a freckle on it, the sideburns and the slightly curled lip. "So, this is Elvis," he thought. "He's a good lookin' lad, all right."

Shad had heard that Elvis had his hair greased back, and had tried the grease himself, but Shad hadn't known that Elvis' hair was so much longer . . . and the sideburns . . .

"The girls are wild about him," said Lillian. "Don't you think he's wonderful?"

"For a girl to look at, maybe," said Shad, and to himself, thought, "I'll have to let my hair grow."

A knock came at the door. It was Lindon Tucker. Lillian let him in.

"You wanna fish this evenin'?" Lindon asked Bill.

"By God, Lindon old buddy, I'm glad you're still about. Do you have a good fishing rod, Lindon?"

"Well, yeah, I got an old one that's seen better days, as the feller says. Seen better days, an old one, yeah."

"Well, I have this Shakespeare I'd like for you to try."

"Sure, sure, the very best. Love to try it. Nice one, nice one, nice one ain't it?"

"Let's go fishin'," said Bill, putting his arm on Lindon's shoulder.

As the two men were leaving the camp, Bill Wallace was saying, "I like you, Lindon! I'd like for you to come down to Stockbridge and visit us sometime! Would you like to have a rod like that, Lindon?"

"Sure, sure, sure, yeah, love to, yeah, nice one, ain't it?"

Bill Wallace stopped at the door, looked at Lillian, gave a quick, dark glance at Shadrack and said, "I'll only be gone for an hour or so, Lillian."

Lillian Wallace knew that the quick, dark glance meant that Shadrack Nash had better not be there when Bill Wallace returned.

Although Shadrack was quite pleased with the situation, he was also somewhat confused. He'd never been alone with a pretty girl before.

Lillian Wallace was tall for her age and was physically well advanced in the transition from girl to woman. She had short blond hair, big blue eyes and an easy smile that revealed perfect white teeth. Earlier, while reading on the veranda, the mosquitoes had found her and she had sprayed her body with repellent. Shad was very fond of the repellent's perfumey smell. Shadrack found himself lost for words.

"You go to school?" asked Shad.

"Yes. I'll be starting high school this September."

"Me, too," lied Shad. Shad quit school when he was twelve.

"How many kids in your class?" asked Lillian.

To Shad, a school was the one room building called the

Brennen Siding School — a blackboard, a woodstove, desks, a bucket in the corner for water and not much more. Shad had never stepped foot in the high school in Blackville. Shad didn't know what a class was.

Resorting to his knowledge of the exterior of Blackville School, he said, "Ninety-two."

"Wow! That's a big class!" said Lillian.

"Blackville's a big place," said Shadrack.

*

And so the conversation between Shadrack Nash and Lillian Wallace continued. Shadrack grew more relaxed as he became more familiar with his luxurious surroundings, with Lillian's accent, tone of voice and smile, but part of him still wanted to get closer. A hug? A kiss? Pass the hand? Shadrack didn't know what to do first.

For ten minutes, Shad sat on the sofa and she in the chair. Then, Lillian moved to the sofa, but sat at the other end.

For another ten minutes, Shad debated whether or not he should move closer to her; then he moved an inch.

He waited ten more minutes for her to make the next move. Finally, she crossed her legs, and maybe (he wasn't sure) moved slightly toward him. He couldn't say whether it was an intentional aggression or not.

She offered him a beer.

"No thanks," he said, "I'm trying to quit."

"You got a girlfriend?" she asked.

"Yeah," he lied, "two or three."

Lillian moved back to her chair.

Ten minutes later, Lillian moved back to the sofa. They both knew they were running out of time. There was a couple of moments when you could hear a pin drop. Shadrack's heart quickened and he made the giant plunge; an unpremeditated, graceful, three-inch glide toward her.

"There's no turning back now," he thought.

Lillian had just had a ten-minute debate with herself, too. The move back to the sofa, for her, had taken a great deal of strenuous reasoning. She had forced herself to favour optimism. At least I can say I was "with" a boy in Canada was the crux of her drive.

She turned slightly toward him.

"What occupation will you eventually pursue?" she asked.

"I don't know," answered Shadrack. "A half dozen maybe."

"I'm considering anthropology, myself. Are you familiar with the Leakeys?"

"No, but I had the measles and the mumps."

"What's your friend Dryfly like?" she asked.

"I like Dry. Didn't use to. Dry's cleaned up a lot."

"You mean he had an addiction?"

"Oh no. Dry's healthy enough. Poor, that's all. Dryfly's pretty near as smart as me and he ain't scared o' nothin'."

"Is he still in school?"

"No, quit a long time ago . . . two years, grade five."

"So, what's he planning on doing?"

"Nothin'. Play guiddar."

Lillian was going to make another move to get nearer to Shadrack, but she changed her mind. She heard Bill Wallace's footsteps on the veranda steps.

"There's Dad," she said. "You'd better go."

"Oh . . . okay."

"But . . . come back tomorrow night"

"Sure," said Shad, rising from the sofa.

"And . . . why don't you bring your friend Dryfly along?"

"Maybe," said Shad.

six

Shirley had become a byword, but Brennen Siding had many bywords, some of which were meaningless adages that would leave an outsider totally confused as to what the insider was talking about. Some of the bywords had been passed down from previous generations, so that even the present day residents of Brennen Siding didn't know why they were using them. For instance, someone might say, "He grabbed the bag o' flour and never 'cried crack' till he hit the top o' the hill." A beautiful woman was described as a "Martha Lebbons." Martha Lebbons had been dead for a hundred years, but obviously she had been very beautiful. Something expensive and new was referred to as a "cream o' tartar."

"I hear ya got a new canoe?"

"Yep."

"Is it a good one?"

"She's a cream o' tartar!"

A conversation outside Bernie Hanley's store might go:

"Would ya like a drink o' rum, Dan?"

"Sure would, Stan. I'm dryer than a corn meal fart."

"How ya like it?"

"(cough) Trip a ghost."

"How ya like that Ford ya bought?"

"She's a cream o' tartar!"

"Fast?"

"Blue streak!" It didn't matter if the car was red or yellow, if it was fast, it was a blue streak.

If anything moved slowly, one might say, "Slower than cold molasses."

After Shadrack fired the .303, the two boys held their breaths and listened to a silent forest. Then they ran a blue streak all the way to the river.

Nutbeam, on the other hand, went into his camp, removed his 30-30 from the wall and went creeping about the forest. He crept as silent as an undertaker's belch, as slow as cold molasses. Nutbeam had heard the two boys running and was very afraid. "That trumpet must've been louder than I thought. The whole country's been listening to me play." Nutbeam was not only afraid, he was also embarrassed. He vowed he'd never play the trumpet again. Like Dryfly, Nutbeam was shy about playing in front of anyone.

Living in the forest was changing Nutbeam. It was making him very timid. He may have been taking on the way of the animal, for, like an animal, the sound of the rifle shot had spooked him into an even deeper hiding, made him even more cunning, and, in a word, wild. He stopped practising his trumpet playing. He stopped boarding the train at Brennen Siding. Instead, he went to Gordon, two miles upstream. He continued to stand in the shadows listening to the radio, but he stopped listening to Lindon Tucker's. Instead, he crossed the footbridge, always on the darkest nights, to stand outside of Shirley Ramsey's house. The Ramseys always played the radio at a much greater volume than Lindon Tucker, and with Nutbeam's acute hearing, he could hear Freddy McKenna sing from thirty yards away.

On some nights, Nutbeam got a very much appreciated bonus. Those were the nights when Dryfly stepped onto the porch with his guitar. Dryfly still had a lot to learn on the guitar, but to Nutbeam, Dryfly was, "The very best! Great! A-1! Couldn't be better! Pretty near as good as Doc Williams! He'll be famous someday!"

*

Doc Williams did not come from Brennen Siding. Kid Baker did not live twelve miles up the Gordon Road. Hank Snow did not include Brennen Siding in his song "I've Been Everywhere." Elvis Presley did not stand on the Brennen Siding footbridge on moonlit nights, singing "Love Me Tender" to Neenie or Naggy Ramsey.

Nobody from Brennen Siding could claim fame or fortune. A store clerk, scaler or a timekeeper was the ultimate goal. Old men and women never talked about what they'd achieved, but instead talked about what they "could have" achieved.

"I could've been a doctor," Stan Tuney said at the store one night, then added, "if I had've gone to school."

John Kaston was "this far" from becoming a preacher. "But Dad needed me to work in the woods with him." "This far" was a very, very long way.

"I could've been a great musician," said Bob Nash. "All I needed was the proper training, practice and something to work with."

It was that way all over the Miramichi area, tributaries included.

David Thornton from Millerton would have been rich if the "nine" (the last number on his sweepstake ticket), had've been a "four."

"That lad from Doaktown . . . what's his name?"

"John Betts?"

"No, not John. That other lad there. You know the lad . . . he would have been the Premier had he won the election?"

"Oh yeah, that lad."

And, of course, Yvon Durelle. Yvon Durelle was never thought of in Brennen Siding as the boxer who was the light heavyweight champion of the British Empire, covering Britain, Canada, Australia, a smidgeon of real estate in South America, and a third, or more, of Africa. Yvon Durelle was that lad from Baie Ste. Anne who would've been the champion of the world, had he beaten Archie Moore.

At the post office one morning, Bert Todder said, "Dryfly, me boy, you could be a singin' star some day, if ya had half a chance."

Dryfly wondered which half of which chance Bert referred to, and if Bert knew. "The Miramichi would've been a great center, only for the Miramichi Fire of 1825."

*

When Shad left the Wallaces' cabin, he met with the warmth of a July evening. He took the path that led from the Cabbage Island Salmon Club to Judge Martin's camp. Judge Martin rarely came to his cabin, and because it was a private and peaceful place, endowed with a terrific view of the river, Shad often went there to think and relax.

Shadrack Nash sat on Judge Martin's veranda to watch the night settle in on what he thought was the prettiest place in the whole world.

Shad couldn't decide whether he felt happy or sad. That he felt different was all he knew.

"God, she's a pretty thing!" he thought. "Got lotsa money, too. Marry that one and a man would never have to cut pulp for a livin', that's for sure."

Shad had a vision of a big white house in the city, a new car in the yard and maybe a pickup truck for him to drive whenever Lillian needed the car to go to work. Shad never thought of himself as ever going to work. "But Lillian'll work," he thought. "She'll be a clerk or a teacher and I'll just look after things. Lillian'll come home from work, all pretty and dressed to kill, and I'll be settin' right back in me big chair, with me feet up, smokin' me pipe, waitin' to tell 'er that I made a hundred dollars sellin' somethin'. I'll be a salesman and not have to work. I'll live in a big city like New York or Bangor . . . or even Wheelin', West Virginia, and play the banjo with Bill Monroe."

"All I have to do is git Lillian to fall in love with me. To do that, I'll have to git her to" — he didn't know — "kiss me? One kiss . . . sure would be a good start. A woman would have to love ya, if ya kissed her . . . wouldn' she?"

It wasn't long before Venus showed itself in the sky, said, "Okay gang, the sky's clear! You can come out now." Pop-pop-pop, pop, pop, pop-pop, the stars commenced to shine.

Thump, came a noise from downstream. Shad recognized it as a pole making contact with the side of a canoe.

"Moooooo!" went Shad.

"Moooooo!" answered Dryfly, from down in front of Sam Little's lodge.

Shad knew that Dryfly was in the process of borrowing Sam Little's canoe for the night. "Borrowin' without askin'," thought Shad. "What's the difference between that and stealin'?" He could hear the plunk, plunk, plunk of the pole as Dryfly pushed his way through the Dungarvon current until he hauled up in front with a scraping sound against the rocks.

"Shad?"

"Yeah, up here."

Dryfly could not see Shad in the shadow of the veranda. He tossed the anchor onto the shore and headed toward the camp.

"How'd ya make out with Lillian?"

"The very best. Kissed her twice. Once in front of the fireplace and once on the veranda."

"On the lips?"

"Course!"

Dryfly sat beside Shad, his breath laboring from his climb up the embankment to the camp.

"Lillian showed me a picture of Elvis Presley," said Shad. "We'll have to let our hair grow more and he's got a little curl to his lip . . . like this."

"Like what?"

"Light a match."

A match was struck.

"Like this."

"Huh! How's this?"

"A little more . . . well . . ." Shad realized that Dryfly could never look like Elvis. Dry had a long head, a big nose, a peaked chin and a very thin upper lip. Dryfly's hair was brown and fine and combed over from a part on the left side. "He's homelier than Shirley Ramsey," thought Shad and chuckled to himself. "The lip looks great," lied Shad, "but you'll have to start combin' your hair back and let your sideburns grow."

"You really kiss Lillian?"

"I was alone with her for four hours! What do you think?"

"You in love with her?"

"I think so."

Dryfly was very disappointed. He, too, was in love with Lillian, although he hadn't spoken to her.

"What do you want to do?" asked Shad.

"I dunno. Go home and go to bed, maybe."

"What d'ya want to go to bed for? It's summer."

"I dunno. Tired, maybe."

"I thought we might pole up to Gordon."

"What for?"

"Somethin' to do. Ya don't git many warm nights like this around here," said Shad.

"You gonna see her tomorrow night?"

"Pretty likely. Me and Lilly would kinda like to git married."

"Kinda young, ain't ya?"

"Not right away. Couldn't now, if we wanted to."

"Why?"

"Lillian's a Cath'lic and I'm a Baptist."

"You could turn with her."

"Lillian said she'd turn with me if I went to church on Sunday," Shad sighed. "But old Bill's gonna be hard to deal with. Would've been easy, if it hadda been you, Dry. I'm the man she loves and we're gonna have to do the best we kin."

Shad hadn't spoken a single word of truth, but what he was saying added a nice wing to his fantasy. Marrying Lillian and moving off to live the life of the rich was the "best" thing that could happen, but simply knowing and being in love with this rich girl was an important attention-getter in itself. Even if they never married, or saw each other again, the intimate contact with her would be good for his reputation.

"Poor Shadrack," people would say, "his poor heart's been broken. He loved that American girl! Never seen him with another woman after. His heart will always be in the States."

"Yes, I know, and him so brave too. Shadrack Nash, the one that shot the Todder Brook Whooper! He would've been a rich man today, if her mean old father, the Fish Hog, had've thought of the poor girl's happiness!"

"Got any more of the dry tobacco left, Dry?"

"Got a new pack. Made fifty cents today pickin' blueberries."
Dryfly handed Shad the tobacco.

"The blueberries ripe yet, Dry?"

"Not quite. They're still red because they're green."

Dryfly really didn't want to spend this warm summer's
night at home in bed. He wasn't really tired. Dryfly was envious, jealous and hurt. "I didn't even get a crack at her," he
thought.

"Lillian wants you and me to go visit her tomorrow night.
Wants you to take yer guiddar. I told 'er you was a good
singer."

"I'll take the guiddar, but I ain't singin'."

"Let's go to Gordon. I'll pole."

"Okay. Why not?"

It took Shad forty-five minutes to pole the canoe to
Gordon. He didn't mind the work. Being on the most beautiful river in the world was all the reward he needed.

Shadrack pushed the canoe ashore; they both jumped out
and pulled it up on the rocky beach.

"So, what're we gonna do now?" asked Dryfly.

"Let's have a smoke," said Shadrack.

Dry started walking back and forth and in circles.

"What're ya lookin' for?" asked Shad.

"A soft rock to set on," said Dry.

"Ya fool!" laughed Shad.

The boys sat on a rock and rolled cigarettes, lit up and eyed
their surroundings. There was the starlit sky overhead, the barns
and houses of Gordon on the hills on both sides of the river
and, here and there, a sport camp. Randall Brook murmured
as it entered the river across from where they sat. They watched
the lights in the houses going out and knew it was bedtime in
Gordon. Everything, other than the murmuring brook, was
very quiet.

The boys sat and smoked until the last light was out and
all fourteen houses and eight sport camps were in darkness.

"The time's about right," said Shad.

"Yep."

"Okay, let's give 'er hell."

"Bark, bark, bark! Yip, yip, yip! Yelp, yelp, yelp!" went the two boys as loud as they could, so that their voices echoed off the hills.

Somebody's dog started barking; then, somebody else's; then another and another until every dog in Gordon — and there were a good many of them — started barking.

A light came on, then another and another. Windows were lifted, doors were opened, dogs were cussed and called.

When the inhabitants of Gordon had calmed their dogs into silence, they switched their lights off and went back to bed.

"We'll give 'er a while," said Shad.

"Here, have another smoke."

"Thanks."

"Know any jokes?"

"Who killed the Dead Sea?"

"I dunno. Who?"

"Same lad painted Red China."

"Lillian tell ya that?"

"No, Dad."

"I like it. Funny."

"Know what I'm gonna be when I grow up?"

"What?"

"Salesman for potato bugs."

Dryfly chuckled. He liked that joke too. "I'll have to re-member that one," he thought.

"Ready?" asked Shad.

"Ready."

"Bark, bark, bark! Yip, yip, yip! Yelp, yelp, yelp!"

Again their voices echoed off the hillsides and started the dogs barking. It took a little longer this time, but again lights came on, windows were lifted, doors were opened and dogs were cussed and called.

"Is that a star up there?" asked Shad, pointing to the Big Dipper.

"I don't know, I'm a stranger around here."

"Ha, ha, ha, ha, ha, ha, ha, ha! You just think o' that?"

"Yep. Just sorta popped into me head. Good one, eh?"

"Yep. It's a good one. Have to remember it."

"They've all gone to bed again."

"Yeah. Give it a few more minutes."

"No hurry. Here, have another smoke."

"Know what I heard, Dry?"

"No, what?"

"Heard yer brother Palidin's a fruit."

"Where'd you hear that?"

"Everybody's sayin' it."

"He might be. He sure does act fruity. Reads all the time."

"Acts like a woman, too."

"He'll get his head kicked in one o' these days."

"I'll kick his head in, if he ever touches me!"

"He won't touch ya. He's my brother."

"Bark, bark, bark! Yip, yip, yip! Yelp, yelp, yelp!"

Lift, lift, lift. Slam, slam, slam. "Git in here you, old sonuvawhore!"

"Here Skippy, Skippy, Skippy!"

"Here Pal, Pal, Pal!"

"Here Spot, Spot, Spot!"

Lights out. Back to bed.

Shad and Dry smoked and played this game for an hour or so, then headed back to Brennen Siding. They didn't paddle but drifted on the current, watching the stars. When they drifted past Helen MacDonald's farm, they did not know that Helen's dog, Rex, was relieving himself for the third time on the kitchen floor. The blueberry pie with the Ex-Lax was taking its effect. Rex was shitting a blue streak.

seven

Palidin Ramsey was different.

He was not just different from Dryfly, but was unlike anybody else in Brennen Siding. If you searched the whole Miramichi area, you would not find a single person like him. Being effeminate was not the only unusual trait that set him aside from the other boys. He was gentle, kind, imaginative and ambitious. Perhaps the greatest difference, though, was his curiosity. He was not superstitious, for he did not fear what he did not understand; he was too curious for that. For instance, he had checked out the Todder Brook Whooper long before Shadrack and Dryfly and had kept it as his very own secret. His trek had been alone at night. He had watched the lonely man trying to play his trumpet and had left him to live his life as he chose. He found the fear, the superstition of Brennen Siding, the stories of Shadrack and Dryfly amusing. The Todder Brook Whooper was a form of entertainment for them all and he chose not to take it away from them.

Palidin went as far in school as Hilda Porter could take him, which was grade eight. To go to high school, he would have had to move to Blackville, to live there and pay room and board, to dress better. Of course, such extravagances were beyond Shirley Ramsey's pecuniary means. So Palidin borrowed what books he could — Hilda Porter was his greatest supplier — and read. John Kaston had felt certain that he had converted Palidin to the Baptist fold when he was approached for the Bible. Palidin read the Bible and returned it, but his face was never seen in the little church.

"Thank you, John. It was interesting," said Palidin and left before John had a chance to preach.

Palidin had taken great pains and much time in the read-

ing of both the New and the Old Testaments. It had been difficult for him, but the crux of his drive had been simple — "At
least it's reading matter." He'd found the Gospel According to
St. Matthew the most interesting of all and read it twice. This
accounted for another difference in Palidin: he was, unlike the
others, aware of the prince of devils and the lord of flies,
Beelzebub.

"You don't have to be Beelzebub, or wicked either, to control flies," he told himself.

Palidin saw nothing wrong or unusual in running naked
through the forest, sitting naked in swamps eyeing birds and
insects. He had a calmness about him, so that when he sat in
the fly-infested swamps of Dungarvon, the blackflies and mosquitoes, as well as the other animals, seemed to accept him
with a casual indifference. He could walk through fields of
goldenrod where thousands of busy bees cluttered the blos-
soms, theorizing, "Take your clothes off and stay calm and
nothing animal will bother you." He liked the bees and the
bees seemed to like him. He never once got stung. "If you fear
them and feel hostile toward them," he thought, "they'll feel
it and not like you. It's goodness, not evil, that helps you
through the field."

Palidin's favourite toy was a dime-sized magnet. "It's like
holding a little planet," he reasoned. He played with it for
hours, picking up needles and nails; spinning it, pondering it,
toying with theories of energy, circles and echoes. He had a
theory that if you shouted at a star, your voice would take
thousands of years to return, but would, eventually, do so.

West of everybody's property line, deep in the forest, was a
valley that everyone in Brennen Siding referred to as "The Big
Hollow." Because the property was government-owned, Shirley
Ramsey often took her family there on picnics. "Nobody'll
bother us back there," she always said. Of course, when Bonzie
got lost just back of the barren beyond The Big Hollow, the
picnics stopped. Nobody in the Ramsey family had the heart to
go back there again. Nobody, except for Palidin.

Palidin liked the barren and went there frequently. The barren was like a lake you could walk on. It was swampy so that

the moss and water would take you to the ankles with every step, but visually it was like a prairie that stretched for several miles, its wild rice and reeds blowing in the wind. There was a huge boulder in the center of the barren where he often sat to think. On that rock, alone, naked, he would tan his body and wait for echoes to return. He fantasized that perhaps a wise old prophet had shouted something from the rock when the barren was still a lake, and that one day the prophet's echo would return. Palidin did not want to miss the prophecy.

It took him a great deal of time and effort, but with a stone and chisel, he hammered out the inscription:

Probe the atom,
  Ponder the echoes of the wise.
    There lie the secrets of the universe.

Palidin Ramsey had but one friend to play with — George Hanley. George was also growing up to be different. When he was a little boy, his hands, feet and ears had seemed too big for his body, but as he grew, everything seemed to take on the proper dimensions. He was developing into a very tall and handsome man and that, in itself, was one difference. Brennen Siding men were rarely good looking. George's teeth were even and white, and that, too, made him different. He was also a good friend of Palidin Ramsey and was more than just a little infatuated with him. They travelled together constantly; their friendship was faithful and true. None of the other boys in Brennen Siding wanted to be seen with Palidin Ramsey.

When he was younger, George spent much of his time playing with girls. He felt girls were more honest and interesting. Girls didn't ask him to be a thief for the sake of buying friendship. He palled around with Max Kaston for a few years, but Max was becoming more and more introverted. Max was scared of everything, would not leave the house at night — had been that way ever since he quit school, and John, fearing Max would never become a preacher, tried to break his spirit by working him long and hard in the woods.

But then, George became drawn by the magnetism, by the

eyes of Palidin Ramsey. Palidin triggered his curiosity, was easy to talk to, told him things about earth, man and the universe — interesting things that whirled his mind to greater heights.

He told himself, "I'll be a friend to Palidin, no matter what anyone thinks!"

*

Lindon Tucker sat by the kitchen table. The kerosene lamp was turned up a little higher than usual. Lindon Tucker was figuring on a used envelope with an inch long pencil. "No sense wastin' good paper," thought Lindon. "No, no," thought Lindon, "and I kin light the fire, as the feller says, yes sir, yes sir, yes sir, I kin light the fire with it in the mornin' and nobody'll ever know what the figures are about. No, no, no, nobody, not a soul, no one will ever know." Lindon was working on the extremely confidential state of his economy.

"Seven dollars a day for guidin'," he figured. "I'll be on the job for seven days . . . seven days, yeah. Seven days on the job, yeah, oh yeah, yeah, yeah. Me pay cheque should be . . . $7+7=14$, $14+7=21$, $21+7=28$, $28+7=35$, $35+7=42$, $42+7=49$. Forty-nine dollars, yeah, yeah, forty-nine dollars, yeah. If I git a five dollar tip . . . $49+5=54$. I'll have fifty-four big ones, oh yeah, yeah, yeah."

Lindon opened his chequebook and thought of his mother. She had passed away the previous spring and Lindon had been very upset. "It cost me nearly" — he looked at the cheque-book — "Damn! Twelve hundred dollars to bury her! Twelve hundred dollars for puttin' somebody in the ground!"

The chequebook read $3962.17. "Add the $49.00 for guidin' and I'll have" — he figured — "$4011.17."

"Damn!" he swore. "When Mom was alive, we had over five thousand dollars!" Clara's senior citizen's cheque once a month and Lindon's penny pinching over a period of fifteen years were the reasons for the five thousand dollars, but Clara's death . . . "Damn! Twelve hundred dollars for puttin' somebody in the ground is robbery, robbery, yeah, robbery!"

To Lindon, five thousand dollars was the magical figure.

Lindon Tucker thought about his riverfront property. "I could sell him all the way to the bottom of the hill. That's about five hundred feet. Me lot's about ninety rods long. Ninety rods by five hundred feet. Wonder what it's worth?"

"If it had good hay on it, it'd be worth a lot more," he thought. "If it had lumber on it, it'd be worth more agin, but thar ain't nothin' on it. No ain't nothin' on it, no, no, no, nothin' on it, no."

"Damn!" he swore at the table, the envelope and his pencil. "I should've had it plowed and seeded! Land ain't worth nothin' if there's no hay on it!"

"Bill Wallace is Amurican . . . he might have a figure in mind," thought Lindon. Lindon eyed his chequebook and wondered if Bill Wallace would give him enough for that old shore to bring the figure $4011.17 back up to five thousand dollars.

"I'll ask him for twelve hundred and let him think he's beatin' me down to a thousand," decided Lindon.

*

Across the river and upstream, another gentleman, Bill Wallace, sat pondering figures.

"That much river frontage on the Connecticut, or the Housatonic would go for half a million. Up here in the sticks, it's not worth a penny more than fifty thousand. I'll have somebody build me a nice cabin on it . . . another fifty thousand."

Bill Wallace wondered if Lindon Tucker was capable of negotiating.

Bill Wallace sipped his scotch and envisioned the Lindon Tucker Salmon Pool. "The Bill Wallace Salmon Pool," he said to himself. "Ninety rods of private rivah frontage. The pool's got hundreds of boulders in it, a strong current, deep water, a gravel beach for landing salmon on . . . it's perfect! One of the best pools on this damn rivah . . . maybe the world. Fifty thousand dollars would be a steal . . . a tax writeoff."

*

Dryfly Ramsey had fine brown hair and a natural part in the middle of his scalp. In Brennen Siding, it was not cool to part your hair in the middle. If Dryfly Ramsey combed his hair over from a part on the left side, it would hide the natural part in the middle. When Dryfly greased and combed his hair back like Elvis, his hair went *flip-flop* and there was the part, like a zipper, streaking back the middle of his head. More grease would hold everything in place, but only until he moved. Although Dryfly didn't know it, he was confronting a problem that would always keep him "homely" and "without confidence" for a great deal of his adolescence. Dryfly knew by the shape of his head, the big nose and the peaked chin, that he could never look like Elvis Presley, but he felt the hair, at least, would help. As Dryfly labored in front of the piece of mirror that hung on the wall above the water bucket, he was very discouraged. If Dryfly had had a closet, he would have hidden in it.

"Maybe I can train it to lay back," he thought, "and I'll hold my head very still."

He turned very slowly away from the mirror.

"How's it look, Mom?"

"Looks good, dear. Don't use up all me lard."

"Well, what am I gonna use, Mom? Ya won't buy me any Brylcreem!"

"How's about the tobacco? Who buys you the tobacco?"

"No argument there," thought Dryfly. "See ya later," he said and left. As he stepped off the porch, his hair went *flip-flop*.

Palidin sat quietly in his bedroom with a book in front of him. He was reading. Palidin was looking in the men's underwear section of the T. Eaton catalogue. He heard Dryfly leave.

"I wish Dryfly would have some sense!" he thought.

Shirley was sitting by the kitchen table, thinking and smoking a cigarette.

"Maybe I should do something with meself," she thought. "The girls are all off and Palidin's the only one home. It's gettin' lonesomer all the time. I should have a man. Maybe I'll wash me hair. Maybe I'll wash all over."

"Palidin!"

No answer.

"Palidin, you go out somewhere. I wanna take a bath."

No answer.

"Palidin?"

"I'll be out in a minute, Mom!"

"NOW, Palidin! I want to take a bath!"

"Why . . . why don't you go to the river, Mom?"

"'Cause I want to take it here!"

"Okay, Mom . . . I'm comin'."

*

When Dryfly met Shadrack at the meeting place, the footbridge, he saw that Shad hadn't forgotten the empty pickle jar. Shadrack and Dryfly had plans for the pickle jar.

"Here, you carry it. You're the one's gonna be usin' it," said Shadrack, passing Dryfly the pickle jar. "Remember the plan?"

"I know, I know, I know!" said Dryfly.

They landed at the Cabbage Island Salmon Club at eight o'clock, Dryfly dressed in his best shirt (a black cowboy shirt with snap buttons), blue jeans and sneakers. Shad had on a blue plaid shirt with the collar turned up and the sleeves rolled in wide, well-ironed cuffs to just below the elbow. Shad's bright red hair was greased back and staying nicely in place. Shad's lip was already feeling tired from holding it in the unaccustomed "curled" fashion.

Lillian was sitting on the veranda in sandals, blue jeans and a red haltertop blouse. She was writing a letter, and when she saw Shad and Dry approaching, she put her pen down and closed the writing pad.

"Hi guys," she said.

"G'day. How's she goin'?"

"G'day."

"How are you boys?"

"Good."

"Good."

"It's a warm day, isn't it?"

"Hot."

"Hot."

"Would you like a soda?"

Both boys, being accustomed to calling it "pop," thought of the Cow Brand Baking Soda, used also for a seltzer for indigestion.

"No, that's all right."

"Not right now," said Dry.

"I have some nice cold soda in the fridge, if you want some," said Lillian.

"I might have a glass o' water, maybe," said Shad.

"You sure you don't want a Pepsi, Dryfly?"

"Yeah, I might have a Pepsi," said Dryfly.

Shad wondered why Lillian hadn't offered him a Pepsi.

Lillian stood and offered Dryfly her hand. "I'm Lillian Wallace," she said.

"Dryfly Ramsey."

Lillian smiled. "I'll get the Pepsi and water," she said and went inside.

"What'd ya do with the pickle bottle?" asked Shad.

"Behind me."

"Remember the plan?"

"Yep. I got 'er."

"Here you go, boys."

"Thanks."

"Thanks."

"So, what's your real name, Dryfly?"

"Driffley," said Dryfly.

Shad chuckled and Lillian smiled.

"There's something about Dryfly," thought Lillian. "Honesty perhaps."

"And you play guitar?" she asked.

"Naw, a few chords, that's all."

"And modesty," thought Lillian.

"You should hear him! He's some good," put in Shad.

"Well, I'd like to," said Lillian.

The three sat in the shade of the veranda, consuming the view and feeling the caress of the warm summer breeze. From here, they could see a man beaching a salmon over on Cabbage Island. They could hear the faint whine of the reel and see the sunlight dancing on the pressured bamboo rod.

"Doctor Saunders," said Lillian.

"Looks like a big one," said Dryfly.

"Do you fish?" asked Lillian.

"Some," said Dryfly.

"Do you catch many big ones?"

"Now and again."

"Do you guide?"

"Some."

"Never caught a salmon in his life," said Shadrack. "Ain't old enough to guide, either!"

"Am too!"

"You're not!"

"Am too! Might go guidin' this fall!"

"Play guiddar's all you do!"

Shad didn't like the way things were going. Lillian was directing too much of her conversation at Dryfly. "Lillian's my girl," he thought. "Surely she can't be interested in Dryfly!"

"There's something mysterious about Dryfly," thought Lillian.

Shad didn't like the way the conversation was going, but he had brought it back to where he wanted it as far as the plan was concerned.

"You should have yer guiddar here. Play us a song," said Shadrack, winking at Dryfly.

"Later, maybe," said Dryfly.

In all actuality, Lillian Wallace was not the prettiest girl in the world. It was just that Shadrack and Dryfly thought she was the prettiest girl in the world. They were like two dogs mooning and sniffing a bitch in heat. They saw magic in her smile, mystery in her accent, wisdom, honesty and sophistication in her eyes.

A dark cloud was creeping up the western sky.

"Looks like we might get a shower," said Dryfly.

"Not for a couple o' hours," said Shad. "The birds are still out."

"Do birds know when it's going to rain?" asked Lillian.

"Birds are like hens," said Shad. "A hen will go under a shed or somethin' when yer about to get a shower. If yer about to get a day's rain, the hen will stay outside, pay the rain no mind at all. Them birds will go and hide in an hour or so, just you watch."

Shad was feeling very wise and grown up. His father had told him about hens, but Shad wasn't sure about birds in general. It didn't matter though. If the birds stayed out, he'd say they were in for a big rain. If the birds took shelter, it was late enough in the evening so that they'd be in for the night anyway.

Shadrack stood up and walked to the veranda railing, sat on it and stared at the river. Shadrack loved the river as much as he loved Lillian Wallace. The angler had landed his salmon and was casting for another. Shad saw a salmon jump, down on the bend.

"That lad landed his fish and I just saw another one jump down on the bend, Dry. Is there a run on?"

"Someone was tellin' Mom that the Renous was full o' fish," said Dryfly.

"That's good," said Shad. "Too bad we didn't have a net."

Shad was commencing to formulate another plan. If it didn't rain all night, he and Dry might borrow a net somewhere and go drifting for salmon — a perfect excuse for being out on the river.

"Netting salmon is against the law," thought Shad, "and that makes it more fun. We'll have lots of cigarettes and whiskey . . . Dry and me will have some fun tonight!"

"Is Helen MacDonald still here?" asked Shad.

"I think she's finished for the day. She'd be down in the kitchen, if she's still here," said Lillian. "Did you want to see her?"

"Oh no, just wonderin'."

"You suppose I could use your bathroom?" asked Shad.

"Of course. Go through the living room and down the hall. It's at the end."

Shad winked at Dryfly. "I'll be right back," he said.

As Shad was going through the door, he stopped. "You didn't find a wallet here today, did ya, Lillian?"

"No."

"I think I left it here last night. It's prob'ly on the sofa."

"Well, take a look around. I haven't seen it, though. Dad might have found it."

"It don't matter. There wasn't any money in it. I'll just take a quick look."

Inside, Shad went directly to the sofa, reached between the cushions and came up with the wallet. He took the opportunity to scan the room. A carton of Lucky Strike cigarettes lay on the table. In the corner, on another table (the bar), sat bottles of rum, rye, gin, bourbon, vodka, scotch, Dubonnet, sherry and Canada Dry Ginger Ale. "All's well," thought Shad, went to the bathroom, peed, then returned to the veranda.

While Shad was inside, Lillian asked, "Shadrack tells me you're not in school. Do you have a job?"

"No place to work around here," said Dryfly. "I might go guidin' in the fall."

"What does your father do?"

"Me father's dead," said Dryfly. "Never saw 'im in me life."

"I'm sorry. Does your mother work?"

"No. Runs the post office."

"Really? There's a post office in the area?"

"At our house, yeah."

"Good, I'll have to mail a letter and some postcards tomorrow."

"I'll come over and git them for ya," said Dryfly.

"Oh, you don't have to do that."

"I don't mind. Ain't doin' nothin' anyway."

"Okay, tomorrow then."

Lillian was thinking of herself and Dryfly being alone without Shadrack. "I could say that I was with two boys, then," she thought.

Dryfly was nervous. He could not look Lillian directly in the eye. He was feeling not so much shy as guilty. He was feeling that maybe Shad's idea was not such a good one. "What if they miss it? What if we get caught?"

"Did you find your wallet?" asked Lillian as Shadrack came through the door.

"Yep," said Shad, holding up his wallet.

Shad sat on the veranda railing once again. "Why don't we go and get your guiddar?" he asked.

"Naw. Not feeling too good."

"Oh, is there something wrong?" asked Lillian.

"No, just tired, I guess. Had a late night last night."

"Maybe me and Lillian could git the guiddar for ya," recommended Shadrack.

"Maybe you don't feel like playing," said Lillian.

"Oh, I don't mind playin', I just don't feel up to goin' after it."

"Me and Lillian will go for it," said Shad.

"I would love to hear you play," said Lillian. "Would you, if we went and got it for you?"

"Yeah, but you lads will have to do the singin', I jist play, I don't sing."

"Ya do so sing!"

"I don't!"

"Ya do!"

"Don't!"

"Wanna go get it, Lillian?"

"How far is it?"

"Just a little ways. Take about ten minutes."

"Well, okay. Will you be all right here, Dryfly?"

"Yeah, I'll just rest here while yer gone."

"Okay. We'll be right back," Shad reassured Dryfly with a wink. The wink said, "It's all there, Dry, just like I said."

When Shadrack and Lillian had gone over the hill and had disappeared into the foliage of Tuney Brook, Dry rose and went into the cabin. Inside he found himself wanting to luxuriate for a while in the richness — the beautiful sofa and chairs, the mahogany tables, the fireplace. Dryfly found himself having to control his fantasies. The plan came first and he didn't want to screw it up.

Dryfly went to the table where Bill Wallace kept his liquor supply. "He must be havin' a party," thought Dryfly, "there's so much of it."

As planned, to make sure that Bill would not miss any-thing gone, Dry poured a little from each bottle until the pickle jar was full of rum, gin, bourbon, vodka, scotch, Dubonnet, sherry and Canada Dry Ginger Ale. He then went to the other table and took two packs of Lucky Strike cigarettes. "He won't miss two packs," he thought.

Carefully, so as not to be seen, Dryfly sneaked out the back door of the cabin. He scanned the surroundings. "All's clear. Everyone's fishin'."

He stashed his booty in the tall grass at the edge of the woods and went back into the camp.

The camp was cool and smelled of pine. He sat in a big upholstered chair for no other reason than to test its quality, wanting to experience for the first time in his life what it was like to sit in a comfortable chair. He sighed, "This is the life!" and tried out the sofa. Then he tried a chair at the table. He ran his hand across the smooth surface of the table, gently, feeling its coolness. He then reluctantly went back outside.

Back on the veranda, Dryfly noticed that the thunder clouds had progressed considerably in their approach. They were deep and fluffy, the horizon blue as steel and periodically swept with lightning. The silence seemed deeper too, between the grumbles of distant thunder.

"It's gonna be a heavy storm," thought Dryfly and checked to see if he was positioned in a safe place.

"In a storm, you should never set near a window," he thought. "People draw lightning, so it's good to git indoors. Stay away from bulb sockets and plug-ins. Stay away from stoves. Lightnin' is apt to come down a stove pipe."

"There's danger all around," he thought. "No escape."

When a lightning storm hovered over Brennen Siding, half the population ran to a neighbor's house. If the storm was particularly heavy, they got on their knees and prayed.

John Kaston always led the prayers, saying things like, "Dear loving Heavenly Father, smite the tempest!" "The voice, mighty in the wilderness," and "Thank thee for removing the cancer from me bowels!" John Kaston loved to preach. John Kaston was "this far" from being a preacher.

"If she's gonna hit, she'll hit," thought Dry. "No sense worrying about it."

Often when a storm approaches Brennen Siding from the northeast, depending on the preceding barometric decline, ahead of it comes the smell of sulfur, the smell of the smoke from the pulpmill in Newcastle. The storm pushes it and spreads it like a monstrous fart over the area. It spread over Brennen Siding this night and reached Dryfly's nostrils.

Dryfly knew what it was; he'd smelled it many times. "The pulpmill," he thought. "You kin always smell it before a storm. Smells like a fart."

Whenever Dryfly smelled the pulpmill on the air, it always reminded him of Shirley's description of the devil, "He's got big horns and a long tail with an arrowhead at the end of it. His eyes are yellow, like a cat's and they shine at night. He smells like . . . like . . . like shit."

"Smells like the devil," thought Dryfly. "Maybe he's comin' to get me for what I just did. The lightning could be the light from the fires of Hell, the thunder could be the sound of the big doors slammin', or the devil's growl. Maybe that's why everyone prays when there's a storm comin'."

Dryfly did not like thoughts of the devil and shrugged them off. He didn't even know if the devil existed — or God, for that matter. Thunderstorms only came at the end of hot summer days and Dryfly loved hot summer days. There was too few of them in this north land, and when they came, he felt obliged to enjoy every minute of them, thunderstorms included. Down deep inside, he liked the thunder. Liking the thunder was one of the few things he had in common with his brother Palidin.

*

When Shadrack and Lillian were crossing the bridge over Tuney Brook on their way from Shirley Ramsey's, Shadrack stopped and looked into the water.

"Sometimes ya kin see trout in here," he said.

"Really!" Lillian moved closer to Shad and peered into the water. "There's one," she pointed, "There!"

"And there's another one," said Shad, inching toward Lillian.

Shadrack eyed Lillian, "God! She's a pretty little thing," he thought.

If there was the smell of sulfur in the air, Shad was not aware of it; all he was smelling was Lillian's perfume.

"If I don't make a move tonight, I might never git the chance," thought Shad. "So, what do I do? Pass the hand? Say something mushy?"

"That's awful good smellin' perfume ya got on there," tried Shad.

"It's fly repellent."

"Still smells good."

The sound of thunder tumbled in from the northeast. The smell of sulfur settled. Lillian sniffed the air and looked at Shadrack with disgust.

"I wish I could say the same thing about you right now," she thought. She turned and walked toward the Cabbage Island Salmon Club.

Shad, carrying Dryfly's guitar, followed.

Lillian was thinking of Shirley Ramsey.

Their visit had been a brief one, just long enough for Shirley to get them the guitar. Shirley had been proud of the fact she had something to give and had shown Lillian great respect and courtesy. Lillian, however, only saw the slop pail, the broken mirror hanging over the sink, the backless chairs.

"How can people live in such a place?" she thought. "I've never seen such a place! And that's where Dryfly lives? Poor Dryfly."

*

"I've had enough fishing for one day, Lindon. Let's go back to the camp and have a drink. I'd like to discuss that property."

"Good, good, good. Gonna rain, gonna rain anyway. Might as well, might as well."

When Lindon and Bill got back to the camp, they found Lillian being entertained by Shadrack and Dryfly. Dryfly was playing guitar and Shadrack was singing, "George Hare shot a bear, shot 'im here, shot 'im there; George Hare shot a bear, shot 'im in the arse and never touched a hair."

"G'day Bill, Lindon! How's she goin', old boys?" yelled Shadrack.

"Good, good, good."

"Hi boys, Lillian."

"Shad and Dry have been singing for me, Dad," explained Lillian.

"Well, don't let me stop you. Lindon and I have some business to discuss. We'll join you latah."

The two men went inside. Bill poured them a couple of stiff scotches and sat across the table from Lindon.

"I should've had that salmon, Lindon. What d'ya think I did wrong?"

"Nuthin', nuthin', nuthin'. Held 'im too tight, maybe. Knot in yer leader. Never did a thing wrong."

"Damn!"

"We'll git 'im tomorrow. Yep! Get 'im tomorrow, we will."

"Let's drink to that," said Bill. "Bottoms up!"

Bill emptied his glass. Lindon put his glass to his lips, opened up and tossed the two ounces back, sloshed it around as if mouth washing and swallowed.

"HEM! AHEM! Trip a ghost!" he said.

"Have anothah," said Bill and replenished the glasses.

"Well, Lindon, I've decided I'd like to buy that property. Do you, or don't you want to sell?"

"Well I've been thinkin', as the feller says, as the feller says, if ya know what I mean, I've been thinkin'. Sell if the price is right."

"Well Lindon, old buddy, let's hear your price."

"Well, I know, I know, I know, I know there ain't no lumber on that old shore; I know that, I know that; and I know there ain't no hay on it, I know that. And, and, and I, I, I, know it might sound dear, but, but, but, I was thinking, I was thinking, I was thinking, I'd sell, if the price was right. Was thinkin' maybe, I know it might sound dear, and all that, but was thinkin' maybe I'd sell it for twelve hundred dollars."

"Twelve hundred dollahs!" Bill Wallace had been expecting fifty thousand.

"Well, I, I, I, couldn't let it go for a cent less than a thousand, no, no, not a cent, not a cent, not a cent less than a thousand, if ya know what I mean, as the feller says, not a cent less than a thousand." Taking Bill's response negatively, Lindon thought, "He thinks I'm askin' too much."

Bill Wallace wanted to laugh and whoop and holler. Instead, he tossed back the second double of scotch. "Twelve hundred is giving it away. I'm getting this property for almost nothing," he thought.

"Are you talking the whole front?" asked Bill.

"Oh yeah, yeah, yeah. Oh yeah, yep. The whole front. No good to me. No lumber on it. No hay, no lumber. Good place to fish though. Good place to fish. Go over the hill anytime at all and ketch a salmon, so ya kin. I wouldn' lie to ya! Ketch a salmon there anytime at all, so ya kin, ya kin yeah."

"How far back you talking?"

"Back about, about, about, about, about, about five hundred feet, five hundred feet back to the top of the hill."

Bill sipped his drink. He had been thinking two hundred feet. "This man doesn't have a clue what he's doing," he thought. "At this rate, I could buy up the whole rivah."

"A thousand dollars, you're asking?"

"Well, I wanted twelve hundred, but like I say, there ain't no lumber on it, no lumber to speak of, like the feller says, like I say, no hay on it either. Guess I could let it go for a thousand."

"Tell me, Lindon, you wouldn't be interested in selling the whole place, would you?"

"No, no, couldn' sell the house and the lumber land. No, oh no. Couldn' sell the house and the lumber land."

"Has the property been in the Tucker family for long?"

"Ever since the, as the feller says, ever since the great fire of 1825, yeah, 1825, yeah, 1825, I think it was. Me grandfather, or me great grandfather, now I ain't sure, I don't know which."

"It was your grandfather that cleared the land?"

"Either him, or me great grandfather, I, I, I, as the feller says, I ain't sure which. All I know is, the old feller, one of them, come here from Ireland after the fire o' 1825 and couldn' find a tree big enough still standin', if ya know what I mean, a tree big enough after the fire, for a fence post."

"Who owns the property next to yours?" asked Bill.

"Well, Sam Little, Sam Little, Sam Little owns across the river from me and Lester Burns owns to me left and Frank Layton owns to me right."

"How about the Lester Burns property? Is that a good pool?"

"Good fishin' yeah, good all along there, yeah, oh yeah."

"And who owns upstream from Lester?"

"Bert Todder. Bert Todder, yeah. Bert ain't got much of a fishin' hole though. Ain't much of a pool in front o' Bert's. Back side o' Cabbage Island. 'Muricans own the island and all this side. Bert just got a little trickle 'tween him and the island."

Bill Wallace poured some more scotch into Lindon's glass.

"Would you consider shaking hands on a deal tonight, Lindon, old buddy?"

"Sure, sure, sure, if you got the money, sure, sure I'd shake hands, if you got the money. Thousand dollars. Wanted twelve hundred, but I'll sell to you for a thousand. A thousand, yeah."

"Well, Lindon, you drive a hard bargain, but I'd really like to have a place up here."

"Okay, okay, okay, we got a deal, got a deal, shake hands on 'er, shake, put 'er there!"

Bill and Lindon shook hands aggressively. Both men were grinning happily. Both men were getting what they wanted and both men were beginning to feel the effects of the liquor.

"We have a deal," said Bill Wallace.

"A deal, yeah."

They drank to the deal.

"You'll be buildin' a camp?" asked Lindon.

"Yes."

"You might be needin' someone to look after yer place when yer not here, if ye know what I mean, someone to look after the place?"

"Yes, by God, Lindon old buddy, maybe I will!"

"Well, sir, I'd do it for ya, so I would. I'm just yer man! I'd do it for ya. Wouldin' mind. I'm right there. Right handy, so I am."

"That sounds like a good idea," said Bill Wallace, then thought, "And so is this Lester Burns fellow whom I'd like to convince to sell."

*

"Gotta have a leak," said Shadrack. "Comin', Dry?"

"Yep. Could do with one meself."

Dryfly put his guitar down and followed Shadrack around to the back of the cabin. This was the fourth time they excused themselves and went to the place where Dryfly had hidden the pickle bottle and cigarettes.

"Startin' to rain," said Dryfly, "We'd better put these cigarettes in our pockets."

"Yeah, but don't make a mistake and smoke one while we're inside. Here, have a drink."

Both boys took substantial slugs of the concoction in the pickle bottle. Both boys were feeling a little woozy and starting to lose their inhibitions. The pickle bottle was only half full.

"Good stuff, eh?"

"Let's get back. I'm gettin' wet."

"Who gives a jesus! I don't care if I git wet! You care if you get wet, Dryfly? A little water wouldn' hurt you, Dryfly! Here, have one more little slug."

"Hem! Ahem! Don't know if I can handle much more of that!"

"I can handl'er. I'll drink'er if you can't, by God!"

"C'mon, let's get back."

"You gonna play us another song?"

"Shhhure, why not!"

Back on the veranda, Dryfly picked up his guitar.

"We should go inside," said Lillian. "The rain's starting to come in here."

"Very best with me, darlin'!" said Shadrack.

"Sure! Let's go in," said Dryfly.

Inside the teenagers found Lindon Tucker and Bill Wallace feeling very happy. Shad and Dry were also feeling very happy. Lillian Wallace, although she wasn't drinking, was picking up on the good time vibrations and was also having fun. A celebration was commencing to brew.

"Ah! Boys! Come in, come in! I see you have a guitar! Let's have another drink, Lindon!"

Lindon Tucker was grinning from ear to ear. "Don't mind if I do," he said. "A little drink wouldn' do us any harm!"

"Sing for us, boy. Sing us a song!" said Bill.

Dry sat on the sofa and strummed a G chord. "What would you like to hear?" he asked.

"Anything you know is fine with me."

Dryfly strummed the G chord once again.

> *Roses are blooming*
> *Come back to me darlin'*
> *Come back to me darlin'*
> *And never more roam . . .*

Dryfly sang loud and clear and strummed smoothly. Dryfly was giving his first performance in front of an audience. He sang, "Roses are Blooming," "Beautiful, Beautiful Brown Eyes," "The Cat Came Back," and "Hannah Won't You Open the Door." Everyone listened and everyone enjoyed.

Much later, Bill Wallace said, "You know, back home in Stockbridge, there's this hotel. The Red Lion, it's called. I know the manager. You'd go over well there, Dryfly. I could arrange to get you a booking."

"A booking."

"Sure! You could entertain there. You could come down and stay with us for a week and entertain at the Red Lion."

"No, I ain't good enough to do that."

"Yes you are, my boy! There's a bunch o' young people playing there all the time that aren't any better than you are. In fact, you're better than most of them."

Bill Wallace, though intoxicated, was serious. He liked

Dryfly's singing, he liked Dryfly's guitar playing, and he liked Dryfly. "He parts his hair in the middle . . . not like all these Elvis Presley freaks. And I could get him a booking."

Dryfly thought of the Red Lion many times, but that was all. He was too shy, too backward, and loved the Dungarvon River too much to leave it for a week.

In Stockbridge, Massachusetts, people like Arlo Guthrie and Joan Baez were starting to get bookings at the Red Lion.

*

The lightning flashed and the thunder boomed and rumbled. There was so much static on the radio that Shirley Ramsey not only turned it off but unplugged it as well. Shirley Ramsey was very afraid of thunderstorms. She sat in the kitchen, smoking and fingering her rosary beads. Palidin was back in his room. Shirley hoped Dryfly was not on the river. "Water draws lightning," she thought.

Nutbeam, on the other hand, was not at all afraid of the storm. He liked it. It added excitement to his life. Nutbeam found the warm summer rain refreshing and often showered himself in it. Nutbeam was standing outside of Shirley Ramsey's window. He had gone to Shirley Ramsey's house to listen to the radio, but had lost all interest in listening when he saw Shirley Ramsey remove her clothes to take a bath.

He moved closer, so that he was actually spying through the window a few inches from the glass. Nutbeam found Shirley Ramsey very exciting.

"The most beautiful woman I ever saw in my life," he whispered to himself.

eight

Palidin Ramsey sat on his bed reading an *Outdoor Life* magazine he'd borrowed from George Hanley. He was reading an article on the Atlantic salmon and was very much interested. "The Atlantic salmon," the article stated, "lay their eggs in the upper reaches of the fresh water rivers such as the Cains, the Renous and the Dungarvon. When the young have grown to about a pound in weight and are called 'smolt,' they take a little journey. They swim a couple of thousand miles to dine in the ocean waters off the coast of Greenland. When they've stuffed themselves to satisfaction, they head back to their place of birth to start another generation. They lay their eggs behind the same rock, or in the same bed where they themselves were conceived."

The questions asked in the article were, "How do salmon find their way to Greenland and back? How do they recognize the same old rock, or the same old bed where they themselves were born?

"Four thousand miles through the dark ocean waters to return to the same nest, on the same river! Why? Why not some other river, or at least some other rock?" One of the article's contributing scientists theorized that salmon may have the ability to sense magnetic forces, that they follow magnetic fields from magnetic rock to magnetic rock, from magnetic coast to magnetic coast. "Salmon do tend to follow coast lines and even river banks," stated the scientist.

Magnetic was the magic word that started Palidin's quick mind to work. Lately Palidin had been thinking that voices, the echoes, were drawn back magnetically. Perhaps one's voice is thrown from a hillside by antimagnetic forces. Perhaps the ear is the magnetic force that attracts it home again. Perhaps

magnetic forces account for the homing instinct in all creatures, for instance, the Monarch butterfly, the swallow . . . and
the salmon.

Palidin had learned at a very early age how to stroke metal
with metal for the purpose of creating magnets. "If salmon
are attracted to magnets," thought Palidin, "why wouldn't a
magnetic hook work better than just your everyday, ordinary
hook?"

Palidin decided to pay a visit to George Hanley.

Palidin found George sitting in the shade of the barn, smoking a cigarette. George always went behind the barn to smoke.

"How's she goin', Pal?" greeted George. "What's up?"

"Was thinkin' I might go fishin'. Was wonderin' if ya had
any hooks."

"Not me, no. There's some in the store, I think."

"Thought maybe you could steal me a couple."

"Shouldn' be any trouble. Where ya goin' fishin'?"

"I dunno. Someplace where it's good."

"Trout or salmon?"

"Salmon."

"Ya need flyhooks and a rod n' reel to fish salmon."

"Thought I might borrow Shad Nash's outfit. You sure ya
need flyhooks for fishing salmon?"

"Yep. That's what everybody's usin'."

"Ya think you could steal me a flyhook?"

"It's hard to say. Flyhooks are a lot more costly than
baithooks. Why don't you just go trout fishin' back the brook?"

"Because I have an idea about catching salmon."

"What idea?"

"Get me a flyhook and I'll tell ya."

"What makes you think the idea is worth it?"

"I don't. I have to experiment."

"Well, I might be able to get you one flyhook. What kind
do you want?"

"It don't matter. I don't know one from the other."

"Okay. I'll see what I can do. Wait here."

In less than five minutes, George returned with a fly called
Blue Charm and handed it to Palidin. George was always giv-

ing Palidin things. George Hanley and Palidin Ramsey were good friends.

"Want to play in the hay?" asked George, gesturing to the inside of the barn.

"I was thinking about you last night," said Palidin.

*

Dryfly found himself pacing restlessly. He couldn't quite figure out what was happening to him, but he knew that something strange was in the making. For the tenth time he found himself pondering the facts. "She spent a lotta the night talkin' to me and hardly spoke at all to Shad. True, they walked all the way here for me guiddar, but they didn' take long in doin' it. They couldn' do nothin' in that short o' time. Shad didn' seem to know what he was doin'. He got drunk, too, and puked off the veranda. Almost didn't make it. Shad drank a lot more than I did. No wonder he got drunk. Lillian was prob'ly makin' fun o' us, but . . . she seemed to like me."

On the way to the Cabbage Island Salmon Club, Dryfly picked a daisy. "Mom says all women like flowers," he thought. "Mom says she carried daisies when she married Buck."

As Dryfly neared the cabin where Lillian Wallace was staying, he found himself thinking that maybe he had arrived too early. "It's still mornin', she might not even be out of bed." He didn't knock on the door but sat on the veranda to wait and watch the river. He heard robins and chickadees and crows. He could see the river and the forest. He could smell the morning, fresh, radiant in the sun, cleansed to sweetness by the recent rain.

"Good morning, Dryfly," greeted Lillian from behind the screen door. "Am I a sleepy head, or are you early?"

"The train goes at eleven o'clock. You said you had a letter to mail and I thought . . ."

"Oh, yes. I haven't finished it yet. Would you like some orange juice?"

"Sure."

"I'll bring it out to you." In a moment Lillian reappeared with two glasses of orange juice, handed one to Dryfly and sat at the table. She was wearing a blue and white checked blouse, blue shorts and sandals.

"I picked you a daisy," said Dryfly, handing her the flower.

"Oh, how nice! Thank you! How thoughtful of you!"

Dryfly was feeling a little bit embarrassed about giving her the flower, but he was glad that he had given it to her. Lillian put the daisy in her hair. She had just taken her morning shower; fresh, clean and radiant, she complemented the morning itself. Dryfly could not take his eyes off her.

"Did you have a good time last night?" she asked, waving at the mosquitoes and blackflies that were already commencing to seek out her sweetness.

"Yeah," said Dryfly.

"My father really enjoyed your singing. It would be nice if you could come down and play at the Red Lion."

"You never know, I might."

"Have you seen Shadrack this morning?"

"Not yet."

"Ouch!" Lillian slapped a mosquito that was feasting on her thigh. "The bugs are terrible! Don't they bother you?"

"Sometimes."

"Only sometimes? I think they're out to devour me. How do you put up with the things?"

Dryfly wanted to tell her what Palidin had told him: that insects were very tiny; that insects had tiny eyes that restricted their vision to but a couple of feet; that insects were attracted to smell and body heat and that, by waving and slapping and getting excited, one was only attracting more of them.

"They don't bother me that much," he said.

There was a can of repellent sitting on the table. Picking it up, Lillian said, "They sure bother me!"

Lillian sprayed her legs and arms. She sprayed some into the palm of her hand, then rubbed the back of her neck and face; she closed her eyes and sprayed her hair, and then she sprayed the air about her.

"Your father gone fishin'?" asked Dryfly.

"He and Mr. Tucker went to Newcastle to see a lawyer. My father's buying some property."

"From Lindon?"

"It's right on the river. Dad tells me it's beautiful."

"Good salmon pool there," commented Dryfly. "Only one left around here."

"What happened to the others?" asked Lillian.

"Oh, they're still there, but us lads can't fish in them."

"But why?"

"Lads from Fredericton and the States and stuff own them. They don't want us lads fishin' in their pools . . . ketch all the fish."

"But there's got to be plenty for everyone, isn't there?"

"Yeah . . . I don't know. I don't fish much anyway. Most of the people around here fish with a net."

"But that's against the law, isn't it?"

Dryfly shrugged. "If you want salmon, that's how ya gotta get 'em if ya don't have a pool to fish in."

"Don't people get caught by the wardens?"

"Sometimes. Hardly ever."

"Well, my father will let you fish in his pool, Dryfly. Don't you worry about that."

"Not worried. I hardly ever fish anyway."

"Dad wants to build a cottage next year."

"That's good. You'll be able to come up more often."

"I guess so. I'd really like to see the property sometime."

"I know where it is."

"Is it far from here?"

"The other side o' the river. Just cross the bridge and down the other side a little bit. See that house down there on the hill?"

Dryfly pointed at the paintless house, barn, woodshed, outdoor toilet, pigpen, toolshed, binder shed, henhouse and well-house that sat on the hill, across and downstream a half a mile or so.

"Could we get over there to see it?"

"No trouble. Cross the bridge and down the path. Wanna go?"

"Sure. I'd love to."

Dryfly and Lillian left the Cabbage Island Salmon Club

115

and went over the hill to the river. They followed a riverside path upstream for several hundred yards until they came to the footbridge.

The footbridge consisted of four steel cables that spanned the river, two on top and two on the bottom. The sides and the bottom were held together by fencing wire. The two bottom cables were crossed with four-foot lengths of two-by-four lumber. Three strips of six-inch board were nailed to the two-by-fours, giving the bridge an eighteen-inch walking space. The cables were connected to pillars of stone and concrete on either side of the river and were stabilized in the middle of the river by a similar abutment. The bridge had to be high to escape the spring torrents and ice flows, so there were stairs of about thirty steps leading to the top of each riverside abutment. The bridge was sturdy enough to hold the weight of, perhaps, a thousand men, but it looked shaky and tended to bounce and sway when walked upon. For Lillian, walking the bridge was a new experience and scary business. She doubted its durability. When she got to the middle abutment she stopped to gather herself.

The morning breeze, cooled by the rains of the previous night, played in her hair and brought gooseflesh out on her arms and legs. Lillian eyed the river, the forested hills in the distance, the little farms, a swooping osprey in the cloudless sky. Dryfly eyed Lillian, her golden hair, her smooth tanned skin, her big blue eyes.

"You scared walkin' the bridge?" he asked.

"Well, it's a new experience," she said. "It's kind of shaky."

"Hold the devil himself."

"Yes, but will it hold two devils?" laughed Lillian.

"In a thunderstorm one night, a lad got beat to death on one of these things," said Dryfly. "Up the river. Above Gordon. The wind came up, started the cables flappin' and beat him to death. You can bang these top cables together hard enough to cut you in two with a little help. It'll bounce, too, and damn near throw you off of it."

"Must be scary."

"Scary enough. See right down there on the bend? There's

a hole down there. You can drop an anchor from a twenty-foot rope and it'll hang straight down. Corpse's Hole it's called, 'cause that's where they always find the bodies of anyone that's drowned. There's a whirlpool there and the bodies just go round and round. Mom says it's prob'ly haunted. Old Bill Tuney said he heard a ghost there one time."

"A ghost? What did the ghost sound like? What did he say?"

"Don't know. He never said, I don't think. He's dead now. Whoopin' prob'ly."

Dryfly looked at Lillian and felt a little bit ashamed; felt he was perhaps sounding like a superstitious old woman, that his choice of topic was perhaps too morbid a thing to have been discussing with a young lady.

Lillian was eyeing Corpse's Hole thoughtfully. "This whole river seems haunted," she said. "Did you and Shadrack really see the whooper?"

"I . . . I . . . no."

"I didn't think so. Shadrack lies a lot, doesn't he?"

"He doesn't mean to lie. He just always does it. And we did hear the thing . . . right in the woods beside us. We were just little kids and ran home."

Lillian turned to face Dryfly. Dryfly turned away to watch the river.

"He's funny looking," thought Lillian, eyeing the worn shirt and jeans, the dirty sneakers, the hair parted in the middle and the long nose.

"Would you hold my hand the rest of the way?" she asked.

"Ah . . . sure." Dryfly looked self-consciously back and forth along the bridge, a little embarrassed that someone might see him holding her hand.

When their hands touched, their hearts quickened. Dryfly's hand was warm and perspiring — so was Lillian's. They walked on, slowly, Lillian being careful to walk the center boards, to minimize the sway. Dryfly, close behind her, reached awkwardly ahead to hold her hand.

When they got to the far side, Dryfly wondered if she would let go of his hand. He left it up to her to make the decision. As they went down the steps and crossed Billy MacDonald's field, Bob Nash's field and Todder Brook, they were still holding hands.

"Do you plan to go back to school?" asked Lillian.

"I dunno," said Dryfly. "Maybe."

"What's your plan for the future?"

"I dunno. Not much to do around here."

"Will you move away?"

"Prob'ly. Everyone else does. Around here, you're either too young or too old to leave, or you're gone. Me brother Digger's livin' in Ontario. I might go and live with 'im in a year or so. Lots to do in Ontario."

"What does . . . ah . . . Digger work at?"

"Don't work hard at all. Packin' tomatoes in a place called Leamington . . . makin' two dollars an hour."

"You could play music for a living."

"Naw."

On the south side of Lindon Tucker's house grew an apple tree loaded with juicy green crab apples.

"Would you like an apple?" asked Dryfly.

Lillian and Dryfly, still holding hands, walked up the hill to the apple tree. Dryfly picked a few and offered one to Lillian.

"They're awfully green, aren't they?"

"Won't hurt ya. Hardly ever give ya the shits."

Lillian giggled a giggle that Dryfly found very pleasing.

"Why ya laughin'?"

"'The shits,'" she said.

Dryfly laughed too.

They stopped laughing when they bit into the apples. They squinted their eyes, the muscles in their cheeks contracted, they wrinkled their noses — the apples were very sour.

They walked around Lindon Tucker's house and sat on the swing.

"It's very pleasant here," said Lillian, "and very quiet."

"Pretty place, yeah," said Dryfly.

"Look! There's a butterfly!" A big yellow butterfly played on an air current that eventually led to the arm of Dryfly's swing.

"Hmm," said Dryfly, "what's this?"

"It likes you," said Lillian.

Dryfly said nothing, thought, "Everything's very pretty."

"How old are you?" asked Lillian.

"Fifteen."

"Do you have a girlfriend?"

"Naw. Ain't many girls around here."

"Shadrack said he had several girlfriends."

"Naw. He didn't mean it."

"Shad lied about girlfriends," thought Dryfly. "Shad lied about everything."

"Do you have a boyfriend?" asked Dryfly.

"No. I'm only fifteen, too."

They were eyeing each other and feeling very warm inside.

"Thank you for the daisy," said Lillian. "You're the first boy to ever give me a flower."

Lillian reached out and gently placed her hand on Dryfly's knee. Dryfly stared into her eyes and saw Heaven.

Something very emotional was sweeping over Lillian — a combination of happiness, sadness and bewilderment. It excited her to the point of tears.

"The butterfly and I both like you," she said.

Dryfly, swept by similar emotions, swallowed, said, "I . . . like you, too."

"The appropriate thing to do," thought Lillian, "would be to kiss him. The appropriate thing to do is for him to kiss me."

A hundred wild horses hooked onto Dryfly's nerve endings. They tugged at his nerve endings, his inhibitions, his shyness and his heart. Every one of the hundred wild horses seemed to be saying, "You haven't got the nerve, Dryfly! She's rich and pretty and you're poor and ugly. She'll laugh at you and you'll feel like a fool! You'll be lucky if she doesn't slap your face." The hundred wild horses pulled so hard that the chains connected to Dryfly snapped and broke.

Dryfly leaned toward Lillian and placed a gentle crab apple- scented kiss on the smooth, cool cheek of Lillian Wallace.

*

Shadrack Nash awakened to his very first hangover. Shadrack Nash didn't feel very well at all. His head was aching, his mouth was dry and he had a guilt complex to no end.

"I made a fool of myself," he thought. "I talked too much, I sung too many dirty songs and to top it all off, I got sick. Lillian Wallace will never want to see me again!"

In the kitchen, Shad sat to a breakfast of tea and toast. He spread some of his mother's fresh strawberry jam on the toast.

Shadrack was very unhappy about something else. Lillian Wallace seemed more interested in Dryfly than she was in him.

"Why? . . . Dryfly was showin' off on the guiddar, for one thing! And he didn' talk too much, or git sick!"

"You home, Shadrack?" The voice of Palidin Ramsey came through the screen of the kitchen door.

"No, I'm in Tracadie fishin' smelts!" said Shadrack.

Palidin entered.

"What're ya up to, Pal?" asked Shadrack.

"Wanna go fishing?" asked Palidin.

"Naw. Don't feel too good," said Shad.

"Would you mind if I borrowed your rod?"

"Fishin' trout or salmon?"

"Salmon."

"How long ya gonna be?"

"An hour . . . two, maybe."

"I don't care. Take it. It's on the porch."

"Thanks, Shad. I'll look after it. Bring ya back a salmon," said Palidin and left, taking Shadrack's rod and reel with him.

Shadrack's mother, Elva Nash, was washing dishes and humming "Rock of Ages." She hadn't spoken to Palidin. Elva Nash did not like the Ramseys. The Ramseys were trash and Elva Nash did not like her son to associate with trash.

"You shouldn't have given him that fishin' rod, Shad," said Elva. "Ya give 'em an inch and they'll take a mile. He'll be back agin, you mark my words! He'll be naggin' ya every day for somethin'!"

"Ah, Pal won't hurt it."

"No odds! I don't want him around the place! They're Catholics! They don't know the word o' God! I pray for you,

Shadrack, darlin'! I pray every night that you will stop hangin' around with the likes o' them Ramseys. They'll jist git you in trouble, mark my words!"

"They're not so bad, Mom."

"NOT SO BAD! NOT SO BAD! THEY'RE TRASH, THAT'S WHAT THEY ARE! Never go to church on Sundays, runnin' the roads like . . . like cattle. 'Pon me soul, Shad, I don't know what's becomin' o' you. Yer gettin' jist like them! That old Shirley Ramsey never took a bath in her life, and I could smell that Palidin as soon's he walked through the door. They'll never see the kingdom o' God, Shad, you kin mark my words!"

Elva Nash was warming up for one of her sermons and Shad knew it. She was washing dishes and Shad was sitting at the table. Through the window over the sink, Elva could see the river. Through the window, Elva could see Lillian Wallace walking down the path with Dryfly Ramsey.

"Now look o' there, would ya! There's that sport's daughter walkin' down the flat with that . . . that . . . that tramp! Boys, she must think a lotta herself! What do you suppose the world's comin' to!"

"Who?" Shad dashed to the window. "Dryfly and Lillian," he muttered through the thick black curtain that seemed to have fallen.

Shad ran outside and around the house. Spying from the corner of the house, he could see Lillian and Dryfly walking through the field, holding hands.

Shad was hungover and a little dizzy. The sight of Dryfly and Lillian almost made him sick. "Damn!" he thought. "Damn! Damn! Damn!"

Shadrack Nash was very hurt and wanted to cry. Shadrack was not hurting so much just because of the girl. There is more to heartbreak than losing a girl. Shadrack Nash was hurting for the same reason all losing lovers hurt. Egomania. How could he face Dryfly?

Shadrack Nash went for a walk through the woods. He needed to think. Shadrack took a walk back to Todder Brook.

*

When Dryfly removed his lips from Lillian's cheek, he could taste her fly repellent.

"She tastes and smells better than the DDT they spray over us in budworm season," he thought.

"We'd better be going back," said Lillian, getting off the swing and reaching her hand out for Dryfly's.

As they walked over the hill and back through the fields toward the bridge, nothing was spoken. Dryfly broke the silence in the shadow of the bridge abutment. There in the shadows, with a thousand blackflies swarming about his head, he stopped and swung in front of her. He looked into her big blue eyes and wanted to say, "I love you." Instead, he said, "Flies like the shade."

Dryfly was hot, inside and out and excited to a single point shy of panic. He forgot Palidin's teachings and waved at the onslaught of flies, attracting a thousand more. But being there with Lillian was a precious moment and he wanted it to last. He wanted to say something, something intelligent, something romantic, anything. "Tell her that you love her," came a tiny voice from deep inside. "Tell her that she's beautiful! Tell her that you think she has the most beautiful eyes in the whole world! Tell her how wonderful she is!"

Lillian was protected by fly repellent and not being attacked, but she was as excited as Dryfly. "Just do what they do in the movies," she thought, parted her lips slightly and closed her eyes.

Dryfly didn't know it, but he was the son of a fabulous lover. Although Dryfly never met Buck, Buck's genes flowed in his veins; the same hereditary instinct was bubbling forth. It was the Buck in Dryfly that took control. Dryfly leaned forward and kissed Lillian gently, as gentle as the butterfly that had rested on his hand. There was no pressure, no desire-driven fondling. Just a gentle, cool kiss — one heartbeat and it was over.

Dryfly withdrew a few inches and looked at the beautiful young girl. Lillian opened her eyes and looked at Dryfly.

"You have awful blue eyes," said Dryfly.

"You have awful brown eyes," said Lillian.

A mosquito drove its proboscis into the back of Dryfly's neck; another feasted on his forehead and another on his arm.

"C'mon! There's plenty for everyone!" yelled the mosquitoes.

One old mosquito zeroed in from the north and jabbed the thin, worn material of Dryfly's shirt, getting him in the back; another — a cowardly bastard of a mosquito — sucked on Dryfly's wonderfully exposed earlobe.

Without taking his eyes off Lillian, Dryfly battled and scratched. He moved in again and kissed Lillian for the second time, and once again tasted her repellent.

Withdrawing and looking at the wonderful girl with the big blue eyes, the same girl who was smart enough to protect herself from the cursed flies of the Dungarvon, Dryfly whispered, "No flies on you."

*

There was another precaution Dryfly could have dwelled upon, "If you keep walking, the mosquitoes and blackflies won't bother you as much."

Shadrack Nash kept walking through the fly-infested forest of Todder Brook until he came to the exact spot where he and Dryfly Ramsey had done away with the panther, or the devil, "or whatever the Todder Brook Whooper was."

For the first time since he left his mother's kitchen, Shadrack was not thinking about his broken heart. Shadrack found himself preoccupied with the Todder Brook Whooper.

"What was it?" he asked himself. "Was it the Dungarvon Whooper? Was the Dungarvon Whooper a devil that wandered from place to place? Where is it now?" It hardly seemed conceivable that the devil, or anything else, could be so wily that a single shot fired into the air by a small boy would scare it off.

"We were standing right here," thought Shad, "and the thing was right down there by the brook. There was moose tracks all over the place . . . or devil tracks."

When Shadrack Nash scanned the rain-drenched clay about his feet, he did not see any moose tracks. What Shadrack did see, though, was the tracks of a human.

"Who else could be back here?" Shadrack asked himself. "Them tracks have been made since the shower last night. Someone must be back here this mornin'."

Shadrack, for no other reason than curiosity, started following the tracks. There weren't many and they didn't go far until they turned down a barely distinguishable path. Shad followed the path for about thirty seconds and came to a place where the path branched off. Now, confronting Shadrack was a path to the right, a path to the left and one down the middle. Each path that lay before him was less distinguishable than the one he was standing on.

The three paths reminded Shadrack of a John Kaston sermon.

"When you die," commenced John Kaston, sounding all the world like a southern American, "y'all will come to a branch in the rewd. Ya won't know which rewd to take unless yer one with the Savior! One path leads to Heaven, one leads to the pits of hell, and one leads to purgatory. Us Protestants don't have to worry about the one to purgatory. Know the Savior and you won't have to worry about the path to hell either!"

Shadrack took the path down the middle, hoping he would at least be accepted into Catholic Heaven. He followed the path for about a hundred yards and came to a dead end — the brook.

"At least it didn't lead to hell," thought Shad and retraced his steps back to where the paths branched.

He eyed the two paths that were left. He had a fifty-fifty chance of going to heaven. He took the path to the right. This path went a little further, three hundred yards or so, but again, Shad found himself eyeing the swift waters of Todder Brook.

"It ain't Heaven," thought Shad, "and it ain't hell either. I wish Dryfly Ramsey would go to hell and leave my woman alone!"

Shad went back to the branch of the path and took the third and last one. Again, he came to the brook.

"Oh well," he thought, "they must be just fishing trails. Whoever made them tracks must be wading down the brook."

Shad was half way back to the junction of the paths when he heard someone sneeze. The sneeze was followed immediately by a bigger sneeze and the word "shit."

Nutbeam was standing behind a fir tree watching Shad. He had heard Shad coming. Nutbeam had stood in the rain for too long on the previous night and had caught a cold.

At first Shad could see nothing, but he knew that the sneeze had come from the vicinity of the fir tree. Examining the tree more carefully, he spotted a big old floppy ear.

"Who's there?" asked Shad.

No answer.

"I can see ya. Who are ya?"

No answer. The ear withdrew from sight. The other ear appeared.

"You got awful big ears," said Shad. "You an elf?"

"What d'ya want?" came a voice from behind the fir tree.

"Nuthin'."

"Then, go home!"

Shad contemplated the words "Go home!" He did not know if he was in danger or not. "Go home," he thought. "Maybe I should . . . but who is it?"

"Who are you?" asked Shad.

Nutbeam was very depressed. He had been found. Out of curiosity, people would visit him. They'd laugh at him and bother him and he'd have to move.

"Why don't you go home?" Nutbeam groaned petulantly. Nutbeam hoped there was still a chance that Shadrack hadn't seen the camp.

Shad could not see Nutbeam's camp, but he heard the whimper in Nutbeam's voice, and he heard the fear. The whimper and the fear in the fir tree's voice restored Shadrack's courage.

"What're ya doin' standin' behind a tree?" asked Shad.

"None of yer bus'ness!" said Nutbeam.

Shadrack had often heard Americans running people out of their salmon pools and in the way of an American, said, "Oh, I don't know about that! My father owns most of this brook and you ain't my father! What're ya doin' back here?!"

"I ain't doin' nothin'!"

"Come out so I can see ya!"

Nutbeam was indeed a timid creature, but he heard the command in the boy's voice. He stepped out.

"Nutbeam!" whispered Shad, amazed. "You're Nutbeam!"

"How do you know that?" asked Nutbeam.

"I don't know," said Shad. He could have added, "There are no secrets in Brennen Siding."

Nutbeam stared at the red-haired, freckled boy. Shadrack was fifteen, but Nutbeam guessed him to be twelve, not a day older. Shadrack was amazed to see Nutbeam and Nutbeam was amazed at the fact that Shadrack was not laughing. It was simple: Shad was too amazed to laugh.

"You back here fishin'?" asked Shad.

"I ain't fishin'."

"What happened to your ears?" asked Shadrack. "You look like an elf, or a monkey, or somethin'." Shad was not intentionally making fun of Nutbeam, he was simply in awe.

Nutbeam didn't answer. Nutbeam simply dropped his head in shame.

Shad gathered more courage and moved closer. "His nose is awful big, too," thought Shad, "and so is his mouth." Shadrack could not imagine why such a big, tall man would seem so afraid.

The next time Shad spoke, his voice was more gentle.

"No one's seen you in a long time, Nutbeam. Where've you been?"

"I ain't been nowhere," said Nutbeam. His voice was barely audible.

"You live around here?"

"Why don't you go home?" Nutbeam's voice had calmed too and sounded mellow and sad.

"Listen," said Shadrack, "if you don't live too far from here, I sure could use a drink o' water. I was drinkin' last night, and I'm sorta hung over. Sure could use a drink o' water."

"Drink from the brook."

"Oh, brook water's bad fer ya. Beaver shit in it."

"Please, go home."

"What's the matter? You ain't scared o' me, are ya? You a criminal?"

"No, I ain't scared and I ain't a criminal! I just want to be left alone. You'll tell everyone where I am and they'll all come to visit the freak!"

"You a freak, Nutbeam?"

"Well, I ain't exactly normal!"

"Look normal to me. Now me, the lad yer lookin' at, I ain't normal. There's somethin' wrong with me."

"What's wrong with you?"

"Well, I had this girlfriend, the prettiest little lady I ever seen, and she left me for a lad as homely as you are. She don't seem that stupid, so there's got to be something wrong with me."

"How much would you take to keep yer mouth shut?"

"What's that?"

"I said, how much money will you take to keep quiet about me?"

Shad thought for a moment, then almost sang, "I wouldn't take yer money, Nutbeam."

*

Palidin Ramsey sat on a boulder at the edge of the water. In his right hand he held a lodestone the size of a dime, and in his left hand he held the flyhook he'd borrowed from George Hanley. He stroked the lodestone across the point of the hook for a few minutes, then touched the hook to the reel of Shad's rod. The hook was magnetized and clung to the reel. "Good," he thought, "now for the experiment."

He kicked off his sneakers and rolled up his pants, carefully crossed the gravel beach and stepped into the water. The water in the Dungarvon is amazingly warm in the summer — about seventy-five degrees — and it felt good on Palidin's feet and ankles. He then waded until the water was encircling his waist.

"If nothing else, I'm getting washed," he thought. He was not very enthusiastic about his experiment. He had thought it up in a moment; it had probably been tried before. "It'll never work in a thousand years," he thought, "but it's worth a try."

Palidin was fishing in Dr. MacDowell's pool. Dr. MacDowell had purchased Graig Allen's shore ten years ago, built a cottage and put the run to every one, local, who tried to fish there. Dr. MacDowell owned one of the five productive fishing pools in Brennen Siding. Three of the other four pools were also owned by Americans. Bill Wallace from Stockbridge, Massachusettes, was in the process of buying the last one, the Lindon Tucker Pool, at that very minute. Graig Allen had sold his pool for five hundred dollars, spent it on moving to Fredericton, and never came back. Times were changing — Lindon Tucker was getting a thousand dollars for his "property."

In 1962, most of the local residents of the Dungarvon River, the Cains or the Renous did not fully appreciate the value of their property. "That old shore ain't worth much to me," was the general attitude. With a million dollars, one could have purchased the whole Dungarvon river valley. "A million dollars for the Dungarvon River!" The locals did not see the approaching change. Bill Wallace would sell the Lindon Tucker Pool in 1986 for three-quarters of a million dollars.

Dr. MacDowell did not allow anyone other than himself and a few friends from back home to fish his pool. Neither did the Americans that owned other pools in the area. Dr. MacDowell was in Florence, trying to get far enough away from the Duomo to photograph it. He wouldn't bother Palidin until September.

Palidin made a cast. A salmon swirled for the fly, a roll, and missed it.

Palidin made another cast.

SPLASH!

Palidin was busy for the next fifteen minutes. He landed a twelve-pound Atlantic salmon. Palidin Ramsey would be hooked on salmon fishing for the rest of his life.

nine

Bill Wallace walked through the field he'd purchased from Lindon Tucker, looking for a suitable site to build a cottage on. On the north end of the field was a knoll that Bill thought had a lot of potential. There was a great view and it was high enough to be above any above-average spring torrents. Lindon Tucker's old house and buildings sat on the hill to the east — quaint, grey, serene and picturesque amongst the elms and apple trees. An old swing sat beside the lilac bushes in front of Lindon's house. It was plain to see the house was going in the ground, falling down.

When Bill Wallace stood on his knoll and looked southwest, he could see at least a mile of river, maybe more. The immediate river was lined on both sides by the green fields of Brennen Siding. In the distance, the river seemed to flow from beneath the forested hills.

"It could be a scene from Vermont," thought Bill Wallace, "but it doesn't have the mountains. Fine with me! I never cared much for mountains, anyway. A rivah's all I need. If the rivah happens to have Atlantic salmon in it, that's a bonus."

Bill Wallace had spent many happy childhood days playing, fishing and canoeing on the White River in Vermont. The White was a tributary of the Connecticut. The Connecticut hadn't had a salmon in it for a hundred years. The Connecticut River had gone the way of all New England rivers, with the exception, maybe, of the Penobscot in Maine. Over-fishing, electrical dams and industrial pollution had turned what used to be some of the greatest Atlantic salmon rivers in the world into sewers for human waste — into dumps for humans to throw their old tires, sometimes whole cars, mattresses, bean cans, dead animals and the occasional human.

"It'll happen here, in time," Bill predicted. "It's the American way. Industry will move in, people will follow and that will be it — bingo, the fifty-first state."

Bill Wallace left his knoll and headed south until he came to the cedar fence that separated the Lindon Tucker farm from the Lester Burns farm.

"The Lester Burns farm," thought Bill, "another gold mine."

Bill Wallace was amazed that nobody had jumped on the opportunity and purchased this land before now. "Unknown to most Americans, thank God," he thought. "And the rich Canadians? Are there any? Sure there are. Do they not know what they have here? Probably not. They probably go to Disneyland on vacations."

"It's an investment that you'd have to be a fool to ignore," thought Bill. "Christ! This is one American that won't ignore it! I'm buying the Lester Burns property, regardless of the cost. The cost — ha! I'll probably get that for nothing, too!"

Bill Wallace wanted to be alone for a few minutes and had convinced Lindon Tucker to "take it easy. Have a nap in the canoe, I'll be just a few minutes." Bill, once he was satisfied with his exploration of the newly-purchased property, went back to where Lindon was waiting, half-asleep in the hot July sun. Lindon climbed from the canoe and held it steady for Bill to climb in the front. Then Lindon stood in the back and poled — plop-swish . . . plop-swish — back toward the Cabbage Island salmon club.

"Newcastle's a nice little town, Lindon," said Bill.

"Oh, yeah, yeah, yeah. Stinks awful bad though."

"I guess they should've built that pulp mill further away from the town."

"Further away, yeah. Should o' built it further away."

"That pulp mill is American-owned, I'll bet on that," thought Bill.

*

Helen MacDonald was making a corned beef and cabbage stew in the kitchen of the Cabbage Island Salmon Club. Although Helen was occupied with peeling potatoes, carrots, turnips and parsnips, she was being more the detective than the cook. She could have been Sam Spade, Sherlock Holmes, or Charlie Chan. Detective Helen MacDonald was fitting together the Blueberry Pie Mystery.

"Somebody took me pie from that window sill," she thought. "And the next day, somebody took the second one — the one with the Ex-Lax in it. Rex, me dog, had a bad case o' the runs, and the somebody that took the pie didn't seem to have a complaint in the world. Seems clear to me that that someone might have fed the pie to poor old Rex. Now that someone has the gall to be hanging around here all day with that young Lillian. Boys, she must think a lotta herself to be hanging around with the likes of that . . . that . . . that tramp!"

"I can't let him get away with it," she thought. "I have to teach 'im a lesson."

Helen MacDonald would get her opportunity to get even with Dryfly Ramsey sooner than she thought. A knock sounded on the kitchen door.

"Come in!" called Helen.

In stepped Lillian Wallace followed closely by Dryfly Ramsey.

"Hello, Miss MacDonald," said Lillian.

"G'day, Helen," said Dryfly.

"Hello. I was just puttin' together your supper, Miss."

"Oh, good! What are we having tonight?"

"We're havin' good old fashion corn beef and cabbage."

"Oh! Good!"

"Your father likes me corn beef and cabbage. I cook it for 'im every time he comes up. What kin I do for ya, young lady?"

"Well, would you mind putting on an extra plate tonight?"

"No trouble. Who's stayin' fer supper? Lindon?"

"I've asked Dryfly to dine with us, and he's accepted."

"Oh! . . . well . . . sure!"

"You don't mind?"

"Oh! . . . well . . . no!"

131

Helen MacDonald thought, "How can they stand havin' that no-good weasel around? I'd put the run to 'im, if it was me!"

"Good," said Lillian. "You sure you don't mind?"

"No, no, not at all."

"Thank you, Miss MacDonald. I appreciate it."

"Does your father know that Dry's stayin'?"

"Not yet, but he won't mind."

"Hmm."

"Will we be having dessert, Miss MacDonald?"

"Well, sure. What would you like?"

"Oh, I don't care. Whatever you decide, is fine with me."

"Well, I don't have any more of the blueberries I spent good money on," said Helen, looking directly at Dryfly, "but I could make some chocolate puddin'. You like chocolate puddin'?"

"Oh, yes, very much."

"Do you like chocolate puddin', Dryfly?"

"Yep. Anything's okay for me."

"Good. You kin have all you want."

*

"See? I told you she wouldn't care if you stayed for supper, Dry." said Lillian.

"I didn't like the way she looked at me when she mentioned the blueberry pie. I think she's out to get me."

"What makes you think that?"

"I dunno. She don't like me very much."

"Dryfly Ramsey, I do believe you have an inferiority complex!"

"Maybe," said Dryfly. Dryfly hadn't the slightest idea what an inferiority complex was, but he liked the sound of the words. "I'll have to remember inferiority comprex," he thought.

The two teenagers went to the veranda of the cabin Bill and Lillian occupied and sat on the railing to watch the river.

"When your father gets his camp built, you'll be able to come up here all the time," said Dryfly. "Would you like stayin' up here?"

"I like it up here very much."

"Are you from a big city?"

"Stockbridge? No, it's a little town . . . not much bigger than Blackville. You'd like Stockbridge."

"Have you ever been to a big city?"

"I've been to New York and Boston. I went to Los Angeles once and Miami a couple of times."

"Ever been to Wheeling?"

"No. Where's Wheeling?"

"Down around where you live somewhere. Wheeling, West Virginia."

"Oh, West Virginia. That's in the south. Who do you know in West Virginia?"

"Nobody. We just hear it on the radio all the time."

"Does anyone around here have a television?"

"No." Dryfly had only heard of television. He would not get a chance to watch a television for another year. Bob Nash would be the first person in Brennen Siding to get a television. "I never saw a television in me life," said Dryfly.

"Television is wonderful. You'd like it," said Lillian. "What do kids do around here?"

"Walk up and down the road mostly. Shad and me spend a lotta time on the river, in the summer."

"You love the river, don't you?"

"Yeah, the river's all there is around here."

"Could you ever leave it?"

"Mostly everybody that ever leaves comes back . . . I don't know, maybe."

Lillian eyed the thin, homely boy. "His hair is greasy," she thought. "A little shampoo would change his whole appearance."

"Where do you take a bath, Dryfly?" she asked.

"In the river during the summer. In the winter, we don't bathe much. Once a month, maybe."

"Can you swim in the river?"

"If ya kin swim, ya kin swim in the river. It's no different than any place else. There's a little bit of a current."

"But it isn't polluted?"

"No. Ain't polluted . . . I don't think."

"Would you like to go for a swim, Dry?"

"Yeah, sure. Okay."

Lillian went inside, grabbed a comb, a towel, some soap and a bottle of shampoo. "I'll clean him up for dinner," she thought. "I'll wash that smelly shirt for him, too. It will dry quickly in the sun."

Lillian and Dryfly walked hand in hand to the river. They swam and bathed and Lillian washed Dryfly's shirt with shampoo, rinsed it and washed it again. They took one last swim, then sat on a boulder to dry off. Lillian combed Dryfly's hair, parting it in the middle.

"I like how you part your hair in the middle," she said.

*

Shadrack had been looking almost directly at it and still hadn't seen it. Then, when he did see it, he couldn't believe his eyes. "A lad could walk by it a million times and never see it," thought Shad, amazed. "It's like a part of the hill."

He asked, "Is that your camp?"

"Damn! Now I'll never have any piece and quiet!" thought Nutbeam. "The little bugger sees it!"

"It's great!" Shadrack was still feasting his eyes on the little half-cave, half-cabin Nutbeam called home. The camp, two-thirds buried into the hill, with the moss-covered roof running parallel to the hill, was the smartest hideout Shadrack had ever seen.

Nutbeam was very proud of the camp. He had put hundreds of hours into its construction. But Shadrack's open, boyish enthusiasm was something Nutbeam had never anticipated. The awe and admiration in Shadrack's eyes was soothing to Nutbeam, and he found himself turning to face what Shad was seeing.

"Made it myself," said Nutbeam.

"Wow! How long ya lived here?"

"'Bout . . . never mind!"

"Some lotta work in a camp like that!" said Shadrack.

"Hard work," said Nutbeam.

Nutbeam sighed. "What's the use?" he thought. "The little bugger sees it. The game is up."

"Just wait till Dry sees this!" said Shadrack.

"I don't want you bringin' no one else here, ya understand!"

"You a criminal?" asked Shad.

"No! I just don't like people around me!"

"You wouldn' mind a few people, would ya, Nutbeam?"

"No! I don't want no people, I tell ya!"

"Just maybe me and Dry and Dad and a few more."

"How much to keep yer mouth shut?"

"Oh, I couldn' take yer money from ya, Nutbeam . . . ," said Shad once again in that singsong how-much-ya-willin'-to-pay voice.

"How much?"

"Well . . . kin I look inside it, Nutbeam?"

"No!"

"What's the matter, Nutbeam?"

"You'll bring everyone back here and they'll laugh and make fun o' me!"

"Because of yer ears?"

"Among other things."

"No one cares about yer big floppy ears, Nutbeam!"

"I'll give ya five dollars to keep quiet."

"No one will laugh at ya, Nutbeam."

"Six dollars!"

"Course, ya never kin tell 'bout some people."

"Seven dollars!"

"Bert Todder's an awful man for laughin'."

"Eight dollars and that's it!"

"It is such a nice place," said Shadrack. "It would be a shame if Graig Allen found out about it being on his property."

"Ten dollars!"

"Well, okay, Nutbeam, but I'll have to tell Dryfly. Bad as I hate him for stealin' me woman, I'll have to tell 'im."

"No! Tell nobody!"

"Him and me will come and see ya once in a while, Nutbeam."

"I don't want you bringin' no one back here!"

"Just Dryfly, Nutbeam."

"What d'ya want to bring 'im back here for?"

Nutbeam knew very well who Dryfly was. He'd heard him play guitar many times.

"For ten dollars, I won't tell a soul yer back here, Nutbeam, 'cept for Dryfly. Him and me will be the only ones to know."

"What's to stop him from tellin' everybody?"

"Oh, ya might have to give him some little thing . . ."

"How do you know he can be trusted?"

"Oh, you can trust Dryfly, Nutbeam. Never did a thing wrong in his life. Leave anything at all layin' around and Dry'd be the last person in the world to ever touch it."

"I don't like it," said Nutbeam. Nutbeam was being blackmailed, and he knew it.

*

When the Atlantic salmon leave the ocean to swim the fresh water rivers to spawn, they stop feeding. They don't feed again until after they've laid their eggs, which sometimes takes three or four months. You can fish over these pregnant fish with all the juicey fat flies, bugs and worms you want, but you might as well try to water a horse that isn't thirsty. They refuse to eat.

Occasionally, these pregnant fish will make a pass at a fly (a roll), and on occasion, they may even go as far as to kill the fly. However, this is really nothing more than recreation. It is these sports-minded salmon, the jocks, that anglers seek. You might say that anglers clean up on the jocks of the school. Palidin Ramsey was sure of only one thing: there had been four jocks in the school that rested in Dr. MacDowell's salmon pool. Palidin Ramsey had four salmon lying dead on the beach.

Palidin was very optimistic. "It could be working," he thought, "but I'm still not sure. There might be some other reason why the fishing's so good today. I'll have to try different flies. Maybe any flyhook, magnetic or not, would take these fish. I need more flies."

Palidin made a little pool out of rocks at the water's edge.

He put three of his salmon in it and covered them up with grass and leaves to keep the sun from spoiling them, then headed for the footbridge with the fourth. He carried the salmon directly to Bernie Hanley's store.

"Boys! What've ya got there!" said Bernie Hanley when he saw the ten-pounder Palidin had with him. "Ain't that a nice one!"

"Just caught it," Palidin proudly announced. "Wanna buy it?"

"Well, by cripes, I could do with a feed o' salmon! How much ya want for it?"

"Want three flyhooks."

"Three flyhooks. Well, that's a little steep. Seventy-five cents apiece . . . seventy-five . . . a dollar fifty . . . two-twenty-five. Well . . . I'll give ya two dollars."

"No, sorry, I'll just take it home."

"Okay. Three flyhooks."

Bernie Hanley paid twenty-five cents per flyhook to Bert Todder for tying them. Bernie Hanley was actually getting the salmon for seventy-five cents . . . a dollar, if you included the flyhook George had stolen from him earlier.

"I want a Butterfly, a Black Bear Hair with a green butt, and a Cosseboom." Three different patterns, along with the Blue Charm George had stolen for him earlier, would greatly enhance the experiment.

Palidin headed back to Dr. MacDowell's pool.

When he got back in the river, he tied on the Butterfly and fished for what he figured to be about fifteen minutes. Nothing happened.

He then took out his lodestone and magnetized the hook of the Butterfly. He made a cast — Bang! Splash! A salmon grabbed the Butterfly.

He landed the salmon and tried the same experiment with the Cosseboom. Fifteen minutes with the regular hook produced nothing. He magnetized the hook and was into a salmon, a grilse, after just a few minutes.

It was a very exciting experience for Palidin. He found himself wanting to run home to tell everyone he met, to share his wealth, so to speak. He fought the urge and tied on the Black Bear Hair with the green butt. He performed the same experiment. He achieved the same results.

He now had four salmon and two grilse. More than he could carry. He would have to make two trips. "I'll give Shad one," he thought, "and take the rest home. If this keeps up, I'll start sellin'. I'll buy me a rod of my own, sell some more and buy a car. I'll fish for a living."

*

Dryfly ate Helen MacDonald's corned beef stew with gusto. He was very hungry. He hadn't eaten all day and it was getting late. "Americans eat awful late," he thought. Helen MacDonald had been very careful not to get Dryfly's bowl of chocolate pudding mixed up with the bowls she had prepared for Bill and Lillian Wallace. Dryfly Ramsey's chocolate pudding was laced with Ex-Lax.

"Not too much," Helen had thought. "But enough to teach him a lesson. Enough to keep him running for a while."

During dinner, everyone was in a good mood. Bill Wallace was happy and so was Lillian. Dryfly, although a little uptight about his own table manners, was also happy. The stew was good and the pudding perfect. Helen MacDonald was a good cook.

The topic of conversation, the common denominator, was the river and the salmon. Bill Wallace asked questions and Dryfly answered the best he could. Dryfly didn't know much about salmon, so most of his answers were inspired by the many stories he'd heard during long winter evenings standing around listening to the men talk in Bernie Hanley's store.

"There use to be a lotta salmon," said Dryfly. "One time Bert Todder was wading the river with a horse and wagon. The salmon were so thick that they were getting caught on the spokes of the wagon. As the wheels turned, the salmon kept flipping up into the box. Bert Todder got enough salmon for the winter, just wading the river."

Bill Wallace laughed loud and long. Both he and Lillian thought it a great story.

Dryfly, liking the laughter, said, "You use to have to get behind a tree to tie yer hook on."

More laughter.

Dryfly blushed, but he was hot. "That was a dry summer," he said. "The salmon used to have to come ashore for a drink."

More laughter.

"What's the biggest salmon you've ever seen?" asked Lillian.

"Well, I don't know how much it weighed, but it was as long as this table," said Dryfly. "It was stuck to an eagle."

"It was stuck to an eagle?"

"Yeah, the eagle had locked his claws in the salmon's back and wouldn' let go. The salmon dived deep and drowned the eagle. The salmon must've been too heavy for the eagle to lift. We found the both of them washed up on the shore down by Tuney's Brook.

"Is that a true story?" asked Bill.

"True as I'm settin' here," said Dryfly, and, indeed, the story was true.

"You know, I haven't caught a salmon all week. I can't imagine what I'm doing wrong," said Bill.

"You'll git one," said Dryfly. "Salmon are funny fish. Once John Kaston fished all week with a sport and didn't ketch a thing. Then, one day they was settin' in the canoe and a salmon jumped right in along side the sport. John killed the salmon and it turned out to be the only one the sport took back with him. That was the only fish they caught all week." That, too, was a true story.

When dinner was over, the three retired to the veranda. Bill gave Dryfly a pack of Lucky Strikes. Bill and Dryfly smoked and talked, Lillian smiled and laughed and looked very pretty. Both Bill and Dryfly loved Lillian Wallace very much.

Ten o'clock rolled around and Bill hinted it was time for Dryfly to go home. Ten o'clock was not late for Lillian, but Bill wanted to discuss a few things with her in private.

"Well, I guess I'd better be goin'," said Dryfly.

"I'll walk a little way with you," said Lillian.

"Good night," said Bill.

"Good night, Bill," said Dryfly.

When they were sure the night was hiding them from Bill's vision, Dryfly and Lillian held hands. They walked to the edge of the Cabbage Island Salmon Club property and sat at the base of a pine tree.

"I had a wonderful day," said Lillian.

"Me too," said Dryfly.

"I like you very much," said Lillian.

"I like you, too," said Dryfly.

"I think my father likes you, too."

"Ya think?"

Lillian leaned and kissed Dryfly one cool little peck on the cheek. It was the first time anyone other than his mother had ever reached out to kiss him. Dryfly was amazed at how good it made him feel. It gave him butterflies and made him feel all warm inside.

"I . . . I . . ."

"Yes?"

"I . . . I . . ." Dryfly wanted to say the magic words, *I love you*, but he couldn't seem to come out with them.

"I'd better be goin'," he said.

"There's no great hurry. Dad won't mind as long as I don't stay too long."

"I know, but it's gettin' late and I . . ."

"I'm really glad you could come to dinner tonight, Dryfly."

"It was good food. I really think I should be goin' now."

"Relax, Dryfly, it's only early."

Dryfly didn't want to go. He would've sat beneath that pine tree with Lillian all night, but he was getting terrible cramps in his abdomen. The Helen MacDonald dosages of cabbage and Ex-Lax were working hand in hand, and Dryfly wasn't sure whether he need to let off gas or indulge in a full scale bout. Either way, he didn't want to do it in the presence of Lillian Wallace.

"I really gotta be goin'," he said.

"What for?"

Dryfly was too backward and shy to tell her the truth.

"Mom wants me home early tonight," he lied.

"Oh, well, okay. Will I see you tomorrow?"

"Sure."

"Will you walk me back to the camp?"

"Sure."

They stood and started back to the camp.

"Want to go on a picnic tomorrow?" Lillian asked.

"Sure. If you want."

Dryfly was beginning to really suffer and Lillian seemed to walk so very slow.

"It's such a beautiful night," said Lillian. "Look, there's a new moon."

"Yep."

"I love moonlit nights." Lillian squeezed his hand and turned to face him. "I'll be leaving Sunday morning, Dryfly. I'm going to miss you."

"I'll miss you too."

It was clear to Dryfly that Lillian wanted to kiss again, but he was not sure he could hold on much longer. A particularly vicious spasm coursed through his bowels forcing him to cross his legs and bend over. He still would not admit to his agony, however.

"What's wrong?" asked Lillian.

"Nothin' . . . thought I saw somethin' on the ground."

"What? I don't see anything."

"Nothin'."

"Are you all right, Dryfly?"

"Yep." Dryfly straightened. "I'm all right."

They moved a few more paces toward the camps. Lillian stopped again. "You know," she said, "it's so quiet here, you can almost hear the silence."

"Yeah, but the flies are eatin' me alive," said Dryfly. "I gotta get out o' here!"

"That's funny, they're not bothering me at all."

"Well, they're botherin' me! I'll see ya later!"

"Kiss me good night?"

Dryfly kissed her quickly. He knew the countdown had started.

"I'll see ya tomorrow," he said, already moving away.

"Good night."

"See ya tomorrow!"

Dryfly walked twenty paces, then ran with desperation into the woods.

*

Shadrack sat on the Tuney Brook bridge until it was too dark for him to see the little trout swimming in the water beneath. Although he was somewhat excited about the events of the day, he kept very still. He did not wave or slap at the mosquitoes and most of them never found him.

"Dryfly stole me woman," thought Shadrack. "Me own fault, though. Should've kissed her when I had the chance. She'd still be with me, if I had've kissed her. Now I got a broken heart and I'm . . . I'm . . . blue, yeah, I'm blue. What's a blue lad feel like, I wonder? What's a man do when he's got a broken heart and blue?"

Shadrack knew what he had told Dryfly. Shadrack knew that he had told Dryfly he and Lillian were lovers; that he and Lillian had even discussed marriage.

"Course, I was lyin'," thought Shad, "but that don't matter, I'll have to show signs of a broken heart, even if I don't care anymore. I could tell 'im I left her for another woman . . . or I left her because I didn't like her cookin'. I'll tell 'im . . . somethin' . . . what's keepin' 'im so long?"

Another hour passed before Shadrack heard Dryfly coming down the path.

> *Beautiful, beautiful brown eyes,*
> *Beautiful, beautiful brown eyes,*
> *Beautiful, beautiful brown eyes,*
> *I'll never love blue eyes again*

sang Dryfly.
"That you, Dryfly?"
Dryfly came to an immediate halt.
"Shad?"
"Yeah. Here on the bridge."
"What're ya doin' here?"

"Waitin' for you!"

Dryfly carefully approached the little bridge. Dryfly was somewhat worried that Shad might be angry. He wasn't afraid. He felt he'd done nothing wrong, but he wasn't up for a confrontation. He still felt somewhat ill, and his spirits were too good to ruin them with an argument, or whatever Shadrack might have in mind.

"Where ya been all night?" asked Shad.

"I . . . I've been with . . . Bill Wallace."

"How's you and Lillian makin' out? You in love with her, Dry?"

"Naw, jist settin' up there talkin', that's all."

"An awful lotta talkin', Dry! You been up there all day!"

"Jist talkin', that's all we were doin'."

"I saw you and Lillian walkin' down the front holdin' hands!"

"So?"

"So, where were ya goin'?"

"Lindon Tucker's."

"Walkin' down the front, holdin' hands in broad daylight! Good thing I left her when I did!"

"You left her?"

"Didn' she tell ya?"

"No."

"Course, I left her! Good thing too, by the looks of it, or you'd be holdin' hands with another man's woman! You think about that, Dry?"

"No."

"No! Course ya didn'! You don't think o' nothin', do ya! You never stopped to think o' me and how I might've got hurt. Course, I didn' get hurt, cause I left the jeezless tramp, but it's a good thing for you that I did!"

"Lillian ain't a tramp, Shad."

"Course she's a tramp! Last night me, tonight you, God knows who tomorrow night! That tramp don't care about us lads, Dry! She's prob'ly up there in the camp right now laughin' her head off at ya. Wouldn' surprise me at all!"

"I don't think so, Shad."

143

"I saw through her, so I did! No woman's gonna make a fool out o' Shadrack Nash!"

Dryfly didn't like what he was hearing. To Dryfly, Lillian Wallace was not a tramp. To Dryfly, Lillian Wallace was the most refined, wonderful, kind, sweet girl in the world.

"I don't care if she laughs at me," said Dryfly.

Dryfly's love for Lillian Wallace was the first real possession he'd ever had. He knew it might not be a possession that would hang around for very long, but he was going to enjoy it and make the most of it while it lasted. He did not want to fight with Shad, though. He would let Shadrack and anybody else say whatever they wanted. He would not give up the precious moments he was spending with Lillian.

"She kin laugh, and you kin say what you want, I don't care!" said Dryfly.

"And you shouldn' care! She'll be gone in a few days and she'll laugh and make fun o' you, all the way home!"

Dryfly endeavored to change the subject. "What've you been doin' all day, Shad?" he asked.

"I've been . . . I've been . . . you'd never guess who I met up with today, Dry."

ten

Saturday night at dusk, Bill Wallace and Lindon Tucker stood outside the Cabbage Island Salmon Club camps. They were saying goodbye. They would not see each other again for a year. Bill paid Lindon for guiding him and tipped him twenty dollars. Twenty dollars was the biggest tip Lindon Tucker had ever received for guiding. Bill Wallace had had a few drinks and was feeling generous. He could afford to be generous. Bill Wallace was a millionaire who had just purchased a fifty thousand dollar salmon pool for a thousand dollars. Lindon Tucker had been drinking too, and was feeling quite good.

"I didn't catch any salmon this year," said Bill, "but I'll be back next year. I want to put up a cottage next year, Lindon, and by God, I want you to be one of the carpenters."

"Yeah, sure, yeah, sure, sure! Done a bit o' carpenter work. Wouldn' mind workin' on it. Yeah, sure, sure! I'll work on it."

"Well, Lindon, I think I'll get my gear together and go to bed. I've got a long drive tomorrow, and Lillian and I will be rising early."

"It's been good doin' bus'ness, yeah. See ya next year. We'll git lotsa fish next year."

"If we could figure out what that young Palidin Ramsey is doing, we'll catch them all right, Lindon. How many do you think he's caught in the last few days?"

"Well, he got six one day, he told me, so he did. Six, yeah. Six one day and four the next. Yeah, yeah, yeah, six one day and four the next and seven today. That makes . . . six and four and seven . . . how many?"

"Seventeen, I believe, Lindon."

"Seventeen, yeah, yeah, seventeen. Did ya buy a few from him to take back with ya?"

"I sure did, Lindon. I bought eight from him. I'll tell the boys back home that I caught them myself."

"Yes sir, yes sir, yes sir. Tell them ya caught them yerself, yeah, yeah yeah. Yeah. Ha, ha."

"Well, good-night, Lindon."

"Yes sir, yes sir. Good-night."

"We'll see you next year."

"Next year, yeah. Yeah, yeah, next year, yeah. Yep. Take 'er easy."

Bill Wallace escaped into the camp.

Lindon Tucker was in a mood for celebrating and headed for Bernie Hanley's store.

Dan Brennen, Bob Nash, John Kaston, Bert Todder and Stan Tuney were all standing around Bernie Hanley's store gossiping, eating oranges and drinking Sussex Ginger Ale. When Lindon Tucker arrived, he pulled a pint — already half empty — from his belt, ordered a bottle of ginger ale and treated the boys.

"Yes sir. Yes sir, yes sir, the best sport I ever guided. Tipped me twenty dollars, so he did. Twenty dollars! And, and, and gimme a fishin' rod. Brand new rod! Give it to me, he did. Twenty dollars and a fishin' rod, jist like that! He said, he said, he said, he said, he said, he said, what he said was I want you to have it, he said. Gimme a rod, jist like that, yeah."

"That old lad I was guidin', didn' ketch a fish all week and didn' tip me a cent!" said Stan Tuney.

"My sport fished from daylight to dark, caught four salmon and a grilse and only tipped me two dollars. I reached right in me pocket and give 'im five. Told 'im he might need it to get home on," said Dan Brennen.

"Remember that old lad I was guidin' in April? The old lad that wouldn' piss in the river?" said Bert Todder.

"Yeah, I remember him. Same lad you were guidin' all week, weren't it?" asked Stan.

"Yeah, that's the same old jeezer!"

"I never heard that story," said Dan Brennen. "What happened?"

"Well, I was guidin' him in April and he wouldn' piss in

the river. I was goin' up the river with that ten Johnson out-board motor and he was in the front. When he needed a piss, he pulled out this pickle bottle and started to piss in it. The wind was blowin' real hard and the piss kept blowin' back all over me . . . jist kind of a fine spray, if ya know what I mean. I snubbed 'er up some quick, I tell ya! I ain't drinkin' yer piss all the way to Gordon, I told 'im!"

All the men laughed.

"Oh yeah, yeah, yeah," commenced Lindon. "Sold that old shore o' mine. Sold it, yeah. No good, that old shore. Got rid o' it, so I did. Got rid o' it. Might sell the whole place, yet. Move to Fredericton, I think. Move to Fredericton and take 'er easy."

There were no secrets in Brennen Siding. All the men knew that Lindon had sold his property. Somehow, Bert Todder had found out.

"You'll get a job lookin' after that lad's camp when he gets it built, won't ya, Lindon?"

"He didn' say for sure. I might, I might, ya never know, I might! I think I'll sell the whole place and move to Fredericton. Lay right back in Fredericton."

"I'd sell that old place o' mine some quick," said Bert Todder. "That old shore, anyway. Them old shores ain't no good to a man."

"Should be able to sell that old shore o' yours, no trouble, Bert. The mouth o' Todder Brook is right there. There's al-ways salmon at the mouth o' the brook. Why don't ya sell it and get a big chunk o' money for it?" said John Kaston. "Them old shores ain't worth nothin'."

"Ain't worth nothin', no," said Lindon Tucker. "Sold mine, so I did. Yep. Think I'll move to Fredericton. Lay right back, take 'er easy, yeah."

*

Lillian Wallace was not laughing. Fifteen-year-old Lillian Wallace had a tear in her eye. Lillian Wallace said, "I'm going to miss you, Dryfly," and meant it.

"Gonna miss you too," said Dryfly.

"I'll come back next year, Dry. We'll get together again next year."

"A year's a long time," said Dryfly.

"You could come down and stay with us, play at the Red Lion."

"Yeah, maybe."

"Will you write to me?"

"If you write to me."

Over the past few days, Dryfly had spent every possible minute with Lillian Wallace. They walked and talked, sat around on the veranda drinking lemonade and "soda"; they swam and went on picnics and kissed and hugged forty-two thousand and one times.

They were very much in love, but the word "love" was never spoken. Dryfly wanted to say it now. Dryfly didn't want Lillian to walk out of his life without her knowing how he felt, and he wanted to know how she felt about him. He wanted to say, "I love you," and he wanted to hear her say, "I love you, too."

He held her close, smelling the fly repellent on her neck, feeling her warm young body against his own. He kissed the tears from her cheek. "This is it," he thought. "This is the last time I'll hold her. I might never see her again." Dryfly wanted to cry too.

Dryfly would never forget her. He would never forget the few short days and nights they'd had together. He was totally in love — in love with Lillian; in love with the stars and the moon; in love with the river and the warm July night.

Dryfly had wanted to say "I love you" so many times during the past few days, but for some reason, couldn't twist his tongue around the three little words. Now, with tears welling from his eyes, while kissing her tears from her face, while looking into the big, tear-filled blue eyes he adored while feeling her warmth with the reality that he might never see her again, he thought he could say it.

"Lillian," he whispered, "Lillian . . ."

"Yes, Dryfly?"

"Lillian . . . I love you!"

There was a silence, during which Dryfly could only hear their heartbeat and their breathing. Then, Lillian pulled away from him. She looked at his tattered sneakers and ragged jeans, the same shirt she had washed for him three days ago, his hair parted in the middle, his long nose and his eyes. He had tears in his eyes.

Crying with all the spirit of a child, she ran into the camp.

*

Dryfly swung and started walking. He didn't know where he was going and he didn't care. All he knew was that he needed to walk. "I'm in love," he thought. "I'm in love with Lillian Wallace and she's gone. I'm alone. I can cry now." He unleashed a flood of tears.

When he got to the Tuney brook bridge, he found Shad waiting for him. He didn't want Shad to see the tears, but there was no stopping them. He approached Shad and stood before him, weeping like a hurt child.

When Shadrack saw that Dryfly was crying, he did not speak. Neither did Dryfly. They stood eyeing each other, Dryfly crying and Shadrack not knowing what to say. Shadrack knew one thing though: he was sorry for the things he'd said about Lillian Wallace.

"You all right?" said Shadrack, when he finally found words.

"I don't know . . . I guess."

"I'm gonna miss her, too," said Shad.

"I love her, Shad!"

"She'll come back, Dryfly. Don't cry. She'll come back."

"Maybe . . . maybe."

"Let me pole you up to Gordon," said Shad. "We'll git some wine at the bootlegger's. We'll have a drink o' wine and talk."

"Wine? I ain't got no money for wine."

"I got that ten dollars Nutbeam gave me. We'll git some wine and have a talk."

"Okay. Might as well."

Shadrack and Dryfly went to the Cabbage Island Salmon

Club and slid off, quietly so that no one would hear them, in one of the club's canoes.

Dryfly found some consolation from being on the river and cheered up a bit. The river reflected the blue of the sky, the stars, the moon and the forested hills. Except for the swish-plunk, swish-plunk of the pole, and the rippling sound of the canoe cutting the water, all was quiet.

"She didn't say it," thought Dryfly. "She didn't say 'I love you.'"

"You know what, Shad?" said Dryfly a little later. "She's the only woman I ever loved."

"Me too," said Shad.

The boys had one more bond between them.

*

Knock, knock.

"Who's there?"

"Shadrack and Dryfly."

"Ah, hell!"

Nutbeam arose from his cot, went to the door and opened it.

"What d'ya want?"

"We got some wine, Nutbeam," said Shadrack. "Thought maybe you'd like a drink."

Nutbeam had just gotten home from his radio listening trip. He had listened to *Saturday Night Jamboree* outside of Shirley Ramsey's house. Again he had crept closer to the house so he could peek through the window at Shirley. Shirley was sewing a shirt for Palidin and looked very beautiful to Nutbeam. Nutbeam wanted very much to meet Shirley Ramsey.

Later, lying on his cot, he had given his predicament thought. "She's a good woman. A man should have a woman. Shirley Ramsey needs a man. I could keep her, look after her . . . but what's the use? She'd never look sideways at a lad like me."

"I'm gonna have to do somethin'," Nutbeam said aloud to the camp. "I'm not gettin' any younger. Let me see . . . I'm forty-six years old. Forty-six and never had a woman. Sweet forty-six and never been kissed."

Nutbeam had spent many hours during the last year, thinking about his lonely situation and had concluded that the loneliness was getting to be too much. He was beginning to talk to himself.

"I'm goin' crazy," he said. "Talkin' to yerself is one of the first signs of goin' crazy."

When Shadrack showed up to unlock his little secret, Nutbeam had been very upset, nervous, yes, and even a little afraid. But now, there in the dark, on his cot, Nutbeam felt that maybe Shadrack's appearance had been a blessing in disguise. Maybe the Good Lord was looking after him and had sent Shadrack to find him, to flush him out, to reveal him to the world that he would either have to face, or go insane. Setting all other predicaments aside, Nutbeam, there in the dark, on his cot, was a very troubled and bewildered man. And then:

Knock, knock.

"If I don't face this young fella and play some sorta game, the young brat will blackmail me. I shouldn' have offered him any money in the first place. And now, he's brought that young Dryfly Ramsey back here in the middle of the night, lookin' to blackmail me. I'll have to face them. I'll have to play some sorta game."

"Mind if we come in?" said Shadrack

"It's awful late," said Nutbeam.

"Ain't late. Ain't even twelve o'clock."

"What d'ya want?"

"Don't want nothin'. Jist came to visit ya. Was tellin' Dryfly here about ya. He wanted to meet ya."

Nutbeam sighed. "Come in," he said. "But just for a minute!"

"Awful dark in here. Ain't ya got a lamp?"

"Yes, I have a lamp."

"Nutbeam struck a match and lit the lamp.

"Nice place ya got here, Nutbeam," said Dryfly.

"Just an old camp."

"I like it."

"Would ya like a drink o' wine?" asked Shad, pulling a bottle of sherry out from under his jacket.

"I haven't had a drink in ten years," said Nutbeam.

"Go ahead, have a drink. It's good stuff. Golden Nut."

"No. I think not."

"Aw, c'mon! Won't hurt ya. Have a drink o' wine. Good for ya. Keeps that lad from starin' at ya." Shad had adopted "Keeps that lad from starin' at ya" from Bert Todder.

Nutbeam stared at the bottle. "Would be nice to have a drink with someone," he thought. He sat by the table and took a small sip of the sweet wine. He thought it was, indeed, quite good.

Shadrack and Dryfly smiled at each other and sat on the cot.

"Bought that with the ten dollars you give me, Nutbeam. Wanted to show ya that I didn't waste the money. Have another drink . . . take a big one, that's no good! Take 'er down! Help yerself!"

Nutbeam took a bigger drink.

"Good stuff," said Nutbeam. "Where'd ya get it?"

"Gordon. From the bootlegger in Gordon. We left another bottle outside, so don't worry about runnin' shy of 'er."

The three sipped from the wine and it wasn't long before they commenced to feel its effects. The conversation flowed a bit easier, and although Nutbeam hadn't really talked any amount in years, he found that the words were coming surprisingly easy. He thought he might even be enjoying himself. The boys weren't making fun of him either, or they didn't seem to be. They actually seemed to like him.

"You play guitar," Nutbeam said to Dryfly.

"How'd ya know that?"

"I know a lotta things."

"Yeah, I play, but not very good."

"You play good." Nutbeam took another drink.

"You sure have some nice rifles," said Shad.

"You like me rifles?"

"Sure do. What's that one?"

Shad pointed at the rifle he fancied most.

"That's a 30-30. Good gun, that."

"You must get a lotta deer and moose and stuff," said Shadrack, still admiring the rifles.

"I get what I need."

"Hey! What's that thing?" asked Dryfly.

"Trumpet."

"Really? What's it for?"

"It's a musical instrument."

"Kin ya play it?"

"Ain't played it much lately."

"Would ya play it fer us, Nutbeam?"

"No. Makes too much noise. Can't play it anyway."

"What do we care if it makes noise? There's only the three of us."

"Not tonight."

"Ya know what we should do some night? We should bring the banjo and guiddar back and play some music."

"Ya could sure let loose back here," agreed Dryfly. "No one would ever hear ya back here."

"I can't play very good," said Nutbeam.

"Sure ya kin," said Shadrack. "All ya have to do is practise."

"They'd hear me all over the country."

"Naw! Never in a million years," said Dryfly. "Never hear ya way back here."

"Play it, Nutbeam," urged Shad.

"Maybe later."

When the three finished the first bottle of wine, Shad went and retrieved the second bottle. With the ten dollars, he had purchased four bottles. He and Dryfly had consumed one on their way from Gordon. If they finished this one, they still had one left. Shadrack was in a party mood.

Soon Shadrack started to sing. He wasn't much for carrying a melody, but he loved to sing, so he bellowed one dirty song out after another. Between songs, the boys told dirty jokes. Nutbeam was forgetting himself. Nutbeam actually laughed at the dirty songs and jokes. This was the best time that Nutbeam had ever had.

Shad got up and danced around the camp. "Yeah-whoo!" he whooped. "Yeah-whoo and her name was Maud!" He grabbed the trumpet and tried to blow into it. Nothing happened.

"Here, Nutbeam old dog, give 'er hell!"

Nutbeam was getting drunk and caught up in the excitement. He took a bigger than average drink of the wine, grabbed the trumpet from Shadrack, stood and commenced to blow. BARMP-BARMP-BEEP-BARMP-BARMP!

Shadrack and Dryfly couldn't believe their ears. At first they just stared at each other. Then, they smiled at each other. The smile turned into a chuckle. The chuckle turned into hilarious laughter. They laughed at Nutbeam's big lips trying to manufacture sounds on the trumpet. They laughed at Nutbeam's big ears and lanky body. They laughed at the awful noise Nutbeam was making. But most of all, they laughed at the reality that there before them, was none other than the Todder Brook Whooper.

Shadrack was already starting to get ideas.

Staggering homeward in the middle of the night, Shadrack said to Dryfly, "What d'ya s'pose a nice lad like that would live his life in the woods for?"

"He's got big floppy ears," said Dryfly.

"Yeah, but there's got to be somethin' else."

"Inferiority comprex," said Dry.

*

At the crack of dawn, Lillian Wallace stirred, rose and got dressed. She put on her blue shorts, pink blouse and sandals. Then, she went to the dresser and peered into the mirror. She combed her hair and looked into her tired, sky-blue eyes. If she had smiled, her full, young lips would have revealed clean, well-kept teeth, but Lillian Wallace did not feel like smiling.

When she was satisfied with her appearance, she picked up a pen from the dresser and jotted down three words on a piece of paper. She put the note in an envelope, wrote "Dryfly" on it, started to lick and seal it, but decided against it. Then she, with envelope in hand, left the room. Three seconds later, she stepped into the grey, pine-scented Dungarvon morning. Every bird that could sing was singing.

Lillian needed to think. To think, she needed to walk. She

went down the path, over the hill and across the little bridge Stan Tuney had built over his brook. A fingerling trout swam beneath the bridge, but Lillian Wallace, there in the cool dewy morning, did not take the time to watch it. She would be leaving the Dungarvon in little more than an hour for Stockbridge, Massachusetts and needed to see Dryfly Ramsey one more time . . . or at least be close to him.

She followed the brook until she came to Stan Tuney's field. Crossing the field, she stopped to pick a daisy. She put the daisy in the envelope with the three word note and sealed it.

By the time she got to the railroad, her feet were soaked with dew. She didn't care. She was almost there. In a minute she stopped in front of Shirley Ramsey's house and peered at the window she thought might be Dryfly's.

In the grey dawn, she eyed the drab, paintless structure before her. She eyed the sandy lawn and the car tires. They were cut diametrically in two and placed at the ends of the culvert. A sandy path led to the front door. In another car tire beside the path, Shirley had planted a geranium.

Lillian went to the door and stood for a moment. She wanted to knock, to awaken Dryfly, to hold him, to feel the warmth of his body, to kiss and hug and love him like he'd never been loved before. Lillian Wallace, young and beautiful, alone in a strange land, standing at Shirley Ramsey's door at dawn, whispered, "Sleep tight, Dryfly, my prince of Dungarvon. I love you."

Quietly, so as not to disturb anyone, she slid the envelope beneath the door. Without looking back, she returned to the Cabbage Island Salmon Club.

Back in her room, Lillian sat on her bed to wait for her father to awaken. She knew she would not have to wait long. Bill Wallace wanted to get an early start.

eleven

When Dryfly found the note from Lillian Wallace, he kissed the daisy. As the daisy touched his lips, a teardrop that had been coursing its way down his cheek dropped to land on the "loves me" petal. The old "She loves me — she loves me not" game would not be necessary.

Dryfly Ramsey was a dreamer.

Dryfly Ramsey had always been a dreamer. When he was a child, he dreamed of cowboys on dynamic white stallions, cacti and coyote calls (there were no coyotes in New Brunswick back then); he dreamed of exotic places like Newcastle and Chatham, Saint John and Fredericton. As he passed through the awkwardness of puberty, his dreams reluctantly changed.

Dryfly didn't have it in mind to give up childhood, but it happened, as it happens to everyone. His dreams had changed from range cowboys to radio cowboys, the guitar being a key implement in the process. He wanted to be like Lee Moore, or Doc Williams. He wanted to live in exotic places like Wheeling, West Virginia or Nashville, Tennessee.

Now, Lillian Wallace had changed things again. The need for the love of a woman stormed in and Dryfly started to experience the cold, ruthless loneliness of adolescence.

Dryfly started taking long walks alone, dreaming of Lillian Wallace. He was seen less often, and whenever he did show up at Bernie Hanley's store to associate with the boys, he was quiet and downcast, always too aware of himself. Shirley Ramsey saw the change in him. She also noticed that Dryfly was paying frequent visits to the piece of mirror that hung above the water buckets. He'd look into the mirror, sigh, comb his hair, look it over and shake his head. When the greased-back hair went *flip flop* he'd sigh again and sometimes left the house for a lonely walk. Dryfly's introverted state passed quickly, but not without leaving a scar — a change had occurred. Dryfly felt he needed a woman.

"It seems to me, to get the women, ya gotta be in with the *in* crowd," said Shadrack one evening.

The two teenagers were sitting on the center abutment of the footbridge. They were facing downstream, watching an American fishing the Judge Martin pool. The American was old and bent and maneuvered his way through the pool with the assistance of a cane.

"The *in* crowd?" asked Dryfly.

"Yeah. That's the new sayin' around places like Blackville these days."

"What's the difference in the *in* crowd and the *out* crowd?"

"Well, the way I see it, the *in* crowd are lads that got a trucker's wallet with a chain that holds it to yer belt, and jetboots."

"And the *out* crowd?"

"Lads like us."

"There ain't no girls around here, anyway."

"There are in Blackville. Everybody goes to Blackville these days."

"Maybe that's what we should be doin'."

"No use. Ain't got a trucker's wallet and jetboots."

*

When Max and John Kaston pulled up in front of Brigham's store in Blackville, the first thing that caught their eyes was a fellow named Lyman MacFee. Lyman MacFee played electric guitar with a country-rock group called Lyman MacFee and the Cornpoppers. Lyman MacFee did much more than play for weekend dances for five dollars a dance. He was also the president of the Blackville recreation council, a right-wing forward for the Blackville hockey team, the Blackville Aces, and the manager of Brigham's Store Blackville Limited. When Max and John Kaston pulled up in front of Brigham's, they saw Lyman MacFee diddling "Mutty Musk" and step-dancing on the step that ran across the front of the store.

Max and John Kaston got out of the truck and approached the diddling, dancing Lyman MacFee. When they reached the step, Lyman quit diddling and dancing, swung and said, "'Mutty Musk!' The best damn tune ever played! Old Ned MacLaggen always said, ya kin tell a good harmonica player when he plays ya 'Mutty Musk' in variations! What kin I do for ya today, boys?"

"I don't know for sure, Lyman, but I was thinkin' I'd like to take a look at yer chainsaws."

"A chainsaw! Now, there's the rig! Come inside! I know just what yer lookin' for! Dee-da-diddle-daddle-diddle-daddle-diddle-daddle-dum."

John and Max followed the diddling Lyman MacFee into what Max thought was probably one of the biggest stores in the world. "It's two stories and must be a hundred feet long," thought Max. "And just look at all this stuff!"

Brigham's Store had everything in it from beds to rifles, shovels to chesterfields, bicycle pumps to phonographs to clothing. Max noticed that they even had a couple of television sets. Max would have loved to have a television, but he knew it would never happen as long as he lived with his father. John Kaston believed that television was the creation of Satan.

Lyman MacFee led them to the corner he had recently cleared to accommodate his newest sales item, the yellow Pioneer chainsaws, the pioneer of the machine that would change Brennen Siding, the Miramichi area, even all of New Brunswick, forever.

"There's what yer lookin' for, right there," said Lyman. "The best outfit to ever hit the woods!"

"Howmuchyouwantfor it?" asked Max, so fast that Lyman wasn't sure if the words were English or not.

Max was a little bit afraid of Lyman, thought he might be lying to them, overpricing the saws, ripping them off. He was also afraid of the saw — it was ugly and heavy. Max had lost twenty pounds working with a bucksaw, but he had gotten used to it. Now this chainsaw would demand even more from him; he'd lose more weight; he'd have more lumber to contend with; he'd be working longer days. He didn't want to get used to it.

"All three of them are the same price, two hundred and forty-nine ninety-five — but they're worth every cent. You kin saw more lumber in a day with them things than ya kin saw with a bucksaw in a week! Randy Carter's young lad's cutting four cord a day with one like this and is home for supper at four o'clock."

"It's a lotta money, though, ain't it?" said John Kaston to Max, the son who was too contrary to go back to school and become a preacher; Max, the son who even refused to read the Bible or lead in prayers.

"Yep," said Max.

"No money at all," cut in Lyman. "No money when ya think of the wood yer cuttin'! That's not one word a lie, John, four cord a day by himself! Let's take 'er out back and I'll show you how it works."

Out back, Lyman MacFee hauled the pullcord of the chainsaw and a sonorous buzzing noise settled over half the village. The other half of the village could also hear the buzzing, but it was somewhat bearable if one was far enough away.

Lyman MacFee cut into a log he had placed out back for the purpose of demonstrating. The sharp new teeth of the chain cut with great rapidity through the bark, knots and wood of the unfortunate log.

The flying sawdust and the buzzing like so many giant insects frightened and depressed Max Kaston to no end.

Again and again Lyman sawed through the log, then handed the saw to John, who gave it a try. When John had zipped off a couple of blocks, he handed the saw to Max.

John Kaston thought that the chainsaw was, indeed, the best outfit for sawing lumber he'd ever seen. Max, on the other hand, was on the verge of tears. He sawed a couple of blocks, but lost heart quickly and handed the saw back to Lyman MacFee.

"What d'ya think, men? Ya ever see anything like it?"

"She's quite the outfit, all right? What do ya think, Max? Ya think you'd like to work in the woods with that outfit from daylight to dark?"

Max, detecting the sarcasm in John's voice, said, "A lotta money."

"A man could pay fer it with four or five cord a day."

"She's an awful heavy outfit," said Max.

"Sure it's heavy," put in Lyman, "but ya'll git used to it. Three or four days o' sawin' and ya won't notice the weight at all. And even if it is a little heavy, it's still a lot easier than pushing a bucksaw all day for half the money. Four cord a day . . . that's forty, forty-five dollars every day you work. I tell ya, John, this outfit's gonna change the whole face of lumberin'! I'll put it on yer bill, you take it home and try it fer a few days, and if ya don't like it, bring it back. I guarantee you won't be sorry."

John Kaston took the chainsaw.

*

To a salmon angler, one salmon a day is considered good fishing. To most anglers, one salmon a week is acceptable. It is not unusual for an angler to fish for a week and catch nothing at all.

But to drive all the way from New York or Boston to Brennen Siding to fish and return with nothing to show for it was looked upon with a certain amount of suspicion by left-behind wives.

"You went all the way to Canada to fish?"

"Yes, my pet."

"So, where's your fish?"

"I didn't catch any, pet."

"Sure!"

While the angler might still be having visions of the Dungarvon River in his memory, the wife was visualizing bars and whorehouses in Montreal or Quebec. An unsuccessful angler, if he was smart, would buy a salmon to take home with him, make up a tale about the struggles he'd had and keep peace in the family.

Palidin, with his magnetized hook, was catching anywhere from two to eight salmon a day. He did not have a freezer. A dead salmon would not last long outside a freezer on an August day. Palidin had to sell his salmon or else give them away. He wanted a car. He did not want to give his salmon away. Palidin Ramsey was in business.

Palidin and George Hanley strolled down the Gordon Road discussing the business.

"I'm ketchin' more than I can sell," said Palidin. "There's just not enough sports around here. I need to be sellin' in Blackville, Upper Blackville, Renous, all over the place."

"Sellin' salmon's against the law. Aren't you scared of gettin' caught?"

"I'll be careful. What I need is a car."

"How much money ya got now?"

"Seventy-eight dollars. I'd have a hundred if I hadn't bought that rod and reel. If I had a couple of hundred, I could buy an old car good enough to get me to Blackville now and again to sell. But I don't have enough money, that's the problem."

"Maybe you could borrow a car."

"Nobody'd ever lend me a car!"

"I kin get one. I kin git Dad's."

"Ya think?"

"Prob'ly. But I'd have to have a cut in the money. You buy me a rod out of the seventy-five dollars and I'll help ya with the fishin', too. We kin be partners."

"I'll think about it," said Palidin, but Palidin was already liking the idea. "I don't have much choice," he thought. "If he can get a car, I'll make him a partner."

David Kaston, Max's older brother, and a girl he was dating from Gordon passed Palidin and George on the road. When they had passed by several yards, Palidin and George turned to watch after them.

"Nice bum," said George.

"She's not bad either," agreed Palidin.

*

Nutbeam was changing, too.

With encouragement from Shadrack and Dryfly, Nutbeam started practicing his trumpet playing again.

"Who cares if they hear me," he said to himself. "I'm

161

not breaking any laws. If they find me out and Graig Allen runs me off his land, I'll move somewhere else. I'd like to have a bigger camp, anyway."

Nutbeam put the trumpet to his lips and unleashed a blast that put the fear of the devil in the hearts of everyone in Brennen Siding . . . except for Shadrack and Dryfly, that is.

Shadrack and Dryfly thought it was the funniest thing they ever heard. They found themselves going to Bernie Hanley's store every night for no other reason than to hear the stories and surmisals.

"I knew that thing was gonna show up again," said Stan Tuney. "I knowd as soon as I saw them tracks in the woods. Hoof tracks, they were!"

"I think meself, now, as the feller says, meself now, I think it's a jeezless fox," said Lindon Tucker.

"Some fox!" said Shadrack. "Weren't no fox we saw in that woods four year ago!"

"Well, just for certain, what did you boys see back in that woods?" asked Bernie Hanley from behind the counter.

"Was awful dark," said Shadrack, "but I do remember seeing a set o' horns like a cow's."

"And it was as big as a moose, but shaped more like a cat," said Dryfly. "What's a panther look like, anyway?"

"They're a big cat," said Bert Todder, "but I never heard tell o' one with horns — you, Bernie?"

"Ain't never been a cat with horns," said Bernie Hanley.

"It's a wonder you boys weren't tore to pieces," said John Kaston.

"I had the rifle, and was about thirty feet away from 'im. Pulled the old gun up and let him have it from thirty feet away. Aimed right for its forward shoulders and let 'er drift. The thing just swung and looked at me as if I was stupid, turned and struck 'er down through the woods," said Shadrack.

"Just seemed to be floatin'," said Dryfly. "Never made a sound."

"Father Murdock blessed the Whooper's grave and it was never heard after. Maybe if I went back in the woods and prayed, the thing would take off out of here," said John Kaston.

"You ain't a priest," said Bernie Hanley.

"No, you're right! I ain't a priest, I'm a good Christian Baptist and that's a lot better than any priest!"

"Prayin' would work just great," said Bert Todder, "but you're forgettin' one thing. We ain't got a grave, or none that we know of, anyway."

"I was out listenin' to it last night," said Bernie Hanley. "Almost sounded like the thing was tryin' to sing, or somethin'."

"Jist sorta sings, so it does," said Lindon Tucker. "Heard it meself, yeah. Jist sorta sings, like."

"Ya know what a crowd o' lads should do? We should load our rifles and go back there and hunt the devil down," said Dan Brennen. "Fill 'im full o' lead."

"That's what a lad should do, Dan old boy. Fill 'im full o' lead, that's what I say. Gun the bugger down, yeah."

"You're movin' to Fredericton pretty soon, ain't ya Lindon?" asked Stan Tuney.

"Oh yeah, yeah, yeah! Movin' in the fall, I think, yeah. Takin' off in the fall, takin' off in the fall."

"Ya can't shoot the devil," said John Kaston. "The good Lord is the only medicine for the devil."

"Young Shadrack scared 'im off with one shot," said Bernie Hanley. "Never came back for four years."

"I wouldn't do that," said Dryfly, recognizing the potential problem for Nutbeam. "I wouldn't go back in that woods again! That bullet didn't hurt 'im one bit."

"But it scared him off," put in Bert Todder.

"And you lads were just a couple o' young lads," added Stan Tuney.

Shad also saw that things might be getting out of hand. "That's the thing," said Shadrack. "We was jist kids back then and didn' know no better. We were lucky, that's all! Knowin' what I know now, I wouldn' take a million dollars for goin' into that woods!"

"Well, I say, somethin's gotta be done!" said John Kaston, "and ya don't need a grave to pray! The power o' the Lord is infinite! I'll go back there with the Lord by my side, and smite that demon. You lads ever think o' prayin'?" It was a rare occasion when John Kaston wouldn't take the opportunity to preach. "Just trust in the Lord and it won't matter if it is the devil back there! Yea, though we walk through the valley o' death, we fear no evil, the Bible says!"

"I'll go back, but I ain't takin' no Bible," said Bert Todder. "I'm takin' the .38-55."

"I'll go too, but I'll have to close the store early," said Bernie Hanley.

"I'll take the Bible. That's the only weapon I need," said John Kaston.

"I'll take me shotgun," said Stan Tuney. Stan Tuney didn't think his shotgun would stand up against the devil, but he had no intention of missing out on anything like this. This would be an adventure to lie about for the rest of his life.

"You lads wouldn't go back there tonight, would ya?" asked Dryfly.

"Too late now. We'll go tomorrow night," said Bernie. "We'll meet here at . . . let's say, nine o'clock." Bernie Hanley very much wanted everybody to meet at his store. The gathering would mean a fairly substantial sale of oranges and ginger ale.

Shadrack and Dryfly knew that these men were cunning hunters and trappers — that they had, in a manner of speaking, been living in the woods all their lives and knew it like the backs of their hands. There was a very good possibility that if these men went back Todder Brook, they would find Nutbeam. Nutbeam was squatting on Graig Allen's property, and although he was somewhat more outgoing than he used to be, he still wanted his location kept secret.

Shadrack and Dryfly slipped away from the crowd and headed for the river.

"What are we gonna do?" asked Dryfly.

"I dunno. Tell Nutbeam to quit playin' for awhile, I guess," said Shadrack.

"Listen . . . I can hear him now."

BLAT, BLAT, BLAT, BARMP-BARMP! Nutbeam was practicing "The Blue Canadian Rockies," but one would have to stretch the imagination considerably to recognize it.

Although the sound of the trumpet may have been inject-
ing fear and bewilderment into the hearts of everyone else in
Brennen Siding, to Shadrack and Dryfly it was what the ear-
torturing grunts of an accordian might be to an Italian, or
what the monotonously unbearable drone of the bagpipes
might be to a Scotsman. It inspired in them a certain nostalgia
— the music that brought back the memory of their greatest
childhood adventure. It was spooky and mysterious, the substance of childhood curiosity.

"I don't want to see him quit playin'," said Shadrack. "It
gives him something to do."

"Me either. I kind of like 'im. These lads around here would
never let it rest."

"They ain't got much to think about, that's for sure."

"It's kinda our fault," said Dryfly. "We're gonna have to
do somethin'."

"Let me think for a minute," said Shad. "We're gonna have
to do something, you're right there."

*

That night the frost paid Brennen Siding a visit and crys-
tallized a million dewdrops. The dewdrops had been eyeing
the northern lights when the frost struck and many of them
were holding a flash within. Like tiny prisms, they shone from
blades of grass and cucumber leaves, on Shirley Ramsey's geranium and Dan Brennen's tomato plants, on Helen
MacDonald's dahlias and Judge Martin's weathervane, on
spider webs and all the tombstones, except for one, behind the
little Baptist church. On the tombstone that did not sparkle,
Clara Tucker's, sat Palidin Ramsey. Clara Tucker had died of
gangrene. The gangrene had started in her toe.

The northern lights soughed like the wind and merged to
the zenith as if drawn by celestial magnets.

Palidin could vaguely remember Bill Tuney. Bill Tuney
smoked a pipe all his adult life, and his lower lip had weakened from the stress and hung loosely from stained teeth. He
had been a lumberman and a guide; he had loved and been

loved; had built a home and raised a family. Bill Tuney had liked molasses in his tea.

"Bill Tuney liked molasses in his tea," thought Palidin. "Right now, people still remember Bill Tuney, but in twenty years, they'll only remember that he liked molasses in his tea. In fifty years, this tombstone will be all that is left. Bill Tuney will have left, memory and all."

The house that Bill Tuney built would never become a museum. The barn was falling down already. His son would never become famous or do anything to be remembered for. Stan Tuney did not even like molasses in his tea.

Palidin Ramsey wondered if he, himself, would pass in the same way, unremembered like Bill Tuney and everybody else in the graveyard . . . his brother Bonzie.

"Bonzie was a great little lad," thought Palidin. "Bonzie might have become somebody, had he lived."

Palidin could hear the murmur of the northern lights. He tilted his head back a bit to listen better.

"The cycle," he thought, "like rain, like water, like magnets, like northern lights, like echoes, bouncing back and forth through time and space. Sometimes you hear it only once; sometimes the echo returns half a dozen times before it escapes into space. But they come back, they always come back. From which star do I hear the hoof fall? Rain falls on Earth to rise again. It falls on me to rise again to fall on God rain, magnets, northern lights, hooves, sandals . . ."

Palidin decided that he would like to watch the Dungarvon River for a while. He slid from the tombstone and headed for the footbridge. He walked to the center abutment and eyed the dark forest, the sparkling fields, the azure above and the reflections below. The foam-speckled water slid smoothly under the bridge.

"Fish farts," he thought. "Bert Todder will be remembered for naming them fish farts."

Palidin was startled by the appearence of two fishery wardens in a canoe. He saw the wardens, but the wardens did not see him, and without a word or gesture of greeting, they slid quietly past in the way of the river.

"It's poachin' season. Hope nobody's out nettin'," thought Palidin.

When he felt the wardens were far enough downstream so that he himself would be safe from being caught as an accessory, he whooped long and loud. The whoop echoed past the wardens like the proverbial bat out of hell, warning poachers for a mile or more that the enemy approached. "If someone hears the whoop, he'll whoop, too," he thought. "The signal could travel all the way to Renous. The wardens will've wasted their run."

In a moment, Palidin heard footsteps falling on the far end of the bridge.

"Could it be the wardens coming back to get me?" he asked himself. "Could they have seen me after all? No. They're talkin' like two fools. It's Shadrack and Dryfly."

Palidin waited.

"We'll have to hide it somewhere till tomorrow night," Dryfly was saying to Shadrack. "Somewhere indoors in case it rains."

"It ain't gonna rain," said Shadrack. "It's gonna be windy and cool tomorrow."

"How ya know that for sure?"

"The northern lights. It's always windy and cool after the northern lights."

"Yeah, I guess you're right. We'll just stash it under a tree somewhere."

"G'day, lads," said Palidin.

"Palidin!"

"What you lads up to?"

"Ah . . . ah, jist walkin' around. What're you doin'?"

"Just standin' here."

"Was that you whooped?"

"Yeah. Saw the wardens."

"Runnin' the river?"

"Yeah, two of them."

"Bastards!"

"What've ya got there?"

"Oh . . . this . . . a trumpet."

*

As Shadrack and Dryfly gave Palidin a five-minute spiel, all lies, on where they got the trumpet and what they intended to do with it, Lindon Tucker left his kitchen to see a man about a horse.

As he made his way to the barn, the chosen building for tonight's annointing, he eyed the northern lights.

"Storm on the ocean," he thought.

Lindon Tucker believed that the northern lights were caused by the sun's reflection off a troubled sea.

"Oh, yeah, yeah, yeah. Be frost tonight and windy tomorrow, yeah."

Lindon stepped into the deep shadows of the barn, sighed contentedly and relieved himself. He sniffed the air — "Yep, gonna be a storm, yeah. I kin smell that pulp mill in Newcastle. Yep. Oh yeah, yep. Pulp mill, yep. Kin always smell that pulp mill before a storm. Yep. Oh yeah, yeah, yeah. Smells like shit, yep."

Clump. Something moved in the field beyond the barn.

Clump . . . clump . . . clump.

Lindon eyed the field. The frost, the stars and the northern lights made it just possible for him to see across the dim field to the edge of the forest. He could see nothing unusual in the glittering expanse.

Clump . . . clump . . . clump. The clumping sound came from the field once again, nearer this time.

"Sounds like a horse walking," thought Lindon, "or a moose."

Then Lindon saw the dark figure standing still about thirty yards away. He thought it might be a cow, or a moose; he wasn't sure. It was hard to see in the dimness of the night. Lindon wasn't even sure that it might not be a tree, although he couldn't recall a tree being in that particular place.

"Yep. Oh yeah, yep. Prob'ly a moose, yeah. Yep. Oh yeah, yeah, moose, yeah. Moose kin be dangerous this time o' year, yep. Dangerous, yeah. Better git in the house, yeah."

*

The next night, every man in Brennen Siding met at Bernie Hanley's store. While they drank Sussex Ginger Ale and discussed the plan, three dogs, eight rifles and four shotguns waited outside in the cool evening. A Gideon Bible got to go inside with John Kaston. The rifles and shotguns were unaccustomed to hunting this time of year, and had never been fired at a devil. The dogs were not trained hunting dogs, but Bert Todder's dog Skip had a fair reputation for chasing cats. The owners of the dogs had brought them along more to sacrifice than to track. "If the rifle don't down the devil, throw the old dog at 'im and run for dear life!"

"We'll all stick together," said Bernie Hanley, "at least until we know what we're dealin' with back there." They were all standing around in Bernie Hanley's store. In Bernie Hanley's store, Bernie Hanley was in charge.

"Okay," said Bert Todder, "Let's go."

"No hurry," said Bernie, thinking that to stall was good for two or three purchases of ginger ale. "The thing never starts yelpin' till near dark."

"Yeah, but we should be over there when it does," said Bert Todder.

"Oh, yeah, yeah, yep. Never shows up till pretty near dark, no. No. No he don't, no."

"If we're gonna wait fer it to start howlin', we should be outside listenin' fer it, I say," said Dan Brennen.

"Oh, yeah, yeah, yeah. Should be outside, we should. Should be outside so we kin hear it," agreed Lindon Tucker.

John Kaston stood fingering his Bible, looking very thoughtful, like a preacher about ready to take the pulpit. Tonight would be a test of faith for him. If he was successful in his exorcism, he would be the talk of the area. He might even get to preach in the church occasionally. "Dear loving heavenly Father . . ." John Kaston was praying for his dream to come true.

"Anyone want anything before I lock up?" asked Bernie.

Several of the men bought ginger ale, then they all went outside to wait and listen. The sun was dropping behind the horizon, splashing the north-west with shades of red.

"That's a cool breeze," said Bob Nash. "Startin' to feel like fall."

"Gonna head to Fredericton in the fall," said Lindon Tucker. "Oh, yeah, yeah, yeah."

Dan Brennen had hidden a quart of navy rum under the rhubarb leaves that grew along the east side of the store. He fetched it and passed it around. "To keep that lad from lookin' at ya," said Dan. John Kaston refused the shot of courage.

They had just tossed the empty rum bottle back into the rhubarb leaves when the Todder Brook Whooper let off his mournful cry. As they reached for their rifles, every man in the group thought, "I wish we had more rum."

When the men were crossing the footbridge on their way to Todder Brook, the noise from the forest stopped. All the men came to an abrupt halt and stood on the bridge and listened.

"It stopped," said Lindon Tucker.

"It's just takin' a rest," said Bob Nash. "It's still back there, you kin bet on that."

When the men were entering the forest on the path that led to Nutbeam's camp, the screaming started up again. This time, however, the noise was not coming from the Todder Brook area. It came from what seemed like John Kaston's farm.

"Bless us and save us," whispered John Kaston, squeezing his Bible tightly in his hands, "the devil's on me very own land!"

"What do we do?" asked Bob Nash.

"Only one thing to do," said Bernie Hanley. "He's up at John's."

All the men swung and headed in the direction of John Kaston's. They crossed the Graig Allen field and climbed over the fence into John Kaston's field. The last man, Stan Tuney, had no more than stepped off the cedar rail when the noise stopped. The men all stopped and stood, closer together than usual, and listened once again. They were more than just a little excited. They now felt they were close. Every man stared into the night for a gigantic cat with horns and eyes the size of ashtrays.

"We'll stick together," said Bernie Hanley. "We don't want to shoot each other."

"If the thing's around here," said Dan Brennen, "it's prob'ly hidin' in the shadows of the barn, or one o' the sheds."

The men formed a line and walked, side by side, toward

the barn. When they were but thirty feet from it, they stopped and all except John Kaston raised their rifles. Bob Nash flicked on his flashlight. Nothing.

They searched every building on John Kaston's farm, inside and out, but came up with nothing unusual. John and Max Kaston went into the house to check on the Mrs.

"John! John! The thing was right out by the barn!"

"I know, I know! You all right?"

"I'm all right, but the thing's right out there by the barn! What are we gonna do?"

"Don't be scared! Max and me will stay here with ya. Max, go and tell the men that we'll stay here, in case it comes back. Tell them to go on without us!"

Max delivered the message and had no more than re-entered the house when the thing screamed from down on Helen MacDonald's farm. Inside, Max found his father loading the rifle.

"He's down at Helen's place," said Bob Nash.

"Helen'll shit herself," said Stan Tuney.

By the time the men climbed the fence into Helen MacDonald's farm, the noise had stopped once again. When it started screaming again, it was coming from Lindon Tucker's farm. When they arrived at Lindon Tucker's, the thing had stopped again. By the light of Bob Nash's flashlight, they searched all the buildings that belonged to Lindon, but once again came up with nothing. Crossing the field, Bob Nash flicked on the flashlight to check his pocket watch for the time and several of the other men spied the hoofprints of the old bull moose.

"Hoof prints!" said Stan Tunney.

"Right in my field, right in my field, right in my field!" Lindon Tucker was nearly in tears.

Then the noise started up again, up by the footbridge.

That night the Todder Brook Whooper haunted every farm in Brennen Siding.

The next morning, a sleepless Lindon Tucker blew out the kerosene lamp that had been turned as high as it would go without smoking.

"That's it! The time's come! That's it, that's it, I'm gettin' outta here! Goin' to Fredericton. Right now . . . soon's I go fishin'. Gotta fish first."

A week later he would walk to Blackville and catch the SMT bus to Fredericton.

twelve

Palidin Ramsey's business took a complicated twist. On the first day of September, Dr. MacDowell returned to his cottage. He would be there for the whole month of September and half of October. Dr. MacDowell did not want anybody but himself fishing his salmon pool.

Palidin had already been run out of Judge Martin's pools. The judge hadn't minded at first, but then he saw that Palidin was catching too many fish, more than his limit. Palidin had been severely reprimanded and was lucky to get away without being reported to the wardens.

Palidin then tried the Cabbage Island Salmon Club's pool. In September, the club's business boomed. For the whole month, all five cabins were occupied by American anglers, paying in the vicinity of a hundred dollars a day each for the privilege of staying there and fishing the productive waters. Frank Layton, the club's manager, did not want Palidin to fish in the pool. It was overcrowded already.

Sam Little, from Hartford, Connecticut, ruled his pool as selfishly as everyone else, but he did not own both sides of the river. Across the river from Sam Little's was the Lindon Tucker pool, which from then on would be called the Bill Wallace Pool.

When Palidin arrived at the Bill Wallace Pool, he found Dan Brennen, Lindon Tucker and Bert Todder, all wading waist-deep, fishing. A little fort of rocks had been constructed at the water's edge, which was occupied by three dead fish — two grilse and a salmon. Palidin sat on a rock to watch and listen. The men were carrying on a leisurely conversation while they fished.

"How big was it?" asked Bert.

"I wouldn' say fer sure, now, but it, now, I wouldn' say fer sure, I wouldn' swear to it, but now it looked to me to be about ten, twelve, fourteen, sixteen pounds. Got 'im right behind his pet rock over there. Gets one there every day, he does, so he does."

"I don't see his car there, now," commented Dan.

"No, no, no. Got his limit. Got his limit twice. Watched him. Got his limit this mornin' and again this afternoon. Got his limit twice and left." It was obvious that Lindon was not happy with the day's activity of Sam Little. Lindon did not like Sam Little one bit. Sam Little fished without a guide ever since he bought the shore from Stan Tuney who lived across the way. Lindon used to guide Sam, but Sam, once he owned river-front property, did not legally need a guide anymore, so Lindon lost out on a month's work every summer.

"G'day, Ramsey. How's she goin'?" yelled Dan.

"Good," said Palidin. "I see ya got some fish."

These men, like all the men and boys in Brennen Siding, did not like Palidin Ramsey. He was fruity. He read all the time. Dan, particularly, did not like him. With all that knowledge, Palidin might learn and surpass Dan's own limited knowledge. But on the river, things were different. On the river, although it had never actually been spoken about, it was customary to be courteous, gentlemanly. A rule that all except for the Americans and Monctonians followed. Local anglers, especially, did not like Monctonians.

In Palidin's case, they would tolerate him with a subtle sarcasm.

"Lindon and Bert got them. I ain't seen a thing," said Dan.

"What did you get them on?" asked Palidin.

"Butterfly. Butterfly. Butterfly. Got 'im on a Butterfly."

"Green butt?"

"Orange. Orange. Orange."

"Got my two on a green butt," said Bert. "The salmon come clean outa the water for it. Jesus, he hit it hard!" Bert was very pleased with his success and started to sing, "My little Blue Charm is better than yer yellow Cosserboom."

"What're ya workin' at, Palidin?" asked Dan.

Bert Todder laughed, "Ha, ha, ha, tee, hee, sob, sob."

The thought that Palidin Ramsey would ever have a job was, indeed, amusing.

"Selling post holes," said Palidin. He did not laugh. He knew the men were making fun of him.

Dan Brennen frowned and spat into the water. He badly wanted to catch a fish — a big one to show the others up. He considered changing flies.

"Only for Lindon and Bert, I might've caught them fish meself," he thought. "Bastards!" Dan didn't like for anyone, other than himself, to catch a fish. He had fished for two hours and was growing impatient with the inactivity. "And now that young arsehole is waitin' to get in!" He made another long, well-executed cast. The fly landed lightly and began its swing on the current. It passed several hotspots, but nothing surfaced or grabbed it.

"The damn nets are ketchin' all the fish," commented Dan.

"'Pon me soul, yeah. Nets are gittin' them, Dan old boy. Nets, yeah. Yeah. Yeah. Couldn' ketch the clap with all them nets in the river, Dan old boy, chummy pard."

"Tee, hee, hee. Sob, tee, sob."

"It's not the downriver nets," commented Palidin. "It's the Russians and the Danes fishing off the coast of Greenland."

"It's them damn Frenchmen! Them lads want 'er all!" Dan was disagreeing with Palidin. "Ain't that right, boys?" He was looking for support.

"Frenchmen, yeah, Dan old boy. Frenchmen. Want 'er all, they do," agreed Lindon.

Bert Todder said, "The damn Frenchmen are tryin' to take 'er over!" He was agreeing with Dan, but deep down, he felt Palidin was right . . . but Dan was older and that was reason enough to agree with him.

Palidin knew their way and shrugged off the conversation.

"I sure put that brat in his place!" thought Dan.

No one spoke for a few minutes. The men fished and scanned the water's surface with well-trained eyes. A salmon jumped upstream.

"You're not fishing clean," yelled Palidin.

No one commented.

"*Ing*," thought Dan. "Fish*ing*! Couldn't say fishin', like everyone else!"

Bert Todder was fishing the upper end of the pool. Lindon and Dan were moving too slowly for him. He decided to take a break and waded ashore.

"You go try 'er, Palidin. I'm gonna have a smoke."

Palidin stood to let Bert sit down.

"How's George Hanley, these days?" asked Bert.

"I . . . I . . . good, I think," said Palidin.

Palidin eyed Bert's countenence for a few seconds, trying to see any expression that might betray Bert's motive for asking about George. Bert seemed to know something. "But how?" Palidin asked himself.

"I'll give it a try," said Palidin and walked to the water's edge. He waded waist-deep into the September water, thinking that he should have waders.

Palidin hooked a fish on the first cast. The salmon weighed about ten pounds and used every ounce, the current and every trick it knew, combined it all with strength and fury, to avoid being beached. The hook was embedded deep in its gills, the leader strong, the fisherman skilled. The salmon lost the battle. Palidin killed it and placed it in the pool with Lindon's and Bert's.

Bert Todder and Lindon Tucker seemed genuinely happy with the action, with Palidin's performance. Dan Brennen had left and gone home.

*

On the twentieth of September, the mail came as usual, but this time when Shirley opened the bag, there was a letter in it addressed to her, from Ottawa. It was a notice from the Director of Postal Services, saying that a change in the postal system was occurring. Her address was being changed. RR #5 was replacing Brennen Siding, N.B. The rural post offices were to be replaced by a rural route. On the first of January, Shirley would be out of a job.

Shirley read the letter, put it down, rolled a cigarette, lit up and began to take inventory.

"Jug is married and living in Renous. Oogan is workin' in Newcastle. I haven't seen Oogan in six months. Bean is married to Mary Francis Shaw and they're havin' their own problems. Bean's outa work and Mary Francis is gonna have their third baby any day. I'll be grandmother again. Naggy's workin' at Eaton's in Moncton. Nagg might be able to help me. She's got a good job, don't do nothin' but clerk in that big store. Neenie and Bossy are married and livin' in Gordon. Junior's married to Mary Stuart and still livin' with old Silas. Junior'll get that place when old Silas dies, which shouldn't be too far away . . . I hope. Digger's in Toronto or Leamin'ton or some place. Last time Digger come home, he stayed drunk all the time he was here. Skippy finally married Joe Moon and is livin' in Quarryville. They finally got married, thank God . . . done it just after Joe's dog got killed. That just leaves Palidin and Dryfly home with me."

Shirley butted her cigarette and went to the piece of mirror that hung over the water buckets.

"Me hair's startin' to turn grey," she thought. "I ain't but forty-five, I got eight grandchildren and me hair's turnin' grey. Me teeth have just about had the biscuit, too. And I'm gettin' fat. I wished I could get rid o' that wart on me cheek."

Shirley sighed. "I won't be gettin' fat this winter when there's nothin' to eat in the house and no money."

Shirley went back to the table and rolled herself another cigarette.

"Palidin's crazier than the birds," she thought. "Don't know where I went wrong with him. All he does is read and fish. I must've salted twenty salmon. Enough to do the winter, but ya can't live on salty salmon, can ya?

Dryfly's no good either. All he does is play guiddar. Well, I got till January. Somethin' might happen before then."

*

By the last week of September, Palidin ran into another complication. He didn't have waders and the water was getting too cold for comfort.

Palidin had clients all over the Blackville area who wanted

salmon; who paid good money to get them. He could afford to buy waders, but it was getting late in the season and he felt that waders at this late date might not be worth the investment. The salmon would be spawning within a few weeks and people would quit buying — the waders might not pay for themselves.

George Hanley, Palidin's business partner, was having the same difficulties; plus, his father was getting suspicious and didn't want him borrowing the car so often. If one got caught selling salmon from a car, one not only got fined and jailed; they'd take the car as well.

Palidin and George sat on two tombstones in the cemetery behind the Baptist church and discussed the situation.

A giant harvest moon lit up the night. From the forest back of Todder Brook, came the sound of a trumpet playing "Red Roses for a Blue Lady."

"We got three hundred and fifty dollars between us," said Palidin. "We could buy an old car for that kind of money."

"Yep. Sure would be nice," said George.

"Mom can't afford to keep me any longer, and I'm no good for woods work, are you?"

"Never worked in the woods in my life."

"What will we do, George?"

"We could get an old car and head for Fredericton, or someplace. We could get a job in Fredericton. We could hunt up Graig Allen, tell 'im who we are . . . he might get us a job in no time."

"I wonder how Lindon Tucker's doing over there?"

"Hard to say. Lindon got a big chunk of money for his shore. He'll be all right."

"A lot of lads from Blackville are going to Toronto."

"That'd be nice. Livin' in Toronto."

"We should think about it, George."

"Sounds good to me."

*

Dryfly had but one thing on his mind: he was not getting any letters from Lillian. He couldn't write her one, because he had been too dumb to get her address. All he could do was wait.

Shadrack Nash had started to work for his father, cutting logs. Shad did not like working with Bob's new chainsaw anymore than he liked peeling pulp. Dry figured Shad would quit his job in a day or two.

Shad and Dry were spending a great deal of time with Nutbeam. Nutbeam was teaching them how to hunt and trap, and the boys were teaching Nutbeam some new songs to play on the trumpet.

"It just seemed to happen overnight," thought Dryfly. "One day he couldn't play a thing, and the next day he was doin' the very best of a job on 'Red Roses for a Blue Lady.'"

Nutbeam had become a good friend of the boys. His camp was a good place to party and play music. Nutbeam never seemed to care how late they stayed, or how dirty they talked. He'd often cook them up a pan of venison and occasionally sent them to the bootlegger in Gordon for Golden Nut. He never wanted them to share in the cost, but he did ask them to run a few errands. Shadrack and Dryfly did much of Nutbeam's shopping at Bernie Hanley's store, thus cutting back on the dreaded trips to Newcastle. They also helped him patch the roof of his camp and gather wood for the winter. The boys did not mind working for Nutbeam. It never seemed like work to them. It was more like play.

Some nights when the boys went to visit Nutbeam, he would not be there and they'd have to wait, sometimes for as much as a couple of hours, for his return. They didn't know where he was going, or for what reason, and he never offered to explain. Nutbeam was spending many evenings listening to Shirley Ramsey's radio.

This turned out to be one of the nights. When Dryfly arrived at Nutbeam's camp, he found it empty. Dryfly sat beside the door to wait.

Dryfly knew that Shadrack might not come tonight, either. Shadrack was rising at six in the morning these days, and working hard. Shadrack would be too tired to play at nights and would not show up until he finally quit his job. "In about three days," thought Dryfly.

It was very pleasant there by Nutbeam's camp. The evening was warm for September and a big moon rose from the forest to keep him company.

"That moon is shining down on Lillian Wallace the same as it's shinin' down on me," thought Dryfly. "I wish I was with her. I wish she was here."

In his mind's eye, Dryfly visualized Lillian sitting beneath the moon somewhere in the States. He could see her big blue eyes and golden hair, the smile on the lips that had kissed him so gently. "God, let her write to me," he thought.

Dryfly didn't know it, but Lillian Wallace was, indeed, writing to him at that very moment.

"G'day, Dryfly," said Nutbeam. Dryfly had not heard Nutbeam approaching, and was somewhat startled.

"G'day! How's she goin'?"

"Good."

"Out for a walk?"

"I got a slug o' wine left. Want some?"

"Yeah, maybe."

Nutbeam went into the camp and returned momentarily with a less than half-full bottle of Golden Nut.

Nutbeam was downhearted. He had just returned from watching Shirley Ramsey take a bath. Shirley Ramsey was looking more beautiful to Nutbeam everyday.

Nutbeam sat beside Dryfly, screwed the top off the bottle and they both took a drink. They did not talk for what seemed like a very long time; just eyed the moon and thought of their lovers.

Dryfly was the first one to break the silence. "Ever been in love?" he asked.

Because Nutbeam had been thinking that he was in love with Shirley Ramsey, Dryfly's question surprised him. It seemed as if Dryfly had been reading his thoughts.

"I don't know," said Nutbeam. "It takes two to fall in love. No woman ever looked sideways at me long enough to fall for me."

"Don't you ever get tired of livin' alone?"

"It's better than being feared, or laughed at all the time. I once went to a dance and asked every girl there to dance with me. Not one said yes. Even the homeliest old woman there, laughed and turned me down. People wouldn' even set close to me."

"I don't think yer that homely, Nutbeam."

"You're jist gettin' use to me, that's all."

"It don't matter, anyway," said Dryfly. "Look at me, I'm in love. But it don't matter none. I'll prob'ly never see her again, anyway. I don't think she loves me as much as I love her."

"Well, you're young and ain't nearly as homely as me. You'll get a woman soon enough."

"Ain't no other woman like this one."

"There ain't no other woman like Shirley Ramsey," thought Nutbeam. "There's lotsa fish in the sea," he said.

Nutbeam wanted to get to know Shirley Ramsey very much, but he didn't know how to set up the opportunity. He had befriended Dryfly, hoping that it might lead somewhere. This was the first private conversation they'd had and Nutbeam sought a way to approach the topic. He drank some more wine, hoping that it would loosen his tongue a little.

"How's yer mother?" asked Nutbeam.

"She's all right."

"Yer father's dead, ain't he?"

"Never saw 'im in me life."

"Yer mother must git awful lonesome with no man around."

"I don't know. Never thought about it."

"She ever look sideways at another man after your father died?"

"I don't know. Not that I know of."

"Yer mother's an awful pretty woman," said Nutbeam.

"She prob'ly was a long time ago."

"Still is."

"I never thought of it before, but Mom never goes any-where. Stays home all the time. Ain't got a friend."

"Sounds like me."

"She should start goin' to dances or somethin'," said Dryfly. "Maybe she'd meet up with some friends."

"You know what I'd like you to do, Dry?"

"What's that?"

"Ah, ah . . . sing me a song."

Dryfly eyed the moon and thought of Lillian Wallace. He sang:

> *Roses are bloomin'*
> *Come back to me darlin',*
> *Come back to me darlin'*
> *And never more roam.*

*

"Get up, Shad, it's time to go to work."

"Day four," thought Shadrack. "Another day in the woods and I'll die. I'll die, I'll die, I'll die! I hate it. I'll starve to death before I pick that chainsaw up again!"

"Shad!"

"I'm too sore, Mom! I can't hardly walk!"

"Don't give me that! You get out here and go to the woods right this minute!"

"I tell ya, I'm too sore! I'm pretty near dead! Ya deaf?"

"Sore! Sore! A big boy like you, sore! Your poor old father's been back there for an hour and you layin' in bed sleepin'! Sore, my arse! Now, get out here and eat yer breakfast before I take a stick to ya! Sore! A big man fifteen years old gettin' sore! Hangin' around doin' nothin' like that . . . that . . . that Dryfly Ramsey. No wonder yer lazy, hangin' around with the likes o' that . . . that . . . that tramp! What's ever gonna become o' ya?"

Shad knew there was no stopping his mother. She had the stage, front and center, and would transmit spiel after spiel, condemning every man, woman and child that Shadrack ever as much as said hello to. She would start with Dryfly Ramsey and end with Dryfly Ramsey, but in between she'd find examples of depression and poverty from both ends of the river. She would bring in her own aging, ailing state, Bob's deterioration, the state of Bob's grandfather who had been no more than a no-good tramp. The Bible would come into the picture and how she'd had hopes for Shad to become a minister some day like cousin Ralph. She would yell through the bedroom door for as long as Shad stayed in there.

Shad arose, dressed, toileted and limped into the kitchen. The hard work, running the chainsaw, had stiffened his muscles. He was not lying about being sore. He checked the time. "Nine o'clock," he thought. "Dad will be ugly at me. I was s'pose to be back in the woods at eight. I'm an hour late." He turned on the radio and sat at the table to listen, to wait for his toast and eggs. The radio was turned to CFNB, and Jack Fenety said, "Good morning, ladies, and welcome to Facts and Fancy. Today we are coming to you from under overcast skies. Our temperature is expected to remain stable at about fifty-five degrees, and we can expect rain, rain, rain." Jack Fenety went on to read some poetry and a prayer; he sent out birthday greetings to Mrs. Smith who was "a hundred years young today"; he played "The Yellow Rose of Texas" and "Bernadine."

Shad eyed the kitchen window as he ate his eggs and toast. "Please, God, let it rain," he prayed. Shad knew that his father would not work in the rain. Shad knew, by the swiftly moving clouds, that chances were very good he'd get the day off.

At nine-thirty, Jack Fenety played CFNB's rattling, ear-torturing news music and said, "CFNB, where New Brunswick hears the news." Shad didn't care about the news. There was nothing happening outside of Brennen Siding that concerned him. Shad gulped down the last of his tea and headed for the woods.

When Shadrack stepped outside, the September morning greeted him with a light drizzle. "It's gonna rain, it's gonna rain," he sang, "ya can't work in the rain, thank God, it's gonna rain." The rain seemed to Shadrack to be a magical rain, for, indeed, the soreness left his limbs with every drop that fell.

On the way back to the worksite, Shadrack met his father coming home.

"Gonna rain," said Bob Nash.

"I figured that," said Shad, "that's why I didn't bother to hurry."

"I covered up the chainsaw and the gas jug," said Bob. Bob Nash didn't want to work that day either. It was mid-September and the salmon, the September run, were here. Bob Nash had it in mind to go fishing.

An hour later, Shadrack announced that he had it in mind to go to Shirley Ramsey's to get the mail. He put on his jacket and headed for the footbridge. The rain was heavier now and slanted in from the southwest. The red checkered Mackinaw did little to keep him dry. Shadrack didn't care if he got wet. "Getting wet is a lot better than working in the woods," he thought.

*

Dryfly awakened to the sounds of Palidin moving about the room, and Shirley talking.

"What are ya gonna be doin' way out there in T'rono?" Shirley was asking Palidin.

"I don't know," said Palidin. "Get a job . . . work. Ain't nothin' to do around here."

"How ya gonna get there?"

"Train."

"Where ya gittin' the money?"

"I got some money."

"Where'll ya live?"

"I'll get a room."

"Way out there in T'rono all by yerself! T'rono's an awful bad place, so it is! No one to cook fer ya, or look after ya. It's not like home, ya know, and you'll be all alone!"

"I won't be alone, Momma! George Hanley's goin' too."

Palidin was packing a cardboard box with his belongings. The box was not very big. Palidin only had one extra pair of jeans, a shirt, a pair of shorts and a pair of socks with the heels worn through to put in the box. He found a white t-shirt in the corner — it was dirty, but he threw it in the box anyway.

"How long ya plannin' on stayin'?" asked Shirley.

"I don't know. A month, six months, a year. If I get a job, I'll send ya home some money."

"What if ya don't get a job? What if ya git lonesome?"

"I'll be all right, Mom!"

The tears were threatening to overflow Palidin's eyes. He was getting lonesome already.

Shirley went back into the kitchen to smoke, to cry, to think things over.

"Poor little Paladin," she thought, "only sixteen, way up in T'rono! I might never see him again!"

Palidin sat on the bed to talk to Dryfly.

"I'm goin' to Toronto," he said.

"No? Yeah! What for?"

"Gotta get a job. Ain't nothin' to do around here."

"When ya comin' back?"

"I don't know for sure."

"Did I hear ya say George Hanley's goin' too?"

"Yeah. We're catching the train in half an hour. Will you stay home and look after Mom?"

"I don't know. I guess."

"Mom's losing the post office. She's gonna need a lotta help. I'll send yas some money soon's I get on my feet."

"You won't be scared up there?"

Palidin shrugged.

"Gonna miss ya, Pal."

"You won't miss me. You'll be too busy courtin' all the women."

"Ain't no women around here."

"Dry?"

"Yeah?"

"'Member me catching all them salmon?"

"Yeah."

"Well, there's a trick to it."

"A trick?"

"Yeah, and I'm gonna tell ya the trick, but I don't want you to tell anybody else. It's a good trick and it could make us rich some day. Promise not to tell it?"

"Sure."

Palidin proceeded to tell Dryfly the ins and outs of magnetizing salmon flies. When he was sure that Dryfly understood completely, he gave Dryfly the little lodestone he'd been using.

"Works every time," said Palidin. "Now, I gotta go. The train'll be here any minute."

"Be good, Pal."

"Yeah. You too."

In the kitchen, Palidin stopped to kiss Shirley goodbye.

"I love you, Mom," he said.

"I love you too, Pal. You know you kin always come home, Pal. You know where your home is."

"I know, Mom. I'll send ya money, Mom. Don't you worry."

Palidin forced back the tears as he eyed the ugly, the laughed at, the forsaken woman. "My mother in Helen MacDonald's hand-me-down dress . . . her hair is starting to turn grey . . . the most beautiful mother in the whole world," he thought.

"Don't cry, Mom," said Palidin, and quickly, so as not to change his mind, he picked up the box and left.

On the way to the Brennen Siding sidinghouse, where he would meet the train, Palidin passed Shadrack Nash on the road. Shadrack was limping slightly and looked soaked to the skin.

"See ya, Shad," were the only words spoken, and Palidin made no attempt to hide the fact that he was capable of crying.

At Shirley Ramsey's house, Shadrack sensed that something dramatic had just occurred.

"What's wrong with Palidin?" Shadrack asked Dryfly.

"Him and George Hanley eloped," said Dry.

thirteen

On the twenty-ninth of October, Shirley opened the mail-bag and found but three letters in it: a bill for John Kaston from Lyman MacFee, a letter from R.M. Crenshaw, Boston, Massachusetts, for Frank Layton, the manager of the Cabbage Island Salmon Club, and a red envelope with Dryfly Ramsey, Brennen Siding, N.B. written neatly on it in blue ink.

Ecstasy is not a strong enough word to describe how Dryfly felt when he saw the envelope. When Shirley passed it to him, he could not contain himself. He jumped for joy. It was one of the happiest moments of his entire life.

His joy was so obviously imprinted upon his countenance that Shirley, too, was stirred by his emotions.

"Thanks, Mom!" Dryfly hurried into his room and shut the door.

As she put the other two letters in their rightful compartments in the post office, she wiped a tear from her cheek and whispered, "Poor little darlin'."

Dryfly threw himself on the bed and eyed the envelope.

"Lillian Wallace," he whispered, "I love you, I love you, I love you!"

He sniffed the envelope and thought he could vaguely smell the scent of fly repellent. "Some kind of perfume, anyway," he thought.

He carefully tore the end off the envelope and removed the pink pages. There were four of them, all folded neatly. "What a girl!" he thought. "What a wonderful, wonderful girl!"

He prolonged opening the letter, wanting to savour the feeling, the moment.

"I just want to see one word," he thought. "The one magic word from the most beautiful girl in the world."

Before he began to read, he sniffed the paper once more
and kissed it.

> *Dear Dryfly,*
> *I'm sorry I took so long to write. I'm the*
> *world's greatest procrastinator!*
> *How are you and what have you been doing?*
> *Did you go to work guiding? How's Shadrack?*

Lillian wrote about going back to school, the turning of
the leaves and the harvest moon; she wrote about her plans to
return to the Dungarvon River, her father's plans for building
a cottage, a recent trip to New York and a new friend, Rick,
she'd met in school. She did not write "I love you" in her
letter, but at the very end she wrote, "I miss you very much.
I'll always be very fond of you. Love, Lillian." It was the "I
miss you very much. I'll always be very fond of you. Love,
Lillian" that Dryfly read over and over and over.

Dryfly showed the letter to Shadrack. Shadrack was no-
ticeably envious and that made Dryfly happy, for that put
him one up on Shadrack in the women department. Shadrack
figured that he, too, had dated Lillian and therefore they were
even.

Dryfly read his letter to Nutbeam and after the "Love,
Lillian" said, "What do you think o' that, Nutbeam?"

"That's a good letter! A real good letter! I think she likes
you a lot, Dryfly. But who's this Rick lad?"

"I don't know. Some lad in school, I s'pose."

Nutbeam sensed that Rick was mentioned for a reason. He
didn't want Dryfly to be overly optimistic. "She mentioned
him twice. Could be a boyfriend," he said.

"Could be." Dryfly had given the same thought consideration, but he didn't want to think about it.

Nutbeam was more impressed with the letter than Dryfly
realized. Nutbeam was not just impressed with what Lillian
wrote, but he was fascinated with the whole concept of letter
writing. Nutbeam had encountered an additional problem in
the Shirley Ramsey venture — not being able to write. If one

can't write, one does not have letters to mail. In Brennen Siding, if one does not have letters to mail, one might never enter the realm of Shirley Ramsey's love nest.

"You gonna answer the letter?" asked Nutbeam.

"Yeah, prob'ly."

"Wished I could write," said Nutbeam.

"Anyone can write. Didn' you ever go to school?"

"I didn't start to school until I was ten years old. I think me father and mother was ashamed of me, thought I was retarded. When I was ten they figured I maybe knew something and sent me off to school where everyone my age had the jump on me by four years. They not only laughed at me being ugly, but they thought I was stupid, too. They use to gang up and play tricks on me, and sometimes even beat me up. I raised a fuss and me parents let me stay home."

Nutbeam seemed very sad. "I couldn' go nowhere, Dryfly," he said.

"If you could write, who would you write to, Nutbeam?"

"Aunt Johannah, prob'ly. She's the only one that was nice to me. I'd like to find out who's dead and how they're all doin'."

"Me or Shad could write letters for ya," said Dryfly. "I ain't a real good writer, but I could scratch something out for ya."

"Maybe . . . maybe."

"You got any paper and a pencil?"

"No. Ain't got anything like that."

"There's paper and pencils in Bernie Hanley's store. I could pick some up for ya."

"Maybe . . . maybe."

"You'll need envelopes, too."

"Yeah. Might work. How's your mother doin'?"

"She's all right. Awful lonesome for Palidin, though."

"A woman like that shouldn't be lonesome," thought Nutbeam. "She ever hear from him?" he asked.

"Not yet. I guess she's worried about him. She's worried about the post office closin', too."

"When's the post office closin'?" asked Nutbeam.

"First o' the year."

"Don't leave much time," thought Nutbeam, "two months and some."

"What's she gonna do for a livin' when the post office closes?"

"Dunno. Somethin'll turn up."

"Maybe," said Nutbeam. "Maybe."

*

Lindon Tucker left his room on Pine Street and walked toward the Carleton Street bridge. This was the second time that day that he had walked "over town." The first time "over town," he'd gone to the bank and withdrawn two hundred dollars. This time he walked toward the hotel. Lindon Tucker always walked — he did not like spending seventy-five cents on a taxi. He didn't like spending seven dollars a week for his room with kitchen privileges, either, and he did not like having to buy things like meat and potatoes. In Brennen Siding, he did not have to pay rent. In Brennen Siding, Lindon grew his own potatoes, and every fall he would shoot a deer or a moose and salt half a barrel of salmon. Lindon Tucker did not like spending money on anything. Lindon Tucker did not like Fredericton very much at all.

Brennen Siding and the people he knew there were his whole life. He thought of them day and night with an aching heart. He longed to be walking on the footbridge, or through the forest; he missed his Sussex Ginger Ale with the boys at Bernie Hanley's store and he missed listening to the radio in his own kitchen and going behind a shed to see a man about a horse. He found the people in Fredericton cold. They rarely spoke to him on the street. On the few times he did manage to strike up a conversation he was as agreeable as he could be — to no avail. They invariably walked away to leave him, once again, alone.

"How kin ya be so alone with so many people around?" he asked himself many, many times. "I'd go home, if I thought that devil would leave me alone, so I would. Oh yeah, yeah, yeah. Home, yeah. Yep."

Another depressing thing in Lindon Tucker's life was his landlord, Arthur McGarrity. To Lindon Tucker, Arthur McGarrity and his wife Monique were something lower than worms. Arthur and Monique McGarrity took great pleasure in beating the living daylights out of their five-year-old son, Bobby. If Bobby whimpered in the night, Arthur or Monique would stomp into his room and SLAM, BANG, THRASH! Bobby would be afflicted with a new set of welts and bruises. Lindon did not know what to do about the beatings. He figured it was not his place to interfere with the goings on of someone else's family. Lindon gritted his teeth and remained silent — silent and alone.

This night, Lindon decided that he didn't want to hear the child being beaten anymore. Last night's beating had been more severe than usual. That day, he had gone to the bank and withdrawn two hundred dollars with the thought in mind to go on a drunk. He decided that the hotel would be a good place to start. "Maybe at the hotel, someone will talk to me."

When Lindon Tucker entered through the glass doors of the hotel, he was met by a good-looking young gentleman in a red jacket with brass buttons.

"Checking in, sir?" asked the bellman.

"You work here?" asked Lindon.

"Yes, sir," said the bellman and thought, "No, no, I'm dressed in this outfit because I'm a monkey grinder."

"Kin ya git drunk here?" asked Lindon.

"There's a bar right in there, sir."

Lindon headed across the lobby toward the lounge. Inside, he sat at the bar and waited for service. The lounge was nearly full and the bartender was very busy.

"What would you like?" yelled the bartender.

"Gimme a glass o' roy whiskey and a bottle o' Moosehead," yelled Lindon and scanned the other people at the bar to see if his order was making an impression. He smiled and winked at a couple of people, but no one seemed to take notice.

"A single or a double?" asked the bartender.

"Yeah, sure," said Lindon.

The bartender poured Lindon nearly a double. He recognized Lindon as a country hick and would shortpour him all evening long.

Lindon tossed the rye down and chased it with a quaff of ale.

"Gimme another roy," he said.

*

Shirley Ramsey took a line-by-line, grey-hair-by-grey-hair inspection of her body. Palidin was gone, and she, for the first time in many years, had the privacy to undress completely without the possibility of being interrupted. Dryfly never came home until at least midnight.

Shirley Ramsey scanned her leg — "varicose veins, but not too bad." She scanned her belly — "bigger than Bert Todder's," she thought.

Bert Todder was a bachelor who did his own cooking. His diet consisted primarily of potatoes. Sometimes he'd cook a piece of salmon or venison to accompany the potatoes, and he ate many, many oranges and drank much ginger ale at Bernie Hanley's store, but primarily, he ate potatoes. For supper, he'd boil as many as ten and would not hesitate to eat the whole lot. If he left any, he'd have them fried for breakfast. He had the biggest belly in Brennen Siding.

When Bert Todder was asked why he let his belly get so big, he replied, "When ya got a good set o' tools, ya should build a shed over them. Tee, hee, ha, ha, sob, sob."

Shirley eyed her breasts. They depressed her. They tapered from chest to nipple like skin hankerchiefs with a marble dropped in each one.

She noticed how brown her skin was. "That's the Indian in me," she said aloud to the kitchen.

Her eyes also indicated Micmac ancestry. Her great-great-grandmother had been a Micmac Indian from the Northwest. Her grandfather had been an immigrant from Ireland. She had the dark eyes, skin, hair, and high cheekbones of the Micmac. Her nose, mouth and chin were Irish. Her great-grandmother had been English; her grandmother Dutch and her mother Scottish. Her children had blue eyes and did not look Indian at all. Shirley bathed, donned her best dress (the Helen MacDonald hand-me-down), and went to the table to smoke, think and take inventory.

"There's one thing I kin say," she thought, "I raised a family."

Shirley was the youngest of nine children. Her mother had given birth to her under the very capable hands of a midwife. The midwife had delivered all nine children successfully. It was not the midwife's fault that Shirley's mother had taken one look at the baby Shirley, said, "It's a girl," and passed away. It was as though she was giving up her space, air and baby-making ability to Shirley.

Shirley spent the first twelve years of her life developing a body. At twelve she had been quite beautiful, with brown hair, dark eyes and an attractive smile. She had developed a sleek young body that yearned to be fondled, caressed and loved, but it wasn't until she reached the age of fourteen that she was able to put her body to the test. After just one night with Buck Ramsey, she learned that her body was as good for making babies as her mother's.

At the ages of sixteen and fourteen respectively, Buck and Shirley married. Junior was born three months later. At first, luck seemed to be with them; Buck's father died and left Buck the crumbling old house and gravel pit. They moved in and waited for someone to buy the gravel, but no construction was applied to the road that year. Buck didn't have a job and couldn't get one. He was forced to seek employment in Fredericton, and then in Saint John, where he found part-time labor loading ships. In Saint John, Buck also found a thirty-five year old widow to live with. As the relationship with the widow grew, Buck returned to Brennen Siding less and less.

Buck had never loved Shirley and Shirley had never loved Buck. They got married because they "had to" — Shirley was pregnant. He didn't love the widow either, but life was a hell of a lot easier in Saint John. As Shirley began to deteriorate under the stress and wear of baby-making, poverty and aging, Buck started to find her too unattractive for his tastes, and eventually even found her repulsive — repulsive, that is, until he got drunk. When Buck Ramsey got drunk, he stayed that way for three or four days. On about the third day, he'd start feeling sorry for himself and Shirley, head for Brennen Siding, stay drunk all the time he was there, make a baby and head back to Saint John, hung over and broke.

After making Dryfly, Buck returned to Saint John to find his thirty-five-year-old widow in bed with another man. With no money and no place to live, he took to bumming on the streets. On this meagre income, he did not eat much. His main source of nourishment became wine.

After several months, he moved to Fredericton, and for a matter of a year or so, it seemed he might pull himself together. He got a job as a janitor, bought himself a guitar and a new radio. He moved into a room on Charlotte Street and even managed to save a few hundred dollars. Then, he started drinking again. On the third day of overindulgence, he thought of Shirley. He would have gone to Brennen Siding, but for one thing — even Buck Ramsey didn't have the gall to face Shirley after eleven years of not being around to help her raise the family. He took some of his money and went to Saint John to see his widow instead.

The Saint John widow saw him coming and locked the door. Buck bought more wine and went in search of his cronies down by the wharf.

Most of the degenerates he knew had either died, or moved away in the year he'd been away and he found himself alone, drunk, cold and without shelter in the middle of February. He lay down by a crate, cuddled himself to keep warm, drank some more wine and passed out. In the middle of the night, a foghorn woke him up briefly. He looked about him to see a ship and an unloaded cargo, a few lights and drifting snow.

"G'day," he said to himself, "I suppose I ain't havin' too hard a time!"

He then went back to sleep, never to awaken.

"At least I raised a family," spoke Shirley once more to the kitchen.

But now, with Palidin in Toronto, or wherever he was, and Dryfly running the roads night and day, Shirley was alone. The loneliness closed in on her like a coffin lid. With her family she had been poor, but never lonely. There had been rough moments when she hadn't known where the next meal was coming from, but there had always been someone to hold onto.

"I'm gettin' old," she thought. "My family's gone and I'm all alone. Nobody loves me, nobody cares. Hail Mary, full of grace . . ."

*

Shadrack Nash was very unhappy. His mother and father nagged him constantly.

"Go to work," they'd yell. "If ya don't go to work, go to school! Ya can't lay around the house and play the banjo for the rest of your life!"

Shadrack was getting so annoyed with the constant nagging that he started playing the banjo just to drown out their voices. The banjo playing did not help the situation. The constant plucking of the sonorous strings was eating at the ends of Bob and Elva's nerves. There was never a moment's peace in the house.

Bob Nash had just read the same paragraph of the *Family Herald* three times. Elva had just added three stitches too many to a sock she was knitting. Shadrack had just played "Will the Circle Be Unbroken" for the twentieth time.

"I could throw something at him," thought Bob.

"I could stab him with a knitting needle," thought Elva.

"John Deere, John Deere, John Deere . . . good tractor . . . John Deere . . . . damn! I'm losing my mind." Bob Nash was reading the John Deere tractor ad on the back cover of the *Family Herald*. He wanted to read the article inside on scabby potatoes, but he couldn't concentrate. The banjo seemed to be getting louder and louder.

Finally, Bob started to roll the *Family Herald* into a tight round tube. His nerves were screaming for help and he was about to come to the rescue. Bob stood. "I'll beat the shit out of him," he thought. "A good thrashin's just what he needs."

Shadrack did not see Bob's approach.

WHACK! went the *Family Herald*.

BOING! went the banjo.

"What the . . ."

WHACK! WHACK! WHACK!

"Stop it!"

"Take that!" — WHACK! — "you little bastard . . . and that!" WHACK!

Bob Nash hit Shadrack on top of the head with the *Family Herald*. To Bob, it felt very good. To Shadrack, it stung and startled him so that he dropped the banjo. Shad knew from experience, from the look in Bob's eyes, that he was in for a thrashing. Shad was uncertain about what he had done to deserve it, but he knew it was too late to discuss it.

WHACK! WHACK! WHACK! WHACK!

Everytime Bob hit Shad, he felt better. The silence of the banjo and the whack of the *Family Herald* on Shad's body was like music to his ears, a pacifying symphony that conquered and replaced "Will the Circle Be Unbroken."

"I could do this all night," thought Bob. WHACK, WHACK, WHACK . . . WHACK . . . a black eye, WHACK, a bloody nose, WHACK, a bruised arm. WHACK on the bum, WHACK on the leg, WHACK on the shoulder. Bob Nash, for the moment, was gloriously insane. The nagging wife and the lazy, banjo-playing boy had removed a brick from his structure; he had been pushed temporarily over the edge.

WHACK, WHACK!

At first, Shad saw it as just another beating, but soon enough he began to realize that things were getting out of control. He realized he was cornered, that there was no escape. He was being attacked by his father and was more than just a little leery about fighting back. He took a couple of more blows. They were getting harder and they weren't slowing down. There was a strange wild look in his father's eyes. Shad knew that he had to do something. "But what? I can't hit my father . . ." WHACK!

Shadrack tensed his muscles and gathered his strength. He made a blind dive at Bob. Thud! It was like colliding with a load of bricks.

WHACK! WHACK!

Elva Nash watched contentedly. The beating was a tension release for her too. "Shad's getting what he deserves," she thought.

Once again Shad cringed and gathered his strength, and once again made a plunge. Thump! Bob Nash was still solid.

"Might as well run into a brick wall," thought Shad.

By now, Shad too had lost all reason. He started counting for his next attack. "One, two, three . . ." He could have been counting bricks.

At the count of three, Shad's foot connected with Bob's crotch, a definite weak point in the wall. On the count of four the *Family Herald* loosened and fell from Bob's hand. On the count of five, Shad saw his father fall to this knees in agony — thump! — like a load of bricks. On the count of six, Shadrack dashed for the door. Seven, eight . . . on the count of nine, Shad glanced over his shoulder to see if he was being pursued. He saw Bob Nash kneeling, holding on to himself. Shad gave a frightened glance at his astonished mother.

"Dad's a brick short of a load!" he yelled, and ran from the house.

*

Dryfly returned to Nutbeam's camp with a pencil, paper and envelopes. He sat at the table across from Nutbeam and the two began to contrive a letter. The letter was to Johanna Banks in Mars Hill, Maine.

"What d'ya want to say?" asked Dryfly.

"You ready?"

"Yep. All ready."

"Dear Johannah, how are you, I am fine, hope you are the same. Dryfly is writing this letter for me. What's going on in Mars Hill? Was it a good year for potatoes? Is Ned dead yet? How's Willy? I am fine and living in Canada. How's Alex and Norah?"

Nutbeam ran out of things to say. "What'll I say now?" he asked.

"Ah . . . how about the weather? Tell 'er how the weather is."

"The weather's good. How's the weather in Mars Hill? It was cold here last night. It will soon be winter."

Dryfly wrote down Nutbeam's dictations with many misspellings and little punctuation.

"Ya think that's enough?" asked Nutbeam when Dryfly had scratched out the word "winter."

"I don't know . . . maybe."

"Put, 'Yours, Nutbeam' on it and that'll do."

Dryfly finished off the letter and put it in an envelope. He wrote "Johanna Banks, Mars Hill, Maine" on it and sealed it.

"Ya want me to mail it for ya, Nutbeam?"

"No, no, that's all right. I'll mail it."

"Wouldn't be any trouble."

"No, that's all right, I'll mail it."

Nutbeam held the letter up and looked at it proudly. He then took it to the shelf beside the stove and laid it down carefully, as if it was breakable, beside a pot. He put a block of birch in the stove and went back to the table. He turned the lamp down a bit. The fire in the stove lulled them with snaps and crackles. The camp was cozy and warm.

"Thanks for writing that letter, Dry. You're a good lad."

"No trouble. Any time."

*

A knock sounded at Nutbeam's door.

"That you, Shad?" yelled Nutbeam.

"It's me, Shadrack," came the muffled voice through the door.

Nutbeam unlatched and opened the door and in stepped the battered and bruised Shadrack Nash. He was limping and had a bloody nose and a swollen eye. The eye was already starting to turn black.

"What you run into, a bear?" asked Dryfly.

"Dad's gone crazy! Beat me up!" panted Shad. "Kicked him in the nuts! I'm done for!"

"You kicked Bob in the nuts?" Dryfly was amazed.

"I'm a dead man! He'll kill me! He'll stomp me into the ground! He'll chew me up and spit me out! He'll . . ."

"Holy dyin'!" said Dryfly, "he'll shoot ya sure as hell! What're ya gonna do?!"

"I don't know, I don't know, I don't know," said Shad, like Lindon Tucker. "I'm dead, I'm dead, I'm dead, I'm dead!"

Shadrack paced back and forth in the tiny camp until Dryfly jumped up and told him to sit down. Shad sat in Dryfly's chair, his breath coming in puffs that caused the lamp to flutter. Nutbeam's ears seemed to flap like wings in the dancing light.

"Take it easy," said Nutbeam, "he'll get over it. He jist got ugly for a while, that's all."

"You don't know my father," said Shadrack. "He'll kill me and not think twice!"

"So, what are you gonna do?"

"Can't go home, I know that!"

"You'll have to hide out at my place," suggested Dryfly.

Shadrack was not thinking too clearly, but he knew immediately he did not want to stay at Shirley Ramsey's. Something like staying with Shirley Ramsey would not be at all good for the reputation. "No, that's all right. I'll think o' something," he said.

"You could maybe stay here with Nutbeam!" offered Dryfly. "This is a great hideout!"

"There's no place for ya to stay here," said Nutbeam.

"He could sleep on the floor," said Dryfly.

"Ya couldn' sleep on that old hard floor," said Nutbeam, "and besides, they'll come lookin' for 'im."

"But they'll never find him here!"

"They'll come lookin' and they'll find him!"

"They never found you!"

"That's different. They're not looking for me."

"I can't go home, I know that much."

"You go home and I bet yer father will've forgot all about it. He ain't out to kill ya. You shouldn't have kicked him anyway! You shouldn' kick yer father!"

"I had to, Nutbeam! He would've killed me!"

"I don't believe he would've killed ya."

"Maybe you'd let me stay for just a while," said Shadrack. "Just until I figure out what I should do."

"They'll come lookin' for ya," argued Nutbeam.

"Just for a couple o' days," said Shadrack.

"They'll find ya sure as hell."

"Just for tonight, then. I'll feel things out tomorrow."

"I don't like it."

"C'mon, Nutbeam, just for the night!"

"I don't know."

"Please?"

"Well . . ."

"Ah, thanks, Nutbeam! You're a pal!"

"Just for the night!"

*

When Lindon Tucker starts feeling his liquor, he likes to talk, or at least, likes to repeat the things other people say. Lindon was sitting at the bar. After the second double rye, he swung and eyed the gentleman sitting on the stool beside him. Lindon thought the gentleman was wearing either a black or purple suit; he wasn't sure, the room was dimly lit. He had a black vandyke beard, but otherwise, his head was as bald as an egg. He had one of those timeless faces. Lindon couldn't tell if he was thirty-five or much older. Oddly, for the lighting was very low, the gentleman wore sunglasses, hiding whatever lines of wisdom, happiness and pain — age — the eyes might have revealed.

Lindon scanned the candle-lit room, then came back to eye the stranger whose glasses reflected the light like cat eyes.

"How come yer warin' smoked glasses in here?" asked Lindon.

"Shade. I like the shade." The gentleman's voice was soft and deep.

"Oh, yeah. Shade, yeah. Okay. Shade."

The gentleman was eyeing Lindon's mackinaw, which he didn't remove despite the room's exceptional warmth.

"Are you cold?" he asked.

"Oh, yeah. Yeah. Cool enough, yeah."

The gentleman removed his eyes from Lindon and lifted his head as if to eye someone across the room.

"Lookin' for someone? What're ya lookin' at? Ya could see better without them glasses on."

"A lovely lady across the way."

"Ha, ha, ha, yes, sir. Yes. Oh yeah, yep. Quite the lady, yep. You from around here, are ya?"

"I'm from . . . the south," said the gentleman.

"Hot country? Hot country? Hot country?"

"It can get hot. It can get very hot."

"What do ya do fer a livin'?"

"I'm a musician. I play the violin."

"Yeah? Yeah? Like the fiddle, you mean?"

"Yes. Like the fiddle." The gentleman nodded toward the corner of the room to where a small triangular stage was located. "I'm here tonight," he said.

"Good, good, good. Like the fiddle. Always liked the fiddle. Play somethin' fer us. Give us a tune. You know 'Mutty Musk,' do ya?"

"I'm not familiar with it. Perhaps I could play you something else."

"Sure, sure, sure. Don't matter. Anything at all."

The gentleman checked his watch. "It's about time," he said. Standing up, he nodded farewell to Lindon, nodded to the lady across the room and headed for the stage.

In a minute the gentleman and two other musicians started to play. Lindon was not familiar with the melody and he thought it was unbearably loud. But as if he were in a Miramichi dancehall, he commenced to stomp his feet and whoop. "Drive 'er!" he yelled. "Walk back on 'er! Whoop! Yeawhooooo! Keep 'er close to the floor!"

Then Lindon felt the eyes upon him. There were more people looking at him than at the men on the stage. He quieted down and ordered another drink.

"Sober crowd," he said. "The music ain't that great, anyway."

The bartender served Lindon another drink, which he tossed back as if it were water. He chased it once again with ale. He was feeling very good and wanted to talk to someone, but he noticed that nobody was sitting near him at the bar. He contemplated moving to another seat and eyed the room for a likely place. He spotted the lady the fiddle player had been eyeing and was surprised that she was eyeing him. He nodded. She nodded back. He winked. She smiled.

"Hm," he thought. "If I had another drink, I'd give that lady a little rub."

He ordered and was served once again. He tossed the rye back, eyeing the woman all the while. He felt he nearly had enough confidence. One more drink and he'd confront her.

But then, to his surprise, the middle-aged woman with the red hair and dark-rimmed glasses left her table and moved to the stool next to Lindon. She ordered a screwdriver and lit a Rothman's.

Lindon eyed her with blurred vision.

The woman saw Lindon staring, smiled and said, "Hi."

Lindon leaned toward her and shouted above the music. "Havin' a little drink, are ya?"

The woman nodded and smiled. "From around here?" she asked.

"Brennen Siding!" he yelled. "Brennen Siding! Blackville!"

"Oh! You're from God's country."

"The Devil's country, devil's country, devil's country, more like it! Ho! Ha, ha, ha! Boys! Ya havin' a little drink, are ya?"

The screwdriver was served and the woman started digging into her purse for money. She removed her gloves, a make-up kit, a package of spearmint gum and a handkerchief. She removed a little black book, her eyeglass case and a ring of keys. The bartender waited patiently. From her purse, the woman removed a pen, a cigarette lighter, several Kleenex, a nail file and a hair brush. Her wallet was the last thing to be removed.

"How much?" asked the woman.

"Same as before — a dollar twenty-five."

"Oh, my goodness," said the lady. "I seem to be out of cash. Would you cash a cheque for me?"

"I'm sorry, Ma'am. It's against the rules."

"Well, what am I to do?"

"I'll have to take your drink back, Ma'am."

"Oh! I'm so embarassed!"

"I'll get that," said Lindon. "I'll get that. Let me buy that. How much?"

"A dollar twenty-five."

Lindon paid for the drink and noticed that the woman seemed impressed with the wad of bills. She inched her stool closer to Lindon's.

"Thank you very much," she said.

"No trouble, no trouble, no trouble. There's lots more where that came from."

"Oh! What do you do for a living?"

"Nothin', nothin', nothin'! Don't have to work. Guide some. Don't have to work!"

Lindon Tucker was wearing heavy woollen APH pants and a plaid Mackinaw coat. Lindon Tucker with his pot belly, unshaven face and missing cuspids, did not look like a doctor, or a lawyer.

"Oh," said the woman. "I'd have thought you was a doctor or a lawyer."

"No, no, no; could, could, could, might, might, ya never know, might. Bartender! Get me and this here little lady another drink."

"You shouldn't be spending your money on me," said the woman sweetly, placing her hand on Lindon's thigh.

"Lots more where that come from! Make them big ones, bartender! Never mind them little sips! Make 'em big ones!"

The bartender poured them two doubles and sat them in front of Lindon and the woman. "Nine dollars," he said.

"Nine dollars!" exclaimed Lindon.

"Yeah, they're triples."

"Oh, oh, oh well then." Lindon paid the bartender.

An hour went by and Lindon grew more and more intoxicated. The woman got prettier and prettier, and very, very friendly. It became quite clear to Lindon that she wanted him to get a room in the hotel.

At first he didn't know how to bring the issue up, but a couple of more doubles looked after that little holdup.

"What d'ya say we get a room, little lady?" said Lindon.

"Oh, my goodness, I hardly know you!"

"Get to know me, git to know me! Git to know me in a room!"

"Well, I guess I could party a little bit. Got any booze?"

"Booze?"

"Vodka, rye, rum, something to drink?"

"No, but there's lot's of it here! Could get it here!"

"Would you be so kind as to sell my friend here a bottle of vodka, bartender?" said the woman.

"I'd have to sell it by the ounce," cautioned the bartender.

"Give us some vodker!" yelled Lindon.

The bartender reached under the bar and sat up a forty ounce bottle of vodka. "Fifty dollars," he said.

The music had been wearing on Lindon. He hadn't liked one tune the band played all evening. But as he left the room with his little lady, he heard them playing the first tune he was familiar with, "The Devil's Dream." Lindon whooped as he was going through the door.

At the front desk, after paying for a room, Lindon noticed that he only had seventy-five dollars left. His only comment was, "Jesus."

He was more than just a little upset, but he decided to worry about the spending later. "Right now, there's something else that needs spending," he thought.

"You know somethin' darlin'?" said Lindon, as they entered room 405, "I don't even know yer name."

"Call me Molly, darlin'."

"MOLLY, MY NAME'S LINDON TUCKER! THE BEST MAN TO EVER SHIT A TURD IN THE DUNGARVON RIVER! HA, HA, HA, WHOOP!"

"You sit on the bed, darlin', and I'll pour us a drink."

Molly found two glasses in the bathroom and poured them each a drink. She poured one ounce in her own drink and topped it off with water. In Lindon's glass, she poured five ounces of straight vodka. She delivered Lindon his drink, they toasted — clink. "Down the hatch," she said and drank her glass empty. Not to be outdone by a little lady, Lindon downed his glass also.

For five minutes, Lindon raved, fondled and boasted; then he went to sleep.

Molly took Lindon's seventy-five dollars. She took his pocket watch and Zippo lighter. She considered taking the rest of the vodka. "Why not?" she said, "I might need it for another sucker at the bar."

As she was leaving the room, she said, "Good-night, Lindon," to the best man to ever shit a turd in the Dungarvon River.

*

Shadrack stayed up as late as he could and talked to Nutbeam. Nutbeam stayed awake much longer than he wanted to, talking to Shadrack. At four o'clock a.m., Shad sat on Nutbeam's cot, yawning. At five o'clock, Shadrack was fast asleep on Nutbeam's cot. Nutbeam only had the one cot and therefore had no place to sleep. He was left sitting alone at the table. The lamp beside him was turned low, so that Nutbeam appeared as a silhouette with an incredibly strange face. His big lips gave him a negroid appearance, although his white skin and blue eyes denied any possibility of black ancestry. His ears in the shadow on the wall behind him made him look like a Labrador Retriever. His nose was so long that two of him back to back would have looked like a pickaxe. Nutbeam was staring at the letter Dryfly had written for him.

Dryfly had tried his best to write well, but the address, crooked and slanted, indicated he needed much practice.

"I wish I could write good like that," thought Nutbeam.

Nutbeam didn't like the fact that Shadrack had stolen his cot, but he figured it would soon be time to rise anyway. Nutbeam knew that Shadrack couldn't possibly stay with him for very long and that Shadrack surely knew that too. With a fleeting inspection, one could easily see that the camp was not designed to accommodate more than one person. Nutbeam had an idea for Shadrack and planned to tell him as soon as he awakened. For the moment, though, going to the post office had to be planned.

"If she laughs," he thought, "I'll just pretend I don't know what she's laughin' at. I'll buy a stamp and tell her . . . tell her . . . tell her I like her dress or somethin'." Nutbeam knew that conversation with Shirley would not be easy. To Nutbeam, Shirley Ramsey was a beautiful woman and he was an ugly man. "No ugly man ever won the heart of a beautiful woman," he thought.

"If I could get that woman," he thought, "I'd be the happiest man in the world. I'd make her happy, too. I'd fix up the house and build a permanent woodshed. There'd be enough room in the shed to keep enough wood to last a year, plus room to hang a couple of deer and a moose. I'd plant whatever land she has with potatoes and vegetables and build a root cellar in the gravel pit. If I could get that woman, I wouldn't care if people laughed at me. I'd take her to dances in the village and to church on Sundays, and I'd get some nice clothes to wear. Maybe I'd even buy that old farm and this woodlot from Graig Allen, build a barn, a new house, the works. Dryfly could live with us and sing to us at nights. Other nights, while Dry's running the roads, we could sit and talk till maybe twelve o'clock and then go to bed."

To go to bed with somebody, to actually feel the warmth of another body next to his, to reach out in the night and find somebody beside him and to make love to somebody had never been anything more than fantasy for Nutbeam.

*

Shadrack awakened to the smell of bacon frying. Nutbeam was cooking them a breakfast of bacon, eggs and biscuits.

"Mornin', Nutbeam. Sorry 'bout takin yer bed. Guess I must've fell asleep."

"Don't matter. Had some figurin' to do, anyway."

The two sat at the table and ate. Conversation was nothing more than an occasional comment. Shadrack had talked himself out during the night and had only slept a couple of hours. He was sore, his clothes were crumpled, he was homeless and broke, there was nothing much to say. Nutbeam had something to say, but the presence of the weary boy sitting across from him, shoulders slumped with the stress of guilt, fear and emptiness, gave the matter a certain delicacy that needed time. Nutbeam would hold off until after breakfast.

Shadrack ate slowly, giving each morsel the consideration of a scrambling mind. Over a bit of bacon, he looked around the tiny camp. "It's mornin' and the sun is high in the sky," he thought, "but it's always night time in here."

When you go to bed at four or five in the morning after a night's rendezvous with the river and sky, you find yourself dreamed out, and so you dream a dreamless sleep. The river creeps into your soul, like a god or a demon, sought on possessing you and holding you in her lush valleys. Shad had been playing on the river a great deal for the past several months and had found great comfort and joy in its grasp, but now the river was starting to reject him. It's just not the same in the autumn. The river tends to give you the cold shoulder after her bout with the frosts and the northeast rains. Shad was losing his friend, the river, and the time spent was being replaced by the restlessness of the idle. He had replaced the river with the banjo and was playing it fanatically. He was plucking fantastic, mind-boggling little melodies from the strings and flew off with them into dreams. Bob Nash found the banjo playing a beautiful thing, an accomplishment for his boy. But in his envy, it was a rasp that constantly filed his nerves, driving him from the house, or more drastically, into the arms of Elva. Bob Nash found that the Elva he once loved was not there anymore. Elva was a bitch, Shad played the banjo and Bob was given to fits of argument and temper — no warmth, no communication, no love — an unfit place to live.

Over a bit of egg, Shad eyed Nutbeam — the mysterious, tall man who looked like an elf, who lived alone in a tiny camp with no windows that smelled of kerosene and woodsmoke — Nutbeam, the Todder Brook Whooper, the man who haunted everyone in Brennen Siding in one way or another. This man was like the river — he summoned dreams from within you. Where John Kaston claimed to know the

Lord, Shadrack Nash could claim to know Nutbeam. Nutbeam was something for Shadrack to hold on to.

Shadrack hadn't held or kissed his mother and father since he was five years old. It was the absence of love, warmth and communication that sent him to the river, Nutbeam and Dryfly.

After breakfast, Nutbeam opened the door to let the light of day in. He cleared the breakfast dishes from the table and replaced them with two tin cups. He poured the tea and sat to confront Shadrack.

"Shad," he began, "I've been thinking."

"Yeah?"

"I've been thinking about letters."

"Letters?"

"Yeah. Writin' letters. Kin you write a letter, Shad?"

"I s'pose, I don't know."

"I can't," said Nutbeam.

"I know. So?"

"So, I wish I had gone to school."

"So, why didn' ya?"

"Because I was weak."

"You was weak, Nutbeam?"

"When I tried to go to school, everyone laughed and made fun o' me. The other kids thought I was a freak and threw rocks at me, wouldn' let me into their games, and I . . . I use to think it was them that was weak." Nutbeam grinned thoughtfully and shook his head negatively. "Wasn't them, Shad, it was me that was weak. I was too weak to stand up to them."

"So you didn' go back to school anymore?"

"You know, Shad, I've been thinkin' a lot lately. I've been thinkin' that I got the best ears of any man in this whole world. I've been thinking that I should've held me head right back and stepped into that school like I owned it; walked around not just like I was as good as everybody else, but better. Hey boy, I can hear a robin sing from across the river! I kin hear a deer walkin' from a hundred yards away! I kin hear yer heart beatin'!"

"So, what are ya comin' at, Nutbeam?"

"I think they would've left me alone after a while if I hadn' been so weak. I think I would've had friends and maybe even a woman. But instead, I crawled back here in this camp, no good to anyone, even meself."

Nutbeam rose from the table and walked to the open door. He stood thoughtfully for a moment, gazing at the generous colors of autumn in the forest around him.

"You like girls, Shad?"

"Pretty likely."

"When I was fifteen I wanted a girl so bad that I use to wish on the evening star and pray to the moon. One night, I was walking and a heart-shaped cloud drifted up so that the moon looked as if it was framed by a heart. I took it as an omen that said, 'Don't worry, Nutbeam old boy, love will come to you.'"

"And did it?"

"A few days later I met this girl I'd never seen before. She was very nice to me; said she was stayin' at a neighbor's house and that she would like for me to come a callin'. She said she'd be waitin' in the kitchen for me at eight o'clock."

"So, did ya go?"

"Yep. I went and knocked on the kitchen door at eight o'clock, feeling on top o' the world. Can you imagine how I felt, knowing that a pretty little lady was waiting for me inside?"

"Yeah, sort of."

"Can you imagine how it felt when I found out that it wasn't a girl at all, but one of a bunch of boys that were playin' a trick on me? The girl opened the door slightly and talked sweet-talk to me for a minute, then threw the door open all the way to reveal six other boys all laughing their heads off."

"So did you hit the bastard?"

"No! I was too weak! I crawled into a deeper hole and cried for two weeks! Are you gonna do that, Shad? Are you gonna crawl into a hole and live in the woods like me?"

"Well . . . I . . . I . . . ."

"Shad, what I'm sayin' to ya is, get off your ass!"

"So, what am I to do?"

"I think you should start goin' to school! You're a smart lad, Shad! You could be an engineer some day!"

"You're starting to sound like me mother!" said Shad.

"Then maybe you should be listenin' to yer mother!"

"My mother don't know nothin'! She ain't never been any-where!"

"Just like you'll be, if ya don't go to school."

Shadrack was beginning to sweat a little. He did not ex-pect this line of talk from Nutbeam and he did not like what he was hearing.

"But why would I wanna go back to school?"

"Because you don't wanna live like me, a hermit for the rest of your life!"

"Ah, you're crazy!"

"A little bit crazy, maybe, and you'll be a little crazy too, if you live alone long enough! What about the girls, Shad? Do you think that a girl wants a man with no schoolin' and lives in a cave in the woods?"

"No."

"You like workin' in the woods, Shad?"

"No."

"You think you're ever gonna git a job doin' anything else, with schoolin' like you got?"

"No . . . maybe, I don't know!"

"Put it this way, Shad: you'd have it easy! As long as you went to school, you wouldn' be expected to work in the woods. You'd be hangin' around with young girls everyday and everyone would look up to you. You'd have 'er made!"

"I don't want to talk about it, Nutbeam. I thought you and me was friends!"

"We are friends, Shad. You and Dryfly are the only friends I got."

"So, leave me alone!"

"Well, you think about what I've said," said Nutbeam.

Nutbeam saw he had talked enough. Shadrack had a con-trary nature; to push him would only make matters worse.

"You think about it, Shad. I'm goin' for a walk."

Nutbeam stepped into the autumn day feeling more confi-dent than he'd ever felt before in his life; his talk to Shad had been good therapy. With the letter addressed to Johannah Banks in his hip pocket, he headed for the post office. He walked to the edge of the forest and, for the first time in nearly nine years, stepped out without concern for who might see him.

On the footbridge, Nutbeam came face to face with Lindon Tucker.

"Hello, Lindon," he said.

"G'day, g'day, g'day, g'day," said Lindon.

Lindon was in a good mood. He was home again. Any other time, he might have been nervous in the presence of Nutbeam, but today, Nutbeam could have been an old friend.

Lindon's pleasantness, his I'm-happy-just-to-see-you attitude, encouraged Nutbeam. "This is going to be a good day," he thought.

fourteen

The Cabbage Island Salmon Club Camps were vacant and closed for the winter. They would re-open on April fifteenth, when the club members and guests returned to fish the black salmon.

Shadrack sat on the same veranda where he'd sat with Lillian Wallace. The river was quiet and uneventful — no swimming or canoeing, no fishermen laughing, talking and wading about. The river, too, was closed for the winter.

Shadrack had the worst case of depression he'd ever had. "Dad and Mom don't love me, Dryfly stole the only woman I've ever loved, and now Nutbeam's turned again me! The homely bastard! They all want me to do what they want," he thought.

Shad knew that Nutbeam's suggestion to go back to school was practical enough and would probably solve most of his problems, but Shadrack Nash did not like being manipulated and told what to do. If he went back to school, the decision to do so would have to be his own. "If I go back to school, I'll have to go suckin' up to Mom and Dad," he thought. "What I really should do is leave. Run away and never come back."

"No sense runnin' away," thought Shad. "I got no money and I got no schoolin'! I might as well be dead! I'll jump in the river and drown. I'll drown and wash up on the shore for someone to find all bird-picked and wormy like Bonzie Ramsey was when they found him. They'll be sorry then, I bet ya!"

Shadrack Nash was very depressed, but he was not suicidal. He was too curious about the future, the cars, the money, the women to seriously consider death.

"Maybe I could get into one of these camps and stay for a while," he thought. "If I stay here and sneak around like

Nutbeam, they might all think I'm dead, anyway. They could look for me all they wanted, but they'd never find me. They'll drag the river and everything. Dad and Mom will cry their hearts out thinkin' they beat me the last time they saw me."

Shadrack rose and started checking the windows. He checked all the windows on three cabins before he found one that was slightly ajar. He opened it and climbed over the sill. He was in! He looked about at the paintings of wildlife, the mounted deerheads and salmon; at the sofas and chairs, at the carpets and fireplace.

"Hello! No house, I suppose! I suppose I ain't got no place to hide out!"

Shadrack inspected the cabin. In the living room, he found dozens of books, a rack completely stacked with rifles and shotguns. A drawer underneath the rifle rack was filled with boxes of ammunition. He found fishing rods and boxes of flyhooks and a full case of various kinds of liquor. In a bedroom drawer, he found three dollars and change that someone had obviously forgotten about.

Shad cracked the seal on a bottle of Glen Livet and took a drink. He sat on the sofa, put his feet on the coffee table and sized up the situation.

"No food," he thought. "I'll have to figure out a way of gettin' food. There's everything else here, though."

Shadrack guzzled another drink. The depression drifted off into oblivion.

"I got 'er made," he thought.

*

Nutbeam walked to Shirley Ramsey's with powerful, deliberate strides. He did not once stop. He did not dare to stop. To stop, even for an instant, might give the old inferiority complex a chance to slip into his plans, to undermine his determination. Nutbeam knew himself very well. He knew the limitations of his confidence. He was following providence. He had no specific course of action. His confidence was holding up quite well as of yet — he hadn't shied away from Lindon

Tucker — but Lindon Tucker was not his concern. Shirley Ramsey would be the ultimate test.

And then there was the house. And then there was the door. His heart was pounding from a combination of walking fast and the excitement of seeing Shirley Ramsey. He knocked.

"Come in."

The voice was muffled from the depths of the house, but Nutbeam could hear it loud and clear. He heard its softness, its femininity — the Goddess had spoken.

"Come in," came the gentle feminine voice once again. Yes, the voice was gentle and feminine, but to Nutbeam it could have been the thunderous bellow of a goddess who could tear him apart.

Nutbeam turned the knob, then let it go quickly, as though it was red hot and had burned him. He heard Shirley's footsteps approaching from inside. She was only a few steps from the door. He eyed the corner of the house and contemplated hiding.

The door opened and there before him stood the Goddess in her hand-me-down dress. The Goddess was as afraid of Nutbeam as he was of her.

When Shirley opened the door to see Nutbeam standing on her step, she didn't know what to do. Her ability to speak leaped from her mouth and into thin air.

"The mysterious man from the woods! He's come to kill me, sure as hell!" she thought.

Nutbeam couldn't find words either, but he was together enough to know that something had to be done. He handed her the letter.

"I . . . I . . . I . . ." tried Nutbeam.

Shirley looked down at the envelope.

"Five cents," she said.

"Fi . . . five cents?"

"The stamp."

Nutbeam started frantically searching his pockets for a coin. There wasn't any. He came up with a five dollar bill, handed it to her.

"I'll get your change," said Shirley and practically ran into the post office. She opened her cash box and fumbled through the few bills and coins. She dropped a quarter, made a dive for it, stumbled and nearly fell. She glanced over her shoulder to make sure that Nutbeam hadn't followed her into the office. She managed to count out four dollars and ninety-five cents, took a deep breath and went back to the open door.

"Your change," she said, but there was nobody there. Nutbeam had vanished.

*

Dryfly removed Lillian's letter from its hiding place under the mattress, unfolded it and commenced to read. He read from beginning to end, then went to the word "love" and eyed it thoughtfully.

He heard a knock on the door.

"Who could that be?" he asked himself. "Nobody knocks around here."

Dryfly was lying on the bed. He heard Shirley responding to the knock, so did not bother to rise.

Dryfly sniffed the letter. When it first arrived he could detect the slight scent of perfume, or perhaps fly repellent. The letter was now ragged and crumpled and the scent of whatever it was was long gone. Dryfly closed his eyes, visualized Lillian's lips, and kissed the letter.

"If you could only read my thoughts," he thought. "I love you, Lillian. I must write to you. But . . . what will I say?"

Dryfly rose, found a scribbler and pencil, then returned to his bed. Lying down, which did nothing to improve his calligraphy, he began to write:

> Dear Lillian,
> How are you? I am fine. Hope you are the same.

Dryfly wanted to spill his heart. He wanted to say: I miss you and I love you, but instead he wrote, "It was good to hear from you." He wanted to say: I'm crazy about you and I need you, but instead he wrote "It's been a good fall. The sun is shining here today. How's your father?" Dryfly wanted to spill his heart, but instead he wrote about Shadrack, his mother, Palidin and Nutbeam. He wrote about the river, the hunting season, the autumn colors and the fact that new boards were needed on the footbridge.

He finished the letter off by saying, "Hope to see you next summer. Love, Dryfly."

"It's a good letter," he thought, "I've managed to squeeze in the word 'love.'"

He folded and fit the letter into an envelope, addressed it and went to the kitchen to give it to Shirley to mail. He didn't have a nickel for a stamp, but he knew that Shirley would send it off for him.

"Who was that at the door, Mom?" he asked.

"You'd never believe it!"

"Who?"

"That Nutbeam fella'."

"Nutbeam? Here?"

"Yeah. Wanted to mail a letter. Give me five dollars and left without his change."

"Did he say anything?"

"No. I came in here to get his change and when I went back to the door, he was gone."

"Odd."

"Yeah. It was."

"Would you stamp this letter for me, Mom?"

Shirley took the letter and read the name and address.

"You think about her a lot, don't you, Dry?"

"Some."

"She's a fine lady. Pretty, too," said Shirley, then thought, "she'll never get caught with the likes of one o' us."

Shirley stamped the envelope.

"What do ya make o' Nutbeam?" she asked.

"Don't know. Wanted to mail a letter, I guess."

"The letter was to somebody in Maine. He's got floppy ears, Dry. You'd have laughed to see him."

"Did you laugh?"

"No, I was too scared to laugh."

216

"That's good."

"Have you ever seen him, Dry?"

"Yeah, I've seen him. He's all right. He won't hurt ya. He's a nice lad, really."

"I wonder why he didn't wait for the change?"

*

The Italians make a cigar that is too strong to inhale. They're about three inches long and tapered. They're hard on the outside. They're good for smoking while you fish. They don't absorb moisture from your hands and when it's raining, they'll stay lit longer. They also smell like the dickens and keep away pesty insects like mosquitoes and blackflies. Parodys, they're called. Shadrack found a box of Parodys on the mantle.

He lit one up and flew into a fit of coughing. "Not bad!" he thought.

Shad puffed on the smelly cigar and nipped straight from the bottle, the Glen Livet. Shad was not a thief at heart. He would never steal anything he thought anyone would care about. He figured the American owners of the Cabbage Island Salmon Club were rich and would never miss the scotch or the cigars and therefore, it was perfectly all right to take it. "They prob'ly don't even know they left it here," he thought.

Shad had sat to think, but something was toying with his concentration. He found himself much too happy to give much thought to being depressed. How could one think seriously about running away or committing suicide while grinning from ear to ear? Instead of thinking about his problems, he carried his scotch to the big window that faced the river, had another nip and bit on the cigar.

"My name's Shaddy Nashville," he said. "I'm a zecative in the nylon industry. I'm from Bangah Maine."

Shadrack started to sing, "I once had a sweetheart, but now I got none! She's gone and left me for somebody neeeeeeeew! La, la, la, la, la, la, la to the red, white and blue! Whoop!"

"Ladies and gentlemen! Star of stage and screen! The great Shadrack Nash!"

Another little nip.

"Hey, boy! Fetch ma wada's and auvis! I'm goin' to the riva!" Shad's fabrication of the American accent was better than he knew. Shad didn't care if his accent was correct or not. Shad didn't give a fiddler's wink about anything.

"Are you mine, rich or poor? Tell me darlin' are ya sure? La, la, la, la, la . . . whoopo! WEEE HAW AND HER NAME WAS MAUD!"

In his mind, Shad was not standing alone in an empty cottage. In his mind, he was facing an audience of thousands of people. He was a powerful performer, with an audience so captivated he could do whatever he wanted and they'd be pleased.

"Ladies and gen'lmen, I don't give a damn about anything," he shouted. "The whole world can go piss up a stump, for all I care! WHOOP! When I was but a little boy before I went to school, I had a fleet of forty sail, I called the ships o' Yule! Ya'll like that, ladies and gen'lemen? Ya'll like me little poem? Thank you, thank you, thank you!"

Then something made a noise in the kitchen. It sounded to Shad like something falling from a shelf. It startled Shad into silence. He stopped to listen.

"Hello?" he called.

Suddenly, although he was glowing from the scotch and a little breathless from his performance, the cabin seemed cold and clammy — too quiet. He had the sensation that someone was looking over his shoulder. The cigar was getting to him, so that when he stopped to listen, all he could hear was his own wheezing lungs.

"Is there someone in the kitchen?" he yelled. "Cause if there is, ya'd better show yerself, 'cause Shadrack Nash ain't scared o' nothin'."

Still holding the Glen Livet, Shad made his way down the hall. The kitchen was across the hall from the bathroom. The bathroom door was shut. Shad debated whether the door had been open or shut when he'd passed it during his earlier exploration of the cabin.

"Had to be closed," he thought. "Nobody here but me."

He stepped into the kitchen.

Nothing unusual. He couldn't see anything out of place. Nothing visible had fallen.

"Must've been a rat," he thought. "A mouse, or a rat in the cupboard."

"Here's to ya, rat!" He toasted and drank from the bottle. The scotch gave him courage. He stepped back into the hall. He opened the bathroom door.

Empty.

He flicked the Parody butt into the toilet. There was no water in the toilet, but he missed anyway and the Parody stood on its end, straight up, on the edge of the porcelain rim.

"Ha! I'd never do that again in a million years," he thought. "Ha! That's even more than you could lie about!"

Shad shrugged, snapped his fingers rhythmically and danced his way back to the livingroom, singing, "Oh, doe, doe, doe, dee, dee; dee yodle dodle day hee hoo; comoss evaw, my name is yodlein' Euclid, dee yodle dodle day hee hoo!" This time he sang louder, with more gusto, as if he were playing to a noisy, difficult audience. He especially chose the song "Yodeling Euclid" as an attention getter.

And when he stepped back into the livingroom, there, staring at him, sad, and undignified, was his audience — the salmon, the moosehead, the deerhead.

Where at first they had looked majestic and beautiful, they now looked grotesque and . . . undignified. They stared at him with unblinking eyes, watching his every move, hating him for what he was; hating him for being human. On the deerhead, you could actually see the seam where the throat had been cut.

"Dryfly," whispered Shad. "I wish Dryfly was here." He might as well have said, "No man is an island."

He was being scrutinized by the mounted animals; he was alone; the cabin was cold and damp; he heard another noise in the kitchen! This time it sounded like something scratching, like a puppy at the door.

Shad knew there were no puppies in Brennen Siding.

He contemplated investigating, decided against it. "I just checked it," he thought.

Shad hurriedly filled his pockets with Parodys, the mounted animals watching him all the while . . . and perhaps other eyes as well, he wasn't sure. He just had the feeling that he might get caught. He felt he had to work quickly.

He took some Parodys, the money and last, but not least, a bottle of Canadian Club whiskey.

He headed for Shirley Ramsey's.

*

Nutbeam entered his camp and shut the door. Lately, he had been lighting the lamp more often, but today he did not. The darkness and gloom of the camp fit his mood. He lay down on the cot.

"I made a fool of myself," he thought. "She must be laughing her head off."

He closed his eyes and envisioned Shirley standing in the doorway, small, somewhat afraid.

"I've ruined it all," he thought. "I should've known that nothin' good would ever happen to me!"

The cot was comfortable and Nutbeam was feeling very tired.

"Why did I run?" he asked himself. "Why was I so afraid of her? Did she see how scared I was? Did I really make a fool of myself? But she didn't laugh, she didn't laugh."

"I'm alone," he whispered to the camp. "I'm all alone."

Nutbeam slept and dreamed of running on a footbridge that ran into infinity. He ran and ran and ran.

Knock, knock, knock.

"Huh?"

"Nutbeam, old boy!"

"Huh?"

"Hey, Nutbeam, chummy pard!"

Still half asleep, Nutbeam unlatched the door and let Shadrack and Dryfly in.

Shadrack was carrying a bottle of whiskey, the contents of which had been half consumed. Both Shadrack and Dryfly reeked of the rye. Dryfly was carrying his guitar.

"What're ya doin' in the dark, Nutbeam?"

"I was sleepin'," said Nutbeam, yawning so that his big, wide-open mouth was like a black hole amid the gloom.

Nutbeam lit the lamp.

"Have a drink, Nutbeam, old dog! Clean 'er up! There's lot's more where that come from!"

"Where'd ya git it?" asked Nutbeam. Nutbeam knew by the size of the bottle and the quality of the rye that they hadn't bought it at the bootlegger's.

"Don't you worry 'bout where we got it, old pal! Here, chummy pard, have a cigar!"

Nutbeam had only slept for two hours and hadn't eaten since morning. The rye shot through his system so that he could feel the effects of the first small drink. It was good. He took another drink, and then a bigger one, and one more. The party began.

When the rye was empty, Shad reached outside the door and pulled in a second bottle, broke the seal and passed it around.

The three were sitting at the table, and as all drunken conversations do, this one too got dangerously personal.

"Ya know, Nutbeam, you're the best lad in the world!" said Shad. "Nobody ever used me any better than you!"

"It's good havin' you boys around," said Nutbeam. "I've been alone for too long."

"You know what I did today, boys? . . . I wrote to Lillian Wallace! I love 'er, you know that?"

"I've been thinkin' over what you've been sayin', Nutbeam," said Shad, "and you're right. I should go back to school. I'm no jeezly good in the woods."

At this point of the party, all three were more or less talking at the same time.

"Do you know what it's like being locked up in a place like this?" said Nutbeam. "What'll happen when a man gets old? No family. No woman. Alone."

"I'm the lonesomest man in the world!" said Dryfly as if stating something so profound that he had to yell it out. "Do you have any, do you have any idea what it's like to not be able to see or touch the woman you love?"

"I know what it's like," said Nutbeam. "You're damned right I know what it's like."

"I'm gonna go back to school and rub all them women in Blackville, become rich and famous and own the Cabbage Island Salmon Club. Lay right back and drink and smoke cigars, do a little fishin'."

"I'm in love with her, I tell ya."

"I'm in love with the most beautiful woman in the whole world!" shouted Nutbeam, as if he were arguing a point.

"If she's nearby, you got 'er made," said Dryfly.

"She's near all right."

"Mine's way the hell down in the States."

"Then go to her, for Jesus sake."

"Can't."

"Go! Go! Tell 'er you love 'er! I would," said Nutbeam.

"I'd have to go to Blackville school," said Shad. "Kin you just see me in that big school?"

"Does she know you're in love, in love with her?" asked Dry.

"No! No! No, she don't know."

"You know what's wrong with you, Nutbeam? You got a feriority comprex."

"I'm goin' home and tellin' Mom I'm goin' back to school," said Shad. "I'm tellin' her right now."

"No! Wait! You can't go now. You're drunk, ya jeezer."

"I went to see her, Dry. Went to see her and failed," said Nutbeam, practically in tears.

"I heard Joe Louis on the radio, Nut. He said the first rule in boxin' is to never give up. You're just down, Nutbeam. Don't let Mom bother ya. You ain't beaten yet."

"How'd you know I was talkin' 'bout yer mother?"

"I know a lotta things," said Dryfly.

*

Elva and Bob Nash sat in the parlour. Elva was knitting Shadrack a pair of mitts. Bob was rocking, thumping his heel on the floor each time the chair rocked forward.

They heard the kitchen door open, Shadrack's uneven footsteps. In a moment, Shad appeared in the parlour door. He was pale, his hair was messed up, he needed a bath and was obviously drunk.

"Mom? Dad? I'm . . . pretty drunk!" said Shadrack.

Neither Elva or Bob commented.

"I know you'll wanna . . . wanna beat me up, but, but, before ya do, I got somethin' to say."

"I don't want no sass from the likes of you!" said Bob.

"I n'ain't . . . ain't gonna ssshass ya. First thing Monday mornin', I'm goin' to ssschool."

"Who in the hell you think you are, comin' in this house smellin' like dirty old liquor!" snapped Elva.

"Goddamned tramp!" said Bob.

"Monday mornin', goin' to school to make somethin' o' meself."

"A little boy like you drinkin' that dirty old liquor! What's the world comin' to?"

"A big boy like you goin' back to school in . . . in grade seven! The other lads will be only half yer size!"

"I don't care," said Shad.

"You don't care! Boys! You don't care!" said Bob, then yelled, "It's about time you started to care!"

"You make me sick!" yelled Elva.

"Get into that bathroom and clean yerself up!" yelled Bob.

"School all right! You'll go to school or I'll skin you alive!" said Elva.

"And you won't be stayin' home and playin' hooky either!" said Bob.

"RIGHT NOW, I SAY!"

"DO AS YER TOLD!"

"NOW!"

Shad staggered to the bathroom, making no effort to hide his tears.

"All he needed was a good beatin'," said Bob.

fifteen

Nutbeam looked down at the fresh deer tracks at his feet. This was the fourth set of prints he'd seen in the last few hundred feet. "Four deer," he thought, "all heading toward the brook. These tracks should all lead to a trail sooner or later . . . a trail that they all follow."

Nutbeam followed the tracks for a hundred yards or so, and did, indeed, come to a path frequently travelled by deer. A lesser hunter would have followed the deer trail, but Nutbeam knew better. He sat to wait . . . Nutbeam knew you don't follow a deer — "Sit and wait and they come to you. Might take an hour, might take as long as two days, but they'll come," thought Nutbeam. Nutbeam sat with his back against a tree. He stood the cocked rifle beside him.

While waiting for the deer to show up, Nutbeam's mind was elsewhere. "The hunt's as good as over," he thought. "Deer are stupid." Shirley Ramsey, on the other hand, was a more perplexing matter. "This whole thing might work. If it doesn't, there's no harm done, anyway. All it'll do is make life a little easier."

There were no leaves left on the trees, so that Nutbeam had a clear view of the trail. The November wind prophesied winter. "It'll soon snow," thought Nutbeam. "Meat'll keep good from now on."

Nutbeam sat there for four hours and the sun was nesting well down in the northwest before he heard it.

Snort, went the deer.

In one swift movement, Nutbeam grabbed his rifle and positioned himself.

"Calm down," he thought. "There's nothin' to be excited about."

He still couldn't see the deer, but he could hear it snort,

and he could hear its hooves falling and crunching the dried leaves on the frozen ground. He waited.

Crunch . . . crunch . . . crunch . . . snort . . . crunch.

The deer approached slowly, cautiously, sensing danger, smelling Nutbeam.

"It could be a human," said the deer, "but I'm not quite sure."

Crunch . . . crunch . . . crunch.

The deer poked its head from behind a fir tree.

Sniff-sniff. "I probably should flash my tail. There's definitely something at the foot of that tree up there. I'll circle around and see if I can get a better look at it."

The deer crunched its way to an easterly point where it could better see Nutbeam. "It's a human, all right," said the deer. "I guess I'd better flash and dash."

When the deer leaped, Nutbeam swiftly shouldered his rifle and pulled the trigger.

A gigantic bell went BOING in the deer's head; the legs buckled, the deer collapsed.

*

"Where ya goin'?" asked Elva Nash.

"To Bernie Hanley's store."

"Got some money?"

"Dad gave me five dollars."

"Don't spend it all foolish."

"See ya later, Mom," said Shad and stepped into the cool November evening. He was feeling good and stepping high; he had a sense of direction; it was Saturday night and he was bound for Blackville.

"I'm in with the in crowd! I go where the in crowd goes. I'm in with the in crowd, and I know what the in crowd knows!" sang Shad, loud, arrogantly.

Shad was not doing great in school; he had a lot of catching up to do. His higher-than-average intelligence and mild interest was helping him along, however, and things were improving. He would not pass at Christmas, but would probably grade in the spring.

His relationship with Bob and Elva was improving, too. It had required a simple solution; stay out of their presence as often as possible.

As he was crossing the river on the footbridge, he noticed that the river was frozen almost completely in. There was but one hole in the ice, about twenty feet long and ten feet wide. It was six o'clock and nearly dark, and the hole appeared black, cold and forbidding in the blue-grey light.

"An air hole," thought Shad. "Could stay there all winter. Dangerous thing, an air hole." Shad was remembering a story about somebody who had walked into an air hole while crossing on the ice on a dark night. There was another story, too, about a child who had skated into one.

Shad made a mental note that the air hole was located just above Dr. MacDowell's cabin, in front of John Kaston's place. "I might be skating there later on in the winter," he thought.

Shad stopped on the center abutment for a minute to take in the twilit scenery. The river frozen had a new beauty to it — a ribbon of ice dividing farms and forests.

"I'd like to build a cabin on the river down in front of home sometime," he thought. "Of course, Dad'll probably sell the shore to a rich American. He could do with a thousand or two."

"See ya next spring, old river," he said. "See ya when you're thawed out again."

*

Eleven men and boys stood around Bernie Hanley's store, eating chocolate bars and drinking Orange Crush.

"Soon be gettin' snow," said Dan Brennen.

"Oh yeah, yeah, yeah. Gonna snow for sure, Dan, yeah. Looks like snow tonight, I noticed, yeah, Dan old boy," said Lindon Tucker.

"Kinda warm, though," said Bernie Hanley. "Might come in rain."

"Rain, yeah. That's true, yeah. Might come in rain, I was thinkin' too. That's right, yeah, Bernie, could come in rain."

"How was Fredericton, Lindon?" asked Bert Todder.

"Quite a place, quite a place. Lotsa women, lotsa women. Lived right there on Pine Street, yeah. Went to the hotel one night, yeah, so I did, one night, yeah. Oh yeah, yeah, yeah. Hotel, yeah. Quite a place!"

"Women ain't much good, if ya can't get yer hands on them," chuckled Dan Brennen. "Did ya get your hands on them, Lindon?"

"Got me hands on them all right! No trouble there! Ha, ha, ha, ha! Got me hands on them all right, Dan old boy. There's, there's, there's, there's no trouble passin' the hand on them ladies!"

All the men laughed. For the moment, Lindon was the center of attention. Everyone knew how Lindon would act when confronted with a female and didn't believe a word he was saying. Lindon was always good for a laugh.

"Everyone should be livin' in Fredericton," said Lindon. "Lotsa women, lotsa women. I, I, I, I, I met up with some kinda fancy woman, I, I, I, so I did. Earrings on, smokin' a big long tailor-made cigarette. Fancy lady, she was. Met 'er at the hotel, I did, yeah, so I did. Got a room. Got a room right there in the hotel, so we did."

"Did ya put the lad to 'er?" asked Stan Tuney.

"Put the lad to 'er, all right! Ho! No I didn'! No! No! No, I suppose I didn't put it to 'er none! Ha, ha! Oh, yeah, yeah, yeah. Put it to 'er, I did! Right there in the hotel room. Drunk a whole bottle o' this stuff she called vodker. There wasn't a drop left in the mornin'! Woke up and I was all alone, yep. Jist as well, though. Jist as well."

"Was she good?"

"Ha, ha, ha! Good! I guess she was good! Ho! No she wasn't! Ho! The very best, so she was!"

"Did ya see Graig Allen while you was over there?" asked John Kaston, who was getting somewhat annoyed with all the dirty talk.

"Never saw Graig, no. No, I never saw Graig. Right there, too, but I never saw him. Been over there for years, Graig has. Workin' at the cotton mill, I think. Someone said Graig was at the cotton mill."

"Never comes back, does he?" said Bob Nash. "Sold his land to Dr. MacDowell and never cried crack till he hit Fredericton. Never came back."

"A man should go and see him, you know," said Dan Brennen.

"Ya'll never guess who I saw on the bridge the other mornin'," said Lindon Tucker.

"Graig?"

"No, no, no, no, not Graig, no. Walkin' cross the bridge I was. Saw that Nutbeam fella. Nutbeam. Nutbeam, know who I mean? Nutbeam. Met him on the bridge."

"What'd he say? What'd he say?"

"Just said g'day. G'day, he said. Just said g'day."

"What'd you say?"

"I said, I said, I said, I said, I said, 'G'day, Nutbeam, old Nutbeam, old boy,' I said. He never said nothin', jist kept walkin'. He's got the biggest ears, look o' here, I ever saw in my life! Ya never saw the like o' them! Big as that pound cake there! Homeliest man ya ever want to meet!"

"I heard, now," lied Stan Tuney, "that he don't cook one thing he eats! Use to being up north someplace. They don't cook their meat in the Yukon, you know."

"How do ya know he don't cook his food?" asked Shadrack.

"Well, if he don't cook his meat he might be from the Yukon, who knows?"

"I heard everything that sticks out on 'im is a foot long," said Bert Todder, "his ears, nose, everything."

"His tool would just look like a young pig with no ears," put in Dan Brennen.

"That's what that Albert Johnson was suppose to look like," said Stan Tuney. "Albert Johnson was from up north, ya know. Shot all them Mounties! I wouldn' be surprised if that's who he is!"

"They captured Albert Johnson, didn' they?" asked Bert Todder.

"They never knew for sure," said Stan Tuney. "They thought they got 'im, but they never knew for sure."

"Homeliest man I ever saw," said Lindon Tucker. "Just said g'day, was all he said."

"You ever hear from yer boy, George, Bernie?" asked Bert Todder.

"Got a letter from 'im yesterday," said Bernie Hanley.

"News from Palidin," thought Dryfly, perking up to listen.

"Said he was workin' in a bakery. Place called Richmond Hill."

"Thought he went to Toronto," said Bert.

"No, no, Richmond Hill. Young Palidin, now, is workin' in Toronto, though. Got 'imself a job workin' with a newspaper, deliverin' papers or somethin'.'"

"And George is workin' in a bakery! Boys! Sounds like a pretty good job to me! I bet ya he's makin' good money, too!" said Bert.

"They'll be back," said Bernie. "Ya couldn' keep that young Palidin away from the river! Best fisherman I ever saw, Palidin was."

"He could ketch 'em when nobody else could," said Bob Nash. "He use to borry that old rod o' Shad's and bring us up a salmon every other day."

"I bought about ten from him," said Bernie.

"How ya s'pose he did it?" asked Dan Brennen. "I fished all one day and never saw a thing. Young Palidin came over the hill, made two casts and bang, got a ten-pounder."

"He seemed to just know how to do it," said Bert Todder.

"He'll be back," said Bernie Hanley. "You'd never get them young lads to stay away from the river for any length o' time."

*

Shadrack and Dryfly left the store and stepped into the dark, windy November evening. It was Saturday night and Shadrack was getting restless.

"There's nothin' to do around here," said Shad. "I'm bored."

"We could take a walk to Gordon," suggested Dryfly. "Might be some girls around."

"No girls in Gordon. Blackville's the place to go. There's about three hundred girls in Blackville school and they all hang around the canteen on Saturday nights. Why don't we see if we can hitch a ride to Blackville, Dry?"

"No, I don't think so. I don't know anyone in Blackville, Shad."

"I do, Dry. I know lotsa lads."

"I don't think so, Shad. We'd never get a ride, anyway."

Since Shadrack started to school in Blackville, Dryfly was seeing a great change in him. Shadrack was beginning to speak differently, to use words like algebra, math, classroom, corridor, cafeteria, and other words that Dryfly had no comprehension of. Shadrack was making new friends at school, too, and often spoke of Gary Perkins, Polly Saunders and David Carlyle. "That Mary Wilson's a cool chick," or "That Don Monroe's a cool cat," Shad would say, and Dryfly would be left feeling totally alienated.

Shadrack stayed over a couple of nights with a new friend called Peter Bower. Peter Bower's parents possessed a television that Shad and Peter watched as much and as often as they could. This new apparatus was inspiring Shadrack to use terms and words like "River Boat, Darin McGavin, Rin-tin-tin, Time for Juniors, Jim Bowie and The Last of the Mohicans."

With school, homework and visits to Peter Bower's house to watch television occupying much of Shadrack's time, Dryfly was finding himself alone more and more. It seemed that the duo were drifting apart.

"We could go to the canteen and get a wiener and chip," said Shad.

"A what?"

"Wieners and french fries."

"Cost a lotta money, wouldn' it?"

"I got a few bucks. C'mon Dry, let's go."

"An awful long ways. What if we got way down there and can't find a way home?"

"We'll walk. Dad said he use to walk it all the time. It's only ten or twelve miles."

"Well, all right," said Dryfly. "I'll go, if we can catch a ride."

Dryfly had conceded for adventure's sake, but he was hoping there'd be no Blackville-bound traffic on the Gordon road.

They had waited on the road in front of Bernie Hanley's store for an hour when Ally Dunphy showed up. Ally Dunphy had hunted the deep forests of Dungarvon until it was too dark to see. On his way home to Blackville, in his 1958 Ford, Ally stopped at Bernie Hanley's store for a snack. When he was getting back into his car, a red-haired lad approached him.

"You goin' to Blackville?" asked the lad.

"Sure am."

"Kin me and Dryfly get a ride with you?"

"Sure can."

In thirty minutes, Shadrack and Dryfly found themselves standing in front of LeBlanc's Canteen in Blackville.

*

With the coming of the chainsaw, more money and cars, came the necessity to improve the byroads. Shirley Ramsey sold a hundred and sixty dollars worth of gravel during the summer of 1962. Cars and gravelled roads made Blackville a center of commerce and entertainment for all the surrounding settlements. Blackville, being more accessible, became a meeting place. Every weekend, young people would crowd on the backs of pickup trucks, or in old cars and head for Blackville. Sometimes there'd be a movie to go to, sometimes a dance, but mostly the teenagers would just walk up and down the street from one take-out restaurant (canteen) to another. There were three canteens in Blackville. No more than five hundred yards separated one from the others.

"What do we do now?" asked Dryfly.

"Let's walk down to the other canteen," said Shad.

When they arrived at the second canteen, Shad suggested that they check out the third. From the third, they walked back to the second, stood around for a few minutes, then walked back to LeBlanc's. They had done everything there was to do in Blackville, except eat. Shadrack and Dryfly completed the social itinerary for Friday night in Blackville by ordering a paper dish full of french fries and three wieners each.

They were just finishing their snack when Peter Bower

showed up with Jim MacNeil, Gary Perkins and David Carlyle.

"G'day, Shadrack. How's she goin'?"

"The very best, Peter."

"Who are you?" asked Peter.

"Dryfly Ramsey," answered Dryfly.

"Dryfly Ramsey! Any relation to Shirley Ramsey?" asked Peter. One of the other boys chuckled.

"Me mother," said Dryfly.

The boys all glanced at each other and grinned.

"What brings you guys out of the woods?" asked David Carlyle.

"Come to chase the chicks," said Shadrack.

"What happened to your hair, Dryfly?" asked Jim MacNeil.

Dryfly scanned the four Blackville boys in their clean black pants, the expensive jackets with the collars turned up, the black jetboots, the trucker's wallets chained to their belts, jutting from their hip pockets, the rings, wrist-watches and the well-groomed Elvis Presley haircuts.

Until now, Dryfly had forgotten that he wasn't very well dressed and that his hair was parted in the middle.

Shadrack scanned Dryfly and saw, maybe for the first time, what the other boys were seeing — the straight brown hair parted in the middle, the ragged jeans that Shad himself had given to him, the mackinaw coat, the black rubber boots with the red soles, the long nose. Shadrack was even more conscious of Dryfly's appearance than was Dryfly, and wished he hadn't brought him along. He had wanted Dryfly for company, in case he had to walk the twelve miles home, alone. He hadn't anticipated that Dryfly might jeopardize whatever chance he might have of being in with the in crowd.

"Where ya get the boots, Dryfly?" asked Gary Perkins, making no attempt whatsoever to hide the mockery in his voice.

Shadrack eyed the grinning Blackville boys and knew he would have to make a decision — go with the in crowd, or be out with Dryfly Ramsey. He decided to try and play it down the middle. He grinned, but not for mockery's sake. He grinned to try and keep it light.

Shy and very uncomfortable, Dryfly blushed and looked

down at himself. The discomfort grew as he compared his own clothes to the others. He said nothing. He wanted to go home to Brennen Siding.

"How's your mother?" asked Peter Bower, nudging David Carlyle and winking at Gary Perkins. Peter Bower, for the moment, was the leader of the pack.

Dryfly wondered how the Blackville boys knew his mother. He didn't know that the byword "Shirley Ramsey" had leaked into Blackville.

People in Blackville took their children on Sunday drives past Shirley's, pointed and said, "Look, kids! There's Shirley Ramsey's house." The kids would all look at the epitome of local poverty: the sagging, paintless house, the dirt lawn, the car tires on each side of the driveway culvert. Ogling arrows of curiosity, they might think, "Shirley Ramsey . . . the woman who invented the culvert ends."

"Shirley Ramsey's boy, boys!" laughed Jim MacNeil. "Great boots, Dryfly!"

Shad made a stab at changing the subject. "What's goin' on, boys?" he asked.

"There's a dance at the public hall," said Peter Bower. "Goin'?"

"I don't know, might."

"Ya might as well. That's where the chicks are."

"I dunno," said Shad, shrugging, eyeing Dryfly.

"C'mon, Shad! Get with it!" said David Carlyle.

"Polly was askin' about ya, Shad."

"Was she?"

"She'll be at the dance, Shad."

"S'pose?"

"Saw her down the road."

"C'mon, Shad."

Shad continued to eye Dryfly. "Dryfly is gonna have to learn to handle it," he thought.

"Great! Let's go," said Shad.

Dryfly wasn't invited, but he had nothing else to do, so he followed the others. He walked behind, ashamed of his clothing and his hair, still wishing he was home. Dryfly did not like

Blackville and he did not like the boys in the in crowd. "At least by walking behind, they don't make fun of me," he thought.

When they got to the public hall, they lined up at the ticket booth and, one by one, paid to enter. From the stage within came the harmony of Lyman MacFee and the Cornpoppers, singing, "Wake Up Little Susie." When it was Shad's turn to pay, he turned to Dryfly, said, "I ain't got enough money for both of us, Dryfly. Why don't you try to sneak in?"

"I'll get caught," said Dryfly.

"No you won't. Just wait till nobody's watchin'. You can do it!"

A lump had suddenly developed in the back of Dryfly's throat. He was being abandoned. He swallowed the lump.

"I'll wait out here," he said.

Shad shrugged and followed the Blackville boys into the hall, leaving Dryfly alone on the steps.

Dryfly waited on the steps of the public hall for what seemed like a very long time. Men and women came and went, but few paid much notice to Dryfly, and Dryfly hoped it would remain that way. As a matter of fact, Dryfly wanted to hide. "How could Shad do this to me! Some friend!"

By the time an hour had passed, Dryfly was feeling very cold in the damp night air. He was also bored and a little bit afraid. Some men had gathered around on the steps to drink some wine and Dryfly sensed that trouble was brewing.

Some fellow by the name of Kelly was displeased for some reason or other with a fellow named Benny Crawford.

"You're nothin' but a rotten bastard!" said Kelly.

"I ain't scared o' no Kelly that ever walked!" said Benny.

"By Jesus, I came here to dance, not fight, but I'll beat the shit outta the likes o' you!" said Kelly.

"C'mon and fight then! I'd just love wipin' the street up with you! C'mon! C'MON AND FIGHT!"

Kelly and Benny threw off their coats and squared off in the street in front of the hall. Someone ran into the hall and yelled, "Fight!" The hall emptied — the fight needed an audience.

Until the crowd gathered, Kelly and Benny were having a verbal fight with the intention that whoever had the biggest vocabulary of swear words would win. Sticks and stones were discussed, but as long as they were only being discussed, nobody would get hurt. But now, they had an audience and the pressure was on.

"Hit him, Kelly! Hit the bastard!" somebody yelled.

"Don't take that off 'im, Benny! Plant the rotten jeezer!"

Kelly made a swing for Benny and missed. Benny made a kick for Kelly and also missed. They stood then, eyeing each other, breathing heavily, obviously very nervous about the showdown, wishing it was over.

Kelly thought that a bluff might discourage his foe, and flew into a spiel of swear words and threats that would make a dead priest turn over in his grave. He touched on the apes and how they were related to the whole of the Crawford family; he spoke of the peculiar smell the Crawfords had picked up doing the only thing that Crawfords were good for — shovelling shit; he recalled that there was never an exceptional mind in the entire history of the Crawford family; he left nothing out that he considered worth a swear word or ten or twelve. At a climactic point of his spiel, for effect, he hit Benny on the shoulder and whooped, saying, "Take that, ya sonuvawhore! Ya think I'm scared o' you?"

Benny Crawford hit back, catching Kelly on the arm.

The two backed off again and yelled a few more obscenities. Kelly made a kick at Benny. Benny took a swing at Kelly. They still remained unscarred.

The crowd were choosing sides a bit, and Dryfly sensed a potential brawl. He didn't like what he was seeing and hearing, and he didn't want to get involved. He looked around for Shad. The crowd was completely encircling the reluctant fighters and Dry saw that Shad was on the other side of the circle, standing, acting cool, with his friends and some fat girl.

"There never was a Kelly any good!" yelled Benny Crawford.

"Look who's talkin', ya yellow bastard!" yelled Kelly.

"Hit 'im Kelly!" yelled somebody from the crowd.

"You stay out of this!" yelled someone else.

The audience was growing. People were coming from their houses to watch the fun, and the canteens emptied. The circle in front of the hall expanded and the whole street was blocked off to traffic. There was a lineup of thirty cars waiting to get through.

Benny Crawford's two sisters showed up and were crying loudly and calling, "Benny, don't fight! C'mon home, Benny!"

"Here," said a man who was standing beside Dryfly, "Hold this! Look after this for me."

The man passed Dryfly a bottle of sherry and stepped into the circle. "You lads want to fight?" he asked. "You lads wanna take on a good man?"

Everyone in the crowd hushed. The fighters shifted their eyes nervously, unable to hold the steady gaze of this new man on the scene.

"We don't want no trouble with you," said Kelly.

"Well, if you're gonna ruin this dance fightin', you're gonna have to do it over me!"

"We got nothin' against you," said Benny Crawford.

"I don't wanna fight with you," said Kelly. "Me and you was always good friends."

"We don't want no trouble with you, Herman," said Benny.

Herman Burns had now taken over the show. Herman Burns was six-foot-four and muscular. He weighed nearly twice as much as either Kelly or Benny Crawford. He towered over them and everyone else. He was like a snake eyeing two unfortunate mice while a horde of other mice watched on. Everyone knew that Herman Burns was a dangerous man.

"We don't want to fight no more," said Kelly.

"But I thought you wanted to fight," urged Herman. "Looked to me that you fellers were lookin' for a fight! Well, if ya want to fight, C'MON!"

Herman Burns kicked Benny Crawford as hard as he could, breaking a rib and leaving him bent and moaning on the ground.

Kelly started crying and begging Herman not to do likewise to him. Herman hit Kelly on the brow, knocking him out cold. The fight was over. Everyone was admiring Herman for his great victory. Herman walked around like a rooster sucking up the sweetness of popularity.

"No, s'pose he can't fight none!" someone behind Dryfly said.

"He beat the both of them, just like that!" said someone else.

With arms and shoulders back and chest thrust out, Herman Burns walked up to Dryfly. Dryfly handed Herman his wine.

"Thanks, lad," said Herman.

Herman unscrewed the cap and took a drink. He then handed the bottle to Dryfly. "Have a drink," he said.

Dry drank from the bottle of sweet sherry.

"What's your name?" asked Herman.

"Dryfly Ramsey."

Other boys were gathering around Herman and Dryfly. Herman looked Dryfly up and down, saw the poverty and the fear.

"You're a friend," said Herman, and offering his hand for Dryfly to shake, said, "Put 'er there."

Dryfly shook the huge callused hand. It looked to the other boys that Dryfly and Herman were the best of friends.

"Better not tangle with Dryfly Ramsey," thought Peter Bower.

"Goin' inside?" asked Herman.

"No, I don't think so."

"C'mon, Dryfly. There's a bunch o' young women in there, and they're lookin' for you."

When Dryfly walked past the ticket booth with Herman Burns, no one asked him for a ticket. When he stepped into the hall with Herman's arm resting on his shoulder, the in crowd did not laugh at him.

*

Shirley Ramsey made a fire and put the kettle on. An inch of snow had fallen in the night and half-melted in the morning sun; it dappled the drab November landscape. Dryfly had walked all the way from Blackville during the night and was still sleeping.

Shirley made a pot of tea, poured some into a mug and a little onto a plate. Into the tea on her plate, she sprinkled some brown sugar, dipped her bread into it and ate. Shirley Ramsey either had bread dipped into pork fat and molasses, or bread dipped into tea and brown sugar, every morning for breakfast. While she ate, she listened to Jack Fenety on the radio. "CFNB — where New Brunswick hears the news," said Jack, then went on to talk about the political dreams and schemes of Hugh John Flemming and John Diefenbaker. After the news, Jack played, "Up on the Housetop," a Christmas song by Gene Autry.

"Christmas," thought Shirley. "'Twould be nice to have some money for Christmas. I wonder if Palidin will come home. I hope the poor little lad is doing well."

After smoking a couple of cigarettes, Shirley put on her coat and boots, tied a red scarf over her hair and went for a walk around the gravel pit.

The gravel pit was getting a little bigger each year. Shirley's land was nearly all dug up. What land was left around the pit's periphery was covered with hawthorn and blueberry bushes, and the occasional fir tree. The Ramsey boys had harvested the land completely and the fir trees had sprouted and grown within the last ten years.

"They're jist right fer Christmas trees," thought Shirley. "Dry could cut them and sell them to Rudy Baxter."

Rudy Baxter, from Blackville, owned a truck. Every November, Rudy Baxter bought a thousand Christmas trees from the locals and trucked them to Boston.

"We'd have a little money for Christmas," thought Shirley. "Not much, but a little. Dry could snare a few rabbits, too, and sell them to the Frenchmen downriver."

With the post office closing at the end of December, and with the selling of Christmas trees and rabbits, Shirley saw the ends meeting until the end of January, no further. After that, times would be tough.

Shirley thought of the tough times in the past. She was thinking of the past a lot lately. She recalled that her father, Bub, had raised his family almost entirely on moose, salmon and potatoes. With no wife and nine children ranging from ages one to twelve, Bub had no time for a regular job, so there was no money for clothes. The children were brought up on hand-me-downs. Shirley had never worn a new dress in her life.

Shirley remembered how Bub would play both mother and father, cook and work the potato field by day, and poach salmon, moose and deer at night.

"There was always something to eat," she thought. "We weren't poor then like I am now, or at least, not as poor as I will be by the time February rolls around."

The bleak gravel pit sprawled before her, a cavity forever threatening her land.

"Another year and that'll be gone, too," she thought. "Never thought ya could run out of gravel."

Shirley heard the distant whistle of the mail train and went to the house for the mailbag. Then, she walked to the siding house for the exchange. When she returned home, Dryfly was awake and sitting at the kitchen table.

"I walked all the way home from Blackville last night," announced Dryfly. "I'm pretty near dead!"

"What took ya to Blackville?"

"Ended up at the dance. Saw a fight, too!"

"Who?"

"Some Kelly fella and another lad. Herman Burns broke it up."

"Herman Burns? He's related to Lester Burns. Use to hang around Brennen Siding a lot when he was a young lad. Nice boy, too. Him and Junior was good friends. Herman could've been a boxer, if he had've got the right trainin'."

"He's some kinda big and rugged."

"He got that from the Pringles. His mother was a Pringle. All the Pringles were big."

"I wouldn' want to cross 'im!"

"There's some Christmas trees around the pit, Dry."

"Yeah?"

"Big enough to cut. You could earn us some money for Christmas."

"Is there lotsa them?"

"Couple o' hundred, maybe."

"That's a good idea, I'll go at it first thing Monday."

"I'll get ya some rabbit wire, too. Soon's the snow gets on to stay, you could snare some rabbits."

"Sure. I might even do some trappin' this year."

"No luck in trappin'."

"What's the difference between snarin' and trappin'?"

"I don't know, but everyone always said that trappers never had any luck. I guess God don't mind if ya snare rabbits, there's so many of them."

"Know what ya kin git me fer Christmas, Mom?"

"What?"

"A new set o' guiddar strings. Them ones on the guiddar are hardly fit to play on. They're startin' to unravel."

"Maybe. The fire's gettin' low, Dry. Would you get me some wood?"

Dryfly groaned as he stood. Both his feet and legs were sore from the long walk from Blackville the previous night. It had snowed a little bit while they walked, which did nothing to make the trek any easier. Dryfly recalled thinking that he wasn't going to make it; that he would never do it again, supposing he did hear the best music he had ever heard. At the dance, Dryfly had enjoyed Lyman MacFee and the Cornpoppers very much. Dryfly put on his coat and limped his way to the woodshed.

"MOM!" he yelled from the shed. "MOM! COME 'ERE QUICK!"

Shirley heard the excitment in Dry's voice and ran to see what was the matter.

When she got to the shed, she found Dryfly standing looking up at the hanging carcass of a deer — gutted, skinned and cleaned.

"Where'd ya git the deer, Dry?" she asked, eyeing the most meat she'd seen in years.

"I didn' get it! It was just here! Don't know where it came from!"

"He was poachin' last night," thought Shirley.

"Nutbeam did it," thought Dryfly.

sixteen

Shadrack and Dryfly were making frequent visits to one of the cabins owned by the members of the Cabbage Island Salmon Club. A dozen forty-ounce bottles of liquor had been left in the cabin in September, and by Christmas, due to Shadrack and Dryfly's little parties, only three were left. The hearth of the stone fireplace was piled up with Parody and cigarette butts and ashes; the sofa cushions were strewn about; the hardwood floors were tracked up with sand and leaves and pine-tree needles, courtesy of rubber boots and gumshoes.

"They got lotsa money," said Shadrack, "they'll never miss the stuff."

"Maybe we should move to the other camp," said Dryfly. "God knows what's in the other ones!"

"I checked them all out," said Shad. "All locked."

"Shit's gonna hit the fan when them lads come back and find all their liquor and cigars gone."

"They won't even remember how much they left."

"I hope you're right."

It was the twenty-fourth of December, and Shad and Dry were having a few drinks to help them get into the spirit of Christmas. Outside the frosty windows that looked down over the frozen Dungarvon River, the temperature was about five below zero; inside, it could have been colder, they weren't sure. They didn't plan to stay long, anyway. "Jist enough to get feelin' good," was their plan.

"I hope I get them jetboots for Christmas," said Shadrack. "I'd like to have a trucker's wallet, too."

"Did you pass in school?"

"Jist failed French and not by much."

"You'll get the boots."

"Maybe."

"Ya like goin' to school, Shad?"

"Not too bad, once ya get used to it. Lotsa girls."

"Yeah. No good for me though. I don't feel like running 'round on Lillian."

"You're crazy, Dry. I bet she hardly remembers who you are. You'll be lucky to ever see her agin."

Dryfly shrugged at the possibility. "Those Blackville women wouldn' go out with me anyway," he thought. He didn't realize it, but he was beginning to sound like Nutbeam.

"You ever think about going back to school, Dry?"

"I'm gettin' too old. I'm pretty near sixteen."

"So?"

"So, I'd be in the same grade with all them little kids. I wouldn' look none too stupid, would I! Me, a big lad o' sixteen, settin' in school with a bunch o' little kids!"

"Maybe you could learn at home and ketch up."

"How would I do that?"

"I don't know. Find out."

"Ya think Nutbeam's home yet?"

"He might be. The train should've come by now."

"Let's go back and check him out."

*

Nutbeam sold six hundred dollars worth of fox, bobcat, mink, weasel and beaver pelts to his Jewish buyer in Newcastle and went shopping. He bought himself a complete set of clothing which included Stanfield's underwear, pants, shirt, woollen socks, another parka and two pairs of boots. He also bought a trucker's wallet, a pipe and tobacco, a half gallon of Lamb's rum, a turkey and six yards of linen, black with red roses on it. Needless to say, when he left the train to make his way to Todder Brook, he was more than just a little burdened. The foot of snow on the ground didn't make the walking any easier, and although it was zero degrees out, Nutbeam was sweating and panting by the time he reached his camp.

He placed everything on the table and proceeded to build a

fire in the stove. He made a pot of tea, poured himself a mug full, spiked it with an ounce or so of rum, then sat to contemplate his situation.

"If the boys show up soon, the better the plan will work," he thought. "If they don't show up, I'll have to play Santa Claus."

From his pocket, Nutbeam removed the three hundred and fifty dollars left over from his shopping spree. He went to his cot, reached underneath and removed a shoe box. He removed the top and added the three hundred and fifty dollars, adding considerably to the bills already in the box.

"One day I'll get Dryfly to count it for me," he thought. "Another day, me and Dry will go to Fredericton and visit that Graig Allen fella; see how much he's askin' for the old farm. Old Doctor MacDowell only bought the shore. There must be a couple o' hundred acres of woodland and pasture left, maybe more. I'll build a house on the old foundation and live normal. No more hiding like a . . . a bear."

He put the shoe box back in its hiding place, added a bit more courage — rum — to his tea and sat once again.

"Let me see," he thought, " . . . deer, a bunch of partridge, a can o' tobacco, and this." He slapped the turkey.

He rubbed his fingers across the linen with the roses on it.

"Ho, ho, ho! Merry Christmas, little lady!" he said. Then, he heard the crunching of approaching footsteps in the snow outside.

Knock-knock-knock.

Nutbeam went to the door, unlatched it and welcomed the boys.

"Come in! Come in!" he said.

"G'day, Nutbeam."

"G'day, g'day."

"How's she goin', boys?"

"We were here earlier," said Shad. "You weren't home."

"Went to Newcastle. Sold me furs."

"Get a good price?"

"Real good."

"See ya got a turkey," said Dry.

"You boys want a drink?" asked Nutbeam.

"Sure."

"Might have a small one."

Nutbeam poured each of the boys a drink and touched up his own. It was evident by the grin on his face that he was in a jolly mood.

"That turkey ain't all I bought today," said Nutbeam, raising his tin mug as if to toast the turkey.

The boys waited.

"Wanna know what else I bought, boys?"

"Yeah."

"Sure."

"Well . . . I got meself two pairs o' boots."

"Yeah?"

"Two pair?"

"Two pairs o' boots. Want to see 'em?"

"Sure."

Nutbeam took the boxes from the table and opened one.

"I bought meself these here jetboots."

Nutbeam took a boot from the box and passed it to Shad.

"Boys! Nice boot!" said Shad, admiring the soft, shiny black leather. "Try it on, Nutbeam."

Nutbeam took the boot from Shad, removed his gumshoe and slid his foot into it. It slipped on easily, a good fit for his oversized foot.

"Nice!" said Dry. "You'll get the women with them on!"

"Boys!" said Shad.

Nutbeam grinned.

"Let's see the other pair," said Dry.

Nutbeam removed the cover of the second box and exposed the second pair of shiny black jetboots.

"They're just the same!" exclaimed Shadrack. "Why two pair the same?"

"Didn' know which ones would fit," said Nutbeam. "Let me try these ones on."

Nutbeam kicked off the first boot and tried on one from the second pair. He barely got the end of his foot into the boot before it tightened. "This pair's too small," he said. "Here, you try it on, Shad."

Shad removed his gumshoe, put his foot in the jet boot and flopped it around. "Way too big for me," he said. "They must be a ten, I take a seven. You try it on, Dry."

Dryfly slid off his red and black rubbers and tried on the expensive leather boot.

"Perfect," he said. "Boys, they're nice!"

"Sure are," said Shad.

"Too bad I didn' have the money to buy them from ya," said Dry. "Too bad ya have to take them back."

"I ain't takin' them back," said Nutbeam. "I got them for you."

Dryfly's mouth fell open.

"They're yours," said Nutbeam.

"Mine?"

"All yours."

"You mean it?"

"They're yours."

Dryfly wanted to whoop a whoop that would echo across the Dungarvon woods. Dryfly wanted to dance and laugh and sing. Instead, a lump lodged in the back of his throat and for a moment it seemed he would cry.

"They're the nicest boots I ever saw in my whole life," said Dryfly. He threw his arms around Nutbeam and squeezed, hiding his tears the best he could behind Nutbeam's big floppy ears. At that moment Dryfly loved the trumpet-playing, Dungarvon-whooping, mysterious hermit as much as he loved . . . Lillian Wallace? . . . Shirley Ramsey?

"Thanks, Nutbeam," he whispered.

"Sit down," said Nutbeam, somewhat embarrassed by the unaccustomed affection. "They're only an old pair o' boots."

Shad was smiling with envy. He tossed back his rum, said, "Merry Christmas, boys!"

"And for you," said Nutbeam, "this here."

Nutbeam handed Shad a small brown paper bag. Shad reached in the bag and pulled out the trucker's wallet — the wallet with the golden chain and belt attachment — the wallet Shadrack wanted.

"Hello! No wallet!" said Shad. "S'pose I ain't gonna look

none too cool or nothin', am I? G'day! S'pose the women ain't gonna like that none! No! No! No they ain't! No!"

"You're a saint, Nutbeam," said Dryfly.

"A real saint! A cream o' tartar!" agreed Shadrack.

"I got a good price for me fur, "said Nutbeam. "Decided to share the wealth."

"Thanks, Nutbeam."

"Yeah, thanks a whole lot. You're a saint and a half."

"Now, for your mother, Dryfly, I got this can of tobacco, that turkey and this pretty cloth."

"For Mom?"

"For Shirley?"

"Yes sir! She's entitled to a good Christmas, too. Merry Christmas, boys! Have another drink!"

The boys and Nutbeam drank the rum straight from the bottle. They were all in very high spirits.

Two hours later, after much talking and laughing, Shad and Dry departed Nutbeam's camp. They followed the moon-lit path homeward through the forest and fields. High on rum, the winter wind did not nip at their heels as it would have otherwise.

Leisurely they walked, carried their goods, talked and laughed until, as usual, they separated at the footbridge.

Crossing the bridge, heavily laden with the turkey, to-bacco, linen and boots, Dryfly stopped to rest and take in the scenery. The moon was full and bright. The river, except for the airhole in front of John Kaston's, was frozen and silent, sleeping beneath the ice and trillions of snowflakes: its blanket.

As Dryfly focused in on the airhole, he thought he could see somebody standing beside it. He was not sure if it was a person; it could have been an animal, perhaps a deer drinking from the open water. It wasn't moving, so Dryfly couldn't really tell if, or if not, the thing was a thing, or just an ex-tended arm of the airhole itself, or perhaps a stake, put there to warn skaters of the thin periphery of ice.

He shrugged off his curiosity, turned and gazed downstream for a while. There, he could see Lindon Tucker's house, its windows reflecting the moon, but no detectable light coming from within. He could also see the sheds and barn, their symmetrical lines jutting from the snow-clad field. "Like something from a Christmas card," he thought.

He could not see the swing, but he pictured it in his mind — the swing, Lillian Wallace, the butterfly, the summer's day.

"All I really wanted for Christmas was Lillian Wallace," he said to the night, turned and walked toward the warmth of home.

*

Max Kaston eyed himself in the mirror. He had a scratch on his thin and sunken right cheek. A wood chip had hurled from his axe and hit him there the previous day while he was limbing a hemlock. His right eye was puffy from the slap he received from John for the incidental oath he had sworn.

It was Christmas Eve and Max was very lonesome and depressed. Earlier in the evening, he and John had quarrelled again when John wanted him to go to church with him. Max had been tired, felt ugly and unpopular, had said, "No! I'm not going."

When John slapped him, Max conjured up every ounce of control he could find to keep from slapping him back.

Max had seen Palidin Ramsey fight at school many years ago. The confrontation had been between Palidin and Joey Layton. Palidin had been so calm and cool and Joey had been so out of control. Joey called Palidin a coward and a fruit and Palidin hadn't batted an eye. He just stared into Joey's eyes, intensely enough to cause Joey to shiver with uncertainty. Joey was backing down when Palidin made his mistake. He dropped his eyes and when he did, Joey slapped him.

It would have been a victory for Joey in the eyes of all the boys watching, but Palidin did something scary, almost eerie. He immediately regained his equipoise and turned the other cheek. It so befuddled Joey that he stepped back as if shocked and ran into the school, shamed and crying like the child he was.

Instead of slapping his father back, Max tried the Palidin Ramsey trick. It infuriated John.

"Blasphemy!" yelled John, slapped Max once again and stormed off to church.

The second slap had been harder and stung, but it hadn't neared his other eye. However, its injury to Max had been far greater than any infliction he had ever before been subjected to. It was that one last slap from his father that accomplished all that John ever set out to do — it broke Max's spirit.

Greatly despondent in the wake of that slap that still seemed to echo throughout the room, Max eyed himself. His eyes filled and tears like rivulets coursed their way down his cheeks. His body convulsed as he released sob after sob.

"I can't!" he sobbed. "I can't become a preacher! Why doesn't Dad understand?!"

One by one, the people of Brennen Siding flashed through his tormented mind. Lindon Tucker: a bachelor, uneducated, going nowhere, half out of his mind. Stan Tuney: alone, a bachelor with no ambition, nothing left to sell, nothing left to live for but lies. Dan Brennen: losing his battle to be better than everyone else, primarily because he was growing old and wisdom was telling him that he would never succeed. Bob Nash: forever in a state of unrest, contrary, never smiling. Bert Todder: who laughed at everything and everyone, perhaps the wisest of all the men in his simplicity . . . but going nowhere as well. Shadrack Nash and Dryfly Ramsey: following along to the same tune, toward the same destiny, as if it were an inalterable direction, a tradition.

"My father," thought Max, " . . . and me. I'm just like my father. I could've been a preacher if I had've gone to school. But I don't want to become a preacher! I couldn't preach to save my soul!"

Suddenly, Max threw his shoulders back as if some unknown power had taken control of him. The fatigue left him; he felt strong and capable. In the mirror, his reflection stared back at him with cold hard eyes — expressionless, the jaw set in determination. A warmth coursed through his body, the hair stood up on his neck; he thought he might even be getting an erection.

The reaction came from the ultimate of negative thoughts — suicide. But the ensuing effects were nothing he'd ever before anticipated. As if in a trance, he walked to the coat-rack, donned his jacket and headed for the river. He was still in the same state when he found himself staring at the airhole. The water rushed, black and cold from beneath the ice on which he stood.

He did not know why he stopped when he did. His full intention had been to walk into it. It was as if he had to size up the eerie, hooded figure of death — and the choice was still his: jump, or remain and fight.

The moon danced on the troubled surface of the water; the wind, stronger here on the river, slapped at his clothing. The cold, exhilarating Dungarvon air and water were having their effects on him, too. If something irrational and demonic had touched him back in the house, the great outdoors was trying to reverse the trance. There were the moon and the stars; the river and the forest, seen through the crystal-clear moonlit air. There were the farms with their lights glowing warmly within ; he could see Lindon Tucker's from the river in front of John Kaston's, and the bridge. There was somebody walking on the bridge.

Max suddenly realized that he was outside, at night, alone. There he was, by himself, on the river at night and not afraid. He looked around as if he'd never seen the night before. It was not all that dark. He always thought the night was black and formidable, that it was occupied with wraiths and evil spirits that blended with the darkness.

But he was standing in a quite different world — one of beauty and serenity — where the stars and moon enchanted the land and all that lived there.

The figure on the bridge walked leisurely along, stopped for a moment, then continued on at a slightly faster pace.

Max shifted his attention to a red, glowing planet, north-east of the moon, its light distorted and exaggerated as it shone through his cloud-like breath.

"Jump, or remain and fight," he whispered.

And then, echoing across the forest from the direction of Todder Brook came the sound of a lone trumpet being played, so far off, so clear in the still night.

Nutbeam, basking in the glow of his rum and generosity, was celebrating still. He was playing "Silent Night" for all of Brennen Siding to hear.

"Stand and fight," said Max, turned and walked slowly home, enjoying his newlyfound world.

*

On Christmas morning, Dryfly awakened to the smell of onions frying. Shirley had already risen and was frying some strips of venison, onions and eggs. Dryfly rose, dressed and went to the kitchen.

"Mornin'," said Shirley. "Merry Christmas."

"Merry Christmas," said Dryfly.

"Cold mornin', must be thirty below. Fire feels good," said Shirley.

Dryfly went to the stove and stood soaking up the heat. "Sure does," he said.

"I'm cookin' us up a great big feed, Dry."

"I see that. Sure smells great. Would ya like your present?"

"You got me a present, Dry?"

"'Tweren't much. Didn' have much money."

"You didn' have to buy me nothin', Dry."

Dryfly went to his bedroom and returned with a gift, crudely wrapped in brown paper.

Shirley unwrapped the rectangular mirror with the white plastic frame.

"It's beautiful, Dry! It's the prettiest mirror I ever saw! It must've cost a lotta money, Dry."

"Wasn't much."

"It's the best Christmas present I ever got, Dry! Thanks! Thanks a whole lot."

"Ya like it?"

"I love it! I'll throw that old thing away and hang this new one up so's you and me kin see how good-looking we are, Dry," said Shirley with a toothless grin.

Dryfly was happy and smiled, too.

"I have a gift for you, too, Dry."

"Yeah?"

"It ain't much," said Shirley, passing Dryfly a small package wrapped in brown paper.

Dryfly ripped the paper off a pair of grey woollen mitts.

"Nice mitts, Mom! Thanks a lot! They fit, too."

"Good. I thought you might need them this winter doin' your snarin', or trappin', or whatever."

Dryfly had a slight twinge of disappointment. He did not get the guitar strings. He knew, however, that the mitts were more important.

"You're right, Mom, ya can't do nothin' without good mitts," he said.

"Glad they fit," said Shirley.

"I got something else for ya, Mom."

"More?"

"Not from me. From Nutbeam."

"From Nutbeam?"

"Yeah. He got ya somethin' for Christmas."

"But why?"

"Don't know. Nice lad. Got me and Shad stuff, too."

Dryfly had hidden the can of tobacco, the turkey and the cloth in the living room where he hoped Shirley wouldn't find it. He went and got them and gave them to her.

"It's beautiful," she said, fingering the black cloth with the red roses on it, " . . . and the turkey . . . and . . . and tobacco . . . why, Dry?"

"Don't know. Nice lad. Give me a pair of boots."

Dryfly had left his boots in the bedroom. He retrieved them for Shirley to see.

Shirley eyed the boots that Dryfly set before her.

"They must have cost a fortune!" she said.

"I know. Nice lad."

"Is that where you go all the time, Dry?"

"Yeah. Me and Nutbeam and Shad is good friends. Nice lad to do that, eh?"

"I just can't figure out why, Dry! Did he leave the deer and them partridge, too?"

"I think so. He never said."

"Strange, eh?"

"Nice lad."

"If we keep all these presents, we'll have to give him something, won't we?"

"Didn' know he'd got them till yesterday. We ain't got no money to get him presents anyway."

"Do you think we should keep them, then?"

"Don't know. Nice boots."

"He lives all alone, don't he?"

"Yeah. Has a little camp."

"Maybe we could invite him over for supper or somethin'."

"Ya think?"

"He's not crazy, or somethin', is he?"

"Kinda homely to look at. Doubt if he'd come."

"Why? Is he shy?"

"Don't like people much. People laugh at 'im."

Shirley sighed. "Know how he feels," she said.

"He's a real nice lad, though, Mom."

"After breakfast, you go talk to him, Dry. Supper's the least we kin give 'im."

Shirley Ramsey was uncertain of what the outcome might be in having this mysterious, but obviously kind, generous and sensitive man in for supper, but she was willing to take the chance. Shirley Ramsey had the Christmas spirit. She wanted to give and share. Shirley saw a can of tobacco here, boots there, venison in the frying pan, the cloth and the turkey on the table.

*

Dryfly Ramsey, as much as he wanted to, did not wear his new boots to Nutbeam's camp. "Walkin' in the snow would ruin them," he decided.

After the brisk walk through the bright, frosty afternoon, he knocked on Nutbeam's door.

"Come in," he heard Nutbeam say, "the door's unlatched."

Dryfly opened the door and stepped into the camp, kicking the snow from his feet as he crossed the threshold.

"No more latching the door," greeted Nutbeam. "Only ones that comes is you and Shad, anyway. I've always kept that door latched, but no more, Dryfly. You kin step right in here any time you like!"

"Cold day," said Dryfly. "Been out?"

"Was out and fed some moose birds earlier. They're around every day lately."

"Yeah, I saw one back the trail."

"What brings you back here on Christmas Day?"

"Mom says thanks for the cloth. She wants you to come and have supper with us," said Dryfly.

To Nutbeam, Dryfly could have just announced him a lottery winner. His heart quickened, butterflies took to flight in his stomach; he felt scared. Never in his wildest fantasies had he thought this dream would come true. Never in his wildest dreams had he thought that this fantasy would become a reality.

"She wants me to come for supper?" asked Nutbeam, afraid he had misunderstood.

"Got that great big turkey. Someone has to eat it," said Dryfly.

Nutbeam stood and ran his fingers through his hair. Decisions had to be made. "Should I, or shouldn't I go? What would I say? How would I act?"

"Dryfly . . . I don't know . . . I don't know if I can."

"Why? You ain't scared o' Mom, are ya?"

"Well . . . I don't know . . . I don't . . . I never talked to a woman before!"

"Mom's not a woman . . . I mean, Mom's just Mom."

Scrambled remnants of forty-two-thousand-and-one dreams unfolded before Nutbeam. He saw himself walking through the forest on moonlit nights, dreaming of having Shirley Ramsey by his side. He saw himself standing at the edge of darkness watching Shirley Ramsey listening to Kid Baker sing. He saw himself shooting a deer, thinking that with each bit of venison consumed, Shirley Ramsey would be, indeed, consuming a portion of his good will for her. He saw dreams of holding her, whispering "Rest, Shirley, take it easy" into her ear.

"What did she say?" asked Nutbeam.

"She just said go get Nutbeam for supper." Nutbeam was beginning to pace and Dryfly could see that he was beside himself. "I think she likes you, Nutbeam. Mentions you every once in a while. She's been wanting to meet ya, I think."

"Then she wants me for sure?"

"Pretty likely! She was just sayin' the other day that she thought it funny that you never drop in."

"That's for the boots," thought Dryfly.

"I don't know, Dry, I . . ."

"She's got that big turkey in the oven already, Nutbeam. Gonna put extra potatoes and stuff on, too."

"I don't know . . . I'm . . . I'm so strange. People act funny when they see me."

"That's because you are strange, ya old jeezer! Get yer coat and c'mon! It must be four o'clock already and supper's at five!"

Nutbeam put on his coat.

"The big test," he thought. "Am I a man or a mouse?"

*

When Nutbeam and Dryfly entered Shirley Ramsey's house, Nutbeam shut the door behind him, stood and waited. He was wearing his parka and the hood was hiding his face. He was reluctant to lift the hood and expose his ears. Shirley Ramsey stood before him. The house smelled of roasting turkey.

"'Day," grunted Nutbeam. Although somewhat slumped, he still towered over her, so that she eyed him as one might eye a giant, with the evidence of wonder in her eyes.

"Take yer coat off," said Shirley. "Supper's almost ready."

Nutbeam removed his parka in one swift movement, watching the delicate little woman to see if she would laugh or scream.

Shirley did neither.

"C'mon. Sit down by the table, Nutbeam," said Dryfly.

Dryfly and Nutbeam sat by the table. Shirley started puttering around the stove.

"You from around here?" asked Shirley.

"No. From Maine."

"You American?"

"I guess so."

"We're all Canadians around here."

"Yeah?"

"Yeah. 'Cept for the sports on the river. You a sport?"

"Just a man," said Nutbeam.

Dryfly sat eyeing his boots. The boots were sitting beside the bedroom door and he was preoccupied with their presence.

Shirley checked the carrots and the potatoes to see if they were cooked. Then she removed the golden brown turkey from the oven.

"Smells good," said Nutbeam.

"It was awful good o' you," said Shirley.

"Good to be here," said Nutbeam.

"Set the table, Dryfly," said Shirley.

Dryfly snapped out of his boot-induced trance and went to the cupboard for plates, knives and forks.

Nutbeam was beginning to relax a little. Shirley, who had been as nervous as Nutbeam, was also beginning to relax.

"He's more funny than scarey, once ya git use to him," she thought.

"Ain't so bad," thought Nutbeam. "She ain't laughin'. I'm doin' okay."

"Kin I help do somethin'?" asked Nutbeam.

"Got everything just about ready," said Shirley. "Bring them plates over here, Dry."

When she was satisfied with the quality of the gravy, Shirley began loading the plates. She sat across from Nutbeam and the three commenced to eat.

"Don't eat with yer fingers, Dryfly, use yer fork."

"Ain't got a fork. Only had two."

"Then get a spoon."

Dryfly went to the cupboard, got a spoon, returned to his seat by the table and dug in.

The three were hungry. Busy eating, the conversation all but died.

"Good stuff," said Dryfly.

"Best meal I had in ages," said Nutbeam.

"There's plenty more on the stove. Have some salt," said Shirley.

When they could eat no more, Shirley made tea and served it in mugs, two of which had broken handles. She gave the good one to Nutbeam.

Dryfly drank his tea quickly. Dryfly was not interested in tea. He was getting restless and wanted to see if Shadrack had gotten jet boots for Christmas. Dryfly was in a dilemma. He felt he shouldn't leave his mother and Nutbeam alone — Nutbeam was shy, his mother nervous around strangers. Dryfly considered leaving and taking Nutbeam with him, but he knew Nutbeam would not want to go to Bob Nash's.

"Have you travelled a lot?" asked Shirley.

"No. Left Maine and come here. That's all the travellin' I ever did."

"I was to Rogersville once," said Shirley. "All French in Rogersville. Burn down the woods so's they kin git a job fightin' fire."

"Sons o' whores!" said Dry.

"Frenchmen," said Nutbeam.

"They paint their houses funny colors," said Shirley.

"Shit brindle," said Dry.

"Frenchmen," said Nutbeam.

Nutbeam eyed the crucifix and rosary beads on Shirley's wall. "You a Cath'lic?" he asked.

"Yeah. Only Cath'lic around here," said Shirley.

"I'm a Cath'lic," said Nutbeam. "Ain't been to church in years, though."

"Me nuther," said Shirley.

"Gotta go all the way to Blackville or Renous to church," said Dryfly.

"John Diefenbaker's a Baptist, ain't he?" asked Shirley.

"Prob'ly," said Nutbeam.

"Baptists don't play cards," said Shirley.

"Some do," said Dryfly, "Shad does."

"Shadrack Nash ain't nothin'," said Shirley. "Devil's gonna get him."

"Devil's already got 'im," said Nutbeam smiling.

Nutbeam had big lips that fringed a big mouth. When Nutbeam smiled, it was like opening up a piano's keyboard. It seemed he had forty-two-thousand-and-one teeth. Nutbeam's mouth was so big that one would not have difficulty envisioning his face disappearing when he yawned. Nutbeam, when he smiled, looked like the sun with floppy ears. When Nutbeam smiled, Shirley Ramsey thought he looked incredibly funny and smiled also. When Shirley Ramsey smiled, which was rare, there wasn't a tooth to be seen. Nutbeam found Shirley's toothless smile amusing and his smile grew even broader. When Nutbeam's smile broadened, so did Shirley's. When Shirley's smile broadened, Nutbeam chuckled. When Nutbeam chuckled, Shirley chuckled also. When Shirley chuckled, Nutbeam chuckled a chuckle that turned to laughter. When Nutbeam laughed, Shirley laughed. The harder Shirley laughed, the harder Nutbeam laughed. Nutbeam was the funniest looking man Shirley had ever seen, and seeing him giggle and laugh — the distorted huge mouth, the big nose, the squinted eyes, the big ears flopping as his head bobbed — was, indeed, a hilarious thing to see. Shirley laughed hysterically, as if she hadn't laughed for forty-two-thousand-and-one years. The more laughter that sprung from Shirley's toothless mouth, the harder Nutbeam laughed. Things were getting out of hand. Dryfly, accustomed as he was to both Nutbeam's and Shirley's features, saw nothing unusual at all and couldn't quite understand all the laughter. Surely Nutbeam's comment about the devil already having Shad was not that funny. Yet, Dryfly had never seen his mother or Nutbeam so out of control ever before. It was good to hear, like music to his ears. Dryfly laughed too. "Ha, ha, ha, ha, ha, ha," repeated itself forty-two-thousand-and-one times, stopped for a brief breather, then continued for forty-two-thousand-and-one more times. The laughter shattered all the fear, crushed the shyness, unlocked forty-two-thousand-and-two inhibitions and broke the ice. The laughter engulfed Nutbeam with a sense of warmth and love and well-being. He had never been happier. He loved Shirley with all his heart. Shirley Ramsey thought that Nutbeam was the funniest, handsomest, most wonderful man she'd seen in her entire life.

seventeen

Bob Nash, Dan Brennen, Bert Todder, John Kaston, Stan Tuney and Lindon Tucker all stood around in Bernie Hanley's store, talking to Bernie, eating oranges and drinking Sussex Ginger Ale.

It was April, and all the men except for John and Bernie were discussing their current jobs, guiding American sportsmen.

Most of them had spent a great deal of the winter looking forward to the day they could go guiding; to the day when the ice had finally cleared from the river; to the day when they could put their canoes in the river and attach their outboard motors; to the day when they could watch and listen to the first spring birds nesting and frolicking about; but now that the day had come, they felt they should complain.

"Boys, it was some cold out there on the river today!" said Dan. "The eyes frosted right up on me fishin' rod."

"Them old sports don't seem to mind it, though, do they?" put in Bob Nash.

"Me? I'd hardly be bothered carrying one o' them old black salmon from the river," lied Stan Tuney.

"Them lads like them though," said Dan. "Pay good money to fish them! Set out there on the river in the wind and rain and like 'er great. I wouldn' eat a black salmon if I was starvin' to death!"

No one in Brennen Siding would admit to eating the spring, sea-bound, spawned-out salmon, except for Shirley Ramsey. Black salmon, as they were called, was poor people's food.

"Them Amuricans like 'em, though, yeah. Yeah. Like 'er great, they do, so they do, yeah. Eat anything at all, them lads," agreed Lindon Tucker.

"'Pon me soul, yeah, that's true. They'll eat anything ya

set in front o' them. I saw a lad eatin' a steak the other day that couldn' been cooked anymore than five or ten minutes. The blood was runnin' right out of it!" said Bert Todder.

"Make ya sick!" said Stan Tuney, who, like everybody else in Brennen Siding, did not like rare meat.

"Yeah, that's right, yeah. Eat anything at all, so they will, yeah," said Lindon.

"That old lad I'm guidin' didn' wanna quit tonight till pretty near dark," said Bert.

"And they'll work yas on Sundays, too!" said John Kaston. "Sinners. Sinners. That's all they are."

John Kaston was not paying much attention to what was being said. He was preoccupied with his new religion. He had applied and gotten accepted to a sub-denominational school in Fredericton and was due to begin a six-week course that would make him a preacher. All he had to do was leave the Baptist church, accept Jesus as his own personal savior and prove that he could read and speak clearly enough to be understood. He had already purchased a new suit, tie and shoes and had presented his twelve-hundred-dollar cheque, the initiation fee, to the master of the school.

It was a drastic step for him. He would've settled for Max becoming a preacher, but when Max sold a freight car of pulp and headed for St. Catharines, Ontario, in March, John was left with no alternative. The worst thing that could happen was to fail the course, and he was told that nobody with twelve hundred dollars in his pocket and the Holy Ghost by his side had ever failed.

"I caught about a ten-pounder this mornin'," said Bert Todder, "so thin and weak, hardly kicked at all when I pulled him into the boat. Give it to Shirley Ramsey, I did. Dropped it off on me way here tonight."

"That Nutbeam lad there, was he?" asked Bernie Hanley.

"That's what I was goin' to tell ya," said Bert. "He was settin' right back, him and Shirley, jist the two o' them. He's there half the time. Great lookin' couple, they are. You ain't careful, Lindon, you're gonna lose yer woman."

"Ain't my woman, so she ain't! No, no, don't need that fer a woman!"

"Tee, hee, hee, sob, snort, sniff!"

"I heard, now, I ain't sayin' who told me, but I heard that Shirley and that lad was thinkin' 'bout gittin' married," put in Stan Tuney. Stan hadn't actually heard it, but he had thought it so much, and had seen Nutbeam crossing the field so often that he actually believed he had heard it.

"Boys! A man would have to be awful hard up for a woman, wouldn' he?!" said Dan Brennen.

"Oh, I don't know . . . she might be pretty nice in the morning," said Bert Todder. "If I was you, Lindon, I wouldn' let her slip away so easy. She'd be a good woman for you, Lindon. Tee, hee, hee, sob, snort, sniff!"

"You could take her fer walks every night in the gravel pit, Lindon," said Dan Brennen.

"Don't need no Shirley Ramsey, I don't! I kin tell ya that right now, don't need no Shirley Ramsey. Got meself a little lady in Fredericton, so I have. Me little vodker drinker."

"Oh, but that Shirley'd be pretty nice, Lindon. All dressed right up, goin' fer walks in the pit, cookin' ya up a nice black salmon every night fer supper. Tee, hee, hee, sob, snort, sniff!"

"She's still young enough to have two or three young lads for ya, Lindon," laughed Stan Tuney.

"I think Lindon might've had a crack at 'er already. That Dryfly kinda looks like Lindon, don't ya think boys?"

"He ain't mine," said Lindon, his face beginning to colour a bit. "He, he, he, he, ain't mine. Might be yours, might be yours, Bert. Ain't my young lad!"

The men could hear the temper rising in Lindon's voice and knew they had carried the joke far enough. Lindon was simple-minded and no one wanted to find out what he'd do if pushed too far. The topic changed.

They talked about cars, gold in the Yukon, the price of pulp . . . periodically, Bert Todder allowed that it was time he went home, but as usual, he was the last to leave.

*

When Dryfly Ramsey and Lillian Wallace met in late June, they did not run toward each other in slow motion across a field of daisies and clover, with open arms.

Dryfly figured that Lillian would be starting her summer holidays any time after the middle of June, and he was checking the Cabbage Island Salmon Club twice a day in anticipation of her return. He missed her arrival. She came late at night. They met on the Tuney Brook bridge the next afternoon.

Her presence startled him. Ten feet apart, they stood motionless, staring as if afraid, their hearts pounding.

"Hello, Dryfly," said Lillian.

"Hi. How are you?" Dryfly's voice seemed timid and weak.

"I'm back . . . ." Lillian smiled.

"I'm . . . I'm glad to see ya."

"How have you been?"

"Good. You?"

"Fine."

Dryfly had dreamed of this moment countless times, had always thought he'd embrace her, kiss her, tell her how he'd spent a year dreaming of how beautiful she looked, smelled, was, and how much he loved her. But now, although he wanted to, he couldn't. He thought she might think him forward, presumptuous. After all, she was a rich American and not some backwoods hussy like the kind Shad Nash courted. This was Lillian Wallace. This was the most wonderful girl in the whole world. He was not sure what to do. He felt shy.

Lillian, too, felt confused. She had often thought of Dryfly, but she'd had a busy year; had gone to school, travelled on holidays, dated other boys — Rick. But here stood Dryfly Ramsey , and there was something about him, not his looks; he was thin, had a long nose, hair parted in the middle; not his expensive boots, and yet (perhaps she saw the adoration in his eyes) there was something attractive about him.

Dryfly was trembling with excitment. He moved closer, looked into the brook for trout, saw one, looked at Lillian, said, "Yer father here?"

"Yes. He's gone fishing."

Lillian moved closer. They could now reach out and touch each other, but instead, they looked into the water.

"And how's Shadrack doing?"

"Good. Don't see him much. Goes to Blackville a lot."

Dryfly moved closer again. They were now standing shoulder to shoulder, gazing into the water. He could feel her warmth and smell that wonderful insect repellent she wore. He was fighting a losing battle trying to contain himself. Another minute and he would embrace her . . . and then, to his surprise and great delight, she touched his arm. It was a touch light as a feather, but it zapped him with energy, unleashing adrenalin from a supply he had never realized was there. Without further premeditation, he swung to her and took her in his arms, holding her close. They hugged for a long blissful moment until, breathless, they parted to gaze into each other's eyes.

"I missed you an awful lot," said Dryfly.

"I missed you, too," said Lillian. "Why do I feel this way?" she asked herself. "What is it about him?"

And then they kissed. It was that gentle kiss they both remembered and they made sure they kept it that way — fragile, the caress of a butterfly, the Dryfly-Lillian kiss.

They embraced again.

Dryfly sniffed the shampoo-scented, silky blond hair. "I love the smell of your hair," he said.

"Do you?" Lillian's voice was like that of a little girl.

Dryfly withdrew far enough so that he could kiss her brow.

"I love your forehead."

He kissed her eyes.

"I love your eyes."

He kissed her cheeks.

"I love your cheeks."

Lillian smiled.

He kissed her nose.

"I love your nose."

He stopped kissing, hugged her instead.

"What about my mouth?" she asked.

"That speaks for itself," said Dryfly.

*

On the tenth of July, Shirley Ramsey and Nutbeam met Palidin at the train. The first thing Palidin noticed was Shirley's new dress, black with red roses on it. The second thing he noticed was her cleanliness, the permed hair and the new dentures when she smiled. He noticed Nutbeam, pleasant-looking enough, but with the biggest ears he'd ever seen. He saw Nutbeam touch Shirley with familiarity and her girlish response, her stimulated spirit, the poise within her he'd never seen before.

Shirley saw a change in Palidin, too. She saw the hair, cut by a real barber; the clothes, snug and clean and new; she saw a far-off look in his eyes and a little grin when he eyed the little red siding house. When he left he had a cardboard box, now he carried real leather luggage: two pieces, a big bag and a small one.

"It's good to have you home, Pal."

"I wouldn't miss your wedding for the world," said Palidin and turned to Nutbeam, held out his hand for shaking and said, "Palidin."

Nutbeam shook the hand and smiled, seemed to lose a great portion of his face behind it, and said, "Nutbeam. Welcome home."

"Are you doin' okay?" asked Shirley.

"I'm doing the very best," said Palidin and gave Shirley a hug.

"Do you mind?" she asked.

"I think it's the best decision you ever made."

"Thanks, Pal."

They started walking, Nutbeam holding her left hand and Palidin her right.

Palidin scanned the fields with their houses and barns. "Everything's so small," he thought. "They used to seem big, but now they're tiny." When Palidin left Brennen Siding, Stan Tuney's barn had been the biggest building he'd ever seen. Now, it looked tiny and shabby, needing paint. The fields that once seemed so large, now all together seemed small in comparison with some of the farms he'd seen east and west of Aurora and Newmarket. He also eyed the narrow dirt road and realized he hadn't seen one since he left home.

As if reading his thoughts, Nutbeam asked, "Big place, Toronto?"

"You wouldn't believe it."

"You must be glad to be back. Are you stayin'?" asked Shirley.

"Only for the wedding. I have a job. I have to go back."

"What're ya workin' at?"

"I work for a newspaper . . . learning to write."

"Sounds like a good job," said Nutbeam.

"Not much money in it . . . in Canada."

"Dryfly got a job."

"Oh yeah? What doing?"

"He's workin' on puttin' up Bill Wallace's camp. Bill Wallace is the father of that girl he's chasin'."

"Ha! Can't he catch her?"

"Oh, I think he can ketch her all right," said Nutbeam, "he's at the club, or out walkin' with her every spare minute he can find."

"Good. He must be happy."

"It'll never come to no good," said Shirley. "She's too far away. He should be chasin' someone handy."

"Ya never know," said Nutbeam.

As they approached Shirley's house, one word echoed through Palidin's mind: Poverty.

And as if Nutbeam had read his thoughts once again, he said, "I bought the old Graig Allen property. Dry and me are buildin' a house on it, soon's he's done workin' on the Wallace camp."

"Great! Good news!" said Palidin.

"You could write about it in the T'rono newspaper," said Shirley, smiling.

Nutbeam and Palidin both chuckled.

"I just might," said Palidin. "I just might. Don't tear this old house down, Nutbeam. I'll need a picture."

*

After unpacking for his three-day visit, Palidin pulled himself away from the many questions Nutbeam and Shirley were asking and went for a walk. He walked through the forest all the way to the big hollow. At the edge of the barren, he removed his clothes, hung them on a spruce tree for a beacon, then ran freely to the boulder that jutted from the barren's center. He stopped in front of the boulder to read his inscription.

> *Probe the atom,*
> *Ponder the echoes of the wise.*
> *There lie the secrets to the universe.*

"There's something wrong with it," he thought. "I don't know what it is, but there's something wrong. I was so much younger when I wrote that, a boy, and it looks just as it did when I wrote it. The only thing I'll ever write that will last, and there's something wrong with it.

"But why did I write it? Oh yes, echoes, the cycle. The echoes and the cycle, the answer to all my fears and superstitions. I guess they had more substance than just accepting everything as being the work of the devil, or ghosts. You can explain everything with echoes and circles, in the same way you can say that God did it, or the devil did it, or ghosts, or fairies. Put them all inside a man and call it fear. We haunt each other."

Palidin sat on the boulder, letting the sun tan his body. It felt good to be back. "My heart's here," he thought. "One day I'll come back to Brennen Siding and retire. I'll sell my idea for magnetizing hooks and retire."

A breeze suddenly came up and swept across his naked body, cool and titillating. He leaned back and lay on the boulder, staring straight up. Looking up, he could not see the grassy barren or the trees on the horizon; he saw only the sky, the sun and a black bird circling far above, far enough away that he could not identify for certain what kind of bird it was, far enough away that he could barely hear its mournful call. It circled higher and higher and got smaller and smaller until it finally disappeared into the azure.

"Circling me like it must have circled Bonzie," thought Palidin. "The cycle. Everything works in cycles — the salmon, the bees, the birds, the Earth, the universe . . . magnets and echoes."

Palidin thought he could hear someone walking, splush, splush, splush, on the barren. He listened to see if he could identify it as being a man or an animal. It would be very embarrassing for him to be caught naked by someone like Dan Brennen or Bert Todder . . . or anyone.

And then a child's voice called out, "Whoop! Over here!" He sat up and searched the barren for a long breathless moment. He heard the call of the bird once again.

There was nobody there.

The Last Tasmanian

About a hundred and fifty miles south of Australia on the other side of the Bass Straight is a hilly little island about the size of what New Brunswick will be after it separates and becomes an independent nation. It has a wet climate like Britain's and looks like northern Europe.

On this little island, you can still see the kind of animals that were there when it was first discovered in 1798 — kangaroos, wallabies, black swans, weird shrimp in mountain pools, crayfish, little pygmy possum, duck-billed platypuses, yellow wattlebirds and, of course, the badger-like Tasmanian devil. Besides much of the dense forests, there is only one thing that does not remain there today: the original Tasmanian people.

Hilda Porter's great-grandfather, Lawrence, went there as a sailor in the Royal Navy in 1876. He claimed to have been there for the exhuming of a little old lady.

The island's name was Tasmania.

The little old lady's name was Trucanini.

Trucanini was the last Tasmanian aborigine that ever walked on the little island — that ever walked on the face of the Earth.

Lawrence Porter stayed on the island for several weeks, during which time he claimed to have befriended a sulking young Englishman. The young Englishman was an anthropologist who told Lawrence much about what happened to Trucanini and her people.

Lawrence Porter went back to England feeling as if he carried the sins of the whole British Empire on his shoulders. "Fee fi fo fum," he said, and puked.

As soon as he could afford it, he moved to North America and settled in a little village on the South West Miramichi River in central New Brunswick, Canada.

Lawrence Porter told the Tasmanian story to Hilda Porter's grandfather.

"Don't ever forget it," he said. "There's very little, if anything, written about it. They want people to forget it happened. It's a lesson about humanity that should never be forgotten."

Hilda Porter's grandfather told the story to her father in the same way her father told it to her.

"No, Father," said Hilda. "I'll never forget it. And I'll tell it — someday."

Hilda Porter was the last relative of Lawrence's ever to walk through the village of Blackville.

one

Dryfly Ramsey spent part of the month of June, all of July and two weeks of August working as a carpenter's helper for a man from Sunny Corner. The man's name was Hugh "Ducky" Shaw. Ducky Shaw was sixty-five years old, strong as an ox, fit as a whip, temperamental as a bull moose in rutting season, homelier than Shirley Ramsey and the best carpenter in Northumberland County. Ducky Shaw had been hired, along with Dryfly Ramsey and Lindon Tucker, to construct Bill Wallace's cottage.

Dryfly had been hired because he was young, strong and Lillian Wallace's friend.

Lindon Tucker was hired because Bill Wallace had purchased the land from him the year before for a thousand dollars. Bill Wallace knew that the land was worth fifty thousand. Lindon Tucker in his ignorance had been pleased with the deal. It had brought his bank account up to five thousand dollars. Bill Wallace gave Lindon the job because he wanted him to remain pleased for as long as possible.

"He hasn't got the brains of a worm," thought Bill, "and he'll be in the way half of the time, but they'll need a draught animal and it will keep him happy."

Bill Wallace was a multimillionaire from Stockbridge, Massachusetts. He had been coming to the Dungarvon River for many years, spending his holidays in Brennen Siding, fishing the Atlantic salmon. He'd always stayed at the Cabbage Island Salmon Club. He'd never liked the club much, so he leaped at the opportunity to have a place of his own. Also, Lillian was growing into womanhood and it didn't seem right that she should have to stay in a club with a bunch of men.

Bill Wallace had an architect by the name of Luke Van Doren

from Newark, New Jersey, design a building sixty feet long and forty feet wide. To Bill, this building would suffice as a fishing camp. To Dryfly, Bill Wallace's fishing camp was the biggest house he had ever seen in his life.

Building Bill Wallace's camp was the first job Dryfly ever had, and it was one of the hardest he'd ever have. Ducky Shaw was contracted to do the job and wanted it done as quickly as possible. He worked Dryfly and Lindon twelve hours a day, six days of the week. He was paying these useless twits, as he called them, a dollar fifty an hour and wanted to make sure he got his money's worth. He would never have hired them, himself. Dryfly and Lindon were Bill Wallace's idea. Ducky Shaw would have hired men who knew what they were doing. He felt that Lindon Tucker was lazy and stupid, with the brains of a worm. He'd not get anything more than labour out of Lindon. Dryfly, on the other hand, could be taught.

He got one more thing besides labour out of Lindon, however. He also got frustration.

Lindon carried a ten-foot length of two-by-six, swung without looking and struck Ducky on the back of the head, knocking his hat off and applying a day's worth of headache.

"Why in hell don't you watch where you're going?" screamed Ducky, rubbing his head.

In his temper and frustration, Ducky kicked a two-by-four, up-ending it into a corner and nearly breaking his toe. Pain shot up his leg.

"You miserable, stupid, foolish sonuvawhore!" he yelled. "God damn it!"

"Hurt, hurt, hurt, hurt yer toe, Ducky old boy?" asked Lindon cheerfully. "Hurt, hurt, hurt yer toe, palsy walsy?"

Lindon Tucker didn't stutter. Lindon repeated himself and everybody else.

"Nnnnnnn . . . " said Ducky. It was a guttural sound that was neither a growl nor a groan.

Dryfly grinned and climbed a ladder to where he was boarding in a gable.

Constructing the camp was hard work for Dryfly, but he often enjoyed it, especially when Ducky and Lindon displayed their respective dispositions. He nailed on a board. The pounding of his hammer did nothing to subdue Ducky's headache.

"Pass me another board, would ya, Lindon?" said Dryfly.

"Yep, sure. Oh, ah, how long ya want it?"

"I might need it all summer," said Dryfly.

Lindon looked puzzled, then saw the humor. "Yi, yi, yi, yi!" he laughed.

"Nnnnnnn . . . " said Ducky.

*

Dryfly needed to get cooled off and he needed a bath. So, instead of going directly home from work, he went for a swim. He'd been working six days of the week, dating Lillian for as late as he could every night and occasionally meeting up with Shad after leaving Lillian. Dryfly and Shadrack loved the river. They often stayed on it, or by it, half the night. Dryfly was nearly exhausted. The cool Dungarvon water seemed to give him some much-needed energy, brought him around a bit. He washed off the day's accumulation of sawdust and perspiration, swam in circles for a few minutes, then waded ashore. Carrying his boots, socks, shorts and shirt, wearing only his jeans, he headed home.

When he stepped into the house, he found Nutbeam and Shirley in the kitchen listening to the radio.

"I'm beat!" said Dryfly, plopping himself down on a chair by the table.

"You might as well get used to it," said Nutbeam. "We've got to build another one before the snow flies."

Dryfly's mother, Shirley Ramsey, had recently married the tall, big-mouthed, floppy-eared Nutbeam. Shirley's old house by the gravel pit was in such bad shape that Nutbeam was determined to build a new one. Nutbeam was already working on cleaning and mending the old Graig Allen basement. Nutbeam had purchased what was left of the Graig Allen farm and planned to use the basement for the new house. The Graig Allen house had fallen down years before, and the basement was nothing more than a weed-infested box of shaky rock. It needed nearly as much work as it would take to build a new one.

"But not that big," said Dryfly. "I'd like to know what Bill Wallace wants with all that room."

"Just be grateful you're workin', darlin'," commented Shirley. "Gonna need every cent we can rake an' scrape."

Shirley had been busy at the stove preparing Dryfly's supper. She set a plate of potatoes and shad on the table in front of Dryfly.

"Careful of the bones," she said. "Want some bread to fill up on?"

Dryfly nodded affirmative.

Shirley proudly set a bag of Lane's white bread on the table.

"I bought that today," said Nutbeam, who was also very proud of the store-bought bread. "No more of that old home-made stuff for us! No more of them old biscuits, either."

"That's the very best with me," said Dryfly.

Dryfly was glad that his mother and Nutbeam were modernizing. However, he wasn't completely sure if he liked the Lane's bread as much as he liked his mother's. He buttered a slice, put some ketchup on it and put half of it into his mouth.

"See Shad around?" he asked

"River's full of them," grinned Nutbeam. "Ya got half o' one in front o' you. Ha, ha, ha!"

Dryfly grinned, too. He had been refering to Shadrack Nash, his friend from across the river. Shirley laughed and laughed and laughed. Her lover had made a joke.

"Well, did ya see him?" asked Dryfly.

"I told ya, ha, ha, ha! The river's full o' them! Ha, ha, ha!"

"C'mon! Did ya see him?"

The laughter subsided.

"Yeah, I saw him. But I wasn't talkin' to him. He looked to be headin' toward Stan Tuney's."

"Are you gonna stay out half the night again tonight?" asked Shirley. "You're gonna kill yourself if you don't get more sleep."

"I ain't got time to sleep," said Dryfly. "Did you wash my shirt for me today?"

"In there on the bed," said Shirley.

A song they all liked came on the radio. They listened.

I've been in here eighteen years
And that's a long long time you know,
But time don't mean a thing to me.
For I still got life to go.

Dryfly finished his supper.

When the song was over, he went to the bedroom to get dressed for his date with Lillian Wallace.

*

When the salmon first return to the river in early summer, they're powerful, silver and so fat that when picked up by the gills their own weight tears them from your fingers. At this time of year, any Miramichier will tell you the Atlantic salmon are several steps ahead of any other fish in the world that is considered beautiful. It is in June and early July that the salmon are the best eating. It is an insult to fry a June salmon. Boiling it in water and a little bit of vinegar and salt is the best way to cook it. It should be served with potatoes and a little bit of chow-chow on the side.

Shadrack Nash wanted to go to Blackville for a wiener and chips and a bottle of pop. He wanted to hang around the canteen and pick up, or at least try and pick up, girls. He wanted to hang around with the in-crowd and follow them to the bootlegger's for beer and wine.

Shadrack Nash was frustrated and broke.

Sitting in his favourite thinking place, the veranda of Dr. MacDowell's cabin, he contemplated his financial situation.

Shad sat on Dr. MacDowell's veranda for two reasons: one, he could see a mile of river in either direction, and two, Dr. MacDowell was rarely there. This day, for instance, the good doctor was in Epidaurus, Greece, seeing if he could hear a pin drop on the centre stage at the theatre.

He couldn't. No such experiment can be executed with

any degree of accuracy with a bunch of yacking Germans and Italians present.

Shad heard something moving beneath the veranda, thought it must be a porcupine. But when the creature sniffed its way into the open to where Shad could see it, it turned out to be a skunk. Shad watched the skunk for several minutes before the skunk picked up his scent and began to eye Shad in return.

There they were watching each other, the skunk trying to communicate, Shad thinking of money.

"Would the hide of a skunk be worth anything?" Shad asked himself.

He shrugged. "Probably not. He shouldn't bother me if I don't move."

Shadrack stared into the skunk's eyes.

The skunk looked for signs of intelligence, found none, turned from Shad's gaze and walked away.

"Ya kin stare down an animal every time," thought Shad.

Out front, a salmon leaped from the smooth Dungarvon, came down with a splash.

"I don't suppose that'd be none too good o' eatin'," thought Shad. "Go some good with a little chow-chow. Can't be bothered fishin' all day for them, though. I could go to the woods, peel a little pulp for somebody, but that's too hard o' work, flies too thick, too hot. A lad could get a good price for a salmon in Blackville this time o' year. Too bad they're so hard to ketch. What a lad needs is a net — get one every night. Trade 'im for a wiener and chips."

Shad grinned at the idea.

"Now, where would a lad get a net? Dan Brennen? Dan wouldn't give ya his net, even if he had one. He'd want to come with me, tell me how it's done. Course, someone will have to fill me in. I don't have a clue how to do it. Lindon Tucker, maybe. No, not Lindon. Stan Tuney? Stan might have a net."

Shad stood and headed over the hill. He walked down the rocky shore, passed Judge Martin's camp and came to the footbridge. He climbed the abutment steps and followed the boardwalk halfway to the centre abutment. Here he stopped and looked into the water below. The sun was high in the sky, he could see the bottom clear across.

There were several salmon beneath the bridge and a few more slightly downstream. Shad spat, the tiny bead of saliva dropped to disturb the water just above the salmon's head. The salmon ignored it. Beside the salmon, a pale green ribbon of eelgrass waved in the current.

Shad moved on a bit, saw two more salmon.

"That's one, two . . . seven salmon altogether," he counted. "Palidin Ramsey made a pile o' money sellin' salmon before he went to Ontario. The wardens never bothered him. But he caught them on a rod. I'd be using a net. The wardens don't like nettin'. I'll need someone to watch."

Shad crossed the bridge and made his way down along the shore to the Cabbage Island Salmon Club. Blades of shore hay took him to the waist. Grasshoppers and crickets gnashed in its midst.

He could hear Todder Brook murmuring across the way. A blackbird guarded its nest on Cabbage Island. He climbed the steps and scanned the cabins, the parking area. He could hear voices coming from inside the dining camp.

"Hello," came a girl's voice.

Shad recognized it. It was the voice of Lillian Wallace. Lillian was sitting on the veranda of Shad's favourite cabin. She was dressed in shorts and a blue blouse. The scene was a familiar one to Shad. He'd seen her there, exactly the same, a year ago, the day that Dryfly fed Helen MacDonald's dog the pie with Ex-Lax in it.

"G'day," said Shad. "How's she goin'?"

Lillian Wallace was sixteen, blonde, tanned, and beautiful. She was an American, the daughter of Old Fish Hog. Old Fish Hog was the name Bill Wallace had earned from the locals.

Confronting Lillian Wallace made Shadrack a bit self-conscious. He hoped his hair was still in place. Shad had red hair combed back, long, greased sideburns, a few freckles.

"I'm fine," said Lillian. "How have you been?"

"The very best. You?"

Lillian smiled and Shad thought her very pretty. He wished

that she was his girlfriend instead of Dryfly's. As he looked at her, his heart quickened and he thought he might even be blushing.

"How's your father?" he asked. "Lindon guiding him, is he?"

"My father's well. I believe he's out with Mr. Todder."

"Gettin' any fish?"

"He caught a beauty this morning."

"Good. Good. Lots of them goin'."

"That's what they tell me. Have you been having any luck?"

"Oh, yeah. Got a twenty-pounder this mornin'."

Lillian smiled again.

Bill Wallace fished a lot. Dryfly visited every evening, but most of Lillian's days were spent alone, reading on the veranda, listening to music. Lillian was grateful to have someone to talk to.

"Would you like a Pepsi?" she asked.

"Yeah, sure."

Shad approached and stepped onto the veranda. Lillian stood and went into the cabin for the Pepsi.

"I'll just be a minute," she said.

Shad waited, watching the river below. A squirrel chirped in a pine; he could hear a hammering in the distance — Bill Wallace's camp was under construction.

Shadrack thought about Lillian. He hadn't seen her in a year. The last time he'd seen her he got drunk and made a fool of himself. "She'd be my girl, only for that," he thought. The memory of her face — even prettier this year than last — stirred the bitter memory of losing her to Dryfly.

He sat on the veranda railing. Lillian returned with two bottles.

"Thanks," said Shad, accepting one.

"So I hear you're doing well in school," commented Lillian.

"Yeah. Passed. Don't know. Might quit."

"Quit? Why would you quit?"

"Don't know." Shad shrugged, drank some Pepsi.

"Do you have a job?"

"No, not right now. Might go to work . . . ah, peelin' pulp."

"A lumberjack," smiled Lillian.

"What do ya do all day?" asked Shad, changing the subject. Shadrack didn't like talking about work. It made him nervous.

"I've been catching up on reading. Dad would take me fishing, but I don't like the flies."

"Want to go swimmin'?"

"I don't think I'd better. I'm expecting my father back soon."

"Oh . . . well . . . "

"But maybe later."

"Yeah?"

"What time would you like to go?"

"Any time . . . "

"How about three?"

"Good. Good. Sounds good."

It seemed there was nothing more to say. Shad finished his Pepsi, set the bottle on the railing.

"Well, I gotta go," he said, standing.

"I'll see you at three," said Lillian.

"Okay. Bye. See ya later."

Shad went down through the woods and over the hill. He came to Tuney Brook, the little bridge, checked to see if there were any trout beneath. Seeing none he continued up the path and through the woods to Stan Tuney's.

Stan was lying in the shade chewing a sprig of grass.

"Saw seven big salmon beneath the footbridge," greeted Shad.

"Good place, that," said Stan. "Got nineteen there last week."

Stan Tuney never told the truth for twenty years. Shad knew it.

"A lad should have a net," said Shad.

When Shad left Dr. MacDowell's, he had been keen on the idea of finding or borrowing a net. He wanted to catch and sell salmon for the money he thought he needed to join the action in Blackville. But now that he had met up with Lillian Wallace, Blackville didn't seem to matter so much.

"I could give Lillian a little rub, and it wouldn't cost me a cent," he thought. "And I wouldn't have to hitchhike or walk any distance at all."

Going to Blackville not only meant that he needed money,

but to get there, quite often you had to walk the Gordon Road. Blackville was twelve miles down the Gordon Road.

"Course, Dryfly'd be madder than sin, but it's every man for himself, ain't it? And didn't she make a date with me?"

"You could get a pile o' them in a net," said Stan Tuney, intruding upon Shad's thoughts. "But there's so many wardens these days."

Stan Tuney had a pot belly, steel-gray hair, two days' growth of whiskers, white against his tanned face; he wore dark-rimmed glasses and smelled of tobacco smoke.

"Wardens don't bother me none," said Shad.

"You ain't scared of the wardens?"

"Nah, wardens could never catch a lad. All ya have to do is run into the woods. They don't know these woods."

"They might surprise you how much they know."

"Don't matter. Ain't got a net anyway."

"Dan Brennen might have a net."

"Wouldn't lend it, though."

"I got an old one that's just as rotten as ever it can be."

"Any good?"

"No good for nothin'! Wouldn't hold a jeezless chub!"

"Ya never know. Might happen to pick one up in it."

"It's pretty bad. Must be twenty years old. An old tideway net, it is. Must be a hundred yards long. Reach clean across the river."

"Where is it?"

"C'mon, I'll show ya."

Shad followed Stan to a shed behind the barn. Stan opened the door to reveal a room cluttered with old rusted harrows, plows, chains and a hundred other odds and ends — remnants of old farm implements. In a back corner, in a burlap bag, they found the net.

"It's not too bad right now," said Stan, bringing it out into the sunlight. "But when it's wet it takes two men just to carry it."

"Can I have it?" asked Shad.

"Sure. I'm not using it. All I want for it is a salmon."

Shad grinned, wondering what Stan had done with the nineteen he said he'd caught recently.

"All right, ya got a deal," said Shad

"You'll have to overhaul it somewhere."

"I'll take it up to Dr. MacDowell's. Never anyone around there."

Stan Tuney had told Shad that the net was a hundred yards long. That was a lie, of course. The net was only half that long. Nevertheless, a hundred and fifty feet of tideway net complete with rope, floats and weights proved to be everything that Shad needed. It took him an hour to lug the bundle back to Dr. MacDowell's camp.

Everyone in Brennen Siding saw him going with it and, somehow, everybody guessed, or knew, exactly what was in the bag.

Now confronting Shad was the task of overhauling it. Overhauling it, in this case, meant unravelling, removing sticks and grass, and spreading it full-length on the ground. Shad did this in Dr. MacDowell's parking area.

When he was finished, instead of putting it back in the bag and hiding it, he left it spread out in the parking area. He figured that in the bag it would just get tangled all over again.

By the time he finished the project, he was hot, hungry and fly-bitten. He thought of going home for a snack, but he had a three o'clock swimming date with Lillian Wallace. He figured it must be three o'clock already. He headed directly for the Cabbage Island Salmon Club.

In Brennen Siding, when you consider yourself too grown up to be playing cowboys and Indians, you start hanging around the river, swimming, canoeing, fishing, skipping stones, making rock formations, whatever catches your fancy. When you're too old to justify these activities, you get a net and a boat and sweep a mile of the river for salmon. In Brennen Siding, this sweeping for salmon is referred to simply as drifting.

Drifting is illegal, frowned upon by the law, the wardens. If you get caught drifting, you could get fined as much as five hundred dollars. They'll take your net and canoe, and if you're a guide they'll take your guide's licence, too. If you have an angling licence, you can wave goodbye to that as well. You don't always catch fish when drifting, so frequently you are risking thousands of dollars for no reason at all . . . other than being on the river . . . playing.

When Shad left Stan Tuney's, Stan said to himself, "I might wander down to the river tonight. He'll need a man to watch."

Bert Todder saw Shad crossing the bridge.

"There goes Shad with a bag," he thought. "Must be a net in it. Must be gonna drift. I wonder if he has anyone to watch for the wardens?"

When Bert mentioned it at Bernie Hanley's store that night, Dan Brennen thought, "Hmm. I could do with a salmon. I'll go watch for him. If he gets quite a few, he might give me one."

Shad was Bob Nash's son. When Bob Nash saw Shad going up the shore with the bag, he said to his wife, "Elva, look what Shad's up to!"

"Drifting!" said Elva. "Ya'd think he'd grow up!"

"I can't afford to pay a fine. I'd better have a talk with him."

If you saw somebody drifting and didn't report it to the wardens, you were considered an accessory. The fine for watching paralleled that of drifting.

It's foolish, even childish to drift, or watch, but the river at night was a beautiful, serene place to be; the possibility of being chased or even caught by the law was an excitement and a romantic adventure that was not otherwise easily acquired in a place like Brennen Siding. Drifting was high-risk adventure, live entertainment, and it was this, not the need for salmon, that drew men to its folds. Most of the males and some of the females were skilled anglers (the legal form of recreation), so the salmon bagged was rarely worth the risk.

So, they would head for the river. If they saw the wardens or heard someone whoop from upstream, they, too, would whoop. If there were enough watchers, the signal would travel for miles and miles. The warden's run would be futile.

When Shadrack Nash saw the beautiful Lillian Wallace sitting on the veranda of the Cabbage Island Salmon Club in a bathing suit, a bikini, his heart as well as several other organs nearly flipped over.

"Beef to the heels," he said to himself. "All that flesh going to waste on the likes of Dryfly Ramsey."

"Hi!" said Lillian, smiling.

"G'day!" said Shad. "G'day, g'day!"

"You're late."

"Ah . . . had some things to look after. Couldn't get away."

"Well, I'm ready. Got your swimsuit?"

Shad had never owned a bathing suit in his life.

"Ah, I forgot it. I'll just go in my jeans."

Lillian smiled again.

"Let's go," she said.

Shad followed her over the hill, unable to take his eyes off her. When they reached the water's edge, he was so hot that he hesitated for only a second before diving in.

Lillian followed.

They swam for half an hour, then sat on the shore in the sun to dry.

"It's a beautiful day and a beautiful river," commented Lillian.

"You ain't nothin' to shake a stick at either," said Shad, grinning. He hoped he wasn't being too forward, that she'd take it as a compliment.

Bill Wallace's best friend was a dentist. Bill Wallace's dentist took good care of Lillian Wallace's teeth. Every time Lillian smiled and revealed her perfect teeth, Shad's heart quickened.

Lillian Wallace smiled.

"Do you think that Dryfly could ever leave this river?" she asked.

Dryfly was Shadrack's best friend. Shadrack was already feeling guilty about associating, swimming with Dryfly's girl.

"Why did she have to bring up Dryfly?" he asked himself. "Dry's homely, tall, thin, a big nose. What does she see in him?"

From the soul of competition came the betrayal.

"No," said Shad. "Dryfly will never do anything."

"Do you think he'll ever go back to school?"

"No, he's no good for nothing, just like all the rest of the Ramseys, poor, living in a shack." Another betrayal.

Lillian looked thoughtful, watched the river. A flock of mergansers dived for fish across the way.

Lillian was feeling a little bit apprehensive about swimming alone with Shad, too, but she wanted to learn more about Dryfly. She wanted to know what he was like when she was not around.

Over the past few weeks she had grown very fond of Dryfly. She thought she might be in love with him. Why? She didn't know. They just had that necessary affinity. She did know, however, that the relationship seemed hopeless. She would have to leave — this year, next year, every year — and Dryfly would never leave. Dryfly belonged to the river. She would not ask him to leave. She loved him too much for that.

Shadrack inched closer.

"Leaving" was a word that was in Lillian's vocabulary and not in Dryfly's. Another word that frequently passed Lillian's lips was "security." Dryfly would never know the meaning of the word.

"Leaving," said Lillian, more to herself than to Shadrack. "You don't know how I hate the thought of it. I get depressed thinking about it." She looked to Shadrack and felt even more apprehensive. "He's competing," she thought. "I'll not learn anything about Dryfly from him."

"I have to go," said Lillian, stood and ran to the cabin.

Shad watched after her, bewildered, heart pounding.

*

Helen MacDonald, the spinster of the settlement, always swept one room at a time, leaving little mounds of dust, lint, sand, and straws from her tired broom in the centre of the room. Then she'd get the dustpan from behind the kitchen stove and gather them all up.

It seemed that every time she made her rounds gathering the dirt, somebody would come, or she'd have to go to the outhouse, or she'd smell a cake burning and she'd have to run to the stove, or perhaps some reverie would occupy her mind. Interrupted, she, without exception, would forget one or more of the mounds. Hence, there was always a mound of dirt in the centre of at least one of Helen MacDonald's six little rooms.

Helen MacDonald was making her rounds picking up the dirt when Bert Todder entered the kitchen.

Bert Todder never knocked, so she would not have known he was there at all if he hadn't slammed the screen door.

"That you, Bert?" she called from the parlour.

Bert Todder had a partiality for potatoes, ate them every meal.

Bert Todder had one tooth in the front of his mouth and the biggest belly in Brennen Siding. When Bert Todder laughed, which was often, one never knew for sure if he was laughing or crying.

"Oh, ah, I can't stay," said Bert, "but, ah, how ya makin' out?"

Helen went to the kitchen. Bert stood in the middle of the floor puffing his pipe as fast as he could, trying to keep it lit. The stem was dirty, the pipe gurgled with every puff. Bert Todder rarely cleaned his pipe. He was wearing gumshoes, black woollen pants and a mackinaw jacket, a package of Forest and Stream tobacco in the breast pocket.

"What's new with you, Bert?" asked Helen. She put down her dustpan and broom.

"Thought maybe you might be needin' a good lookin' man," said Bert, smiling.

Helen saw his single tooth, grinned.

"Now who might that be?" she asked, playing along.

"Tee, hee, hee, sob, ha, ha, ha, sob, sniff, puff, puff, puff!"

"Ya lost out on Shirley Ramsey. Now yer chasin' me, are ya Bert?" laughed Helen.

"Never say die," said Bert.

"Would you like a piece of cake, Bert?"

"No, no. No thanks. I jist et and come. Did ya see young Shad going up the shore?"

"Yeah, I did. Looked like he had a net."

"Yeah. Stan Tuney's old net. Must be gonna drift."

"Boys, a nice June salmon would go some good, eh Bert?"

It was July, but all the silver beauties would be considered June salmon for a while yet.

"Oh boys, I tell ya!" winked Bert. "Puff, puff, puff."

Having no teeth to grip the stem caused the pipe to slip full length into his mouth occasionally.

"Takin' an awful risk, though, ain't he?" said Helen.

"He'll be needin' someone to watch."

"Does he know how to throw a net?"

"Doubt it."

"Who's polin' the boat? Dryfly?"

"Prob'ly. 'Magine."

"Didn't I see Shad an' that Wallace girl swimmin' a while ago?"

"I believe ya did, yeah. Yeah."

"So what d'ya suppose is goin' on there? I thought she was Dryfly's girl?"

"Maybe she smartened up."

"I hope so. Nice young thing like that hangin' around the likes o' them Ramseys. I hope she has more sense! Tch! Tch!"

"That young Dryfly might have what it takes," grinned Bert. "He might have a great big . . . "

"Now, Bert!"

"Tee, hee, hee, puff, sob, sniff, puff, puff, puff! I soon gotta go."

"That old net o' Stan's can't be much, Bert."

"Sail a canoe right through it. Salmon would have to weigh fifty pounds to get caught in it. There's lots of them goin', though."

"I used to watch when Dad drifted."

"I mind that. You was a young, pretty thing back then!"

"I was homelier than Shirley Ramsey and you know it!"

"Tee, hee, hee, sob, snort, sniff, puff, puff, puff! I gotta be goin'. Where's yer dog?"

"Oh, he's down at the club, eatin', prob'ly. I gotta get back myself shortly. I'm just home for a couple of hours," said Helen.

Helen MacDonald cooked for the Cabbage Island Salmon Club. Bert Todder guided there. Bert was guiding Bill Wallace. Bill Wallace's liquor supply had vanished sometime during the winter and he was off to Newcastle for more. Bill Wallace hadn't been in the cabin all winter, and it was evident that someone had robbed him — another reason why he wanted a place of his own.

"Have to be back myself at seven o'clock," said Bert.

"He'll want to fish till dark, I suppose."

"Old Fish Hog, yeah. Should be slapped with an old nylon full o' . . . "

"Now, Bert!"

"Tee, hee, hee, sob, snort, sniff, puff, puff, puff! Well, I should be goin'."

*

Dryfly was tired, but he was going to see the most beautiful girl in the world, the girl he loved with all his heart. He felt good. He crossed the field, went through the woods and approached the Tuney Brook bridge.

Shadrack Nash was standing on the little bridge gazing into the water. Shad was watching a little trout swim below.

"What's up, Shad?" said Dryfly.

"You gonna be girlin' all night?" asked Shad.

"Don't know. Why?"

"I got a net."

"Yeah?"

"Stan Tuney's."

"Many goin'?"

"River's full o' them. Must've seen fifteen or twenty of them beneath the footbridge."

"Net any good?"

"Got a few holes in it. The very best, all ya need."

"Know how to throw it?"

"Pretty likely. Want to pole?"

"Never did it."

"You know how to pole, don't ya?"

"Pretty likely!"

"Then just pole!"

"What time ya goin'?"

"Soon's yer done girlin'."

"Might be late."

"Don't matter."

"I suppose we could. Got anybody to watch?"

"Not yet. Thought I'd get Lester Burns."

"Good," said Dryfly. "I'll see you later."

"Meet ya at the club . . . at the canoes."

"Usin' their canoes?"

"Thought we should. Wouldn't want to lose somebody's we know."

"Good. See ya later."

"About eleven?"

"Sounds good."

*

Dryfly climbed the hill to the Cabbage Island Salmon Club. Lillian Wallace, dressed in blue jeans, red-checkered blouse and white sneakers, waited on the veranda. When Dryfly saw her, he waved. Lillian waved back. Dryfly approached.

"G'day!" he said.

"Hi," said Lillian.

Dryfly had been expecting a smile. Lillian Wallace was not smiling.

"Want to go for a walk?" asked Dryfly.

"Ah . . . okay."

Lillian stood, stepped from the veranda.

Dryfly reached for her hand. Lillian declined the offer, put her hands in her pockets. She started over the hill. Dryfly followed her to the river. He sensed a change in her — she hadn't smiled; she wasn't holding his hand; she was walking faster than usual.

"What ya do all day?" asked Dryfly.

"Nothing," said Lillian.

Lillian Wallace was not happy. She felt she had to break it off with Dryfly, had to tell him it was over, had to tell him in a way that wouldn't hurt him.

"I have to tell him he can't come over anymore, and I can't even face him," she thought.

Sometimes when there was little to talk about, one would tell the other a story. Dryfly thought that this might be one of those times.

He looked upstream toward the bridge — someone was fishing just beyond in Judge Martin's pool.

"Judge Martin, prob'ly," thought Dryfly.

He swung his gaze downstream, faced the sunset. It was a very beautiful sunset — the reds and yellows, the sun itself glowing on the summit of the hazy forest, the river reflecting.

Dryfly's stories were just about exhausted. He couldn't think of any he hadn't already told her.

Then he saw a daisy and thought of his brother Palidin's story.

"See that daisy over there?" said Dryfly.

Lillian looked, nodded.

"Daisies used to be twice as pretty. Know what happened?"

Lillian nodded negative.

"It used to be the prettiest flower in the whole world. Then, a man came along one day. He thought it was the prettiest flower he'd ever seen, couldn't take his eyes off it. Know what happened?"

"No." Lillian's voice was very small, not much more than a whisper.

"He got tired of lookin' at it. The flower got plain, homely, just because he saw it too much."

"I don't think it's plain," said Lillian.

Dryfly looked at Lillian — her lips, her nose and eyes. He looked at the silky blonde hair, her ears and the tiny diamond studs. He wanted to reach out and hold her, to kiss her.

"Neither do I," he said.

Lillian turned to face him.

"Why did you tell me that story?" she asked

"I don't know," shrugged Dryfly. "Was lookin' at the pretty sunset, I guess."

Lillian smiled, kissed him on the cheek.

*

"Oh yeah, yeah, yeah. Uh huh. Yes, sir. Wouldn't mind havin' a feed o' baloney, yep," thought Lindon Tucker.

Lindon was on his way home from work, changed his mind

and went to Bernie Hanley's store. He wanted to get some baloney for supper.

"Hot. Hot. Hot. Warmish, Bernie old boy!" greeted Lindon.

Bernie Hanley was behind the counter sucking on a peppermint. He wore a hat, wire-rimmed glasses, a white short-sleeved shirt, navy pants with suspenders, black shoes. An electric fan hummed, a refrigerator rumbled. The store smelled of produce and peppermint. Lindon Tucker was the first customer of the evening.

"Sure is," said Bernie. "But it won't last long. It'll rain half the summer, no doubt."

"That's, that's, that's for sure, Bernie. Rain. Could, could, could git up tomorrow and find it rainin'. Oh, ah, where's everybody tonight, Bern? All, all, all settin' in the shade are they?"

"I don't know . . . fishin' maybe, I don't know."

Bernie Hanley was slightly concerned. At this time of the evening the store was usually full of men and boys eating oranges and drinking Sussex Ginger Ale. Lindon Tucker was not a good customer, rarely bought anything. Lindon Tucker didn't like spending money.

Lindon Tucker wore a green shirt with the sleeves rolled up to the armpits, green pants and gumshoes. He had a pot belly and missing cuspids. He frequently repeated himself and everybody else. He didn't know how to laugh. For years, he tried to learn the right syllable for laughter. He used "Ow!" for a while. He tried "Snee." Lately, he'd settled on "Yi!" Most of the time Lindon just grinned, tight-lipped. Lindon Tucker was self-conscious about his missing cuspids.

"Business is, business is, business is, as the feller says, business is pretty scarce," said Lindon, sensing Bernie's concern.

"Ya'd better give me a ginger ale, old pal, yeah, palsy walsy."

While Bernie opened the refrigerator door to get the ginger ale, Lindon sang, "Di, di, di, di, di; di, di, di, di, di; for tomorrow never comes." He tapped his heel as he sang. He counted out what he hoped was ten cents for the pop.

"Great, great, good run o' fish on, Bernie, Bernie, old boy."

"That's what they tell me," said Bernie.

"Gittin' any?"

"I couldn't ketch a salmon unless it came up over the hill. Can't leave the store long enough."

"Would have to, have to, salmon would have to come up over the hill, eh Bernie? Yi, yi, yi yi!"

"The flies don't seem to be so bad this year," commented Bernie. "And the hornet nests are right on the ground. Gonna be a good winter, I think."

"Oh yeah, yeah, yeah. No flies, no. Hardly a fly. I was thinkin' that, too, yeah. Might be a good winter."

Bernie sighed.

"No sense talkin' wisdom to Lindon Tucker," thought Bernie.

At this point in the conversation, Lindon had forgotten why he came to the store. He didn't remember until eleven o'clock, at which time he bought a half a pound of baloney. Then he said, "Well, Bernie old pal, chummy pard, if I was down the road, over the hill, 'cross the bridge, up the hill, had this baloney et an' was in bed, I'd be all right."

Bernie said nothing. He was afraid that Lindon might not leave. If he said anything to Lindon, Lindon might want to repeat it and stay and stay and stay.

Lindon Tucker went down the road and over the hill. He was crossing the bridge when he heard the call of a bird. He'd heard the bird before, but didn't know what kind of bird it was. It had a lonesome call, more of a "coo" than a "hoot."

"Coo!" went the bird.

Lindon echoed the bird.

"Coo! Coo!"

"Coo!" went the bird again.

"Coooo!" hooted Lindon.

*

When Shadrack and Dryfly poled up the river toward Dr. MacDowell's cabin to pick up the net, they did not see Helen MacDonald standing by the footbridge abutment. They did not see Dan Brennen and his two boys standing by an alder bush on Cabbage Island. Bert Todder was standing in the tall grass at the mouth of Todder Brook, and Stan Tuney watched from a rock on Judge Martin's shore, but Shadrack and Dryfly did not see them. Lester Burns was the only one they knew for sure to be watching. On this dark night, all they could see of Lester Burns was the glow from his cigarette. They thought they could hear someone walking on the footbridge, and further upstream they thought they heard someone coming over the hill, but they could not see Lindon Tucker or Bernie Hanley. It was so dark that Shadrack and Dryfly could barely see each other.

When Dryfly and Shadrack approached the net, they could not see the skunk, but they could smell it. The skunk had been heading across Dr. MacDowell's parking area and had gotten tangled in the net. It was in a state of panic. You could smell it for a hundred yards.

"So, what do we do now?" asked Dryfly.

"We'll have to get it out somehow," said Shadrack.

"How we gonna do that?"

"Heard a skunk can't piss if you pick him up by the tail. Needs to have his feet on the ground."

"Yeah, I heard that too, but who's gonna do it?"

"You."

"Oh for sure! I ain't gonna do it!"

"Here, I'll toss a coin."

Shadrack pretended to toss a coin.

"Heads or tails?" he asked.

"Heads," said Dryfly. He could not see the coin.

"Tails!" said Shadrack. "You lose!"

"Ya stupid jeezer!" said Dryfly. "C'mon, we'll both do it! One lad's gonna have to hold the skunk up while the other untangles him. We'll both get pissed on if it doesn't work."

The skunk watched the boys approach. It was nearly exhausted from strangulation, dying. It let itself be lifted, untangled, biting only once, and carried to the edge of the parking area. It scurried off into the woods.

It didn't matter. The net had been well-sprinkled, and the boys could not carry it anyway. They threw it into the alders and went back to the canoe.

"Should have killed that jeezless skunk!" said Shad. "Saw him today — should've knowed!"

"It don't matter. I kin ketch fish, anyway. Palidin told me how."

"Lotta good that's gonna do me!"

They shoved the canoe off and drifted down the river. They didn't paddle; they didn't make a sound. All they could see was the sky, the river and the dark shores.

They approached the footbridge.

"Coo! Coo!" went Lindon Tucker.

Helen MacDonald was standing in the ebon shadows of the footbridge abutment. When she heard the bird, she took it to be nothing more than a bird.

Then she heard Lindon's "coo!" and his footsteps on the bridge. Although it was too dark to see Lindon on the bridge, she could distinguish the shape of the canoe coming down the smooth Dungarvon.

Lindon cooed again.

"Whoever that is on the bridge might be trying to warn the boys," she thought. "Can't whoop much, whoever it is. I'll have to show him how it's done."

"WHOOP!" went Helen and took off up the shore, homeward.

The whoop echoed up and down the river.

Bert Todder heard the whoop and whooped just to make sure the boys heard it.

Stan Tuney whooped, too. After all, why else was he there?

Dan Brennen also whooped. How else could he earn a salmon?

Lindon Tucker repeated every whoop he heard, then repeated himself. He found great delight in whooping and cooing, whooping and cooing. He occasionally laughed at the absurdity of it all. "Yi, yi, yi, yi! Whoop! Coo! Yi, yi, yi, yi, yi!"

Everyone else just whooped once and ran, making sure they didn't get caught and charged as accessories to Shadrack and Dryfly's terrible crime.

The shore of the little river echoed with whoops. Lindon Tucker echoed the echoes . . . and laughed.

To avoid confrontation with the wardens, Shadrack and Dryfly paddled quickly to the shore and ran up over the hill.

They heard someone running toward them. It was Helen MacDonald, but they could not identify her in the night. They thought it might be the wardens. They turned and ran toward Todder Brook. When Helen heard Shadrack and Dryfly coming, she, too, thought she was hearing the wardens, swung and ran toward Dr. MacDowell's.

Dan Brennen and his boys had a similar experience with Stan Tuney. Bert Todder ran from Bernie Hanley.

Lester Burns encountered Helen MacDonald, who quickly yelled, "Run! The wardens are after me!"

Lester Burns ran as fast as he could until he ran into Shadrack and Dryfly, who by this time were running from Bert Todder.

Feet were thumping the ground all over the place.

Finally, everyone made it home, went directly to bed and listened to their pounding hearts, content with the adventure. They hadn't been caught.

"The wardens could never catch us on our own turf."

Before Lindon Tucker went to bed, he fried up half a pound of baloney.

two

Shad climbed out of bed, dressed and went downstairs. He didn't know what time it was, but he thought it must be noon — his father was eating beans at the kitchen table. His mother sat at the other end of the table sipping from a cup of tea.

"Look!" said Elva. "Just look who crawled out! Old, old, old Buck Ramsey himself. It's too bad the wardens hadn't caught ya, I say! Out on the river breaking the law, like, like, a common criminal!"

"Mornin', Mom," said Shad.

"You just gettin' up?" snapped Bob.

Shad didn't answer, entered the bathroom, closed the door, pissed, washed his face and hands and combed his hair. He gave particular attention to his hair, making sure it was just right, well greased.

"They're in a great mood today!" he thought. "Wonder what's up?"

Bob Nash was wound up tighter than a banjo string.

"What's up?" he snapped. "You have the gall!"

Shad shrugged, got himself a cup from the cupboard, poured it full of black tea, sat at the table.

"What were you out on that river for?" barked Elva.

"For fun. Paddlin' around."

"Paddlin' around all right! You were driftin', that's what!"

"I wasn't driftin'."

"Don't you lie to me!"

"I ain't lyin'!"

"You are!"

"I wasn't driftin'!"

"You were!"

"We didn't have a net!"

297

"What about the net you got from Stan Tuney?"

Elva was attacking Shad for a reason. Elva Nash had given John Kaston, her brother the preacher, fifty dollars, a donation for his new church. She just handed it over, didn't tell Bob anything. Bob Nash was thoroughly irked. It took Bob a week of hard work in the woods to earn fifty dollars. The money could have been used for fixing the roof of the barn. They already had a church to go to, and who did John Kaston think he was? Attacking Shad was Elva's way of evading the issue.

"How'd you know about that?" asked Shad.

"Everybody in the country saw you goin' up the shore with it!"

"Well, we didn't use it. A skunk got in it."

"You lads didn't have a net?" asked Bob.

"No. I told ya. A skunk got in it."

"There. Case closed," said Bob. "Now what about my fifty dollars?"

"It's not the end of the world! Although the Lord knows the end is nigh."

"The barn leaks."

"Give and you shall receive."

"Receive! What the hell are we gonna receive from John Kaston, tell me that? Is he gonna fix the barn?"

"He's doin' God's work. He wants to build a church. The least we can do is help him out. Don't you ever think of your soul?"

"Soul? Lotta good yer soul is if the barn falls down."

"I, I, I never saw anyone more like old, old, old Buck Ramsey in my life!"

"Buck Ramsey was not old. He was not much older than forty when he died."

"He was an old tramp is what he was. A Catholic! That Dryfly makes me sick. That Wallace girl must think a lot of herself." Elva was evading the issue again.

Bob aggressively slid back his chair. He was too upset to continue his meal. He stood, started to say something, scratched his head instead. He went to the window, looked through the glass at the valley, the river.

Shad knew his mother's way. He decided to help his father out — Shad needed money for a wiener and chips.

"You gave John Kaston fifty dollars?" he asked his mother.

"Yes! Yes, I gave it to him. John's a minister now, needs a church. And if you two know what's good for your, you'll go to it! If you need money so bad, why don't you sell that old shore?"

"Why don't John sell *his* old shore?"

"He's going to."

"I worked hard to keep that old shore," grumbled Bob.

"And what's the good of it? Ain't worth one red cent. Bill Wallace would buy it in a minute. Don't you know he's after Bert Todder's shore? You could get ahead of Bert. You could get two or three thousand dollars for that shore."

"I want the shore," said Shad, meekly.

"Ha!" was the reply he got from Elva.

Bob, however, turned from the window and stared down at this son. He didn't say anything, just stared. Shad didn't know whether he was about to get hugged or smashed in the mouth.

"We could build a camp on it," said Shad.

Like most Miramichiers, Elva was a master of sarcasm. Here, she deployed its powers.

"Yes, that's right," she said sweetly. "That would be just lovely. It would be so nice to have a little shack by the river for you and dear little Dryfly to get drunk in. He's such a good boy, Bob. Gets up early in the morning and works with you all day. Goes to church on Sunday. Why don't you build your good Christian son a camp, Bob? Ha!"

Bob removed his eyes from Shad, started for the door.

"Ah . . . Dad?"

Bob stopped, waited.

"You got five dollars?"

Bob reached into his pocket, removed five dollars and tossed it on the table in front of Shad. He looked down at Elva, daring her to react. She didn't. Bob was master of the house. He swung and left without farewell.

*

"Cooooo!" went Lindon Tucker.

Lindon Tucker, Dryfly Ramsey and Ducky Shaw were driving nails, boarding in the roof of Bill Wallace's camp. The relentless, cacophanous hammering could be heard all over Brennen Siding.

"What's that all about?" asked Dryfly.

"What's that?" asked Lindon.

"What're ya cooin' for?"

"Cooin'? Did you, did you, did you hear it, too, chummy pard?"

"Yeah, just now. You cooed."

"Heard it last night myself, so I did. Yeah. Yeah. Oh yeah, heard it myself, yeah. Last night. Heard it crossin' the bridge. Coooo! Yeah. Must've been some kinda bird, I believe, yeah, Dry old boy. Bird. Bird. Went coo, yeah, so it did."

"Did you see it?" asked Dryfly.

"No. No. No, I couldn't see it, no. No sir. Too dark, if ya know what I mean. Last night, yeah. On the bridge, yeah. Cooo!"

"If ya couldn't see it, how d'ya know it was a bird?" asked Dryfly.

"Could, could, could've been a bird, yeah, Dryfly. That's fer sure, yeah. Could've been a bird all right, yeah."

"There's all kinds of strange animals around, you know," said Dryfly. "Could've been a beaver, or a muskrat. Could've been a bat."

"Well, yeah, yea, it could've been a bat, Dry, pal, buddy, could've been a bat, yeah. Never thought o' that."

Dryfly remembered the story about the snakes that grab their tails, making their bodies into hoops and rolling around the ground like a wheel. He grinned at the thought.

"Could've been a snake," said Dryfly. "You hear it whoop, eh?"

"Whooped, yeah. Jist sorta whooped, so it did, yeah, Dry, palsy walsy."

"That's what it was, then," said Dryfly.

Ducky Shaw was listening in on the conversation, half annoyed that Dryfly and Lindon could talk and work at the same time. If they had stopped to talk, Ducky would have told them to get back to work, executing his authority. But as long as they kept working, he couldn't find any reason to tell them to stop talking.

"A snake?" asked Ducky, annoyed with the absurdity of Dryfly's reasoning.

"Yeah, you know, a whoop snake," said Dryfly.

"A whoop snake, yeah. Oh yeah, yeah, yeah. A whoop snake, yeah. Yi, yi, yi, yi, yi!"

"Goddamned foolish talk," muttered Ducky. "Ya'd think grown men would have more sense. Now who's that comin' to bother us?"

Bob Nash was crossing the field walking slowly, thoughtfully. He approached and looked up at the men on the roof.

"G'day, g'day, Bob, old boy! How's she going'?" greeted Lindon.

"The very best," said Bob. "She's an awful big camp, ain't she."

"Sixty by forty," said Dryfly.

"Too goddamned big if ya ask me," snapped Ducky.

"Big, big, big," said Lindon.

"Ya can't build too big a camp in this country," said Bob.

"No, no, no, you're right there, Bobby old boy. Ya can't put up too big a camp in country. No, sir. No," agreed Lindon.

"I tried to tell 'im that," said Ducky. "I tried to tell 'im that when he showed me the plans. Ya can't tell an American nothin'."

"What'd he say?" asked Bob.

"He said, yeah, you're right. Ya can't build too big a camp. Then he went on about all the guests he planned to bring up here and all the room he'd need."

Bob shrugged. "Do you think there's enough support?" he asked.

"I don't give a damn!" snapped Ducky. "I didn't draw the plans. I just follow them. I tried to tell 'im. Ever talk to 'im?"

"A few times," said Bob.

"He doesn't listen to a word ya say. Thinks there's nobody

up here that knows a thing. Ya might as well talk to that saw over there. I tried to tell 'im."

"Well, I won't hold ya up any longer. I gotta be goin'. See ya later."

"Yeah, take 'er easy, buddy, pal!" yelled Lindon.

*

Shadrack Nash rummaged through his dresser drawer, found a t-shirt, put it on.

"Damn!" he thought.

The t-shirt had a hole in it just below the neck.

"Right in the front where everyone can see it," mumbled Shad.

He took the t-shirt off and tried it on backward. He checked how it looked in the mirror. The logo on the back of the neck was now at the front. Shad cut the threads with a Wilkinson Sword razor blade and removed the logo. The fabric was slightly whiter where the logo had been, and he could see the little rectangle of thread holes.

"Will have to do," he thought and reached for his shirt.

When Shad finished dressing, he was wearing a t-shirt on backward beneath a black cowboy shirt with pearl-like buttons, a white rope design on the shoulders, collar turned up, sleeves rolled to wide cuffs just below the elbows. He was wearing black pants with a three-by-two-inch Mack truck buckle that belonged to his father. He had grown out of his pants somewhat so that when he sat, one could see his white socks above the top of his black jetboots. He had a black trucker's wallet with a gold chain running from it around front to follow the hem of his pocket up to where it was connected to his belt. The wallet had five dollars in it.

After applying a liberal supply of Brylcreem to his red hair, he combed it straight back, grinning, curling his lip a little bit into the mirror.

He liked what he saw.

"This shirt's gonna be too hot," he thought, "but I look good. That's the main thing."

He went downstairs. Elva was crocheting a doily in the

parlour. She looked sad. Bob hadn't returned. She thought he might be off getting drunk.

"Dad back yet?" asked Shad.

"No. I don't know where he is."

"Fishin', prob'ly."

"Didn't take his rod. Where're you goin'?"

"Blackville."

"Well, don't you go near that sand bed. The water's forty feet deep there. And there's an undertow."

"Yeah, I know."

"And don't you stay out all night. Bob'll want you to help him in the woods tomorrow."

"I ain't workin' in the woods!"

"Shad, how can you be such a bad boy? Your poor old father works his fingers to the bone. And we try to do so much for ya. I pray for you all the time, Shad. Why can't you be more like Freddy Donovon, or Mark Hanson? Mark dresses all up and goes to church every Sunday. Such a nice lookin' boy in his black suit and tie."

"Yeah, well, I'll see ya later."

As Shad went over the hill and crossed the bridge, the sun glared down on his black clothing with all the heat it could muster.

"Some o' the guys are wearing black leather jackets. Must be murder on them," he thought. "Besides the black leather jacket I need a red Chevy with a 327 four-barrel, dual exhaust, a four on the floor, spoke wheels. First I'll go to Bernie Hanley's store to get a package of Export A for forty cents. Then I'll have sixty cents for jingling in my pocket. Cool, daddy-o! The most!"

> *It's not the way you look*
> *That breaks my heart, na, na, sha, na, na, na, na!*
> *It's not the way you smile*
> *That tears me apart, na, na, sha, na, na, na ,na, na . . .*

Shad sang all the way to Bernie Hanley's. At the store, he purchased a package of Export A and had Bernie break down a quarter to two dimes and a nickel. Then he started walking to Blackville, the clickers on his jetboots wasted on the dirt road, the change jingling.

Na, na, sha, na, na, na, na . . .

He walked three miles before he got a ride. Clive Connors picked him up. Clive had been up the Gordon Road delivering bread, donuts, jelly rolls and yoyo cookies to Danny O'Hara's store in Gordon and Bernie Hanley's store in Brennen Siding. Clive drove the Lane's bread truck.

Shad asked Clive to drop him off at the village line. He didn't want to be seen getting out of a bread truck — there was nothing cool about a bread truck.

"Although it might be cool to *drive* a bread truck," thought Shad. "Truck drivers are cool. Elvis Presley was a truck driver."

Shad walked the remaining half mile up through the village to Biff's canteen. Biff's was closed, would not open until seven o'clock. It was only four-thirty in the afternoon. Shad continued on up the sidewalk to LeBlanc's.

LeBlanc's canteen was closed, too. Shad went around back. Sitting in the shade on two orange crates were Gary Perkins and Milton Bean. They were taking turns sipping foam from a bottle of warm Moosehead ale. The Moosehead had been out in the sun, tasted skunky.

"G'day, boys," said Shad.

"Shad," said Gary.

Milton nodded.

Gary and Milton were cool as Fundy. They were wearing black leather jackets. Shad was glad he met up with them.

"What's up?" asked Shad.

"Drink?" asked Gary, offering Shad the warm Moosehead. Shad took the bottle, drank.

"Good," he said. "Thanks. That all ya got?"

"We're short on cash, Nash," said Milton.

"They're so cool!" thought Shad. "I can't believe how cool they are!"

"I got the means, Bean," said Shad, grinning, curling his lip the best he could.

They were all cool. They all grinned, curling their lips.

Shad figured to himself, "I got four dollars and sixty cents. I can get six quarts of beer for four dollars. I'll have sixty cents left for a wiener and chips."

They walked to the bootlegger's, then to the sand bed carrying the six quarts of beer under their jackets and belts, in their sleeves.

Several other people were at the sand bed swimming, getting a tan.

It was a very hot day. All were thirsty. They shared the beer. All six quarts were emptied in a matter of minutes.

The river, the hot sun and the beer made them lazy.

All the people that lived in Blackville soon left, went home for supper. By six o'clock, only Shad and Gary Perkins remained.

Gary yawned.

"Did I tell ya I got a new electric guitar?" he asked.

"No."

"Yeah. Bought Neil MacLaggen's guitar and amplifier. Fifty bucks."

"Yeah?"

"Might start up a band, do some *in* stuff. Hear you play the banjo."

"Not much good for *in* stuff."

"Better than nothin'. Gotta start somewhere."

"Who else ya got?"

"Need a drummer, rhythm man and a singer."

"Should have a good-lookin' singer."

"Yeah, I know, but I can't sing all that good, you know."

"Me either. Dryfly Ramsey can play rhythm *and* sing, but . . ."

"Yeah. We'll find somebody."

"I'll think about it."

"Yeah, well, I have to go, beat the feet, put on the feed bag," said Gary. "Gonna be around tonight?"

"Yeah, I guess."

"Okay, Nash, see ya later."

"Take it cool," said Shad.

Alone, with nothing to do, Shad walked up the hill to the village. He sat behind LeBlanc's canteen until it opened at seven, went in and ordered a wiener and chips. He smothered the food with salt, vinegar and ketchup and ate it quickly. He was hungry from all the walking. He checked the clock on the wall.

"Half-past seven," he thought. "The gang won't gather till about nine. And I'm broke. Not much sense hangin' around broke."

He decided to go home.

It took him better than three hours to walk home to Brennen Siding.

*

Bob Nash did a lot of walking that day, too. Bob had an old rickety and rusty pickup truck that he could have driven up to Gordon, but he felt he needed the exercise. Bob Nash worked as a lumberjack six days of the week, running a chainsaw, up-ending eight-foot lengths of boxwood to the yard, piling it — Bob Nash did not need exercise. Bob Nash needed to walk off his frustrations. He walked to Gordon because that was where the nearest bootlegger lived.

Ben Brooks was thin, unshaven and smelled slightly of vomit. His skin was orange, his head was bald and he was blinder than the proverbial bat. He lived alone in a crumbling tarpaper shack, stayed drunk most of the time, sold very little. Ben Brooks was the epitome of man's affinity for alcohol. The young people of Gordon and Brennen Siding referred to Ben Brooks as Barf Breath — coincidental initials.

"Hello, Ben," said Bob. "Got any liquor?"

"I . . . I . . . who's this?"

"Bob Nash."

"Bob Nash? Not Bob Nash! YOU OLD HOUND DOG!"

"How ya been, Ben?"

"The very best, Bob. You?"

"Fair. Fair."

"Yes. Yes. Yes. I got a little whiskey. What did you want?"

"Oh, rye, I guess."

"Yeah, I got a little rye. How many you want? How's Elva? How many did you want?"

"Oh, I don't know . . . "

"I just got the four pints left."

"I'll take the four," said Bob, knowing the custom was to drink one with Ben.

Ben fumbled his way to the only other room in the shack. Bob waited, wanted to hold his breath, such was the smell of the place. The shack hadn't been cleaned or aired out for twenty years. Dirty clothes, paper, beer and whiskey bottles, dried bread, dirty dishes, empty tobacco packages, and other stuff lay all over the place.

"It's a wonder the place don't catch on fire," thought Bob.

Ben returned with the liquor.

"That's the last of it," said Ben. "Shoulda kept one for myself. But bein' it's you . . . well! Bob Nash! I haven't seen you in ten years! How've ya been, ya old hound dog? Where ya headin'?"

"Nowhere. Just thought I'd have a little drink."

"Then sit down! Stay for a while! How's Elva? Playin' any music?"

"No, haven't played the banjo in ten years."

"Boys, we used to have some times, didn't we? Sit down! Open a pint o' that stuff and have a drink."

There were only two chairs in the place. One of the chairs had molasses drippings on it. Bob reluctantly sat in the other one. Ben sat in the molasses drippings.

Bob opened the pint, drank half of it in one quaff, handed the pint to Ben.

"Here, have a shot," said Bob. "Right in front o' ya."

Ben drank from the pint leaving Bob but a mouthful in the bottom. Bob finished the pint and stood. He felt he had to get out of this disgusting place.

"How much do I owe ya?" he asked.

"What? What? You're not leavin'! Ya just got here. How's Elva. What've you been doin'?"

"Here's twelve dollars," said Bob.

"You know, Bob, that was my last four pints. Gonna have to send Marvin on a run tomorrow. Sit down, sit down! Stay a while! How's Elva. What've ya been workin' at? Have ya been playin' any music?"

"I'm puttin' the money right here, Ben. Right here in your shirt pocket."

"You leavin', Bob?"

"Yeah. You take it easy, Ben. I gotta go."

"Ah, don't leave, Bob. Playin' any music these days? Ya can't go. Mind all the playin' and singin' we use to do? God, Bob! Where's the time go? How . . . you married Elva Kaston, didn't you? How's Elva? Where have you been? It must be ten years since I saw ya."

"Yeah, well, I have to go, Ben. I might see ya later," said Bob and left.

Ben kept talking, his voice fading with every step that Bob took.

"Ya gotta stay and have a little drink, Bob, old hound dog," were the last words that Bob could distinguish. He walked as fast as he could back to Brennen Siding. He opened the second pint on the footbridge.

"Where to now?" he asked himself. "I can't go home. Not yet, anyway. I should go and see Shirley. Haven't talked to Shirley in years."

Elva Nash wouldn't associate with Shirley Ramsey and convinced Bob to ignore her also. Shirley Ramsey was poor and a Catholic, a bad influence on good, clean-living Protestants. When Elva first met Bob, he had been good friends with Buck Ramsey — in the same way that Shad and Dry were buddies. When they got married, Elva put an end to it. After marrying Elva, Bob only got together with Buck and Shirley when he was drunk. Then Buck left and returned only about once a year, stayed for a few days and left again.

"It must be fifteen years since Buck and Shirley came in that night with the guitar and the three of us drank and partied," thought Bob. "Elva wouldn't speak to me for a week. It wasn't worth the bother, but I wish Buck Ramsey was still livin'. Always liked Buck."

Bob Nash finished his second pint and headed for Shirley Ramsey's.

Shirley Ramsey was always a little nervous around people. Her new husband, Nutbeam, was self-conscious, shy. Shirley was not used to having anyone visit other than Bert Todder. Nobody in Brennen Siding would associate with the likes of Shirley Ramsey. Bert Todder only visited her because she made good gossip — she was always good for a laugh.

"Look. Look at that. Buck's old guitar. Well, well, well," said Bob. "Does anyone play that these days, Shirley?"

"Dry. Dry plays it. He kin sing real good, too."

Nutbeam agreed, nodded.

"Where is Dryfly?" asked Bob. "I could do with a little song."

"Ya jist missed 'im," said Shirley. "He's off every night, chasin' that Wallace girl."

"Don't blame 'im," said Bob. "He an' Shadrack are good buddies, eh?"

Nutbeam nodded, smiled. Nutbeam's mouth was very big. His smile was an arc of lips from ear to ear. When he nodded, his big ears seemed to flop. Bob had to grin to see him. It was the first time Bob had grinned in a long while.

"Your family's all grown up, eh Shirley?" commented Bob.

"Yeah, all o' them. Just got Dryfly left. Palidin was the last to leave." Shirley said this, looked at Nutbeam, smiled.

"Palidin! Palidin! Palidin was the best damn fisherman on this river. He could ketch a fish right out from under your nose. What's he doin'?"

"Pal's doin' real good," said Shirley. "Workin' in T'rono, so he is. Workin' for a big newspaper."

"Ah, yes. Him and George Hanley. He was down for the wedding, wasn't he?"

"Could jist stay three days."

Bob Nash found the memory of George Hanley and Palidin Ramsey distasteful.

"Fruits!" he thought. "Goddamned fruits!"

Bob opened another pint, took a drink, offered the bottle to Shirley and Nutbeam. Shirley declined the offer. Nutbeam accepted, took a drink. Nutbeam was in a celebrating mood. Shirley was pregnant.

*

Lillian Wallace's eyes were fixed on the sunset. She seemed to be searching for something. Dryfly could see that they were not happy eyes. Dryfly and Lillian hadn't spoken for what must have been five minutes. Lillian was the first to break the silence.

"Another sunset," she said.

"Not much of one," said Dryfly.

"It's beautiful," said Lillian. "It's different every night."

"It's trying to show up the northern lights," said Dryfly.

"Dad was on an island once where every evening all the people went to the east end to watch the sunset. He said that there were as many as a couple of thousand people standing on the cliffs, facing the sun. He brought back pictures — the island was beautiful, like a mountain in the sea. The sunset, the whole island was like a . . . like a robin's breast."

"Where was it?"

"Greece, I think. One of the Greek Islands. Would you like to travel someday, Dryfly?"

Dryfly looked at the sunset, the bank of billowy clouds like mountains adorned with crimson snow, their glow.

"I don't know," said Dryfly. "Maybe."

Lillian sighed.

"It's gonna rain tomorrow," said Dryfly. "I wonder if Ducky'll want to work."

Lillian didn't know. She shrugged. Shrugging was a habit she was beginning to pick up from the Canadians.

"You should go to school, Dryfly," she said.

Lillian Wallace couldn't have hurt Dryfly more if she had slapped his face. She saw the peace flow from his eyes, the turmoil replace it.

"What's wrong?" she asked.

The word "school" had lodged in Dryfly's solar plexus like a potato.

"Nothin'," said Dryfly. "Keep talkin'."

310

"You could go to school, even to university if you wanted. I bet Dad would help you. I know he would. He likes you. He never likes for me to have boys around, but he never says anything about you."

The potato in Dryfly's solar plexus grew. The first growth had sprung from the word "school." Dryfly hated school, was maybe a little afraid of it. He didn't have good clothes to wear. He'd been out of school for four years and going back would mean that he would be that much older than the rest of the class. It would be embarrassing for a sixteen-year-old to be sitting in a class with a bunch of twelve-year-olds. The word "school," spoken by Lillian, meant that she thought he should go, that she thought he was ignorant, that education was a necessary ingredient in their relationship.

Dryfly Ramsey was very poor, but he never felt poor or noticed being poor unless he ventured out of Brennen Siding. Now, all this talk about the sunset in Greece, the travelling, the Dad-would-help-you stuff increased the size of the potato and shrouded him with the realization that Lillian was seeing his poverty, that their relationship needed a second ingredient: money.

Lillian Wallace knew that she was handling a delicate matter, but she felt it something that needed to be discussed. She had intended to bring the topic up the night before, but Dryfly had side-stepped it. Now, she was into it and intended to unveil the whole issue regardless of the consequences. To Lillian, it was a matter of facing reality and dealing with it.

They looked into each other's eyes. Dryfly saw blue, wisdom, knowledge, wealth, the world; Lillian saw brown, honesty, sadness, hopelessness.

"What are you going to do?" asked Lillian gently.

Dryfly didn't answer. He turned away, looked at the river.

"I read somewhere that here in Canada everyone will have to be bilingual pretty soon. You should learn to speak French." Lillian was trying to be gentle and helpful, but it seemed she was saying all the wrong things.

"I'm gonna keep my mouth shut," said Dryfly. "With my mouth shut, I'm as bilingual as the next lad."

Dryfly thought he sounded bitter, turned to her, faked a smile.

Lillian Wallace was more than just a girlfriend to Dryfly Ramsey. For the past year Lillian Wallace had been Dryfly's crutch to lean on, his ego booster — the mere thought of her caused him to walk taller, gave him dignity, pride. Receiving her letters gave him joy; reading them gave him happiness. There was nothing unique about this — men and women often make each other feel that way — it's called love. Dryfly Ramsey had never permitted himself to think about the day that Lillian Wallace might not love him, or at least write to him. Lillian Wallace was the only girl that Dryfly had ever had. Not having any other girl to love, he loved Lillian Wallace.

Last year, when Lillian returned to her home in Stockbridge, Dryfly had been very lonesome. But he was not empty, he still had Lillian Wallace in his heart. Lillian Wallace was not just a girlfriend to Dryfly, she was a religion. The old adage, "absence makes the heart grow fonder," never missed a tick of Dryfly's clock or a stroke of his hand. His love grew stronger and deeper every day.

Lillian hadn't exactly said that she was cutting off the relationship, but Dryfly knew that that was what she was trying to say. In his mind he could hear the words, "You're too poor, you don't have any education, you'll never leave this river." They could have been the words of Elva Nash.

"I'm very fond of you," said Lillian.

Lillian had chose her words carefully. She hadn't used the word "love." She didn't want to make it any harder. She didn't want to lead him on. She moved to kiss him on the cheek.

Dryfly turned away. He wanted to remember her as she was last night, the night before, last year. He did not want to remember them as they were now. He did not want a goodbye kiss.

"I'll love you for the rest of my life," he said and walked away, heading he didn't know where.

"Dryfly!" called Lillian.

He did not turn to answer. He did not even hesitate. He just kept walking until he disappeared into the crimson forest.

Neither Dryfly nor Lillian was very happy.

*

Shadrack Nash walked the footbridge and gazed up at the starlit sky. Bob Nash was standing thoughtfully on the centre abutment. It was so dark that Shad came to within inches from running into him.

"Dad!"

"Shad?"

"What're ya doin'?"

"You really want that old shore, Shad?" Bob's speech was slurred. Shad knew he was drunk.

"Maybe," said Shad.

"That old shore wouldn't be there five minutes if anything were to happen to me," said Bob.

"Why's that?"

"Why? I'll tell ya well. That woman o' mine would sell it and anything else she could the her hands on in five minutes, that's why. She'd sell everything and travel the roads and preach, give the money to John. Give it to John or some other fuckin' preacher!"

Shad had never heard his father say "fuckin'" before. Shad was set back a bit. Bob was almost sounding like a normal human being.

"Shad?"

"Yeah, Dad?"

"Tell me this and tell me no more." Bob threw his arm over Shad's shoulder. "Did you have a net last night, or not?"

"Skunk got in it, pissed all over it. Left it up at Dr. MacDowell's in the alders."

"Me and you should go for a little drive," said Bob.

"Me and you?"

"Sure! I know how to throw a net. You can pole, can't ya?"

"Yeah, but . . . "

"Let's go for a little drift. Here."

"What?"

"Have a drink o' whiskey."

Shad grinned, took a drink.

313

"Tonight?" asked Shad.

"Right now! Don't you tell your mother about this, will ya, Shad? She'd skin the both of us, wouldn't she? Ha, ha, ha! She would, Shad."

"Right now?"

"Pretty goddamned likely! Why not?"

"Shh."

"What?"

"The wardens might hear us talkin'." Shad had lowered his voice to a whisper.

"I don't give a damn for the wardens!" yelled Bob. "The wardens never bothered Bob Nash, the cowardly bastards."

"What'll we use for a boat?"

"We'll use the club's boat. C'mon, let's have one more little drink and give 'er hell. Yahooooo!"

"Coo! Coo!" went a bird from somewhere east.

"What bird is that, Dad?" asked Shad.

"What bird? I don't hear any bird. Buck Ramsey always said that that cooin' jeezer was the devil. Yahooo! The devil's all over these woods, eh Shad? Just ask John Kaston, eh Shad? He'd tell ya, wha', Shad? Old John would tell ya soon enough."

"You're awful drunk, Dad."

"I ain't drunk enough. I ain't *half* drunk enough. Let's go for a little drift."

"But the net's all over . . . "

"I got a brand new net. Fine-twine, four-inch mesh. She'll pick up every salmon in the goddamned river. Ya hear that? Ya hear that, Elva? Ya hear that, devil? Yahooo!"

Bob's whoop echoed up and down the river. Bob and Shad listened. Bob had another drink, gave some to Shad.

"You know somethin', Shad? We could build a camp, you and me."

*

Before Nutbeam married and moved in with Shirley Ramsey, he lived in a little half-cave, half-camp in the forest on Todder Brook. The camp was so well camouflaged, so well hidden in the hillside with so few of its logs showing, that one could walk right past it and never know it was there. The roof of the camp was cleverly designed to look like part of the hill, actually *was* part of the hill. A deer once walked on Nutbeam's roof.

Although Dryfly was tired, he was too depressed to consider going home to bed. Instead, he went to Nutbeam's camp. He lit a match, found the lamp, lit it. He stretched out on the cot, hands behind his head, looking up at the poles, the ceiling. The poles still had much of their bark left on them. Nutbeam hadn't had much to work with when he built the camp.

Dryfly didn't know whether he was sad or angry, whether he wanted to cry or fight. It was very quiet in the camp — he could hear his heart beating. His heart was unaccustomed to carrying such a heavy load and drummed out messages of distress, perhaps despair.

"She's the only girl I ever loved," he thought.

There was something wrong with the word "loved." The tense was wrong. Dryfly knew very little about grammar, tenses and the like, but he knew that he didn't like the word "love" with a *d* on it. He didn't know about the word "ego," but had he known he wouldn't have liked it much either — "ego," the word that adds *d*s to words like "love" and often changes them completely, to words like "hate," "hurt," and "revenge."

Dryfly did not want revenge. If Dryfly was feeling any hatred, it was for himself for being so poor and backward. He could never hate Lillian Wallace. If Dryfly was feeling anything, it was hurt.

"I should've knowed," he thought. "I should've knowed I could never have something as good as Lillian. The best thing I can do is forget about her."

He tried forgetting her, but he couldn't stop envisioning her; she could have been standing direcly in front of him.

"You look sad," he whispered. "Don't look sad."

Tears welled from Dryfly's eyes.

"I love you. No need to look sad. Please? Just go off and be happy. I'll be sad for the rest of my life, but you be happy, okay?"

But at the moment, he didn't want her to go — be happy, yes, but not go. He didn't want her *ever* to leave, and he felt that perhaps she wouldn't leave — not his heart, anyway.

An hour passed before he had rationalized his predicament to any kind of tolerable compromise.

"I'll love her forever," he thought. "That's number one. I'll love her and keep her in my heart forever. And number two, I'll try for her. I'll try to do something with my life, make her proud of me. If she doesn't want me, at least she can like me, be proud of me, remember me. Maybe I can work something out. Maybe I can go to a school for older lads, or somethin'. I'm only sixteen. Maybe I can have her yet. Maybe I gotta earn her."

That was the end of his reverie, but he should have added, "Maybe she's gotta earn me," for ego's sake.

"I gotta go home," he thought. "I gotta work in the mornin'. I gotta work and earn money so I kin do somethin' with my life."

Dryfly was not happy, but he felt a little better. The tears had been good for him. He blew out the lamp and headed home. Clouds were creeping up from the west, but a few stars still shone — a breeze played in the trees, the mosquitoes hummed.

Dryfly was approaching the bridge when he heard something in the direction of the river, upstream. He stopped to listen. He heard a sound like that of a paddle thumping on the side of a canoe.

"Someone's drifting," he thought.

Then he heard a splash. A big salmon was trying to escape Bob Nash's four-inch mesh fine-twine net.

Then the lights came on. Two wardens were on the foot-bridge, and two more were in a canoe not more than thirty feet away from Bob and Shad. All four had lights as big as a man's face.

Dryfly could see the confused and vexed Bob Nash, the frightened Shadrack.

"Oh God!" thought Dryfly. "They're caught, surer than hell!"

"You lads are under arrest!" yelled a warden. "Just leave the net and take yer time and paddle ashore. No sense trying to escape. Keep that light on them, boys!"

Dryfly took refuge behind a chokecherry bush so he wouldn't be seen and suspected of watching.

Shad poled the canoe ashore, and he and Bob stepped out. Bob had been drunk, but the presence of the wardens waiting for him on the shore sobered him a bit. Shad was trembling like a leaf.

"They'll be charged for stealing a canoe, they'll lose their net and they'll have to pay a fine," thought Dryfly. "It'll ruin them. Bob'll lose his fishin' licence, guidin' licence. Something has to be done. But what?"

"Bob Nash, ain't it?" said one of the wardens.

"And his young fella," said another.

"Now, Bob, you should know better than to be out driftin'," said another warden. "I never thought I'd ketch you doin' the likes o' that!" This warden was getting out of his canoe.

"Evenin', Fred," said Bob.

"Don't you evenin' me! You're under arrest!" said Fred.

Dryfly had to think fast. He didn't know what he was going to do, but he knew he had to do something. Then, as if there was some kind of devil about, set on encouraging this sort of activity, an idea was driven into Dryfly's head. Dryfly suddenly knew exactly what he had to do.

"It might work," he thought as he ran to Helen Mac-Donald's. "It might just work."

He ran past Judge Martin's camp and up the hill. He pounded ten times on Helen MacDonald's door. He didn't wait for a response, but headed back to the river. When he ran past Judge Martin's again, he pounded on that door, too — just for safety. When he got back to the river, the wardens had already scolded Bob and Shad and had read them their rights.

"So, ya got anything to say for yourselves?" Fred was asking.

Bob started to say something.

"Bob! Shad!" yelled Dryfly on the run. "Bob! Shad!"

Dryfly approached.

"Dryfly! What?" Bob and Shad were looking at Dryfly as if

317

they thought he was crazy to be taking such a risk. Shad was trying to speak. Above all, Dryfly couldn't let Shadrack speak. Dryfly could only hope that Shad hadn't said too much already.

"I couldn't get Helen up!" yelled Dryfly. "And Judge Martin's not there. But I see that the wardens are already here." Dryfly sighed as if relieved.

"What in Judas cram'ny is goin' on here?" snapped the warden called Fred.

"Thank God, you're here," said Dryfly. Dry was puffing and panting from all the running. "Did ya git the net?"

"You're damned right we got the net. Who are you?"

"Dryfly Ramsey, sir. Did ya git the lads who was driftin'?"

"Right here. We got them all right. What business is . . . "

"No! No!" Dryfly was getting into character now: acting. "You got the wrong lads!"

"What do you mean, we got the wrong lads? We caught them in the act. You been watchin'?"

"No! No, I ain't been watchin, but I was goin' home from girlin' when I saw them lads driftin'!" Dryfly gestured upstream. "I've been trying to report it, but nobody around here has a telephone. While I've been runnin' around from house to house, Bob and Shad here have been chasin' the drifters and takin' up their net before anything got caught in it. Ain't that right, Shad?"

"That's the god's truth," said Shad.

"Look," said Dryfly, pointing to Helen MacDonald's. "Helen's light is on. She's up. She can tell ya that I was pounding on her door."

Helen MacDonald was standing, a silhouette against her open door, wondering what all the commotion was about. She could see the warden's lights, the men.

"What's goin' on down there?" she yelled. "Can't a woman get any peace and quiet around here?"

"It's all right, Helen! The wardens are here!" yelled Dryfly.

Shadrack Nash wanted to grin, but controlled it. He also controlled his desire to whoop and kiss Dryfly.

Bob Nash, drunk as he was, picked up on it, too.

"Dryfly's right," said Bob. "But I'm afraid we're all too

late. A salmon's already been caught. Struck 'er jist as we got to the net, and the lads, the drifters, got away. I'm sorry to have to tell ya in this way, Dryfly — I know how you always feel so bad about salmon dyin' in nets." Bob swung on the wardens. "Where the hell were you lads, anyway?" he snapped.

"Well, we . . . we . . . " stammered the warden. "Why the hell didn't you tell us this in the first place?"

Bob evaded the question, turned, put his hand on Shad's shoulder, looked at Dryfly.

"It's all right, boys," he said, shakin' his head. "It's just not a fit country to bring a young lad up in anymore."

The warden called Fred knew that this was a total, complete fabrication, but Fred hadn't really wanted to catch anyone. In Fred's opinion, there was nothing wrong with a man catching a few salmon . . . so long as he didn't try to sell them. Selling them was a different, more serious matter — it indicated greed. If Bob Nash was on the river drifting, he was probably just trying to get a salmon for the table. There was nothing wrong in that. And besides, the story was smart; Fred liked it. Fred was the boss.

"Ya don't believe that, do ya, Fred?" asked one of the younger wardens.

"Well, we don't know for sure," said Fred. "They could be telling the truth. And the real drifters could be gettin' away."

"That's crazy. These lads were driftin' and you know it."

"Yes, yes! Blame us!" snapped Bob. "Sure, we're to blame. Yes, these poor boys and me will always feel to blame for not savin' that poor little salmon, one of the good Lord's creatures! But, while you're blamin' us, them lads . . . them crim'nals are half way to Renous. Git after them, for Christ sake!"

"C'mon boys. We got no time to lose," said Fred, getting into the canoe.

"But, but . . . but . . . " The other wardens were totally awed, amazed.

"Karl and Ned, you lads go back to the truck, get to the next bridge below here. C'mon Sam, we ain't got all night."

Karl, Ned and Sam all looked at one another in disbelief, but shrugged and obeyed their boss.

In a minute, Bob, Shad and Dryfly were alone on the shore.

They all had a little drink from Bob's last pint. Bob and Shad were feeling very good. They had lost the net, but that was a small price to pay. Dryfly felt . . . not too bad, considering.

three

Dryfly awakened the next morning to the sound of music. It was coming from the other side of his curtained door, the kitchen. He could hear it raining, too. The light coming from his curtainless window was so grey and dim that he took it to be an hour earlier than it actually was. He snuggled down beneath his sheet and stared at the curtain.

The music stopped, an announcer took over, a commercial was played.

> *You'll wonder where the yellow went,*
> *When you brush your teeth with Pepsodent!*

Then, without a word of introduction, Hank Thompson sang:

> *There's a salmon-coloured girl,*
> *That sets my heart awhirl,*
> *Who lives along the Yukon far away . . .*

Dryfly tried to picture a salmon-coloured girl. He saw a scaly, silver face with red dots, a green forehead. "Maybe it's a Cains River salmon," he thought. The red dots tripled in size, the nose grew a bit, the chin hooked, the facial skin took on an orange tint.

Dryfly grinned at the thought of lifting some lady's fur-lined parka hood to see such a face.

He heard Nutbeam cough in the kitchen. Nutbeam was up listening to the radio, putting the kettle on. He came to the curtain, poked his head through the opening. Dryfly could not see the big, happy face smiling in at him, or the big nose,

321

but he could see the shape of the head and the big floppy ears silhouetted against the light of the kitchen.

"You awake, Dryfly?" asked Nutbeam.

"Yeah."

"You gettin' up?"

"Early yet."

"Time's comin' around . . . almost half-past seven."

Dryfly realized what was happening. The morning was so dark and grey that it only *seemed* early.

"Yeah, I'm gettin' up," said Dryfly.

Nutbeam disappeared, went back to the kettle, yawned. He hadn't slept well. He'd been too excited to sleep. Thoughts of a baby, a child, a son, a daughter, twins, triplets — the baby, Shirley and himself, the new home, the family occupied his thoughts most of the night. He thought of Dryfly, too. Dryfly didn't know yet. Nutbeam was very anxious to tell Dryfly. When Nutbeam told Dryfly that it was nearly half-past seven, it was really only quarter after.

Nutbeam emptied yesterday's tea into the slop bucket, spooned some Salada into the pot and added boiling water. He could hear Dryfly moving about his room. Shirley was still sleeping and that was good — he wanted to talk to his good friend, Dryfly, alone, man-to-man.

"Bringing the time around to twenty minutes after the hour," said the radio announcer. "We're under overcast skies; and it's raining here on Pleasant Street, so put on those rubber boots before you go tippy-toeing downtown to Stedman's big two-for-one sale! That's Stedman's, right here in beautiful down-town Newcastle."

Jim Reeves took over, sang:

> *When your lover cries, hold her close and*
> *   whisper low,*
> *Tears are only rain to make love grow.*

When Dryfly heard this song, his heart sank to the depths of his being.

"Lillian," he thought. "Damn!"

He had finished dressing and had intended to enter the kitchen. He sat on the bed and listened to Jim Reeves instead. Suddenly, he thought the room very gloomy, the rain depressing.

The salmon-coloured girl he had envisioned was replaced by the blonde, blue-eyed and beautiful Lillian Wallace. The salmon-coloured girl had lifted his spirits; Lillian Wallace had both hands on his aorta. His heart begged to have its contents released. Dryfly sighed deeply.

"What am I ever gonna do?" he thought. "What am I ever gonna do without Lillian? How am I ever gonna work, feelin' like this?"

The song ended. Dryfly stood, sighed again, entered the kitchen.

"Mornin', Dry," said Nutbeam, smiling. "You look like you lost your best friend. Have a hard night?"

"Tired, that's all," said Dryfly.

Dryfly went to the washstand, wiped his face with a damp cloth. Nutbeam poured him a cup of tea.

"Want some beans?" asked Nutbeam.

"No . . . tea's all right."

"You should eat something."

"Not hungry."

Nutbeam sat at the table. Dryfly joined him.

"Bob Nash was here last night," said Nutbeam.

"Yeah?"

"Yes, sir. Drinkin'."

"I saw 'im down by the river."

"I suppose a man has to have the odd toot. How's Lillian?"

"Good."

"Your mother's still in bed."

"Yeah."

"Gonna have a baby."

Dryfly nodded, sighed.

Nutbeam watched Dryfly for any indication that he was pleased with the announcement.

A minute went by, the radio playing.

"Well, I gotta get to work," said Dryfly finally, stood and went to the door. He stopped for a few seconds, turned. He had a broad smile on his face.

"Yeah!" he exclaimed.

Nutbeam beamed.

*

Hilda Porter had lived in Brennen Siding most of her life, teaching grades one to eight in the little one-room school. She taught Bob Nash when he was a boy, and she had taught Shadrack as well. But, like all the one-roomers, the Brennen Siding school closed its doors in the early 1960s, giving its occupants to the rural school in Blackville. From then on, all the Brennen Siding children had to travel to and from Blackville every day on a bus to get to school.

Hilda Porter was not qualified to teach in the rural school. She was forced to retire.

She boarded for twenty-five years in Brennen Siding with Dan Brennen, but her home, a fairly big house and several sheds and barns, was on the south side of the river across from Blackville. With no job, or reason to stay in Brennen Siding any longer, she moved home.

Hilda Porter was a spinster and a teacher. Everyone supposed she knew nothing about sex. Everyone knew, evidently by the condition of her farm, that she knew nothing about maintenance.

Hilda Porter needed a man.

At the age of seventy-five, she was not very interested in sex. She just needed a man to help around the place.

"I couldn't pay him much," she thought. "But, there'd be room and board; I could keep him in tobacco, give him money for a haircut."

Hilda was sitting in a rocking chair on her veranda. When she rocked, the floor creaked. She rocked slowly, afraid she might go through.

"I'm all alone in the world, and I need someone to look after me in my old age. Now who could a person get? Who could a person trust? I don't want some old coot you can't trust. Somebody young and able is what I need. Young enough to marry some young thing and have children. To tell the story

. . . to tell the story. Why didn't I tell it before now? Why didn't I make it a lesson in school? It wasn't part of the curriculum, but I could've told it and nobody would have known. I just kept putting it off, procrastinating as usual. Now, I'm getting old . . . I could have told lots of people, but now I'm getting old. Time goes so fast. When you're one year old, that one year is your whole lifetime; when you're ten years old, a year is only one-tenth of your life. I'm seventy-five. Time goes so fast. A day, even a week is but a moment in time. I should have written my book, written down the story, just in case . . . "

Hilda Porter thought about how she would tell the story.

"'Once upon a time among the shadowy ferns and trees of a little island called Tasmania, there lived a race of people like no other race on earth. These people hadn't a clue about the outside world.' Yes, yes, that would be a good beginning, just like Father told it. Then, I'll go into how they were nomadic, never building a village or a town; how they looked — small, long-legged, red-brown in colour. They had funny brows, deep-set eyes, big mouths and noses; both the men and women had beards. Must've been odd to see a woman with a beard. They weren't very strong and ran on all fours. And I might be the only person in the world who knows about them. I have to tell somebody. Father always said that if the story had've been told with enough conviction, Hitler might have thought twice about starting World War II. Surely, there must be somebody around that could look after the place, someone I could tell the story to, someone who could take the place over when I'm gone . . . "

*

Walking to work, Dryfly was soaked to the skin in the rain. When he arrived, neither Ducky nor Lindon was there. He waited in the building under the unshingled roof. Water poured through the cracks and holes above him.

He stood in the door cavity, waiting. He could see the misty river, the footbridge and the forest. Lindon would simply come over the hill when he saw Ducky coming. Ducky would come via the footbridge.

"A baby," thought Dryfly. "Mom's gonna have a baby, another Dryfly . . . or maybe Nutbeam."

Dryfly's thoughts fed him a picture of a baby with big floppy ears, a big mouth and nose. He grinned.

"No baby could ever look like Nutbeam," he thought. "But if it did, and had my chin, my stupid hair that always wants to part in the middle, and maybe some o' Mom's looks . . . "

In the words of Stan Tuney, Shirley Ramsey was "a hard-looking ticket." She was bent and figureless from having her first twelve children. Her hair was starting to turn gray and her mouth was wrinkled at the corners from the years of having so few teeth. Now that she had dentures, her smile looked unatural — the teeth seemed to leap out at you. Her lips had never been designed to accommodate such a store of ivory. Her eyes, ringed with what could have been exhaustion, or worry, were as dark as the molasses droppings on Ben Brooks's chair.

"Poor little baby," thought Dry. "Don't stand much of a chance for lookin' good. If ya don't look good, ya don't stand much of a chance of having it easy. Nobody wants ya."

Dryfly heard distant thunder. The rain slanted in. He stepped back a bit.

Across the river and upstream sat the Cabbage Island Salmon Club. Dry could see someone on the veranda dressed in a yellow raincoat. Including the dining camp, there were six camps in all. Bill Wallace and Lillian were staying in the lower camp, the first one. The person in the yellow raincoat was standing on the veranda of the lower camp.

Dryfly's heart began to ache. He thought he might be looking at Lillian from afar. He looked down at a mud puddle outside, in front of him. There was an angleworm in it.

"I just feel like you must feel," said Dryfly to the worm. "All white and wrinkled, like a wet toe. Gotta do something with my life. But what can I do? A little bit o' carpenter work — I'm learnin', anyway. I can pole a canoe. I know Palidin's trick for ketchin' salmon, if it really works. I could guide. I can play guiddar, and sing a bit. Wished I could sing like Jim Reeves, soft."

Dryfly thought of the song he'd heard earlier. Jim Reeves singing those words so deep and mellow had nearly brought tears to his eyes.

"Tears are only rain to make love grow," sang Dryfly. His voice sounded tiny in the empty shell that would be Bill Wallace's camp.

"There just ain't no future for me," he thought.

There was another roll and tumble of distant thunder.

"Thunder in the mornin', sailors take warnin'," thought Dryfly. He looked back to the club. The person in the yellow raincoat was running over the hill. He, or she, slowed to a walk at the bottom and started up the shore toward the footbridge.

"It's Lillian," thought Dryfly. "It's got to be Lillian. Nobody from around here would have a raincoat."

Lillian walked the shore to the footbridge, mounted the abutment and slowly (she was a little bit afraid on the bouncy bridge) made her way across. She had seen Dryfly walking to work earlier and needed to talk to him.

Lillian Wallace hadn't slept much all night, thinking of Dryfly, of their relationship. The night before, when he left and walked into the forest lit by the crimson sunset, she thought she would never see him again. The thought that she would never see this tall, thin, funny-looking boy again thoroughly depressed her.

"It had to be done," she whimpered, and, "Why do these things have to happen to me?"

The tears flowed. She went to her room and tried to reason things out, tried to convince herself that she had done the right thing. By the time midnight rolled around, she was thinking that "time" was the answer. Everything would get better with the passing of time. All this would just be a memory, or even forgotten about. This line of thinking didn't help. She didn't want to forget Dryfly Ramsey.

At one o'clock she was thinking how wonderful it would be if this chinny, big-nosed boy was to become successful, of how they could live somewhere, anywhere . . . here, even.

327

"It shouldn't matter where we live so long as we're not poor and unhappy. We could live in Dad's cottage, or build one of our own. I bet Dad has a million, maybe even many millions of dollars. Mom left him. She's living with an artist. Money didn't make Dad any happier. But, he has it — a whole bunch of it. We wouldn't always be poor."

At two o'clock Lillian was wondering if she had ruined everything.

"He might never come back. Why did I have to be so hasty? Why couldn't I just enjoy having him around and not worry about the future? Dryfly and I are adolescents. When I get depressed, Dad tells me that I'm not to worry, that what I'm feeling is only the pain of adolescence, that adolescence is one of the most lonely and difficult times of life. I guess the secret is to not do anything stupid, like have a baby. The secret is to not think about marriage and the future. The secret is to enjoy what we feel . . . "

At three o'clock, Lillian went to sleep.

At four o'clock, a Dungarvon mosquito found its way into her room.

"Hummmmmm."

It hummed about, up, down, all around the room, spotted Lillian.

"Hummmmmm," it went. "A delectable prospect, to be sure."

It zeroed in on Lillian's exposed neck, gorged itself and flew, on labouring wings, to the wall. There it sat to digest and remember the joy of feasting. It watched Lillian, wishing it had brought its friends and family along. There was plenty of blood for everyone.

At five o'clock, Lillian awoke, scratched her neck, turned on the light, thought of Dryfly. She could hear the rain on the roof and the window.

"I hope he didn't go into the woods and get lost," she thought. "I love him very much."

At six, her father arose and immediately went to fish with Bert Todder. Old Fish Hog didn't even bother to have a cup of coffee. He thought the fishing was better in the rain.

Lillian killed time until, at seven o'clock, she gave a sigh of relief. She saw Dryfly crossing the footbridge on his way to work.

She put on her raincoat. She had to talk to Dryfly.

Dryfly watched her approach, heart pounding in his chest. He felt wet and miserable and knew he looked that way. Strands of hair clung to his forehead; you could see his skin through the thin material of his soaking-wet shirt. The worn, denim jeans felt tight on his hips and thighs.

The hood of Lillian's raincoat was up, her head bent forward, he could not see her eyes. All he could see were her hands and her tanned, sandalled feet.

There was no doorstep. Without greeting, he offered his hand to assist her into the camp.

She threw back her hood and graced him with her big blue eyes.

"I'm all wet," said Dry. He half chuckled, half whimpered.

Then, they didn't say anything. They just hugged each other for ten whole minutes. They hugged away all thoughts of time, the past, the present and the future; they hugged away money and sophistication; they hugged away material values and security; they hugged away loneliness and fear. Lillian and Dryfly hugged until they were both smiling.

It was raining. When they pulled apart, they saw no need to dry their tears.

An hour later Lillian Wallace was back at the club and Dryfly Ramsey was home. It was obvious that he had the day off. They had made plans to meet later, after the rain.

Lillian left her raincoat and sandals on the veranda. Her jeans were wet. She went to the bedroom to change.

The mosquito was still on the wall. It saw her enter the room, sit on the bed. It saw her remove her clothes to reveal the shapely body, the virgin-pink nipples. It heard her speak to the room.

Lillian was thinking about Dryfly and his daisy story. She smiled a smile that would inspire Bill Wallace to tip their dentist.

"You can't see the one you love too much," she said.

"Hummmmmm," went the mosquito, which translated meant: "Good blood in that girl."

*

Bert Todder didn't know for sure how much land he owned, but thought it was somewhere between two and three hundred acres. Ninety percent of the property consisted of lumberland; the other ten percent made up the field where his house, barn and sheds sat. The hillside that sloped to the river was part of the field. He owned the shore in front and the mouth of Todder Brook.

The lumberland wasn't worth much — mostly budworm-eaten fir and spruce, many of which had already fallen in the wind. The field wasn't worth much either — there wasn't enough hay on it to keep a cow alive.

Standing looking out from the mouth of Todder Brook, you face the upper end of Cabbage Island. Bert, unfortunately, owned the wrong side of the island for good fishing. The salmon only ran Bert's side of the island when the water was very high. Also, a few came into the cool waters of his brook when the water in the river was very warm, but not many — not enough to give the shore much value.

Bill Wallace put a ten-thousand-dollar value on the shore and made Bert an offer. Bill Wallace was standing in the river fishing when he made the offer.

"Say, Bert!" he called. "How's about selling me that shore of yours? I'll give you a thousand dollahs for it. You could do with a thousand dollahs, huh Bert?"

Bert was standing on the shore. He had his chest waders on, but he couldn't have been wetter, from the top up. Bert Todder didn't have a raincoat like the green fifty-dollar L.L. Bean special William Wallace had. Bert Todder didn't have a raincoat at all.

Bert could hardly see Bill for the falling rain. Bert Todder couldn't keep his pipe lit and was getting dizzy from sucking the juice out of the stem.

"Puff, puff, puff, puff, puff!" On the last puff the stem slipped clear to the bowl, into his mouth.

There was so much moisture in the air that Bill was having trouble getting his line out — he had to wade deeper, shorten his cast.

The rain was beginning to find its way into Bert's waders. It trickled down his back, tickle-tickle-tickle, all the way down, down, down, to his boot. Bert Todder did not answer or respond in any way to whatever it was that Bill Wallace had said. Bert Todder was so angry about his situation that he wouldn't have answered Bill, even if he had heard him over the din of falling rain and the river rushing through Bill's legs.

When Bill didn't get a response, he thought, "I guess this is not a good way or time to discuss business. Bert's probably madder than a wet . . . guide."

Bill looked into the water. Several chubs played around his feet. The water was beginning to look smoky, a bit sandy; Bill was picking up the odd strand of grass on his line.

"It's not too bad yet," thought Bill and moved downstream a few steps, made another cast.

Bawny Google,
With the goo-goo-googly eyes!
Bawny Google had a wife three times his size!

Bill Wallace sang "Barney Google" in a deep, nasal, arrogant Yankee baritone. Bill Wallace was very much enjoying fishing in the rain.

"Maybe I should change flies," he thought. "A bigger fly might work bettah now that the watah's rising. I'll consult Bert."

Bill reeled in, waded ashore.

Bert was glad to see Bill coming in.

"Finally!" thought Bert. "Finally, we can go home!"

"Bert, old buddy, you should get yourself a raincoat!" Bill was saying as he approached. "That coat you have on must leak like a basket! What fly do you suggest, Bert? I was thinking maybe I'd try a big Buttahfly."

"Don't matter what you try now that the water's raisin'," said Bert. "Ya ain't gonna git anythin'."

Bert Todder could smell garlic on Bill Wallace's breath. Bert hadn't smelled garlic before and didn't know what it was.

"Got a fart in yer waders, have you?" grinned Bert.

Bill didn't know what Bert was referring to. He thought that Bert must have been hearing his waders squeaking, rubber on rubber, as he waded ashore.

"That's my wadahs you're hearing, Bert," said Bill.

"Somethin' like that'll rot yer waders!" said Bert. "Tee, hee, hee, sob, snort, sniff. Let's go home."

"Home! What do you want to go home for?"

"Gittin' wet, water's raisin'; no fishin' . . . water's raisin'."

"Ah! Yeah . . . well, yes . . . ah, maybe just one more run-through . . . ah, hell, okay, let's get out of here, go back to the camp." Bill was thinking that it might pay to be very nice to Bert Todder. "Maybe we'll have a game of cahds latah."

Bert hadn't expected Bill to agree so quickly. He thought that maybe he had over-emphasized his desire to leave. Bert thought that there was a chance that he was being rude, and Bert would never be rude to anyone intentionally.

"I mean, ya kin stay at 'er if ya want, now, but there's not much sense, if ya know what I mean." Bert was sounding apologetic.

"C'mon, Bert! You'll catch pneumonia!"

"It don't matter to me none, now. I'm all wet anyway, if ya know what I mean. And the water's raisin'. There won't be no sense in comin' back out later. This rain will tie up the fishin' for two or three days, like. Ya might as well git 'em now before the water gets too dirty. Put on a Butterfly! A big number six."

"Well, Christ! I don't know . . . "

"Go ahead! Give 'er hell! Ya never know! Ya might pick one up!"

"Well, Okay, Bert, if you insist. Let's see." Bill checked his watch. "Lunch is at noon. We have an hour."

"Not much sense of tryin' it just for an hour, though," said Bert. "And I'm gettin' cold, if ya know what I mean. It's not the wet so much as the cold . . . puff, puff, puff. Maybe we should head back to the camp. I don't see anybody else out. Look. I guess that tells us somethin'."

"Well, whatever you say, Bert. You're the guide."

"I guess we'll head 'er back then. Wanna quit?"

"Whatever you want to do, Bert."

"I'm gittin' cold, wet. Let's go, wha'?"

"I'll just give it one more quick little run," said Bill. "Then we'll go back to the camp, have a drink, play some cahds. Dryfly will be there, I imagine — I doubt if they're working today — and maybe Lindon would play. Can't do much else in this rain. I'll just give it a few more minutes, okay, Bert?"

"Sure! Sure! Sure! Go right to 'er! Fish! Put on a big Butterfly! Fish! That's what yer here for!"

Bill Wallace tied on a number six Butterfly and waded back into the river. He made a few casts, rolled a salmon.

"I can't leave for a while yet," thought Bill.

Bill thought he could hear Bert Todder laugh about something on the shore. "Tee, hee, hee, sob, snort, sniff!"

"Or is he crying?"

Bill shrugged, made another cast. He fished until one o'clock.

*

Dryfly went home and changed into his dry jeans and shirt. He changed his socks, one of which was heelless, and pulled on his jetboots. Then he began to pace around the house, wishing that the rain would ease enough for him to get to the club to see Lillian.

It rained as hard as it could until one-thirty in the afternoon, then eased to a drizzle and stopped. Dryfly hurried to the club, knocked lightly on Bill Wallace's door.

"Come in!" yelled Bill.

Dryfly entered.

Lillian was in her room, heard Dryfly knock and enter. She went to greet him.

"What are you two planning this afternoon?" asked Bill.

"I thought we might listen to some music," said Lillian. "I thought Dryfly might like hearing the Beatles and the Dave Clark Five."

"I was going to fish," said Bill. "But the watah's rising so fast you can't see the bottom for sand and grass. Bert Todder's gone home to change. I told him to go and get Lindon Tucker. We thought we'd have a game of cahds. You two are welcome to join us, if you want. Sit down, Dryfly."

Bill Wallace was sitting on the sofa, sipping from a glass of Teacher's Highland Cream. He preferred Glen Livet, but he couldn't get it in Newcastle. He was dressed in a blue shirt, plaid shorts and sandals.

Dryfly sat in an armchair, Lillian sat beside her father.

"I don't play much cards," said Dryfly.

Dryfly was feeling a bit nervous and self-conscious. To Dryfly, Bill Wallace was a complete mystery; he could have been from outer space. Bill talked loud, often used words that Dryfly didn't know the meaning of; he bubbled with confidence; he seemed to be forever in a hurry, never relaxed; he had travelled the world and had so much money. Dryfly quite often found himself staring at Bill to see if seeing so much of the world might have left some sort of aura on or about his face. Bill Wallace had been to Greece — might Dryfly see the Acropolis in his eyes? Was that the shadow of the pyramids on his cheek? The Empire State Building on his nose? St. Peter's Basilica on his ear? Also, Dryfly was more than a just little embarrassed to see a grown man in short pants.

"I've been wanting to talk to you, Dryfly," said Bill.

Dryfly slumped, thinking that he must have done something wrong, that perhaps Bill didn't want him around Lillian.

"I've been thinking about you," continued Bill. "How old are you?"

"Sixteen," said Dryfly. He looked to Lillian for support.

"Dryfly, my boy, I like you. You've been good company for Lillian. I like your attitude. You're not, shall we say, influenced by this superfluous bullshit of the big city. In short, I think you might be able to assist me in a little matter. Dryfly, how would you like a part-time job?"

"Ah . . . sure," said Dryfly.

"Lillian tells me that you don't go to school."

"Quit . . . a long time ago," said Dryfly.

"Well, I was thinking I'd make you a proposition. As you

know, I'm building a cottage. And when that's finished I plan to put up a guest house, maybe two. Last winter, someone came into this one and drank all my liquor, smoked all my cigars, partied, left the place in a mess. Christ! You can't leave anything around here! If they'd steal from the Cabbage Island Salmon Club, they'd steal from my own place. Get it?"

"Yeah." Dryfly nodded and hoped he wasn't blushing or giving any indication that it was he and Shad that had consumed Bill's liquor and smoked the cigars.

"So, how would you like to look after the place for me?" asked Bill.

Bill Wallace suspected that it might have been Shadrack and Dryfly who were doing the stealing, and to hire Dryfly, to make him responsible, was a sure way of preventing it from happening again.

Dryfly didn't know what to say. The job of looking after Bill's property should actually go to Lindon Tucker. The land had originally belonged to Lindon.

Dryfly took a chance and asked, "What about Lindon Tucker?"

"What about Lindon Tucker! Poor Lindon couldn't look after a chicken coop. He's too damned agreeable! Picture it, kids: Lindon catches a thief going into my cottage . . . the thief says, 'I'm just going to take some of this stuff, Lindon, then I thought I'd burn the place. Got a match, Lindon?' 'Oh, yeah, yeah, yep! Got a match, yep, yep, yep, yep.'" Bill Wallace grinned at his own ability to impersonate Lindon Tucker.

"You see? I need someone young and smart . . . and educated. I'll be sending some clients of mine up here. They'll need things, a guide, someone to get them this and that. I need someone that can mend the shutters, that can paint, patch the roof, mow the grass."

Dryfly nodded.

"Now, here's my proposition," said Bill. "I'll give you a hundred dollars a month for looking after my place and going back to school. You'll make more when you're guiding in the summer, of course."

"I . . . I . . . " Dryfly didn't know what to say. A hundred dollars a month was more money than he had ever dreamed about earning. Looking after a place like Bill's would be the best job in the whole world. But go back to school? How could he go back to school? Dryfly needed time to think.

Lillian didn't know if she liked the idea or not, either. She knew her father to be a hard man to work for. He was hard on everybody. He had been hard on her mother and was hard on her. She didn't want her father to give Dryfly a hard time.

"But school would be good for Dry," she thought. "And the money . . . "

Bill Wallace couldn't have cared less if Dryfly ever went to school. School would simply occupy Dryfly's idle time, give him something to do other than hang around the cottage all the time.

"You don't have to give me an answer today," said Bill. "I'll be around for another week, and I'm coming back up in September. If you're in school in September, I'll write you a cheque."

Dryfly nodded. "Okay," he said.

The conversation ended just in time. Bert Todder knocked on the door. He had Lindon Tucker with him.

Bill poured Bert and Lindon a drink. Lillian went to the kitchen and returned with some Pepsi for Dryfly and herself. Bill found a deck of playing cards, and they all sat around the dining table.

"So, what games do you know?" asked Bill.

Bill knew many card games, but he thought hearts or bridge or some of the games he liked would be too difficult for Bert and Lindon to learn. He liked to play with knowledgeable players and had little tolerance for anyone who played stupidly — it was a waste of his valuable time. He preferred dealer's choice himself, but he didn't want to play poker with his daughter and these poor people who might get upset if they lost a few dollars.

"Auction," said Bert. "We generally play auction forty-five around here."

"Okay," said Bill. "I've never heard of it, but I'll learn it. How's it played?"

"Nothin' to it," said Bert, shuffling the deck.

"Nothin', nothin', nothin' to it, nothin' to it. Auction, yeah. Forty-five. Auction, yeah. Anyone, anyone, anyone kin learn auction, eh Bert, pal?" said Lindon Tucker.

Bert dealt three and two to everyone, then put four cards in the centre of the table.

"That's the kitty," said Bert.

"So how do we play this?" asked Lillian.

"Well," said Bert, "it's highest in red and lowest in black. The five is the best trump. The second best trump is the jack, the third is the ace of hearts. After that comes the ace of trump, the king and the queen. In red, the best trump after the queen is the ten, in black it's the two, then the three and the four, like that. Now when you're off trump, the ace of diamonds is the poorest card in the deck, but remember the ace of hearts is always trump and always beats the ace of trump, but not the five or the jack of trump. When you're off trump, a five is just like any other card and won't beat a red six, although it will beat a black six, know what I mean?"

"Ah . . . we'd better take it one step at a time," suggested Bill. "What do we do first?"

"Well, the first thing you have to do is look at yer cards. If you got a pretty good hand, say a five and a few trumps, you put in a bid to the dealer. The bidding always starts at the left of the dealer. You can bid twenty, twenty-five and thirty for sixty. If you lose a hand on a thirty for sixty bid, you go back thirty; if you win them all, you go ahead sixty. If you're in the hole, you can bid sixty for a hundred and twenty . That works the same way, back sixty ahead a hundred and twenty. The best trump is worth ten, everything else is worth five."

"So, the five is always worth ten?" asked Bill.

"Only when it's trump, old buddy, pal, only when it's trump," put in Lindon.

"Now, you have to pick your best suit and bid," said Bert.

"Okay," said Bill. "Twenty."

"All right," said Bert. "I'll let you have it this time, jist fer learnin'. Now you take the kitty."

Bill picked up the four cards from the centre of the table. He now had nine.

THE BRENNEN SIDING TRILOGY

"Now you pick a suit," said Bert. "Throw the rest of your cards away and draw what you need to bring you up to five. Remember, they run five, jack, ace, king, queen, like that. Except when you're off trump, the two of black beats the three and the red ten beats the nine. Lowest in black, highest in red, except for the face cards, which run pretty much the same all the time. When you're off trump the king beats the queen and they both beat the jack."

"You'll learn, old boy! Nothin' to it, nothin' to it! You'll learn, learn it, you'll learn it, won't he, Bert? No trouble, no trouble, nothin' to it," said Lindon.

The game began.

Dryfly had a hard time concentrating on the card game.

Dryfly had a great deal to think about.

*

Elva Nash spent the morning doing things.

When Elva Nash washed the dishes, she set a cup down so hard that she broke the handle. When she put it into the garbage, she did so with such virulence that she shattered the rest of it. When she put the last dish up, she slammed the cupboard door so hard that it sprang back open again. When she put the last knife away, she slammed the drawer shut.

She knew that Bob and Shad were hanging around the house because of the rain, but she preferred to think that they were just being lazy. Bob was reading a filthy magazine in the parlour, and Shad was listening to filthy music on the radio.

"They'd have to be sitting around the parlour on the very day I want to clean it!" she thought, and grabbed the broom.

She stomped into the parlour. Bob was sitting in his rocking chair reading *Outdoor Life* — an article about trout fishing in Arizona.

Elva started sweeping around and under the rocking chair. "Move," she said.

Bob moved the chair two feet to the right.

When Elva finished sweeping the area where the chair had

been, she moved to its new location and once again started sweeping around and under it.

"Move your feet!" she snapped.

Bob lifted his feet.

Sweep, sweep, sweep.

Elva needed the chair moved again.

"It's too bad you couldn't get stuck in the way a little more!" was how she asked Bob to move it.

Bob was hung over and irritable.

"What are you doing, woman?" he snapped.

"I'm trying T-R-Y-I-N-G to clean C-L-E-A-N the house!" yelled Elva.

"Well, why can't you C-L-E-A-N somewhere else?"

"Why don't you read your filthy paper somewhere else?"

"You never thought o' sweepin', until you saw me readin', did ya?"

"Listen to 'im! Listen to the old, old, old, old devil comin' out of him! Out runnin' the roads, drinkin' that dirty old liquor! You're a good one to complain about givin' money to a church!"

"Give money to a church, yes! But John Kaston ain't my church!"

"What did ya do, spend the evenin' with Shirley Ramsey? She's good enough for ya, I say."

Shad was on the sofa, trying to hear the radio.

"Why don't you two get yourselves a set o' boxin' gloves!" he yelled.

"Look!" said Elva, pointing the broom at Shad, as if she had just spotted a turd on the sofa. "Look! Look at old, old, old Buck Ramsey, would ya!"

She lost control, hit Shad on the leg with the broom.

Shad sprang to his feet.

"Sit down, Shad!" yelled Bob.

"What's wrong with you?" Shad yelled at his mother.

Elva didn't know about menopause. She yelled, "What's wrong with me? I'm a good God-fearin' woman, that's what's wrong with me!"

"Jesus!" spat Shad.

"DON'T YOU SWEAR IN THIS HOUSE!" screamed Elva.

"Shad! Go to your room!" yelled Bob.

Shad started to retaliate, saw the futility in it, sighed and went to his room, flopped down on the bed. Round one was over and he had lost. He could hear Bob and Elva battling round two in the parlour.

"Gettin' worse all the time," thought Shad. "I can't handle it anymore. I gotta git out o' here."

Shad closed his eyes and tried to shut out the sound of his parents fighting. He thought of the only thing he knew that would pacify him: the river.

He pictured himself poling a canoe up the calm Dungarvon in the moonlight, fireflies flickering, the scent of lilac in the air.

Shad knew the time was coming when he'd have to leave, get a job in the woods, or the mill in Blackville, maybe in Fredericton or Moncton. He had no misgivings about leaving home. It would be better all around for everybody if he left. But he wished he could take the river with him.

"It was nice being out on the river with Dad last night," thought Shad. "It was like he was a friend, Dryfly, or somebody. . . and we'd have been caught, only for Dry. Dry's a good lad. He's got Lillian and everything."

Shad heard a door slam, then quietude.

Bob had left the house.

"Escapin' Mom," thought Shad. "Gone to Bernie Hanley's store, prob'ly . . . or maybe to get drunk again."

Shad got up from the bed, went to his dresser and inspected himself in the mirror. He combed his hair for ten minutes.

"I'd go to Blackville," he thought, "but I ain't got no money." Comb, comb, comb.

A knock sounded on his door.

"Yeah?" yelled Shad.

"Your lunch is ready," said Elva.

four

When Lindon sold his shore to Bill Wallace for a thousand dollars, he had had looking after the camp in mind. He thought he'd have money in the bank and another fifty dollars or more coming in every month. Everyone else who ever sold their property to an American got to look after their place, so Lindon assumed it would be that way with him and Bill.

He mentioned this several times at the store and on the job, so Dryfly knew it.

"Oh yeah, yeah, yeah! I'll be lookin' after this place, yeah. Oh yeah, yeah," said Lindon, then sang, "Shave and a haircut, pea soup!"

It was Saturday and they were shingling the cabin. They usually quit early on Saturdays and they didn't work at all on Sundays. They also figured they might get paid today. Thus, Lindon and Dryfly were in a good mood.

Ducky, as usual, was not in a good mood. The rain had held him back a day. He worked Dryfly and Lindon as hard as he could, and he kept them on the site until six o'clock, at which time he reluctantly paid them. Dryfly went home with the most money he ever had in his life — three hundred and six dollars for three weeks' work.

When Dryfly got home, supper was on the table — canned beans and bakers' bread.

"No more of them old home-made beans," Nutbean declared.

There was also a bottle of store-bought mustard pickles on the table.

"You know what I'm gonna start doin', Dryfly?" asked Nutbeam.

"No. What?" asked Dryfly with a mouth full of beans. He was hungry, eating ravenously.

"I'm gonna start makin' cows and ducks and stuff!"

When Dryfly heard this, his mouth full of beans spurted all the way across the kitchen to land and sizzle on the stove. He took it that Nutbeam had it in mind to make enough meat for the winter — canned beans, store-bought bread and pickles, wooden meat.

"Lawn ornaments," explained Nutbeam. "Cows, moose, ducks, windmills, stuff like that for the lawn! The new house is gonna have a lawn in front!"

"Always wanted a lawn with nice ornaments on it," said Shirley.

Nutbeam was getting excited about building the house. He was making plans. With a purple crayon he had drawn a picture of what he thought the house should look like.

"I was thinkin' we'd put in an indoor toilet and a sink," he announced. "Maybe later, even a tub or a shower. Shirley's got a good idea with the car tires cut in two, the culvert ends, but I think they should be painted white, or maybe red to match the trim on the house. Did I tell ya that I'm gonna paint the house orange?"

"Yeah," said Dryfly.

"A nice orange or yellow with red trim," said Shirley.

"Should be all right," said Dryfly. "I got paid today . . . three hundred and six dollars. Good money, eh?"

"That's real good, dear. What're ya gonna do with it?" asked Shirley.

Dryfly shrugged. "Don't know," he said. "Give some to you lads and spend the rest, I guess."

"I hope you don't start spending money like your father used to. I remember one time I gave him ten dollars from my family allowance check. He went and stayed away all night. When he came home in the mornin', I asked him what he'd done with it. Know what he said to me?" Shirley grinned. Her dentures looked too big for her mouth. "He said, 'I bought a case o' beer, a package o' tobacco an' spent the rest foolish.'"

Nutbeam laughed heartily. His mouth looked like a watermelon wedge with teeth. Dryfly laughed, too, and dished himself up some more beans.

"Two hundred and fifty all right?" he asked.

"That'd be a great help, dear," said Shirley. "You'll have fifty-six dollars left to buy clothes with."

"Yeah, and I'll be makin' another three or four hundred, I figure."

"And I got a thousand put away in the shoe box," put in Nutbeam. "We should be able to build quite a house with fourteen or fifteen hundred dollars."

"Hope so," said Dryfly. "Know what else? Bill Wallace wants me to look after his camp, said he'd pay me a hundred dollars a month, year round."

Nutbeam grinned, reached his arm clear across the table and messed up Dry's hair.

Shirley looked pleased, too, but the first thing that entered her mind was Lindon Tucker.

"What about Lindon?" she asked. "I would've thought that he'd get the job."

"I don't know . . . guess he thinks Lindon can't do it, or somethin'," said Dryfly.

"Lindon'll be awful ugly about that. He's s'posed to have an awful bad temper when he loses it. Someone teased him too far once, and I heard he choked 'im pretty near to death, right black in the face." Shirley told Dryfly this with great conviction. She didn't know that the story originated with Stan Tuney and was all lies.

"I don't know," said Dryfly. "There's a ketch, anyway. He wants me to go back to school."

"I wouldn't let Lindon Tucker stand in my way," said Nutbeam seriously. "This is a good chance for you, Dry."

"I know, but I'd have to go to school with a bunch o' kids," said Dry. He stopped eating, pushed his chair back.

"That wouldn't be much fun for you, would it, dear?" asked Shirley.

Dryfly gave a little negative shake of his head, stared at his plate.

"Would you be going to Blackville School?" asked Nutbeam.

"I guess so," said Dry.

"Well, there now! Shad goes to that school. You and Shad'll be together!"

"Shad's in a lot higher grade than I am. I've only got grade five."

"So?"

"So, I'd be in a room with a bunch o' little kids."

"So?"

"So, that'd look pretty stupid, wouldn't it?"

"That don't matter! Look stupid! You'll get learned . . . and you'll get the last laugh!"

"I don't know. "

"And a hundred dollars a month! You should do it, I say."

"What d'ya think, Mom?"

"Do what you want, dear. There's lotsa smart men with no learnin'."

＊

Hilda Porter sat in the rocking chair on her veranda. She was a little bit afraid — she had just returned from the bathroom.

"I'm feeling pretty well," she thought. "A little bowel problem, but at my age. I don't like blood, but at my age. When my grandmother had that, the doctor gave her a year, and sure enough . . . I'm a lot like my grandmother, dark, small, thin, withered. I don't think I ever saw her smile. She always had a look . . . amusement, but never a smile. Grammy was the homeliest woman that ever walked, and I grew up looking just like her. Everybody thinks I'm a hundred. I'm only seventy-five . . . wrinkled . . . "

Hilda looked at the thin skin on the back of her hand, the arteries and veins, the tan.

"I was always tanned, even in the winter. Maybe old Lawrence Porter did have a special interest in Tasmania, more than just the story of some young Englishmen. He saw them dig up Trucanini, the old woman. Gracious sakes, how he must have felt!"

There was a hornets' nest beneath the veranda. Hilda watched a hornet clip the wings of a housefly and carry it to the little hole in the floor.

"Gonna be a good winter," she thought. "The nests are low."

From the direction of the river came the lonesome call of a bird. Hilda thought it might be a cuckoo? a pigeon? an owl? She shrugged, not knowing.

"They ate roots and berries, lizards and snakes," she thought. "They carried heavy spears and fought funny little battles. When a man got killed, the battle was over — no more fighting. Seems civilized to me. But they couldn't talk very well, had a funny language — no linking grammar: moon, fire, dance. Autumn, happy time. Bodies all painted in red ochre, dancing, sleeping in hollow trees like elves, or in little lean-tos with seashells stuck on top to keep the rain out. The English thought they were abominations. "

Hilda Porter dared to rock, the floor creaking beneath the runners of her chair.

"Have to get this floor fixed. Need a man," she thought.

"Maybe it's all meant to be, and a person is crazy to be thinking about it . . . meant to be . . . everything that is, is meant to be. That rules out the abomination part of it. And the prisoners, the killers, rapists, thieves the English sent there, were meant to be. Or were they? Would a sane man behead another man and tie the head around his wife's neck? Would sane men hunt other men like animals in the name of Christ, in the name of land, in the name of taking over? The prisoners were sent there. The prisoners never meant to be prisoners. They meant to be free, rich. Tasmania was a prison."

Hilda Porter made a quick decision, stood.

"Meant to be or not, things happen," she said aloud to the chair that was still rocking.

She went into the house and found her writing paper — the stuff with the violets across the top and the bottom — picked up a pen and sat at the kitchen table.

"I could write a story, maybe even a book. Always wanted to write a book. I could write the story of Trucanini's life. What a story that would be! The story of a lonely old woman, the last of her people."

Hilda wrote: "Once upon a time," sighed, thought for a moment, then added, "there was a little girl."

"One is only little for a little while," she thought. "Youth is so . . . fleeting. When you're young you think you have so much time to do everything. My father used to say, 'I'll just work at the mill for a few years and then *do* something with my life.' Poor father . . . did a million things . . . but nothing that he *wanted* to do. He wanted to sail, but never got around to it. He wanted to live in the city, but procrastinated until it was too late. We all have our dreams when we're young. I wanted to write a book, be a famous author."

Hilda stared at the words in front of her. "Once upon a time there was a little girl," she read, added a semicolon, wrote: "A little girl who wanted to do things — a little girl with dreams of faraway islands and men."

"That wasn't all that difficult," thought Hilda. "I've started my book. I could have started it years ago. I could've gotten a man, too. I spent all those years in Brennen Siding teaching snotty-nosed kids, reading. I must have read a thousand books. Not that reading is bad, but I wasted so much time. All I had to do was put down the book I was reading, pick up a pen and start writing. Maybe if I had started writing it would have used up my dreaming time . . . my free time could have been used for experiencing, doing other things I wanted to do. People would have seen a spark, a glimmer of ambition, an interesting person."

*

When Dryfly went to the outhouse, the first thing he saw was a roll of toilet paper. He couldn't recall ever seeing toilet paper there before — catalogues and newspapers, yes, but never *real* toilet paper.

"Store-bought bread and pickles, canned beans and now toilet paper," he thought. "What next?"

Dryfly dropped his pants and sat over the hole. The flies buzzed beneath him. He was feeling good. He hummed a little tune.

"What tune is that?" he asked himself and hummed it again.

"Kinda ketchy, kinda different. Never heard it before, I don't think. Jist made it up myself. Kinda like it."

Later, in his room, Dryfly hummed and diddled his new melody again and played his guitar. He gave it some rhythm and picked up a pencil.

He wrote, "Here I am again, standing in the rain" on a piece of paper. He sang the words ten or fifteen times, then wrote, "It's what I get for being such a fool."

He was getting excited.

"This is great!" he thought. "My very own song! There's nothing to it! This is how it's done! I'm a song writer!"

"Mom!" he called. "How do you spell 'teardrops'?"

"T-E-A-R-D-R-O-P-S," yelled Shirley.

A half-hour later, he yelled out again.

"Mom! How do you spell 'evilest'?"

"I don't know, dear!" yelled Shirley.

Shirley and Nutbeam were in the kitchen. Shirley was darning the heel of Dryfly's sock, Nutbeam was making a rabbit out of a piece of board. They could hear Dryfly's great new composition coming from behind his curtain door. They couldn't make out the words, but they could hear the music.

"What's that song he's singin'?" asked Shirley.

"Ooga ooga wishka," said Nutbeam.

Shirley nodded, recognizing it.

"'The Squaws along the Yukon,'" she said.

*

Shadrack Nash went through every pocket in the house. He found thirty-five cents in Bob's suit pants and a quarter in Elva's winter coat. He found eleven cents in Elva's purse and three more in her pins and needle basket. Then, dressed for the in crowd, he headed over the river.

He went to the Tuney Brook bridge where he waited for Dryfly.

Dryfly came later than usual. By the time they met, Shad had grown impatient. Time was an important factor — the later he left, the fewer chances he'd have of catching a ride to Blackville.

"Where were you?" asked Shad.

"Home. Where you goin' all dressed up?"

"Where ya think?"

"Dance tonight?"

"Lyman MacPhee and the Cornpoppers."

"Public Hall?"

"Gary Perkins got a new guiddar and amplifier."

"Kin 'e play?"

"We're startin' a band."

"When?"

"Want to be in it?"

"Don't know."

"We kin practise in Gary's basement."

"Don't know . . . "

"Oh, ah . . . Dry?"

"Headin' to Lillian's."

"You couldn't lend me five dollars, could ya?"

Dryfly didn't hesitate, reached into his pocket and gave Shad five dollars. Dryfly was glad to be able to do it. It made him feel good.

"Well, I gotta be goin'," said Shad.

"Gonna be around later?"

"Might."

"See ya," said Dryfly.

They separated, Dryfly heading for the Cabbage Island Salmon Club, Shadrack for the Gordon Road. When they were about twenty yards apart, Shad turned and called to Dry.

"Dry!"

Dryfly stopped, turned, waited.

"Ah, thanks for the other night!" said Shadrack grinning.

Dryfly grinned, too. "See ya later," he called.

The moon rose like a bubble, a sperm whale fart from the sea. The whiskers of Acadian fishermen grew erect. It crept up the river, quarreled with the rapids. Silver maples tittered. It swept inland to light up the garbage dumps and swamp puddles. Aluminum pie plates challenged it. It twinkled in beads of dew on spider webs, glimmered in moose eyes. It sent frogs, grasshoppers, salmon and the hearts of young lovers and lords a-leaping.

Dryfly saw the breeze sweeping the smooth Dungarvon,

spreading moonlit ripples here and there; he saw the forest kissed with moonlit haze, the moon itself. He saw the dew-laden fields tapering from river to forest between their rail fences — fireflies flickering. He saw the footbridge, the little homes, their windows. He saw the moon reflecting like stars in Lillian Wallace's eyes. He saw her lips and hair.

Lillian, too, could see the summer, smell its perfume, feel its breath. She could see Dryfly, blue in the moonlight, staring out at the river.

"His hair is too long," she thought, "and so is his nose. He looks like a fairy tale prince. He's looking at the river . . . *his* river. Lord of the river."

Dryfly was thinking of an old joke, wondering if Lillian had heard it.

"It was on a night like this that Dan Brennen's pig disappeared," he said.

"A pig disappeared? What happened to it?"

"Nothin' around the sty was disturbed or anything, and there were no tracks. But Dan knew right away that it was a bear that done it."

"How did he know that?"

"The pig squealed on him."

"You're incorrigible, Dryfly," said Lillian and Dryfly didn't know whether she thought his joke funny or not.

They sat in silence for a few minutes.

Dryfly could see a school of salmon moving up the river, a V moving up the otherwise flawless surface. One jumped just above the footbridge.

"We have four nights left . . . and then the moon shall behold the night of our solemnities," said Lillian.

"What's that?" asked Dryfly.

"From Shakespeare," said Lillian. "Do you like poetry, Dry?"

"Never read much. 'The Ships of Yule,' 'In Flanders Field' . . . that's about it."

For a second a bird gave its wings to the moon, then disappeared into the azure.

"Some folks spoon in parlour chairs, some in Ford sedans, but Lillian and me, we had other plans. We had no parlour chairs, or Ford sedans, you see, so every night you'd find Lillian and me . . . down by the footbridge," recited Dryfly.

Lillian smiled.

"Where did that come from?" she asked.

Dryfly shrugged.

"Mom . . . something Dad used to tell her, I guess. Come from an old primer, I think. Don't know for sure. I made up the Lillian and the footbridge part. It's Annabel and the railroad track, the way Mom tells it."

"What's the great Canadian poem about?" asked Lillian.

"Don't know. Moose, prob'ly . . . or whoopin'."

Lillian smiled again.

"You should be a poet, Dryfly. Ever think about it, about writing a poem?"

"Naw. I wrote a song. I s'pose that's sorta like writin' poems."

"So, how's it go? Sing it for me."

"No."

"Why not?"

"Well, I sorta wanted to sing it for ya sometime, but now I think it's pretty bad. Some other time, maybe. I have to learn it better. I shouldn' have brought it up."

"You wouldn't have brought it up if you hadn't wanted to sing it. So, sing it," said Lillian, and Dryfly knew she was right. He *had* brought it up because he wanted to sing it. But now that the opportunity had arisen, he was feeling self-conscious, shy, nervous.

"I don't know the words very well," he said.

"Well, sing what you know."

"Why do you want to hear my old song so much?"

"Because I want to hear it. You sang for me before."

"Yeah, but this is my own song. It's different, it's stupid, you'll laugh."

"I won't laugh! Sing it. I'll do something really nice for you, if you do."

"Well, okay . . . ahem!"

The song was new to Dryfly and he had to think for a moment about the words and the melody. He wished he had his old friend the guitar with him, and a good slug of rum would help, too.

"I guess it don't matter if you laugh," shrugged Dryfly. "It's kind of meant to be funny . . . least I thought it was a bit funny. It was never meant to be a great song. I mean, I ain't no poet."

Lillian said nothing, waited.

Dryfly took a deep breath and began to sing. Earlier, when he was writing it, he sang it fast, up tempo, with arrogance. But singing his own words to Lillian, here in the moonlight, caused him to slow down, to sing softly.

> Well, here I am again
> Standing in the rain —
> It's what I get for being such a fool.
> On the ground in front of me,
> A lonesome angleworm,
> Stares me down from a muddy little pool.

Dryfly's eyes were fixed on the river, trying to ignore the fact that Lillian was there, listening.

He was nervous.

Lillian sensed it.

She put her hand on his.

He looked at her, beheld her eyes, sang on.

> My hat is leakin' teardrops,
> I hang my head and cry
> To think that you would push me to the edge.
> Well, the river's still arisin',
> Cabins goin' by —
> I guess it's floodin' Nelson Hollow bridge.

Lillian inched toward Dryfly ready to reward him — their noses but an inch or two apart.

Inhaling for strength, Dryfly began singing the chorus. His voice trembled with emotion, his eyes saw only Lillian.

Well, remember little darlin',
How we use to go a-walkin'
In our parkas on Yukon summer nights —
My salmon-coloured girl
With scales all a-glitter,
Reflectin' both the moon and northern lights.

That was all he had written. He stopped singing, waited
for his reward.

Appropriately, they rubbed noses.

*

By the time Shad arrived in Blackville, the moon was high
in the sky. He had walked five of the twelve miles. Leslie Dunn
picked him up in his 1962 GMC pickup truck, and Shad had
ridden the rest of the way on the back. Leslie dropped Shad
off at LeBlanc's canteen.

None of Shad's gang were at LeBlanc's, nor were they at
the other two canteens.

"Must be at the dance," thought Shad and headed for the
Public Hall.

He bought a ticket and entered.

Lyman MacPhee and the Cornpoppers were on the stage
singing, "Put Your Sweet Lips a Little Closer to the Phone."
About fifty couples were waltzing and thirty men and boys circled the dance floor trying their best to look macho, cool, passing time and time again any girls that weren't dancing. The
girls that weren't dancing, the wallflowers, watched the men,
giving them their best side, hoping they'd get asked to dance.

Mona Childs watched Ken MacCormick pass her by thirty-
eight times before; half way through the last waltz, he asked
her to dance.

Dances in Blackville on Saturday night were mating ritu-
als, a game. The name of the game could have been "Average" or "Mediocrity." The wallflowers waited for the right
man to quit circling the room long enough to ask for a dance.
The men circled until they saw the right girl, the girl that

best complemented their level of mediocrity. If a girl was very pretty, she might not get asked because there was the very good possibility that she might say no; she might be waiting for someone better-looking than herself. If a girl was ugly, she would not get asked because nobody wanted to be seen with her. If a girl was too rich, she would not get asked because she might be wanting a man with a big new car and lots of money. If a girl was very poor, she would not get asked because . . . what was the point? A girl would not get asked to dance if she danced too well or not well enough, if her hair was too blonde or too black, if she dressed too flashy or too drab, if she talked too loud or too soft. A girl might spend the whole evening waiting for someone as average as herself to ask her to dance.

Shad spotted Gary Perkins across the way. Gary was making his eighteenth lap around the room. When he approached, Shad joined him.

"G'day, Gary! How's she goin'?" yelled Shad, contending with the amplified music.

"Shad."

"How long ya been here?"

"From the start! Ya missed the fight!"

"Yeah? Who fought?"

"Two lads from Quarryville! Big crowd, eh?"

"Have ya danced yet?"

"Yeah . . . Maryann Crocker! Where were you all night?"

"Late gettin' away! Got any beer?"

"No! You?"

"Wanna go to the bootleggers?"

"What time is it?"

"Lotsa time . . . got two hours. We kin be back here in half an hour. Got any money?"

"Four dollars."

"Me too."

"Let's go."

Shad and Gary left the dance and walked to Rodent Davidson's. Rodent Davidson was the nearest bootlegger, and because of the dance was having a very busy night. He was nearly sold out.

"I ain't got no beer or wine," said Rodent.

"What've ya got?" asked Gary.

"Panty remover, and I only got three pints o' that left. I sold a dozen flats o' beer tonight, and twenty-four bottles o' wine."

"But, lemon gin?"

"Take it or leave it. That's all I got."

"Well, what d'ya think, Shad?" asked Gary.

"Might as well get it. Ya can't go to a dance sober."

Shad and Gary each bought a pint and headed back to the dance. On their way back they had several drinks of the panty-removing lemon gin.

"Should save some for whatever chicks we might pick up," said Shad.

Gary curled his lip into a little smile, snapped his fingers.

"I don't need lemon gin to remove panties," he said.

"God, he's cool!" thought Shad.

Back inside the hall they fell into the ritual of circling the dance floor once again. Occasionally, they stopped in a dark corner to sip some gin, but that was all. They carried the gin under their belts next to their skin, hidden, except for the bulge in their black shirts.

They walked around the room a dozen times, passing the same two blondes, three redheads and twenty-seven brunettes. It was on the thirteenth lap that Shad saw something the like of which he had never seen before in his life.

A man with long hair.

Shad was amazed.

"Who the hell is that?" he asked.

"Milton's brother. Billy Bean," said Gary. "Home from T'rono."

"He looks like a jeezless bean!" said Shad.

"Hippie."

"Hippie? What d'ya mean, hippie?"

"Beatle."

"Oh. What's all them girls hangin' around a homely jeezer like that for?"

"Somebody new. That's the *in* thing now-a-days, I guess."

"Who in hell would want to wear their hair all hangin' down like that?"

Gary shrugged.

Shad was feeling the gin.

"He should be thrown outta here!"

"Can't do that!" said Gary.

"Why not?"

"He's our drummer!"

Later, Gary invited Billy Bean outside for a drink. Shad reluctantly tagged along. Shad wasn't sure he wanted to be seen with this lad with long hair.

They went behind the hall, pissed and had a drink of gin. They mixed the gin with Seven-Up.

Gary made the introductions. The three talked a while about the band.

"I was talkin' to Dryfly Ramsey," said Shad. "He might want to join up with us."

"Can he play rhythm and sing?" asked Billy.

"Yeah, but he . . . " Shad was going to say that he looked awfully bad, but looking at Billy, he changed his mind.

Then the conversation exploded.

"I got a van and most of the equipment we need," said Billy. "Do you think this Dryfly lad will let his hair grow?"

"I . . . I don't know," said Shad. "Does he have to?"

Gary saw the bewilderment on Shad's face, explained, "We're gonna be doin' new stuff. We're all letting our hair grow . . . you too."

"Oh," said Shad.

The times they were a-changing.

*

Sunday morning, the sun came up with the intentions of baking Brennen Siding pie. It sent salamanders in search of cool moss by spring brooks; snakes grabbed their tails and wheeled for grassy havens; insects fled to the forest; bees hovered at the tiny entrances of their hives, buzzing, fanning, cooling the queen within. The timothy ripened that day. The moon got a sunburn, would remain red half the night.

Dryfly went to Bernie Hanley's store and persuaded Bernie

to sell him a package of chocolate cupcakes and some strawberry Kool-Aid. Bernie believed it was a sin to work on Sunday and was reluctant to let Dryfly into the store.

"What do ya need in the store?" he asked.

"I need a box of aspirins," lied Dryfly.

"Oh! Oh, well then . . . ."

Bernie knew that Dryfly was probably lying about needing the aspirins, but if it were true, surely selling something for pain could not be a sin. Also, Bernie knew that Dryfly had a job and could pay cash for the aspirins.

Bernie opened the store and he and Dryfly entered. He gave Dryfly the aspirins and Dryfly pretended to have second thoughts.

"I hate to have you open the store on Sunday just for some aspirins," said Dryfly. "I'll just get these cupcakes to make it worth your while."

"Well, you're here, you might as well," said Bernie.

"It's gotta be the hottest day this year," said Dryfly. "Gimme a couple o' packages o' that drink stuff . . . make it strawberry. And I might as well get a package o' Export A from ya, too."

Dryfly paid for the articles and headed for the club. He found Lillian Wallace in the kitchen preparing their picnic lunch. She was packing rolls and fried chicken into a bag. She also put two apples and Dryfly's cupcakes into the bag. Dryfly made Kool-Aid in a thermos, and after getting a blanket from Lillian's room they headed for the river.

"Do you know a good place?" asked Lillian.

Dryfly shrugged.

"I don't know," he said. "Some place in the shade, I suppose."

They took one of the club's canoes, and Dryfly poled them up to Dr. MacDowell's shore. Here, they went up the hill, passed the doctor's cabin to the Graig Allen farm. The Graig Allen farm now belonged to Nutbeam and was where Nutbeam planned to build his new house.

When they got to the old basement, Dryfly was amazed at how much progress Nutbeam had made. The weeds had been removed, the fallen rocks fixed back in place and mortared; the alders and sumacs had been cut.

"This is where Nutbeam is buildin' his house," commented Dry.

"It's pretty here. I hope he doesn't cut the trees," said Lillian.

"He won't . . . except for that one. He'll want to see up and down the river. He's gonna put nice pretty lawn ornaments all over the place, too," boasted Dryfly.

Lillian smiled.

They continued on, crossed John Kaston's farm and came to the woods. They were now at the upper end of Brennen Siding. Here, two miles of forest separated Brennen Siding from Gordon. They followed a path into the forest until they came to a brook. They followed the brook for a little way, then spread the blanket and sat.

"I like picnics," said Lillian.

"Me too," said Dryfly. "When I was a kid, we used to picnic back at the big hollow in the woods back o' home. One Sunday my brother Bonzie got lost. We sorta quit after that. Found 'im dead five weeks later."

"That's terrible. I'm sorry."

Dryfly shrugged, removed his shirt, stretched out on the blanket. Lillian tickled his arm with a blade of grass. From the direction of the river came the call of a meadow hen sounding like someone driving a stake with a maul. Tall trees stood about. Dryfly stared up through the boughs at the sky.

"Are you considering Dad's offer?" asked Lillian.

"I don't know . . . kind of old for goin' to school," said Dryfly.

"You're not old, Dryfly. Everyone your age goes to school."

"Old for goin' with a bunch o' kids."

"Yes, but you could take a correspondence course."

"What's that?"

"You send away for books and things and teach yourself at home."

"Yeah . . . that'd be all right."

"Why don't you consider doin' that?"

"Ya think Bill . . . yer father would settle for that?"

"You could ask him."

"Any idea where ya send?"

"No, but they must have them in Canada."

"Don't know."

Dryfly rolled over on his side, propped his head with his hand, elbow on the blanket.

Lillian slid from her sitting position, took a similar pose, faced him. She ran her fingers over his chest, gently, ever so gently.

"Would you like to make love to me?" she asked.

Dryfly swallowed.

"Y . . . y . . . yeah," he said.

Dryfly's heart began to pound. His body responded.

"How come you never try . . . or ask me?" asked Lillian.

"Scared ya might say no," said Dry.

"So, what if I did? You'll never know until you ask."

"You'd say no, wouldn't ya?"

"Yes."

"But, you'd want to."

". . . yes."

"Well, I wouldn't want you to lie."

They stared into each other's eyes, kissed.

"Want to?" asked Dryfly.

"Yes," said Lillian.

"Will you?" asked Dryfly.

"No," said Lillian.

Dryfly was trembling with desire. Lillian could see how it was affecting him.

"I can't make love to him," she thought. "That would be the worse thing I could do. It would be stupid, but . . . "

She reached out and touched him.

"I love you," she said.

Dryfly had lost his ability to speak. He swallowed. He was so excited and his heart was beating so fast that he thought he might explode.

"You're teasin' me," he managed to say.

"Just lie back and close your eyes," said Lillian.

*

John Kaston was born, raised and married in Brennen Siding. He would live there for the rest of his life. He raised two boys there, both of whom left for Ontario as soon as they were old enough to do so. Neither boy would become a preacher, and that meant that John considered himself a great failure.

So, what does a man do when he's got his back against the wall? He fights back. John fought tooth, nail and tongue. He became a preacher himself.

There was one little Baptist church in Brennen Siding that John had attended regularly until just recently. He did not attend now because to become a preacher he had to leave the Baptist church, join and pay into a subdenominational one. John didn't have much education. John had to accept Jesus Christ as his own personal Saviour, spend twelve hundred dollars and attend a school in Fredericton for six weeks to become a preacher.

Now, John had a problem. He lived in Brennen Siding and he didn't have a church. Money was dwindling, too. Being a preacher, he could not be expected to work in the woods. Rita, John's wife, was beginning to worry.

"What's the answer to everything?" she asked.

"God," replied John.

"You should get on your knees and pray," said Rita piously, softly.

"I know that," said John and went into the woods where he prayed for an answer, a sign, a message, something that would tell him what to do about his problem.

He didn't have to wait long.

When he got home a few minutes later, he found Rita rolling around on the kitchen floor. She was making funny noises, yipping and yacking and going on in such a frenzy that it frightened John at first. Then she grew quiet, lay on her back and stared up at the ceiling. Then she snapped out of it and stood.

"You must build a church of your own," she said.

That was a good enough sign for John. He started raising money. He raised $432.67 — enough money to buy one of the little stained-glass windows he wanted.

He couldn't ask for more money. He'd already knocked on every door in Brennen Siding and Gordon.

So, he sold his lumber land for ten thousand dollars, all his farm equipment, animals and chainsaw for two thousand dollars, and had it in mind to sell his shore for whatever Bill Wallace, or some other rich American, would give him for it. He figured his shore was worth at least a couple of thousand.

Things were moving along nicely.

He had kept his house, barn and enough land to build a church on. He was half considering changing his barn into a church. If he did that, the land he'd intended for the church could be used for a graveyard.

But there was a minor detail to consider. John didn't have a congregation — he was working on Lindon Tucker and Elva Nash — and that meant perhaps he'd have no one to bury there.

"A minor detail," he thought. "They'll all start coming once they hear me preach. But I need practice. The instructor said to practise, that practice makes a good preacher. I should be practising now."

John grabbed his Bible and left the house, headed for his favourite preaching place, the woods. It was a very hot Sunday morning.

As he followed the path into the woods, he was in deep thought. He had learned a new word recently that he thought might sound good in a sermon.

"Lambent," he thought. "Brothers and Sisters, how ya gonna account for yourselves when your wretched souls are being covered by His lambent eyes? Yes, that's pretty good. That's how I'll say it."

When he came to the brook, he didn't notice the salamander on a rock, nor did he see the snake doing wheelies in the grass. When he came to the brook and started up along it, he was so preoccupied with "lambent eyes" that he nearly stepped on Dryfly Ramsey and Lillian Wallace.

Lillian saw him first. She jolted upright.

Dryfly had his eyes closed, did not see him at all.

"What's the matter?" asked Dryfly.

"What's goin' on here?" snapped John.

Now it was Dryfly's turn to jolt.

Dryfly jumped to his feet with the intentions of escaping, running. He and Lillian had been doing nothing more than some heavy petting, but he figured that that was enough to have himself condemned for life in the eyes of John Kaston. He knew that John Kaston would disapprove and could find reason to preach about a lot less. However, Dryfly did not run. Instead he faced John, guiltily.

Lillian thought she might run, too, but decided against it.

She did not know John Kaston and felt that she was doing nothing wrong, anyway. The thought of running had been nothing more than a response to being startled. She threw her head back indignantly, met John eye to eye.

For a few seconds John was at a loss for words. He knew he was obligated to say something, but he didn't know where to begin.

Dryfly was overwrought. His eyes flicked back and forth from the arrogant girl to the fanatical preacher.

"John, I, I, I . . . " he managed to say.

"Ah ha!" went John. "Ah . . . you . . . if the good Lord could only see you now!"

"We . . . ah . . . " Dryfly tried again.

"It's a wonder he don't smite you both with lightning!" said John.

"We were having a picnic," said Lillian calmly. Her voice was so strong and calm that it pulled Dryfly around, gave him strength.

"Yeah," said Dryfly. "Ah . . . hope you don't mind."

Lillian's self-assurance affected John as well.

"It is a wicked world we live in," he said.

John decided that because Lillian was so calm about the whole thing he should start his inevitible sermon with a certain degree of calmness as well. "Start calm," he told himself, "and build into a dramatic ending."

"How you gonna account for yourselves when yer wretched souls are being covered by the lambent eyes of Jesus Christ? Can you tell me that, Dryfly Ramsey? Miss? Don't you ever ask yourselves that question?"

"Well, I . . . " tried Dryfly.

"You know what I want to see, Dryfly? You know what would give me joy?"

"Well, I . . . "

"It would give me great pleasure to see you on your knees praising the Lord. He can set you free, Dryfly! You too, Miss."

"I am free!" snapped Lillian. "I'm an American!"

"Yeah, me too!" said Dryfly. "I'm a Catholic!"

"A Catholic," thought John. "Yes, yes, he's a Catholic, but he could very well belong to the . . . the . . . Church of John Kaston."

"You know, Satan has been watchin' you today, and he's smilin' his wicked smile. You've made him very happy. The good Lord has been watchin', too. But the good Lord is not happy at all. He weeps for his poor lost lambs, tears in his lambent eyes. And what about Shirley, Dryfly? How's she gonna feel about this? And Mr. Nutbeam? How's he gonna feel?"

"Good, I think. He knocked Mom up!"

Lillian giggled.

The giggle seemed to mock the whole affair. The conversation had been so intense that the giggle seemed to be like a rock hurled into a very delicate stained-glass window. Dryfly had to laugh, too.

"You laugh, Miss Wallace! You laugh! But how's your father gonna feel?"

Lillian's smile vanished. If Bill Wallace found out about what she had been doing, he would never forgive her. She would never be allowed to see Dryfly again. He would probably put her in an all-girls school. She would certainly never be allowed to come back up to the Dungarvon.

"And you're going to tell him?" she asked.

"Oh, you can't keep a great sin like this a secret! You have to bring it out in the open! Deal with it! You must confess your sins! You must ask forgiveness! Pray! Go to church! I'm afraid, for the sake of your soul, that I'll have to speak to your father, miss."

"Why? What good would that do? It would only cause unrest, conflict! Hurt!" reasoned Lillian.

"He doesn't need to know," put in Dryfly.

"Yes, yes! Yes, we can keep this little secret from Mr. Wallace, but you can't keep secrets from the Lord. You must repent, Dryfly! I'm not blaming this young girl! It's you that's to blame! You might think that what you were doing here was innocent enough, but in the eyes of the Maker you're guilty of adultery! It's adultery to as much as look a woman . . . to even think about, ah, what you were thinking about! The sin rests heavy on your wretched shoulders! I can see it in your eyes. You must ask forgiveness, Dryfly! Pray! Go to church! You must repent! That's the only alternative you have! Repent and see the light o' God! . . . and I can make that happen for you, Dryfly. I'm starting up a little church, son." John Kaston tried to look lambent. "You can call me Shepherd."

"I was just wonderin' when you were gonna git that church started," said Dryfly. "I've been thinkin' a lot about helpin' you with it, lately."

"You have?" asked John.

"Yeah. I ah . . . was thinkin' a man should have a good church to go to. Can't go to that Baptist one, me bein' a Catholic. Ah, yeah, I thought I might like to give you a hand."

"Really! Well, now."

And that was how Dryfly Ramsey became the first member of the church of John Kaston.

five

On her way up the road and across the bridge to the post office, Hilda Porter noticed that she was feeling more tired than usual. It was a brilliant Monday morning, and the heat seemed to be drawing her energy. She stopped on the bridge to rest: to luxuriate in the cool breeze that came up the river, to watch the water below.

"I'm getting old," she thought. "And I'm the last of my family. I came close to getting married once, if he had only asked me."

Downstream, on the northwest side, sat the mill. Hilda could see the tall brick chimney, white smoke rising.

"I'll put one of these posters up in the mill office," she thought. "There might be someone working there that needs a place to stay."

She had five posters in a shopping bag. She removed one, read it.

NOTICE

MAN WANTED FOR ODD JOBS.
ROOM AND BOARD PROVIDED.
WILL DISCUSS WAGES.
SEE HILDA PORTER.
THE OTHER SIDE OF THE RIVER.

The settlement across the river from Blackville did not have a name. It was always referred to as "the other side of the river."

"That's all I need to say," she thought. "One in the mill office, one in the post office, one in Brigham's store, one in LeBlanc's canteen and one in Biff's."

A shiny new Plymouth crossed the bridge. Somebody tooted, waved.

"Looked like a Rapider," she thought. A Rapider was a person from the Gray Rapids, several miles downstream. She didn't know why, but for some reason she could always tell a Rapider. She could always recognize a Renouser and a Howard Roader, too. She could tell a Blackviller from an Upper Blackviller, a Gordoner from a Brennen Sidinger. They all had some distinctive characteristic: the way they wore their hair, turned up their collar, laced their boots, trimmed and shined their cars, the width they rolled the cuffs of their pants.

"Clans," she thought. "Little clans living in the woods, accepting life as . . . as something . . . conditional? Provisional?" She was thinking about Tasmania now. As always lately the Tasmanian aborigines had taken over her reverie.

"They abandoned their old and their sick," she thought. "Left them behind like some useless thing. Later, they'd find them dead and burn them without ceremony, without watching, or they put them in hollow trees with a spear through their bodies to hold them in place."

Hilda shuddered at the thought of being similarly abandoned, alone, pinned to a tree.

"And once a person died, they were never mentioned again, forgotten as one might forget a common insect. Funny people, not to remember their dead. But I guess nobody is remembered for very long. That's why we need religion, afterlife, education.

"Most of the aborigines couldn't count beyond two or three; some, a few, could count to five. Worse than half the children I taught in Brennen Siding."

Hilda grinned at this, chuckled. "They must have been very meek. Meek. Blessed are the meek: for they shall inherit the earth. Blessed are they which are persecuted for righteousness' sake: for theirs is the Kingdom of Heaven."

Hilda looked toward the northeast bank of the Miramichi, fixed her eyes on a particular place, a grassy glade. She was gazing at the place where she had picnicked years ago.

"I was with Jerry MacLaggon," she thought. "And we were so young and strong. He kissed me. We had white wine . . . Chablis, I believe, and chicken.

"It was a day like today, but there was a refreshing breeze that played in the tall grass, the flowers, our hair. And there were bees and robins. I love the song of a robin. Wished I could hear better, wished I could hear the song of the robin just one more time, and I suppose I could if I were close enough, there in that glade.

"Poor Jerry. I was awful, so cold to him, bored him with foolish, childish stories. Pretended to be upset with him when he kissed me. What a stupid, backward fool I was! Oh! If I only had that day to live again. A picnic in that same glade with a boy. I wonder where poor Jerry is today, if he's still living? He'd be old now, even older than me, And you can't relive the past. All those years alone. A schoolmarm. I'd have been happier a pauper."

Hilda sighed and continued on her way to the village. She put her posters up. Then she bought a few groceries. Then she went home to wait.

*

Nutbeam arose at five o'clock in the morning, breakfasted and headed for the Graig Allen farm. The radio predicted an extremely hot day, and he wanted to get his work done before the temperature reached its full intensity.

He sized up the basement.

"Should be able to finish it today," he thought. "Then, the sills, the joists and the floor. I can do that all without help. I won't need Dryfly to help me do that stuff. Course, Dryfly will have to be here for the rafters and stuff. 'Magine he'll know all about how to do that stuff by the time he finishes the Wallace camp. Lucky break, that — him getting that job. Now I got me very own carpenter. All I'll need after today is some lumber. I'll have to get Dryfly or Shadrack to go to the mill and order the lumber."

Nutbeam was shy, didn't like going very many places. It was just recently that he gathered enough courage to enter Bernie Hanley's store.

He began mixing some mortar, enough to secure a half-dozen rocks or so. He didn't know if he would need any more than that — the job was nearly finished. The floor of the basement was still dirt, but he intended to leave it that way. Someday, he'd do the floor, but dirt was good enough for the time being.

Working with sand, mortar, rocks, in the basement, he attracted hundreds, thousands, millions of blackflies and mosquitoes. They swarmed about him. He had a hat on to protect his head; he buttoned his sleeves at the wrists, his shirt at the neck. He didn't have fly repellent, there was little more he could do.

"I'm a pretty lucky man," he thought. "There was a time when I thought a homely man couldn't be happy. But look at me now — a nice woman, a baby comin', Dryfly. I can't help but think o' myself as Dryfly's father, even though I know I ain't. This house . . . sixteen by twenty — bigger house than I ever thought o' ownin'. Enough room here for us all, for sure.

"If it's a boy, I'll call him Mathew Nutbeam the second, after myself. If it's a girl, I'll call her Shirley."

Shirley.

"What a wonderful lady she is! Never tells me what to do, never asks for anything. I'm gonna be awful good to Shirley. My Shirley, smart woman, kin read and everthing. Likes my lawn ornaments, too.

"What was the word she read to me last night, the big long one, about all the money them lads were makin' outta . . . parn . . . pern . . . pernography . . . something like that. Dirty pictures. Millions! Millions o' dollars fer takin' pictures o' naked women and puttin' them in a magazine."

He lifted a rock into a cavity and secured it with mortar. He did not have to search for rocks. He was using the originals. All he had to do was fit the rocks back into their original spaces on the wall.

"I paid a dollar once to see a picture of a naked woman. T'was worth it, too. Learned what I was up against.

"Shirley sure liked that blue rabbit I made. Put it out front soon's the paint dried. Said I should be in the business.

"Ha! Sure would be an easy way to make a livin'. None o' this huntin' and fishin' and trappin. Never liked trappin'. A man could make a couple, three, four lawn ornaments every day. Make a pretty good livin'. Everybody's got them, wants them.

"What was that one I saw last week? Had a propeller on it, a little man splittin' wood. Every time the propeller turned in the wind, it turned a crooked rod and the little man tapped a little block o' wood with his axe. Something like that would be worth a fortune. Wouldn't be that hard to make, either. All ya'd need is a crooked rod, some plywood, a nut or two, maybe. A lad could make all kindsa things. A little man choppin' wood. You could have him runnin', sawin' off a board, wavin' his arm. You could even have him bendin' over and standin' up, his bum movin'. Ha! You could have him screwin'! Ha, ha, ha! He'd have good stayin' power, too, so long's the four winds blew. Ha, ha! Pernography lawn ornaments!

"I bet ya Dry and Shad will laugh when they hear that one! Ha! Pernography lawn ornaments. Them lads are prob'ly crazy enough to make them . . . ha!

"Shirley'd not care . . . or would she? Wouldn't want to rub her the wrong way — not my Shirley. I miss Shirley. Wonder what time it is? Wonder if she's outta bed. Needs a lotta sleep with that baby, I suppose — with Mathew or little Shirley the second."

Nutbeam started working a little harder, faster.

"Git this done and get home," he thought. "Home to Shirley. Maybe I'll go to the store on my way home, buy her some nice tailor-made cigarettes. No woman o' mine should have to smoke them old makin's . . . not while she's carryin' a young lad, anyway."

*

William Wallace climbed the steps to the Cabbage Island Salmon Club. He was carrying his four-hundred-dollar, nine-foot bamboo fishing rod. Bert Todder puffed and panted along behind. Bert carried the scoop net. He was sunburned, hot and about ready to strangle Bill for keeping him on the river for so long.

Bert knew that the water in the river was much too warm for good fishing. In hot weather the salmon move to the mouths of brooks, seem to sleep there, won't take a fly.

Three hours ago, Bert told Bill, "There's no fish when it's hot like this."

"The wind's in the west," was how Bill Wallace answered him. "When the wind is in the west, the fish bite best," was Bill's reasoning. Bill Wallace also theorized that salmon are very apt to take a fly when the sun's at the zenith. Morning, midday and evening were the best times to fish, according to Bill Wallace. Lunchtime was not that productive, but what's the sense in going home for an hour or two and coming back out again? Bill wasn't in need of lunch and had little regard for Bert's needs. Bert Todder had one of the biggest bellies that Bill had ever seen. Bert Todder, according to Bill, was a walking cardiac time bomb — a little fasting could only do Bert Todder some good.

So, here it was three o'clock and they were just coming in off the river.

"A man could starve to death," mumbled Bert as he climbed the steps behind Bill.

"What's that?" asked Bill.

"I could use a cold drink," said Bert.

"So could I," said Bill, stepping up on the veranda.

Lillian Wallace was inside listening to music. She came out to greet her father. Bill was removing his waders.

"Hi, Dad," she said. "Hi, Mr. Todder."

"G'day, g'day," said Bert.

"Any fish?" asked Lillian.

"No . . . I don't think there's a fish in the damned river," said Bill.

"That'd be the only way ya'd ketch a fish in this heat," said Bert, swabbing his brow. "If ya had the river dammed. Tee, hee, hee, sob, snort, sniff. Well, I gotta go."

"Are you not having a cold drink with us, Bert?"

"Well, I might just have the one." Bert hung the scoop net on a nail on the side of the camp and sat in the shade of the veranda.

"What would you like, Bert?" asked Bill.

"Oh, I don't know . . . anything a'tall, water, anything a'tall."

"Anything cold?" asked Bill.

"I'll make us some lemonade," said Lillian.

Bert had been hoping for a beer, or a scotch.

Lillian went inside. Bill hung up his waders and sat in a chair near Bert.

"So, have you thought of a price?" asked Bill.

"Well, now . . . yes, I have . . . " Bert removed his pipe and tobacco, began filling it.

"And?" asked Bill.

"And . . . " Bert finished filling his pipe, found a match, struck it on his zipper. Puff, puff, puff. "Yes, sir" — puff, puff, puff — "I was thinkin' maybe a hundred thousand dollars."

"What!"

"Tee, hee, hee, sob, snort, sniff!" Bert was joking, of course. "No" — puff, puff, puff — "I might not sell it at all. Then again, I might."

"Well, I wouldn't want to rush you, Bert, but did I tell you that John Kaston came to visit me last night?"

"No, ya never mentioned it, no."

"Yes, well, he dropped in last evening. Tell me, Bert, what's that watah like in front of his place? Is there a pool there?"

"Not many salmon there, no. A few, not many. You know, you can pick up the odd one, but it's not as good as, oh, let's say here or . . . or over in front o' your place. Not as good as mine, either."

"Well, he wants to sell it to me."

Lillian came out with two tall glasses of lemonade.

"Thanks, love," said Bill.

"Great, great, great, the very best," said Bert, taking the drink. He feasted his eyes on Lillian's young body, wished he was twenty-five years younger.

Lillian went back inside to get her own drink. It was cooler inside — she decided to stay.

"How much is he askin'?" asked Bert.

"Christ, Bert, he wants an arm and a leg! Six thousand dollars!"

"Too much!"

"That's what I said, Bert old buddy. I'm glad you agree with me. Do you know how long it takes to make six thousand dollars?"

Bert thought maybe a year. Bill was thinking a day.

"Yeah, well, I wouldn't want that much," said Bert. "If I decide to sell, I'll prob'ly let ya have it fer . . . oh, let's say, five."

"That's still a lot of money, Bert."

"Yeah, but . . . it'll be there. Land never rots. Next year, or in ten years, I might get a lot more than five, if ya know what I mean."

Bill Wallace knew that the land was already worth as much as fifty thousand, but he did not mention it to Bert.

"Well," said Bill. "I'll have to think it over, Bert. I haven't really sized up that John Kaston property yet."

Bert said nothing.

Bill grinned at the scheme he had in mind.

*

Ducky Shaw quit work for the day at four-thirty.

"It's too hot," he said. "Be back here an hour earlier in the morning."

Getting off early pleased Dryfly very much. This would be his last night with Lillian Wallace this year.

Lindon Tucker was also happy to get off early. He had it in mind to take a walk through his lumberland, check it out. Dan Brennen had mentioned that the budworms were destroying his spruce and fir, that anything bigger than six inches at the butt was either rotten in the middle or already toppled by the wind. Dan was thinking about hiring a crew of men to clearcut his land.

"Might as well," he said that night at Berney Hanley's store. "It ain't growin'. I'll lose money if I wait."

Lindon Tucker could very well be having the same problem. He didn't know for sure. He hadn't been back in the woods for a couple of years. He went directly home from work, ate some potatoes and salted salmon and headed for the woods.

He thought his trees looked pretty good, not nearly as bad as Dan Brennen's. But he also thought he'd get it cut in the fall.

"Dan Brennen said he'd get ten, said he'd get ten thousand dollars for his logs. Ten. Yeah. Ten thousand dollars. He doesn't have to do a tap o' work. Gettin' a crew. Ten thousand dollars, just like that."

Lindon Tucker never thought of hiring a crew to cut his land before. He always thought he'd have to cut it himself. Lindon didn't much like working in the woods and, therefore, his land hadn't been harvested in years. Lindon had never thought of his lumber being worth ten thousand dollars, either. He liked the sound of it. Lindon Tucker was very fond of money.

Because of the fact that Lindon seldom walked through his woods, the trail that ran through it was nothing more than a path — a path seriously threatened with extinction. Occasionally, brambles and ferns, alders and brakes had taken it over completely. Frequently, Lindon had to guess where he was going.

He was nearly to the back end of his property when he heard the bushes stir beside him.

Being an old hunter, he stopped immediately, thinking the disturbance might be caused by a deer.

He stood as if frozen, for a minute or maybe more.

Nothing happened.

He decided to check it out, moved to the bushes where he'd heard the rustling.

There was nothing there.

"Coo! Coo!" came the call of the bird.

"That, that, that's that cooin' jeezer," said Lindon. "Must, must, must . . . must have been . . . must have been that cooin' jeezer."

"Coo! Coo!" came the call again.

Lindon was curious. He didn't know what kind of bird it was. He walked stealthily toward the sound. The sound moved away. Again Lindon moved toward it. Again it moved.

"The hell wit' it!" said Lindon and started to turn back to the path.

"Coo! Coo!" came the call, closer again.

Lindon made a sudden dash into the bush. He hoped to spook it to flight and thus at least get a glance at it on the wing.

He found nothing there.

"Hmm," thought Lindon.

He looked at the ground.

"Hoof prints," he murmured. "Moose."

"Coo! Coo!" went the bird.

"It's just down by that big spruce," thought Lindon, headed toward it.

"Like a game. Like a jeezless game o' fox an' geese," he thought. "Maybe it's a goose."

"Honk! Honk!" he called.

The bird answered. Lindon wasn't sure if his ears were playing tricks on him or not. When the bird answered, it came more like a delayed echo than an actual answer, and it seemed to honk.

"It's the same bird I heard on the bridge that night," he thought. He grinned at the memory. His missing cuspids gave him the appearance of a defanged vampire. He stood still for a while, waiting to see if his goose call would get another answer.

Nothing happened.

Lindon shrugged, gave up the quest, headed back to the path.

Lindon walked for quite a while but did not come to it. He thought maybe he'd walked too far. He thought he might have crossed the path at a place where it was not identifiable. He turned back, walked even further. No path.

"Maybe if I, if I, if I, if I walked . . . walked . . . if I walked in a circle," he thought.

He walked in a big circle. Nothing. He sat to think.

Lindon Tucker was not a complete fool when it came to the woods. He had hunted and had heard stories.

"I'm almost, almost, almost lost," he thought. "Yeah. Yes, sir. Yeah. Lost, yeah. But when I left home, the sun was sorta at me back. At me back, yeah. There . . . 'cept, which way was I facin'?"

He looked about him. There were brakes and alders, firs and spruce, ferns and shrubs. "I . . . I . . . I'm lost, fer jeezless sure!" he thought.

"What now?" he asked himself.

Lindon Tucker tried with all his might to think of all the stories he'd heard about the woods, being lost. He knew all the stories and could tell them in detail, just as he'd heard them. The problem in all of this was that in order to tell them he had to start each one at the beginning.

He thought of one — the Bonzie Ramsey story. Bonzie had gotten lost back at the Big Hollow, in the barren. They found him eaten and pecked a month or two later.

Lindon gave up on this one. Lindon Tucker wanted to be found alive.

He thought of the story of the card game in the lumber camp. It was in the middle of the night, the middle of a storm, somewhere on the Dungarvon.

"Near here," thought Lindon. "A knock came to the door. And, and, and a tall, dark stranger came in, played, never lost a hand. Bill Tuney was there. Poor old Bill. Dead now, Bill. Liked molasses in his tea. Somebody dropped a card, reached fer it, saw the lad's feet. Feet, yeah. Yeah, yep. Feet. Weren't feet, no. Hooves, they were, yeah. Hooves. Jumped up he did. Scared. Upset the table, the lamp, burned the camp down."

Lindon was only halfway through the story, but he realized it was not about being lost. Thinking of this story was doing him no good.

"Someone said, when a man's lost, he should sit, wait, wait and sit till someone comes along, comes lookin'. Sit, yeah. Coo! I'll just wait right here.

"Well, the sun is down, the moon is up, the larks are singin' freeeeeee. Come listen while I sing about my old brown coat and me!" sang Lindon.

"Doc Williams sings that song. Good song that. Always liked Doc. The best. Wonder how long I'll have to wait?"

*

Dryfly didn't have much to say. There were no words to describe how he felt.

If the world was a game of auction forty-five, the US of A would be the five of trump, the Soviet Union, the jack, and England, the ace of hearts. The ace of hearts is always trump. In a game where cards are ranked according to colour — highest in red, lowest in black — Canada would rank some where around the seven of diamonds. There are red twos and black tens to look down on, but any trump can beat you.

To an American, Canada is the cold, barren land north of Boston. When an American plays a card, the Canadian follows suit. Lindon Johnson physically shook Lester Pearson for disagreeing, set him drunk and took him on a tour of his ranch when there was important business to discuss. When Paul Revere yelled, "The British are coming!" the phrase became a household word.

Who, on the other hand, knows the story of Laura Secord?

"The Americans are coming! The Americans are coming!" yelled Laura.

A battle was fought, a war was won. The Canadians beat the shit out of the Americans and remained something other than (more than? less than?) an American state.

Fred Davis hosted a TV show once and lost his cool. He had an American Senator for a guest. Someone asked the Senator if he thought Canada would ever become a state.

"You should be so lucky," answered the Senator.

Fred told the Senator where to go. Fred, no doubt, thought that somebody cared.

Canada. Ten provinces and two territories.

What's happening in the Yukon these days? Is Sparks Street the main drag in Ottawa, or Metcalfe? Is Gordie Howe a Canadian? Isn't Gordie's wife a politician in Connecticut or some place? Is Gordie's bar in Regina, or Hartford? Do any Canadians live east of Montreal? West of the Ontario border? How far from the American border do ninety percent of the Canadian people live? Who was Sir MacKenzie Bowel?

James Eayrs said, "Franklin Delano Roosevelt was the best president Canadians ever had."

The American capitalist J.P. Morgan said, "Canada's a very nice place and we intend to keep it that way."

J.F. Kennedy said, "When I ask Canada to do something, I expect Canada to do it."

How many Canadians would rather be in Philadelphia? How many Canadians know the meaning of true patriot love?

"Where are you from?"

"New Brunswick."

"So, what's happening in Jersey these days?"

How many Quebecers, Maritimers, or Albertans get on their knees at night to thank the Lord for Confederation?

"Does everyone in Ontario drive a truck for a living?"

"No. Some drive buses."

Is the province of Newfoundland an island?

Does Prince Edward Island have its own licence plate?

"Ever been to Canada?"

"Oh, yeah. I've been all over dem providences."

Why do all Canadian country singers sound like they're from Tennessee? Why do Canadian evangelists talk like they're from the South?

"When you die, y'all will come to a branch in the rewd," said . . . guess who? John Kaston.

Dryfly Ramsey was a Canadian boy and Lillian Wallace was an American girl, but there was no border between them yet. Dryfly was very sad — so sad that he could say very little. Lillian was sad, too, but she was also angry — angry at the fact that even though she had anticipated this moment, she had allowed it to happen. However, she was not going to permit her anger to spoil these last few moments. Her intention was to play it out to the end, to savour and enjoy every last second. And then? She would never let it happen again.

Dryfly was thinking of not seeing her for a whole year, writing letters and being true and faithful. Lillian thought she would never return, never write; she intended to keep Dryfly as a pleasant memory, nothing more. Brennen Siding was a very nice place and she intended to keep it that way.

"In a little while he'll walk out of my life," she thought. "And he'll be nothing more than a memory . . . but not *just* a memory . . . a very fond memory."

"I just wish I could die!" said Lillian.

Dryfly heard the pain in her voice, had his own pain to deal with. "We could both die," he said.

"Leaving is dying, almost," said Lillian.

"If we die, it would mean being together for the rest of our lives," said Dryfly.

"I have something for you," said Lillian. "Wait here."

She ran inside the cabin, came out with a book.

"Here," she said. "Shakespeare."

Dryfly was too overwhelmed to say anything. Lillian saw the tears of thanks trickle down his cheek. She kissed them away. Then, she ran into the cabin to her room.

Dryfly remained where he was for several moments, holding the book, gazing at the empty space where Lillian had been.

"I love you," he whispered.

Dryfly was thinking that he loved her very much, but she was an American — too good for him. He was only the two of diamonds, Lillian was the queen of hearts.

Dryfly wasn't even trump.

*

The evening passed, the sun went down, the stars came out, the moon came up red-faced, then yellow, then finally glowed like a white marble, high over Lindon Tucker.

Mosquitoes hummed, an owl hooted, the strange bird cooed, a jet passed overhead rumbling, a tiny light blinking thirty thousand feet up.

"I, I, I, I must've been here for three, four, five hours. Maybe . . . maybe . . . maybe if I whooped someone, someone, some-one might hear me, if I whooped."

"Awhooooo!" whooped Lindon.

He listened to see if anyone was answering. He thought he heard a movement in the shadows off to the right. A mos-quito hummed.

"Lotsa flies," thought Lindon. "Gettin' et up pretty good. If I walked a bit, they wouldn't bother me so much. But s'pose to stay where you are, wait. Could wait, could, could, could wait for a week."

The mosquito landed on his neck, bit. Lindon slapped it to death. He sniffed the air, thought he could smell the pulpmill. If you could smell the pulpmill, there was a good chance a storm was approaching from the east. The sulphuric smell of the mill could sometimes be detected all the way to Brennen Siding twenty miles away. Looking up, Lindon could not see a single cloud. But the smell of sulphur was definitely present.

"Sometimes a swamp smells like that," reasoned Lindon. "Must be a swamp nearby. That's, that's, that's why there's so many flies. S'posed to wait, though. But would it matter where a man waited? Nobody knows I'm here under this pine. I could be waiting over there, or down at, down at, down at Todder Brook . . . or up back o' Bob Nash's . . . or over back o' Frank Layton's . . . " Lindon tried very hard to make sense of it all.

He thought once more about the fact that the sun had been behind him when he left the house. "That's all the very best," thought Lindon, "but how does the sun know which way I might be gonna face? And when it comes up in the mornin' . . . ?"

"Awhooooo!" he whooped again.

He heard movement in the bush once again. Whatever it was had now moved to the bushes behind him. Lindon gave the movement his full attention, listened.

"Something walkin' on the leaves. Could be a deer, or a moose, or a bear. Maybe I should move, get to hell outta here. Maybe I should put on a fire. Ain't cold, but, but, but the smoke might keep the flies away. And someone might see the smoke, the flames.

"Awhooooo!"

Lindon was sitting at the base of a pine tree. He had chosen this place because it was dry, had been a shade from the sun. He stood, found he was a little stiff from sitting so long. He looked around for a birch — birch bark made excellent kindling for a fire. He saw one a hundred feet away, lit by the moon. He went to it, gathered some of its loose paper-like bark and took it back to his pine. Then he went to several other locations, breaking the dead, dry limbs from the fir, spruce, alders, whatever sources were available, convenient.

He searched his pockets for a match, found one, ignited the bark. Immediately, there was light, reflections, heat. He added some sticks. The fire consumed them greedily. He added more.

Time passed.

"I'm out of wood already," he thought. "Better get some more."

He left the fire and was breaking off a few more sticks when he came upon an old dead spruce, dry as a bone, lying on the ground.

"I might, might, might be able to drag the whole tree to the fire," he thought. He grabbed the butt of the tree and tugged. The tree gave a little. He tugged again. The tree was old, rotten and dried. It broke halfway up. He could manage his half quite easily, pulled it through the woods to his fire.

The recent exertion, the heat of the fire and the warmth of the summer's night had Lindon perspiring profusely, but he found the light comforting, worth it.

"Coo! Coo!" sang the strange bird.

"Coo! Coo!" went Lindon.

Then, suddenly, a breeze came up, caused Lindon's fire to dance and roar to life. The remains of the old dead spruce were too close. The fire reached out and ignited one of its limbs. In a minute, Lindon had a roaring inferno on his hands. The heat reached up, singed the pine needles above his head. The pine burst into flames. Within ten minutes, Joe Morris could see Lindon's location all the way from his forestry tower. Joe Morris was in the Department of Forestry's look-out tower three miles away.

*

The next day, Dryfly did not spend much time dealing with his aching heart; Nutbeam did not get any work done to his house, did not make any lawn ornaments; John Kaston did not preach and Bob Nash did not bicker with Elva; Shadrack Nash did not go to Blackville. The next morning, Ducky Shaw did not boss anyone around — he, himself, took orders from the game wardens just like everyone else. Everyone else consisted of men and boys from Brennen Siding, Gordon, Renous, Blackville, Howard, Keenan, Upper Blackville. Two hundred men from the area were all back of Brennen Siding fighting fire.

At the end of the day, with help from water bombers and an almost breathless evening, they put the fire out. The winds had been coming from the west — a lucky break for Brennen Siding. It was not a lucky break for the Dungarvon woods, however. The fire managed to destroy several hundred acres of budworm-eaten forest.

Lindon Tucker was delivered home on the back of a forest ranger's red pickup truck.

"G'night, pal! See ya! Take 'er easy, now! Thanks! Be good! Take 'er easy, old boy!" Lindon called to the game warden.

Lindon Tucker had only lost about an acre of land at the extreme back end of his property. Lindon Tucker was a very lucky man.

six

It was two weeks before Hilda Porter got a response to the little notes she had posted. A local derelict paid her a visit. Hilda was polite, tolerated his half-drunken state, his barf-breath smell, but did not hire him. She lied, told him she had already hired someone.

Her second applicant arrived a week later in the middle of the night.

Shadrack Nash had come to the end of his rope as far as living at home was concerned. It ended in one great, final blowup.

"Get out!" screamed Elva. "Get out of this house!"

Shad had been to the mill in Blackville. He went to order lumber for Nutbeam.

"Do you want it delivered?" asked the clerk.

"Ah . . . no . . . I'll see," said Shad.

It wasn't until he got home that he realized he'd made a mistake. Of course he should have had it delivered — Nutbeam didn't have a truck.

"I'll either have to go back to Blackville or fix it up some other way," thought Shad.

An hour later, he asked his father if he would get the lumber with his pickup.

Elva overheard the request.

"Yes! Yes! For sure!" she yelled. "Now you're runnin' errands for the Ramseys, are ya?"

One thing led to another. Bob yelled that he was an independent man and would make his own decisions; Elva screamed back; Shad got into it; Elva momentarily lost her cool completely and told Shad to get out. Shad didn't care — neither did Bob. Shad left.

He went back to Blackville, went to the mill and told the

clerk to deliver Nutbeam's lumber. While he was there, he saw Hilda Porter's note.

At first, he didn't give the note much thought, but as the day wore down to evening and evening became night, the idea became more and more appealing.

"It's just what I need," he told Gary Perkins. "Room and board, the odd buck for booze, handy to the action. Maybe we could even practise there once in a while."

Gary reassured him, saying, "Sounds good to me. Go for it."

Shad went for it.

Knock, knock, knock. Knock, knock, knock.

Shad knocked again and again until finally Hilda woke up and came to the door.

"My goodness! What's goin' on?" she exclaimed when she saw Shad.

"Remember me?" asked Shad.

"You look like a Brennen Sidinger to me. What do you want?"

"Ah . . . my name's Shad Nash. You used to teach me. Ah, I saw your note at the mill, and . . . "

"Note? What note?"

"The note . . . you needed someone to . . . ah . . . work."

"Ah! Yes! Yes, the note! Come in! You're Shadrack Nash! You're Bob Nash's boy! I taught you in school!"

"I'm lookin' for a job, yeah," said Shad.

"Oh, well, I, well now . . . why so late? Don't you know how late it is?"

"Ah, I . . . I left home thinkin' I'd get a drive. I had to walk all the way."

"Well, you must be exhausted. You look exhausted! Sit down here by the table. I'll fix you a cup of tea. Do you like carrot cake?"

"Yeah. The very best. Anything at all is good enough for me."

"And did you say you want a job?" Hilda began busying herself making the tea.

"Yeah. Hope it's not taken. I saw the note today and got here as soon as I could."

"Well! I don't know! I . . . do . . . I don't know. How much were you thinking you'd get paid? I mean, it's not really a job;

it's sort of part-time, for room and board. I couldn't pay you much. Goodness knows, you're Bob Nash's son and you'd be . . . " Hilda stopped her business at the stove and looked down at Shad.

Shad looked pale and tired. His hair was too long, parted in the middle.

"Pay me anything at all," said Shad.

"Don't you go to school?" asked Hilda.

"It don't matter. I can quit."

"Quit? You can't quit school!"

"Well, maybe I could go to school and do whatever it is you want done in the evenings, or something."

"Hmm. Well . . . give me a chance to think about it. How's Bob?"

"Good."

"And Elva?"

"Good. The very best."

"Have you seen Dan Brennen lately?"

"Yeah. Oh, yeah. He's around, just waitin' around for the fall guidin', I think."

"What was all that I heard about Lindon Tucker burning the woods down?"

"Oh, you know Lindon."

"Here's your cake. The water'll be boilin' in a minute. You know, it might just work."

Shad shrugged, bit into the cake.

"You could split the wood, carry it in, mow the lawn, shovel the snow, do odd jobs in the evening."

She was thinking: "And I'll have time to myself."

"Anything you want," said Shad.

"I'll tell you what. I'll give you room and board, tobacco and ten dollars a week."

"Sounds good."

"When can you start?"

"I'll go home and get my stuff right now," said Shad.

"No! No, you don't! You can stay here tonight, get your things in the morning."

"Good, good, good."

*

Ducky Shaw and his crew completed their job in early August. The construction of Bill Wallace's cabin was transferred to the capable hands of drywallers, cabinet-makers, carpet layers, masons, plumbers, electricians and painters. Dryfly Ramsey went to work with Nutbeam. After his experience with Bill Wallace's gigantic lodge, Nutbeam's little house seemed almost comical to work on. Everything was so small — the rooms, the roof, everything.

Dryfly found working with Nutbeam much more pleasant than working with Ducky Shaw — Nutbeam never bossed him around and frequently asked for advice. Driven by nothing more than personal ambition, they worked when they felt like it, quitting some days at two o'clock in the afternoon.

The first thing Dryfly did every day when he got home was check the mailbox. Every day he was disappointed to find no letter from Lillian Wallace. He blamed it on the postal system and tried not to let it get him down.

"I love Lillian and Lillian loves me," he thought. "She'll write."

But the days ran into weeks, the weeks became a month. No letter came.

"I know her address — maybe I should write her. I'll get some good paper and a pen from Bernie Hanley's store and write a nice long letter."

He bought the paper and pen and spent two evenings sitting on the abutment of the bridge composing a letter. Both evenings he took his little book of Shakespeare sonnets, and both evenings he looked to it for inspiration. He found it nearly impossible to read. Dryfly was not a great reader of even the simplest literature, but when it came to Shakespeare, he was totally confused. He thought that maybe Shakespeare was in the habit of making up words, or deliberately saying things in a way that a person couldn't understand. "Makeless," for instance, seemed like an odd word; "swart-complexioned" and "vouchsafe," "equipage" and "foison."

He wrote a twelve-page letter anyway, and sent it off.

Then he found himself waiting for an answer.

"Surely, she'll answer me," he thought.

But the summer that had started out so wonderfully was ending in lonesome, miserable waiting.

It was nearly September when the familiar red envelope appeared in the mailbox. He ran into the house to his room, pulled the curtain for greater privacy and sat on the bed. He carefully opened the envelope, sniffed it and kissed it, held the same paper that Lillian had held to his face. Then with trembling fingers he removed the single page. The page had a card of matches attached to it.

He read:

Dear Dryfly,

I was talking to a professor friend of Dad's and mentioned your predicament. He told me that a correspondence course should get you started on the right foot, but that you should probably consider a tutor. You'll be happy to know that Dad thought it was a good idea and will do all he can to help you out.

Take the course, get the job! That's Dad for you. Ha, ha!

You'll find a card of matches attached. It has the address of a place in Canada you can write.

Hope all is well with you. Was glad to hear you'll soon be moving into the new house.

Take care of yourself, Dryfly.

> *Your good friend,*
> *Lillian*

That's all she wrote.

Dryfly read the letter five times, looking for more, the word "love."

"When I wrote my letter to her, I told her that I loved her twelve times," he thought. "A dozen times. I guess that means I love her a dozen times more than she loves me."

Dryfly sulked for two days. Nutbeam could hardly get a word out of him. Nutbeam knew there was something wrong but chose not to interfere.

"If Dryfly needs to have a talk, he'll talk," he thought.

Dryfly needed to have a talk, but he thought Nutbeam might think him stupid, some kind of a wimp. He remained silent, preoccupied.

Then one day he ripped the matches from their folder, addressed it and sent it off. The move was a positive one, made him feel better.

Then he went looking for Shadrack Nash.

"Shad's not home," said Elva.

"Ah, do you know where he is?" asked Dryfly.

Elva was talking to Dryfly through the screen door. She had no intentions of letting Dryfly into the house.

"He's got a job! He's lookin' . . . ah, he's workin' for Hilda Porter . . . ah, runnin' the farm. He stays there with her."

"Ah, okay, thanks," said Dryfly and left.

He went home to his room, opened his little book of sonnets. He began to read, skipped a few pages, tried again. He did not settle into any kind of real comprehension of the great Shakespeare's work until he read sonnets number twenty-nine and thirty.

"He can't write very good," thought Dryfly. "But I kinda like this, a little."

Dryfly picked up his pen and paper, wrote:

Dear Lillian,

Thanks for your letter. I love you very much and think of you very often. Funny — when I think of you, I feel I should be happy that at least I knew you for a little while — that thy sweet love remember'd such wealth brings that then I scorn to change my state with kings . . .

"That's stupid," he thought. But the writing was making him feel better. He continued his plagiarism, wrote:

But if the while I think of thee, dear friend, all losses are restored and sorrows end . . .

"That's probably all old Shakespeare meant to write in the

first place," thought Dryfly. "All that other stuff was prob'ly just somethin' to fill up on."

Dryfly reread what he'd written, crumpled it up and threw it into the corner.

"If she don't write to me, I'll not write to her," he thought. "I get a one-page letter in a month, sayin' nothin'! What's a tutor? Nutbeam plays the trumpet. Does that make him a tutor?"

He stood and went into the kitchen. Nutbeam was sitting by the table. He had a steel rod and was bending it, first to the right, then to the left.

"What're ya makin?" asked Dry.

"Lawn ornament," said Nutbeam.

"With a rod?"

"Yep. With a rod."

Dryfly could have asked, "Modern art?" But Dryfly was unaware of modern art, as of yet, so asked, "What is it?"

Nutbeam had whittled out a little propeller. He picked it up, showed it to Dryfly.

"This is gonna turn the rod," he said. "Make a little man split wood. Know what I mean?"

"I'm not sure," said Dryfly.

"I figured out the works, and it ain't hard at all. With the right tools I could make two or three every day, sell them for ten, fifteen dollars apiece."

"Crooked rods?"

"Little men splitting wood, milkin' cows, sheep, other things. Wind-driven lawn ornaments. Ya ever hear of parn . . . punography?"

"No."

"Well, let me tell ya all about it."

Nutbeam told Dryfly about all the money that was being made on pornography, then revealed his idea for lawn ornaments. Dryfly laughed for the first time since Lillian Wallace left. It felt good to laugh.

Nutbeam and Shirley laughed too. Shirley had been eavesdropping from across the room.

"You should advertise," she said.

*

Before becoming a preacher John Kaston had been a hard-working man. But now that he was a preacher, hard work, manual labour, didn't seem to fit. What self-respecting preacher would be seen working in the woods or ploughing a field? It was a preacher's job to preach and pray, save souls and comfort the dying. With no church and only one sixteen-year-old boy, Dryfly, in his fold, John Kaston was getting bored.

He decided that something had to be done. He decided to start work on his church. He would build it himself. Doing carpenter work would be acceptable — Jesus was a carpenter.

John designed a very small church, one that would accommodate fifty people. There were fewer than that in Brennen Siding, but he allowed room for a few stragglers from the Roman Catholic community of Gordon.

He decided that he could do most of the work, but that he might need a little help with the basement . . . and maybe putting down the sills and floor joists. Possibly, he'd need a little help with the walls.

"And the rafters," he thought. "I might need some donated time putting up the rafters and boarding and shingling the roof. Maybe I'll get some young lads to help me put the windows in and paint, but that's about all. Oh, maybe a few men to help with the inside, but I'll do most of it. It's my church after all. The electricity — I'll need someone to wire the place. I should be able to make the pews myself. And the steeple . . . I'll get someone that kin climb for doin' the steeple. But right now all I need is someone to help me with the forms, the basement forms, and pouring cement."

"It's God's work, so, surely, nobody'd want to get paid. Surely, they must know that I'd pray for them."

He brought the matter up to Rita.

"I want to start the church," he said. "But I'm gonna need a little help getting started. Just a hand or two to help me with the basement. How do you think I should go about asking everyone?"

Rita was making a big stewpot full of mustard pickles. The

smell of vinegar in the kitchen was strong enough to make you sneeze.

"How many men will you need?" asked Rita.

"Well, not that many, five or ten, that's all. Just enough to dig the hole, put up the forms and pour the cement. Shouldn't take that long."

"Well, what's the answer to everything?"

"God, of course."

"Then, what should you do?"

"Pray, of course."

"You're so smart, John."

"It's the Lord speaking through me, my love."

John Kaston left the house and went into what everyone else in Brennen Siding called "the woods," into what he himself called "the wilderness."

He came to the place where Dryfly and Lillian had had their picnic. He knelt by a boulder and began to pray.

"Dear loving Heavenly Father," he began. "I'm in dire need of your wisdom; thus, I kneel to humbly beseech thee, to cower before thy lambent eyes."

John Kaston had been practising, had been studying both his Bible and his dictionary.

There was another rock near him that was big enough to sit on. He closed his eyes and envisioned Jesus there.

"So, what do you need?" asked Jesus, as if he didn't already know.

"My church. I need help with my church," explained John.

"Your church?"

"I'm sorry. I meant your church."

For a brief moment, John's inner eye shifted from Jesus to something he had seen earlier in the summer — to Dryfly Ramsey and Lillian Wallace embraced and fondling on their picnic blanket. John shuddered. Jesus returned.

"Cold?" asked Jesus.

"Ah . . . yeah, it's a bit chilly here."

"How would you like to have been in Dryfly's shoes that day?"

"What do you mean?"

"You think about it often enough."

"No, I . . . well, I . . . please, I'm just a poor sinner."

"Do you think I didn't see you looking at Helen MacDonald?"

"But not like that . . . I mean . . . I'm sorry . . . please forgive me."

"Maybe you would rather serve the antichrist."

"Never!"

"Maybe you'd be happier in pursuit of the flesh."

"Never!"

"You weren't thinking of Rita when you looked at Helen."

"I . . . I . . . I know. Please forgive me."

"What about adultery? You've read the commandments, haven't you?"

"Yes, but . . . "

"One commandment is not meant to be taken more lightly than another! Break one, you might as well break them all! Or have we found a loophole?"

"Please . . . "

"Please what? Please you, or me?"

"Please you."

John opened his eyes to make sure he was alone.

Across the way, a salamander watched him from a rock; a snake in the grass sniffed its tail with its tongue, grabbed it and wheeled away.

"Coo! Coo!" a bird called.

John noticed that there were hoofprints on the ground about him.

"Moose tracks," he thought. He stood, looked about him, saw nothing unusual.

Then, suddenly, he was feeling very warm. He began to perspire, removed his coat.

"Funny," he thought. "I was chilly just a minute ago."

He sat again, sighed. He was very depressed.

"Why am I such a sinner?" he asked himself, closed his eyes.

This time when he closed his eyes, he did not envision Jesus. This time he envisioned Helen MacDonald.

"No," he whispered.

Helen gave way to the Dryfly and Lillian scene.

"No!" he yelled, his voice echoing down through the wilderness.

"Coo! Coo!" came the call of the bird.

He once again envisioned what he took to be Jesus.

"I feel like a worm, or a snake in the grass," said John.

The eyes looked sternly at John — they did not appear to be lambent anymore.

"You must preach a sermon in the wilderness. Talk about the absurdity of pleasing me."

"Yes," said John.

From the woods, John went to where Nutbeam and Dryfly were building their house.

"I see you don't have it partitioned off yet," said John.

Nutbeam smiled nervously, was too shy to answer.

"Yep," said Dryfly. "We're doin' that next week, movin' in the week after."

"Well, before you put up the walls, I'd like to have a little gatherin' here. You understand, don't you, Dryfly? I must talk about pleasing the Lord."

"You want to preach here?"

"It's big enough."

"Yeah, I suppose so."

"And I'd like for y'all to be there."

"But we're Catholics," said Dryfly.

"Catholics, Protestants, we're all the same in the eyes of the Lord."

"Yeah . . . yeah . . . you're right there," managed Nutbeam.

John took that for the permission he sought.

Then John went to see Dan Brennen, Billy Campbell, Bernie Hanley, Stan Tuney, Frank Layton, Lindon Tucker, Lester Burns, Bert Todder, Bob Nash and, last but not least, Helen MacDonald.

He interrupted Helen MacDonald's sweeping. She left a little pile of sand and lint in the middle of the parlour floor.

*

Shadrack Nash mowed Hilda Porter's grass on Monday. On Tuesday he split enough wood to last a week. That wasn't that much — Hilda had a hotplate and seldom cooked on the stove in the summer. On Wednesday he found a saw and a couple of boards and began to fix the veranda floor.

He had just begun to remove one of the boards when he got stung several times by one or more hornets.

"I'll have to tear down the nest," he told Hilda as she treated his stings.

"They're right under the veranda. Do you think they might get into the house?"

"They might. It's a big nest, a lotta hornets."

"And they might sting you again if you fool around with the nest," said Hilda.

Hilda was treating Shad's stings with cold cream. Hilda Porter did not want for Shad to get stung again.

"Do they hurt?" she asked.

"A little. They'll be all right."

"You should get yourself a haircut."

"Yeah . . . can't, though. Gotta look like a Beatle."

"Ha, ha, ha! A beetle! What do you want to look like a beetle for?"

"For the band. Me and Gary and Milton and Billy Bean are startin' up a band. Gotta look like them Beatle lads from England."

Hilda smiled.

Shadrack Nash had red hair, pale skin, a few freckles. As she dabbed the stings, she couldn't help seeing the contrast of their skins. Hers was tan, his was white.

"You ever hear of Tasmania?" she asked.

"The Tasmanian devil," said Shad.

"Yes. Yes, the Tasmanian devil comes from there. Tasmania is a little island south of Australia. There are many weird animals there, and there once was a people. They lived in the forest, ran on all fours. They were red-brown in colour. The women were as bearded as the men. Would you believe that? They had beetle brows."

Hilda Porter told Shad how the Tasmanian aborigines were

nomadic: how they lived on roots and berries, lizards and snakes; how they had no religion, but believed in spirits and goblins; how they stuck feathers and berries in their hair, wore human bones around their necks and painted their skins with red ochre; how they fought their battles and buried their dead; how happy they were until the English came along.

"What happened to them?" asked Shad.

"They made Tasmania a penal colony and . . . but I shouldn't be bothering you with them old stories . . . do the stings feel better?"

"Yeah, the pain's easin' up pretty good. Thanks."

Shad was sitting at the table, Hilda was standing, treating his stings. Shad was seeing a wrinkled, grey-haired old woman in a blue dress and a frilled white apron. Hilda was seeing Shad's thick red hair, pale blue eyes, youthful skin. She was suddenly possessed with an irresistible urge to reach out and touch him.

"You're so young," she said. "You have your whole life ahead of you." She reached out, touched his brow, fingered some loose hair to its rightful place. "What would you like to do with your life, Shad — I mean, after you graduate from school?"

"Don't know. Thought I'd like to become a barber."

"I bet you're a real heartbreaker with the girls around the village."

"Naw . . . I ain't very good with the women."

Hilda straightened Shad's collar, smiled, turned away, went to her chair beside the stove, sat.

"You know, when I was a girl, I wanted to write a book," she said. "I procrastinated all my life. Time just slipped away and I ended up doing nothing."

"You became a teacher," said Shad.

"Yes, sort of, but I should have become a better one, a professor or something. I guess I had no confidence. But you know, I'm not dead yet — I think I will write my book."

"Yeah?"

"I'll write it about the Tasmanian aborigines."

"Well, I'd sure like to read it."

"Would you, Shad? Really?"

"Sure! I bet you could write a great book."

Knock, knock, knock.

"Now who could that be?" said Hilda.

Hilda stood, went to the door and opened it to find Dryfly Ramsey standing on the other side of the screen.

"G'day," said Dryfly.

"Hello," said Hilda. Hilda did not recognize Dryfly, but she knew he was from Brennen Siding.

"Is Shad here?" asked Dryfly.

"Yes. Yes."

"Kin I see him?"

"Ah, yes, I guess. Come in."

"G'day, Dry!" yelled Shad.

Dryfly followed Hilda into the kitchen. He found Shad seated by the table, a dot of cold cream on his face, several on his arms.

"You have a visitor," said Hilda to Shad, then swung to Dryfly. "Now, whose boy might you be?" she asked.

"I'm, ah, Dryfly Ramsey," said Dryfly.

"Dryfly Ramsey . . . Dryfly Ramsey. Oh, yes! Palidin's brother. Dear, dear Palidin! He was the nicest boy. Smart in school, loved to read. You were one of my pupils, too, weren't you?"

"Yes, Miss Porter."

"Well! So how is Palidin these days?"

"Good, good. He's in T'rono."

"He is! Well!"

"What's up?" asked Shad.

Dryfly shrugged. He had a parcel under his arm. He sat the parcel on the table.

"Bought some clothes," said Dryfly. "Got the band goin' yet?"

"Sort of. Practised the other night. Hard gettin' a place. Nobody wants us to plug in the amplifier."

"How about some tea and pie?" put in Hilda.

"Sure," said Shad.

"Good, good," said Dryfly.

"How'd ya get here?" asked Shad.

"Walked."

"Get yer lumber?"

"Yeah, thanks. Yer father brought it. Wouldn't take a cent either."

"Huh!"

"Got the house all up. Almost ready to move in."

"Gonna have a housewarmin'?"

"Sort of. That's what I wanted to talk to you about."

*

Elva Nash was making chow-chow. Bob was whittling an axe handle, a mound of curly shavings at his feet.

"You want to make sure to sweep them old shavin's up good before you go trackin' into the parlour," said Elva.

"Hmm," said Bob. "What's for supper?"

"Well, it ain't salmon, I can tell you that!"

"I know it ain't salmon! All I did was ask a civil question."

"Beans is what we're havin'. You haven't caught a salmon all summer."

"What am I supposed to do, go to the river and tie them on? There hasn't been any good fishin' all summer."

"A lotta sense me makin' chow-chow when there ain't a salmon in the house."

"You don't have to have salmon with chow-chow, and you don't have to have chow-chow with salmon."

"Ha! Pork an' beans, love and marriage, salmon and chow-chow," said Elva as if she were going over some sort of litany, some sort of internationally known proverb.

Bob shook his head negatively.

"No sense talkin' to you," he said.

Elva decided to change the subject.

"I wonder if poor bugger Shad is gettin' enough to eat an' drink?"

"I don't know why you'd care," said Bob.

"Of course I'd care. He's my son after all."

"Then why'd ya kick 'im out?"

"Yes! Yes! Blame me! Blame me!"

"Well, ya did!"

"I did not! He left of his own accord!"

"You kicked him out!"

"Did I? Did you see me kick him out? Did you see me as much as lay a finger on him?" Elva was bringing the volume up a bit.

"Well, ya told him to get out!"

"Well, he didn't have to just up an' leave! I just needed some peace an' quiet!"

"You just needed to argue an' fight, is what you needed."

"Me? It was you an' Shad that were always fightin' like cats an' dogs!"

"You're just as stubborn an' contrary as ever you can be!"

"Yes! Yes, old snoozer! Blame it on me! It's little wonder a person rants an' raves!"

Elva was stirring the chow-chow. Her face and arms were getting hot from working over the stove. The conversation with Bob had her equally hot under the collar.

"Do you think poor little Shad knows the difference between right an' wrong?" she asked.

"If he don't, he must be deaf an' dumb! You've been prayin' an' preachin' over him enough."

"Well, I only wanted him to be aware of the ins an' outs of life."

"What about the ups an' downs?"

"Believe in God and there shouldn't be any downs. That's about the long an' short of it."

Elva tasted her chow-chow. She was not sure if it contained the right amount of herbs and spices.

"Taste this," she said to Bob, handing him a spoon with a bit of chow-chow on it.

Bob took the spoon, blew over its hot contents, smelled and tasted it.

"What's it need?" asked Elva.

"Salt an' pepper," said Bob.

"Have you ever thought about goin' an' gettin' him? He might not be very happy down there with Hilda. And what d'ya think people are thinkin an' sayin'? He's runnin' around Blackville day an' night, rain or shine. The first thing he'll be gettin' into that old liquor an' dope."

Bob sighted along the axe handle. He was pleased with the fact that it was perfectly straight.

"I wouldn't blame 'im if he never came home," said Bob. "The way you scream an' holler, always goin' on about what's good an' what's evil."

"Well, I didn't see you givin' 'im any overflow of love an' affection!"

They fell silent for a while.

There had been an unfamiliar silence in the house lately. They were both aware of it. They could hear the house creaking, the wind blowing, the rain falling, the fire crackling in the stove — if there was a sound, they could hear it. Shad was away — no radio, no banjo. When Shad was home, he played the banjo and the radio constantly, morning, noon and night, often the same tunes over and over again. They were beginning to think that his obsession with music would drive them crazy. But now that he was gone, they found they missed it, that there was a void.

"Maybe I'll go see 'im . . . have a little man-to-man. He wants to build a camp. He could keep a few sports."

Satisfied that her chow-chow was cooked properly, Elva set it aside, then sat at the table to watch Bob sandpaper the axe handle. Bob Nash took great pride in his axe handles. To whittle a handle smoothly, to select the right wood with the right grain — one end had to have a perfect grip, the other end had to fit the axe. Making axe handles was a delicate craft.

There was something almost erotic in the way Bob Nash handled his axe handles.

Elva took a deep breath, needing extra energy for what she was about to say.

"Let's go to bed," she said.

Bob looked up from his work. He saw a very unhappy woman staring back at him. He saw other things, too — simplicity, mediocrity, time, the reflection of the girl he once had loved, fear . . .

"We're like black an' white," he thought. "But what is it that keeps us together? I guess we're together because we've done this to each other. We're a man and a woman. The man makes the woman and the woman makes the man."

At that moment a feeling came over Bob Nash.

"That's good-smellin' chow-chow," he said.

"Ah . . . nothin'," said Elva.

"It is," persisted Bob.

"That's a pretty good lookin' axe handle ya got there, too," said Elva.

Bob Nash didn't know whether to laugh or cry.

*

After they ate their fill of Hilda Porter's pie, Shad said, "I should show you that hornets' nest, Dry, see what ya think."

"Okay," said Dry.

"Now, you boys be careful!" said Hilda.

"We will," said Shad. "Don't wanna git stung agin."

Shad and Dry went outdoors to the front of the house, knelt and peered into the shadows under the veranda. They could see the nest, grey, the size of a man's head. The hornets held a quick conference to see which of them would sacrifice itself and warn the monsters that they were getting too close. A few were already zipping by Shad and Dry, seeing if the vibrations were threatening or not.

"So, what do ya think?" asked Shad.

"A bad outfit," said Dry.

"Too close to the house to pour gas on," said Shad. "Throw a cigarette butt down and the house would go up like a torch."

"Knock it down with a long board and run fer your life," suggested Dryfly.

"Can't do that, they might all get into the house. There's already a few goin' in. . . see them on the windows all the time."

"You could just stay away from them, wait for fall, then tear it down."

"Yeah . . . I don't know. C'mon, I'll show ya all the stuff she's got in the sheds."

The two boys rounded the house and went to the barn. They swung back one of the big doors and entered. Sunlight streaked from cracks between the boards; they could smell the stale hay; startled swallows swooped about. There was a wagon, an upside-down canoe spattered with bird droppings, a bunch of pitchforks. Shovels and hay rakes stood in the corner.

"We need a name for the band," said Shad. "And you're gonna have to find some way to practise with us. Then, we need a place to play, a dance or something."

"John Kaston wants to preach a sermon in the new house."

"Yeah?"

Both boys grinned at the thought.

"Saturday evening, seven o'clock."

"That should be good."

"Ha, ha! He's askin' everyone to come . . . even went up to Gordon and passed the word around."

"Anyone gonna go?"

"Not a soul."

"Ha! Mom'll prob'ly go."

"Me and Nutbeam thought we might have a party that night, after the sermon."

"Yeah?"

"People would come to the party."

"S'pose?"

"Sure. And you lads could play fer it."

"You too."

"Whatever. It'd be a good practice."

"Sure would."

"No electricity yet, though."

"Wouldn't need no amplifiers in a little place like that."

"That's what I thought."

"What's John think of it?"

"Don't matter. It's our house. Think Gary and them will do it?"

"Sure. Gotta start somewhere."

"Nutbeam said he'd supply the band with wine."

"Do ya think he'll show up at the party?"

"Don't know. He's pretty shy. We should go to the sermon, Shad."

"What for?"

"For a laugh. Should be awful funny, shouldn't it? Anyway, he shouldn't preach for very long. Should be done at eight or so. Then we kin party."

They left the barn and went to a long, garage-like shed, entered.

This shed was cluttered with old farm machinery.

"All you need is a horse," said Dryfly.

"Yep. A man could have quite a farm, if he wanted."

"There's an old sleigh . . . and what's that thing?"

"Threshing machine, I think," said Shad.

"What are all the other bands callin' themselves?" asked Dry.

"Well, there's Lyman MacPhee and the Cornpoppers. The big name bands seem to be named after, well, there's the Animals, the Beatles, the Monkeys, Jerry and the Pacemakers."

"Pacemaker an animal?" This was a stupid question delivered with a grin.

"Don't know, worm maybe," grinned Shad. Shad slapped Dryfly on the back. "Good to see ya," he said. "How've ya been?"

"Good, I guess."

"Mom kicked me out."

"Yeah? Gonna stay here?"

"I don't know what to do," said Shad.

Shad sighed, climbed into the sleigh, changed the subject.

"Any word from Lillian?" he asked.

Dryfly's heart sank with the mention of Lillian.

"Yeah," he said. "Get letters all the time."

"You should have yourself two women," said Shad. "One for the winter."

That statement did not deserve a response. Dryfly dropped his eyes.

A little whirlwind moaned its way through the shed.

"Do you like stayin' here?" asked Dryfly.

Shad shrugged. "Yeah, I guess," he said. "Pretty good setup."

"How about the Whoopsnakes?" asked Dry.

"Hoopsnakes?"

"Whoopsnakes . . . with a *w*."

"Ha!"

seven

About a mile below Brennen Siding, the Gordon road branched. Here, a lesser road ran out to the Dungarvon river to a place where the water was shallow enough, and the gravel on the river's bottom was smooth and stable enough, to wade a vehicle across. Once across, you could drive up through the woods to Brennen Siding's east side. This was an OK access for six months of the year, and in winter you could drive across on the ice. For a month in the spring and another month in the late fall, however, John Kaston, Bob Nash and anybody else that wanted to get to the Gordon Road had to leave their vehicles on the west side of the river and cross in a canoe.

Billy Bean waded the river with his old GMC cargo van. On the seat beside him sat Shad Nash. Shad was navigating.

In the back, amongst the drums, guitar, banjo, two spare tires, a shovel, battery cables, an old coat, a cardboard box full of paraphernalia, empty beer and pop bottles, girly magazines, somebody's shoe, a jack, a bicycle pump and an old mattress, sat Gary Perkins and Billy Bean's brother, Milton.

The Whoopsnakes were headed for their first gig.

John and Rita Kaston, Bob and Elva Nash, and Dryfly Ramsey waited at Nutbeam's house for a crowd to show.

"I told everybody to come at seven o'clock," said John. "It's almost nine. I guess nobody wants to hear the word o' God."

"You could preach to us," said Elva.

"I'll give it a few more minutes," said John.

Dryfly was growing impatient. He hadn't counted on John waiting for so long for a crowd to show. Now, when the Whoopsnakes and the party people showed, John would think they were coming to hear him preach.

"Are you sure you told everyone that it was tonight?" asked Dryfly.

"Yes! Yes, I'm sure! Do you think I'm stupid?"

"Praise the Lord!" said Rita, looking out at the river.

Everyone looked to see what she was looking at.

Two canoes were being pulled up at the shore. Six party people were getting out and heading up the hill to Nutbeam's house-warming.

"Damn!" thought Dryfly. "What am I goin' to do now?"

"And here comes Bert and Lindon," said Bob.

"Hallelujah!" said John.

"And here comes the Whoopsnakes," moaned Dryfly.

"The what?" asked John.

"Ah . . . Shad and them," said Dryfly.

"Whose van is that?" asked Elva.

"Ah . . . that's, ah . . . ah, Billy Bean's," said Dryfly.

"Well! Imagine that, John! They're coming all the way from Blackville to hear ya!" put in Rita.

John Kaston smiled lambently.

There was a car coming up the flat, too, and they could see a pick-up truck coming in the distance. Within fifteen minutes there were twenty-five people standing around outside of Nutbeam's little house, and more coming. By the time nine o'clock rolled around, there were sixty people there from all over Brennen Siding and Gordon.

John Kaston was overwhelmed with joy. He had never dreamed so many would turn out.

Dryfly called the Whoopsnakes out behind the van and over a drink of wine stated the problem.

"You mean he hasn't preached yet?" said Shad.

"No, and he thinks everyone is here to hear him."

"Good scrape!"

"Well, get him started and get it over with," said Milton. "He can't preach all that long, can he?"

"Ya never know."

"Ladies and gentlemen!" yelled John Kaston. "Brothers and sisters!"

Everyone looked toward John.

The Whoopsnakes took one more drink and, grinning, headed for the sermon. They were expecting this to be a laugh and a half.

"It's such a beautiful evening!" yelled John. "I'm inclined to think that the good Lord had it in mind that we remain outside. Outside in the good land He hath bestowed upon us."

It was, indeed, a nice evening. The sun had set, the stars were coming out, a moon was rising, lanterns were being lit, the air was warm. Everybody looked about, agreed with John's observation and turned back to their conversations.

But John was just beginning.

"Brothers and sisters!" he yelled. "I am pleased to see so many of you here, and it's a great feeling to know that the good Lord has the attention of so many!"

People were gathered around in little groups, talking, laughing and nipping at pints of rum and quarts of wine. Some of them swung their attention to John, wondering why he was so adamant about making a speech. If anyone were to make a speech, it should be Nutbeam or Dryfly, not John Kaston.

"What's he got to do with the new house?" someone asked.

John was somewhat annoyed with the lack of attention, blamed it on his vantage point. There was a pile of boards beside the house. John went to it, climbed up on them. He could look down on everybody.

"Tonight!" he yelled. "Tonight, I'm gonna speak to you about pleasing the Lord!"

"We'll never get him out of here," said Shadrack.

"Let him go," said Billy Bean. "This should be good for a laugh. Anything will sound good after he rants for a while."

"I'd like to ask y'all a question," said John. "How many of you get down on yer knees every day? How many of you get on your knees, and when you do, just what do you say?"

John looked over the congregation. The board pile idea was working. More and more people were giving him their attention. They were curious about what he was up to.

"Do you think that getting on your knees once a day is enough to please the Lord? NO!"

A few people thought that this was a joke, chuckled.

"Yes, yes, it's funny to think that you could please the Lord," said John. "You'd have to be perfect to do that! Is there any of you that are perfect? Well? NOOOO! There's nobody perfect! Do you think that goin' to church on Sunday pleases the Lord? NOOOO! You could go to church every day and it would not please the Lord!

"Brothers and sisters, there once was a man who had five dollars. He met up with another man who asked him if he could borrow just one dollar. Wanting to please the Lord, the man gave his friend the whole five. Just reached into his pocket and gave the man the whole five. He said, 'There! That should please the Lord!' So, what do you think? Do you think the Lord was pleased? Eh? NOOOO, HE WASN'T PLEASED! The Lord wasn't pleased because the man didn't offer his friend his clothes, his house, his car!"

Elva Nash was beaming with pride.

"My brother John, the preacher!" she thought. "Bless us and save us, thank you, Lord!"

Bob Nash, however, saw the reality of the situation and felt like crawling under a rock. He was sorry he came, would have given anything, another fifty dollars, just to be away from there.

He was looking for an escape route when he saw Shad standing with Dryfly and three other boys.

Shad saw Bob looking at him, nodded.

Bob approached Shad.

"Let's go for a little walk," he whispered.

They moved away, went behind the van.

"How've ya been, Shad?" he asked.

"Good," said Shad.

"Now, ah, ah, listen, Shad . . . you, ah . . . I want, ah, you, ah, to know that, ah, I, ah, oh, ah, you kin come home anytime ya want."

"I'm all right," said Shad.

"Yeah, well, ah, I, ah, oh, ah, you and me kin go at that camp."

John Kaston was really getting into his sermon now. "Nothing less than your soul is good enough for the Lord," he was yelling.

"Oh, ah, Elva and me, ah, talked it over and, well, we'd like fer ya to come home, Shad."

"Mom wants me to come home?"

"Yeah, well, she misses ya, Shad. She thinks a lotta you, you know."

"Go to Rome!" yelled John Kaston, as if he'd been there. "Go to the Vatican and see all the wealth stored there! That's not right, ladies and gentlemen!" John was attacking Roman Catholicism now. "It's not right, because all that wealth should be given to the poor! To Jesus! To the church!"

"Well, I don't know," said Shad. "I'm doing okay. I'll be around. I'll help you build a camp."

Bob nodded.

"Would ya . . . would ya like a little drink?" asked Shad.

"You got somethin' to drink?" asked Bob, grinning, proud of his son.

Shad opened the back of the van. Bob could see the wine, the drums, the banjo and guitar.

"Holy jeez . . . dyin'!" he exclaimed.

They had a drink.

"And now, brothers and sisters, let me tell you about Zaccheus," John Kaston was saying to a very anxious crowd as Bob and Shad rejoined them. "There was a man that was so short that he had to climb a sycamore tree to see our Lord . . . " This story had to do with money and so did John's next story about Solomon, and the one after that about the eye of the needle. "Do you think that any one of you people with money in your pockets kin manage to get through the eye of a needle?" yelled John. "Well, that's how hard it's gonna be! That's how hard it's gonna be to get into the kingdom of God!"

"And now ladies and gentlemen, let's sing an old hymn, a favourite of mine, 'In The Sweet Bye and Bye.'"

John started singing: "There's a land that is fairer than day . . . " He was a terrible singer and it was a very funny thing to listen to. "In the sweeeeeeeeeet bye an' bye, we shall meet on that beautiful shore!"

Elva Nash and Rita Kaston joined in.

Bert Todder and Lindon Tucker were feeling their rum, felt

like singing and joined in. Billy and Milton Bean and Gary Perkins were drinking and felt like making fun — they joined in as well.

Soon everyone was singing and laughing.

Shad ran back to the van and returned with the banjo and guitar, gave the guitar to Billy and began, to the delight of everyone, to accompany the singing. Dryfly's guitar was standing against the house, and when he saw what Shad was up to, he, too, began to play.

"Most of John's sermon was about money," thought Dryfly. "He prob'ly should be singing 'In the Sweet Buy and Buy.'" Dryfly began to grin to himself, sang "In the sweet buy and buy, we shall meet in that beautiful store."

The Whoopsnakes had it in mind to keep the music rolling and not give John Kaston a chance to continue his preaching. When "The Sweet Bye and Bye" ended, Shad immediately started playing "Will the Circle Be Unbroken." John Kaston was slightly uncomfortable with what was happening, but sang along.

When the song ended, he yelled, "Brothers and sisters . . . !"

"Good idea!" yelled Shad. "Try this one. 'There's a singing waterfall in a mountain far away.'" The music had already started, the people were already singing. Again, there was nothing John could do. He started to sing, but it suddenly occurred to him that this song was not a hymn.

"Stop!" he yelled, "Stop that singing!" but nobody paid him any attention. His congregation was out of hand and, what was worse, he hadn't even taken up a collection. He waited for the song to end.

"Yes, yes," he said then, "'There's a Singin' Waterfall' is not a hymn, but it's so good to hear all you fine singers." John looked about at what he considered to be his congregation. Everybody was mingling and conversing, some singing; he saw a quart of wine being passed around. He knew his sermon was over.

Dryfly started singing a song that many of the people seemed to know. He sang "Your cheatin' heart will tell on you, you'll cry and cry . . . "

"Whoop!"

Elva Nash saw John and Rita walking across the field toward home. She grabbed Bob's arm. "C'mon!" she snapped. "Let's get away from these awful, awful . . . " She could think of no word bad enough to describe the sinners.

"Oh, I don't know," said Bob, pinching her behind. "I think I'll stick around and have some fun. We haven't been at a real party for twenty years."

"But this is supposed to be a sermon!"

"Well, I guess old John just ain't meant to be a preacher."

"What about your soul?"

"My soul is here," said Bob. "There ain't much I can do about that."

"Well, I'm stayin' right here with you," said Elva.

"That's my girl," said Bob.

"Oh, don't get me wrong! I'm stayin' to keep an eye on you. You're not gettin' into that dirty old liquor tonight! I saw you and Shad go behind that van. Did you talk with him?"

"Yeah, he's doin' just fine. Sound pretty good, don't they? Don't him and Dryfly remind you of Buck and me when we used to sing and play?"

"They've ruined John's sermon."

"Ah! He'll get over it."

"Who's that big, tall lad with the big ears? Is that Nutbeam?"

"Yep. Shirley's lookin' good, ain't she?"

"I see Helen MacDonald's here, too. I suppose Bert Todder will be chasin' her half the night."

"He'll never quit chasin' Helen."

"I think I'll say hello to her," said Elva.

"Yeah, yeah, you do that. I think I'll just go over and sing along with the boys."

*

On their way across the field to home, John Kaston walked ten feet in front of Rita. He told himself he needed to be alone, but in the back of his mind he knew he was ashamed to face her. He was ashamed to face anyone. His debut had been a joke. He felt he had been used.

"Those people weren't there for my sermon," he thought. "They all had liquor with them. Nobody showed for the sermon. That's why they were all two hours late. Dryfly Ramsey! Dryfly's the culprit here!"

When they got home, John's thoughts continued well into the night. He paced and scratched his head, mumbled and grumbled, went to bed, got up again, had a drink of water, paced some more, went back to bed, got up again, went outside. He could hear the party across the field at Nutbeam's.

"The devil's got the whole bunch o' them," he thought. "Here it is past midnight — it's Sunday and they're still at it, singing, whoopin' and hollerin'. Sinners."

John went back into the kitchen. Rita was up having a drink of water. Her hair was down, black, hanging to her fat bum. Rita believed that it was a sin for a woman to cut her hair.

"Can't sleep either?" asked John.

"It's the noise of that party over there," said Rita.

"I should have known not to expect any better from that, that Dryfly-Ramsey-old-Buck-boiled-right-down!" said John.

"Well, just forget about it."

"Forget about it! How can I forget this? Ever!"

"Forgive and forget and pray, John."

"I'm not done with him yet," mumbled John. "They're not gonna live like a bunch o' heathens next door to me, next door to my church! They're not gonna make a fool outta me, either! If that Dryfly was my son, I'd take a stick to 'im!"

"You're talkin' just like the devil would want ya to talk! Why don't ya just go to bed, pray, forget!"

John sighed, sat at the table.

"I . . . I . . . I don't know what to do," he said.

"Everything's gonna be all right, dear. The Lord's on our side."

"Why do you think everything's goin' wrong?" asked John.

"Everything's goin' the way the good Lord wants it to go."

"Do you think the Lord wants them heathens singin' and partyin' like that?"

"The Lord works in mysterious ways."

"My sermon . . . what did you think of my sermon?"

"Elva liked it."

"Yes, yes, my dear sister Elva."

"What was that about not being able to please God?"

"That was good, eh?"

"Yes, you talked well, and yes, it's truly hard to live up to His wants, but that story about the five dollars . . . where'd that come from?"

"Just a story. Made it up."

"Then it was a lie."

"No, just a little . . . a little parable."

"It was a lie, John."

"The Lord used parables!"

"C'mon to bed, John. We'll pray."

"You go to bed. I need to think. I'm goin' into the wilderness for a little walk."

John left the house and headed across the field to the woods. He had a flashlight with him, thought he might need it for the path. The moon was up, however, and he could see the path quite well. He made it to his rock, to the place where Dryfly and Lillian had had their picnic, without switching on the light. He sat on the rock.

Moonbeams filtered through the tree branches and danced with the troubled waters of the little brook.

"Things aren't looking too good," thought John. "It seems so useless. What am I to do, Lord? What would you do?"

Somebody at the party whooped. It carried across the field and into the woods to John's ears.

"How do I fight this sin?"

"To fight a battle one must step into the battlefield."

"Must I go back to that party?"

"The sinners are there."

"Yes, I must go back and mingle with the sinners. That's where I'm needed most."

John left the woods and went to Nutbeam's. He stood in the shadow of the house watching the dancing, the singers; hearing the steady flow of laughter, blasphemy, arguments.

THE **BRENNEN SIDING** TRILOGY

Everyone there seemed drunk and loud. Bob Nash was still there, singing and drinking. Lindon Tucker staggered about from group to group, agreeing with everyone, repeating what he'd heard from the previous group.

"Oh yeah, yeah, yep. Great, great, great time, yep."

Bert Todder was there, hot on the corned heels of Helen MacDonald.

"It's gettin' late, Helen. Maybe you'd better let me walk you home."

"Bert Todder, I've lived here for fifty-five years and kin find my own way home, thank you very much!"

Bert grinned. Helen could see his lone tooth.

"An awful waste," said Bert. "That thing's gonna dry up if you're not careful."

"Now, Bert! Don't you start!"

"Tee, hee, hee, sob, snort, sniff!"

Somebody had built a fire and was burning up bits, ends and pieces of boards and two-by-fours. The Whoopsnakes were standing around the fire and were singing what songs they knew for the second and third time. Bob Nash was with them, "the special guest." Every now and then he'd take the banjo from Shad and play a song or two, but he was much too drunk to play well. He was having great fun, however.

"Bye, bye love! Bye, bye happiness," sang the Whoopsnakes.

The area in front of Nutbeam's little house was aglow with light from the fire and lanterns. John Kaston stood in the shadows debating his approach.

"Should I stand on the boards and address the whole crowd?" he asked himself. "Or should I approach one at a time? Prob'ly one at a time would be the best. They're too drunk, they'd never listen to a sermon." He took a deep breath and stepped into the light.

A few people looked his way, but paid him little attention.

He approached Dan Brennen.

"Evenin', Dan," said John.

"John! How'shhh she goin'?" Dan staggered, grabbed John's sleeve for stability.

"You're drunk!" said John.

"Oh, jush a little bit. Where's Rita?"

"Home in bed where all good Christian women belong!"

"Here! Have a little nip o' rum, John!"

John was about to speak his mind on the evils of liquor when someone grabbed his arm from behind.

"John Kaston!" said Helen MacDonald. "You've come back!"

"Evenin', Helen."

"Where's Rita?"

"She's home . . . in bed."

Dan Brennen shrugged and staggered off toward the music.

"That was a great little sermon you preached, John."

"Why, I'm glad you liked it, Helen."

"It's too bad the party and the sermon were both on the same night, but everyone thought you were just wonderful."

"I . . . I didn't know . . . I didn't think they . . . did they for sure?"

"Oh, yes. Elva just loved it. I'm sure they all did."

"Well, now!"

"It's mighty neighbourly of you to come back to the party, John. Poor Shirley's finally getting her new home. There's always something good comes of everything, eh? And I didn't know that Dryfly and Shadrack could sing and play like that!"

"Hmm."

"Remember the party we had when you built your house, John?"

"Ah, yeah, I remember."

"I was so happy for you and Rita."

"I didn't think you were."

"Well, I was . . . is everything going well for you and Rita, John?"

It had been five years since Rita had decided that making love was a sin unless one had procreation in mind, but John did not mention this to Helen MacDonald.

"We're doing okay," said John. "I've started my church."

"Well, isn't that just wonderful! You can bet that I'll be the first one to go to it. I think about you a lot, John. Even after all these years."

"You should've found yourself someone else, Helen."

"I told you, John. You were the only man for me. Rita's a lucky woman. I've remained an old maid all these years. Do you remember why you left me for Rita, John?"

"I was young and foolish."

"You mean you think you made a mistake?"

"No, I mean I was young and foolish to be thinking about . . . what I was thinking about."

"When you came in the other day to tell me about your sermon, for a while I felt young and foolish again."

"You did?"

"I've needed you for years, John."

"That's a terrible sin," said John.

"I s'pose it is, but I'm fifty-five and gettin' older every day. I've never had a lover, John. That old Bert Todder keeps hangin' around, but ya can't take 'im serious, and besides, I wouldn't have him for bear bait."

"You poor, poor sinner."

"That dog that's barkin' sounds like my Rex. I should go home, I suppose, and see what he's into. He hardly ever barks like that."

"Yeah, well, I'll pray for you, Helen."

"Would you pray for me tonight, John?"

"I would."

"Come. Walk me home and pray for me."

Helen MacDonald led John away from the party. As they approached her house, they could hear Rex barking so ferociously that he seemed to be in some serious trouble.

"Now, what do you suppose that old dog's barkin' at?" said Helen.

John was thinking of the party, the sinners staying up until Sunday morning and still partying. He was thinking of what might happen if he were to follow Helen into the house. It had almost happened before. Helen had always wanted him, had never let him forget it, even after twenty-five years. If he were to follow her into the house, he was sure she would make advances, want him to sit close beside her on the sofa, tempt him.

"The devil's about, no doubt," he said.

*

The party lasted until three o'clock in the morning. The Whoopsnakes were the last to leave, and when Billy Bean's van pulled away, only Dryfly remained. He checked out the house to make sure that nobody left any live cigarette butts lying around, then blew out the lantern, picked up his guitar and headed for home. He took the shortcut over the hill and through the Judge Martin property to the bridge. On the centre abutment he paused to look at the river. The moon was racing the stars to the horizon.

"It was a good party," thought Dryfly, "even though it started off with a sermon. It would have been a better time if Billy hadn't sung that song. At least there were no fights. Usually, there's a fight when Brennen Sidingers get together with Gordoners. I never sung so much before in my life. We must've sung every Beatle song ten times. Know most of the words already. It was good to be playin' music with the boys, though I wish Billy hadn't sung that song. Nice lads, though. It's funny how they're all wearin' their hair combed down in the front. Not much trouble for me to wear my hair like that. All I have to do is shake my head."

It had been a successful party, and Dryfly had enjoyed himself most of the night. The fun had ended late for him when Billy Bean sang the Jim Reeves song, "Tears are only rain to make love grow." Billy's voice had been shaky and weak, but he had followed the melody quite well. Well enough. Well enough to blanket Dryfly with a gigantic blue shroud with Lillian Wallace's initials on it.

The song had taken Dryfly back to that rainy morning beneath the leaking roof of Bill Wallace's camp, to the morning that he and Lillian had hugged and kissed away their heartaches. The song had churned up memories of tears and laughter, full cups of love.

Songs.

The last thing Dryfly needed was to hear a song of heartache. He did not need to be reminded of how lonely he was, of how much he missed Lillian Wallace.

Songs.

"What selfish, egotistical bugger for punishment, loser, sucker for abuse, sulk, wimp, thought up the first song of heartache?

"Who caused more pain, more people to cry? Adolf Hitler, or Hank Williams?"

Dryfly Ramsey was not crying there on the bridge. There were no tears in his eyes. Dryfly did not think that tears would contribute significantly to his love for Lillian Wallace. Dryfly Ramsey did not think that Lillian had a cold, cold heart. Dryfly Ramsey didn't give a shit about honky tonk heaven. Dryfly Ramsey did not have a telephone to put his sweet lips to.

Dryfly needed one single little letter with "I love you" written on it. Dryfly needed Lillian Wallace. Dryfly did not need to listen to the woes of Hank Williams, Jim Reeves, Patsy Cline and George Jones. Dryfly Ramsey needed to know the man who put the bomp in the bomp-sha-bomp-sha-bomp.

"I'm trying for you," said Dryfly. "I'm takin' the correspondence course."

Dryfly's recollection of Lillian Wallace was so vivid that she could have been there beside him on the bridge or sitting on the moon smiling down at him, legs crossed, chin resting in her palm. He was seeing her with the sharp-sighted vision of a lover.

"I'll get educated . . . for you. I'll become a doctor or a lawyer . . . for you. I'd do anything for you. Anything I can do."

If you're living in the same neighbourhood as your lover, there are things you can do to win her heart — send flowers, stand beneath her balcony and sing your little heart out, recite poetry, get on your knees and beg her to be yours, seduce her and make love so wonderfully that she could never again consider doing it with anyone but you; you can date someone else to make her jealous, ignore her to make her curious, change your way to fit her needs, show her the fun side of you, make her laugh; you can beat up that other guy that's been seeing her, let the air out of his tires, put sugar in his gas tank, poop on his car seat. If you're living in the same neighbourhood as the apple of your eye, there's always the possibility that you can woo her to save you a bite of the core. The core of the apple of love is the best part. That's where the seeds are.

When Dryfly thought that he'd do anything for Lillian Wallace, what could he have had in mind? "When Nutbeam and Shirley move into the new house, you and I can move into the old one with the plastic windows, slop pail, outdoor toilet and tarpaper roof."

"Let's go on a shopping spree way up at Bernie Hanley's, darling."

"Why don't we splurge and go to Brigham's in Blackville?"

"Okay. We can go out for dinner afterward. We'll go to Biff's canteen for a wiener and chips."

"Or we can come home early and have a nice dinner of black salmon and potatoes. I'll get the chow-chow."

"It sounds so romantic, darling. Do I get to listen to *Hay Shaker's Hoedown* on the radio?"

"The sky's the limit, my love. We can even go to a dance, if you want. As you know, I never danced in my life, but there's just about always a fight to watch."

"What do you say we have Lindon Tucker over some night for a little intellectual debate?"

"And possibly Bert Todder. Bert could talk to us about fish farts."

But whoever said that reality and futility made any difference to a young man's heart?

In Dryfly Ramsey's situation, he might as well have been flapping his arms in an attempt to reach the moon. Telling him that he could never have Lillian Wallace for his own would be like telling a Miramichier that he should go to Venice, even though the salmon are running; would be like telling genitalia that sex is not important.

It was three-thirty in the morning. Dryfly was standing on the centre abutment of the Brennen Siding footbridge. The moon was on the horizon. The river swept beneath his feet.

At three-thirty on a Brennen Siding morning there should not have been anybody else around. All the houses, except for

Helen MacDonald's, were in darkness. There was a light in Helen MacDonald's bedroom. At three-thirty in the morning, Dryfly should have been the only person not having sweet dreams between the sheets.

When someone steps onto one end of a footbridge, the whole bridge responds to the stress: the cables creak, the bridge sways, waves, rocks.

Dryfly heard the cables creak, felt the bridge respond to somebody's footsteps. Whoever it was, was used to walking the narrow boardwalk — the footsteps were loud and confident. He looked in their direction. He could see the dim ribbon of boards all the way to its end. He took the fact that he could see nobody as an illusion played by sounds and echoes, shrugged and looked toward the other end.

There was nobody there, either.

Clomp, clomp, clomp, came the footsteps.

"What's goin' on here?" thought Dryfly. "Why isn't somebody there?"

Clomp, clomp, clomp.

The footsteps grew louder, approached to where they seemed to be but a few yards away, stopped.

The phenomenon had Dryfly baffled, but he did not feel afraid. What he felt was more of an exhilaration, a chill. Gooseflesh coursed over his body.

A sense of anger possessed him.

All the warm, loving thoughts of Lillian Wallace fled from his heart and took up residence in his loins, partied there. Dryfly's vision of Lillian Wallace took a dramatic shift from a sweet young girl sitting crosslegged on the moon to a shifty-eyed slut begging to be taken.

He took her, abused her, raped her, forgetting gentleness, pleasure, love.

"Fuck you, Lillian Wallace!" he panted. "Fuck you and the whole world! I'm all that's important! I'm all that matters! What gives you the right to play with me? Who the hell do you think you are?"

He spat at her, slapped her. The perspiration came out on his brow.

"See what I think of you! See what I'm doing! See what you did to me!"

At the climax of it all, only hate, egocentricity, narcissism rained on the river below.

And then, as sudden as the hate had come over him, it left and he was standing looking at the river, holding his manhood, heart pounding. Tears welled from his eyes.

"No," he said. His voice was a murmur. "No . . . " He pulled himself together and continued across the bridge on shaky legs, trying to not think of what he had just been thinking, what he had just done.

"I've had too much wine," he thought. "That old Golden Nut will drive you crazy."

eight

Nutbeam and Dryfly clapboarded and painted the front side, the side facing the river, and both ends of the new house. They were running low on money, so the back side had to settle for tarpaper.

"Nobody'll ever see the back o' the house, anyway," said Nutbeam. "We need some furniture and stuff, and we have to make ends meet till trappin' season. That's two months away."

"Bill Wallace is back," said Dryfly. "I'm gonna go and see him tonight or tomorrow. Gonna take that job he offered me."

"That'll sure help, Dryfly."

"All right, so we'll do the front and both ends this year and do the back when we have the money. That's okay by me."

They painted the clapboards pumpkin orange, the finishing red. Shirley had selected the colours. She had seen a similar combination in Rogersville years ago. They were French colours.

Nutbeam bought a chrome table and chairs for the kitchen. "No more old wooden stuff for my Shirley," was his reason.

The new house was actually smaller than the old one. It had a door and a window on the north end and a door and a window on the front. There were two windows on the south end. A window was planned for the back, but that was put on hold, boarded in and tarpapered over. Windows were expensive. They bought them small — just big enough to crawl through, but that was about it. There was nothing wrong in having small windows. Many Dungarvoners put small windows in their houses. Small windows indicated that you were a good, hardworking, conservative sort. Small windows were less expensive and warmer — saved on drapes and curtains, too.

If Nutbeam hadn't found a two-for-one sale on second-hand doors, he would not have put a door on the front side of the house at all. On the Dungarvon front, doors were pretty much ornamental, the kitchen door being the preferred exit. The front door was used only when somebody died. On the Dungarvon you could always tell where the old people lived. Old people were the only ones with a doorstep at the front door. They waked their dead at home on the Dungarvon.

"We're gettin' old, Nellie. No tellin' when they might have to carry a coffin through that front door. Better build a step."

Nutbeam and Dryfly did not build a step at the front door.

They put up two stoves — a cooking range in the kitchen and a furnacette in the tiny living room. They did not build a chimney. Pipes protruded from the roof above the kitchen and the living room. The pipes were teed at the top.

Bob Nash moved them in his pick-up, wading the river over and back twice, the pick-up laden with everything useful that they owned — beds and mattresses, dishes, backless chairs, a mirror, clothes, lawn ornaments.

Nutbeam pinned twenty-one lawn ornaments in various places in front of the house, in what he called the lawn. He put a black and white cow on the right side of the door, a black moose to the left. He put two black cats under the window, a white chicken at each of the two front corners. He had a spotted fawn and a mother goose with three young baby geese trailing behind, and a white horse with a black harness pulling a wagon; he had a giraffe and a zebra and two billy goats. Shirley Ramsey had painted the walls of her living room pink and had a cup or so of the paint left over. Nutbeam took advantage of the situation. He put the two pink flamingo-like birds on the lawn right in the centre, one on each side of a car tire he had placed there. The car tire, which he had painted pumpkin orange, was intended to become a planter when the spring rolled around again. The pink flamingos looked more like long-legged hens than anything else, but Nutbeam was happy — the pink gave his zoo variety. On the north side of the house at the base of a spruce tree, away from the critical scrutiny of John and Rita Kaston, Nutbeam placed his first wind-driven pornographic lawn ornament. The propeller turned in the breeze, the little man banged his sheep, a twinkle in his eyes, a grin on his pink little face.

*

Shadrack Nash was splitting wood in front of Hilda Porter's woodshed. He had been at it all morning. It was a Saturday morning and he was thinking about the school dance he had attended the night before. Bamby Dudley had been there, and Shad had circled the auditorium for three hours before he decided that she was better than nothing and asked her to dance.

Bamby Dudley was a tall, fat girl with orange hair, big breasts and sleepy eyes. Bamby Dudley was not the prettiest girl at the dance, but as far as Shad knew, she was the prettiest girl there that was interested in him. Every time he walked past her, she smiled, nodded, said "Hi."

They danced.

Bamby was bigger than Shad. The dance was a waltz. She held him close, crushed her breasts against his face. She was chewing gum, snapped it frequently in his ear. Her breath smelled like Juicy Fruit, her breasts smelled like onions.

They talked very little, just enough to learn that they were both heading to the canteen after the dance. They danced the last waltz, then headed to the canteen together. Shad had a wiener and chips, Bamby had two. Shad walked her home. She lived in Swingtown, Lower Blackville. He walked her to the front door, kissed her goodnight. When he left, she had to walk around to the side door in order to get into the house. Her parents weren't that old — they didn't have a front doorstep.

Shad walked home to Hilda Porter's, happy that he had had his first date, thinking that his very first kiss had tasted like deepfried wieners.

Shad chopped into a stick of dry, knotty pine. The axe wedged itself so tightly into the wood that he could not remove it without help. He had to get a second axe to hammer the first axe through the block.

"Bamby," thought Shad. "The first girl I ever kissed. My first date. Nothin' to it. I'll try it again. I'll practise on Bamby."

"Shad! Lunch is on!" called Hilda.

Shad left his work, entered the house, sat by the kitchen table. Hilda sat a bowl of steaming-hot creamed corn in front of him. She also placed bread and butter on the table. He began to eat.

"How's things in school?" asked Hilda. "You finding grade nine hard?"

"Not yet. Haven't got into much yet."

"What are you studying? Algebra? History?"

"Yeah, math, geography, all that stuff."

Hilda was feeling tired. She sat across the table from Shad to rest. She watched him eat.

"How's the woodpile coming?" she asked.

"Half done. Another two or three days should finish it."

"That's wonderful, dear. Wished I was young enough to help you. I hope I'm not working you too hard."

A hornet buzzed on the window, trying to escape.

Shad noticed it, felt that it was his fault that it was there, that he should comment.

"It's been a warm fall," he said. "If them hornets would just die or go to sleep, I'd tear down that nest."

"It'll get cold soon enough," said Hilda.

"I can't fix that veranda floor until I tear down that nest."

"I know that, dear. Don't worry about it."

"I just want ya to be careful, that's all."

Shad and Hilda had very little in common. Their conversations were limited to the few chores that needed to be done. Frequently, there were long moments of silence. Often, Hilda would break them with comments about Tasmania. Shad was learning the story in bits and pieces.

The last thing she had told him was how the aborigines liked touching the white skin, a curious look in their eyes, never smiling, but somehow amused. The Europeans did not notice that the aborigines did not caress each other in the same way. The Europeans didn't learn for quite some time that the native Tasmanians took the white Europeans as ghosts of their own dead.

So Tasmania just about always entered the conversation

and Shad didn't mind. He liked hearing about the strange people, often questioned Hilda about them, encouraged her to tell him more. It was always something they could talk about when small talk fell to silence.

"Tell me more about the Tasmanians," said Shad, pushed back his chair and lit a cigarette.

"The Tasmanians," said Hilda. "You like hearing about them, don't you?"

"Yeah. Did everyone think they were animals?"

"Not animals so much as abominations, freaks of nature. It's a strange thing. At first, when boats pulled ashore on Tasmania, they only *heard* the natives, just human sounds from the forest, gongs and things. And when they finally encountered each other, the Tasmanians attacked with stones and spears. The whites, as you can well imagine, fired back with guns and killed one of them, wounded several more."

"So, what did they do?"

"They were astonished and afraid, ran back into the forest howling like dogs. You see, they believed that to lose a single man was to lose the battle, the war. They were defeated and that was the end of it."

"Ha!"

"Captain Cook met up with them and liked them all right, and so did Captain Bligh. They found they could trust the aborigines the very best, that they often were met with cries of joy and a strange stamping of the feet."

"They stamped their feet?"

"Well, I suppose that was how they paid their respect to their victors."

Hilda fell silent for a minute trying to recall the many stories her father had told her. Shad waited, knowing she would eventually continue.

"One group of whites were doing something or other one day and looked up to see a whole line of the aboriginal people coming out of the woods, crossing the field as if they intended to surround them. There were hundreds of them, men, women, children, old people, everyone. Nobody could say for certain just what they were planning to do."

"So, what happened?"

"The whites were accompanied by soldiers. The soldiers jumped to conclusions, opened fire and killed a bunch of them, took one little wounded boy prisoner."

"Did the aborigines fight back?"

"No, it turned out that they were just coming to greet the ghosts of their dead. The soldiers thought maybe they were carrying weapons, but instead they were carrying gifts, boughs, shells and stuff like that."

"So what happened to the little boy?"

"The whites took him home, kept him, drove their religion into into his head, baptized him."

"Ha!"

"That was where the trouble began. From that day on, the aborigines distrusted the whites, and the whites distrusted the aborigines. The whites thought that there could only be one answer to the problem: convert them all to Christianity."

"Sounds like maybe my uncle John could have been there."

"Who?"

"My uncle, John Kaston."

Hilda nodded trying to remember who John Kaston was. "Kaston," she thought. "A Brennen Siding name, but what has he got to do with Tasmania? I guess Shad is tired with my stories. Perhaps he doesn't want to hear that old stuff at all. But he asked me, didn't he? And he seems so . . . "

"Ever go on a picnic, Shad?" she asked.

"A few times when I was a little kid," said Shad.

"I would love to go on a picnic some day. I'd love to get closer to nature, hear the robins singing, feel the grass beneath my feet. You'd think a person like me, living in the woods, would be able to hear robins enough. But you have to get out in the field to really hear them picnic in some glade by the river where there's lots of flowers and bees. I'm just a little hard of hearing, you see, and it helps to get close to the bushes and trees. They sing in the bushes and trees, the robins do. I haven't heard one for a long time."

"Then we should go on a picnic some day . . . just pack a lunch and go," said Shad.

"I'd like that," said Hilda. "I'd like that very, very much. I know a place not far from here."

"Any time at all is fine with me."

"Do you really mean that, Shad? Would you really take me on a picnic?"

"Why not? Sounds like fun to me."

"Then we'll go. In the spring when everything is lush and there's lots of birds."

*

John Kaston worked on his church from daylight to dark six days of the week. He had been a hard worker all his life, but never had he driven himself like he was driving himself now. Hammer, hammer, hammer. Saw, saw, saw. Sweat, sweat, sweat. While he worked, he sometimes preached to himself, or prayed, or wept. Bitter turmoil occupied his heart. He knew that God had all the answers, that He could remedy the problem with a single lambent look or a wave of His mighty hand — God had always told him what to do. But sometimes God did not speak to John himself. Sometimes, more often than not, God spoke through Rita. Rita had always been the crystal, the speaker, the radio, the transmitter, the direct line. As long as John could confide in Rita, he had an open line to Heaven. He needed Rita's open line now. He himself was getting a constant busy signal. John, of course, knew what he had to do, anyway. There was only one thing he *could* do. To remain a Christian, he'd have to tell Rita. But how to do it remained a bit of a problem.

"Why did I let it happen?" John asked himself. "Why did I have to do it? Why didn't I just say no? Am I so weak? I allowed myself to be seduced, lost all reasoning. It just came over me suddenly. All I could think about was the flesh. Would Rita forgive me for such a sin? Would life with her have any meaning, trust, happiness after that? She might tell me to get out, tell others what I did, make me a symbol of hypocrisy, a pharisee. Who'd ever take me seriously? Who'll ever go to my church?"

424

He had comitted adultery. That was a sin. "Thou shalt not commit adultery" was one of the commandments handed down to Moses. To break one commandment was as bad as breaking them all. He might as well have murdered Helen MacDonald as far as God was concerned. John also figured that by not telling Rita he was nurturing a lie, another sin.

"You just can't please God!" thought John. He put a nail in place, hit it hard enough with his hammer to sink it out of sight.

"Why does life have to be so difficult? Old Beelzebub has designed his labyrinth, weaved his web, and I'm the sacrificial fly.

"My sin is no less than Dryfly Ramsey's, no less than that of a thief, than Adolf Hitler's. I walk the same path as a common whore. What do I do, what do I do? All men and women are sinners; one's as bad as the other.

Thus . . . thus, we are all equals in the eyes of the Lord."

This was a lesson that John should teach. If John were to preach this sermon in his church, God might very well reopen his line.

"All I have to do is stand in the pulpit and tell the whole story, step by creaking step, and God would forgive me, release me from Satan's web. But I can't do it. That makes me an adulterer, a liar, and to become a minister is to become a hypocrite. God have mercy on my soul."

John stopped hammering, thought he heard something.

He had.

"A bird," he thought.

*

"Let me tell ya, son. This great big old world of ours is a lonely place. There's only two ways a man can walk — you can walk with loneliness and be a star, or you can walk with your friends and be the little man that stars shine upon. Tell me, Dryfly, are you lonesome tonight? Do you miss her tonight? Are you sorry you drifted apart? I'm a lonely man, Dryfly, just like you. I'm the king, but I'm lonely. Sometimes when my memory strays to those bright summer days, I don't know if I will be able to handle it, know what I mean, son? The loneliest man in the world is the man that has everythang."

"Or nothin'," said Dryfly.

Elvis Presley was wearing a white suit with glittering designs on the shoulders and cuffs. He was sitting in the kitchen, talking to Dryfly and Shirley Ramsey.

"Let me tell ya, son. It's lonely at the top," he was saying. "Never forget that. The happiest man is the man whose pleasures are simple and few. When a man wants to get to the top, he's never happy until he gets there. Once a man reaches the top, he finds he's burdened with the task of trying to stay there."

"But you can have anything you want."

"Not everythang, Dryfly. I cain't have love, I cain't have freedom, I cain't have what you have, Dry. You're a lucky man to be working for Bill Wallace."

"I don't understand," said Dryfly.

"I'm a star! I cain't let nobody down. I cain't walk with the simple folk, the people I love; the chairs in my parlour are empty and bare, if you know what I mean, son."

"Why? Why can't you? You're a big star! You're Elvis Presley! You've been all over the world! There's nobody that don't know you! What if you were me? I can't even have the girl I love!"

"You can have anything you want, son, but don't give up happiness for fame. Don't be cruel. Don't have a wooden heart, son. Do you know how long it took to arrange this trip for me? To find a place where I could be alone, myself, free? You don't know, you cain't know how wonderful this place is. If I were you, I'd not move to America at all. I'd stay right here in Brennen Siding. As a matter of fact, when I die I'd like to haunt this neck of the woods."

"But I have to leave! I have to go and see Lillian! I have to! Don't you understand, Elvis? I have to! I have to!"

"Mind if I have a pickle bottle of tea, Shirley?" asked Elvis.

"Help yourself, Elvis dear."

"Thank you, ma'am."

Dryfly woke up.

He had been dreaming.

He had dreamed he was in the old house talking to Elvis Presley. When he awoke, he was confused, disoriented.

Reality moved in.

"I was dreaming," he thought. "It was just a dream . . . and I'm in the new house."

Daylight shone through his tiny window. He decided to get up.

He dressed and went into the kitchen.

Shirley was alone, sitting by the table, smoking a Rothmans.

"Mornin', Dry," she said.

"Mornin'. Where's Nut?"

"Took Pal's rod and went fishin'. Wants to salt down a barrel o' salmon."

"Did he take Pal's flies, too?"

"I guess so."

"That's good. He'll catch fish, then."

"Hope so. What're you doin' today?"

Dry shrugged. "Go over to the club, maybe. I got some work to do on that arithmetic."

"How's it comin'?"

"Pretty easy so far."

"Gonna talk to Bill Wallace?"

"Yeah . . . anything to eat?"

"Nutbeam picked a bag o' crab apples. I stewed some, if ya'd like a few."

"Sure. Don't get up. I'll get them."

"I'm startin' to get big," said Shirley, rubbing her pregnant belly.

"Yeah, I noticed. This is only September. You're gonna be awful big come March."

"Guess the baby'll be big like Nutbeam."

After breakfast, Dryfly put on his jacket and headed across the footbridge to the Cabbage Island Salmon Club. He had it in mind to talk to Bill Wallace about the caretaker job. He didn't know if he should bring the subject up to Bill, but thought that if he hung around for a while Bill might mention it himself.

When he got to the club, he was unprepared for the feeling

that rushed over him. The club, Bill's car in the yard, the camp, the furniture, the smell, Bill, everything reminded him of Lillian. When he knocked and entered on Bill's request, he found he was both excited and emotional.

"Dryfly, my boy! How the hell have you been?"

"Good. Good. You?"

"Great! Great! The cottage is coming along beautifully. How's school?"

"Ah . . . I'm not in school . . . correspondence . . . "

"Ah, yes, yes. Lillian told me about that."

"Ah . . . how is Lillian?"

"Oh, Lillian's fine. Back to school. Christ, she'll be in college before you know it. Sends her regards. So, what can I do for you?"

"Ah, I was just passin' by, thought I'd say hello. How's the fishin'?"

"Great! Great! I landed two nice salmon this morning. There's nothing like September fishing. How about you?"

"Don't fish much."

"You don't fish much! How the hell could you live on the Dungarvon Rivah and not fish?"

"Ah, Mr Wallace?"

"Yes?"

"I was wonderin' about what you said last summer about me lookin' after yer place."

"Oh, yes . . . I . . . well, it's something I've tossed around. I do believe that the place is, ah . . . in need of some sort of casual surveillance."

Bill was sitting in an armchair. He had been reading a *Time* magazine. He put down the magazine and stood. He ran his fingers through his hair, searched for tactful words.

"You see, Dryfly, I've been bothered lately with your ghost," was how he began.

Dryfly didn't understand, waited.

Bill Wallace was a businessman, owned one of the biggest construction industries in the New England states, perhaps in the whole United States considering many of his contracts came out of New York City. Bill had a crisp, deep voice and a vast vocabulary which he pronounced with a honed accuracy — the Yankee accent did nothing to reduce its power. He addressed his board of directors every other day, had been guest speaker at hundreds of conferences.

Now he was addressing Dryfly Ramsey. Dryfly had always been nervous and self-conscious when confronting Bill Wallace, found even trivial conversation difficult. He was always aware of his own ignorance, poverty, accent, Bill's dominance. Bill was the cat, Dryfly the mouse — Bill the lord, Dryfly the peasant.

"My daughter speaks of you a lot," explained Bill. "As a matter fact, she's not very happy because of you."

Bill was staring directly at Dryfly now. Dryfly was beginning to cower, dropped his eyes.

"Have you been writing to her?" asked Bill.

Dryfly searched for his voice, found a tiny piece of it amid the saliva in his throat.

"I wrote to her once, yeah," he said.

"Well, I don't know what you two had going, and I don't know what you wrote to her, but she's been a very unhappy young lady lately."

"Now don't get me wrong, Dryfly. I'm not opposed to my daughter experiencing puppy love, but I want her to see it for what it is and not be pushed into thinking it's anything more than that. Do you have any idea what the Dungarvon Rivah means to me?" asked Bill.

The Dungarvon River ran in Dryfly's veins, but he did not reply.

"A couple of years ago, even more recent than that, my daughter and I spent a great deal of time thinking about and discussing this area. It's a retreat like no other. I would rather fish salmon than do anything else. Lillian looked forward to coming up here with me. She loves it up here. The Dungarvon was a much-needed bond between us. But now? Now she's stopped talking about it. Christ, I'm spending a fortune on a place for us to come to, and the last time I discussed it with her the most I could gather was that she didn't want to come up here anymore."

Dryfly was devastated, wanted to leave, didn't want to hear any more.

But Bill Wallace hadn't dismissed Dryfly Ramsey yet.

"Now, about you working for me. I just don't think it's a very wise move. The only reason I considerd it in the first place was to keep the thieves out, and I doubt if you could stop that. What do you think? Do you know who broke in here last winter, Dryfly?"

Dryfly knew. He and Shadrack Nash had entered the cabin many times, smoked the cigars, drank the liquor. Dryfly sensed that Bill Wallace knew too.

"No," said Dryfly. "But Lindon Tucker's the lad you should have anyway. It don't matter."

"Ha! Lindon Tucker's a jackass. No, I've been thinking that I might get Reverend Kaston. I'm going to talk to him tonight."

"Yeah . . . well, okay then. Just thought I'd mention it, case you thought I was still lookin' for the job . . . I, ah, wanted to tell you that I was, ah, too busy with my correspondence course, ah, I wouldn't have time. So, anyway, I, ah, gotta be goin'." Dryfly swung to leave.

"Ah, Dryfly?"

Dryfly stopped his departure, turned back to Bill. Dryfly was humiliated and wanted to get out of there more than anything else in the world, but Bill was in control. He swung to cower before Bill as if he were a puppy.

"About Lillian . . . I doubt if there's any reason for concern, but would you mind not bothering to keep in touch? You understand what I mean? We don't want her to be unhappy, do we?"

Dryfly had too big a lump in his throat to answer. He nodded.

Bill Wallace smiled, winked. "You're a good man, Dryfly. Give my regards to your folks."

"Yeah. See ya later," said Dryfly.

Dryfly left, easing the door shut behind him. He wondered to himself which of Bill Wallace's faces he disliked the most.

Dryfly didn't know where he was going, but over the hill

seemed appropriate. He went to the Tuney Brook bridge, stopped, gazed into the little stream below. His thoughts were jumbled. He searched for something rational to hold on to. He looked up and down the path making sure he was alone. Then he whimpered and let the tears flow. His thoughts may have been jumbled, but he did have it enough together to know that he didn't think that he was crying for Lillian. He was simply just feeling sorry for himself. Bill Wallace had humiliated him, had made him feel like he was some kind of a dog to be commanded or reprimanded at will. Dryfly hadn't been able to defend himself, hadn't been able to demonstrate any kind of manly qualities; he had cowered without dignity — this was the sting that brought tears to his eyes.

When it came to Lillian, he thought that he might even be encouraged by what Bill had revealed. Apparently, Lillian was very unhappy. Apparently, Lillian talked about him frequently. These were clues that revealed how she felt about him.

"I don't know why I ever doubted her," he thought. "She loved me when she left. Why wouldn't she still love me? I still love her, don't I?" He sighed deeply. "But if she's so unhappy, why didn't she write? Maybe old Bill's talkin' to her in the same way he just talked to me. The old bastard sure changed since the summer. Why? In the summer he seemed to like me, he offered me a job, said he wanted to help me out. What happened, do you suppose? Could his change have come from the fact that Lillian didn't want to come up here any more? And why doesn't she want to come up here? God! What a state for a lad to be in! Not knowin'. I don't know what's goin' on and I doubt if I'll ever know, but I can try to find out. It would make me feel better to find out. I'll write to her. I have to write to her. I have every reason in the world to write my lover. The greatest reason I have to write is because Old Fish Hog told me not to."

There on the bridge Dryfly made a decision. He didn't know for sure if it was a right decision, but he knew it made him feel better.

Dryfly went home, found a pen and paper, went to his room, wrote:

431

Dear Lillian,

If you think of me every time I think of you, then you must think of me a whole lot, because I think of you all the time. If you never think of me, then I am off balance. If you think of me and find yourself sad, then I feel I must have done something wrong. Please be happy when you think of me. That's all I ask. It makes me happy to think of your smile. I love you.

Yours,
Dryfly

*

John Kaston continued to work on his church and search his mind for answers. He was thoroughly confused. He thought himself a condemned, tormented man, a hypocrite; his life was a shambles, a sadistic play, and he found himself going over the script time after time, trying to make sense of it.

"If I could deal with the route to the problem, it might solve everything," he reasoned. "The route to the problem was mapped by the devil. To deal with the route to the problem I must deal with the devil.

"Now let me see . . . the party . . . Helen MacDonald. It started with Helen MacDonald at the party. The devil possesses people. He was no doubt possessing Helen, and through Helen he got to me, tricked me, found my weakness, seduced me into sinning. I'd been upset . . . he took advantage of my down moment. He used Helen to get to me. I'm no good. He doesn't want me around. He torments me yet. He tempts me with thoughts of her. He interferes with my thoughts of the Lord. He's a crafty devil, that. He's taking advantage of my situation with Rita.

"Helen!

"Poor Helen must be in terrible misery, bein' possessed by the devil like that. She probably doesn't even know it.

"Now, let me see . . . what to do, what to do. Deal with the route to the problem. The route to the problem is across that field, past Nutbeam's house, to Helen's. I must go to see Helen

. . . take it one step at a time. The first step is to go to Helen's. The second step is to smite that demon that dwells within her poor, weak, female soul. Yes, yes, the females are weak, more susceptible to evil. That's common knowledge. Look at Eve in Eden. Yes, I'll smite the demon, and once that's done the Lord will reign once again and I'll be able to confront Rita. Rita will forgive me in the eyes of God. It's all Helen's fault for being a woman, weak, treacherous. Behind every bad man there's a woman."

John waited until Helen took her afternoon break from the Cabbage Island Salmon Club. He watched her cross the bridge and field, climb the hill and enter the house. He grabbed his ever-present Bible and went to see her, knocked on her door. She came to let him in, she was smiling.

"John!" she said. "Come in, John! It's so good to see you!"

John entered. He did not return her smile, his lips busy with prayer. He didn't even look at her. He would not allow the devil within her to get the upper hand a second time.

"You're possessed!" he said bluntly. "I've come to save your soul!"

"Oh, for God's sake, John, I . . . "

"Yes! Yes! For God's sake, I've come."

Helen reached out to take him in her arms. John stepped back, avoided her. Helen was excited with his visit, she looked warmly into his eyes. John's eyes were not looking back. They were gazing at a spot just over her head, lowering no further than her brow at any time.

"John dear," said Helen, "are you all right? Would you like a cup of tea?"

"Tea? Do you think I'm stupid? Do you think I've come here in the full light of day to drink tea? First you offer me tea, then you'll offer me your body! You have a smooth tongue, devil!"

"You're such a little devil, yourself, dear."

"Shut up, Helen!"

"John, I . . . this is not funny! What's gotten into you?"

"No! The saving of a soul is never a laughing matter! You must know that, devil."

"John. Will you stop! I am not the devil."

"No, Helen, you're not, but he's there inside of you. I can
. . . I can almost smell him!"

"John, will you stop looking at me like that. It spooks me!"

John thought that if he looked into Helen's eyes he might
see the devil there. He glanced quickly, saw only Helen's.

"Helen," he said, "we have been tricked by Beelzebub. He
has tricked us, caused us to commit a great and terrible sin. I
am in dire need of salvation and whether you know it or not,
so are you. Get on your knees, Helen!"

"Oh, John! It's the middle of the day. I'm glad you came
over, but here in the kitchen? It's the middle of the day! What
if Bert Todder comes snoopin' around? You know how Bert
Todder never knocks, how he always walks right in!" Helen
was blushing, excited.

"Get on your knees, Helen!"

Helen sighed, grinned devilishly, knelt. "You've always had
such a vivid imagination," she said.

John looked at the ceiling, closed his eyes. "Dear, loving
Heavenly Father," he began. "Rid our sister Helen of the dirt,
the filth that dwells within her."

John looked down at Helen, reached out and clasped her
head in his strong right hand, squeezed.

"BEGONE! BEGONE, SATAN!" he yelled.

"John! You're hurting me! You don't have to be so rough!
I'll play your game!"

"What? What did you say?"

"I said, you don't have to . . . ouch! Stop it, John! I'll do
it! I'll do it!"

"You slut!" yelled John. "You poor lost soul! Begone, Satan! Leave this poor, weak woman! NOW!"

Helen was frightened now. She was seeing insanity in John's
eyes. She tried to rise. John pushed her back to her knees.

"John, I . . . " she tried. "I'll . . . I'll do anything for you."

"Yes! Yes, you will, as long as that devil remains inside you.
You'd be my slut, wouldn't you?"

"Oh, John, please! I don't like this game . . . "

"The devil's inside of you! Admit it! Surely you can feel
him! That lust that you feel! That's the devil, Helen!"

"No! No! No, I think it's gone! I don't feel it anymore!"

"No! No! No, I can tell it's still there! Poor Helen. Lord, smite the demon! Cleanse this poor humble soul!"

"Please, John! You're hurting my head!"

John released his hold, raised his arms piously.

Helen started to get up from her knees.

"Stay there!" he warned. "We must pray."

Helen disregarded this, stood.

John aggressively pushed her back to her knees. He hurt her arm doing it.

"John, please don't do this," she said.

"You think that this is easy for me? This is only the beginning, Helen! First, I deal with you! Then, I deal with myself! Don't you understand that we've sinned? Don't you understand that we've fornicated without the consent of the Lord?"

"No, John . . . I mean, yes, John . . . but don't make matters any worse!"

"Worse! How could matters get any worse? You've made me succumb to the will of the devil! You've made me a pharisee! How can I base a church on such evil? We must beg the Lord for his forgiveness!"

"All right, John . . . all right. Pray with me, but don't hurt me. Please!"

"Dear, loving Heavenly Father . . . "

John Kaston prayed for an hour. He prayed until he redeemed both himself and Helen. He prayed until he found justification. Justification meant bliss, freedom. He prayed until he felt he had God's blessing, consent. Then, with bliss and freedom in their hearts and self-married, they locked the doors against a possible intrusion by Bert Todder and retired to Helen's bedroom to begin their honeymoon.

All was well. God had blessed John with a second little woman.

nine

For the first time in months, Dryfly Ramsey found himself idle as an autumn hornet, useless as an impotent crone, inactive as a Blackville cop, a sloth on pogey. There is nothing more vulnerable to melancholy than an idle sixteen-year-old. Idleness is exhibit A in the devil's trial; it kicks the winds of inspiration out of life; it is the serpent, the hoopsnake in the garden. Idleness, one of the seven deadly sins, tempts you to experiment with the other six. Bigotry is the brainstorm of an idle mind. Idleness transforms adolescents into irrational brats. God created art, music and literature to combat idleness. When Jesus said, "He that is without sin among you, cast the first stone," He looked about and was grateful that there wasn't an idle teenager in the group.

Dryfly employed himself for two hours a day working on his correspondence course; he played guitar for two hours a day and averaged nine or ten hours eating and sleeping — the other ten, eleven hours were spent staring into the empty eyes of idleness.

While Bert Todder, Lindon Tucker, Bob Nash and Dan Brennen teased the Atlantic salmon by placing flies here and there on the deep and dark Dungarvon waters, Dryfly spent the last days of the fishing season wandering aimlessly through the fields, skipping stones on the water, loafing about the house, waiting for a letter from Lillian Wallace.

One day, Nutbeam hung a flycatcher from the ceiling in the kitchen, and Dryfly spent many hours gazing intently on the coiled, sticky, yellow ribbon — the activity, or the inactivity, there. He watched the gullible flies light on it to eat, rest, copulate, or for whatever reason and too late find themselves irretrievably glued, imprisoned — legs, wings, body, everything.

"Except for the eyes," thought Dryfly. "The eyes can still see things, and the heart. They're still alive, watching me. It must be kind of like being crucified, but you wouldn't bleed to death or anything. You'd just be there, stuck to the paper, unable to move, until you starved to death or died of thirst or boredom or somethin'."

Occasionally, Dryfly took a stroll over to Bernie Hanley's store for a Coke and to listen to the men talk. The stories and yarns would sometimes give him food for thought, but more often he quickly became bored and returned home or to someplace he could be alone. The men never talked about anything other than fishing, hunting, planting and the various other activities common in the everyday life of Brennen Siding anyway, and Dryfly felt that he'd been listening to something he had already heard a hundred times before.

Boring, boring, boring. Sigh, sigh, sigh.

One day, Dryfly thought he might like to give John Kaston some help building his church, just for something to do, but decided against it. In the state of mind he was in, he figured he'd never be able to tolerate the rants and raves, the religious fanaticism of John Kaston.

Dryfly learned through Bert Todder that John Kaston had sold his shore to Bill Wallace and was put in charge of it and the rest of Bill's property. Dryfly couldn't have cared less. Lindon Tucker, on the other hand, was greatly disappointed, fit to be tied, angry as a bull moose in mating season, hot under the collar, red in the face. Dryfly prophesied that Lindon Tucker lightning might hit Bill Wallace's camp before very long. Dryfly didn't care about that, either.

Although Nutbeam and Shirley never commented on his current behaviour, Dryfly couldn't shake the fact that he might be starting to become a burden. This concept caused him to eat less and ramble more, added apathy and alienation to his idleness. He lost some weight, and the last semblance of boyhood fled from his appearance and took refuge behind the mask of a young man. The fuzz on his face darkened, became hair. His thin, boyish frame became lean and virile. His hair lengthened to his shoulders, and he found that the only way to keep it looking good was to wash it. So he washed it every day and had the cleanest hair in Brennen Siding. His voice deepened — Nutbeam and Shirley noticed it in his singing.

Of course, all these changes had been happening gradually over the past year, but they seemed to have been boosted with the coming of autumn. By the middle of October, if Dryfly had been a birch tree, his leaves would have been red, just like all the others — Nature was having her way.

In November, Nutbeam shot a deer and a moose, which meant that they had more than enough meat for the winter. Nutbeam was a master hunter and trapper, knew he could always get more, if needed, so he bartered with the neighbours.

"I'll give you a hindquarter of moose meat for a keg of salty salmon, Lindon."

"The, the, the very best, Nut, Nut Nutty old boy. Yes, sir. Great, great, good, good, good."

"Moose meat? Sure, I'll give you some potatoes for it! I've been eatin' nothin' but potatoes and point lately. Tee, hee, hee, sob, snort, sniff! Puff puff puff."

When you are poor and have but a tiny piece of meat left to eat, instead of eating it you hang it from a string over the table, eat your potatoes and point at it. In this way the meat will last all winter. This is what Bert Todder meant by potatoes and point.

Nutbeam went to Dan Brennen.

"I'll trade you half a deer for a bag of turnips," he said.

"Turnips? I don't know. I'll have to take a look. C'mon way down in the basement . . . you never know what might turn up. Ha, ha."

"You've given away all the venison," said Shirley.

"I know. I'll get more," said Nutbeam.

He did. The very next day he shot a large, antlered buck.

Nutbeam kept busy, and by the time the pink flamingo was knee-deep in the snow he had accumulated enough provisions to keep them all winter. Then he started trapping. Trapping meant that there'd be money for finer things in life — canned beans, store-bought bread and pickles, things like that.

"You need a good warm winter coat, Dry," Nutbeam commented one day.

"No, I'm all right," said Dryfly.

"Here's twenty dollars. Get yourself one."

Dryfly looked at the twenty dollars. All his apathy and idleness climaxed with the sight of it.

"I can't take your money," he said.

"You need a coat."

"Yeah, but you don't have to buy it."

"I know I don't have to buy it, but I know you ain't got no money. You gave it all to us in the summer. This is your money, Dry. I kept it for ya."

"You did?"

"Yeah, well, I sort of did, here in my head. Go to Blackville. Buy yourself a coat."

"Well . . . you sure?"

"Yes, I'm sure. Go!"

"Thanks, Nutbeam."

"Oh, Dry?" Nutbeam was reaching into his wallet again. "Here's ten more. Go to the dance, get drunk, chase them girls."

They were in the kitchen, sitting at the table. Shirley was sitting by the stove, feet on the oven door. She was knitting and eating a yeastcake.

"Nut . . . I . . . " Dryfly didn't know what to say. He was overwhelmed with Nutbeam's good will and tolerance. Tears threatened to flow.

"Don't say nothin', Dry. Jist go and have a good time. Get yourself a new coat."

"You should go and visit Shadrack," said Shirley. "Go to the dance with Shad."

Dryfly nodded, but said nothing. He was afraid to speak. He thought that his manly voice might give away the fact that he was crying inside. He did not want to remove the mask and reveal the boy.

*

Shadrack Nash split the wood and piled it in the shed, raked the leaves and burned them; he picked apples and banked the house, tore down the abandoned hornets' nest under the veranda floor. Then he tore up the floor itself and repaired it with newer boards he'd found in the barn. He also went to school, practiced the essentials of sexual foreplay with Bamby Dudley and played music with the Whoopsnakes. Every Friday night he went to a dance, and every Saturday night he attended a movie. The movies were either commercial-like films for various states of the USA (starring Elvis Presley), or vampire flicks. After the Elvis movies he'd walk Bamby home, singing "Love Me Tender," "Blue Hawaii," "Wooden Heart," or whatever; after the vampire movies he'd walk her to Swingtown, frequently glancing over his shoulder, checking to make sure he wasn't being shadowed by the Count.

Bob and Elva visited him and asked him to move home. He decided against it. Brennen Siding had little to offer him, especially now in the late autumn, now that the river was cold and bleak, inhospitable. The reason he gave Bob and Elva for not moving home was school-related. He told them that his studies were improving. Being so close to the school, living with Hilda gave him the privacy and books he needed. Hilda herself, the retired teacher, was helping him with a very difficult grade nine. He did not tell them how much he admired and loved the old woman, nor did he tell them how much he felt she needed him to be there. He didn't have to. Bob and Elva were amazed to see how much the aging process had shrunken Hilda.

"Hilda's failin'," commented Bob after they left and were driving up the Gordon Road in Bob's pickup.

"Somethin' awful altogether," sighed Elva. "I never saw the like of it. Good thing she has Shad with her."

Hilda Porter had lost weight, was getting more wrinkled every day, was becoming more and more absent-minded. There was something else, too. Shad noticed that even though she could remember the past, her childhood fifty years ago, with great detail, at the same time she might forget to eat or brush her teeth; she was frequently forgetting Shad's name. He'd be raking leaves, for instance, and when he came into the house, she'd ask, "What boy is this?"

"It's me. Shad."

"Oh, yes. My darling boy. Shad."

She would sometimes prepare him a lunch, forgetting that they had just eaten an hour ago. Ask her who she taught forty years ago and she'd remember everyone in the class. Ask her who the man was that brought the mail this morning and she would have forgotten.

So they talked mostly about the past.

One cold Saturday afternoon in November, Shad finished eating his lunch, pushed back his chair and asked, "How come your great-grandfather went to Tasmania? Seems like an awful long way to go, back then."

"Well, he went there in 1876. He was in the navy. But his interest in Tasmania had been kindled years before that. In 1876.

"You see, for a period of about a hundred years, there, the aboriginal population dwindled. They were being hunted and killed for sport. The whites wanted the whole island, didn't want these smelly, strange people around. The whites, as you know, didn't believe that the aborigines were people. The aborigines had beetle brows, couldn't walk very well, moved better on all fours. The whites murdered the men and raped the women. Did I tell you about them killing a man and tying his head around his wife's neck?"

"Yeah. Somebody wanted her for a pet."

"Can you imagine what kind of a pet you'd be after something like that?"

"Hmm."

"Did I tell you that they thought the whites were ghosts?"

"Yeah."

"Did I tell you how they were like ghosts, themselves?"

"I don't think so."

"Well, one year it was realized that the natives were facing extinction, and that if that were to happen things would look pretty grim for the authorities of the island, for the British government.

"Yet it was plain to see that the natives had to be gotten rid of."

Hilda Porter was sitting in a rocking chair beside the stove. She was gazing dreamily into her Tasmanian world. Shad sat at the table smoking a cigarette, listening.

"So," continued Hilda, "they decided to move them all to another island, a little barren, cold, damp place out in the ocean, forty or fifty miles away.

"The Tasmanians were hiding in the woods and wouldn't come out. So the Army decided to form a line of men and comb the island from end to end, thinking that they could herd them all out to one tiny peninsula. Soldiers and civilians alike gathered for the search, and just before the harvest they set out . . . twenty-five-hundred men. The civilians, of course, took it to be a hunt and came prepared for shooting. But they were told that it was not a matter of sport or amusement but an absolute necessity to gather the creatures alive to be transferred to Flinders Island."

"So, did they get them all?" asked Shad.

Hilda chuckled, then thought for a moment.

Shad waited, puffed his cigarette.

"The line of men started out and made this great big arc, like a noose. Each man was about fifty yards from the other, and they were in constant contact with each other, shouting and blowing their bugles.

"Once in a while they spotted a native. Once they spotted forty. They searched the island for nearly two months and thought they'd find the lot, captured at last on the tiny peninsula.

"There wasn't a one, Shad. They hadn't captured a single one. Walked right by the whole lot. It seems they had a way of hiding, that they could hide behind a rock that was much smaller than themselves . . . some strange way they had."

"So, did they ever catch them?"

"Yes, yes, they got them. They hired a man that could speak the native language, who went to their camps, gave them gifts, played them music on a flute. He won over a few of them, who went to work persuading others and so on. It took him five years, but he got the whole bunch of them. Of course, there weren't many of them left by that time, anyway, maybe a couple of hundred. And they all thought they were going to heaven, to the place that the white ghosts had prepared for them. When they boarded the ship, they were smiling and happy.

"But when they arrived at Flinders Island, I guess they began to tremble, their whole bodies drooped, they cried like babies. The winds were strong and cold, there was rain and sleet. They believed that Flinders was where they had been sent to die."

"And did they?" asked Shad.

"Most of them," said Hilda. "They thought they had been taken there to die, so they stopped doing things, grew idle, pined away. I guess some of them used to sing a real mournful song, over and over . . . and . . . " Hilda shook her head, negatively, as if with disblief in what she was about to say. "And they believed that when they died, they'd go not to some paradise in the sky, but to England."

"Ha!"

"Anyway, they wasted away and grew more and more melancholy, and, finally, they even stopped loving each other, stopped having babies. The population dropped to forty-four."

"Just forty-four? There's that many people in Brennen Siding."

"That's all that were left. Forty-four people of an entire race . . . twelve men and twenty-two women. The rest were children."

"Didn't anybody try to help them?"

"Well, nobody knew what was going on, but some fellow did arrange to take them back to Tasmania, thought he was helping them by putting them in a penal settlement at Oyster Cove. It didn't help. The natives had given up. They just lay around, ate scraps with the dogs. By 1855, there were only sixteen left.

"In 1868, Prince Alfred visited the island and asked to be introduced to the chief of the Tasmanian people. Of course there was no leader. The Tasmanians never had a leader. But

443

some men went to Oyster Cove and took one of the men, dressed him in fine clothes like the English would wear and showed him off to the Prince. The Prince praised them for succeeding in developing such a primitive race into such a noble people. It made the newspapers in England. I guess the Prince must have talked about it. Anyway, that's where my great-grandfather heard about them. I'm not sure why he took such an interest in them. Some of the people in Tasmania used to adopt one now and again and keep it as a pet. It could have been that someone might have taken one back to England. My great-grandfather Lawrence wanted to see them so bad that he joined the navy just to get there."

"Couldn't he have just gone?"

"Well, he was poor, I suppose, couldn't afford to take the trip.

"The man they took to be the Prince, his name was William Lanney. The boys used to have great fun with him afterward. They set him drunk and called him King Billy. He only lived about a year. Have you eaten, Shad?"

"Just finished. How you makin' out writin' down your story?"

"What story, dear?"

"You, ah, I thought you were gonna write a book about all that stuff, about Tasmania."

"Well, you know, the thought has crossed my mind. It seems to me I even started it once years ago. Did I ever tell you I wanted to write a book?"

"Yeah, you told me. I thought you had already started it, or were about to start it. It's something you always wanted to do. Why don't you do it?"

"You know, Shad, you're a lovely boy and you're absolutely right, I should write all that stuff down. There's other stuff I could write about, too — like the time Willy Dunn scraped his knee, or the time Joe Bryenton turned the handspring and lost all his change. There's lotsa things a person could write. Why, I remember when there was no hydro on this side of the river and there was only about three telephones in the whole Blackville area."

"You shouldn't put it off, Hilda. You should get right at it. I'd even help you, if you wanted. You could tell me what to write and I could write it down for you. It would help me with my English, too."

"It would be fun, wouldn't it. Yes, yes, we should do that, and you know, we should go on a picnic, too. I'd love to get out in the woods and hear the robins singing. I know a glade not far from here."

Shad sensed that Hilda was tired. She was always more forgetful when she was tired. "Some days she's worse than others," he thought. "This is not one of her better ones."

"I've got a few more things I have to tend to," he said. "You prob'ly should have a little nap."

"Yes. Yes, I'm tired, Shad. I think I'll lie down. Would you keep the fires on?"

"Yep. You have a snooze. I'll look after the place."

Hilda stood, started to her room, stopped, turned, said, "You know, Shad, I think I've got some Tasmanian blood in me."

"Ha! How do you figure that?"

"I don't know . . . I don't know. Fix yourself a lunch, Shad dear, I'm going to have a little nap."

"Yeah, I will. Don't worry. I'll have a lunch."

Hilda went to her room humming "Rock of Ages."

*

John Kaston maneuvered the Gordon Road in his 1960 Vauxhall. He was on his way to Blackville. When John Kaston first became a preacher, one of the first things he did was trade his pickup for a 1960 Vauxhall. "It wouldn't be right for a preacher to drive a pickup, would it?"

Life for John Kaston had improved. His church was coming along nicely — the roof was boarded in and shingled and he had spent the last week drywalling the interior. He sold his shore to Bill Wallace for three thousand dollars, and was collecting a hundred a month for looking after Bill's cabin. He was at peace with himself, Rita and Helen — God had blessed him. All he needed now was a congregation, and he figured that would come through word of mouth. He was planning to preach a mighty sermon somewhere in Blackville to start the ball rolling.

"I'll preach now and again in Blackville throughout the fall and winter. By spring I'll open up my church to a capacity crowd."

Besides building the church, John had one other thing on his list of accomplishments. He had wielded a mighty blow to the drinking class of Brennen Siding and Gordon. In only eleven visits to the blind and lonely Ben Brooks, John had converted Ben to his fold.

"It was amazing," thought John. "I just walked in and prayed and before long poor old Ben was on his knees, too. He quit drinkin', quit bootleggin', became a Christian. Wants me to stay longer every time I visit him. Always asks about Rita. Said he'd be a regular churchgoer. Hallelujah! . . . Now if he could only figure out a way of makin' a livin' . . .

"My next trick is to convert Lindon Tucker. That shouldn't be too hard. Lindon will go along with whatever anyone tells him, except he's got this hate on for me lately, I think. But I'll get him. He won't be able to resist, to yield beneath my perspicuity."

The discovery of the word "perspicuity" was something else that John Kaston could have added to his fall list of accomplishments. He'd had a feeling that he was over-using the word "lambent" and sought a synonym. He found the word "perspicacious," liked it. He planned to use it in his up-coming service in Blackville.

"How small are you gonna feel when you're cowering before the perspicacious eyes of the Lord?" was how he planned to use it.

John negotiated the Vauxhall around a bend, and there on the road, a few hundred yards ahead, on foot, heading for Blackville, was Dryfly Ramsey.

John picked him up.

"G'day, John," said Dryfly.

"Afternoon, Dryfly. Headin' for Blackville?"

"Yeah. Cold, eh?"

"Winter'll soon be here."

"I see your church is comin' along good," said Dryfly.

"It's the work of the Lord — can't help but be good," said John.

"I should never have mentioned the word church," thought Dry. "He'll preach all the way to Blackville now. Maybe I can change the subject."

"Ever hear from Max?" asked Dry.

"Not lately. So, you like how my church is coming along, eh?"

"Yeah. What's Max doin', anyway?"

"I'm not sure. He's in a paper factory in St. Catharines . . . I'm gonna paint that cross over the door red. Think that'll look all right?"

"Might be all right. Ever hear from Bill Wallace?"

"Yep . . . oh, about once a month. Wonderful man, Bill Wallace. A good God-fearing man. Donated a hundred dollars to my church, said he might even consider buying a stained-glass window. Do you ever go to church, Dryfly?"

"Ah . . . once in a while . . . I saw two otters on the river today."

"It'll be good for you and your folks when I get the church finished. All you'll have to do is cross the field."

"Yeah, otter skins must be worth quite a lot, don't you think?"

"Otters are God's creatures. All God's creatures are worth a lot."

"You headin' for Blackville?" asked Dryfly.

"Yes, yes. Goin' to see Reverend MacBride. Thought I might get his hall for a sermon I've been meaning to preach. Maybe a week from tomorrow."

"Why don't you ask him for the use of his church?"

"Can't preach in another man's church."

"Ha!"

"I think he'll probably let me use the hall, though."

"There must be ten churches in the area. Must be one you kin use, without havin' to preach in a hall."

"Can't preach in another man's church."

"Why not?"

"Cause ya can't."

"Ha!"

Dryfly thought about the concept. He didn't necessarily want to talk about religion with John Kaston, but he couldn't understand why so many churches were needed. He counted to himself. "One, two, three, four . . . two in the Rapids, four in Upper Blackville, one in Howards, one in Renous. There'll be two in Brennen Siding. That'll be fourteen churches . . . "

"How often do they use them?" asked Dry.

"Use what?"

"The churches."

"Well, every Sunday, of course. Then there's the odd funeral and wedding."

"Seems to me they should all take turns in the same buildin'. All them churches must cost a lot of money to build, must be an awful big up-keep. They'd save an awful lotta money if there was just the one."

"What's money got to do with it?"

"Well, there's fourteen churches in the area. Cost a lotta money to build fourteen churches."

"It's all for God's work. Money don't mean anything. We, each religion, has their church, their pride. How would you like it if there was no Catholic church?"

"Wouldn't matter to me. With just one church you could give all that money to the poor. God would like that, wouldn't He?"

"Well, you gotta spread the word."

"Well, that wouldn't be a problem . . . take turns. Catholics at ten o'clock, Baptists at noon, Pentecosts at two, like that. One church would do for the whole crowd."

"Dryfly Ramsey, do you think I'd play second fiddle to . . . to a . . . to a Catholic?"

"Why not? They believe in God, don't they?"

"They believe in God, but they also use beads and pray to the Virgin Mary, kneel before graven images."

"So, what about the Anglicans?"

"They believe in the Trinity. They're all different. You take Reverend Haley, now. He reads his prayers from a book. Me, now, I make up my own prayers as I go along . . . and ya gotta stick to the Bible. Not all religions stick to the Bible, you know."

They were approaching Blackville. From the summit of a hill they could see the smoke from the mill rising pink, the snow-clad fields blushing like a wild rose petal in the waning sun.

"Bill Wallace told me you wanted the job looking after his property," said John.

"He asked me in the summer, I asked him this fall. You got the job. It don't matter . . . not to me, anyway."

"He wants me to put signs . . . No Trespassing signs . . . he doesn't want anyone fishing his pool."

"Figures."

"Not even Lindon."

"Figures."

"I can't do that."

"No."

"Ah . . . Lindon's not speaking to me."

"He's being a little strange to me, too."

"Why's he mad at you?"

"He doesn't know who to blame, I guess."

"Bert Todder's a little, ah, angry, too."

"Why Bert?"

"Well, he sort of had his mind set on selling his shore to Bill. Bill doesn't want it now that he has mine. Lindon used to guide him . . . then Bert . . . now that he has a place, he doesn't need a guide."

"So you gonna put up the signs?"

John sighed, slowed down.

"You and Max, young Shadrack, George Hanley, Palidin, you all used to play together, skate, play hockey on Tuney Brook."

Dryfly smiled, remembered the hockey games.

"Yeah . . . used Eaton's catalogues for shin pads."

"Max never writes. Ever hear from Palidin?"

"Mom gets letters all the time. He's doin' real good, but he'd rather be home."

"What're you gonna do, Dryfly? You gonna leave, too? What're ya gonna do all winter?"

"I don't know."

"You could help me with the church."

"Yeah."

"You could do anything, you know, if you turn to the Lord. Would you like to pray, Dryfly? You can do anything, be anybody, if you pray. I tried to tell that to Max."

Dryfly was beginning to feel a little hot under the collar.

"Here?" he asked.

"Sure. It don't matter where you pray! God will hear you. Take Jesus into your heart, Dryfly."

"If it don't matter where you pray, what do you need with a church?"

"We gotta be shepherds, bring in the lost sheep."

"Then you pray for yourself in your church, and I'll pray for myself in mine."

"But . . . "

"Drop it, John!"

John Kaston sighed, accelerated, mumbled something. Dryfly thought he might have said, "Catholic."

*

Dryfly bought a coat at Brigham's Store. He removed the tags and put it on. He threw his old coat into the garbage. He was now dressed like Bert Todder — red mackinaw, green pants, gumshoes. He left Brigham's and went to Biff's canteen, sat on a stool and ordered a wiener and chips. A pretty blonde girl was both waitress and cook. She smiled at him pleasantly.

"You're new around here," she said. "What's your name?"

"Dryfly Ramsey."

"I'm Charley."

"Charley?"

"Charley."

Charley smiled. Dryfly liked her.

"Is there a dance tonight?" he asked.

"At the Public Hall. Lyman MacPhee and the Cornpoppers. Where ya from?"

"Ah . . . Renous."

"Where in Renous?"

"Ah . . . " Dryfly didn't know much about Renous, realized he shouldn't have lied. Dryfly was ashamed to say he was from Brennen Siding. "Brennen Siding," he said, blushing.

"Brennen Siding's up Dungarvon, ain't it?"

"Yeah. The Dungarvon runs into the Renous."

"Oh."

Charley removed the wieners and fries from the grease, served Dryfly. Dryfly paid her, began to eat. Other than Charley, Dryfly was the only other person in the canteen. Charley went to the jukebox, put a quarter in the slot and punched some buttons. The Righteous Brothers began to sing "You've Lost That Loving Feeling."

"Where is everybody?" asked Dryfly.

"At the rink, I imagine. The Aces are playing Doaktown."

The clock on the wall read seven. The dance wouldn't start until nine. Dryfly considered going to the rink to kill time. A fellow from the Rapids came in and sat two stools down from Dryfly, ordered a Pepsi, started up a conversation with Charley. He was obviously drunk.

"You see that jeezless bunch of long-haired bastards around?" he asked.

"What's wrong with you?" asked Charley.

"The son's o' whores passed me on the road!"

"Maybe they didn't know ya."

"Maybe they're all on dope, too! Goddamn hippies! That goddamn Billy Bean should be shot!"

"Oh, Billy's all right. He couldn't have seen ya."

"Seen me all right! Has Shad Nash been around?"

"Haven't seen him."

"That's another one o' them bastards I'd like to get my hands on! Who are you?"

Dryfly was eating.

"I said, who are you?"

When Dryfly realized he was being spoken to, he looked up.

451

"Dryfly Ramsey," he said.

"Why the hell don't you get your hair cut?" snapped Tommy Nolan.

"Can't afford it," said Dryfly.

"Probably too goddamn lazy to work! You a friend of them jeezless Whoopsnakes?" asked Tommy.

Dryfly tried to remain calm, concentrated on his food. He didn't want anything to do with this guy, but he didn't like the way he was being ogled, spoken to. He didn't like the way the guy was being loud, the swearing in front of the girl.

"Might be," said Dryfly.

"Might be! Might be! What d'ya mean, might be? Charley! Charley! What's this jeezless long-hair doin' in here?"

"He's tryin' to eat, Tommy! Leave him alone!"

Tommy stood, stared down drunkenly at Dryfly. Dryfly bit off a wiener, looked at Charley. "She asked him to leave me alone," he thought. "Does she think I'm afraid? That I can't look after myself? She's pretty. Her eyes are asking me to avoid trouble." He swung on his stool, stared up at Tommy.

Dryfly didn't have a lot of street savvy, but having been brought up the only Catholic in Brennen Siding, the son of Shirley Ramsey, had taught him the art of survival and the craft of congeniality at a very early age. He knew what he had to do. He knew he would have to speak this guy's language.

Dryfly reached for a cigarette.

"Got a light?" he asked.

Tommy, without thinking, gave him a card of matches but kept staring at him. Dryfly lit the cigarette, stared back, released a rich little cloud of smoke, sucked it up his nostrils.

"Why in Christ don't you get a haircut?" asked Tommy.

"You don't know me, do ya?" asked Dryfly.

"I don't know ya, and I don't want to know ya, ya jeezless long-hair!" said Tommy.

Dryfly could smell his aftershave mingled with the barf on his breath. "You must know me," he said. "I'm the lad that can turn a flyin' handspring with his arms crossed." Dryfly crossed his arms, as if he might demonstrate. "I hit a man in

. . . in Stockbridge one time and he just bled like a jeezless pig. Where ya from, anyway?"

"I'm a Nolan . . . from the Rapids." Tommy had lost some of his spark, his voice had lowered, softened. He didn't know this tanned young man in the mackinaw. Tommy had seen a pig bleed, the flow from the jugular. Dryfly had, indeed, found the right language for the local boy to understand.

"From the Rapids," said Dryfly. "You must know Herman Burns."

Dryfly had seen Herman Burns fight at a dance about a year ago. Herman Burns was a giant of a man, had defeated two men in a matter of seconds, had befriended Dryfly on that same night.

"Yeah, I know Herman. How do you know him?"

Dryfly slowly unfolded his arms, held up two fingers. "Me and Herman's just like that," he said. "We used to do a lotta fightin' in Boisetown."

Dryfly knew that Boiestown was a key word, too. Boiestown was somewhat of a mystery place for Blackvillers, populated with big Swedes and Irishmen. Most Blackvillers avoided Boiestown dances — there was always a fight at the Boiestown dance. Herman Burns would perhaps hold his own at a Boiestown dance, but few others.

"Gimme a cigarette," said Tommy.

"I only got a few left," said Dryfly. "Buy your own."

"You going to the dance, are ya?"

"Might. You?"

"Yeah. Thought I might."

Dryfly swung back to his wiener and chips, butted the cigarette and began to eat. A few seconds later he heard Tommy Nolan leave.

Charley smiled appreciatively.

Dryfly felt warm inside, realizing, perhaps for the first time, that Lillian Wallace was not the only pretty girl in the world.

"You workin' all night?" asked Dryfly.

"Yeah, till closin'."

"What time is closin'?"

"One, two, when everybody leaves."

"Got a boyfriend?"

"No. Who do you go with?"

"Nobody."

The record on the jukebox had changed. Now, Nino Temple and April Stevens were doing a great job on "I've Been Carrying a Torch for You So Long That I've Burned a Great Big Hole into My Heart." Charley had made a mistake punching up the song. She had meant to play the flip side, "Deep Purple."

"You handled that guy pretty cool," said Charley.

Dryfly smiled. "I don't even know where Stockbridge is," he said.

"Would you like a Pepsi to go with that? On me."

"Sure."

Charley uncapped a bottle and sat it beside Dryfly. "Do you go to school?" she asked.

"Takin' a correspondence course. Might get educated in about twenty years."

Charley smiled.

Dryfly's heart quickened. "Blonde, blue-eyed, pretty, great smile. I'm gonna ask this little lady out," thought Dryfly.

"So you work every Saturday night?" he asked.

"Every other. One week I get to go to the dance, the next week I get to go to the movie."

"I never get to go to the movies," said Dryfly. "I've never been to one."

"Holy dyin'! Where have you been?"

"No movies in Brennen Siding."

"Well, you'll just have to go some Friday."

"Yeah . . . ah . . . maybe I'll go next Friday. Ah, you goin'?"

"Prob'ly. Nothin' else to do on Fridays."

"Yeah. Where you from?"

"Blackville. Out the lane . . . "

"Ah, maybe I'll see ya next Friday . . . at the movie . . . "

"Yeah, prob'ly . . . "

"So, what's your last name?"

"Underwood."

"You gonna be around later?" asked Dryfly as he stood to leave.

"I just go home after work."

"Ah . . . maybe I could walk you home."

"Well, it could be pretty late."

"Don't matter. I got nothin' else to do."

"Well, I guess . . . "

"Great. I'll see ya later . . . "

"Sure."

*

Dryfly left the canteen at seven-thirty with an hour and a half to kill before dance time. He considered going to the rink or one of the other canteens, but because he knew so few people in Blackville he decided against it.

"No sense hangin' around some place where you don't know anybody," he thought.

With this in mind, he walked up the road and across the bridge to Hilda Porter's. He knocked, entered, found Shad sitting in the kitchen by the table. Hilda sat in a rocking chair by the stove. She was having a cup of tea, had just arisen from a nap.

"G'day, Dry."

"Shad."

"What boy is this?" asked Hilda.

"It's Dryfly Ramsey!" announced Shad.

"Dryfly Ramsey, Dryfly Ramsey . . . now, who's boy might you be?"

"Shirley's boy," said Dryfly. "From Brennen Siding."

"Brennen Siding . . . Brennen Siding . . . oh, yes! Dryfly! Sit down, Dryfly!"

Dry sat at the table across from Shad.

"What're you up to?" asked Shad.

"Nothin'. Thought I'd go to the dance. Goin'?"

"Yeah. Get a new coat?"

Dryfly smiled.

You could not buy much in the line of clothes in Blackville. If you needed clothes, you'd be wise to go to Newcastle. In Blackville, you could buy a mackinaw coat, APH pants, underwear, socks and gumshoes, but that was about it. Bert Todder always wore a mackinaw coat, APH pants and gumshoes; thus, he never had to go to Newcastle.

"Borrowed Bert Todder's," said Dryfly.

Shad grinned, appreciating the humour. "Bert not goin' to Bernie Hanley's tonight?"

"Bert's stayin' home tonight. Killed his pig today. Wants to study the milt."

"Ha! Is it big on one end?"

"Yep. Gonna be a mild winter."

Shad grinned thinking of Bert Todder studying the spleen of a pig for signs of the weather. "I knowed right well it was," said Shad, impersonating Bert. "The moon came up right over Helen MacDonald's barn last night."

"Gonna be dry, too," said Dryfly, continuing the play. "The moon was on 'er tip."

"Ha!"

Shadrack and Dryfly had no idea what these signs meant — they were simply making fun. Hilda, however, was dead serious when she said, "I knew it would be a mild winter when them hornets built their nest under the veranda. Hornets will build their nests high up if there's gonna be deep snow."

"If a lad only knew where Bert was standing when he saw the moon coming up over Helen's barn, he'd be able to tell the weather right on," said Shad. "Very many around the village?"

"Hardly anyone yet. Almost got in a fight at the canteen. Lad from the Rapids. He's got a hate on for the Whoopsnakes."

"Ha! Who was he?"

"Tommy somebody."

"Did ya thrash 'im?"

"Didn't have to. But you might. It's you he don't like. Said you lads passed him on the road."

"A lotta people don't like us lately."

"How come?"

"They're sayin' that Billy Bean's on dope."

"What kinda dope?"

"Grass, nutmeg, stuff like that."

"Do you know Charley, the girl at the canteen?" asked Dryfly.

"Charley Underwood," said Shadrack.

"Yeah. Walkin' her home after she's off for the night."

"For sure?"

"Said she'd let me."

"Ha! Never thought o' givin' her a rub."

"You goin' out with anyone?"

"Bamby."

"What's she like?"

"She looks a lot like Bert Todder," grinned Shad. "But she can't tell the weather."

"Eats a lotta potatoes, does she?"

"And onions."

"Good to see ya," said Dryfly.

"Yeah. You haven't been around all fall."

Dryfly shrugged.

"How'd ya get down?" asked Shad.

"Old Shep," said Dryfly.

"Who?"

"Old Shepherd. John Kaston."

"Ha! Did he save ya?"

"Ba-a-a!"

"I gotta wash my hair, get dressed," said Shad.

Shad left the room. Dryfly waited quietly. Hilda rocked, hummed "Rock of Ages." The runners of her chair squeaked. A clock ticked.

"The Ramseys were very poor," said Hilda. Hilda had forgotten Dryfly was there. She thought she was talking to Shadrack.

"Yeah," said Dryfly, surprised that Hilda would mention such a thing so openly in front of him.

"That Buck left poor Shirley alone with twelve kids. It's a wonder they didn't starve to death."

Dryfly didn't know what to say. He had never known his father. Dryfly didn't know about his father leaving.

"Buck died," said Dryfly.

"He left long before he died. Couldn't stand the hard times, I guess. They had a son, a young lad that . . . now what happened to him? His name was Bonzie."

"He went for a shit and the crows got him," said Dryfly.

"What's that?"

"Nothin'."

"Oh! Dryfly!"

"It's all right," said Dryfly.

"I'm . . . I'm sorry . . . I . . . I'm . . . "

"You got a nice place here," said Dryfly, changing the subject.

"Oh . . . yes, yes. I don't know what will ever become of it, though."

"Ain't you got a family?"

"All gone, every last one of them. It's good to have Shadrack here."

"Shad's a good lad."

"A good boy. All I have. Should go and straighten things out, look after him in my will."

"Yeah."

"Shad listens to me. He's good around the place, too. Have you ever been alone, Shadrack?"

"My name's Dryfly."

"Dryfly . . . oh, yes, Dryfly. Have you ever been alone, Dryfly?"

"Yeah, I guess so." When Dryfly thought of the word "alone," he immediately conjured up visions of Lillian Wallace. He felt he knew very well what it was like to be alone.

"It's no fun being alone . . . having nobody to talk to. I've been alone all my life."

Shad re-entered the kitchen, towelling his hair.

"You should get married," he said to Hilda.

Hilda didn't smile but somehow looked amused.

"All the men I knew were either married, or drunk, or both."

"A little wine never hurt anyone," said Shad.

Hilda smiled. It was this kind of conversation that had deepened her affection for Shadrack. She liked the way he never talked to her like she was an old lady. Everybody else was so careful about what they said to her.

"I'm too old," she said.

"Never too old for a little lovin'," said Shad. "What you need is to do a little partyin'."

"I haven't been to a party in twenty, thirty years."

"Well, let's have a party!"

"Oh no, Shad! We couldn't do that!"

"Why not? There's you and me and Dryfly."

"Oh Shad! I'm too old for that!"

"I'll get some wine," put in Dryfly, liking what he saw Shad doing. "And you can go get Bamby, Shad."

"Dryfly'll go get some wine, I'll get some people and some potato chips and stuff and we'll have a party," announced Shad.

"Oh, we couldn't!"

"Why not? You need to have some fun!"

"Oh, but, Shad . . . wine, people . . . we . . . "

"You get dressed in your nice black dress, and Dry and me will look after the rest."

"Well . . . well, we couldn't party very late . . . I . . . "

"We'll just stay until you're ready for bed. You just say the word when you're ready for us to go, and we'll get the crowd out of here."

Shadrack was very keen on the idea of having fun with this old woman. He was seeing a light in her eyes he hadn't seen there before.

Hilda went upstairs to change her dress and put on some make-up. For days now she had been feeling very tired. The thought of partying with young people excited her, erased her fatigue, started her adrenalin flowing.

"I'm old," she told herself, "but I'm still alive. I'll have to be careful not to make a fool of myself. They're so young . . . and beautiful . . . "

ten

The Whoopsnakes started out as a band with five members. Billy and Milton Bean, Gary Perkins, Shadrack Nash and Dryfly Ramsey were the original Whoopsnakes. Because of the popularity of guys like Billy, Milton, Gary and Shad, within three months the Whoopsnakes had a following of half the teenage population of the Blackville area. You could always tell a Whoopsnake, or a Whoopsnake follower, by the length of his hair. Before the advent of the Whoopsnakes, the popular boys in the area wore jetboots, trucker's wallets, checkered shirts with the sleeves rolled up two wide folds of the cuff, undone three buttons from the collar. Brylcreem and cars with big engines sold very well before the advent of the Whooopsnakes.

The Beatles conceived, spawned, laid, gave birth to, inspired and influenced the Whoopsnakes. The Beatles were changing the Western world — the Whoopsnakes were changing the Blackville area. A long-haired teenager in Schenectady, New York, Olivehurst, California, or Flamborough Head, England, might be referred to as a hippie or a flower child. In Blackville, if a lad had long hair, he was labelled a Whoopsnake. To a Whoopsnake, it was cool to wear ragged bell-bottomed jeans, flowered shirts and mackinaw coats.

The Brylcreemed, jetbooted boys in the big-engined cars were labeled "greasers" by the followers of the Whoopsnakes.

Greasers drank Golden Nut and Hermit Sherry. Whoopsnakes and their followers drank Cold Duck.

Tommy Nolan was a greaser. Tommy Nolan suspected that the Whoopsnakes were on dope. If a greaser could get his hands on anyone who took dope, he'd beat him up. If a Whoopsnake could get his hands on dope, he'd take it.

Marijuana was locally referred to as "dope." Occasionally, you could buy a nickle of marijuana in Newcastle, or Fredericton, for five dollars, a dime for ten, an ounce for twenty-five.

Billy Bean was the first drug pusher, dope dealer in Blackville. Occasionally, Billy Bean would go to Newcastle in his van, buy a dime of marijuana, take it back to Blackville and sell it to Whoopsnakes. He made his profit by dividing the dime into three nickles. Most Whoopsnakes hadn't a clue about the quality of marijuana — they could have been smoking nutmeg for all they knew. Billy Bean figured that, anyway.

Shadrack and Dryfly were crossing the bridge on their way to get Cold Duck, potato chips and Bamby when Billy Bean's van pulled up and stopped beside them. The side door was slid open and a cloud of nutmeg smoke escaped into the frosty evening.

The van had eight people in it — two girls and six boys. All the boys had long hair, wore ragged jeans.

"G'day boys!" yelled Billy. "Climb in!"

Shadrack and Dryfly squeezed in, the door was slid shut, the van took off.

Other than Shad, Dryfly only knew Billy, Milton and Gary — all the rest were new to him. Shad knew everyone.

Someone passed Dryfly a cigarette. All he could see was its glow in the dark van. He thought the smoke smelled like nutmeg.

"Toke?" said the person.

"No thanks," said Dry.

"C'mon, man! Have a toke!" persisted the fellow.

"Pass 'er here," said Shadrack.

Shad was handed the nutmeg joint. He puffed on it deeply, the glow lighting up his pale, freckled face. He flew into a fit of coughing.

"Eh!" he said.

"Where you lads headed?" asked Gary Perkins.

"Goin' to get Bamby," said Shad.

"Goin' to the dance?"

"Don't know. Later, maybe."

"Why don't you come to Newcastle with us?"

"Can't. Told Bamby I'd pick 'er up."

Shad didn't think it would be very cool to tell these guys that he planned to party for a while with Hilda Porter.

"We'll pick 'er up," said Billy from the driver's seat. "She can come with us."

A girl in the back of the van began to sing: "Bows and flows of angels' hair, and ice cream castles in the air . . . "

"What's goin' on in Newcastle?" asked Shad.

"Don't know. We'll check it out," said Billy.

"Want to go to Newcastle, Dry?" asked Shad.

"No . . . what about Hilda?"

"No, I guess we better not," said Shad to Billy.

Someone passed a bottle of Cold Duck to Shad. Shad drank, passed it to Dryfly.

"Take us to the bootleggers, will ya?" said Shad.

"Carl Eagle wants us to play for his New Year's party," said Milton.

"Yeah? When?"

"New Year's, ya arsehole!"

"Ha!"

"He'll pay us thirty bucks. Ain't much, but it's a gig."

"Sure! I'll play."

"Wanna be our singer, Dry?"

"Might. New Year's?"

"New Year's Eve."

"Sure. Might."

"Have another drink o' wine."

"Bows and flows of angels' hair . . . ," sang the girl in the back.

"Ha, ha, ha, ha, ha!" someone laughed.

"What's the difference between a sports car and a cactus?" asked somebody.

"Don't know. What?" replied a girl.

"With a cactus the pricks are on the outside."

"Ha, ha, ha!"

They went to the bootleggers. They picked up Bamby. Bamby wanted to go to Newcastle.

"What about Hilda?" Dryfly asked once again.

"She can hardly remember her own name. She's forgotten about the party already," said Shad.

They went to Newcastle.

*

Shad didn't think that Hilda had taken his "party talk" very seriously, and even if she did, he believed that she would forget what she was doing before she got to her room. Yet he had deceived her and was somewhat preoccupied by the thought of her possibly waiting for his and Dry's return with wine, potato chips and Bamby.

Hilda did not forget.

She went to her room to change her dress, fix her hair — she put on lipstick and rouge, rhinestone necklace and earrings. Shad had told her to put on her black dress — "Black is not a party colour," she thought and put on a pink silk one instead. Then she went back to the kitchen.

"They might be as much as an hour," she thought. "I should prepare something. I have at least half an hour."

The clock read eight-thirty.

"Sandwiches," she thought. "Elegant little sandwiches."

She went to the cupboard and the pantry, busied herself making Kam and mustard sandwiches, cutting them small for the sake of elegance. She prepared a plate of crackers, dill pickles and baloney. She turned on the radio to CFNB, lit candles and turned out the electric lights. She sat by the table to wait, contented with the cozy room.

At nine-thirty, she added some wood to the fire and sat in her rocking chair beside the stove.

"An hour and a half. They've been gone for an hour and a half. I wonder what's keeping them. Hope they didn't get into any trouble. They might not . . . "

Not wanting to concede to any possibility that the boys and Bamby might not show up, she allowed herself to drift into a reverie. She thought of spring, robins plucking worms from freshly turned furrows, fishing trout in the eddy.

"I caught an eel once," she thought. "I couldn't bring my-self to remove it from the hook. It frightened me. It was like a snake. I ran home. How it must have suffered there on the shore with the hook and line attached. I hated it. Then I hated myself. My greed had lured it to me; its greed urged it to take my hook. It died there on the shore. We all die on one shore or another . . . with hooks and lines attached . . ."

The radio announcer said, "Bringing the time around to ten minutes after the hour of ten o'clock. It's Saturday night, and John, Paul, George and Ringo are sending all their loving to you."

The Beatles sang "All My Loving."

"Ten after ten," thought Hilda. "They must have. . . what? No . . . they'll be here. They'll come, surely . . . I hope they come soon — the sandwiches will dry out. I'm getting tired. I'm too old for this anyway. At least my body is old . . . I should be in bed."

"You old, stupid, undignified fool!" she said aloud, sighed, stood and walked to the window. The breath of her passing dis-turbed the flame of the candle. The rhinestones glittered. She gazed out at the moonlit, snow-clad yard. What she took to be Venus shone above the barn. She swallowed. Her throat felt sore, irritated by the battle raging there — she was trying not to weep.

The lights of a car flickered on some trees across the road.

"Maybe they hitched a ride," she thought. "Maybe that's them coming."

But the car came and went as did several more before she turned away from the window.

Hilda was certain, now, that nobody was coming, and the reality confused her somewhat, tossed her between anger and sorrow, dignity and humility, hate and self-pity.

"I'm too old to have to deal with such unchained senti-ments," she thought. "Too old and too tired to be sitting here hoping beyond hope. At what point does one give up hope? What is hope? Is hope just another word for fear? Hope is a dream. Hope is a delusion . . . the state of mourners. When one stops hoping, one still hopes. Oh, Shad, Shad, Shad. Can one persevere without hope? Maybe Shad was just being nice to an old woman, having fun. Maybe he didn't have a party in mind at all. And then again, maybe he did and something happened. Maybe he will still show up. He always does come home, sooner or later. How's that for hope? To give up hope and wants and needs is to be. God. I'm old . . . but what's the old adage? The fruit ripens as the shadows lengthen?"

"I'll make some tea," she thought. "Tea will keep me awake. Not that I'm intending to wait all night, mind you. But I have nothing else to do, to wait for, to hope for. I'll give him another hour."

*

The Whoopsnakes went to Newcastle, drove around for an hour and returned to Blackville in time to catch the last half of the dance.

"I don't think I want to go to the dance," said Shad. "Let's go to my place for a while. I'll get a bottle of wine."

"Your place? What's goin' on at your place?" said Bamby. Bamby was chewing gum. Shad noticed that she continued to do so, even as she spoke.

"Nothin'," said Shad. "I just sorta told Hilda I'd . . . ah . . . be home early."

"She's not your mother."

"I know, but . . . "

"We're goin' to the dance!" Bamby had spoken her mind. She had snapped her gum for effect.

Shad sighed. He and Dryfly and Bamby were standing on the street outside the Public Hall. The rest of the gang had already entered.

"What're you gonna do, Dryfly?" asked Shad.

"Don't matter to me. Thought I'd stick around till the canteen closes, that's all."

"Oh, yeah, Charley Underwood."

Dryfly shrugged.

"Well, you two can go to the dance," said Shad. "I'm goin' to the bootleggers."

"But aren't you comin' to the dance?" asked Bamby.

"Yeah. I'll get somethin' to drink and come back. No sense you walkin' to the bootleggers."

"But you won't come back!"

"Yes I will!"

"No you won't!"

"I'll come back."

"What time?"

"Soon's I get the wine."

"How long's that gonna take?"

"I don't know! Five minutes, an hour. I don't know!"

"You won't come back."

"I told ya! I'll come back!"

"You'd better!"

"I will! I'll come back in time to dance with ya. Then I can take ya out to eat."

"You better! I'm hungry already!"

"I will!"

"Pay me way in."

"Jesus!"

"What?"

"Here! Here's two dollars. I'll be back."

"Sure you will."

"I'll be back!" Shad swung to Dryfly. "You comin'?"

"Well, ah, yeah, sure."

"You'd better come back," Bamby was saying as they walked away.

At the bootleggers they found out it was eleven o'clock. They each bought a bottle of Cold Duck and headed for Hilda's.

"Hilda gonna be up?" asked Dryfly.

"Don't matter. I can't spend another minute with Bamby, anyway. She's gonna drive me crazy! If Hilda's not up, we'll drink this wine, anyway. We'll have a say till its time for you to walk Charley home. You can come back later, stay the night. You'll never get a drive back to Brennen Siding tonight."

"Hilda won't mind?"

"She won't care."

As they approached Hilda's, they could not see the candle-light in the kitchen. The house appeared to be in darkness.

"Funny," said Shad. "She usually leaves a light on for me."

"Maybe she's mad at us for not comin' back earlier," commented Dryfly.

"No . . . hope not."

They hurried up to the door, quietly opened it and stepped inside.

Across the hall they saw the candlelit door, the kitchen. The house seemed very warm. The radio was playing. Shad and Dry gave each other a quizzical glance and crossed the hall, entered the kitchen.

They saw the candles on the table, the sandwiches, the plate of baloney, crackers and dill pickles. They saw Hilda Porter, lipsticked and rouged, wearing her pink party dress, the rhinestones. She was asleep in the rocking chair beside the stove. A pot of tea boiled on the stove.

Shad sank to a chair as if he'd just been told some horrible news. He looked at the little white-haired lady, the tanned skin with the dots of rouge on her cheeks, the lipstick.

"She waited up for us," whispered Dryfly. "What're we gonna tell her?"

Shad was still watching Hilda, speechless. All he could do was sigh.

"Are you thinking that maybe you might be the biggest asshole that ever walked?" asked Dry, feeling Shad's chagrin.

Shad thought for a moment, then went, "Ahem!"

Hilda did not stir.

"Ahem!" went Shad again.

Hilda opened her eyes.

"You were havin' a nap," said Shad. "We got tied up, but we're here. See you made some sandwiches . . . look good. Want some wine?"

"Well . . . I . . . " Hilda did not look very happy. She could not look Shad straight in the eyes. "I thought you weren't coming."

"Yeah, well, we, ah, Billy Bean picked us up and on our way to the bootleggers, we, ah, somethin' happpened to the van . . . motor or somethin' . . . "

"Well, you're here, safe, that's the main thing."

Shad handed Dryfly his bottle. "Pour us all a drink, Dry," he said.

"I'm very tired, Shad. I think I need to go to bed."

"Hilda . . . I . . . I'm sorry . . . please . . . I . . . "

"I made a lunch for you . . . enough for both of you . . . Shad, I'm sorry . . . I . . . I'm so old."

If Hilda had slapped Shad's face, it would not have hurt him much; if she had kicked him in the crotch, he would have recovered quickly; if she had stabbed him in the heart, he would have felt he deserved it and died peacefully, but she laid a much worse punishment on him — she began to cry.

"Don't cry," said Shad. "Throw me out, do anything, but don't cry."

"Throw you out? Why would I throw you out? Because I'm a foolish old woman . . . I can cry if I want to . . . but what's your excuse?"

"I'm not crying . . . I've . . . sniff . . . got a hair or somethin' in my eye. And you're not a foolish old woman! You're not old at all! And who cares if you're old . . . I . . . I love ya . . . "

They embraced.

Dryfly didn't know whether to pour the wine or not. He picked up a glass, sat it down again, decided to have a drink, drank straight from the bottle. "Ahem! I, ah, I guess I'll be running along . . . I, well, you two might want to be alone. "

Shad and Hilda released each other, not knowing at this point whether to laugh or cry.

"Don't go . . . " said Hilda. "I'm just . . . "

"Stick around," said Shad. "I've been drinkin'. I can't trust myself around this young lady when I'm drinkin'. And if she has a drink, God knows what might happen — I might even try to give her a little rub."

"Oh, Shad! Have some sense!"

"Well, I think we should drink a little toast," said Dryfly.

"Well, maybe . . . just a little."

Hilda smiled and somehow looked very pretty in her pink party dress.

Dryfly poured, being careful not to let his tears drop into the Cold Duck.

*

Later, Dryfly went back to the canteen and spent the last of his money playing pinball, waiting for everyone to leave. By the time Charley turned out the lights and locked the place up, it was one-thirty in the morning. She'd had a long, busy night and was tired, but she still looked pretty and managed a smile for Dryfly. They walked hand in hand out the lane toward the large old town house Charley called home.

"You were busy tonight," commented Dryfly.

"Yeah, we're always busy. I didn't think you'd come back."

"Why not?"

"I thought you'd probably take a ride home, if you could . How you getting home this hour of the night?"

"Stayin' with Shad and Hilda."

"Well, thanks."

"Thanks for what?"

"For showin' up."

"You're a pretty girl. I'd have waited all night."

"You're funny."

"You know Shad, eh?"

"Yeah, I know 'im."

"Was Bamby in tonight?"

"Yeah, she was in, sulking. I don't know what he sees in her."

"She's the only girl he ever bothered with. He don't know no better. But he's comin' around. I think he left her tonight. I doubt if he takes her out again."

They walked along for a minute, not talking, the electric wires humming, the snow crunching beneath their feet.

"So, what do you do?" asked Charley, after a while.

"I . . . ah . . . I'm not doing anything these days. The boys and I are planning to start a band."

"What boys?"

"The Whoopsnakes."

"You're in with that crowd?"

"Sort of."

"You don't seem like them."

469

Dryfly shrugged, tightened his hold on her hand.

"They're all right lads, aren't they?"

"Yeah, they're okay. You're just different, that's all," said Charley and stopped.

"Is this your place?" asked Dry, looking up at the big yellow house.

"This is it."

Dryfly sighed. He'd waited all this time to walk just a few hundred yards.

"Is something wrong?" asked Charley.

"No, I'm fine."

"Are you sure?"

"Yeah, I'm fine."

"You seem a little . . . quiet. Are you sure you're okay?"

"Yeah, I'm sure. I'm fine."

"You can tell me, you know."

"Tell you what?"

"If there's something botherin' you."

"I'm okay. There's nothin' botherin' me."

"You're sure."

"I'm sure."

"There's probably something wrong and you're not telling me."

"No, honest, I'm okay."

There was nothing wrong with Dryfly — he'd never felt better. He was a little tired from all the walking and waiting, but he'd had a nice time with Shad and Hilda, and now he was with a pretty girl. Being with Charley made any amount of walking and waiting worth it. If Charley was detecting any change in his demeanour, it may have sprung from the fact that he was pondering how he'd go about asking her out. He wanted to take her to the dance next Friday night.

"It's pretty cold, eh?" said Charley.

"Yeah. Winter's coming. Soon be Christmas."

"Would you like to take me to the dance next Friday night?" asked Charley.

"Ah, yeah, sure, I'd love to!"

"Is something wrong?"

"No, I'm just surprised you'd ask me, that's all. I was gonna ask you."

"So, why didn't you?"

"I was just about to."

"There's nothin' wrong?"

"No, no, I'd love to take you to the dance."

"You don't think I'm too forward?"

"No."

"I'll meet you at the canteen."

"Good! Great!"

"You sure?"

"Yeah, I'm sure. At the canteen."

"You'll come?"

"Yeah, I'll be there."

"You sure?"

Dryfly sighed.

"What's wrong?"

"Nothin'."

"You sighed."

"I'm fine, I'm fine."

"You don't seem very happy."

"I'm real happy. What time would you like me to show up?"

"Seven-thirty?"

"Okay. I'll be there."

"And you're sure there's nothing wrong?"

"I'm real good, couldn't be better."

"Well, I'd better be goin' in."

"Yeah, I s'pose I'd better be runnin' along."

"I like you, Dryfly."

"I like you, too."

"You can kiss me goodnight if you want."

Dryfly didn't hesitate, took her in his arms and kissed her cool lips.

When they parted, Charley smiled.

"You sure there's nothing wrong?" she asked.

"Yeah, I'm fine. Wasn't the kiss okay?"

"Yeah, it was nice."

"Wanna try it again?"

"Just one more and then I gotta go."

Dryfly kissed her again.

"Well, see you next Friday."

"Uh huh. Seven-thirty."

"Goodnight."

"Bye."

"See ya."

"Yeah."

As Dryfly walked to Hilda Porter's, he had mixed feelings about his little affair with Charley. She was the only girl, other than Lillian, he'd ever kissed. He was feeling very good about her, but deep inside he felt he shouldn't be dating her, that his devotion, his heart, belonged to Lillian Wallace.

"But Lillian's not here," he argued with himself. "And she doesn't even write."

He walked through the little village, passed a church, grave-yard, morgue, a few stores, a few houses. Other than a few young men sitting around in cars talking, drinking and smoking, the village seemed asleep. On the bridge, he stopped, gazed down at the frozen river, up at the crescent moon, the stars.

"I don't want to fool around on you," he whispered. "I still love you with all my heart."

Lillian Wallace, six hundred miles away, didn't reply.

She may have been six hundred miles away, but Dryfly could see her there before him, close enough to touch, to kiss.

The smoke from the mill veiled the moon, created a halo, presented a spectrum, blue, yellow and red.

"If I look at the moon and speak your name, a pot may fall from your cupboard, or your guitar might topple, or your door might blow shut. I don't mean to bother you. It's just my way of saying 'I love you,'" thought Dryfly and continued on his way.

eleven

Dryfly Ramsey wasn't the only one in Brennen Siding who had an idle fall. Lindon Tucker wasn't exactly overworked either. But where idleness rapes, plunders and has its way with the spirits of people like Dryfly Ramsey, it is usually accepted, or even expected, by people like Lindon Tucker. Idleness dwelt in the mind of Lindon Tucker as comfortably as a bug in a rug, a pig in mire, a snake in the grass. Lindon Tucker was idle every fall . . . and winter . . . and spring. The only time he considered himself *not* idle was when he went guiding in the summer. A guide's job is to sit eight to twelve hours a day on the shore watching somebody else fish. Lindon Tucker often said that he'd cut a little pulp, "if the snow don't get too deep, or if it don't rain, or the flies don't get too thick, or if it doesn't get too hot, or too cold, or too dry.

"Oh, yeah, yeah, yeah. Take 'er easy, yeah. Set right back and take 'er easy."

This fall, however, he spent most of his time watching Bill Wallace's cabin. This fall there was something bothering Lindon. Where usually the devil couldn't be bothered with it, this fall Lindon's mind became the devil's workshop.

Lindon Tucker never disagreed with anyone in his life. So, all the devil had to do to stir up trouble and unrest within Lindon was to implant one tiny contradiction.

"How come you didn't get the job of looking after Bill Wallace's camp?" asked the devil, and Lindon felt he had a thorn in his brain.

When Lindon Tucker heard that John Kaston had taken the job of looking after Bill Wallace's cabin — the cabin that sat right in front of Lindon's own house on property that Lindon himself used to own, on the field where Lindon's own

473

father and grandfather used to scythe — he clenched his fist, reached up and hit the ceiling. Like Bert Todder, he didn't know whether to laugh or cry. Unlike Bert Todder, however, he did not go "Tee, hee, hee, sob, snort, sniff!"

"Ouch! I hurt my hand!" was his first verbal reaction.

Then he took a walk back to where he'd set the woods on fire. The devil had planted his thorn well — Lindon Tucker needed to think.

"I blame Bert Todder for the whole thing," thought Lindon. "Bert, yeah. Bert guided him. Bert prob'ly told him somethin' about me. Bert Todder's a sonuvawhore, yeah. Told 'im somethin', he did, so he did, yeah.

"Course that young Dryfly was around that girl all the time. Could've been Dryfly. Dryfly was prob'ly after the job, yeah. Must've been that damned Dryfly, yeah. Can't, can't, can't, could never trust 'im, no. Yes, sir. Yeah.

"Then, again, John Kaston, the jeezless Bible-thumper that he is, got the job. John might o' been out to get me.

"God knows who told 'im somethin'. Could o' been that, that, that, that, oh, ah, anyone. Dan Brennen, maybe, the cute bastard! Thinks he knows 'er all. Or maybe that jeezless, lyin' Stan Tuney. Stan would have to lie. Ya couldn't trust Stan Tuney, that's for sure."

One by one, Lindon accused every man, woman and child in Brennen Siding of plotting against him for the job. Then he accused a few Gordon people. At one point he accused them all as a group, thought maybe they were ganging up on him, that there was some kind of conspiracy against him.

This thought depressed him greatly.

"I thought they were all my friends," he thought. "But, ya, ya, ya can't trust anyone. They were all ugly, prob'ly. Ugly cuz I got to 'im first, sold me land to 'im. Thought I'd get the job lookin' after his place. Jealous, they were, so they were. Jealous.

"Thought the jeezless Fish Hog was a good lad. Jealous, they were, thought I was gonna get ahead of the rest o' them. They were just actin' smart. They all think they're so goddamned smart. There's one thing I can say. I might be stupid, but I ain't smart. I'd tell them that, too. I might be stupid, but I ain't smart, I'd tell them. I'd like to see the look on their faces when I told them that. Yi, yi, yi! The jeezless bastards!"

The acreage that Lindon had set on fire that ill-fated summer's night was now referred to as the "Burnt Woods." Lindon came to the edge of the Burnt Woods and gazed out upon the charred, black expanse.

"I could've lost, could've, could've lost every stick o' lumber I got," he thought. "The wind blowed right to save me land. The fire went back instead of out. A fire kin do a lotta damage some quick. Yes, sir. Yeah. Fire, yeah. Fire. Kin do a lotta damage, yeah. Change 'er all in one night.

"If a man put a match to that jeezless camp, it would change things quick enough. That'd learn 'im for foolin' around with a man. Be jist a, jist a, jist a jeezless pile o' ashes, that's all that'd be left. Yes, sir."

Lindon tossed this idea around in his head all fall. Occasionally, he'd head over the hill and size up the cabin, trying to calculate what the fire might do should it get away. Would it cross the field and burn his own house, barns and sheds? He kept thinking about it, the consequences, the possibilities.

But he kept procrastinating. It seemed it was either too hot, or too cold, or too dry, or there wasn't enough snow or . . .

It wasn't until the snow fell in late November that he thought there might be a possibility of getting away with it.

*

On Monday, the first of December, Dryfly got out of bed, dressed and went to the kitchen to join Nutbeam and Shirley.

"Snowin'," said Shirley.

Shirley was standing by the stove frying pork strips. They'd have pork strips and bread dipped in fat and molasses for breakfast.

"Big flakes, small storm," said Nutbeam.

Through the little kitchen window Dryfly could see the big, feather-like flakes falling. "Kinda Christmasy," he said.

"Don't talk about it," said Shirley. "It'll be here and gone before you know it."

The radio was on and Jack Fenety was reading a poem written by a lady from Jemseg.

> *Walk by my side, oh saviour divine,*
> *Don't snip us free from thy heavenly vine . . .*

"I have to figure out a way to make some money," said Dryfly.

"Why don't you cut some pulp?" asked Nutbeam. "This old farm has got quite a stand of lumber on it."

"I'd have to get a saw."

"That's true. It'd cost more than you'd make between now and Christmas," said Nutbeam.

"How about Christmas trees?" asked Shirley.

"Now, there!" said Nutbeam. "We got thousands o' Christmas trees. You could cut a load or two every week, and all ya'd need is an axe."

"You wouldn't mind me cuttin' yer trees?"

Nutbeam seemed to be a little annoyed with Dryfly's comment. "You're family, Dry. Ain't we?"

"Yeah, I just wouldn't want to rub you the wrong way, that's all."

"Don't you worry about it. You helped build this house. Who do you think bought that door? You did! If you want to cut a few Christmas trees, go ahead. You don't even have to ask me. We're family!"

"I know we are, Nutbeam."

"I'll even give you a hand," said Nutbeam. "It's good fun cuttin' Christmas trees. I tell ya what I'll do, Dry. You help me with the trap line and I'll help you with the Christmas trees. We can be partners."

"I don't know much about trappin'. What could I do to help you?"

"Help me carry the animals, the bait. I'll teach ya the tricks. Any idea how much a beaver weighs?"

"No."

"An old beaver can weigh as much as a hundred pounds. Try carryin' a couple o' them up over a hill sometime."

"Ah, okay. Ya think we could make some money, like, this week?"

"We should be able to get a load in this week. Why do ya need money this week?"

"Well, I'd sorta like to go to the dance Friday night."

"Aha! You got yerself a new girl, have ya?"

Dryfly grinned, looked away.

Nutbeam winked at Shirley. Shirley chuckled.

"It's good to see ya grin, Dry, darlin'," she said.

"What's her name?" teased Nutbeam.

Dryfly was blushing but still grinning — it was nearly impossible to watch Nutbeam smile and not grin yourself. "Charley," said Dryfly.

"Is she a pretty little thing? Eh?" Nutbeam was still teasing.

"She's a cream o' tartar," winked Dryfly.

"Well, let's eat and get at it," said Nutbeam. "Ya can't waste time when yer dealin' with a pretty girl."

Dryfly didn't like trapping. No matter how deadly the trap, he couldn't bring himself to believe that animals did not suffer both severe pain and unendurable fear in their moments, or even hours, of expiration. He could not have accepted the occupation at all if it hadn't been for Nutbeam's great skill at setting traps in the most deadly and inescapable manner.

Although Dryfly did not have the same anthropomorphic problem with plants, cutting Christmas trees was not a job he liked much, either. The weather was cold and miserable; it snowed every day, covering the trees so that no one could not identify their quality without shaking them first. Whenever Dryfly shook a tree, he was not sure whether most of the snow fell to the ground or went down the back of his neck to melt and trickle in little rivulets all the way to his bum.

Nevertheless, by Friday they had several hundred trees, which they sold to Rudy Baxter for $73.15, all of which Nutbeam insisted Dryfly keep for himself. Nutbeam had had a good week trapping as well.

Friday night, Dryfly stepped into the Public Hall with more money in his pocket than perhaps any other teenager there — if not the most money, he at least had the prettiest girl.

*

Charley Underwood turned out to be a good dancer. She and Dryfly did the twist, the limbo, the foxtrot, the Mexican hat dance, and late in the evening when Lyman MacPhee closed both eyes and began to sing "The Tennessee Waltz" for ten minutes, she pulled Dryfly onto the floor once again.

Lyman MacPhee was a seasoned musician, had played for a thousand dances, had watched a couple of hundred thousand feet scuff and shuffle past him, had seen every boy in Blackville hustle every girl. He'd seen a thousand fights where drunken and anxious young men tore each other's shirts and swore a hundred thousand swearwords. Since nobody ever danced at the beginning of the night, Lyman MacPhee and the Cornpoppers would start out playing songs that weren't necessarily good for dancing, but songs that they themselves liked. Lyman MacPhee's favourite songs were "Honky Tonk Heaven," "I'm Walking the Floor over You" and "Your Cheating Heart."

Lyman MacPhee knew that people didn't go to these dances just to dance. A man would approach a woman, ask her to dance, dance, talk for an hour with someone he hadn't seen for a month, then dance again. Lyman MacPhee knew that these dances were social events where people went to meet, to talk, drink, make fun, interact. Lyman MacPhee knew that nobody ever seriously hustled up dates until the last waltz.

He also knew that his songs lasted approximately three minutes and that three minutes was not giving a man much time to meet, talk to, get to know and ask a girl if he could walk her home, or buy her a wiener and chips. It was good business for Lyman MacPhee to play the last waltz for ten minutes.

For the first minute, Dryfly and Charley danced at arm's

478

length. Then they edged closer. By the time the waltz was half over, Dryfly had his face buried in Charley's hair, was pressing himself against her, was smelling her soap-scented neck, was trying his darnedest to enter her through five layers of cloth. When the music finally stopped, he hesitated to step back from her, such was the extent of his arousal.

After the dance they went to the canteen, shared a Pepsi, then went for a walk. The night was warmer than usual, a wet snow falling.

"Heard on the radio we're gettin' a big storm tonight," said Dryfly.

"Yeah, you prob'ly should start home before it starts coming down too hard."

"I had fun tonight," said Dryfly. "How would you like to go to the movie with me next week?"

"Yeah . . . I s'pose."

"Good."

"The Horror of Dracula."

"Any good?"

"Scary, prob'ly . . . everyone screamin'."

"Sounds good."

They passed the church, a few houses, the morgue.

The storm was coming from the west, an almost too-warm-to-snow storm that stuck to the sides of buildings and trees, clothing, everything. The graveyard beside the church appeared as if so many ghosts had arisen and left their shrouds draped over the tombstones.

It was the first major snowstorm, and being the first it was perhaps the only one all year that everyone might appreciate. Children would roll in it playing snowball, building forts, igloos and snowmen; adults would shovel it, snowshoe paths on it, bank their houses with it, appreciate its cleanliness.

Dryfly was not a winter person, but like most New Brunswickers he could appreciate this first mellow storm — it was the second, third, tenth or twentieth storm that he'd grow to hate: the storm that came in January, so cold that people would feel obliged to bring their brass monkeys in; the one that came in February that would last for three long, depressing days; the storm that came in March, during which time bored, idle people, frustrated and out of patience, blew their heads off with .303 rifles.

This was the *first* storm and Dryfly could actually *like* it — it fell softly, warmly, silently, cleanly; it changed the rough edges and drab colours of late autumn to gentle mounds, asymmetrical walls, drifts and waves. Unlike the cold January storms, the long-winded February ones and the March mind-busters, this storm was not a test of human endurance — this storm was filled with the essence of children's dreams: dreams of snuggling in cozy dens with friendly bears, dreams of joining cuddly wolf cubs in a fire-lit lean-to. Christmas day should always fall simultaneously with the first fall of snow.

Dryfly turned his face upward and felt the cool flakes upon his cheek and brow.

"Is something wrong?" asked Charley.

"No . . . just the snow."

"You're sure?"

"Yeah . . . just the snow."

"Maybe we should turn back. You'd better start home."

"Yeah, okay."

They turned back, headed for Charley's.

"The wires are hummin' awful loud," said Charley.

"They always do before a storm . . . must be the snow hittin' them, I guess."

"Gonna be a white Christmas."

"Yeah."

"It's awful wet, though. Could turn to rain."

"S'posed to snow."

"Shad was back with Bamby tonight."

"I saw that. Do you think he likes her?"

Dryfly sighed. "I don't know. He spends most of the time with the lads."

"Is something wrong?"

"No, why?"

"You sighed."

"I did?"

"You can tell me if there's something wrong."

"I'm okay. I like you."

"I like you, too."

"Yeah?"

"My friends . . . they think you're cute."

"Yeah?"

"Gloria, anyway."

"Gloria?"

"The redhead."

"Ha!"

"What's wrong?"

"Never thought anyone would think me cute."

"I think you're cute."

"You're cute, too."

They approached Charley's house, stopped out front.

"You think so?" asked Charley.

"Yeah."

"What makes you think so?"

"You have nice hair."

"Is that all?"

"No, you have nice eyes and a nice nose."

"You can tell me if there's something about me you don't like."

"Everything's just great. I like you."

"I like your nose," said Charley.

"Ha!"

"What's wrong?"

"Nothin'."

"You sure?"

"Nothin's wrong . . . I'd like to kiss you."

"So why don't you?"

"You didn't ask me to."

"A girl's not supposed to ask."

"You asked last time."

They kissed three times.

"You be careful walking home," said Charley.

"Yeah."

"You don't get scared walkin' that road at night?"

"Nothin' to be scared of."

"Moose."

"No moose this time o' year. Wouldn't hurt ya anyway."

"Well, just be careful."

"I will."

"Well, goodnight."

Kiss-kiss.

"See ya next week."

"Yeah."

Kiss-kiss.

"Bye."

"See ya."

Dryfly started out on his three-hour trek to Brennen Siding.

The moon was somewhere up, so that even though it was snowing and cloudy, the night was fairly bright, and Dryfly could see where he was going. He followed the Gordon Road around bends, up and over hills and through valleys. The walking was tiresome and he got wet with snow, but he was warm enough and was feeling good inside. He decided he liked Charley very much, that he wanted to see a lot more of her.

"I'll even buy her a Christmas present," he thought. "It's good to have a girlfriend. It keeps your mind off the one you love."

When Dryfly arrived home at three o'clock in the morning, there were already six inches of heavy, wet snow on the ground. All he could see of Nutbeam's pink flamingo was the neck and head.

*

Lindon Tucker spent the evening listening to the radio and eating. Although he never worked a tap in the winter, there was one exercise he was dedicated to, and that was going to Bernie Hanley's store six nights of the week. Bernie Hanley was a Baptist, closed his store on Sundays.

But now, Lindon thought he had no friends, that he couldn't trust anyone; he didn't want to be with them, quit going to Bernie Hanley's store. He spent every evening in the same way

482

that he spent this one — eating and listening to the radio. As far as he went was over the hill to Bill Wallace's cottage. He gained ten pounds.

Lindon Tucker wanted to do something about his problem, but was unable to make a decision all by himself. Usually, he would bring up his problems to his friends, get them to decide, then repeat what they said until he forgot who told him and took the decision for his own.

The devil had whispered, "Burn the camp! Burn the camp!" into his ear, but the devil refused to tell him how he should go about doing it. Lindon couldn't go to his friends because he didn't trust them — they might tell him the wrong thing, might tell on him after he did it.

Lindon Tucker spent many hours standing, staring at Bill Wallace's cottage, wondering how he'd go about burning it without catching the hay on the field afire. If the hay caught on fire, the wind might spread the flames to the trees, the house, the barn, the sheds. He'd already had one bad experience with fire that year.

He thought he almost had it figured out when the snow came and solved the problem for him. He had decided that he would have to do it on a rainy day, but now that it had snowed, that part of the problem didn't matter — fire would not burn snow.

After the first snowfall he grabbed a few matches and went over the hill to Bill Wallace's cottage.

He was about to light the match when he noticed that he was leaving tracks in the snow everywhere he walked. There was a direct line of them all the way back to the house.

"They'd track me back to the house, know it was me burnt it."

With this thought in mind, Lindon had to start figuring all over again.

Lindon Tucker went over the hill, leaving a trail behind him . . . every time it snowed. He tried dragging a shovel behind him, filling in his tracks as he went. But that didn't change things much — you could see where he had dragged the shovel. He tried taking long hops in zigzags and circles, but, of course, that didn't work either.

It wasn't until this night — the night of the big storm —
that he, with great delight, came up with the solution.

"I, I, I, I'll go *during* the storm!" he thought. "The snow
will fill up me tracks!"

He repeated this sixty-two times just to make sure it was a
good idea, lit the lantern and went over the hill.

He circled the camp a couple of times wondering where he
should set the fire. At one place he lit a few matches and held
the flame to the boards, but nothing happened. The matches
soon went out.

"Inside, prob'ly. Yeah. Inside would be the best place, yeah."

He searched for an open window, not wanting to break
one. The bathroom window — a high, little window with
translucent glass — was the only one unlocked.

He had to reach up to pry it open, then used a stick to
push it up the rest of the way. Then, like doing a chin-up, he
pulled himself up and halfway through the window. The window was small. He got jammed at the belly.

Big, wet flakes of snow fell on his bum, his eyes looked
straight down into a toilet.

He teetered in the window for quite some time, trying to
grasp his predicament. Then he went, "Yi, yi, yi, yi!" his voice
echoing through the big forty-by-sixty-foot cottage.

He had left the lantern sitting outside on the ground, the
light of which shone through the pane above him just enough
to light up two objects in the corner. They could have been the
taps of the sink or the bathtub; they could have been the eyes
of the devil.

Lindon heard something move, a sound like that of someone stepping on a loose board, a creak. The bathroom door
was easing shut, gained momentum, slammed. Lindon didn't
think that the door had been activated by the wind coming
through the window, through the open space beside him. The
slamming of the door startled him so that he flailed his legs
frantically and managed to force himself back out. He dropped
to the ground, heart pounding.

"I think, I think, I think I'll, I'll just just go up the hill, go
to the house and think this over," he thought. "There's no

hurry. Be lots of storms. Got the whole winter. Oh yeah, yeah, yeah. Lotsa time, yeah. Better think this over some more, yeah. Uh huh, yeah. Go way up the hill, lay right back and take 'er easy, Lindon old boy, yep, yes sir."

*

As far as tracks were concerned, Lindon couldn't have picked a better time to burn a camp. It snowed all that night and all the next day. Thirty-four inches of snow fell. Then it began to rain.

*

Luke Van Doren was from Newark, New Jersey. When Bill Wallace said that he was building a cottage in New Brunswick, Luke Van Doren didn't know that Bill was talking about New Brunswick, Canada. Luke Van Doren was the architect Bill Wallace commissioned to design his cottage. Luke Van Doren designed a cottage with New Brunswick, New Jersey, in mind.

On Sunday, the seventh of December, Bill Wallace's cottage creaked and groaned beneath three feet of heavy, wet snow. Then it collapsed.

On Monday, as soon as the road was plowed, John Kaston drove tearfully to Blackville. He went to the only phone booth in the village and phoned Bill Wallace.

"Don't worry," said Bill. "It's not your fault, John. It's that goddamned carpenter I hired. I should've known better! It's insured, but I intend to give that Ducky Shaw a piece of my mind!"

"God bless you," said John.

"I'll get back to you," said Bill. "We'll start reconstruction as soon as we can."

Then Bill Wallace phoned Ducky Shaw.

"You stupid asshole!" he screamed into the receiver. "What kind of a carpenter are you? My cottage collapsed! You couldn't build a shithouse!"

Ducky had a short temper, retaliated.

"I told ya!" he screamed back. "You can't build too big a camp in this country! You wouldn't listen!" and hung up.

Ducky forgot about the whole thing, never mentioned it after and never spoke to or laid eyes on Bill Wallace again.

Bill Wallace phoned his insurance agent, who told Bill that his policy did not cover acts of God, that the only way he'd get any money was to sue Luke Van Doren. Bill Wallace phoned his lawyer and sued Luke and got his money. Luke Van Doren was insured against such things. Everyone involved was happy with the outcome except Luke's insurance company.

Back in Brennen Siding, Lindon Tucker was happy and even a little optimistic — everything had worked out perfectly.

"Bill will blame John Kaston and Dryfly," thought Lindon, "and Bill will hire me to look after his place. He'll build another camp. I'll get a job there . . . make more money than ya kin shake a stick at."

John Kaston cried and prayed for two days. John Kaston believed the storm and its results were, indeed, acts of God, that God was punishing none other than himself for being a sinner.

"Dear loving Heavenly Father, I've sinned," he prayed. "I am burdened with guilt and shame, my cup is empty, all is lost."

John was in his cold, empty church, kneeling before a little homemade cross.

"I am not worthy of space in Paradise. I realize, now, that my future lies in the hands of Providence."

John composed prayer after prayer, but nothing he could say made him feel any better.

"It's all my fault," he prayed at last. "What more can I say?"

Dryfly Ramsey was not having it so well either. The thirty-four inches of snow on top of the foot or so that was already down made cutting Christmas trees virtually impossible. Nutbeam had snowshoes and could continue with his trapping, but without snowshoes there was no way that Dryfly could follow him through the woods. Dryfly was forced to stay home. He split wood, helped Shirley when she needed him, but otherwise he was back to being idle.

Shirley saw that he was unhappy, tried to cheer him up. Her attempt did not work very well, however.

"You look down in the dumps, Dry dear," she commented.

Dryfly was staring through the kitchen window at the snow-clad landscape. He did not reply.

"You must have some money left from that load of trees," she persisted.

"Fifty dollars," sighed Dry.

"That'll do ya fer Christmas, won't it?"

"Yeah . . . I'm all right."

"Palidin might come home for Christmas."

"I doubt it."

"He said he might."

"Yeah, I read the letter."

"How you makin' out with that girl?"

"She's okay."

"Charley, wasn't it?"

"Yeah . . . Charley Underwood."

"Underwood?"

"Yeah."

"Who's her father?"

"Jim."

"You're going out with Jim Underwood's daughter?"

"Yeah . . . sort of."

"From out the lane in Blackville?"

"Yeah . . . big yellow house."

"Do you know who her mother is?"

"No."

"She's . . . she was a Ramsey. She's Buck's sister."

"Dad's sister?"

"I'm afraid so, Dry darlin'."

"You mean . . . ?"

"Charley's mother's your aunt, Dry. Charley's your first cousin."

Dryfly sighed disappointedly. "You could've told me," he muttered.

"I didn't know."

"It don't matter . . . nothin' matters," said Dryfly and went to his room.

An hour later he wrote a long letter to Lillian Wallace.

twelve

The train clickity-clacked all the way from Toronto to New-castle. Aboard it were a hundred people or more heading home for Christmas. For a mile in every direction rabbits and deer, moose, weasels and owls alerted themselves to the eerie whis-tle, then settled back knowing the train to be a human thing: a thing that left steel tracks, a thing without freedom to stray, a great serpent with humans in its bowels.

Palidin Ramsey was one of the humans in the train.

Palidin Ramsey was fair-skinned, had mysterious brown eyes and a little beard slightly lighter in colour than his long, brown hair. He was heading home for his three-day visit with Nutbeam, Shirley and Dryfly.

Palidin stared out the train window. The great wintry forest, Eastern Canada, had been rolling by for such a long time that its monotony was having somewhat of a hypnotic effect on him.

"Have you seen any indication that it is round?" asked the man in the seat facing him.

Palidin swung his attention to the man.

The man was big and fat, bearded, had naughty eyes mag-nified by thick, dark-rimmed glasses. Palidin had learned ear-lier that the man's name was Al and that he was a poet.

"What's that?" asked Palidin.

"I think it's corrugated," said Al.

"Why not round?" asked Palidin.

"It just doesn't *seem* round," said Al.

"What about Columbus?" asked Palidin.

"Well, if the ocean was corrugated, the sails would disap-pear all the same."

"I never thought of that," said Palidin. "But when I think of it, sound is corrugated. Echoes go and come in waves. Now you hear it, now you don't. But what about the pictures from outer space?"

"All lies. Trick photography. The moon's a disk, too."

Al chuckled, removed a flask of gin from his coat, passed it to Palidin. Palidin drank, passed it back. Al drank.

"Cosmic law," said Al. "It's true that if you fly in one direction long enough, you'll return to the place you started from . . . but, as you said this morning, so do echoes."

"That leaves us with the question, do echoes travel in circles, or do they rebound?" said Palidin.

"Rebound, of course. The world is flat," said Al.

"They could be travelling in circles," said Palidin. "There's a chance they could be rebounding from the back of our heads."

Al sighed, took another drink.

"Do you think that it's possible to meet oneself on the rebound?" asked Palidin.

A smile appeared from within the great red beard — Al liked the question.

"There's always the mirror," he said.

"Reflections and echoes." Palidin shook his head, sighed an exaggerated sigh. "There's no end to it."

"We'll reach our destination soon, and then, I suppose, we'll go back," said Al.

"Like a hockey puck . . . "

"A disc . . . "

" . . . inside a big saucer . . . "

" . . . perpetual motion . . . "

"If we knew enough, we'd have no need of rockets and diesel engines," said Palidin.

"It reminds me of the time I found a bug in my watch," said Al. "The watch had never been opened. Know how it got in there?"

"Between the ticks?"

"Precisely."

"Are you a Liberal?" asked Palidin.

"No, I'd say I was more of an eccentric."

"I never voted eccentric," said Palidin. "but I'd like to."

"Ha!"

Palidin returned his gaze to the passing forest, wondered what Al had meant by "Ha!" Mesmerized by the passing scenery, he did not know if a minute, ten minutes or an hour had passed before Al spoke again.

"We're in New Brunswick now," said Al. "We'll soon be home."

"We'll probably never meet again," said Palidin.

"We will under cosmic law."

"I feel I've know you a long time."

"I suppose we keep meeting on this same train."

"Like, we're on the same wave length."

"If we meet again, I'll remember you. You have a certain . . . charisma I will never forget. I expect one day I will read your works. You are a poet, I can tell that."

"Does it take a poet to know one?"

"Maybe."

"I haven't written any poems yet. I have a rhyming problem."

"Well, don't get discouraged . . . I had a problem with Os I couldn't shake for years. I had an affinity for Os, you see."

"How do you mean?" asked Palidin.

"When I wrote any more than one O, I couldn't get stopped. Like in the words 'look,' 'boot' and 'door' . . . I'd write 'looooooooooook,' 'booooooooooot,' 'doooooooooor,' like that. A man once went down to the broooooooooook, with a fishing line, sinker and hoooooooooooooook . . . " Al brooed the brook, hooed the hook, sounded like an owl or a coyote. People looked at him curiously. "Sometimes I'd not be able to control it and write thousands of them. Pretty little Os, on and on and on, page after page. I wrote my first three novels that way."

"Everyone must've thought you were crazy," said Palidin.

"No, not really. Not many read my works. The academics liked it; I punctuated well," said Al, thought for a moment, added, "they printed fifty copies, three sold and the rest burned in the publisher's warehouse. The burning of a poem . . . poetic, isn't it?"

"I thought you said they were novels," said Palidin.

"Yes, but novels are not as poetic as poetry. It was good to see the warehouse burn, but I'd rather burn poetry."

Palidin smiled.

"Let's drink to that," said Al, handing Palidin the flask once again.

"To the burning of poetry!" said Palidin.

*

Hilda Porter's face had more lines on it than an Illinois road map. Dark around the eyes, frail, growing weaker and more forgetful every day, she spent more and more of her time beside the stove.

One day just before Christmas she fell, and Shad had to help her into the chair. She made light of it, chuckled, but Shad knew there was something terribly wrong with her. She had forgotten to flush the toilet on a few occasions and Shad had seen the blood.

"I think we should get you to a doctor," he said.

Hilda knew that Shad was right, but she also knew that if she went to a doctor, she'd be hospitalized and kept, perhaps for weeks. She did not want to spend Christmas in the hospital.

"I'll be all right, dear," she said. "Maybe, if things don't improve, I'll go after Christmas. Will you be going home for Christmas, darling boy?"

"Don't know . . . s'pose I should."

"Well, do what you have to, dear. Don't let me stand in your way."

"Maybe I'll just go home for a little while, see the folks and come back again."

"Christmas don't mean anything to me, dear. I haven't celebrated Christmas for years. It's just for kids, young people. Is it tomorrow or the next day?"

"Day after tomorrow. Thought I'd get a tree."

"For here? I . . . my goodness, we don't need a tree. "

"Just a little one. We can put it in the parlour."

"But your parents will have a tree. That's good enough. I don't need a tree."

Shad could have been a philosopher, a psychoanalyst or an ecologist when he said, "Everyone needs a tree."

He grabbed the axe and headed out.

"But we haven't any decorations," said Hilda.

There was no more arguing — Shad was already heading for the road.

The snow was too deep to go into the woods any distance without snowshoes, so Shad walked along the road searching the ditch for something suitable. He didn't go far until he came to a little fir, sparse, but with a certain uniformity, slightly better than a Charlie Brown tree, but not a caricature. He cut it and carried it home.

He took it in through the front door and stood it in the parlour. Then he went to the kitchen to find Hilda standing by the table — she was making gingerbread.

Shad watched the thin little white-haired person for a moment before he spoke. She wore a white apron, blue dress and pink knitted slippers. She was humming a melody with a shaky voice. For some reason she reminded Shad of a little girl playing house, making mud pies.

"Makin' gingerbread men?" he asked.

He sat on a chair by the table to watch, to talk.

Hilda began to sing the words to what she was humming —

Put me in your pocket,
So I'll be close to you . . .
No more will I be lonesome
And no more will I be blue.

"You never hear them old songs anymore," she said.

"That a Christmas song?" asked Shadrack.

"No, just a song. I was thinking some gingerbread men would work for the tree. We don't have any decorations. Got thrown out, I guess. We used to make strings of popcorn and cranberries. I don't think we have either. I was thinking you might go to the store."

"Yeah, sure. Maybe I can find something to make a star out of."

"Have I given you any money lately?" asked Hilda.

"No, but that's all right."

"You need money. Christmas coming up and all. Goodness me, I'm getting stupider every day. Go into my purse there by the door and take fifty dollars."

"Fifty dollars!"

"I've been saving it for you; I just never got around to giving it to you. And here it is almost Christmas! Go get it, and go shopping. Bring back some popcorn and cranberries!"

"But, fifty dollars?"

"You earned it. Go get it."

Shad went to the purse, took fifty dollars, came back, sat.

"Tell me more about the Tasmanians," he said. "You haven't talked about them for a long time."

"The Tasmanians? I told you about the Tasmanians?"

"Yeah . . . the last thing you told me about was a lad called King Billy."

"King Billy . . . the last male Tasmanian."

"Only women left?"

"And not many of them. It wasn't long before there was only one — Trucanini . . . " Hilda sighed, growing tired with the work. She had finished cutting out the gingerbread men and placing them on a cookie sheet. She carried the cookie sheet to the stove and slipped them into the oven. Then she sat in her rocking chair.

"By this time, these lads, anthropologists, I think they were called, were studying her."

"Studying her?"

"She was the last of her kind, you see, and they were realizing it for the first time. All of a sudden she was very important to anthropologists . . . men who study man. She was the only living specimen of what was probably the most primitive people on Earth. Not only were they studying her, but they had done something that was very taboo to her way of thinking — they dug up King Billy and dissected his body. They had been dissecting the bodies of the Tasmanian aborigines for quite some time, but Trucanini hadn't known it. When she found out, she was terrified. "Don't let them cut me up," she cried. "Bury me behind the mountains!"

"So, did they?"

"Yes."

"And that's it?"

"No. They took her to the woods in the cheapest coffin they could find, on an oxcart. They buried her . . . the premier and some other big shots were there. It was supposed to be very secret. They did it in the night."

"Well, they did that much for her, anyway," commented Shad.

"Well, yes, but they dug her up. Imagine! They dug her up and wired her bones in a sitting position, put them in a museum."

*

Palidin Ramsey rode the Ocean Limited from Toronto to Montreal, the Scotian from Montreal to Newcastle. In Newcastle he boarded the little, single-unit Oil-Electric which dropped him off in Brennen Siding.

Dryfly was waiting at the siding. Although Shirley didn't know when or if Palidin was coming, it was drawing near to Christmas, and she insisted that Dryfly meet the train every morning — "Just in case Pal might be there." Dryfly was surprised when he saw his thin, handsome brother step down to the platform.

"G'day!" said Dryfly.

"Dry! How are ya?"

"Good. Good. You?"

"It's great to be here!"

"You look tired."

"I'm not. I slept on the train."

Palidin had two bags, one of which he gave to Dryfly. The two boys started walking out the Switch, the snow crunching beneath their feet, a cold wind in their faces.

"How'd you know I'd be here?" asked Palidin.

"Been comin' every mornin'. You let yer hair grow. I like the beard. How long you been growin' that?"

"A couple of months. Your hair is long, too. Smokin' a little dope, are ya?"

Dope was generally a taboo topic in Brennen Siding as of

yet, and Dryfly was surprised that Palidin would bring it up so openly.

"Not much dope around here," said Dryfly. "A little grass. Some lads are smokin' nutmeg."

"Nutmeg?" Palidin laughed. "Can you get high on nutmeg?"

Dryfly shrugged. "Guess so," he said. "How's T'rono?"

"Busier than a hen hauling wood," said Palidin.

"Got a good job?"

"It's all right. I'm learning."

"Newspaper?"

"Still there."

"Good money?"

"No. What's that over there in front of Lindon Tucker's?"

"Bill Wallace's camp . . . what's left of it."

"Ha! What happened?"

Dryfly laughed. "Me and Lindon Tucker built it. It fell down."

"And there's the new house," said Palidin noticing Nutbeam's little place. "Red and orange?"

"Ya'll have to come home in the summer to see the lawn ornaments."

"What's that up by John Kaston's?"

"A church. John built a church."

"Ha! Who goes to it?"

"Rita, Helen MacDonald . . . Elva Nash."

"I like it," said Palidin. "Maybe I'll go Christmas Eve."

Palidin was glad to be back, liked everthing he saw. As he walked across the bridge and fields to home — they followed a snowshoe path across the field — he took in every little change, regardless of its subtlety.

Watching the boys cross the field and climb the hill, Nutbeam and Shirley were overwhelmed with anxiety. When Palidin entered the house and set his bag down, the very pregnant Shirley kissed him thirty times, while Nutbeam affectionately slapped him on the back and ruffled his hair.

When things calmed down, Shirley said, "You must be starved darlin'. I'll fry you up some pork. I got some stewed apples, too."

"No, no, no!" exclaimed Nutbeam. "None o' that old stuff for a city slicker! We got a nice can o' Kam there, some store-bought bread and pickles! Let's go all out!"

"If you don't mind, I'd prefer the pork," said Palidin.

"Well, suit yourself. I suppose you get nothin' *but* store-bought stuff in T'rono. Old pork and stuff would be sort of a treat for ya."

"Yeah . . . that's it." said Palidin.

"You still living with George Hanley?" asked Dryfly.

"No. George is up in the north end, I'm downtown. I see him once in a while, though."

"You seem to be doin' good," said Shirley. "Nice clothes."

"I'm doin' all right."

"Makin' a fortune, are ya?" said Nutbeam.

"No . . . just surviving."

"Any thought on comin' home to live?" asked Shirley.

"I'd like to. Someday, maybe."

"What's it like, anyway?" asked Dryfly.

"T'rono? Big. You can drive from here to Newcastle and never leave the city."

"What's everybody work at?"

"Driving trucks, mostly."

"Everybody drives trucks?"

"No," smiled Palidin. "Some drive buses."

"Must be a pile o' big shots up there," said Nutbeam. "I don't think I'd like bein' around all them big shots."

"If there is, I never see them. Got a girlfriend, Dry?"

"No . . . had one . . . turned out to be my cousin. My luck!"

Shirley prepared lunch for them all, and while they ate Palidin was told all the latest news of Brennen Siding.

"So, how'd you find out about Helen MacDonald and John Kaston?" asked Palidin.

"He never misses a night," said Shirley. "Ya kin see him goin' in her place every night."

"Does Rita know?"

"I think she thinks he's prayin' in the church, or somethin'. He always turns the lights on in the church before you see him crossin' the field," said Nutbeam.

"Ever see Max?" asked Dryfly.

"He's down around Niagara. Never see him. What's John working at?"

"Nothin'," said Shirley. "They're poorer than we are. At least we got wood and food."

"Maybe Helen MacDonald's keepin' them," said Dryfly.

"Let's go get a tree," said Nutbeam, changing the subject. "I know where there's a beauty. I've been makin' ornaments all fall for it. It's time we put them to use."

"You get the tree," said Dryfly. "I gotta go to Blackville, do some shoppin'."

"You got anything to wear other than them overshoes, Palidin?" asked Nutbeam.

"These are all I brought with me. I'll just stick around here and talk to Mom."

"Well . . . well, okay," said Nutbeam. "I guess one lad can handle it. I won't be long."

Nutbeam put on his snowshoes and went into the woods. He wished the boys were with him, had wanted the tree-cutting to be a family affair.

It was a cold, crisp day, the wind from out of the north.

"A nice day," thought Nutbeam. "Too nice a day to let little things get ya down. We're a family, it's Christmas time. We can trim the tree together, at least. Glad I made them ornaments."

All the time Nutbeam was making lawn ornaments, he had saved the leftover pieces of wood, shaped them into stars and quarter-moons, angels, little reindeer, Santa Clauses and wreaths, painted them red, pumpkin orange and pink. He had made sixty of them, enough to decorate a big tree.

"No scrawny little tree for *my* family," he thought.

He came to the tree he had chosen, looked up at it, looked down, began to chop.

"Bammy balsam," he muttered. "The best!"

The forest was cold and silent, a winter wonderland, a scene for Hallmark.

Chop, chop, chop.

Nutbeam was the only one to hear the tree fall.

He grabbed it by the bottom limb and began to haul it homeward. It was too big to carry.

Fifteen minutes later, he stood it up against the house, sized it up. It was taller than the house, eight feet too tall for the living room.

"I'll have to shorten it," he thought. "But it's so pretty . . . "

He sighed. "Well, if it has to be done, it has to be done."

He laid the tree on the ground, chopped four feet off the bottom, stood it up again.

"Still too tall . . . hate to ruin it."

He chopped four more feet off. This time he took from the top, so as not to ruin it.

When he showed the square tree to Palidin and Shirley in the living room, he was smiling his broadest Nutbeam smile.

Shirley chuckled.

"I love you," she said.

*

John Kaston delivered several sermons to empty halls in Blackville. He made a fool of himself there — a few drunken teenagers showed up to make fun of him, but that was all. Nobody cared, people avoided him, turned away when he approached. He felt persecuted, lonely, discouraged. He didn't have enough wood for the winter, his boots were worn, Rita needed things, and because food was scarce, John was growing thin. He found he couldn't put a bit of food in his mouth without thinking that he was somehow eating up provisions that might be needed later on in the winter when things got *really* tough.

"What's the matter, John? Don't you like your porridge?" Rita would ask, and John would stand and leave the room.

John was liking his wife less and less. He was jealous of her. She still had a relationship with God. She was free from lust; she was not fornicating; she was not having an affair with Bert Todder or Lindon Tucker, or even with John, himself.

Rita would sometimes stand in the middle of the room and sing "In the Sweet Bye and Bye," or "When the Roll is Called Up Yonder." John never tried to harmonize.

Every night John went to the church, turned on the lights and built a fire. One of the reasons he was low on wood was that he was keeping the church heated too much.

Alone in the church he could pray and preach and weep and not be heard by human ears. What was tremendously depressing to him, though, was the feeling that God was not hearing him either. He felt that God's space within him was empty, void.

On the twenty-third of December, John was on his way to the church when he met a young man on the path. The young man was smoking a cigarette and gazing up at the stars.

"Evening, John," said the young man. John could not recognize him in the night, but thought he sounded like Dryfly.

"Dryfly?" asked John.

"Palidin," said Palidin.

"Palidin. I didn't know you'd come back."

"This morning," said Palidin. "I like your church."

"Ah, thank you . . . it . . . it was a lot of work, but it's comin' along."

"Know anything about the stars, John?"

"The stars?" John looked up at the Milky Way, the Dippers, the North Star. "I know they're God's creation," he said.

"Even Solomon in all his glory was not arrayed like one of these," quoted Palidin.

"What's that?"

"Do you think it's a sin to love, John?"

"Jesus was talking about flowers, of course."

"Why . . . no. Love is God's creation, too. I love it here," said Palidin. "I love the woods, the animals, the insects. I'll move back one day. The air's so fresh."

"You always appeared to be a little strange, Palidin, but I never thought you were *that* strange. Look how cold it is; look at the snowshoe paths we have to follow; look at the poverty. In the summer you have the flies . . . "

"Yes, it's never easy, but you have nature. I had a brother die in these woods. What could be more natural than that?"

"Your brother Bonzie . . . I remember."

"The main thing is to not fear it."

"We have to fear God."

"I don't think so, John. I think we have to love God."

"Yeah, but He . . . "

"The best way to love God is to love God's things. I'm one of God's things . . . so are the snails and snakes and bees and stars. To fear God is to fear his things. You should preach about that sometime, John."

"Yeah, well . . . "

"Well, goodnight, John."

"Goodnight, Palidin."

thirteen

Christmas Eve, Bob and Elva Nash went to Blackville to do some shopping, then dropped in to Hilda Porter's. Hilda sat in her chair by the stove; Bob, Elva and Shad sat by the table.

Hilda had very little to say. She knew they had come to get Shad, to take him home for Christmas.

"Are you feeling pretty good, Hilda?" Elva asked this so loud she could have been heard upstairs. Hilda was looking very tired and old — Elva assumed she was deaf.

"Oh, pretty well," said Hilda.

"Ya can't kill them old Porters," said Bob. Bob was nearly shouting as well.

Shad saw the amused look appear on Hilda's face. "She has a way of smiling . . . without smiling," he thought.

"I'm the last, you know," said Hilda. "Would you folks like a cup of tea?"

"No. No tea, no!" said Bob. "I said, ya can't kill them old Porters! You could live to be a hundred yet! Women always live old!"

Elva chuckled, then grew serious. "You gonna try to get to church?" she asked.

"I don't think so," said Hilda.

"You should try to go to church, dear!" said Elva. "I hope you pray, dear!"

"I might try to go tomorrow if I can find a way . . . if it doesn't snow," said Hilda.

"Your father lived old!" said Bob.

"Yes, yes, he was nearly ninety when he died," said Hilda.

"You got a good many years ahead of you yet, then!" said Bob.

Hilda knew by the way Bob and Elva were shouting that

they thought she was deaf. She also knew that they thought she was dying. It amused her. She decided to play along.

"Eh?" she asked.

"I say, you'll live to be a hundred!" shouted Bob.

"I hope you've been saying your prayers," said Elva to Shad. Shad looked away.

"I got your present," said Elva. "Couldn't afford very much. You like them laminated jackets, dear?"

"Yeah," said Shad.

"You should get your stuff ready and come home with us," said Elva. "We'll be going to church tonight."

"If you call John Kaston's church a church," grumbled Bob.

"John Kaston's havin' a sermon tonight?" asked Shad.

"He wasn't gonna, but come around this mornin' and said he was. You'll have to come home with us, dear, and go to church like a good boy."

Shad could only sigh. He didn't want to leave Hilda Porter. He did not want for Hilda to spend Christmas alone.

"You taught me in school!" shouted Bob to Hilda. "Must be thirty-five years ago! I guess that makes you . . . I'd say you were pretty near eighty!"

"Shad got us a tree," said Hilda, changing the subject.

"I saw it as I came in!" yelled Bob. "I think he must have got it in an alder swamp."

Hilda looked at Shad and smiled.

"I say, I think he must've got it in an alder swamp!" repeated Bob.

"I think it's a beautiful tree," said Hilda.

"Your mother didn't live that old, did she?" asked Bob.

"She was sixty-five . . . "

"Old enough! Old enough! A person can't expect to live much older than sixty-five!" said Bob. "My mother died when she was in her sixties. How old are you, Hilda?"

"I'm older than that. You folks sure you won't have a cup of tea?"

"No! No, can't stay." said Bob.

"We just came to get Shad, dear! We don't want to bother you with tea!" said Elva.

Shad grinned at Hilda, winked.

"I can't go home with you," he said to Elva.

"Oh, you'll *have* to come home, dear! It's Christmas. John's havin' a sermon."

"Well, old Hilda here is pretty near dead. Gittin awful old. think I'd better stay with her tonight. I'll try to get home tomorrow."

"You not feelin' too well, are ya Hilda?" asked Elva.

"No . . . no, I'm pretty near dead, dear," whined Hilda. "I'm not long for *this* world."

"Maybe Shad should stay the night with you!" said Bob. "He kin come home tomorrow!"

"Oh, no," sighed Hilda. "He'd better go home . . . when's Christmas?"

"Today's Christmas Eve! Tomorrow's Christmas! Shad's gonna stay the night with ya!"

Hilda looked at Shad, searched his eyes for the truth. "Don't you want to go home?" she asked softly.

Shad smiled, nodded a quick, barely distinguishable negative. "That okay, Mom?" asked Shad.

"Well, I . . . I suppose . . . you . . . well, I do have your present in the truck . . . "

"I have yours here, too. I'll come home tomorrow."

"Well, all right, dear. You still wear a medium jacket, eh?"

"Yeah," said Shad.

*

Christmas Eve, the Ramsey-Nutbeam family decided to trim the tree.

"We should put a star or an angel on the top before we do anything else," said Palidin.

"I didn't forget that," said Nutbeam. "I have, right in this box, made speshly for the top o' the tree, one genuine angel!"

From the box, Nutbeam removed an object that looked for all the world to Palidin and Dryfly like a turtle with a rabbit-wire halo.

Palidin and Dryfly grinned at each other, wanting to com-

ment but, for some reason, not saying anything. Shirley, however, was not so kind.

"It looks like a turtle with a rabbit-wire halo," said Shirley.

Nutbeam defended his work. "Well, I only had one colour
left. The body's there, see . . . these are his wings . . . "

"It's perfect!" said Palidin.

"Couldn't be better!" said Dryfly.

They mounted the turtle-like angel on the top of the tree and
began hanging the other peculiar objects Nutbeam had made.

There were little clothespin reindeer, a Santa Claus with a
clump of cotton glued to his face for a beard; there were two
harness bells Nutbeam had found in the field; there were pine
needles wrapped with ribbon and balls wrapped with red or
green yarn; there were wooden triangles and squares and stars
made from pie-plate tin foil.

When they finished the decorating, they stood back to ad-
mire their work, Nutbeam's creativity.

"It's a great tree," said Dryfly softly.

Shirley dabbed a tear of joy from her eye.

Palidin stared beyond the tree, saw another tree stained with
blood from thorn-inflicted wounds, the first Christmas tree.

"Calls for a drink, I'd say," said a very happy and proud
Nutbeam.

"I'll pour them," said Shirley.

"No, no, I'll do it," said Nutbeam and went to the kitchen.

Dryfly's thoughts wandered to Lillian Wallace. He wondered what she might be doing at that very moment. He saw
her sitting before a bigger and better tree, her eyes reflecting
coloured lights.

"And she's thinkin' of me," he thought. "I know she is."

Lillian Wallace was not sitting before a bigger and better
tree with coloured lights — Dryfly was wrong about that.
Lillian Wallace was in Sarasota, Florida, sitting on the beach
gazing at the moon above the Gulf of Mexico. There was a
party behind her, laughter and singing. A warm breeze played
in her hair. She was thinking about Dryfly Ramsey.

"I don't know what it is about Christmas," said Shirley. "I
always feel good at Christmas."

"Some of God's good will is bound to rub off with so many rubbing shoulders with Him," said Palidin.

When Nutbeam went to the kitchen to pour the rum, he had to stop and count his blessings. He picked up the bottle of rum and cradled it in his arms, tilted his head back, stared at the ceiling, closed his eyes.

"I was getting used to being alone," he thought, "and getting used to being alone is . . . what? Goin' crazy? God! In that old camp I lived in I used to welcome the sound of a mouse. Even when I heard that thing walkin' around the camp at night, it was better than nothing, better than silence."

Nutbeam shuddered, opened his eyes, looked down, poured the drinks. He went back to the living room.

"I have to tell yas somethin'," he said.

There was a sadness in his eyes — his family saw it. He passed the drinks. Everyone gave him his time.

Nutbeam had always talked slow, was always shy. Now, in the presence of the citified Palidin, he found himself even more lost for words. He looked at the tree, the floor, the ceiling, looked at Shirley and found his courage.

"It's my first *real* Christmas," he said. "If someone was to tell my story, this would be the happy endin'. But there's the baby."

Dryfly was amazed at the fact that Nutbeam could smile and have his eyes flooding with tears all at the same time.

"It's not right that he should have to struggle so hard at sayin' somethin'," thought Dryfly, and he reached out and clicked his mug against Nutbeam's.

"There's the baby," whispered Nutbeam.

When Shirley smiled and went to him, hugged him, no one but Palidin saw that her dentures looked unnatural. Palidin saw the dentures and the plain, grey dress, the swollen ankles and the straight hair; he saw the goodness and the joy of Nutbeam and the loneliness of Dryfly; he saw the square tree in the tiny room, the pink walls and the tiny window through which shone a tiny star. Palidin saw all this, raised his mug and said, "Merry Christmas."

*

505

At eight o'clock Shad told Hilda that he was going over to see Bamby, but that he wouldn't be gone for long.

"Will I wait up for you?" asked Hilda.

"Yeah, I'll just be gone for a little while."

As he walked across the bridge, he whistled "Jingle Bells." It was a frosty, clear night; Shad figured it must be twenty below zero.

He found the village quiet, uneventful — there would be church services to attend later, but, otherwise, everyone stayed in on Christmas Eve. He passed the post office, a church, the mill, crossed the Bartholomew River bridge, entered Swingtown.

He walked up to Bamby's door, knocked. Bamby's mother greeted him and showed him through the kitchen where Bamby's father sat blurry-eyed drunk.

"She's in there," said Bamby's mother, gesturing to the living room.

Bamby was watching TV, her eyes shifting periodically from the screen to the presents beneath the tree. She was wondering if Santa, her father, had somehow managed to get her all she had asked for.

She was wearing a pink blouse, unbuttoned at the neck; Shad could see her cleavage, the straining bra. She had one foot in her hands, rubbed her fingers between her toes. She was positioned in her chair in such a way that the black polyester of her slacks threatened to come apart at the seams as it stretched around her nearly obese thighs. She had a piece of ribbon candy protruding from her mouth.

When she saw Shad, she reluctantly removed the candy and placed it on the coffee table in front of her.

"What're ya watchin'?" asked Shad.

"Church service."

"Nothin' else on?"

"No . . . only got one station, can't get CHSJ. Ya hear that, Dad?" she yelled. "We can't get CHSJ!"

"Brought you a present," said Shad.

"Put it under the tree," Bamby yawned.

"Don't you wanna open it?"

"No! It's only Christmas Eve!"

Shad shrugged.

"Did you get your hair dryer?" he asked.

"How should I know? I think it's in the one with the green paper."

Shad put the box of chocolates, Bamby's present, under the tree.

"What's Santa bringin' you?" asked Bamby.

"Laminated jacket, I think."

"MOM! I'M HUNGRY!" yelled Bamby to her mother, who was in the kitchen.

"For God's sake!" yelled her mother. "You just ate!"

Bamby sighed. "What'd ya bring me?" she asked.

"Can't say. It's only Christmas Eve."

Bamby stood, sighed once again and went to the tree, picked up the chocolates, shook the box. "I know what it is," she said.

She picked up and handed Shad a little present wrapped in red paper, ribboned. "Here's yours," she said.

"Thanks," said Shad.

"You'll never guess what it is," said Bamby.

Shad shrugged.

"C'mon!" said Bamby.

"C'mon, what?"

"Guess!"

"I don't know what it is."

"Well, guess!"

"It's a pair o' socks."

"No."

"A tie?"

"Hardly!"

"I don't know."

"See? I told ya you couldn't guess."

"Well, anyway, I gotta be goin'," said Shad.

"I love you, you know," said Bamby.

"Do ya?"

"You know I do."

"That's good."

Bamby took Shad in her arms, held him to her massive breasts, kissed him.

"You love me?" she asked.

"You're a cream o' tartar. You're my little heifer."

"What's that supposed to mean?"

"Jerseys have the prettiest eyes in the world."

"Silly."

They kissed again.

"Well, I'll see you tomorrow," said Shad.

"Promise?"

"Yeah, if I can. I have to go home sometime tomorrow."

"I hope you like what I got ya."

"I will."

*

When Shadrack returned home at nine-thirty, he found Hilda Porter sitting in the living room. All the lights were out except for a couple of candles. He could hear the radio in the kitchen, Bing Crosby singing "White Christmas." There was a pot of tea and a fancy plate of fruitcake on the coffee table in front of her. She looked very old, fragile, cozy.

"I'm glad ya waited up," said Shad.

"You said you wouldn't be long," said Hilda.

Shad sat, poured himself a cup of very weak-looking tea. He did not like fruitcake much, but took a piece anyway — after all, it was Christmas.

"We should be drinkin' wine," he said.

He sipped his tea. It was not tea but brandy. He realized there was a whole teapot full of brandy. He couldn't help grinning from ear to ear.

"Bamby says hello," he said. "She gimme a present."

"You like Bamby a lot, don't you?" said Hilda.

"She's all right," shrugged Shad.

"So, what did she get you?"

"Don't know. She won't let me open it till Christmas, till tomorrow mornin'."

"Of course," smiled Hilda.

Hilda wore a blue satin dress; her cheeks were rouged to a bubblegum pink.

"She's kinda nuts," said Shad. "But I like nutty people. She eats a lot."

"See what's under the tree?" asked Hilda.

Shad looked under the tree. There was a small package there wrapped in blue paper, red ribbon, a bow.

"You can open it tonight, if you'd like," said Hilda. "I'm planning on sleeping in tomorrow, and later you'll be off. I thought we'd celebrate Christmas tonight."

"I have a present for you, too," said Shad. "I'll open mine, if you'll open yours. I'll even open Bamby's."

Shad drank from his cup, sat it down, stood. "That's good tea," he said, and ran to his room for Hilda's present.

While he was gone, Hilda replenished his cup. Shad was only gone for a moment, came back with a present the size of a shoe box.

"Here you go," he said. "Open 'er up!"

"You first," said Hilda.

"Well, okay." Shad removed the little gift from under the tree, went to Hilda and sat on the arm of her chair. "What is it?" he asked.

Hilda had an overwhelming urge to reach up and scratch Shad's back. She stifled it, said, "Open it and see."

Shad untied the ribbon and fingered open the pretty paper, trying not to rip it. He opened a little velvet box and feasted his eyes on the contents — a very ornate pocket watch.

"A gold watch," he breathed. "A beautiful gold watch."

"It was my grandfather's," said Hilda. "It's very old. My father gave it to me years ago. That's a real diamond. It comes from South Africa."

"A real diamond! It must be worth a fortune! Hilda, I . . . "

"I want you to have it, Shadrack," said Hilda, touching his arm. "You're my darling boy."

"But it's worth a fortune."

"It's only worth something to me if you keep it and look after it. When you get old, give it to your son or grandson. Give it to him and tell him the story I told you."

"Yes, but . . . "

"Say no more."

"Thanks, Hilda." Shad kissed the old woman on the bubble-gum-pink cheek. "It's the nicest thing anyone ever gave me."

"Oh, Shad, don't start. You'll have me in tears."

"Ain't no time for cryin', little lady! Here. Open yours."

Shad passed her the present he had bought her.

Hilda sniffed and began to unwrap her gift.

"Now, I wonder what this could be?" she mused. "Did you wrap this yourself?"

"Well, I wasn't much good at it. I had the lady at the store do it."

"I thought so. No man could wrap a gift this well."

"I hope you'll like it," said Shad.

"It's . . . it's a make-up kit! Shad . . . look! Rouge! Lipstick! Perfume! Eyeshadow . . . !"

"Like it?"

"Yes, but . . . "

"I thought we might take a drive to Tasmania next summer, steal Trucanini's body from that museum. Thought you'd need a disguise."

"Ha, ha, ha, ha, ha! Shad, you're crazy! But . . . I love you . . . and thanks very much."

"I must see what's in this thing," said Shad, picking up his gift from Bamby.

He unwrapped it, stared at its contents, first with disbelief, then with a broad grin.

"You ever hear tell of a girl givin' a man a pair o' shorts for Christmas before?" he asked.

"Now, Shad, don't make fun of her gift. What's in it, really?"

"I'm serious," said Shad, grinning. He held up a pair of red men's briefs.

Hilda was amazed. "Well, I never!" she said, chuckled, laughed.

"I guess you'd have to call her practical, anyway," laughed Shad.

Hilda took a deep breath in an attempt to stifle her laughter. She didn't think that it was right to laugh at someone's gift, but she couldn't help herself.

"I should lend that woman to Dryfly for a while," laughed Shad. "I imagine he could do with a new pair of shorts!"

"Now, Shad! Ha, ha, ha, ha . . . it's the thought that counts! Ha, ha, ha, ha!"

"I think we should have some more tea," said Shad.

Hilda was laughing so hard at her last remark that the tears were running down her cheeks. She held out her cup. Shad poured.

*

At ten o'clock, the gaunt and grey John Kaston found himself standing at the pulpit gazing down on his congregation.

Up front sat Rita, Bob and Elva Nash and Helen MacDonald. That was usually the extent of John's audience, but tonight, Christmas Eve, John was looking down on Stan Tuney, Mr. and Mrs. Dan Brennen and their three children. Behind them sat the single-toothed Bert Todder and the mackinawed Lindon Tucker. There was Lester Burns and his family and Mr. and Mrs. Bernie Hanley, Frank Layton, the manager of the Cabbage Island Salmon Club, and his wife, his sister and her husband and children from Fredericton, his kids, his sister's kids and his mother. There was Mathew Nutbeam and his wife Shirley, Dryfly and Palidin Ramsey.

The presence of all these people excited John, stirred dozens of butterflies to flight in his stomach. He wasn't sure if he had prepared himself for such a crowd; he wasn't sure he had the nerve to preach in front of so many — and there was Palidin Ramsey. Palidin Ramsey's eyes unnerved John to no end; they were dark and animal-like; they had a calmness about them, and yet they seemed to see not just your exterior, but your interior as well.

"Ahem!" went John.

"Cough! Cough!" went Lindon Tucker.

"Sniff, sniff," went Bert Todder.

Dryfly Ramsey yawned.

Then, the door opened at the back of the church. A stranger entered, closed the door behind him and took a seat. The stranger was tall and dark, wore a black suit, had a little goatee for a beard. His dark glasses suggested that he might be blind.

"Ahem!" went John again.

All eyes were upon him — except for the stranger's. John wasn't sure about the stranger's.

John's metabolism was low. He took a deep breath as if attempting to draw energy from the air. The air in the little church was a drop in the bucket, a breath in a vast land, a fart in a twenty-below-zero wind; it was damp and chilly; it did nothing to boost his energy supply. Clams pissed on his metacarpus; his ears were as cold as hoopsnakes.

John wanted to say, "All rise and praise the Lord," but thought somehow, now, that it might be too dramatic, that Palidin Ramsey or the stranger might detect a grammatical flaw, that Bert Todder might think him pretentious and laugh "tee, hee, hee, sob, snort, sniff." Not knowing what to say was a new experience for John — he felt like Adolf Hitler facing the devil. His legs began to shake.

He looked to Rita for strength, saw a greying, pale, tired, unhappy woman. This was *his* moment, not hers — she could not help him. He looked to Helen MacDonald and visualized little mounds of dirt in empty rooms; he saw her naked, panting, begging shamelessly. She beamed up at him, stupidly, without spirit. She couldn't possibly have spirit — she had been banged, raped, used.

All eyes were upon him and all eyes saw a very sad, poor man; all saw a man lost, a little boy in the great Dungarvon woods. These eyes were the eyes of his friends. He had preached to his friends all his life, had damned each and every one of them for blaspheming, for stealing, borrowing, canoes on summer nights, for playing auction forty-five, for not reading the Bible, for not going to church. They were still his friends, however — they were there in his church on Christmas Eve.

John had always thought that Palidin Ramsey had lambent eyes. Now, as he gazed upon his congregation, he noticed that *all* the eyes were lambent.

And then, to his surprise and great joy, he was jolted with

the realization, the salvation, the words. When John began to speak, he did not use words like "lambent" and "metacarpus"; he did not speak with the accent of a southern American. He spoke softly, kindly, from the heart.

"I've been trying to tell you how and where to find God," he said. "That was not very smart of me. I didn't know . . . I didn't know where He was, myself. I . . . I kept praying. I didn't know where to look!"

John Kaston began to cry.

The congregation looked to each other, not knowing what to do or say.

"I'm a fool!" snapped John and slammed his fist into the Bible, one, two, three times. He wanted to run, but he felt there was more to say and knew he must say it.

He sniffed, straightened up, the tears rivulets on his face.

"He was here . . . right here! I never thought He might be staring at me from you lads! I never thought that I had to love you in order to love God! I'm sorry. Forgive me. Forgive me, Max — Max was not in church. Forgive me, Rita. Please . . . all of you, forgive me."

Rita Kaston dropped her head and began to cry, silently, convulsively. Elva Nash held her and began to cry too. Bert Todder scratched his neck, Lindon Tucker coughed, Palidin Ramsey reached and held Dryfly's hand. Shirley Ramsey's baby gave a little kick in her belly, Nutbeam stared at the cross.

"That's all," whispered John.

There was a long painful silence.

Bob Nash took the initiative. He was sitting in the front; it was easier for him to reach out and pick up the collection mug. He put five dollars in it and handed it back to Dan Brennen, who contributed and passed it to Stan Tuney. From person to person the mug was passed, and all contributed. Lindon Tucker gave a dime and passed it to Palidin Ramsey. Palidin Ramsey swung to give the mug to the stranger.

The stranger was gone.

Palidin swung to Dryfly.

"Sing a hymn," he whispered.

"Me?" Dryfly whispered back.

"Someone's got to sing a hymn."

"Then you sing it."

"You start, I'll join in."

People could hear them whispering, began to stare.

"I don't know any hymns," whispered Dryfly.

"Then sing something, anything!"

"You better sing, too."

"I will. You start."

"I can't think of anything."

"Something! Anything! Something everyone knows."

"How do I know what everyone knows?"

"Just sing something."

"Do I stand?"

"Yes, stand! I'll stand, too."

When Dryfly and Palidin stood, Shirley and Nutbeam stood. When Shirley and Nutbeam stood, everyone else stood.

"Sing," whispered Palidin.

Dryfly couldn't think of anything. The first song that came into his head was "The Squaws Along the Yukon," but he knew that that wouldn't work. And then, from a jumble of words and melodies, he chose one, sang:

> *Roses are bloomin', come back to me darlin',*
> *Come back to me darlin' and never more roam . . .*

It turned out to be an excellent choice. Everyone knew it and everyone joined in.

Outside, after the service, Bert Todder offered Stan Tuney a drink.

"Have a drink o' rum, Stan. Merry Christmas," said Bert.

"You know, Bert?" said Stan. "I've been known to lie a little."

fourteen

Carl Eagle threw a BYOB New Year's Eve party. Carl's little kids, Brian, Susan and Noreen, decorated the living room of his Howard Road house with ribbons and balloons. His big kids, Sharon, Karen and Nancy, made hors d'oeuvres and sandwiches. Carl invited sixty people, so the girls made sixty Kam sandwiches, sixty deviled ham sandwiches, and sixty egg sandwiches. The hors d'oeuvres consisted of several heaping plates of baloney and dill pickles. Carl's wife Henrietta made a punch — sweetened Kool-Aid and Alcool.

Carl Eagle invited every friend, old and new, he had, most of whom showed up at nine o'clock. Carl had hired Billy Bean and the Whoopsnakes to play for his party. However, he had not invited the twenty-seven Whoopsnake followers that showed up between ten and eleven o'clock.

The Whoopsnake followers were soft-spoken, wore long hair, beards, their heads bobbed a lot. Their colourful flowered and checked clothes clashed with the blacks and whites of Carl's invited guests; their long hair did not tickle the fancy of the Brylcreemers; the invited guests did not wear bell-bottomed trousers and beads — the Whoopsnakes did not wear jetboots and trucker's wallets.

Tommy Nolan was there.

Tommy Nolan did not like the music or Cold Duck wine.

Tommy Nolan drank Hermit Sherry and could whoop louder than the devil in a bear trap.

"She loves you, yeah, yeah, yeah," sang Dryfly Ramsey. Shad and Clinton harmonized. The Whoopsnakes did not have a Ringo Starr, but otherwise sounded pretty good.

"Whoop!" went Tommy Nolan for attention, then yelled, "Stop the music!"

The music did not stop.

Tommy faced the band, watched for a moment.

"Look at them!" he yelled. "Look at the jeezless sheepdogs, would ya!"

Shad smiled.

Billy Bean winked.

"She loves you and you know that can't be bad," sang Dryfly.

"Sing 'Honky Tonk Angels!'" yelled somebody from the back of the room.

"'Honky Tonk Angels'!" yelled Tommy. "These assholes couldn't sing 'Honky Tonk Angels'!"

"Cool it, man," said Joe Carson, a nearby Whoopsnake follower. "They're good heads, Tommy. Leave them alone."

Tommy swung to Joe, eyed his long hair and beads, his pink shirt and yellow bell-bottomed jeans.

"You're a Carson, ain't ya?" said Tommy. "You're Newt Carson's young lad?"

"That's right," said Joe Carson.

"Look at 'im, boys! Look at the jeezless hippie, would ya!"

A few of Tommy's friends, invited guests, chuckled.

A chuckle or two was all the encouragement Tommy needed.

"What're ya wearin' beads for? You some kinda fruit?" yelled Tommy. Everyone in the house heard him, a hush intruded upon what had been a near cacophony of talking and laughter. The music, however, continued.

"She loves you, yeah, yeah, yeah," sang Dryfly, thinking that perhaps Lindon Tucker had had a hand in writing the song. "She loves you yeah, yeah, yeah, yeah . . . " The song ended and Gary Perkins twanged his guitar and without missing a beat, as if in medley, started playing "Because."

"Give me one chance and I'll be happy . . . just, just to be with you," sang Dry.

"How can you stand there wearing beads and them fruity clothes, with hair half way to yer arse like that?" asked Tommy. "What's yer poor father think?"

"Leave my father outta this," said Joe Carson.

"Ha!" went Tommy, "If I was yer father, I'd beat the shit outta ya! AND STOP THAT GODDAMNED MUSIC!"

"Well, you're not my father . . . and cool it, man! This is a party. We're here for a good time!"

"Man! Man!" mocked Tommy. "You'd better call me *man*! How in hell can a *man* have a good time when he has to rub shoulders with the likes o' you?"

"Well, don't rub shoulders with me, then. Go some place else."

"I was invited to my good friend's party, I'll rub shoulders with whoever I want!"

Carl Eagle had not invited the Whoopsnake followers, but he did know them all — their mothers and fathers, families. Carl Eagle did not want any trouble at his party. He made his way through the crowd to confront the potential fight. His intention was to nip it in the bud. He was carrying a bottle of wine.

"C'mon boys, settle down, have a drink, let's party," he said.

"You mean you invited this jeezless dick?" yelled Tommy.

"No, I didn't invite him, but . . . "

"You didn't invite 'im! You didn't invite 'im! Then what the hell is he doin' here?"

"It's all right," said Joe Carson. "I'll leave. I don't want any trouble."

Tommy Nolan hated bell-bottomed jeans and beads, despised long hair and Whoopsnakes; he did not like the Beatles, Rolling Stones, or change. Tommy Nolan believed marijuana was a harmful, addictive drug, thought it was the root of all evil, that one could overdose and die from taking it. He had been more than just a little concerned about its recent influx into the Miramichi area and had vigorously opposed it from the first time he'd heard of it. There was no doubt in his mind that the long-haired, bell-bottomed, bead-wearing Joe Carson was apt to be on it, might even be a pusher, might give it to children.

In his ignorance, Tommy Nolan had no intentions of letting Joe Carson walk away. He was slightly dizzy, the wine gave him an unreasonable courage.

"You'll leave when I'm through talkin' to you!" said Tommy.

"Now, that's enough, Tommy," said Carl. "C'mon, boys, have a drink. We're all friends here."

"Drink! Do you think I'd drink from anything that these sons o' whores might've slipped dope into?" yelled Tommy.

Carl Eagle sighed, frustrated.

"I think it's time you both left," he said.

That was not the right thing for Carl Eagle to say. Tommy Nolan had been thinking he'd have an ally in Carl, but these words indicated that Carl was not choosing sides.

"Are you asking me to get out?" he snapped.

"I just don't want no trouble at my party!" said Carl.

"Well, there's the arsehole that's leavin', and he's leavin' right now!" yelled Tommy and violently grabbed Joe Carson and started for the door.

"Leave Joe alone!" yelled a big long-hair from the corner, rushed to Joe's defence. In doing so he upset a table on which sat a plate of Kam sandwiches.

"You stay out of this!" yelled a Brylcreem.

"Settle down!" yelled Carl. "You'll break something! Settle down, I say!"

Joe Carson didn't like how he was being manhandled, swung and hit Tommy Nolan, staggering him back against Jerry Layton. Jerry Layton was so taken by surprise that it was nothing more than a reflex action that caused him to hit Joe Carson.

Several men anticipated a potential brawl and moved in to police the affair.

Others thought that the men were taking sides and moved in to police the police.

Within seconds, no more than a minute, every male in the room was fighting, and every female was hollering, screaming and crying.

Someone got thrown through a window.

The band played on. Dryfly got hit on the brow by a piece of baloney but kept on singing.

Gradually, after many things were broken, wine spilled and food trampled, the fight moved outdoors.

Everyone was either fighting or watching the fight — everyone except the Whoopsnakes. This was a valuable rehearsal for them, too valuable to spend watching a fight that they themselves would probably end up in if they went to watch. And, besides, with everybody outdoors there was all that unattended Cold Duck and Hermit to be looked after, all those sandwiches to be eaten.

At one point, Shad checked his golden, diamond-studded pocket watch.

"It's time," he said and struck a chord on his banjo. "HAPPY NEW YEAR!" he yelled.

The music started.

"Should auld acquaintance be forgot, and never brought to mind . . . " sang Dryfly.

Clinton, Billy, Gary, and Shadrack joined in, sang along. They sang "Auld Lang Syne" to an empty house.

*

Dear Dryfly,

I've had a miserable fall and winter. I spent the Christmas holidays in Florida and it was the pits — Dad had a great time with old friends and lovers, but there were no kids around and I found myself somewhat lonely most of the time. There's nothing like being home for Christmas. Then, we spent New Year's in New York and that, although fascinating to see, was not so good either. New Year's Eve we went out to dinner and had a nice time, but later, Dad went to a ball and I was left to spend the magic hour with Aunt Christine, in our suite, thirty floors above where Dad was kicking up his heels.

I love my father very much and he thinks that I'm the salt of the earth, but he is a lonely man, needs friends, needs a lover (I think he has one, by the way), needs to be with these friends and lovers. It is my misfortune, I guess, to tag along.

You might have guessed by the tone of this letter that I've been moping around a lot. If so, you've guessed right. School is a great enjoyment for me, and I'm doing very well, but otherwise, life seems to be offering few pleasures.

And then there's you, Dryfly.

When I left you last summer, I knew I was leaving part of me behind, but I had no idea how much. I was very unhappy, but I thought it would just go away eventually and everything would return to normal. I thought I could forget you . . . and that's why I only wrote you one letter — the one with the matches. I knew you were unhappy, as well, and I thought that writing to you would only lead things along in a painfully hopeless direction. It was very selfish, immature and unkind of me. I'm sorry.

Dryfly, my love, I've learned that a void is a void. Since the summer, since I left you in Brennen Siding, there has been a great void within me, a void that only you can fill.

If these words are causing you pain, I'm sorry. I have no right to play with your feelings, your heart. You may be over it; you may have another lover. Whatever's happening with you, I hope you are very happy. Your happiness is my happiness.

Maybe a letter such as this is the whim of one who is young and foolish, but I just had to let you know how I feel. It makes me feel better to tell you that I love you very much; that the mere thought of you gives me strength.

Take care, my love.

> *Your good friend,*
> *Lillian Wallace*

*

Hilda Porter sat knitting beside the stove. She was making Shadrack a pair of mitts.

Shadrack Nash sat at the table doing homework. On a page in front of him was written: "Define Oxymoron and give ten examples that aren't found in the text."

"Oxymoron," thought Shad. "Words together that contradict each other." He wrote this beneath the question and tried to think of some examples.

He looked out the window. A dirty, twelve-foot pile of

snow blocked his view of the road, the yard was hued with twilight blue, the sky a slate grey.

"Will spring never come?" he thought. "Here it is March and we haven't had a warm day. Won't be long till the robins are back, though. When it warms up, I'll take a week off from school and do . . . nothin'. Watch the Stanley Cup playoffs, walk on the crust in the mornings, listen for the first robin, pick Hilda some mayflowers, take her on a picnic."

He turned back to his page, wrote "mild winter." After a few minutes more of thought, he wrote "smart cookie," "New Brunswick highway" and "honest politician." Then he drew a blank, mused for several minutes and, finally, turned to Hilda.

"Know any oxymorons?" he asked.

"Oxymorons . . . oxymorons . . . ." said Hilda. "'Bittersweet' is an oxymoron . . . I always thought that the term 'faithful husband' was one."

Shad grinned, added "bitter-sweet" and "faithful husband" to his list. He now had six. "I need ten altogether," he said.

"What do you have so far?" asked Hilda.

Shad told her what he had. Hilda chuckled at "New Brunswick highway" and "honest politician." She doubted that his teacher would consider these true oxymorons, but said nothing to that effect.

"How about 'worldly American'?" she suggested.

Shad had complete confidence in Hilda, wrote "worldly American" on his page.

"Would 'Miramichi optimism' work?" he asked.

"If you think so," said Hilda. To Hilda, this was a game. She very much enjoyed helping Shad with his homework.

"That's eight," said Shad.

They sat silent for a moment, thinking.

"'Maritime fashion' might be a good one," chuckled Hilda in a while.

Shad wrote down "Maritime fashion," sighed, reviewed his list, sighed again. "I don't know," he said.

"You don't know what?" asked Hilda.

"I don't know if they're any good or not."

"I think they're kind of good, shows imagination, but your

teacher will probably give you a better mark for words like 'cruel kindness' and 'laborious idleness.'"

A knock sounded on the door.

"Come in!" shouted Shad.

Dryfly Ramsey entered, sat across from Shad. He slumped, looked unhappy, seemed not himself.

"What's the matter with you?" asked Shad.

"Nothin'. What're you up to?"

"Know any oxymorons?"

"Don't know . . . where are they from?"

Hilda chuckled.

"Oxymorons!" said Shad. "Back-to-back words that have opposite meanings."

"Like 'bitter-sweet,'" put in Hilda.

"Oh. No."

"What're you doin' down here on a Wednesday?" asked Shad.

"Well . . . Billy Bean came to visit me . . . "

"What's new with Billy?"

"Not too much. He got another gig, the Easter dance at the school."

"Yeah? He never mentioned it to me."

Dryfly sighed, looked away. "I . . . I . . . he told me he was cuttin' back on band members."

"Why would he do that? You're the only one that can sing!"

"Yeah, well, he wasn't talkin' about me."

"You mean . . . "

"He doesn't think the band needs a banjo for rock 'n' roll, I guess."

Shad sat silent for a moment, his expression revealing his disappointment. "What's Billy Bean know?" he said softly.

"He don't know nothin'!" said Dryfly. "I told 'im that, too. I thought 'Eight Days a Week' sounded great with the banjo."

Shad sighed. "But he doesn't want me," he said.

Dryfly shrugged. "I guess not."

"That's a good gig, too," said Shad.

"I know," said Dryfly.

"Well, at least you'll be able to do it."

"No."

"No, what?"

"I ain't doin' it."

"Why?"

"Told 'im it's all of us, or I ain't playin'."

"Why?"

"Cause you're a part of the band."

"I know, but . . . so, what'd he say to that?"

"Nothin'. He didn't seem to care. He thinks there's more money in a smaller band, wants to use the extra money for buying equipment. He said he was thinking about getting a girl singer, anyway — thinks a girl will add class to the group."

"A girl! Girls can't sing!"

Hilda chuckled at this.

"I know that," said Dryfly, "but that's what he wants. You and me are out. . . on our own."

"So, we'll start our own band."

"That's what I was thinkin'. I was thinkin' maybe just the two of us, like the Everly Brothers, or Ian and Sylvia."

"Which one of us will be Sylvia?"

"You know what I mean."

"Might work."

"Yeah, well . . . " Dryfly shrugged. "Worth thinkin' about."

"But the Whoopsnakes were so damn popular," sighed Shad.

"We can still use the name," said Dryfly.

"How?"

"Cause Billy wants a new name for his group, too."

"How come?"

"Cause it was us thought of it. He wants to call the new band the Earwigs."

"The Earwigs?"

"That's what he said."

"Ha! Competition!"

"We can do it," said Dryfly, tapping himself on the chest. "Ain't nobody can resist this golden voice."

Shad grinned. "We can throw in a little bit o' comedy, too," he said.

"That reminds me," said Dryfly. "I got this letter from

Palidin." He removed a piece of paper from his pocket, handed it to Shad. "He must've been talkin' to Nutbeam. It's funny. Ha! Maybe Pal could write jokes for us."

Shad read:

PORNOGRAPHIC LAWN ORNAMENT AD

Ladies and gentlemen! Be the envy of your block! Get one of these genuine, hand-made and locally painted pornographic lawn ornaments. A product of this our very own province of New Brunswick!

Get a shepherd attending to his sheep! See Little Boy Blue do it to Little Bo Peep! Here's one you'll enjoy, the precision-crafted and wind-driven reminder of how man loves his dog.

No quickies here! You can tease the fantasies of your neighbours all day and into the night, for as long as the four winds blow. What a man! What a concept!

Afternoon, dusk or dawn
You'll have action on your lawn.
Morning, noon or late, late night
You'll be spellbound with delight!

And ladies? We haven't forgotten you! We have here the perfect playmate — a wind-driven vibrator. No cords or batteries needed, no distracting hum. All you need is the wind. Try it on for size! I guarantee, you'll be tickled pink!

"What's it say?" asked Hilda.

"Ah . . . man talk," said Shad.

Two hours later, after much planning, laughing and general foolishness, Dryfly left. Shad swung back to his oxymorons, wrote "rock 'n' roll banjo."

*

It all began in the kitchen on the twentieth of March, and it all happened very quickly.

Shirley was sewing a button on the flap of Nutbeam's long underwear when she felt a spasm. Shirley was an experienced baby maker and knew exactly what was happening, that it was time.

Nutbeam was greasing the leather tops of his gumshoes, Dryfly was in the bedroom trying to get a handle on arithmetic. Because he had received a letter the day before from Lillian Wallace, he was unable to concentrate on arithmetic or anything else. He was sitting in an aura, a state of emotional bliss.

"It . . . it's time," said Shirley.

Nutbeam looked up from his gumshoe. "Time for what?" he asked.

"The baby's comin'."

Nutbeam jumped up so fast that he left his shadow where it was, that his blood had to rush to catch up. He nearly fainted from the sensation, had to sit down again. He tried to grasp the reality of the situation, couldn't. He jumped up again, started for Shirley, changed his mind, started for the door, changed his mind, started for the bedroom to get Dryfly, changed his mind and turned back to Shirley.

He tried to say "What do I do?" but couldn't.

"Wha, wha, wha . . ." said Nutbeam.

"Helen MacDonald," said Shirley.

Nutbeam nodded, started for the door.

"You'd better put your boots on," said Shirley. "There's four feet of snow on the ground."

Nutbeam went back to his chair, pulled on his gumshoes, tried to lace them up. His hands were so shaky that he missed several holes. Nutbeam didn't care about that. He had to get Helen MacDonald. He tied the laces.

"You got them on the wrong feet," said Shirley.

Nutbeam didn't care about that, either. He left the house and ran all the way to Helen's, pounded on her door. Helen took a long time coming. He knocked again, louder. When Helen finally did open the door, Nutbeam found himself speechless. He had forgotten how shy he was, and the appearance of Helen left him gaping stupidly.

"Yes?" said Helen.

"I . . . I . . . Shir . . . she . . . ba, ba, ba . . . "

"For Heaven's sake, what's the matter, Mr. Nutbeam?"

"The ba, ba . . . the ba, ba," explained Nutbeam.

"The baby!" Helen understood, rushed to the closet, donned her coat, hat and fur-topped high-heeled boots. This took her only a minute, but it seemed to Nutbeam to be a very long process. Then Helen picked up a bag and began to check its contents. Nutbeam was beside himself. "Shirley could die while she's here checking the goddamned bag!" he thought.

On the way to Nutbeam's, Helen yelled, "Slow down! I can't keep up with ya!" They were following a snowshoe path, and Nutbeam cursed the fact that Helen would not leave it. He, himself, would shortcut, wade through the snow.

Shirley went to her room, shouting to Dryfly as she went.

"The baby's comin'!" she called. "Dryfly, boil some water!" Inside her room with the door shut, she found the box she had prepared, the one with all the sheets and towels in it. She sat on the bed to wait.

Dryfly put the kettle on and was adding wood to the stove when Helen and Nutbeam came through the door.

"How often are the pains?" Helen was asking.

"Don't know," said Nutbeam, and then to Dryfly: "Where's Shirley? What's happened to Shirley?"

"She's in the bedroom! Where were you?"

"I was gettin' Helen!"

"I know, but you took long enough!"

"Hot water, Dryfly! I'll need lotsa hot water!" ordered Helen. She removed her coat and kicked off her boots.

"The kettle's on and I filled the tank," said Dryfly.

"That's good. And keep that fire roaring hot. I want it so warm in here that you can hardly stand it! I'll need all the towels and sheets you can get your hands on."

Helen, with bag in hand, hurried to Shirley's room.

Nutbeam and Dryfly stared wide-eyed at each other, two very excited, ignorant and scared men.

"What do we do?" asked Nutbeam.

"Boil water, I guess," said Dryfly.

"What if something goes wrong?"

Dryfly shrugged, looked away. He didn't want to think about it.

"Maybe I should get a doctor," said Nutbeam.

"I don't know . . . "

Nutbeam went to the bedroom door, tapped lightly. "Helen? Should I go for a doctor?"

"Go away!" said Helen. "Everything's all right! I'll let you know if we need a doctor!"

Nutbeam sighed and began to pace.

*

"How often are the pains?" asked Helen.

"The first one came about ten minutes ago," said Shirley. "I just had the second one."

"How long are they lasting?"

"About half a minute . . . seems like an hour."

"That gives us about two hours," said Helen. "Try to relax and don't worry about a thing. I've delivered a good many babies. Brennen Siding, Gordon, all over the place. How many is this for you?"

"Thirteen . . . never had a problem before . . . but it's been a while . . . sixteen years . . . "

"Well . . . you know as much about this as I do."

"Mom died havin' me."

"Well, you're all right . . . healthy . . . you'll be all right."

"I knew this morning it was coming," said Shirley.

"The shows?" asked Helen.

"It sorta let go this mornin'. Let's hope it's a girl; girls are easier."

"Yes, leave it to a boy to be difficult."

An hour passed, during which Helen timed the contractions. Now they were coming every five minutes, lasting between forty-five and fifty-five seconds. It was eleven-fifteen — Helen figured the baby would be born at midnight. She inspected the towel and sheet supply. "Not enough," she thought, "but we'll make do." She removed a pair of scissors from her bag and went to the kitchen. "Boil these," she told Dryfly. "Boil them until you hear the baby cry, then bring pan and all to me . . . knock and don't dare enter. I'll come to the door. I don't want no squeamish men in there botherin' Shirley." Helen swung to Nutbeam. "Get me a piece of rope about four or five feet long," she ordered. "Tie a piece of broom handle to one end of it. Don't stand there gawkin'! Hurry!"

Helen went back to Shirley and in a few minutes the rope and stick were delivered. One end was tied to the broom handle. She tied the other end to the bed post. She handed the broom handle end to Shirley. "You can tug and haul on this," she said. "You'd better remove your dentures. Let me look at your tongue."

Helen examined Shirley's tongue, eyes, skin, pulse — then she examined the vagina. "At this stage it should be four fingers," she thought. "Five, just before the baby's due." She made the examination, the measurement, chuckled. "Six . . ." she thought to herself.

"How's the pains?" she asked.

"Oh, you know," said Shirley. "I sorta go outa my head once in a while. How long do you think it will be?"

"It's doing well," said Helen, removing a rubber sheet from her bag. "You'll have to lift your bum. I have to put this and a couple of linen ones under you."

Helen prepared the bed, then dumped the rest of her bag's contents and checked once again to see if she had forgotten anything. "Twine, pins, diaper, the scissors are boilin', I've made up the bed, she has the stick, there's the towels and sheets, there's lots of warm water, the room is good and warm. I'm ready."

Helen sat to wait. Shirley moaned and pulled on the broom handle. Helen would not have to wait very long.

Things began to happen. Helen worked steadily, keeping things clean, occasionally swabbing Shirley's brow with a damp cloth. She gave Shirley reassurance, held her hand.

At the first glimpse of the baby's head, Helen breathed a sigh of relief. It would be a normal birth.

Helen gently assisted the baby into the world, cradling its head, using her finger to remove mucous from its mouth, and at the very last, tapping the bottom of its feet. The baby gasped, breathed. Helen had delivered as many as fifty babies, but it never ceased to amaze her how beautiful was the umbilical cord, or how the body turned from blue to pink. She wept at the sight of it. Helen carefully placed the baby on Shirley's abdomen to assist the release of the placenta.

"Everything's just wonderful, Shirley, dear," she said, weeping with enjoyment. "It's a girl!"

Nutbeam heard the baby cry, was at the door with the water and scissors. Helen opened the door just wide enough to allow him to pass them through to her. "It's a girl," she said and shut the door again, quickly, leaving Nutbeam on the outside gasping with excitement.

When Helen thought the time was right, she tied the umbilical cord a half-inch from the baby's belly, then snipped it a half-inch back.

Everything had gone very, very well, and Helen was very pleased that she had another successful case to add to her list.

"It was five to twelve when I first saw the baby's head," she thought. "It was five after twelve when the rest of her came out. Now, what shall her birthday be?"

It was a little bit of a dilemma, but Helen shrugged it off. "The twenty-first," she decided. "She can be an Aries, same as myself."

*

"You can come in, now!" called Helen.

Nutbeam looked to Dryfly for confirmation, support. Dryfly nodded.

They were in the kitchen where it was so warm they could hardly stand it. Dryfly had removed his shirt. Nutbeam's shirt was unbuttoned; he wore a white linder underneath.

"You comin' too, Dry?" Nutbeam managed to ask.

"Maybe you should be alone with her . . . with them for a few minutes," said Dry. "I'll come in shortly."

Nutbeam nodded, took a deep breath, started for the bedroom. Nutbeam had ears the size of pie plates flopped at the top; his mouth was big enough to accommodate a softball. He was six and a half feet tall with large hands and feet. He had spent most of his life being too aware of these peculiarities. He'd been laughed at, mocked, driven to misanthropy — only in the last couple of years had he learned that having such an unusual appearance was not such a great handicap, that having big ears meant that he could hear better than most people. In the last couple of years he had stopped being so aware of himself, had met up with Shadrack and Dryfly, and the ensuing chain of events: Shirley, the courtship, the wedding, the building of the house and this moment.

The baby in Shirley's arms whimpered so softly that only Shirley should have been able to hear it, but big-eared Nutbeam heard it as if it were a booming voice making some great announcement. He slowly approached the bedroom door, heart pounding. Helen was there smiling at him.

"C'mon!" she whispered, a little impatient with his hesitancy. She grabbed his hand and pulled him into the room.

Shirley was lying in bed, holding the bundle. She smiled up at Nutbeam, revealing her toothless gums — she had forgotten to replace her dentures. She looked grey and tired, but beamed all the same.

"The prettiest woman in the whole world," he thought, and knelt before her.

"It's a girl," said Shirley, removing the linen from the baby's face.

Tears began to flow from Nutbeam's eyes. "Normal." he whispered. "She's normal!" He began to sob.

"What's the matter, dear?" said Shirley, feebly. "Were you expecting a puppy or something?"

"No, I . . . I . . . " He had been expecting big ears, or maybe a big mouth like his own. The sleeping baby had nothing of the kind. "It's beautiful!" he managed.

"She's your daughter," said Shirley reaching out and brushing the tears from his cheeks. "You kin name her."

"I love you," said Nutbeam and kissed Shirley's hand. "Smack!"

The baby made a little stretching movement, yawned.

Nutbeam, with blurred vision, noticed she had no teeth. He made a noise that could very well have come from Bert Todder — a sob? a chuckle?

"She looks like you," he said.

"So, do you have a name?" smiled Shirley.

"Shirley," said Nutbeam.

"Oh, no, don't name her after me. She needs a name all of her own. We don't need two Shirleys in the house."

"Then, you name her. You did all the work. You should name her, anyway."

"I'd been thinkin' 'bout Sarah," said Shirley.

"Then, Sarah it is," said Nutbeam.

"We'll put an *l* in it," said Shirley. "We'll call her Sally."

"Sally . . . Sally Nutbeam. It's got a good sound to it, but her middle name will be Shirley."

"S.S. Nutbeam," chuckled Helen MacDonald, who had been watching from the door. "Dryfly! Come and see Sally!"

fifteen

"John Ferguson, two minutes for high sticking!" announced the radio.

It seemed that Stan Makita and Bobby Hull were everywhere. And now John Ferguson was taking a stupid penalty.

"You stupid jeezer!" yelled Shad. "You wanna lose this game?"

It was the seventh and deciding game of the Stanley Cup finals. The Montreal Canadiens were battling it out with the Chicago Black Hawks. It was the third period, the Black Hawks were leading. Shad Nash was on the edge of his chair, rooting for the Canadiens. The only other person in the world more excited about the game than Shad was Danny Gallivan, the announcer.

"A scintillating drive!" yelled Danny. "The save! What a save! The Gump came up with a spectacular save on Hull's hundred-and-sixteen mile-per-hour slapshot! This forum crowd of sixteen thousand one hundred and ninety-seven are going wild! There'll be a face off to the left of Worsley. And may I remind you that this hockey game is being brought to you by Imperial Oil and its dealers and distributors from coast to coast!"

"Shut up and get on with the game!" yelled Shad. "Who in hell cares about who brings us the game?"

"Shad?" called Hilda from her room.

"Not now!" Shad called back. "The Black Hawks are on a powerplay!"

The Canadiens had a tough act to follow that year. They still had Toe Blake coaching, but the majority of players were aging, playing as shadows of their former selves. Their former selves, along with forwards Maurice "Rocket" Richard, Bernie

532

"Boom Boom" Geoffrion, goalie Jacques Plante and defenceman Doug Harvey, had been, just a few years before, the greatest hockey team in NHL history. Now, with these four greats gone, Shad doubted that the still-dynamic but aging Jean Belliveau, Jean Guy Talbot, Henri "Pocket-Rocket" Richard, Ralph Backstrom and Bobby Rousseau could pull it off. He didn't have a lot of faith in Gump Worsley either — he was too short. Shad felt that he himself would put Charlie Hodge in the net.

The puck was dropped, Belliveau won the draw, passed it back to J.C. Tremblay, Tremblay circled back behind the net, waited for the boys to get into position; he was also cheating the Black Hawks of valuable power-play time. Tremblay passed up to Bobby Rousseau who nearly lost it to Stan Makita. Rousseau quickly laid it out to Yvan Cournoyer. The Black Hawks, because they were on a power-play, were playing offensive hockey, had only one man back. Cournoyer crossed the Black Hawk blue line. He was on the right wing and had drawn Moose Vasco to him; he could see Belliveau moving up the center. Yvon made the swift accurate pass. Belliveau connected, shot. Glen Hall got a piece of it, but not enough. "He shoots, he scores!" yelled Danny Gallivan. "A short-handed goal!"

"A short-handed goal!" yelled Shad.

"We have a tie game!" yelled Danny.

"It's tied up! It's tied up!" yelled Shad.

"Shad!" called Hilda.

"It's tied up!" yelled Shad.

"Come here, Shad!" called Hilda.

Shad was so excited that he didn't hear the desperation in Hilda's voice at first. But this last time he heard it and rushed to her room to see what was the matter.

Hilda was in her bed, looking grey and tired; her eyes were glossy and barely open. Shad knew immediately that there was something terribly wrong.

"Hilda? Are you all right?" he asked.

"Shad," she whispered. "Shad, my chest, my eyes. Are you there, Shad?"

Shad rushed to her side, took her hand. It was cold, clammy.

He could hear her breathing. It sounded as though she was having great difficulty breathing. "You're freezing!" said Shad. "I'll build the fire up."

"No! No, don't leave, Shad, I . . . I think I'm going . . . "

"Going! You can't go! What's the matter? Are you all right? What happened?"

"I . . . I can't see . . . I'm . . . " She gripped Shad's hand, gasped as if in pain. "Hold me, Shad, " she breathed.

Shad positioned himself so that he could put his arms around her shoulders. She seemed so small, thin, fragile. "I'd better go for a doctor," he said.

"No. No, there's no doctor . . . Shad?"

"Yes, Hilda?"

"You're so young. My boy. My darling boy. So young. Do things, Shad. There's so much to do. I'm leaving you this old place, but don't waste your life. Don't spend it like I did. Never walk away from experience, Shad. Don't put things off until it's too late. I . . . I wanted to write a book. Now, it's too late."

"No, Hilda! Your not gonna. . . . it's spring, Hilda. We have to go on our picnic! The flowers will be out soon. You can't . . . we'll write the book. We'll write a bunch of them!"

"Don't, Shad. Everything that's mine is yours. You've been very good to me . . . No! Let me talk. I . . . I have a few thousand. See that I get a good burial. Maybe behind that little church in Brennen Siding. And don't bury me in black. I don't want to be buried in black."

"Aw, Hilda! Don't die! I love you! You can't leave me now! Not now!"

All of a sudden Shad was crying, his tears falling upon the old woman's hair. He nuzzled her, kissed her. She felt him convulse.

"Don't cry," she whispered. "Don't cry for an old woman that's going to a better place . . . Shad?"

"Yes . . . "

"That old story. It was foolish. Do you remember it? It was foolishness. Remember? It was dwelling on the past. It was a crutch, or something. I've always talked about things that had no place, that nobody cared about. A person gets strange when they spend so much time alone."

"You're not strange, Hilda. And I remember the story, and it was a good story. It was about a people, a race of people like no other race on Earth. They lived on an island called Tasmania, till the whites came . . . "

"Darling boy . . . hold me . . . darling boy . . . "

"We gotta go on that picnic, Hilda, just you and me. There will be green grass and flowers just like you said, and bees, and birds. Wrens and moosebirds and robins, lots of robins. You like robins most of all, don't you? And the warm sunshine. And we'll have chicken and that wine you mentioned . . . Chablis. And we'll talk and sit in the sun until it gets too hot and then we'll move to the shade where it's nice and cool. And maybe I'll catch some trout. I know a place where there's lots of trout. And you can tell me stories and I'll write them down word for word."

"Yes, darling boy . . . the sun . . . and the birds . . . I love you, Shad . . . "

"I love you, too, Hilda."

Shad held Hilda Porter for what seemed like a very long time, listening to her sleep, to each laboured breath, wondering if it would be her last. And then it came and he could hear the radio in the kitchen and sixteen thousand one hundred ninety-seven Canadiens fans celebrating a victory.

Later, he tucked Hilda in, noticed her peaceful expression. She was not smiling, but somehow looked amused. Then he left the house, stepped into the rainy April night. He walked across the bridge to Blackville. The street lights shone on the wet pavement, there was the smell of thawing dog shit in the air, the sky dark as a witch's pocket.

Never had he felt more depressed and alone, confused, inadequate. He needed help, needed to talk to someone, Bamby, anyone. He headed toward Swingtown, went to Bamby's, found the house in darkness, all were in bed. He knocked anyway, several times before Bamby's mother came and let him in.

He explained that Hilda was dead. "I don't know what to do," he said.

"I'll call the doctor, the coroner" she said and went to the phone.

Bamby heard the commotion, came down the stairs to investigate.

Shad went to her, embraced her, cried in her big onion-scented breasts.

"Now, now," said Bamby. "She was an old woman. She's better off. As soon as Mom gets off the phone, she'll make us a nice cup o' tea. Everything's gonna be all right. I'll look after you real good."

*

Hilda Porter taught everyone in Brennen Siding everything they knew about reading, writing and arithmetic, so it wasn't surprising that everyone in the settlement showed up for her funeral. A good many people from Blackville, Gordon, the Gray Rapids, the Howard Road and Renous came, too. John Kaston's little church was full. People sat, stood in the aisle, around the pink coffin that Shad had chosen; they found room to stand in front, beside and behind the pulpit, in the doorway and outside.

John Kaston had been awake most of the night studying his Service Book. He was nervous but grateful that Shad had called upon him, and confident. On the pulpit he looked tall, thin, grey. His blue suit was faded, shone at the knees and elbows. He scanned the congregation—all the familiar faces, innocently indifferent children's faces, saddened adult faces. There was coughing, sniffing, the shuffling of feet, whispering — but when John raised his arms and spoke, the little church fell silent.

"Hilda Porter was our sister," began John. "And although we will forever miss her presence and are saddened by her departure, we must also rejoice. She is at home with God. The Lord said, 'Let not your heart be troubled. In my Father's house are many mansions.' Let us pray. Our Father, who art in Heaven . . ."

There was no organ in the little church, so when it came

time to sing, John, himself, in a dull and wavering baritone had to start the hymn off.

"Earnestly, tenderly, Jesus is calling," he sang.

Rita Kaston and Bob and Elva Nash were the first to join in, but soon all the people were either singing or humming along — not everyone knew the words.

Shad stood beside his mother and father. He had slept little in the past few days, looked pale and tired beneath his long, red hair. He had held up well, managed to actually enjoy his responsibilities. He and Dryfly had sat with Hilda all the previous night. They had talked, planned, even laughed. They had smoked every bit of tobacco they could get their hands on. Never once had Shad allowed himself bo be shadowed by emotion.

"I knew it would happen sooner or later," he told Dryfly. "She was getting pretty old and sick. She wouldn't go to a doctor, kept putting it off. You know, she left me the place."

Hilda had been waked in her house. Bob and Elva stayed there with Shad, slept in his room. Dryfly also came and stayed, was there by Shad's side to shake hands with people who came to pay their respects. Both nights the two sat in the kitchen until dawn, talking. Hilda was laid out in the parlour in her pink party dress, in her pink coffin.

"It's a great old farm," Shad told Dryfly. "I think there might even be a piece of shore, maybe a pool to fish in."

"You gonna live here?" asked Dryfly.

"Mom and Dad don't want me to, but I think I will. I'd like to keep the place up, if I can. You know, Dry, you could stay here with me if you wanted. We could practise our music, get a band together."

"I don't know . . . might work. You're a lucky lad to have a place like this for your very own. Not many lads around here have a place this nice."

"Hey! If you helped me fix up the place, I could give you a piece of land, across the road or somewhere . . . there's acres and acres of land here and I'll never use it all! You know about carpenter work. You could help me do a lot of things!"

"Yeah . . . "

Shad was puzzled why he wasn't feeling more despondent. It was as if Hilda were still there beside the stove in her rocking chair. Neither Shad nor Dryfly sat in the rocking chair — an unspoken agreement between them. It seemed that Hilda had merely excused herself for a moment and, as she often did, would rejoin them after a short nap or something.

"I was thinking I might go to Fredericton in the fall," said Dryfly.

"What're ya gonna do there?"

"Don't know for sure . . . somethin'."

"Ha! Lillian comin' up this summer?"

"Hope so."

"Get your hands on that one and you'll never have to worry."

Dryfly shrugged.

"There's one thing I learned, Dry," said Shad earnestly. "If you got something you want to do, you should do it. Don't put it off."

They talked through the night.

And then the next day Nutbeam and Shirley came to visit, to pay their respects. They had the baby with them and seemed very happy. Nutbeam had called Shad aside, said, "Shad, you know me. Eh . . . anytime ya need a . . . anything, you jist come and see me. You know where I am. If I kin help ya I will," and Shadrack knew that Nutbeam was, indeed, a genuine friend.

Now, in the church, with the singing, the prayers, John Kaston's words of walking through valleys of death, Shad realized that Hilda was not just having a nap, that she would never again hum in her rocking chair beside the stove or tell him stories about Tasmania.

A marble-sized lump expanded in Shad's throat, tears appeared in his eyes.

"This is crazy," he thought. "I'm cryin' and singin' all at the same time. It's like . . . what's it called? Oxymoron."

Shad, for the first time since the night with Bamby, allowed himself to weep. Those people that could see him watched him compassionately. They saw him as the son that

Hilda Porter never had, the one that looked after her in her last days, the one that was with her when she died. None saw him as the founder of the dreaded, mysterious, long-haired Whoopsnakes. Shad didn't care if they watched him cry. Before now, he had been thinking himself abnormal for not showing more emotion. Now, his tears were a catharsis; his cup was full of love and respect for Hilda Porter.

Later, outside, Shad stared at the coffin being lowered into the grave. He remembered hearing his father saying that the digging of the grave had been very hard work, for although the snow had left the fields, had receded to the forest's edge, the ground was still frozen.

"Forasmuch as it hath pleased Almighty God of His great mercy, to take unto Himself the soul of our sister, we therefore commit her body to the ground, earth to earth, ashes to ashes, dust to dust . . . " read John Kaston. He scanned the graveside gathering for Rita, found her. Everyone else had a look of sadness on his or her face, but not Rita — Rita was a Christian; to Rita, death was a joyous occasion, a reunion with God, the Maker of all things. She was smiling and looking at John with admiration. She was happy for Hilda and she was happy for John, the man she loved, the man who had finally found himself.

John switched his gaze to Helen MacDonald and saw what he thought was a good woman — not a *true* Christian, perhaps, but a good woman nevertheless. She was standing beside Bert Todder — friends? lovers? It didn't matter to John, they seemed happy and together. "They'd be good for each other," thought John.

Lindon Tucker hadn't known Hilda Porter very well, hadn't spent enough time in school to get to know her. Nevertheless, he looked very sad and even wept a little — not so much because he would miss Hilda, but because he'd seen Shad weeping and felt that he should follow suit. He was not angry with any of his neighbors anymore and was actually proud of the fact that John Kaston the preacher was a friend that he had grown up with. John Kaston looked at Lindon Tucker, too, and liked what he saw; John liked what he saw in every face there by the grave. "They're my friends," he thought, "and I will look after them as they looked after me. I will never again talk to them negatively. I will make them aware of the Coming, but I will also make them aware of the future."

A robin sang.

Shadrack Nash removed his gaze from the grave and looked at the river, the cold, dark ribbon winding through the drab April landscape. It looked high and swift, and here and there sheets of ice made their voyage to the Renous, the Miramichi and, ultimately, the sea.

"The deep and dark Dungarvon," thought Shad.

The robin sang again.

The sound of sand being tossed onto the coffin brought Shad back to the moment.

Sally Nutbeam cried.

"I had a real good time living with you," thought Shad, spirit to spirit to Hilda. "I'll never forget you. And I'll come here real soon and we'll have a picnic, just you and me. And maybe I'll get Dry and Bamby and I'll tell them your story. Goodbye, my old friend . . . "

"Shad?"

"We'll meet again . . . in Heaven or someplace . . . "

"Shad?"

"Oh, Dryfly . . . "

"Let's me and you go to the bootleggers. I got a few bucks. I've written this new song. Want to hear it later?"

"Yeah . . . sure."

The two boys left the grave and headed for the river.

The Lone Angler

No one knows for sure what the names were of the people who killed the last Arabian ostrich, dodo bird or carrier pigeon. It is known, however, that the Barbary lion, the Bali tiger and the eastern elk vanished primarily because of overhunting. It is believed that three guys by the names of Jon Brandsson, Sigourer Isleffson and Ketil Ketilsson saw the last two great auks that ever enjoyed Earth's climate. Brandsson and Isleffson killed the adult birds while Ketilsson smashed their eggs with his boot.

The last heath hen was seen on Martha's Vineyard. A typical tale of humanity — this bird was hunted down to where there were but a few left. Then, the compassionate hunters started shooting cats in an attempt to save it.

The last one narrowly escaped getting run over by a car and lived to die of old age.

Way to go, hunters!

one

From the grimy window of his third-floor apartment, Palidin Ramsey watched the falling snow. It fell on Dundas Street, its sidewalks and buildings; it fell on shoulders, police caps and hair; it fell on tulips, daffodils and grass. The scrotums of squirrels, bassets and other short-legged animals withdrew and clung to their owners' bodies like crabs or marsupial pups; budding shrubs and trees yawned, pulled the drapes and went back to bed.

An April storm.

Palidin turned away from the melting, clammy ugliness of the day, sighed, picked up his bags, double-checked the room with a single glance and left. In a minute, he was heading south toward Bay Street, the slush splatting like Cream of Wheat beneath his feet. A large snowflake fell to rest on one of his long eyelashes, momentarily blurred his vision, tickled his eye. He brushed it away quickly before it had time to melt — to transform itself into anything that might resemble a tear.

"No tears for Toronto," he whispered.

Palidin Ramsey was heading for Texas.

*

Eight hundred miles away, in the wilds of New Brunswick's Dungarvon River, Palidin's brother Dryfly was experiencing his first day on the job as a guide. He was in the Snake's Coffin with David O'Hara, anchored about fifty yards below Cabbage Island.

The Cabbage Island Salmon Club had eighteen Chestnut canoes of various lengths and widths, one of which was labelled the Snake's Coffin. The Snake's Coffin got its name from the fact that it was long (twenty-two feet) and narrow (thirty inches at its widest point).

"You might as well try and stay in Martha Lebbons as that outfit," Bert Todder once commented.

This was Dryfly's first day on the job and he was given the Snake's Coffin because anyone who knew anything about the river, guiding and canoes wouldn't touch it with a ten-foot pole.

Dryfly Ramsey was hired to guide David O'Hara for three reasons: one, David O'Hara needed a guide, no one else was available, and Frank Layton, the manager of the Cabbage Island Salmon Club, was desperate; two, David O'Hara was thought to be a cheap and ornery son of a bitch and anyone with any experience would rather work in the woods or be the handyman around the place than guide him; and three, the Snake's Coffin was the only canoe that Frank had left and only a novice like Dryfly would be stupid enough to try and manoeuvre it about the rushing spring currents without questions and complaints. Frank Layton figured that if Dryfly upset the Snake's Coffin and drowned both himself and David O'Hara, that if the Snake's Coffin were lost in the process, it would solve a few unpleasantnesses for himself. He'd be getting rid of a sport who complained about everything from the food cooked by Helen MacDonald to the fact that he could only legally keep five fish a day (David O'Hara didn't like the rates, the guides, the river, Frank Layton, or Canada), he'd be getting rid of Buck Ramsey's son Dryfly, who wasn't worth the sweat on a boar's nipples, according to Frank, and with any luck the Snake's Coffin would never be seen again, would spend the rest of its days somewhere on the bottom of the North Atlantic.

"Oh, yes! I have a job for you, Dryfly me boy! I need someone to guide David O'Hara. Take that canoe right there . . . no, no, no, not the green one . . . the blue one, number thirteen, the one with the 7.5 Elgin on it."

To operate the obsolete 7.5-horsepower Elgin outboard motor safely, you needed three hands: one for steering, one for holding the choke open (it wouldn't run without the choke being on), and one for throttling. The 7.5-horsepower Elgin just about always started somewhere between the thirty-third and the one hundred and seventeenth pull of the pullcord — it had to do with the malfunction in the choke.

David O'Hara was on the Dungarvon River to fish for the black salmon. He was a fifty-eight-year-old, six-foot-three-inch, two-hundred-and-sixty-pound, bald-headed lawyer from Albany, New York. He had pale blue eyes, jowls, and yellow, cigar-stained teeth. He was dressed in expensive, heavy, bright yellow woollen clothes and knee-length fleece-lined leather boots. He talked loud, with never a hint of kindness or gentleness in his deep, booming voice, even while fishing. He sat in the bow of the Snake's Coffin, totally unaware that any sudden shift of his massive body could quite possibly upset him and Dryfly into the slightly-above-freezing waters of the rushing Dungarvon.

So he kept moving — throwing a leg up to rest on the gunwale, shifting his weight from one numb butt to the other, turning to watch other canoes coming and going, the actions of other fishermen, to scratch everything from his bald head to the bunion on his toe.

Dryfly, who was thin as the proverbial rake, ill-dressed against this cold April morning and nursing a cold to boot, had to be extremely alert. Every time David O'Hara moved, Dryfly had to move even further, but in the opposite direction, to counterbalance the weight.

"Maybe I should be casting," said David.

"No, no, don't cast. Just let your line out a hundred yards or so, then reel it back in slow . . . lift your rod when ya feel — a . . . a . . . achoo! — a tug."

David O'Hara's response to this was a long, thin bean fart.

A nearby merganser took to flight. Dryfly grinned.

"Sounded like a pencil being pulled out of a balloon," said Dryfly.

"What's that?"

"Nothin'."

"For Christ's sake, speak up, Dryfly!"

"I said, that . . . that — achoo! — that bird looked like a loon!"

"A merganser. "

"Eh?"

"A goddamned fish-eating merganser."

"Oh."

Dryfly knew the minute he stepped into the Snake's Coffin that it was ticklish and required delicate handling, for even though this might have been his first day on the job as a guide, he'd been around canoes since he was a child. There were grown men on the Miramichi, the Cains and the Dungarvon who couldn't pole a canoe, but Dryfly could pole one at the ripe old age of eight. He knew the river, too — the rocks, holes, crosscurrents, eddies, bars. He knew it better than anyone else, with the exception of his good friend, Shadrack Nash, perhaps. The river was Dryfly's park, zoo, playground, life. What Dryfly Ramsey didn't know about the river wasn't worth talking about and when asked about something that wasn't worth talking about, he, like all good, fun-loving river people, could come up with a fabrication that even the good Lord himself would not frown upon. If fishermen were liars, guides were greater liars.

Dryfly Ramsey wasn't the biggest liar in the guides' camp. The biggest liar was a fellow by the name of Stan Tuney. If you were gullible enough to believe everything that Stan Tuney told you, you might be inclined to think that he was Superman. Stan boasted catching nineteen salmon in one afternoon . . . on a fishing rod. "Beached every one o' them!" When walking through the woods with Stan Tuney, you'd be stopping every hundred yards or so to hear him say, "Boys, I shot a lotta deer right here." He was so good at lying that he might even make you believe that you, yourself, had been a part of it. "Mind the time you and me tied the two cats together by the tail and threw them over the clothesline." Or "Mind the time you almost shot me with Lindon Tucker's old .38-55." He'd bring things up so casually and with such conviction that you'd have to stop and think quite a while trying to remember just when and where the incident had occurred.

Dryfly would never be so pretentious as to compare his lying ability with that of the great Stan Tuney, but (in fun, or by necessity) his imagination had a pretty good set of wings.

David O'Hara hooked into a grilse (an adolescent salmon) about an hour — a long, cold, old April hour — after Dryfly choked the 7.5-horsepower Elgin to death and dropped the anchor in the safest place he knew, just fifty yards below Cabbage Island. It was cold, even for April, and the thin, starving grilse was about as lethargic as a fish could possibly get. It grabbed the big Golden Eagle fly that David had tied on his twelve-pound-test German leader and was immediately reeled up to the canoe and netted. It didn't jump or kick or give David any struggle at all and seemed almost relieved to be pulled out of the water, to have its misery put to an end. A worm would have been as active. It was thin, bug-eyed and blackened from spending the winter in the swampy waters of the Dungarvon. Dryfly thought it the poorest specimen of Atlantic salmon flesh that he had ever seen. He figured that its inner flesh, which would have been a rich pink in the fall, would prove to be as pale as a farmer's armpit — and about as tasty. Nobody from Brennen Siding would ever keep such a fish.

"Congratulations!" said Dryfly. "Nice fish!"

David O'Hara was trembling with excitement. "God! You know, I've been waiting a whole year to get into one of these beauties! Thank you, Dryfly! You did a fine job scooping it. You've made my day! How much do you think he weighs?"

Dryfly figured about two pounds.

"Four, four and a half, five — achoo! — pounds," said Dryfly, grinning.

David O'Hara didn't hear the jest in Dryfly's voice. "Well, how much do you think it would've weighed when it came up last fall?" he asked.

Dryfly sobered, shrugged. "Not much more. A little maybe."

David O'Hara scratched his scalp and gazed upon the grilse with both pride and curiosity. Dryfly thought, "This fool is gonna *keep* that fish."

"Now, I read somewhere that these things don't eat all winter, that they live off their body fat until they get back to the salt water. I'm almost certain it was the Atlantic salmon I was reading about and I recall something about them losing as much as half their weight."

"Oh, no," said Dryfly. "They eat three squares a day just like everything else. Nothin' could live that long without eatin' — achoo! Sniff, sniff. Ahhhh!"

"It seems to me that you don't find anything in their stomachs in fresh water. You should take something for that cold. Let's open it up and check it out, Dryfly."

The grilse was cold and wet. Dryfly was holding it and his hands were just as cold and he wasn't excited about handling it any more than he had already. What Dryfly wanted to do was release the fish and get off the river for a while and warm up.

"Oh, you won't find anything in its stomach," said Dryfly. "They eat invisible food, here in the river, anyway."

"Come again?"

"The salmon eat invisible food. But of course when they get back to the ocean they eat regular seeable food."

"Invisible food."

"Sure, little tiny things that can't be seen with the human eye. That fish, now, looks a lot smaller than it actually is. That fish is really quite . . . quite . . . ahhhh . . . fat. Achooo! But you or me can't see it, if you know what I mean. Sniff, sniff."

"Uh, I'm not sure. Tell me more, Dryfly." David O'Hara was just now beginning to see where Dryfly was coming from, but Mona Lisa still had the broader smile.

"Well, ya should be able to figure that one out easy enough. The salmon eats invisible food, right?"

"If you say so. You're the guide."

"Well, it's only logical that if ya can't see the food it eats, ya can't see the weight it gains, either. Ya can't really see how big this here fish is until it gets back to the ocean and starts eatin' food like clams and stuff that ya kin see. You ever eat salmon?"

"Oh, yes, many times. I prefer it smoked, although I must admit it gives me the heartburn."

"Well, then you know that you can't eat very much of it.

I've heard people say all my life that salmon's so rich they can only eat a little piece and they're filled right up."

"Yes, I have to admit that it's very rich food."

"Well, it's not really. It only seems rich because you kin only see half what you eat."

"I see. So, this grilse might indeed be an adult salmon." David was smiling now. "It could maybe weigh as much as ten or fifteen pounds?"

"Sure. Maybe even bigger, if ya want it to be. You could release this small-looking fish and tell everyone you landed a twenty-pounder and nobody'd know the difference. You're a lucky man."

"You know, Dryfly, I think I'm going to enjoy my holiday with you," said David O'Hara, and for the first time in his life he released a salmon.

Dryfly was glad that David released it. He would have been ashamed to go back to the camp with such a small grilse. Nobody in Brennen Siding would eat such a fish. The other guides would have laughed their heads off.

David O'Hara started letting out another line, pulling it an arm-length at a time, his Hardy reel harshly reporting each pull. David would release as much as a hundred and fifty yards of line. Then he would reel it all back in again, slowly, as Dryfly had suggested.

"So, will you guide all summer?" asked David.

"I don't know. Prob'ly. Maybe. I doubt it. Me and Shad have a band goin'. Might play around with that a bit."

"A band? You're a musician?"

"Play guiddar a bit."

"What do you call your band?"

"The Whoop Snakes. Achoo! Sniff, sniff."

"Hmm. Will you go back to school in the fall?"

"No. Quit school. Takin' a correspondence course. I'm up to grade eight now."

"I see. Well, stick with it, an education is very important. Do you have a girlfriend?"

"No. Not really. Sort of . . . " Dryfly always hesitated to call Lillian Wallace his girlfriend. True, he was in love with her, and, yes, she was a friend and she was certainly very much a girl, but she was only really his *girlfriend* for a week or two of the year. Lillian Wallace lived in Stockbridge, Massachusetts, and she and Dryfly were carrying on a long-distance relationship. If it hadn't been for the few letters they managed to write, the relationship would not have been a fancy more than a summer romance. Dryfly wasn't sure if he would see her this summer at all, and for all he knew, he might never see her again.

"What's her name, Dryfly?"

"Ah . . . she's not from around here. I only get to see her in the summer. She's Bill Wallace's daughter, Lillian."

"Bill Wallace . . . Bill Wallace . . . where have I heard that name before?"

"Bill's one of the club members. Or at least he used to be. He could still be, I'm not sure. He built a cabin down there . . . the one down there . . . he built one two years ago that fell down, then built another one last summer. I don't imagine he belongs to the club anymore."

"Bill Wallace's place fell down?"

"Yeah. Couldn't have been braced right . . . for the snow . . . "

"Ha, ha, ha! The snow, huh! Well, well, well!" David O'Hara seemed quite pleased with the fact that Bill Wallace's cabin had collapsed under the weight of snow. David O'Hara didn't get along very well with the club members. They were a bunch of snobbish jerks as far as he was concerned, and he figured their manager, Frank Layton, was no different. David had only been coming to the Dungarvon for three years, but each year he'd ended up fishing from this same old excuse for a canoe and with a novice guide. David O'Hara did not remember how he had complained about the food, the beds, the weather, the poor fishing and everything else that might have entered his mind on his first year there.

"Do you know 'im?" asked Dryfly.

"Heard of him. A Hahvard man, I think. He's in the construction business, isn't he? Ha, ha, ha!"

"Don't know . . . might be."

"You met his daughter up here?"

"Yea. She comes up every summer."

"Hey! Another one!"

"Hold your rod up! Let 'im run!"

"This is a good spot, Dryfly! How is it that nobody else ever brought me here to fish?"

"Don't know. There's always black salmon below the island."

"If we keep this up, we might win one of the contests. Ha, ha, ha! Look at it go!"

"It's a big one! Achoo!"

"Ha, ha, ha! And just think, we can't even see it all! Ha, ha, ha!"

*

For the Cabbage Island Salmon Club, the third week of April was the busiest week of the year. This was the week of the annual gathering of the clients, friends and executives of the American Electronics Association. It was not a conference. No shop talk here — just fishing, drinking, stories, laughter, good times. This was the one week of the year when these men could honestly call themselves sportsmen. The people of Brennen Siding called them "sports" for short.

Each sport had a guide.

Bob Nash guided the president of the company. Bert Todder was guiding the governor of Connecticut and Dan Brennen guided Mr. Rockefeller. Lindon Tucker guided a five-star general. Lindon could never remember his name, but because he wore a little mustache, Lindon called him Old Cooky Duster. "Old, Old, Old Cooky Duster. Never, never, could, could, couldn't ketch a, a, a, salmon, if ya know what I mean, now, couldn't ketch a salmon, now, with a jeezless tank! Yi, yi, yi, yi, yi!"

Dryfly Ramsey was guiding one of the company's top lawyers, and Stan Tuney was guiding a man very few had heard of, a new guest, the ex-vice-president of the United States. "He and me made up our minds what they should do with them lads in Vietnam, yeah. Send in the boys in khaki, I told 'im. Blow the jeezers right outta the swamp! Yessir! Sparrow, they call 'im. Should be a good tipper."

Eighteen of these powerful, rich men were staying at the club, and the whole settlement buzzed with their presence. Helen MacDonald couldn't possibly do all the cooking for that many sportsmen and guides, so Frank Layton hired Mrs. Bob Nash to assist her. John Kaston, the preacher, gave up his sermon-writing for the week and went guiding. John didn't like having to do it, but his wife, Rita, said that God would okay the move so long as he didn't guide on Sunday. John told this condition to Frank Layton, and Frank fixed the matter by teaming John up with a cardinal from Boston. Business at Bernie Hanley's store boomed, too. Bernie's was a small store and could not supply everything for the club, but it did have a good supply of things like bread, catsup, pop for mix, milk, eggs, and, most importantly, flyhooks. Bert Todder tied flyhooks all winter, sold them to Bernie Hanley, who, in turn, sold them to the Cabbage Island Salmon Club and anyone else in the area who wanted them. Bert was one of the best fly tiers in New Brunswick, perhaps Canada, perhaps the world. Bert didn't know this, of course.

*

"There's no use in talkin', there's no use in talkin', that boy has lost his mind!" said Shirley to Nutbeam. "He had himself a real good job in T'rono and he jist quit and struck 'er fer Texas."

Shirley Ramsey Nutbeam was seated by the kitchen table, reading a letter from her son Palidin. Her husband, Nutbeam, was stretched out on the floor with their thirteen- month-old daughter, Sally. Nutbeam was a giant of a man, as far as height goes, and his body seemed to take up a great deal of the little kitchen.

"Dada, dada, mom mom mom . . . " sang Sally.

Nutbeam tickled her little belly with his huge index finger, and Sally lit up, smiled.

> I had a little rooster way down on the farm,
> My little rooster don't do me no harm.
> My little rooster goes cockadee do,
> Deedoodle, deedoodle, deedoodle deedoo,

sang Nutbeam.

"Daddadadadadadadada . . . mom, mom, momma, mommamomma . . . " said Sally.

Shirley sighed. She was slightly frustrated at the reality that when her tall, big-mouthed, big-eared husband got playing with the baby, he sometimes threw all other communication to the wind.

"Way down there in Texas. What's he wanna be, a cowboy?" she asked.

Nutbeam got on his hands and knees and crept under the table.

"Peekaboo! Peekaboo! You can't see me, baby, but I can see youooo."

"Dadda . . . Mom, mom, mom . . . "

"It's a wonder a person don't worry to death."

Nutbeam put his hand over his eyes. "You can't see me nowow," he said melodiously.

"Palidin in Texas and Dryfly guidin' out on that big old river, the ice runnin'. In the cold wind — and him with a cold. Even if he don't get drownt, he'll die of pneumonia."

Still on all fours, with knees thumping the floor, Nutbeam scurried awkwardly across the kitchen and hid behind the stove. "Peekaboo!" he said and bobbed his head.

Whenever Nutbeam bobbed his head, Sally laughed.

Everyone always laughed when Nutbeam bobbed his head.

Whenever Nutbeam bobbed his head, his big floppy ears seemed to wave at you several times after his head stopped bobbing. It was a hilarious sight to see.

"I don't even know where Texas is. He's leavin' on the twenty-fourth." Shirley studied one of the eight calendars that hung on the kitchen walls. Nutbeam liked the dogs, the pretty girls, the wilderness scenes and the other pictures on the calendars very much. Nutbeam rarely looked at the numbers on the calendars. Most of them didn't even display the right month. To Nutbeam, the calendars were works of art. He had turned the kitchen into a calendar gallery. "That's today. He's on his way to Texas this very minute. He might even be there already."

Nutbeam pretended to yawn, and for a moment his face seemed to disappear behind the massive black hole that was his wide-open mouth. Sally grinned.

"Can you say Dadda?" asked Nutbeam.

"Mom Mom Mom Mom."

"Can you say Momma?"

"Dadda Dadda da da da."

"Can you say Dryfly?"

"Mom Mom Mom Mom Mom." said Sally.

"Oh, you're such a smart girl!" Nutbeam proudly exclaimed.

Shirley put down Palidin's letter, stood, went to the window and watched the river for a moment. There was still some ice along the shore and patches of snow here and there in shady places, but for the most part the fields were bare. The forest separated the fields from the sky, its evergreens dark as phantoms, its leafless birches, alders and maples the colour of strawberry-rhubarb pie. She could hear a boat coming, the outboard buzzing in the distance. When it appeared, she recognized the guide — he was fat, wore a green mackinaw.

"Bert Todder," she thought. "Bert must be glad to be back on the river. Thank God it's spring. Wonder where Dry is? It's his first day. Surely they'll tell him what to do. Foolish to worry, I s'pose. He knows the river better'n anyone."

Suddenly she felt Nutbeam behind her. He put his arms around her, kissed her scalp.

"My lovely lady," he whispered.

Shirley had had twelve children for her first husband, Buck Ramsey, and one more, Sally, for Nutbeam. She was extremely out of shape as a result of having all these children — wide buttocks, a plump belly, sagging breasts; her emery-grey hair was straight and sheenless. When Nutbeam first met her, she had only about two or three teeth in her head. She now had dentures, but they seemed to be crowding her mouth; they looked unnatural, as if they belonged to another mouth, a bigger mouth. For years, Shirley had been the neighbourhood pauper, the epitome of poverty and ugliness — "If I don't get some work pretty soon, I'll be poorer than Shirley

Ramsey"; "I've been sick all winter. I look worse than Shirley Ramsey."

Nutbeam had been a lonely hermit living in a tiny camp in the woods beside Todder Brook. The extent of his social life had been visiting various houses in the late evening. He'd go to a house and stand outside in the dark. He did this not to eavesdrop on whoever lived within, but to listen to their radio. If they didn't have their radio on or turned it off, for whatever reason, he'd move to the next house and the next until he found someone listening to *The Saturday Night Jamboree* or *Hay Shakers' Hoedown, Doc Williams and the Border Riders* or *Lee Moore*. With his big floppy ears, he could hear a pin drop, so he didn't have to get very close to the house. Thus he never got caught and accused of being a Peeping Tom.

This was how he first laid eyes on Shirley Ramsey. Nutbeam, himself a freak of nature, had seen only beauty where all others saw ugliness. He fell in love with her.

"My lovely, lovely lady," he whispered.

two

When you hired a guide on the Dungarvon, you not only employed a man knowledgeable about the river, its pools and fish, but you acquired a servant as well. In the mid-sixties, for eight dollars a day, a guide would do just about anything for you — rig your tackle, carry your gear, patch your waders, cook beans, bacon and trout over an open fire on the shore; he'd pour your drinks and help you up the hill and into the camp when you had one or more too many; he might, if he wasn't too shy, entertain you with stories and songs, and he might become your friend, that shoulder to lean on when you needed it. And when you needed to be alone, the guide had an uncanny ability of knowing it, and perhaps because guides knew better than anyone else the value and importance of reaping strength and peace from the river and the forest, he'd slip away as nonchalantly as a two-faced hotel manager. And if you did not respect your guide, did not listen to his simple directions, you might find yourself as lost as a pirate in the maze of Mikonos, for your guide was not just your buddy and servant, he was also your master. When it came to catching old Salmo Salar and surviving on the swift and frigid waters of the deep and dark Dungarvon, even corporation giants, generals and governors took orders from the likes of Stan Tuney, Bert Todder and Lindon Tucker. David O'Hara would not have survived five minutes in the Snake's Coffin without the savvy of Dryfly Ramsey.

When Lindon Tucker was told that the gentleman he was about to guide was a general, he said, "Good, good, good." And when he was told that the general was not just *any* general, but that he was nothing less than a *five-star* general, Lindon scratched his head and wondered, "Which five?" and

"What, what, what, what's a man, what's a man, what's a man do with a star?"

He asked Dryfly about it.

"He doesn't own the stars in the sky," explained Dryfly. "He's into country music. The stars he's talkin' about are lads like Doc Williams, Johnny Cash, Kid Baker. The general sets up shows for them."

Lindon believed it.

One morning when Lindon was sitting behind the general, fishing from their canoe, Lindon asked, "Oh ah, oh ah, oh ah, how well do ya know Hank Snow? Do ya know 'im, do ya?"

"Hank Snow? Never met the man," said the general.

Ten minutes went by before Lindon spoke up again.

"That, oh ah, that Johnny Cash is quite a singer, ain't he? Sings way down low, deep, low, way down, if ya know what I mean. You like Johnny Cash?"

"I hardly ever listen to country music. Classical, now, is wonderful. It gets me here." The general gestured to his heart. "Vivaldi, Bach, Mozart, Beethoven, Chopin . . . "

Lindon had never heard of these singers, but he was satisfied. The general was from the States after all and might not know of the same country stars that were popular in Brennen Siding.

Lindon pulled in the anchor, let the canoe drift a hundred yards or so downstream to an eddy he knew about and anchored there.

"Dryfly Ramsey plays guiddar and sings," said Lindon. "I don't know now if he knows any songs of them lads you mentioned or not. He knows a lotta them though. Prob'ly does. Yeah, prob'ly does, yeah. Oh, yeah, yeah, yeah . . . probably does, uh huh. Yep. Yep! Oh, yep! Regular Hank Snow, that lad, yep."

The general made a sloppy cast, the wind caught the line and the big, two-inch-long Mickey Finn flyhook struck Lindon, whack! on the back of the head.

"Oh, Christ, Lindon! I'm sorry. The wind caught my line. You okay?"

"No, no, no, no, okay, yeah . . . Oh! A little flyhook in the side of the head never hurt anyone! The very best, yeah! Fish!

Fish! Fish! I'm okay! I'm the very jeezless best! Give 'er hell! Go to 'er! No, no, no, a little flyhook in the side of the head never hurt anybody . . . fish, take 'er easy, fish!" To make sure that he had sufficiently stressed the fact that he was unharmed by the needle-sharp flyhook, Lindon sang, "Oh, she jumped in bed and covered up her head and thought I couldn't find 'er, but I was quick and di di di and jumped right in behind 'er! Whoop!"

A few minutes later, the general hooked into a salmon. He was a big one, twenty, thirty pounds, and aided by the heavy spring current it greedily stripped line from the general's reel as if he couldn't get enough, as if he had been hooked before and knew from experience that if he swam fast enough and far enough the line would run out, snap and give him his freedom. The reel squealed like a possessed piglet, or the devil's clock set for the end of time.

"What the hell have I got on here, a freight train?" exclaimed the general.

Lindon's experience immediately told him of the salmon's intent.

"We'll have to go ashore," he said, already pulling the anchor.

Lindon paddled the canoe in backwards so that the general was facing his foe at all times. There were large cakes of ice, sometimes nestled, sometimes precariously perched along the shoreline, and Lindon found himself having to drift a bit in order to find a safe place to dock.

The salmon leaped five feet into the air, and the general whooped with delight at the sight of it.

Finding a convenient place between two cakes of ice, Lindon slid the canoe safely onto the washed sand and wintered hay. He stepped out, grabbed the canoe and swung it in, offered his hand to the general and assisted him ashore.

"You got a big one there!" said Lindon, grinning yellow teeth and missing cuspids.

The salmon stopped for a moment, hung on the current. The general's rod was a dancing crescent against the sky.

"Don't, don't, don't hold 'im too tight," cautioned Lindon. "You'll lose 'im!"

"He's a long way down there . . . I haven't got much line left," said the general, his words more of a plea than a boast.

Lindon winked and diddled, "Di di diddle daddle diddle daddle diddle daddle dum!" He reached down and grabbed the scoop net from the canoe. "We'll have to follow 'im down along the shore, palsy walsy," he said. "Careful, careful, careful ya don't, ya don't stand on the ice . . . be, be, be, be, be careful of the ice."

It was nearly lunchtime, and Bob Nash and the president of the AEA were motoring upstream, heading back to the club. When they saw the general's salmon jump, they pulled in to watch the action. Dryfly Ramsey and David O'Hara watched, too, from the Snake's Coffin just upstream at the foot of Cabbage Island.

"Looks like he might have the winning fish on there," commented David.

"Hope not," said Dryfly.

Every spring, while at the Cabbage Island Salmon Club, the American Electronics Association ran a pool — a hundred dollars for the biggest fish hooked and landed. If you released the fish, you had to have at least one witness other than yourself and your guide. It was decided that a witness was needed because every fisherman from the Reverend John Kaston and the Boston cardinal to the prince of liars, Stan Tuney, tended to exaggerate. Bob Nash pulled ashore, not just to watch the excitement, but to act as a witness as well. Bob was not looking out just for his sport, but for himself as well, for, traditionally, the sport split the winnings with the guide, and sometimes, as in the case of Sparrow during the years he enjoyed the vice-presidency, the guide was given *all* the money.

There weren't that many salmon in the river that exceeded the weight of the one that the general was now playing, and Dryfly, wanting very much at least a share of the money, found himself on the side of the salmon, hoping the salmon would win the fight and get free.

The general would never have become a general if he hadn't long ago learned to follow orders. And the orders came, you can bet on that. He had three of the world's greatest fishermen with him . . . or so the three that were with him thought.

When Bob Nash said "Hold 'im high," the general held his rod high.

When Lindon said "Back up a little," the general backed up.

When the president of the American Electronics Association said "Let it run," the general let go of his reel and gave the salmon all the line it wanted.

And there were more orders, "Try to swing him," "Don't horse 'im," "Move down," "Reel like hell," "Don't hold 'im too tight," "Get 'im out from behind that rock," "Careful of the bushes," and "Don't give 'im too much slack," just to mention a few. The general gave it his best, and the salmon, an old fish, spawned-out and famished from eating invisible food all winter, was clearly tiring.

Amongst all the orders he was receiving was the most important order of all, and it was an order that the general did not quite understand: Lindon Tucker's "Careful, careful, careful ya don't, ya don't stand on the ice . . . be, be, be, be, be careful of the ice."

It was a common-sense thing for the general. "Of course one has to be careful about slipping on the ice," he thought. But what was common sense for the general and what was common sense to Lindon Tucker were two different things. Lindon wasn't talking about *slipping* on the ice.

A few weeks earlier, a warm spring rain had swept in from the south, melting most of the snow in its path. Water, water everywhere. The water in the river rose twelve feet straight up, and what ice it didn't carry off seaward, it pushed high and dry upon the shore. After the rain stopped and the water level began to drop, the ice was left there to melt in the warm afternoon sun. Of course, the ice melted faster where it was sheltered from the wind, so many of the huge cakes had melted away at the bottom so that they sat precariously on pinnacles that you could only see if you were on the river looking shoreward. The top of the ice had melted some, too, and its surface resembled hail or coarse salt, not in the least bit slippery — the general's observation.

Lindon's observation did not include the haily surface of the ice; Lindon had seen the brittle pinnacles beneath and knew that the extra weight of a man could cause the pinnacles to break, sending both the ice and the man sliding into the frigid water.

"Be, be, be, be, be careful of the ice," he had warned.

The general and his followers were making their way down along the shore, and when a huge cake of ice blocked the general's path, he sized it up, saw that it wasn't slippery and stepped up on it.

"I wouldn't stand on that ice, if I were you," said Bob Nash.

"It's safe," said the general.

The salmon swung and started to swim upstream toward the general, who was frantically reeling to keep up the pace.

"Try and bring 'im in down there," suggested Lindon, pointing at a grassy slope that ran into the river. "He'll be easy to net in a place like that."

"You're right," said the general and stepped off the ice with the agility of a much younger man, reeling and reeling all the while. He came to a second cake of ice blocking his way and, with the confidence enhanced by his first experience, he stepped up on it.

KERTHRASH! SPLASH!

The general was wearing enough clothes to keep him warm on the coldest of days — long insulated underwear, heavy woolen pants, a shirt, a sweater, a winter parka, and knee-length rubber boots. So, when the ice slid into the river and he with it, he sank immediately. The water temperature was just two degrees above freezing and shocked him so much that he lost all rationality and couldn't figure out what to do first. The current was sweeping him along under water, and he was doing absolutely nothing to save himself. He was a general, however, and was not giving up his battle — he still clutched his fishing rod in his stiffening fingers.

Then he felt something pulling on the hood of his parka.

When Bob Nash saw what had happened, he removed his coat and boots and jumped into the river. He was a little more prepared for the shock than the general had been and somehow had maintained his sanity. Here, the water was about ten feet deep, and the Dungarvon river is dark even on the brightest of days, so the fact that he found the general almost immediately was sheer luck. He swam the general to safety with the strength of a man on the verge of panic. Lindon Tucker was at the edge of the water, waiting. He offered his hand and pulled both the general and Bob to safety. Bob Nash emerged redfaced and puffing; the general was the colour of an old and dried-up beet sandwich, red and moldy. The way he was coughing and gagging, it seemed he may have tried to eat the sandwich.

"Gotta git 'im to the camp, git 'im to the camp, git 'im to the camp!" yelled Lindon, already running up the shore toward the canoe.

Dryfly and David O'Hara saw it all happening from the Snake's Coffin.

"Reel in!" said Dryfly. "They'll need help!"

David reeled in quickly, and Dryfly pulled the anchor. He pulled on the pullcord of the 7.5-horsepower Elgin outboard.

By the time Dryfly got the 7.5 Elgin started, Lindon Tucker and the president of the American Electronics Association had the general and Bob Nash safely in the camp back at the Cabbage Island Salmon Club.

Dryfly and David headed for the camp anyway, and when they stepped inside the first thing they noticed was that both the general and Bob Nash were stripped naked. Lindon was coming from the bedroom with blankets to wrap them in, and the president of the AEA was pouring brandy into two snifters at the bar.

Bob took a blanket from Lindon and with teeth chattering, immediately wrapped himself in it. The general was lying on the sofa, and just before Lindon threw a blanket over him Dryfly noticed something — the general's genitals. They had shrunken in the cold water to the point where they resembled a shrunken and shrivelled deep-fried clam. Dryfly gazed on this phenomenon with amazement. He'd never seen such a meagre endowment on a full-grown man, and he could not help grinning. "Just looks like a young swallow peekin' out of his nest," he thought. He had been unable to take his eyes off the spectacle, and with the grin on his face he could have been a smug Priapus or a washroom cruiser.

Bob Nash saw Dryfly staring down on the general and, with just a bit of irritation in his voice, asked, "What's wrong with you?"

Dryfly snapped from his bemusement.

"Oh! Ah . . . I was just lookin' at the general's privates," he said.

The general coughed and drank his brandy, and while Lindon tucked him snugly into a warm blanket he said, "I let go of the rod at the last minute. I lost the fish."

"And the rod, too," said Bob. "But it could have been your life."

"And yours," said the general. "I owe you my life."

"In the water . . . my hands were too cold . . . "

"What do you mean?"

"I couldn't hold on to anything . . . we'd have both drowned if Lindon hadn't been there."

Lindon was grinning and winking at everybody, happy to be part of the group, happy that he was being allowed in the cabin with the Americans (usually the guides sat around outside on the grass, while the Americans went inside for food and drinks) and happy that Bob had given him some recognition. He was hoping that he had perhaps earned a drink of brandy.

*

The first major stop the bus made was in Columbus, Ohio. They had stopped briefly in Niagara Falls at the border. They'd had a fifteen-minute pee stop in Erie, Pennsylvania, and another one in Cleveland, Ohio, and when Palidin stepped from the bus to enjoy the scheduled one-hour dinner break in Columbus, he felt stiff-legged, numb-bummed and a little bit blurry-eyed from watching Interstates 90 and 71 roll monotonously by.

The bus was pretty much full, and Palidin had been sitting

beside a young fellow from Little Rock, Arkansas, a shy, boring, fuzzy-faced kid who, when he spoke at all, used the word "friggin'" to describe everything from his father's "friggin' chickens" to the "friggin' watermelons" he planned to steal when he got back to "friggin' Little Rock."

However, the kid, Jake Lucas, hadn't liked cold old Toronto very much and therefore didn't much care for Palidin, so they had only carried on brief conversations, had only talked for perhaps fifteen minutes during the whole nine hours on the road.

Palidin, always the thinker, had had plenty of time to think, his mind wandering in strange and confusing circles — from his invention of the magnetic flyhook and Brennen Siding, to Ptolemy's conception of the universe, from the Druids to the Romans; he crisscrossed Christianity as wearily as a homosexual priest or a frustrated and rebellious woman. He at one time thought, "We use buses to travel in, and we know no more about the roads we travel than the bus does."

At one point — at the stop in Cleveland — he had come within a hair's breadth of exchanging his ticket and heading home to Canada, to Toronto, or even to Brennen Siding.

"Man has forgotten his roots," he theorized. "We're in the hands of scientists, of specialists — educated men and women, yes, but they lack the wisdom to recognize magic. God is magic. All the gods have been magic. Where's Pan today?"

The bus exited from Interstate 71 at Columbus, stopped at a service station restaurant, and everyone, including the driver, disembarked and entered the restaurant end for a much-needed break. The bus driver knew the waitresses. They gave him his coffee for free. They seemed to like him a lot, and even though he was twice their age, balding and overweight, they joked and flirted with him. "Perhaps it's his uniform," thought Palidin. The bus driver wore a blue suit with black stripes down the legs and a captain's cap with a plastic visor, black socks, shoes and tie, white shirt.

Palidin sat on a red, revolving stool at the counter and ordered a hot eastern sandwich (no onions) and a coffee. On the wall was a picture of a big-titted blond country singer with a massive hairdo. Palidin thought that it might be the same singer whose child-like warble blared from the juke box. He grinned, thinking that considering most hair sprays were flammable, the girl in the picture probably never got within ten feet of a smoker.

A thin, brown-haired, tired-looking woman came in and sat beside him, ordered a coffee, and, as if she had been reading his thoughts, lit up a stinking Pall Mall cigarette. She had smoked so much all day (nothing else to do on the bus) that she was wheezing, and Palidin observed by her lack of sheen that much of the smoke had settled on her skin.

"Where ya headin'?" she asked of Palidin.

"Texas."

"Oh yeah? Ain't never been to Texas. Y'all from Texas?"

"No, I'm a Canadian. Toronto."

"Oh! I've been to Canada!"

"Oh yeah? What part?"

"Ah . . . Canada. Across the river from Detroit. You know, where you're from. What did you call it?"

"I'm from Toronto. I believe you were in Windsor."

"Whatever. Why ya goin' to Texas, handsome?"

"Business, I think."

"Ha! Don't ya know?"

"Depends on what happens when I get there," Palidin smiled.

"You some kind of a big shot?"

"Why you ask me that?"

"Well, if you ain't, you sure seem like you are. What you do for a livin'?"

Palidin had quit his job. He had been writing for *The Sun*. He had to stop and think. "Ah . . . right now, I guess you could call me an inventor," he said and immediately regretted saying it, for now she was bound to ask him what he invented.

"Oh yeah? What'd you invent?" she asked.

"Ah . . . nothing important. I'm working on something. Where are you from?"

"Didn't ya see me get on back in Cleveland? I sure as hell saw you! I'm headin' fer Nashville."

Palidin's sandwich was served. It came thick and hot with enough french fries for three people.

"I didn't expect such a big meal," he commented.

"You ordered it, didn't ya?"

"Yeah . . . but there's so much of it."

His new acquaintance shrugged, not knowing that in Canada Palidin was used to getting half as much for twice the price.

"What's your name?" asked the girl.

"Palidin. What's yours?"

"Palidin! Ha! Sure it is!"

"That's my name. Is there something wrong with it?"

"No, nothin'. My name's Amelia."

After eating, Palidin went back to the bus. This time he sat with Amelia — a much pleasanter travelling companion than that friggin' Jake Lucas. They talked and laughed all the way to Cincinnati until Amelia fell asleep with her head on Palidin's shoulder.

From the dim interior of the bus, Palidin watched the lights of Cincinnati skyscrapers, complex highways, bridges, their reflections on a river that he thought must be the Ohio.

"A few short hours ago this girl did not exist. Now she is as real as the warmth I feel from her, the scent I smell, the breathing I hear. By tomorrow she'll be gone . . . a memory apt to be forgotten — like so many gods, fairies, ghosts, settlements . . ." and this thought fit very well with Palidin's purpose.

three

Hilda Porter was born and raised across the river from Blackville. She went to Blackville school for a number of years, then went to normal school in Fredericton and became a teacher. At the age of nineteen she moved into the Dungarvon woods and started teaching in the little one-room school in Brennen Siding. She held down the job for forty-four years.

She was an only child, and when her parents died she was left the farm near Blackville. She didn't move there, however, until she retired in June of 1963, the year the Brennen Siding one-roomer closed and the kids began being bused to the larger school in the village.

The farm hadn't been worked in twenty years — the house was shabby, needed paint, shingles, a new veranda floor, interior renovations from top to bottom; the barn needed shingles and sills; one shed was beyond repair; the fields had been neglected; poplars, alders, little spruce, pine and fir were springing up all over the place — chores and responsibilities that an old woman like Hilda couldn't possibly contend with on her own.

So she decided she'd hire someone who would work for room and board and very little cash, someone who needed a place to live, someone who could help around the place and look after her, preferably someone young, because she didn't want to have to put up with some old fart who'd be forever curious about the colour of her bloomers. She put up posters at the post office, the mill office, Brigham's store and in the two canteens, LeBlanc's and Biff's.

The poster read:

NOTICE

MAN WANTED FOR ODD JOBS.
ROOM AND BOARD PROVIDED.
WILL DISCUSS WAGES.
SEE HILDA PORTER.
THE OTHER SIDE OF THE RIVER.

Shortly after, Shadrack Nash applied for the job.

Shad Nash had been living at home, where he drove his parents, Bob and Elva, to the verge of insanity with his constant flailing, picking and plucking of the banjo, to the point where one day in a fit of menopausal irrationality Elva kicked him out.

Shad needed a place to stay, saw Hilda's posters, applied for the job. He knew Hilda, she had taught him in school. She hired him on.

It was a perfect setup for Hilda: Shad was young, energetic, imaginative, personable; he could split the wood, shovel the driveway, repair the veranda floor, the roof; he listened to her stories, flirted with her a bit, made her feel young again, made her laugh and cry. She never felt more alive.

And she was good for Shad, too. She helped him with his homework, inspired him, created an appreciation and a curiosity within him for things other than banjo playing, gave him a gold watch for Christmas, gave him spending money — and when she died, less than a year after he moved in, she gave him the farm and twenty-five hundred dollars above the cost of her burial expenses.

Shadrack Nash and his friend Dryfly Ramsey had decided, after an unsuccessful stint with a rock 'n' roll band called the Whoopsnakes, that they wanted to combine their talents and form a comedy duo. Shadrack played the banjo and told jokes and stories; Dryfly played the guitar and sang — a combination they felt would work. So, when Shad got his hands on the twenty-five hundred dollars, he immediately invested in a guitar, a harmonica, some sound equipment and a 1959 VW minibus. They started writing songs and comedy material they could call their own, and because Shad lived alone in Hilda's old house, Dryfly started spending most of his time there help-ing Shad with the place and rehearsing the act.

They launched the act at various parties where they got paid in "All-the-beer-you-can-drink." Then, they did a show at the Blackville Legion, got paid ten dollars each. They rented the Public Hall, performed and lost ten dollars each — their songs were crudely written and their jokes more than a little risqué for a small-town audience. They realized the problem right away and cleaned up the act. However, they already had a reputation. Nobody called them, nobody offered them any jobs. Their greatest concern became the big M — Money.

Then, one night in April Dryfly showed up to rehearse and to fill Shad in on the Brennen Siding news. Dryfly had landed a job guiding at the Cabbage Island Salmon Club, and his feature story was the one about Bob Nash, Shad's father, res-cuing Old Cooky Duster, the general.

"It just looked like a baby swallow peekin' from his nest," concluded Dry.

"Bet it made you big-feelin'," said Shad with a grin.

"Just like a horse! Got an awful cold, Shad. Hope it don't turn to pneumonia."

"Hope Dad don't get pneumonia after jumpin' in that river."

"The old general'll prob'ly give him a big tip. Bob saved his life."

"Hope so. I could sure do with some money and Dad ain't had none for the last little while. I'm down to my last can o' beans. Been savin' it. Ain't been eatin' nothin' but whole wheat bread and honey for the last week."

"You that broke?"

"Ain't got a cent."

"So, what're ya gonna do?"

"Don't know." Shad fingered his long red hair. He looked worried. "I might have to quit school," he said.

"Can't do that. School's where the girls are," said Dryfly. "Why don't ya start bootleggin' or somethin'?"

"I couldn't bootleg, ya stupid jeezer! I ain't old enough to get in the liquor store."

"Oh yeah. Never thought o' that. Ya gotta be twenty-one."

"I don't know what to do," sighed Shad.

"You could take a week off from school and go guidin'."

"Naw. Havin' a tough time as it is. Don't even know if I'm gonna pass. Ya think Nutbeam could lend a lad a few bucks?"

"Don't know. Prob'ly needs every cent he's got."

Shad sighed again, deeply concerned.

"You could sell the van. Ya might as well. Ya can't afford to put gas in it."

"Yeah, and I could move home, too, but that would be like givin' up. Shad Nash ain't givin' up!"

"You could cut some pulp, or logs or something. Any lumber on this land?"

"Yeah, lotsa lumber," said Shad. He seemed to consider the possibility for a moment, then added, "Ain't got a chain saw. Got an axe and an old bucksaw, but a man would kill himself workin' with a bucksaw. Too hard o' work, anyway. And besides, I don't want to cut me land all down."

"Maybe ya got something here you could sell. What about that old rifle in the parlour?"

"Yeah, s'pose I could sell that to somebody. Wanna buy it?"

"What with, sawdust? Might be able to buy it when I get paid, but you need money right away. What calibre is it?"

"Its a .38-55." Shad went to the parlour, returned with the rifle. "Not too bad a shape. There's bullets, too, up in the cupboard."

"Do ya know if it works?"

"No. Was always scared to try it."

"We'll have to show it to Nutbeam."

"Maybe Nutbeam would buy it."

"No harm in givin' 'im a try."

*

"Long barrel, full magazine, Rocky Mountain sights, lever action. The gun that won the west . . . " Nutbeam seemed to be thinking out loud as he aimed the rifle first at the pink flamingo, then at the black and white cow, the black cat, the goose and the giraffe — the lawn ornaments.

Shad handed him a bullet. "Try 'er, Nut. See if ya can hit anything with it."

Nutbeam slid the bullet into the magazine slot and levered it up into the barrel; then, all in a single second, he snapped the rifle to his shoulder, aimed at a fence post a hundred yards away and pulled the trigger. BANG! It all happened so fast that both Dryfly and Shadrack jumped, startled.

"It works!" yelled Shad.

"It works real good," said Nutbeam.

"What'd ya fire at?" asked Dryfly.

"That post. Dead center."

"Really?"

"Yes sir, a good old rifle, that. Ya wanna sell it, eh?"

"Well, I'm not sure. I mean, I don't know. I mean, yeah, I guess so." Shad hadn't realized that the rifle was any good. Now that he had seen Nutbeam shoot it and actually hit something with it, he wasn't so keen on selling it. He had been thinking that it might perhaps be worth ten dollars, enough money to buy him beans, bread and cigarettes for a week. But now he didn't know what to think. "It could be worth a lot more. Maybe I should keep it. I could hunt with it in the fall. A man should have a rifle . . . " and stuff like that was how his mind was working.

But he needed money.

"Yeah. Yeah, I wanna sell it. Think it's worth anything?"

"Bullets are hard to get for it," said Nutbeam. "You'd have to keep the empties for refillin'. You ain't got a rifle, Dryfly. Why don't you buy it?"

"Can't till I get paid. Shad needs the money now."

"Ah! I see."

Nutbeam sized Shad up. "Thin, pale, his hair's too long, his clothes need ironing. Shouldn't be livin' alone. Too young to be livin' alone. Livin' alone ain't good. If anyone knows about livin alone, it's me. But he's Bob Nash's son, so might be braver than most," he thought to himself, then said, "Ya want the rifle, Dryfly? I mean, I could give Shad the money, and you could pay me when ya get your guidin' pay."

Dryfly had never hunted in his life and really didn't want the rifle, but he too had observed Shad and his predicament. Dryfly wondered if Shad was not just prolonging the inevitable, that he would have to move home to Bob and Elva sooner or later, regardless, if he sold the rifle or not. "Well, I guess that'd be all right with me. I mean, if ya have the money. If ya don't mind."

Nutbeam figured the rifle was worth twenty dollars. "I'll give ya twenty-five dollars for it," he said to Shad.

"Twenty-five dollars? I, ah . . . "

"All right, thirty! Not a penny more!"

"Well, I . . . sure! Ha! Great!"

Nutbeam tossed the rifle to Dryfly, reached for his wallet and gave Shad the last thirty dollars he had. "Don't spend it all on rum," he said with a wink and went into the house to tell Shirley that he had spent their last thirty dollars on an old rifle, but that it was okay because the money had gone to the son of Bob Nash, the man who risked his life to save an American general.

"What d'ya wanna do now?" asked Dryfly.

"Well, I should go to the store," said Shad. "I need cigarettes and food."

"So, let's go to Bernie Hanley's. Your father will be there."

"Yeah. Yeah, I guess he probably will."

Because there was no road up the back side of the river, the side where Nutbeam lived, Shad had left his van at the Cabbage Island Salmon Club, and they had crossed the footbridge. Shad hadn't crossed the footbridge or walked about Brennen Siding in any kind of leisurely frame of mind for quite some time. The last time he had been in Brennen Siding the ice had still been in the river, and it was cold, with four feet of snow on the ground. Now that the ice was out and the exposed river rushed angrily beneath the bridge, the ground bare and the transient robins singing, black birds chirping and the thirty dollars in his pocket lifting his worries for a week or two, he found he was enjoying the walk very much. Living near the village and spending all his time with friends there was great, but he was now looking forward to seeing his father and the good old boys — Lindon Tucker, Dan Brennen, Stan Tuney, Bert Todder and John Kaston — who spent their evenings raving, gossiping and bantering with Bernie Hanley at the store. Since Shad purchased the van, he had walked very little, drove even if he had but a hundred yards up the road to go. For this reason, Dryfly was surprised that when they came back over the bridge, Shad chose to leave the van at the club and walk to Bernie Hanley's.

Bernie Hanley stood behind the counter sucking on a peppermint. Bob Nash leaned on the outside of the counter, positioned so that he did not have his back to Bernie, but yet could also face his fans.

"Shad!" shouted Bob. "Come in! Come in! How've ya been, boy?" When Shad was near enough, he slapped him warmly on the shoulder. "Jesus! Why don't ya git that hair cut!"

Shad's red hair was very long, halfway down his back. Long hair on a male seemed very odd to all the men in the store. Lindon Tucker could not stop grinning at the spectacle.

"Hippie," muttered Dan Brennen, but nobody heard because everyone's attention was divided between Bob-the-hero and his son Shad.

"The first thing, they'll be callin' ya hippie!" said Bob.

"Yeah," said Shad, grinning.

"They'll, they'll, they'll, they'll be callin' ya hippie, won't they, Shad, codger, manikin, palsy walsy, eh?" put in Lindon Tucker, smiling his missing cuspids.

"Heard what happened," said Shad to Bob. "You all right?"

"Me? I'm the very best! A little cold water never hurt anyone!"

"It almost done in the old general," commented Stan Tuney. "It wouldn't surprise me if the old bugger never gets over it." Stan was, of course, exaggerating.

"Old, Old, Old, Old Cooky Duster might never get over it, eh Stan?" said Lindon.

"How's she goin', Dryfly?" greeted John Kaston the preacher. He had changed from his guiding clothes (mackinaw, APH pants, rubber boots and cap) and was now dressed in a worn blue suit, white shirt and tie.

"The very best," said Dryfly. "You?"

"Good, good, good." John was bored and wanted to break the spell, the hero worship that had been dominating the conversation for more than two hours. Acknowledging the long-haired and slightly bedraggled son of Shirley Ramsey had done the trick. Before now, nobody had even noticed that Dryfly was there.

Dryfly's hair was as long as Shad's, but brown, thinner and needed washing. Where everyone had barely noticed Shad's long hair, Dryfly's hair was a different matter. Dryfly was not the son of the hero Bob Nash. Dryfly was the son of Shirley Ramsey.

Bert Todder, who had been unusually quiet until now, chuckled and said, "Looks like old Leon Gratin! Tee, hee, hee, sob, snort, sniff!" When Bert Todder laughed, one never knew if he was laughing or crying. When Bert laughed, or cried, you could see the lone tooth in the front of his mouth and his big belly jiggling.

All the other men chuckled. Dryfly began to feel uncomfortable.

"It's the style," he said, attempting to make light of the matter. "To get the women, this is how ya gotta look."

Dan Brennen repeated himself for emphasis, "I don't know why, I don't know why, I don't know why everyone feels they have to look so bad! Every young lad ya see has his hair way down his back. I don't know what the world's comin' to! Ya look like a jeezless wimp, Dryfly! Why in hell don't ya git yer hair cut?"

"I told ya," said Dryfly. "It's how ya . . . "

"You can't tell me that any woman with a head on her shoulders likes a man in long hair! I'll pay for the goddamn haircut, if that's yer problem!"

Bob Nash the hero came to Dryfly's defence. A couple of years ago, Dryfly had schemed and rescued Bob and Shad from some Fishery wardens who had nailed them for illegally netting salmon. Bob would have had to pay a stiff fine and would have lost both his fishing and his guide's license. Bob Nash owed Dryfly Ramsey a lot.

"Ah, it's jist a passing thing. A few years ago, every kid in the country wore his hair all greased back, now they're wearing it long. Ten years from now, kids will shave their heads or something. There's always something."

Dan shook his head in disgust, but he did not pursue the argument with the hero of the day.

John Kaston had grown to like Dryfly, too, and being a preacher who liked to preach everywhere he went, he seized what he thought was a golden opportunity. "Our blessed Savior wore His hair long," he said, then quoted, "And His raiment became shining, exceeding white as snow; so as no fuller on Earth can white them." And everyone looked to each other, wondering what the hell that was all about.

"Well, I soon gotta go," said Bert Todder. "I'm fed up with this old foolish talk, I am!"

"Ya know, they claimed that's what happened to Phil Langdon," said Stan Tuney.

"Phil Langdon! Phil Langdon's been dead for twenty years," said Dan Brennen.

"Yep, and that's why," said Stan. "He jumped in the river in the spring o' the year and about two weeks later he started to get this sore just inside his arse, like . . . jist barely inside, if ya know what I mean. They claim it was the cold water that got up there. He died in less than a year."

"I thought he died of colitis," commented Bernie Hanley.

"Well, yeah. Yeah, that's what it was, but it was the cold water what give it to 'im," said Stan.

"You wouldn't lie to a man, would ya, Stan?" asked Bob Nash, and Bert Todder laughed, "Tee hee hee sob snort sniff."

"'Pon me word to God, that's what I heard, now."

"Yeah, yeah, oh yeah, yeah, yeah. Cold water got up his arse and killed 'im stone dead, yeah," said Lindon Tucker, taking Stan's word for it.

"What in the name of God is yer brother Palidin doin' in Texas?" Bernie Hanley asked Dryfly.

"Couldn't tell ya," said Dryfly, truthfully. "Mom just got a letter from him sayin' he was goin' to Texas."

"Boys! She'd be hot weather way down there, wouldn't she?" commented Dan Brennen.

"Bet, bet, bet, bet the water'd be warm down there," said Lindon, who was still thinking of the problem of getting cold water up his ass.

"I guided a lad from Texas once," said Dan Brennen. "Kind of a fruity lad, if I recall correctly."

This was a slur about Palidin, and everyone including Dryfly knew it.

"Well, it'll soon be time to go," said Bert Todder. "I suppose a man'll have to try and get home before dark. Break yer neck on that bridge after dark, so ya might. Went through it comin' over and damn near broke me neck!"

"So why in hell don't ya carry a lantern or a flashlight?" put in Stan Tuney.

"I'll carry a flashlight if I want! If I don't want, I won't! A man shouldn't have to carry a flashlight! The gov'ment should keep that bridge fixed up!"

"They're not gonna keep a bridge fixed up for three or four people to cross," reasoned Dan Brennen. "It costs a lotta o' money to keep up a bridge. "

"So what are we s'pose to do, swim across the river?" shouted Bert, reddening.

"Well, ya don't have to yell at me!" said Dan. "I was just sayin' a . . . "

"I don't give a damn what you were sayin'!"

"Well, no sense in arguin'," mumbled Dan.

It was obvious to all the men that Bert Todder was angry. He was raising his voice and that was not characteristic of anyone from Brennen Siding. Brennen Sidingers talked soft, easy. "No sense in arguing," could very well have been their motto. And so they changed the subject and avoided any topic that they thought might possibly rub Bert the wrong way. And although Bert kept repeating that it was getting late and that it was time to go, he stayed and stayed and stayed until all the others left and just he and Bernie remained in the store. Bert Todder needed to talk privately to his old friend, Bernie Hanley.

When they were finally alone, Bert asked, "So . . . ah . . . oh ah, how ya makin' out, anyway, Bernie?"

"Oh, you know how it is, Bert. Ya have to live on. I get lonesome, but, well . . . ya have to live on, keep goin'."

"Think ya'll ever get married agin?"

"Ha! I don't know who'd have the likes o' me! No, Ilene was all the woman I ever wanted, Bert. I'll be buried beside her when I die. Right up there in the old Baptist cemetery. We'll all be buried there, I figure. What's on your mind, Bert?"

"Oh, well, I ain't been feelin' myself lately, Bern."

"Ha! You've been feelin' yerself too much, if ya ask me!"

"You know what I mean. I mean, I feel good, but, well, sorta not good. Lonesome or somethin', I guess. We used to be the best o' friends, eh Bernie? Well, I thought that after Ilene died, you know, I thought we might . . . do things . . . you know, like we used to. Drift, shoot a moose, maybe go way down to Saint John on a toot — you know, like we used to."

"We're a little old for that, ain't we, Bert?"

"Yeah, well, that's what makes me lonesome. I'm lonesome about everything, you know? Don't go nowhere, ain't done nothin', never got married. Time's runnin' out. All that stuff. You know, lonesome."

"Well, that's no way to be, Bert. Don't you know that God's always there beside you, that you're never alone. I mean, I don't want to sound like John Kaston, but it's true. You can't turn yer back on God."

"I know that, I know that! But we ain't all that old, Bernie. We got a few good years left in us, and I ain't turnin' me back on God, anyway! But a man's gotta live! Doin' somethin', havin' a good time ain't turnin' yer back on God!"

"Pleasures of the flesh ain't worth snuff in the eyes of the Lord."

Bert sighed, knowing the conversation would go nowhere as long as they continued to fence around and about God and religion.

"You ever get the feeling you're being watched, Bernie?" he asked.

"Of course! God keeps a constant watch over his flock."

"No, but I mean, like a deer. You know, like a deer who's

bein' stalked by a big cat or a sly hunter. I can't see or smell anything, but I just feel there's somethin' there! Like somethin's followin' me everywhere I go!"

"Well, I . . . "

"And ya know what I think it is?"

"I . . . no, I . . . "

"Well, I don't know what it is for sure, but it seems like it's like my past or something. It's hard to put a finger on, but it's like myself as a young lad bein' pissed off at me for not doin' any of the things that I wanted to do. I don't know, I don't know. It's all up here in my head! I think I'm alone too much! I think I'm goin' crazy! I'm just as foolish as ever I kin be! I laugh, I cry — and I don't mind that. It's my temper I don't like. I get ugly at the drop of a hat! And you know yerself, that's not like me! I never used to get ugly at anything! But now. I don't know. I was crossin' the footbridge tonight, and by damn, me foot went through one o' the boards. Bernie, I felt like settin' fire to the fuckin' bridge! You know what I mean? I was fit to be tied! And all the time I feel like I'm bein' watched, like as if by the old devil or something!"

"Ah! It's all in yer head, Bert! Don't let it worry ya!"

"I tell ya, it's gettin' so that I'm scared to go outside at night!"

"C'mon, Bert! You've rambled around in the dark all yer life! You ain't scared o' nothin' and you know it!"

"I don't know, I don't know nothin' anymore. I mean, like, I keep lookin' over my shoulder like a kid that's afraid of the dark! Like a coward! I just get this feelin' there's some-thing there!"

"Well . . . pray! That's all I can say! Pray!"

*

Shadrack and Dryfly parted at the Cabbage Island Salmon Club.

"See ya, Shad," said Dryfly. "Hope ya don't run out of gas on the way home."

"It's on the empty mark. Should make it."

"Maybe I should go with ya."

"Nothin' you can do. If I run outta gas, I run outta gas. No sense in you walkin' half the night when ya have to get up and guide in the morning."

"Yeah. Well, okay. See ya later. Take 'er easy."

"You, too. Be good."

Shad pulled away and left Dryfly standing in the darkness of the club's parking area. After watching the lights of the van, Dryfly waited for a couple of minutes giving his eyes the necessary time to adjust to the night. The parking area was surrounded with pines so that all he could see were the lights in the farthest cabin where the Americans loudly laughed and talked, partied; all else, except for the sky above, was darkness.

When his eyes finally opened for the darkness, he could distinguish the veranda and the end of the nearest cabin, the cabin where Bill Wallace and his daughter Lillian always stayed when they visited the Dungarvon. Dryfly knew that this year when they came up, they would be staying in their new place on the land they bought from Lindon Tucker, but, as of yet, it was this cabin belonging to the Cabbage Island Salmon Club that meant the most to him.

He yearned to step onto the veranda and sit for a while. He often sat there by himself when nobody was around. It was a link to Lillian.

There he would sit, sometimes with his eyes closed, envisioning the blond beauty that occupied so much of his heart — her hair, her brilliant smile, her big blue eyes. There on the veranda he'd sometimes feel so close to her that he could smell her perfume, hear the music in her laughter, or feel the warmth of her breath as she whispered the magic words — *I love you*.

He sighed, knowing that tonight was not the night to sit there. The club was completely occupied by the American Electronics Association group, and although everyone was in the upper cabin, it was getting late and they might return any minute. Dryfly knew that if they found him on the veranda, even if he was just sitting there doing nothing, they'd feel intruded upon, so he took the path over the hill to the river and followed it upstream toward the footbridge.

The night was cold, as April nights on the Dungarvon often are. Dryfly could hear a dog barking, the voice coming on the clear frosty air, perhaps following the river from as far away as Gordon. The settlement of Gordon was two miles away. He could also hear a car maneuvering its way up the Gordon road, coming, then going, sounding like a stagecoach on the gravel.

He followed the path more from memory than from sight, came to the footbridge, climbed the abutment steps, followed the boardwalk, gray against the dark water below. When he got to the center of the river, he stopped on the abutment there and gazed upstream. The river slid beneath him like the hem of a gigantic wizard's gown. From here he could hear the rush of a brook entering the river — "Tuney Brook? Todder Brook? Both?" He wasn't sure.

"How many times have I stood on this bridge thinking about you?" he asked.

"A thousand times," answered Lillian from her place in his heart.

"This year when you come will be the fourth year for us. Three years you've been here. A total of . . . you were here for nearly a week that first year, before I met you . . . so, five weeks . . . I've spent five whole weeks with you. And this summer will make seven weeks, maybe even eight, if you can talk old Bill into staying a little longer. I'll get at least two weeks with you and then *this* all over again. Why do I keep on loving you . . . day after day, week after week, year after year? — I *do* love you, you know."

"I know. I love you, too. "

Dryfly sighed, then shrugged.

"Wishful thinking," he said aloud to his old friend the river.

four

Amelia talked and talked and talked and talked. By the time she got off the bus in Nashville, Palidin felt he knew everything there was to know about her, her family, in-laws, boyfriends, friends, enemies, neighbours, employers, pets, the dog catcher whom she hated and the boy she liked until she found out that he spent a great deal of his leisure time hanging out in a mall washroom.

"He had a little hole whittled in the wall, and he'd sit on the toilet and peek at the guy in the next stall! Imagine! Ever' time they patched the hole he'd just whittle another one! Imagine! Then one day some guy that worked at the mall walked in and kicked the stall door in. There was Billy, his payants to his knees . . . doin' it! Can you imagine? He never got back in that mall, I tell ya! I heard about it soon enough, and the next time I saw him, I puked!"

"How old was he?" asked Palidin.

"Well, he was, oh, he must have been sayeventeen, eighteen . . . he had grayaduated. Imagine! He was a real corker, too. Tall, black hayer, blue eyes . . . did I tell ya about what happened to Silver King, me sister Karen's husband's brother? Of course I didn't. Well, he got in trouble with the preacher's daughter Louise, or so he thought. Louise went to 'im, said she was four weeks preyegnant. "No problem," he said. "I'll take ya to Cincinnati for an abortion." So off they wayent in Caroline's old green Buick, the one with the balls in the windows and the whip aerial, Caroline was his sister. Anyway, they went and God Almighty, she wasn't four weeks preyegnant at all, but twelve weeks! Imagine! Poor little Silver hadn't even known her twelve weeks before that! Imagine! Am I boring you? Of course I am. Anyway, poor little Silver had committed himself, and he has a heart about as big as that silo over there. And guess what — what's your name again?"

"Palidin."

"Palidin. Ha! Guess what Silver did! He married her! Imagine! Turned out he fell in love with her in Cincinnati when they stayed overnight in the motor hotel. That was great for her, of course. Saved her face, made her look like the Virgin Mary in the eyes of her father. She left poor Silver a week after she had the baby! Not only that, she left poor Silver *with* the baby! Ha! Imagine! Now, poor Silver is raisin' somebody else's kid! Ha! Crazy world!"

"I thought she had an abortion."

"Oh, no! No, no, no, no, no! She was twelve weeks preyegnant! They only had enough money for a four-weeker! Now, Aunt Mary said that Louise wasn't really the preacher's daughter at all, that she was adopted. I always said, ya never know what kind of tramp you're getting when you adopt somebody. And that's what irks me to the long and curlies! Poor little Silver is left with the kid of a tramp! Another tramp! You ain't adopted, are ya?"

"No. My sister had me."

"Huh?

"Nothin'."

"You're a strange one. You a sanger?"

"No. You?"

"Me sang? No, can't sang a note, but I play the fiddle a bit."

"Is that why you're goin' to Nashville?"

"No, I'm from Nashville. I was livin' with Bob Joe Randall in Cleveland. Sonuvabitch kicked me out! Said I was abusin' him. He weren't no bigger than a mouse's dick. Weren't no more than five feet tall when he took off his cowboy hat and boots. He wears one of them big Mack truck belt buckles? Everytime he took his clothes off, you could see the shape of that big buckle on his belly, like a tattoo. I couldn't help but laugh when I saw it! Ha! Maybe I did abuse him, now that I think about it. Might as well have a chicken in bed with ya! Belly spotter, I called him. Made him so mad when I called him that! Don't know what I ever saw in that little fart! He had money, I can say that for him. He was a good provider, but money ain't everythang. Drives truck, he does; has more money than you can spend in Indianapolis in a week! My God, here we are in Tennessee. Home sweet home! Kentucky's such a bore compared to Tennessee. Look at those hills! The Volunteer State. I can almost smell the dogwood!"

Forty-five minutes later, the bus stopped at a terminal in downtown Nashville.

"Well, it's the end of the road for me, honey. It's been real good talkin' to ya."

"Yeah. You've been good company. Maybe we'll meet again sometime."

"Not much chance of that, darlin'. Give me a big kiss, honey."

Palidin kissed her.

"Hope y'all do well in Texas, babe."

"Take 'er easy."

"Sure will, honey. Bye."

"Bye."

*

For the last year and a half or so, Dryfly had spent much of his time studying, applying himself to getting an education by means of a good old Winnipeg-based correspondence school. He was beginning to enjoy the textbooks that accompanied the course and found that he was beginning to read other books as well. He worked hard, and in just a year and a half he had increased his education by three grades. He was now wrapping up grade eight.

Another thing that he was doing was writing many of the jokes, skits and songs for his and Shad's act. Writing and studying demands a certain amount of thinking, and Dryfly was beginning to think more and more. He hadn't slept well this night for two reasons: one, it seemed unusually quiet, and two, he was thinking.

He had gone to bed with Lillian Wallace on his mind, dealt

with it in the same way that most normal young people deal with sexual concerns when they're alone, then found himself thinking about other things.

Lying on his back, Dryfly thought about his brother Bonzie. One Sunday afternoon a number of years ago, all the Ramsey family, including little Bonzie, were having a picnic in the woods just back of the Big Hollow near a barren. Dryfly, Palidin and Bonzie had been running around the woods mooing, stomping and pretending they were moose, when, as is often the case when in the woods with no toilet paper, Bonzie needed to have a poop. He left the company of his brothers and went down through the woods in search of some privacy and was never again seen alive. Later that day, they found a couple of turds beneath a broken-down birch tree, and five weeks later they found a crow-pecked, worm-eaten, very dead Bonzie.

Lying on his right side, Dryfly thought about the story that Shad had told him about breaking into one of the Cabbage Island Salmon Club's camps. Shad said that he'd felt a presence there, that something was making noises in the kitchen, but when he checked it out, he found no cause for it. Shad had been smoking a Parody cigar that he had found in the camp, and when he tossed the butt in the toilet bowl, he missed and it stood straight up on its end on the rim. The presence grew stronger; the stuffed animals on the wall started to stare at him pathetically, rebelliously.

Lying on his belly, Dryfly thought about Lindon Tucker. "A jeezless bird got me lost!" Lindon repeated time after time in Bernie Hanley's store. "I could, I could, I could hear it right there beside me, so I could, but couldn't, couldn't, couldn't, if ya know what I mean, couldn't see it. No trace, no sign, not a thing, not a jeezless thing! I couldn't see it, if ya know what I mean. I could've follied it all day, jist makin' his noise right there outta sight!"

Lindon got lost pursuing the bird and built a small fire for comfort. "Then, all of a sudden a gust of wind come up and the next thing I knew the whole damn woods was burnin' down! Yep, yeah. Yes sir! A forest fire, it was. Damn near burnt the whole country down, I did! Yep. Yes sir. Dum de dum dum di di di ..."

Lying on his left side, Dryfly thought about the time he'd been walking home from a party and was standing on the footbridge thinking about, who else? Lillian Wallace.

"I heard someone walking toward me on the bridge," thought Dryfly as he rolled over to face the ceiling. "But, when I looked, there was nobody there. I could see the very best; the moon was up, but there was nobody there — just the sound of someone or somethin' walkin'. The footsteps kept coming until they stopped right there beside me. I was too drunk to be scared, but I remember it, and I think I've heard that bird that Lindon heard. Did the same thing happen to Bonzie? Did poor little Bonzie get lost chasing a bird? And why is it so quiet here tonight? It's too quiet to sleep!"

Over and over, Dryfly thought of these things, and over and over he rolled.

Little things entered his head, like the abundance of hoofprints that were always all over the place, although one rarely saw a moose and they were too big for a deer. He tossed around the tale of the Dungarvon Whooper, the story of a murdered cook or cookee, who from his grave, by means of ferocious screaming and howling, whooping, put the run to a whole crew of lumberjacks. He kept it up, too, until Father Murdock dug him up and reburied him in consecrated soil.

Lying on his belly once again, with his head under his pillow, Dryfly thought, "A guy in Blackville — or was it Renous? — told the story about playin' cards in a camp in the Dungarvon woods. A stranger showed up in the middle of the night. Someone dropped a card on the floor, and when he reached to pick it up he noticed that the stranger had hooves instead of feet. Damn near scared the shit out of him. He jumped, upset the table, the oil lamp, burnt the camp down. And sometime during the racket the stranger disappeared. Where'd he come from? Where'd he go? Just yarns, prob'ly. But what was that on the bridge? Was it just me being drunk? Will liquor do that to ya? And why is it so quiet? It's never *this* quiet!

"Maybe there's something out there, something haunting the whole area. I should bring it up at the store sometime, to hear what lads like Bob Nash, Dan Brennen, Bert Todder. No, not Bert — Bert would make fun of a lad. And not John Kaston — John would want to preach about it. Lindon Tucker? Ha! Lindon would have a bright conversation about it, I'm sure! Oh, yeah, yeah, yep! The devil, yep. Heard 'im meself, yep! On second thought, I might as well keep my foolish thoughts to myself. After all, they thought Nutbeam was the devil — the Todder Brook Whooper. Ha! Course, Shad and I didn't help matters much with our running around through the fields blowin' on the trumpet and with our yarn about shooting the monster in the woods, a thing the size of an elephant, with horns like a cow and eyes the size of pie plates. I could talk to Nutbeam about it. Nutbeam never laughs at your foolish thoughts, and he sure as hell lived long enough in the woods. Alone in that old camp half buried in the hill. If anyone knows what's out there, it's Nutbeam. What I should do is go out and check things out, like Palidin used to do. Palidin used to wander around in the night, used to spend more time wanderin' around in the night than he did in the day. All he did in the daytime was read. I'd like to talk to Palidin about my foolish thoughts, too. It seems to me that I've heard that strange-sounding bird right in the middle of the winter. I should get up, go for a walk like Palidin used to . . . check things out — just to see."

It was four o'clock. Dryfly got dressed and went to the kitchen, brewed a pot of tea and ate a piece of Shirley's chocolate cake, using the tea as a chaser. In the quiet little house he found himself sneaking from stove to table, sipping his tea as a Parisian dandy would a fine cognac, minimizing the resounding slurp that might awaken Nutbeam, Shirley or, more importantly, Sally. When he finished the last cud of the somewhat undercooked cake, he donned his warmest coat and a pair of rubber boots and turned off the kitchen light. Easing the door shut behind him, he stepped into a night as dark and cold as a black salmon's bowel.

The great outdoors turned out to be as quiet as the little house had been — no owls hooted, no loons fluted, no canines pined; no wind in the trees, no traffic on the road, no burps, farts, squeaks, squalls or squawks — quiet.

"It's too quiet," thought Dryfly. "I can't even hear the brooks. Why? There'd have to be something awful powerful in the woods to make even the brooks hush."

Dryfly didn't know what he wanted to do, which way to go. "Which way?" he asked the night. He could have been a prophet making a humble plea to a god, and in this case the god was Darkness.

"Down through the field," answered Darkness. "It's easier going that way."

So down through the field he went, slowly picking his way along, for though he knew the path well, the starless sky offered very little light. He came to John Kaston's house and barn, one as dark as the other, and just beyond sat John's little but somewhat more visible church, for its walls were whiter than the weathered cedar shingles of the house and barn. Beside the church sat the lone grave of Hilda Porter, the woman whose house and property Shad now owned. Dryfly shivered as he passed the cold marble stone, knowing it was inscribed "The Last Tasmanian." That particular inscription had been Shad's idea.

Years ago, on his way home from the forest after he and Shad had allegedly shot the Todder Brook Whooper, Dryfly had heard the strange bird. It frightened him so that he ran all the way home, through the most populated route he knew. He was just a little boy back then, and when he heard the mournful coo, it seemed to be almost human, or some human-like thing that could in a simple "coo" express warning, alert, prophecy, or something like, "You can't see in the dark, kid. I'm a bird in a tree and you can't see me. I'm only ten feet away from you and you can't even smell me! What manner of creature are you?" For many years after that, Dryfly considered himself a coward to have run like that from the coo of a bird.

When you fly over New Brunswick, perhaps on a trans-Atlantic flight from Montreal to Athens, you see below you a vast forest that begins somewhere in Quebec and is uninterrupted until it reaches the sea. If you look carefully, you might spot Moncton, Bathurst, Campbellton and Fredericton like a distant galaxy in the azure, but places like Newcastle, Chatham, Plaster Rock and Sussex might only be a glimmer here or a puff of smoke there, little more. Places like Blackville, Juniper and Harvey Station you'll miss completely. Such flights, such observations were never designed to boost the ego of the individual New Brunswicker — unless, of course, you are inclined to be more turned on by trees than concrete.

If the Pope had given John Kaston's Boston cardinal the province of New Brunswick for his diocese, he would probably have done so to punish the guy for failing to say his ten Hail Marys every night.

No different from the rest of Canada, really.

Although Dryfly had not taken any transatlantic flights at that point in his life, there in the night, in Brennen Siding, twelve miles up the Gordon Road from the metropolis of Blackville, in the middle of a great forest, a hundred yards or so from the deep, and on this night particularly dark, Dungarvon River, he was in some way or another infiltrated with that Lilliputian complex.

The realization entered Dryfly's keen young mind like a midge through a gaspereaux net — the forest ejaculated it, the little church oozed it, the darkness spewed it; it soared on the wings of time and swam on the currents of space; the wilderness screamed it and the spirits of long-gone aborigines drummed it; it reached from the cold April earth like a spook from a Boris Karloff flop. Not much more than a germ but profound enough to be a whisper from Calliope the Muse, it brought Dryfly to an abrupt halt halfway between the Church of John Kaston and the home of Helen MacDonald.

"Coo!"

Dryfly knew immediately what it meant.

"You don't belong here, man."

No argument. Still the child. Perhaps a coward, perhaps a wise man, Dryfly turned on his heels and headed home. When he entered Nutbeam's little house, he didn't even bother to turn on the lights. Instead, he went straight to his room, sat on his bed in the dark, and with all the patience of a peach in a rusty can awaited the light of day.

*

Palidin had absolutely nothing to do with the fact that the bus arrived in Texarkana, Arkansas, at nine o'clock in the evening and left for San Antonio, Texas, a half hour later. If the itinerary had been planned by Palidin, he would have stayed the night in Texarkana and travelled that last three hundred and fifty-three miles the next day so that he could see the rolling hills, the magnolia trees, tulip trees, hanging trees, sagebrush and cactus — the terrain of Texas. "There were cowboys in Texas, I'm sure of that. The Lone Ranger was in fact a Texas Ranger, and he was a cowboy, wasn't he?" thought Palidin. "In the Lone Ranger comic books the famed masked man and his sidekick Tonto rode Silver and Scout beside, or on or across mesas, whatever mesas were, and they moodily fried bacon over sagebrush fires. Or was it buffalo poop they used for fire? And there were tumbleweeds and cactus. Everything was arid and there were always big boulders for them to hide behind when bandits ambushed them. Silver — Amelia's sister Karen's husband's brother. That would be her sister Karen's brother-in-law was Silver . . . Silver King? I wonder if he was named after the Lone Ranger's horse? And King could be the name of a horse, too."

His thoughts rambled, but the Lone Ranger's Texas was the Texas that Palidin wanted to see.

Now, however, all he could see were a few lights in the distance, the occasional billboard and truck stop, other vehicles passing. He might as well have been travelling through India, or Saskatchewan. When he entered Texas, he had been dozing and missed the welcome sign, and when he woke he would not have known he was there at all if it hadn't been for the telltale lone star that shone high in the southern sky.

One of the things that Palidin was learning on this trip was that he was not a good sleeper sitting up. He hadn't slept more than a couple of hours in the two days since he left Toronto. Every time a baby cried from somewhere else in the bus or someone sneezed or coughed, every time the bus was passed by a transport truck or a car horn blasted, he tensed and became alert. That he slept at all was strictly because at times he was just too exhausted not to.

He was exhausted now. And satisfied with the fact that the lone star in the south somehow, even facetiously, indicated that he was in Texas at last, he closed his eyes and slept for three hours. In that three hours, the bus manoeuvered a hundred and eighty miles of Interstate 30, and it was the din of heavy traffic in a huge city that awakened him. He sat up and gazed out the window at the spectacle before him. There were lights everywhere — the highways and skyways, the skyscrapers in the distance, even the sky itself was busy with the flashing lights of planes coming and going.

"So many lights. No wonder you can only see one star. Why so many, I wonder? What does so many lights say about life here? A lot of crime, I suppose. A great many people afraid of the dark. A great many people wasting energy. Lots of money. It's like . . . hell. Man pays homage to the hell he's created — destroys nature, replaces it with hells like this. Adorns his hell with electric lights . . . buzzing, mind-rotting electric lights. We build walls against the wind, roofs against the sky, floors against the earth — crowd out nature — as if it was something vile, alien, evil. Create darkness . . . light our creations artificially. God created one forbidden fruit — man's created a bunch." Palidin thought this, grateful that he was just passing through and that he had the walls and windows of the fast-moving bus between himself and the city of Dallas.

*

Sally Nutbeam finished peeing in her diaper, and because it was starting to cool and feel uncomfortable, she decided she would do something about it, decided she would go for a walk.

"If someone as tall as Dada can stand upright, anyone can," she thought. "Creeping's all right around the house, but a carriage on these fields, that footbridge and especially on the pebbly surface of the Gordon Road is a pain in the ass. And besides, I'm tired of being pushed around! Not only that, but if I could walk, I could do things for myself, progress, get the important things that one needs in life. Like that nice shiny hunting knife of Dada's that he'll never let me have. Nice guy but, boy! He sure is mean with his possessions! Won't let me play with his matches, his hunting knife or his old trumpet; every time I put a piece of bark, a rock, a bottle cap or a penny in my mouth, he freaks right out and reaches right in with his grubby finger and takes it from me. And Mama is every bit as bad! So I'm going to learn to do things for myself, and I'm going to start by learning to walk."

She was sitting on the kitchen floor looking up at the giants Nutbeam and Shirley. As usual, they were talking. "Talk, talk, talk! Doesn't anyone change diapers any more?"

Sally gave walking a try and learned almost immediately that it was not as easy as it looked. Standing was the problem. She managed to get only halfway up, and she tumbled back on her soggy bum. She tried as many as eight or ten times, and each attempt ended with the same result. Thump! Back on her bum.

After giving the situation some careful deliberation, she came up with what she thought could be the solution to her problem. It had to do with standing. "If you're ever going to get anywhere, first you have to learn to stand on your own two feet," she thought, and if she had been a writer, she probably would have jotted that bit of wisdom down.

"I know that if I can get to my feet, I can do it," she reasoned, and tried again.

Thump, back down she plopped.

"It's the getting up off my ass that's the problem. I need help. Sometimes a person needs help in getting started. Now, whom should I approach, Dada or Mama? Sometimes Dada pulls me up with his fingers, lets me hold onto them while I stand and look around . . . and the view up there! You can see so much when you're standing. I really must do it."

"Dada! Dadadadadadada!"

"It was either Naggy or Neenie," said Shirley. "One of the girls, anyway, and she, whichever one it was, wanted my scarf to wrap around her head so that she'd look like me, I suppose. God forbid, that she'd ever look like me! Anyway, it was the only scarf I had, and I wasn't about to give it to her to get all sticky with the jam on her fingers or wear around the dooryard and get dirty. So I wouldn't give it to her. No way!"

Nutbeam listened intently to Shirley's story.

"Dada! Dadadadadadada!"

"Well, she hollered and she cried and went on somethin' awful! Nothin' would do but she'd have that old scarf! And I wouldn't budge! 'No,' I said. 'Ya can't have it and that's that!' Well, she give up after a while and started playin' wit' her doll. She had an old doll that Ruby Underwood gave 'er, and she used to put Dryfly's old nightshirt on it. Dryfly was just about the age of Sally and he had this little nightshirt. Come to think of it, he was wearin' the nightshirt at the very time that Naggy wanted it."

"Dada! Goo goo baba bababa!" said Sally. Translated, it meant, "Nutbeam! Give me a hand! I want to walk!"

"So, what'd ya do, take the shirt off of Dryfly just to please Naggy?"

"No, I just let her scream and holler, 'I want Dryfly's shirt! I want Dryfly's shirt!' And she cried and went on like that for what must've been a half hour. Finally, Digger, who was a pretty big junk of a lad at the time, and he was gettin' pretty fed up wit' all the racket, said 'Naggy, I have a shirt for ya, the very same as Dryfly's 'cept it's invisible, ya can't see it. Ya might say it's a magic shirt.'"

"I'll have to pull the old scream and holler act myself, if they don't soon start paying attention to me," thought Sally. "Dada! Goo goo goo!"

"That Digger could make anyone believe anything. 'This kin be your very own shirt and you kin dress yer doll wit' it every day,' he said to Naggy. Naggy jist looked at him kinda curious, and Digger reached in his pocket and pulled out what could have been somethin', the way he handled it, but there weren't nothin' at all — he was jist makin' out that he had somethin', holdin' it up, givin' it a shake like he had a real shirt and was tryin' to git the wrinkles outta it. He even went as far as to unbutton it. Then, real careful like, he started to dress the doll wit' it. He was like one of them . . . what d'ya call them? Mimmies? Mimics?"

"Yeah, yeah, like a mime." persisted Nutbeam.

"Dada! Give me a hand!" Wah! Wah! Wah! Whimper, whimper, whimper!

"What in the name of God is wrong wit' that child?"

"Sally's all right. Needs her diaper changed. So, Digger put the shirt on the doll and what then?"

"Well, he got it about half way on, or what seemed to be about halfway on, when he said, 'Oh, darn! I got it on inside-out! Don't you think that shirt's on inside-out, Naggy?' And, by God, didn't Naggy light right up and say, 'Yes, Digger, it's inside-out. Boy, you're careless, Digger!' Ha, ha, ha! And Digger took it off the doll again, went through all the actions of pulling the arms free, unbuttonin' it and then pullin' the arms agin as if he was rightin' an inside-out shirt. Then he put it on the right way and said, 'There ya go, Naggy! Ya got yer very own shirt!'"

"And did Naggy believe 'im?"

"She never asked for Dryfly's shirt again. Played wit' that invisible shirt day after day and learned to do that mimic stuff just as good as Digger."

"Kids are like that," said Nutbeam. "When I was a kid, I'd pretend I was ridin' big white stallions. Ha! No real horse could be as big and white as the ones I rode. And I remember not having a toy gun. I'd pretend I had a gun, use my finger. The difference between my gun and the toy guns that all the other boys were using was that my gun seemed real, like Wyatt Earp's or Daniel Boone's. No piece of cheap tin or wood for me. My gun, the gun I had right up here in my head was made out of steel and had pearl handles. The imaginary toy is always the best."

"They're more real than the toy ones."

"Now, what's my little darlin' want?" asked Nutbeam, going to a very unhappy Sally. "Oooooh, Sally baby, what's the matter? Poor baby! Want yer diaper changed? Oh! Poor baby! Hold on! Daddy'll fix you right up! Now, now, now, now, now. Hold on. Daddy's doin' it."

It wasn't until an hour later that Nutbeam, not knowing why Sally was being so petulant, offered her his big index finger so that she could pull herself to her feet.

"Finally!" thought Sally. "Now, hold on, Dada old dog, I'm going to give this walkin' stuff a go. Now let me see.

Which foot first? I'll try the right one . . . oops! That's right, hold on to me. One step at a time . . . "

*

Labrador sent New Brunswick a gift. It was not a gift that New Brunswick wanted to keep, or even accept. It was a gift that New Brunswick would try to give away to Maine, Prince Edward Island, Nova Scotia or Quebec just as soon as Labrador, that practical joker from Newfoundland, turned its back. It was a white, feathery, cold and wet gift that Labrador had purchased at a spring clearance sale from a North Atlantic surplus store. It had been a two-for-one sale. Labrador kept one for itself; the other it wrapped and sent to its southern brother via the northeast wind.

"No, no, no, no, I couldn't!" said New Brunswick.

"I insist," said Labrador. "Share the wealth, I always say."

New Brunswick knew there was no arguing with temperamental old Labrador, so with a sigh of resignation it gracefully accepted the six inches of wet, slushy snow.

Dryfly Ramsey sat huddled behind David O'Hara in the Snake's Coffin. The wind swept the snowflakes up the river directly into his face, and he was using the warmly-dressed David O'Hara as a shelter.

"No wonder it was dark this mornin'," thought Dryfly. "This darn storm was coming. Any person that wasn't crazier than a tickled hyena would stay in the camp on a day like this! No sleep last night. I'm tired, I'm wet, my throat's sore, I got a cold. I've already spent most of the money that I'm earning for doing this shitty job on a rifle I will prob'ly never use. Where in life did I go wrong? Why am I doin' this? Or better still, why is this crazy, jeezless old American doin' this? If I had his money, I'd be settin' right back in the sun somewhere, drinkin' tall drinks with ice cubes in them and watchin' half-naked women wiggle their bums. Well, I gotta do somethin'."

When David O'Hara reeled in his line and was about to let it out again, Dryfly said "How about trying somewhere else?"

"All right with me. Got any place in mind?"

"Yep. Good place down there on the bend."

"Let's go."

Dryfly pulled the anchor and very carefully, so as to not upset the Snake's Coffin, eased his way back to the 7.5 Elgin. He choked it, throttled it and pulled and pulled and pulled and pulled and pulled on the pullcord. "Start, you goddamned son of a whore!" he yelled. "Start!"

"Maybe it's flooded," commented David.

"Flooded all right! The miserable, stinking mailbox of a no good . . . " Dryfly had exhausted himself cranking the stubborn engine, stopped to rest. His hands felt as if they might soon freeze. He flew into a fit of coughing. On another day, a calmer day, he would not have to start the motor to get to where he wanted to go. On a calmer day, the current would carry him down to the bend he had chosen because there it would be windier and colder, and David O'Hara might decide to head back to the camp; but not today! Today, the same wind that carried Labrador's generous little gift to New Brunswick also carried the Snake's Coffin upstream against the current. They were sailing!

Lindon Tucker was anchored just upstream from them, and Dryfly had to stop cranking the 7.5 Elgin, grab the paddle and steer the Snake's Coffin away from Lindon's canoe. He avoided a collision by a mere ten feet.

"G'day, g'day, g'day! How, how, how, how, how's she goin', Dryfly, buddy, pal? How, how, how, how's the fishin'?"

Dryfly had to laugh. It was an emotional release. Better laughter than tears.

"Out of gas?" asked the general as they drifted by.

"Maybe, maybe, maybe she's out of gas," added Lindon.

"No, I filled the tank this morning. I only came about a half mile . . . lotsa gas."

"Well, yer headin' in the right direction. You'll, you'll, you'll be back to the camp in no time!"

But the wind was not steady, came in gusts. As soon as it eased, the Snake's Coffin drifted downstream again.

"Back, back, back again, are ya, Dryfly, pal?"

David O'Hara was growing frustrated with the fiasco.

"Let me give you a hand," he said and started to rise, to make his way back to where Dryfly laboured.

"No! No!" yelled Dryfly. "Stay where you are, you fool! You'll drown the both of us!"

Hearing the sincerity in Dryfly's voice, David settled back into his seat. "What kind of a goddamned piece of junk is that?" he asked. "Where the hell did they get that motor, Dogpatch?"

They were now thirty feet below Lindon and the general again, and the wind, which had shifted a bit, had carried them to a spot directly over the general's twenty-five dollar pink Cortland 444 double-tapered floating fishing line, and it was here that the 7.5 Elgin decided to cough, sputter, and in a cloud of smoke swiftly consumed by Labrador's courier, start.

"Thank God!" said Dryfly, swung and headed down toward the coldest place on the river he could think of. His mind was on a single objective: freeze David O'Hara into going back to the camp. At no time, at least until he got back to the camp several hours later, did he know that the general's flyhook had hooked into the bottom of the Snake's Coffin and that he was pulling all three hundred yards of line from the general's reel with all the power and speed of seven and a half horses.

"Stop! What the hell is going on? Stop!" yelled the general.

In the notheast wind and with the motor running, Dryfly could not hear the general and Lindon shouting, nor could he feel the tug of the line when it snapped tight and broke from the general's reel.

His scheme to freeze David O'Hara off the river worked, however. When they went back to the camp for lunch, it was still snowing, and David declared the weather unfit for fishing. Dryfly got the afternoon off.

He went home, went directly to bed and within minutes he was sleeping as peacefully, as soundly as a . . . Labrador duck.

five

Palidin Ramsey checked into San Antonio's most dilapidated hotel. It was situated in the heart of the downtown area, and how it had escaped the claws, hammers and balls of the demolition squad was anyone's guess. Above the front desk in the lobby was a dusty eight-by-ten autographed photograph of Bob Hope. The expression on his face indicated that he felt pretty ridiculous in a ten-gallon hat, chaps and cowboy boots. Below the picture, on the yellowing border, someone had typed, "Bob Hope stayed here." This was the Vogue Hotel, and the truth of the matter was that Bob Hope had never graced its shabby interior. One of the original owners of the Vogue had stolen this particular photograph from the Rogers Hotel in Wheeling, West Virginia, and placed it here in the lobby of the Vogue because he thought it would be good publicity. It fooled a lot of people; it might have been the one reason why the hotel had managed not to get torn down.

"Oh, we can't tear down the Vogue! Bob Hope stayed there!"

To get to his room Palidin had to take a clunky cage-like elevator to the fifth floor. The elevator came to a halt a good eighteen inches above the level of the floor so that Palidin had to hop down to get out. He walked down a narrow corridor on a worn carpet to Room 509, unlocked a door that was at least eight feet tall and entered the musty-smelling room. The room was small with a high ceiling, had an old-fashioned bathroom off to the left, a double bed with a commode beside it, a closet and a fifty-foot, one-inch-in-diameter rope coiled beneath a tall, dirty window. The rope, of course, was the fire escape. There was a telephone but no radio or television.

Upon scanning the room, Palidin was immediately reminded of the gun-slinging, bounty-hunting Paladin of "Have Gun Will Travel," played by Richard Boone. "He stayed in rooms like this," thought Palidin. "Ha! That's why Amelia thought my name was strange. Probably thought I was making it up." He went to the bathroom to wash his face and hands. Turning on the water, he sang a bit of the theme song from the TV series. "Paladin, Paladin, where do you roam? Paladin, Paladin, far, far from home . . . " His voice sounded small and hollow in the tall-ceilinged room. He reached for the soap. "Ha! This is different," he thought. "Soap on a rope!"

He washed, went back to his bed, kicked off his shoes and lay back on the white bedspread. "God, it feels good to lie down and stretch," he thought. "In my mind, I'll be travelling on that bus for the next week. And then, I'll be travelling back. To where? Toronto? Brennen Siding? If my plan doesn't work, I won't have two cents to rub together when I get to . . . wherever it is that I end up. My plan *has* to work . . . I can't afford to start thinking negatively. No plan just works — you have to *make* it work. That's why I'm here."

Palidin was very tired, too tired to sleep. He sat up, picked up the phone book, looked under the letter *W*, found West Wind Sports. There were three numbers: a store number, an administration number and a 1-800. He memorized the administration number. "555-1234 . . . 555-1234 . . . easy enough. Now, let's see . . . West Wind Sports, 1098 Bowie Boulevard East. I'll shower, have a little nap so that I feel better, shower again, put on my good clothes and head out to 1098 Bowie Boulevard East. No sense in wasting time."

Several hours later, Palidin stepped into the massive West Wind Sports store and office complex on Bowie Boulevard. The store occupied the bottom four floors, administration the remaining six. Here was the headquarters of a chain of over a hundred and sixty stores dealing exclusively in sporting goods throughout the Western world. The latest store to be opened was in Zurich, Switzerland. The owner of the company was a Texas tycoon by the name of Malcolm "Brandy" Burgess. Palidin had read about old Brandy and his conglomerate —

Brandy was also into oil, cattle, shipping and real estate — in *The Business Journal*. Palidin wanted very much to meet Brandy Burgess.

Palidin was nervous; the palms of his hands were wet with perspiration — especially his right hand, the one that twiddled with the little plastic box in his pocket. He approached a tall man who was standing behind a glass counter in which was displayed a number of very expensive hunting knives. The man was thumbing through a West Wind Sports catalogue, and it wasn't until Palidin went "Ahem!" that he bothered to look up. He had seen Palidin approaching from across the room and knew by his clothing, the green corduroys and t-shirt, that he didn't have enough money to bother dealing with.

"What can I do for you?" asked the tall man, emphasizing the " you" as if to say, "the likes of you."

"I'd like to talk to . . . ah . . . Mr. Burgess."

"Mr. Burgess?"

"Ah . . . ahem! Yes. Mr. Malcolm Burgess, please."

The man with the catalogue grinned. "Oh! *that* Mr. Burgess!" he drawled. "Well, you're not about to find him here. You probably want to talk with the store manager."

"Doesn't Mr. Burgess have an office in this building?" asked Palidin.

"Well, he does at that, but I've never seen him in all the nine years that I've worked here. His daughter comes in occasionally, but not the old man."

Palidin sighed, fearing that perhaps this whole trip had been a waste of time and money.

"I've come a long way to see him. Ah, any idea where he lives?"

"He lives just about anywhere he damn well pleases. I hear he has fifteen or twenty houses, one in just about every major center in the whole United States of America. Where y'all from?"

"Ah . . . Toronto, Canada."

"Never heard of it. Up north, ain't it?"

Palidin didn't like this guy very much. "Wisconsin," he said. "I guess maybe I should talk to the manager. Is he in?"

"He's on the tenth floor, but you'll probably need an appointment."

"Well, thanks very much. Ah . . . the elevator?"

"Over there."

Palidin headed for the elevator, pushed the up button and waited what seemed like a long time for the doors to open. When they finally did, he stepped in beside a huge black woman.

"Up or down?" she asked.

"Yes, please," said Palidin, smiling. "I doubt if it goes any other way."

The woman just rolled her eyes as if she'd heard that minuscule attempt at humour a million times before.

"Ten," said Palidin.

On the tenth floor he was greeted by a very beautiful red-haired, blue-eyed secretary. She looked Palidin over, her eyes roaming boldly up and down his body as if he were a Cajun sausage and she was starving to death. Palidin half expected she might start drooling and lick her lips.

"What can I do for you?" she asked, slowly. She seemed to be using but half her voice and filling the other half in with a whisper.

"Throat damage," thought Palidin and almost chuckled when he said he'd like to see the manager.

"The store manager, or the general manager?" she asked.

"The . . . I guess I wanna see the general manager."

"Do you have an appointment?" she asked.

"No, but I'd like to make one," said Palidin.

"Mr. Wilson . . . ," she checked her daytimer. "Mr. Wilson is tied up for the rest of the day with meetings. Won't be in tomorrow. And then he's off to Seattle. I could fit you in for a week from Friday. You looking for a job? A salesman?"

"Well, yes, I suppose you could call me a salesman. But a week from Friday is no good to me. I've come all the way from Toronto, Canada, and I'll only be here for a few days."

"Oh, that's too bad. You should have called ahead. Perhaps if you told me your business I could fit you in with Mr. Lowery." She checked her daytimer again.

"Mr. Lowery?"

"The store manager. I could fit you in with him tomorrow afternoon. Two o'clock okay? But what are you selling?"

"Ah . . . a new line of flyhooks. Two o'clock tomorrow would be fine. Thanks."

The secretary scribbled something into the daytimer. "Your name?" she asked.

"Ah . . . Palidin. Palidin Ramsey."

What she had scribbled into the daytimer was "flyhooks." She wrote, "Mr. Palidin Ramsey from Canada" below the word "flyhooks."

"Do you have a card or a phone number? You know . . . in case of cancellation?"

"I'm at the Vogue Hotel."

"Okay," she said. "Tomorrow at two."

"See ya," said Palidin, and when he had turned to leave the secretary stared at his behind and licked her lips.

*

The next day at two o'clock, the horny secretary ushered Palidin into a large, luxuriously furnished office and closed the door behind him, leaving him alone with the manager.

The manager, James Lowery, was one of those guys that can't keep his mouth shut. Not that he talked so much, or stood around like a person in awe of everything, or like a thoughtless idiot, but more like one who knows the power of a smile but has forgotten how to execute it — a smile that isn't a smile, a questioning, scheming smile, a smile that, even when broadened to include the eyes, seems somehow poisoned with intimidation, distrust. He had red, curly hair, a bit too long, Palidin felt, for a man his age. Palidin guessed Lowery was about fifty. He was clean shaven, had bright blue eyes, wore a diamond ring on the little finger of his right hand.

When Palidin entered the office, James Lowery stood and looked him straight in the eye, smiled that unsettling smile and offered his hand.

"I'm James Lowery," he said.

"Ahem! Palidin Ramsey, sir." Palidin shook the hand. James Lowery sat but did not offer a chair to Palidin.

"What's your line?" asked James.

"Ah, well . . . I, ah, have this flyhook." Palidin pulled the little plastic box from his pocket and handed it to the manager, who took it and gazed at the little salmon fly within.

"I see . . . so?"

"It's a valuable fly, sir."

"It is? Looks like a salmon fly to me . . . a . . . a Blue Charm, I believe."

Palidin laughed.

"What's funny?" Lowery asked. There was the perpetual great white smile, the scheming eyes that darted to a picture on the wall or something, then back to Palidin.

Palidin had his own eyes for power-wielding, sobered quickly, said, "I see you know your flies."

"It's my business to know about everything I sell. Why do you say this fly is so valuable?"

"Because, even though it looks like an ordinary Blue Charm, it's not. There's something special about it that salmon can't resist."

"I see." James Lowery gave the fly a closer inspection. "So, ah, what is it you refer to?"

Palidin took a deep breath. "That I can tell you for a price."

James Lowery was sitting in a leather swivel chair. He swung around, stopped, and with his back to Palidin, thought for a minute. Then, as he swung to face Palidin once again, he said, "How productive is it?"

"I can catch any migratory fish that swims, with this fly. It never fails."

"Do you spray it with something?"

"That I can tell you for a price."

James Lowery smiled, smiled, smiled. Palidin thought he might laugh right out loud. "You've come all the way from Canada for" — he gestured at the flyhook with his eyes — "for this?"

"I'm from eastern Canada, the province of New Brunswick. You probably have no idea where that is."

"I know where that is. The Miramichi, right?" Palidin would have thought it impossible, but Lowery's smile broadened.

"You've been there?" asked Palidin, trying a smile of his own.

"A number of years ago. But not all the way from Texas. I'm originally from Springfield, Massachusetts. I was up there five times in my life and never caught one single salmon. If you have a fly that will catch a bunch of them, you might be talking something valuable. Who sent you to me?"

"Well, actually, I didn't come here to see you. I really came here to see Mr. Burgess."

"Ha, ha, ha, ha!"

"I suppose that was aiming a bit high," said Palidin, somewhat embarrassed.

"Ha, ha, ha, ha! No! Ha! It's . . . it's just that you might as well talk to a bird as that old coyote pup!" James Lowery composed himself, rotated his index finger about his ear. "I'm sorry. It's just that old Brandy is rather . . . shall we say, eccentric. He hasn't been active, as far as business goes, for years."

"So, who runs things now?"

"Well, his daughter's involved. She's the company president; there's a board of directors, a general manager. But never mind, you've come to the right person. Tell me about it."

"If it works, how much do you think it's worth?"

"Depends on how well it works . . . *if* it works. I've never seen anything work yet. Do you have any idea how many people approach us every year with their magic worms and super lures and their turn-on bait, buck scent. We talked to one guy a while back who claimed he had invented a fish call. Turned out to be an ordinary old corn-cob pipe, a dirty old pipe that gurgled when you puffed it. Ha! Another guy designed a boot with the likeness of a bear's paw on the soles. He never thought for a moment that every hunter in the forest would be tracking him instead of the real bear. 'Camouflage! I've designed a papa-bear boot, a momma-bear boot and a baby-bear boot,' he said, setting right there where you are now. He said that the bears would hunt for you instead of you having to hunt for the bears. You wouldn't believe some of the people that I've talked to! And the gimmicks are all alike. The fishermen buy them for the novelty of having them in their tackle boxes. We make a few dollars and that's as far as it goes. The things don't work, never did work and never will work, but just about anyone will give it a try."

"I must tell you," said Palidin with a sigh, "that this, what I do to the flies, is not just a gimmick. For now, you might say that I kiss the fly. It's just that simple, you know. And whatever I do to it works on every fly, not just the Blue Charm, and I think it's worth a whole bunch of money."

"Well, don't you worry about that. Just tell me what you call this magical thing you have. We'll consider the name, maybe give it a better one, for marketing, you understand. And I guess, we could risk . . . oh, let's say a thousand for the time being. You got a thousand with you?"

Palidin shook his head, searched for words. "You don't seem to understand where I'm coming from. I can take any fly at all, do something to it and, yes, in sort of a way it is like a magic kiss, because that fish will take that fly the second it hits the water! What I want to sell you is not a thousand flies, or a million for that matter. What I want to sell you is the idea, the kiss. What you'll be doing is manufacturing those things." Palidin pointed at the little plastic box that was now on the desk between them. "You'll have exclusive rights to a product that everyone in the whole world will want. People would have to be crazy to buy a fly anywhere else than in your stores — selling those things."

James Lowery sighed. He had a meeting with the general manager in a few minutes and needed to get rid of what he figured was just another kook.

"All right. Tell me what you do to these flies and I'll discuss it with the board, and we'll see what happens," he said.

Palidin looked down at his feet, wished he were sitting. "If I tell you the idea, if I tell you what I do to the fly, this whole business will be a waste of time for me. You'd know what I do. The secret would be out. Why pay me for something that you already know? I don't think you can patent the idea, you see. The whole business depends on its secrecy. What I propose is,

I guess, is that I take you, or somebody in this company, fishing somewhere. When you see what this fly is all about, you'll understand that it's . . . "

"If we can't patent it, what the hell's the good of it? Our competitors will simply analyze the fly, copy it, and that will be the end of our exclusivity," said Lowery, rising. "I'm sorry, I have to run. It's been an interesting chat, and I wish you all the luck in the world with your idea. What's the name again?"

"Palidin."

They shook hands.

"You will mention it to the board, then?"

"Yes, yes, of course. I promise."

"You might mention that no analysis will reveal its secret — I don't think."

"Yes, yes. Now, if you'll excuse me, I'm already late."

"When might I hear from you?"

"Ah, real soon. I'll call you. You're at?"

"The Vogue."

Lowery's smile broadened. "Yes, of course. You'll be hearing from me."

That was it. Palidin left. He was halfway down in the elevator before he realized that he had left the Blue Charm on Lowery's desk. He shrugged. "The hell with it," he thought. "I'm not about to face that secretary again."

*

Every spring, on the Saturday before the Sunday that the AEA boys packed up to head back to their homes in locations all over the United States, and if it didn't rain or snow, they held a picnic on Cabbage Island.

It was a massive affair by Brennen Siding standards, for the picnic was attended not only by the AEA members and their guides but also by a few of the Cabbage Island Salmon Club members, guests and members of other clubs and outfitters in the area; former guides, executive members of the Miramichi Salmon Association, local dignitaries like the mayors of Blackville, Newcastle, Chatham, Doaktown, Boiestown and

Fredericton, a couple of the local MLA's, the premier and a band
— Lyman MacFee and the Cornpoppers — were invited as well.

In the words of Stan Tuney, "It's the best time in the dear
world!"

This year's Saturday turned out to be a warm, sunny day.

Because the affair was taking place on the island and also
because he figured everyone would be drunker than a skunk by
the end of the day, Frank Layton, the manager of the club, was
obliged to hire a couple of men to canoe everyone to and from
the island. Both Bob Nash and Dryfly Ramsey recommended
Shad for the job. So Frank hired Shad and gave the other position to young Timmy MacCormick from Gordon. They'd each
get paid twenty dollars, and it was worth every penny because
not only did they have to transport all the guests (over sober,
back drunk), and the four women in charge of the barbecue,
but it was their responsibility to deliver the food and drink as
well. What made the job even more difficult was the fact that
they weren't permitted to have a motor. An outboard motor is
a noisy contraption and all that transporting would have
played havoc with the ambiance.

That was all right with Shad and Timmy. The job paid
twenty dollars. They needed the money.

The first thing they delivered to the island was Helen
MacDonald and Rex, Helen's dog, Rita Kaston, Elva Nash
and Kate Brennen, the cooks. Helen MacDonald was in charge,
and when Shad dropped her off she gave him and Timmy
their orders for the next two hours before they were to start
delivering the guests.

"Everything's in the kitchen," she said. "Bring the pots and
pans first. They're on the floor right beside the dishwasher. If
ya got room, bring the plates, glasses, cups and saucers, forks
and knives . . . that stuff. If not, ya'll have to make another
trip. Then, I want you to bring all the stuff that's in the can-
isters — that's the tea, the coffee, cakes, cookies, bread. You'll
see it all there on the counter by the sink. Then bring the sal-
ads. There's five bowls of it in the big fridge. After that, I want
you to bring the salmon and the lobsters. Ya'll have to be careful with the lobsters because they're alive and in them big pots

in the shed. The both of you will have to carry them one pot at a time, 'cause they're heavy. The salmon are all filleted and on boards in the ice house. You kin bring them any time after we start the barbecue. I suppose you should bring the liquor and beer, mix and stuff right away though, 'cause they'll be drinkin' a full two hours, maybe three before they eat. After you get everybody here, I'll give you the word and you kin go for the beans. They're still in the oven and should be ready about the time everybody gets around to eatin'. If ya can't find somethin', come and ask me, I'll be up there by the tables or by the barbecue."

"Good 'nough," said Shad, and he and Timmy shoved their canoes off and paddled like hell for the club.

Within two hours they had everything but the beans delivered to the island. Helen had everything timed perfectly, for they had just dropped off the salmon when the guests started to arrive. They taxied the men over three at a time and had to make thirty-five trips. The distance between the mainland and the island was only about thirty yards, but it took them a full hour to deliver everyone. The only one they didn't have to deliver was the premier. The premier came by helicopter.

The party began.

Just as a lobster trap on the roof of an Ontario car is one of the first signs of summer, in Brennen Siding the AEA's annual picnic on Cabbage Island is one of the first signs of spring. The music of the Cornpoppers and the loud talking and laughing of the drunken men celebrating spring could be heard for a half a mile in any direction. Even John Kaston could be persuaded to have a little sip of rum on this particular occasion. Joke after joke, yarn after yarn, story after story were traded, concepts were discussed, deals were signed.

"De American people are de friend of all Canada," said the premier after several stiff drinks. "I tink we, de people of Nouveau Brunswick, will name a park after your illustrious dead president! Maybe in Fredericton, hey? How's dat for comradeship, no? Oui."

"Ha, ha, ha, ha, ha! What a man! Ha, ha, ha, ha, ha!"

"Aaaaaaawhoop!"

About halfway through the afternoon, Frank Layton stepped up onto a picnic table and shouted "Gentlemen!" several times, demanding attention. Everyone hushed. It was the moment they were waiting for, the highlight of the party.

"This is it, boys!" he yelled. "This is the moment you've been waiting for! But before I tell you who caught the biggest fish, I'd like to call on Mr. Young here to read a little poem!"

"Yea! Yahoo! Give 'er hell! Whoop!"

"Thank you, Frank! This little poem was written by my good friend Charlie here from Jemseg. You worked on this all winter, didn't you, Charlie?"

"Ha, ha, ha, ha!"

"If any of you gentlemen don't know Charlie, he's the Cabbage Island laureate . . . "

"Ha, ha, ha, ha!"

"Ahem! It goes like this:

> The moon was up, the stars were bright,
> The toads were harmonizing . . .
> Could've been the fiddle symphony I heard about
>   from Pa;
>
> With the dew like beads of lace
> On the webs about the place
> Where I was hiding in the alders from the law.
>
> I was drifting on the river
> With a net I took from Joe,
> For he said that I could have it if I caught him three
>   or four.
>
> Wasn't hurting anyone,
> Just trying to have some fun.
> I had thirty-seven kicking on the shore.
>
> Thought I'd make one last maneuver
> To score an even fifty,
> I do better on the river than working at the mill.

Then I heard the wardens comin',
There must have been a dozen
And a dozen more awatching from the hill.

When the lights lit up the river,
Thought I was on TV,
Could have been in Montreal, instead of Miramichi.

Well, you could say I flew
When I leaped from the canoe.
The hunt was on, the law was after me!

Well, every warden showed up from Juniper to
                    Chatham,
There was one lad from the Nashwaak
With a hundred dollar hound.

They took my old canoe,
My net and paddle, too,
And my thirty-seven shad from off the ground.

Now, they're searching door to door,
The hillside and the shore
And every dog's abarking from Boiestown to Renous —

Who's the criminal so bad
On the river netting shad
Was the headlines in Cadogan's weekly news.

That's it boys!"
"Yahoo! The very jeezless best!"
"Whoop!"
"A cream o' tartar!"
"Couldn't be better! The very best! A hunderd percent! A-one!"

Frank Layton got back up on the table. "Let's hear it for the laureate of Cabbage Island! Great, eh? Couldn't have written a better one myself! And now — the moment you've all been waiting for! This year's big salmon weighed sixteen and a half pounds and was caught late yesterday at Corpse Hole by none other than — wait for it! It was caught by none other than our good buddy from Albany, New York — Mr. David O'Hara!"

Everyone whooped and hollered and cheered.

"And as is the tradition here at the Cabbage Island Salmon Club, the cheque of one hundred dollars will go to the man who pointed the fish out to the winner! Come up here and get your money, Dryfly!"

Giving the hundred dollars to the guide was not necessarily the tradition. It was usually up to the sport to keep, divide or give all the money to the guide. Frank Layton figured that David O'Hara was cheap and might not share the money with Dryfly. From that day on, however, giving all the money to the guide was indeed the tradition.

Dryfly stepped up to the table and was given the cheque.

"Speech!" yelled Shadrack Nash.

Everyone cheered and shouted, "Speech! Speech! Speech! Speech!"

"Thanks a lot!" said Dryfly. "I'm speechless!"

And the ha ha ha's could be heard all the way to Gordon.

"Shad?"

"Yeah?"

"Mrs. MacDonald wants us to get the beans."

"Does it take two of us to get a crock of beans?"

Timmy MacCormick shrugged. "I dunno. She said to get you."

"Okay, let's do it and get it over with."

Ten minutes later when Shad and Timmy opened the oven in the club's kitchen, they were glad that they both had come for the beans. The pot was huge, practically filled the whole oven.

"We're gonna have to double up on the oven mitts to handle this thing," said Shad. "It's hot as hell."

"We better get a board or somethin' to set it on so's it don't burn the bottom of the canoe," suggested Timmy.

"We'll get a rock off the shore."

So, together they carried the big cast-iron pot full of beans to the river. They sat the pot down, found a flat rock, put it in the bottom of the canoe, then sat the pot on the rock. Being anxious to get back to the party, they paddled quickly over to the island.

Timmy was about fourteen years old, and although he was bright enough, he did not have a lot of river savvy, had not spent half of his time around the river as Shad and Dry had. His mother used to say to him, "Don't go near that river and get drownt, Timmy dear!" Because of this, he wasn't all that familiar with the Americans, either. This event was a very thrilling experience for him. He liked to hear the Americans talk, liked their accent. He was in a rush to get back to hear more. When they reached the island, he jumped out, grabbed the bean pot, for he knew he was strong enough to lift it at least out of the canoe. He managed the lift all right, but in his haste he had forgotten how hot the pot was. When it started to burn his hands, he exclaimed, "Ouch! Damn!" He quickly set the heavy pot on the gunwale of the canoe and let go. The pot tipped over, spilling its entire contents into the Dungarvon. A strip of beans a hundred yards long went floating down the river.

Many of the men on the island had been watching the river and witnessed the occurrence. A great din of laughter sprang up.

"There ends the fishing for the next week!" someone joked.

"Don't worry about it, son, the fish will eat them up!" yelled someone else.

"Hello fer fish farts tomorrow!" yelled Bert Todder.

Helen MacDonald didn't actually see the incident, but she heard about it soon enough, and she was immediately thrown into a state of thorough pissedoffity. She took great pride in her beans and had spent a great deal of time making sure that they turned out just the way she liked them.

Timmy MacCormick was an Irish Catholic from Gordon, so naturally he took the brunt of her wrath, her scolding. Shad said, "I should've yelled out to him, I just let him do it, it was as much my fault as his!" But Helen didn't seem to hear. "You scoundrel!" she whispered. "You clumsy oaf!" she screamed.

"You brute!" she growled. "You dum-dum!" she whimpered. "What a racket! What a waste! I might as well have fed them beans to Rex! Timmy, Timmy, Timmy! What in the world possessed you to do a trick like that? No! No! Don't tell me! I don't want to know! Get out of my sight! GET OUT OF MY SIGHT! I should wring your neck! Ohhh! You've ruined my day! So? So what're ya standin' there for? Get out of my sight, I tell ya! Go!"

And that was that. No cuts or bruises, no sticks or stones. Timmy slunk away, periodically licking and blowing his burned palms to ease the pain.

Bob Nash stood with his eyes closed, dreamily listening to Lyman MacFee and the Cornpoppers. The boys were in good form today and Lyman in his best voice was singing, "I'm Walking the Floor Over You," one of Bob's favourite songs.

Having his eyes closed and singing along to himself, Bob did not notice Old Cooky Duster's approach.

"Mr. Nash."

"Oh! Oh, g'day, General! Quite a party, eh?"

"Bob, I don't know how to properly thank you for what you did for me. You saved my life."

"Anyone would've done the same, General. Ya can't just let a man drown. Think nothin' of it. You know, I used to play some music . . . the banjo, believe it or not." Bob had changed the subject, knowing the general wanted to talk about their little dip in the Dungarvon River. To talk about such a thing seemed unnecessary. He knew he had saved the general and he knew that if the roles had been switched the general would have saved him. If the general *had* saved Bob from such a fate, Bob would have found it close to impossible to show any kind of verbal gratitude. There was no need to talk about such things. Bob would find other ways to express himself. He'd give him the occasional salmon, help him get the hay in the barn before a threatening storm, help him slaughter his pigs, perhaps doing the dirtier work like pulling the trigger, slitting the throat and gutting. But to talk about it would be just . . . too hard.

The general was taller than Bob by about a foot, and today

Bob thought he looked particularly old and grey. Although he had known him for five years, Bob had never guided the general — the general was Lindon Tucker's sport. However, they had talked occasionally, usually about fishing: what fly Bob had been using when he caught a big salmon when nobody else was catching any — things like that. But mostly, Bob had just listened to the general talking to the other Americans about things like how he believed that it should be compulsory for every American to serve in the armed forces for at least one year. The general was always serious, never good for as much as a single chuckle. Bob thought the general was arrogant. "Big-feelin', an old fart." But today the general was not nearly as intimidating, looked humbled, sad.

"You risked your life for me, Bob. I will never forget that." The general pulled a piece of paper from his shirt pocket and handed it to Bob. "This is so little in comparison to what I owe you, but I do hope you will accept it as a token of my appreciation."

Bob took the cheque, opened it. "A thousand dollars . . . "

Tears welled from the general's eyes, and Bob could tell that the old man was fighting a great battle within himself — that it was probably not *right* for a general to cry, to show such childish emotions. Bob agreed. Men shouldn't cry. Crying was an emotion shared by women and children. A man that cries is a blubbering idiot.

"God!" thought Bob. "I'm gonna have to save him again."

"General . . . I . . . "

"Bob . . . I . . . "

"A thousand dollars . . . "

"Please."

"I don't know what to say," said Bob and thought, "He's not gonna take no for an answer. Ya can't say no to a man at a time like this. He knows what a thousand dollars means to me."

"I . . . I . . . if . . . when I come back here . . . you'll be my guide," said the general.

Bob nodded, stuffed the cheque into his shirt pocket and turned back to watch the band.

The general breathed a great sigh of relief.

six

"Hi again!" said the secretary. "You're back." She swallowed to control the excitement she always felt when Palidin entered her office.

"Have you been talkin' to Mr. Lowery?"

"I'll check with him now, okay?"

"Great. Thanks."

The secretary picked up the phone, punched a single button. She wasn't wearing a bra, and the white satin blouse she was wearing did little to hide her nipples.

"Mr. Lowery . . . Mr. Ramsey . . . yes, again . . . but . . . tomorrow? Yes, sir." That was all. She hung up.

"Tomorrow," she said to Palidin. "He said he might have something to talk to you about tomorrow."

Palidin sighed. "That's what he said yesterday and the day before. I'm running out of time."

"Have you had lunch?"

"Lunch? I ah . . . "

The secretary grabbed her purse, stood. "Let me buy you lunch," she said.

Palidin shrugged. "Sure. Why not?"

"There's a nice little place right around the corner," said the secretary. "Like Mexican?"

Palidin shrugged again. "I guess so."

They went down in the elevator, hurried through the lobby and stepped out into the glaring, hot Texas sun.

"It's awfully hot," commented Palidin as he hurried to keep up with her, her high-heeled shoes tapping down the sidewalk and around the corner.

"It gets hotter. June and July are unbearable! My name is Jessy, by the way. Friends call me Jucy for some reason . . .

618

Jucy McLeod. I spell it like Lucy, sounds like in . . . Juicy Fruit?"

"Hmm."

"Here we are."

"Already?"

"I told you it wasn't far."

They entered a small, dimly lit restaurant. An easy melody played on a Mexican guitar came from the speaker in the ceiling. Jucy headed directly for a booth in the back corner. Following, Palidin noticed the seductive sway to her hips, the stretchy material of her white slacks tight like another skin. "Like boxing gloves," he thought. "Sparring, boxing . . . knockout bum!"

When she reached her booth, she threw her purse on the bench and slid in beside it. Palidin sat across from her. They lit cigarettes and waited for the waiter to wipe off the table. It was obvious by the crumbs and drops of liquid on the table and the still warm seats that some earlier diner had just left.

"What's my favourite señorita having today?" the waiter said to Jucy.

"Oh, I don't know. What do you think?"

The waiter looked Palidin over, smiled. "I think you will eat well, Jucy, my friend," he said. "Would you like a menu?"

"Tacos and beer will do. We'll share," said Jucy. She seemed in a hurry to get rid of him.

"Si, Señorita." He nodded at Palidin — "Señor" — and left for the kitchen.

"So, Palidin, what's so important that brings you all the way from Canada and keeps you coming back to our office? You're not just coming to see little old me, are ya?"

Palidin sighed. "I'm wasting my time with Lowery, aren't I?"

Jucy pouted her beautiful painted lips and looked directly into Palidin's dark eyes with her big blue ones. "Mista Wilson would probably be a better man to see, although he's an old pisser, too. What y'all selling?"

"A . . . fly . . . for fishing."

"Is that all? And he wouldn't buy a few?"

"It's not quite that simple. Wilson's the general manager?"

"Have y'all thought about going out to see Linda Burgess?"

"That's the daughter?"

"The president."

"I thought about trying to see the old man, but I guess he's . . . not well or something."

"Crazier than a turkey vulture on loco! Thinks he's Billy the Kid or someone, the way he goes on! Got millions of dollars! Lives in a little old shack way up in the hills of his ranch. Refuses to live with his daughter, refuses to do business. Couldn't care less if the business collapsed and left him without a penny."

"Ha! What's the chances of getting to see the daughter?"

"Linda's kind of . . . you know, a big shot. A tart, mind you, but a big shot, wears furs like her mother used to? Minks and stuff? Think she was the Queen of England! You know, the old man kicked his wife out for wearin' furs."

"Ha!"

"He tried to kick Linda out, too, I guess, but the lawyers and whatnot decided he was crazy. They hate each other, Linda and the old man, but Linda knows the business and is sure out to make a buck. Y'all might get to see her. But we don't want to talk about silly old Linda, now, do we? Y'all still staying in that hotel, what's it called?"

Jucy toyed with the red bobble, the earring that dangled from her right lobe. Palidin noticed that it matched the colour of her long fingernails.

"The Vogue. Yeah, I'm still there."

"Oh, poor boy!"

"It's all right."

The tacos and beer were served, the tacos on a large platter in the center of the table, the beer in large mugs.

Palidin tried one of the tacos, found it very hot, spicy. He washed it down with a generous quaff of beer.

"You know, y'all don't have to be staying in that silly old hotel. I have a spare room." Jucy was ogling now.

"It's all right. Is there something wrong?"

"Not a thing. You're just so handsome, Palidin! You know that? Y'all got a girlfriend back home?"

"Ah . . . Ahem! Not really. I ah . . . "

"I bet you got a whole bunch of them! They're lining up at your door, aren't they?"

"Not exactly, I ah . . . "

"You just make me feel all tingly, honey. I liked you from the moment I set eyes on you! I said, 'Now there's a good looking man!' And when I heard you were all the way down here from Canada, I just couldn't sleep thinking about you being all alone in that old hotel with nobody to talk to. Why don't y'all let me keep y'all company?"

"Oh, I'm ah . . . quite all right, really. You could help me get to see this Linda lady."

"Why, yes! I just might be able to help you, at that! I don't know her that well, mind you, but I know where the ranch is. You know what we could do? Tomorrow's Saturday. We could take a ride out there! You could spend the night with me in my apartment . . . in my spare room, of course. That way, we could get an early start and I could drive us out there first thing in the mornin'. S'posin' we never did get to see her, we'd be out in the country, you'd be seeing Texas and we could maybe stop for a picnic! Oh, it sounds so exciting! That's just what I'll do! I'll pack us a picnic basket!"

"But . . . "

"No buts!"

"But . . . "

"Y'all want to see Miss Linda, don't you?"

"Yes, I certainly do."

"Then you just go back to that old dumpy hotel, pack your bags and check out! Ya hear? I'll pick you up just as soon as I get off work. I'll leave early, say, three o'clock, okay? And to-night I'll show you the town! You are about to get a taste of good old Southern hospitality! José! José! Bring my Canada friend another beer!"

*

When Bert Todder said, "Hello fer fish farts" and laughed, "Tee hee hee, sob snort sniff!" as he always did, leaving people confused about whether he was laughing or crying, everybody who heard the comment laughed heartily. The ha ha ha's could be heard all over Brennen Siding. Because everybody laughed, Lindon Tucker figured he should laugh, too, but he was a little late getting around to it, so that his "yi-yi-yi-yi-yi" seemed very alone and alien amid the afterglow. Lindon Tucker didn't know how to laugh, could never figure out what syllable to use for laughter and had settled on yi-yi-yi-yi-yi as being "good 'nough."

Bert Todder had only one tooth, a yellow incisor that appeared fair in the center of his mouth on his top gum. Lindon Tucker had two teeth missing, his canines, and in a comical sort of way they made him look like a defanged vampire. Perhaps the condition of their teeth embarrassed them a little, because as soon as Bert and Lindon stopped laughing they closed their mouths and remained tight-lipped until the next bit of hilarity came along.

Mildly curious, Dryfly Ramsey watched this little phenomenon for a while, then moved on to watch Dan Brennen. Dan was talking to the Premier and Sparrow, telling them about how rough the road was and that it wouldn't take more than a few loads of gravel to make all the difference in the world. The Premier and Sparrow smiled and listened; Dan was frowning and seemed half angry.

"Strange," thought Dryfly. "I don't think I've ever seen Dan Brennen smile. Maybe he's got bad teeth, too. But a lad would have to smile sometime, s'posin' he had no teeth at all, wouldn't he?"

Dryfly moved on.

Stan Tuney was talking to several Americans who were staying with an outfitter from Doaktown on the Miramichi. With all the conviction of a praying pontiff, he was telling them about a salmon he had caught.

"'Pon me soul to God, yeah, ain't one word a lie, it weighed sixty-two pounds! When he grabbed the hook, he snapped the rod right out of me hands!"

Dryfly could tell that the Americans knew Stan was lying by the way they chuckled and smiled.

"They smile so easy . . . almost without even knowin' it, like it was natural to smile all the time," he thought, then moved to watch Bob Nash having what seemed to be a very serious conversation with Old Cooky Duster. It was a short conversation, and when it was over Bob swung to watch the band play, stood listening with his eyes closed. Bob was not smiling. If anything, he seemed to be on the verge of tears. The general seemed sad, too, but as soon as he walked away to join several other Americans in a nearby group, he smiled, shook hands and was soon talking happily about primary this and political that and how he doubted that Joe Blow had ever seen a field of battle. "No American will elect anybody who never saw action," he said. He seemed dead serious, but there was the smile.

Dryfly was not looking for attention, for someone to talk to. He was simply moving from group to group observing. He could have been a dog, or even a ghost whose presence was felt but not realized. He could have been a social anthropologist studying the difference between the rich and the poor, comparing the people from Brennen Siding with the people from elsewhere.

There was a difference. He was sure of that. "But it's not just money. There's something else. Maybe all these outsiders are different because they've travelled, seen a lotta stuff. No doubt that's why they can smile all the time. Does smilin' mean that yer happy? Does being from somewhere else other than Brennen Siding make you smile? Lillian used to smile all the time. God! She had the most beautiful smile in the whole world! There's something about a smile . . . "

He approached David O'Hara and John Kaston.

"It's a beautiful place," John was saying. "Five bedrooms, two baths, a living room that must be as big as my whole house, a big kitchen."

"Does he come up often?" asked David.

"Comes up every summer with his daughter and again in the fall by himself."

"From Stockbridge, you say?"

"Yes sir."

"That's just down the road from my town, can't be much more than an hour away. Hello, Dryfly! How's it going?"

"Good."

"We were just talking about Bill Wallace." David O'Hara smiled warmly. "I guess you're familiar with that family."

"Yeah . . . we won the hunderd dollars," said Dryfly. "You want half?"

"No, Dryfly. It's all yours. You're a good guide, Dryfly. This has been the most successful fishing trip I've been on in years."

"He'd be a better guide if he'd go to church once in a while," said John.

David smiled again.

"The difference," thought Dryfly. "There's a difference. They smile. All these outsiders *smile* at you. They all seem to have a little flame burning inside them that makes them smile. Whether they are or not, they seem so . . . so *nice*. Lillian smiles all the time — seems so *nice*. I would like to smile right now, but I don't feel like smiling. I'm lonesome for Lillian's smile. I'm lonesome all the time."

"I think the general would have won, if he hadn't fell in the river," said Dryfly.

"Dem's da breaks," said David. "You know, I think I'll get myself a little drink. How about you guys?"

"I don't drink, thanks," said John.

"Ah . . . maybe later," said Dryfly. "I gotta see Shad for a minute."

The three separated.

"Maybe everybody from around here is lonesome all the time," thought Dryfly. "Lonesome for lovers; lonesome for the summer when the winter comes; lonesome for the past, for when they were little kids, or young men and women. We all laughed when Bert Todder cracked his joke about fish farts, and now maybe we're lonesome for the laughter. Brennen Siding is a lonesome place. As soon as ya get old enough to meet someone like Lillian, who smiles and makes ya feel good and happy, ya get lonesome. The guides are lonesome today, because the sports are going away. And when you're lonesome, ya don't smile . . . and when ya stop smiling, you might as well turn out the lights."

Dryfly found Shad down by the river. He was sitting in his canoe and seemed not at all happy.

"He's not smiling," thought Dryfly. "He's from Brennen Siding and he's not smiling. I must smile at him and see what happens."

"G'day, Shad!" said Dryfly, flashing his broken ivories.

"What's wrong with you? Drunk?" asked Shad.

"No . . . not yet. What's wrong with you?"

"You know that half them old bastards won't use the shit house here on the island? I've been paddlin' back and forth across this river more times than a jeezless duck after a smelt run! I ain't even had time to get at the food."

"Not the beans, anyway," said Dryfly, smiling. "Where is Timmy?"

"He's got an old lad over there right now. What're ya doin' down here? Why ain't ya partyin'?"

"I gotta go home for a while. Take me over?"

"What're ya goin' home for?"

"Ah . . . I got this hundred dollars. Thought I'd put it away. Wouldn't want to get drunk and lose it."

Shadrack sighed. "Hop in," he said.

Shad dropped Dryfly off in front of Nutbeam's and, with a "See ya later," headed back to the island. Dryfly watched him paddle away for a few minutes, then headed up over the hill. Nutbeam was splitting wood beside the house, but Dryfly didn't acknowledge him. Instead, he kept on walking as if in a daze, past the house, across the field, over a cedar rail fence and into the woods. Here, he found a path, followed it and came to a brook. He went up the brook until he came to the place where he and Lillian Wallace had had their picnic two summers ago. There was still some snow in the woods, but in the little opening where they had spread their blanket the ground was bare. Dryfly found a rock and sat to think.

A crow cawed, a chickadee sang, a red squirrel chattered, the brook murmured, the breeze whispered in a pine like two Anglicans in a back pew. And Dryfly, perhaps the only alien in the scene, sighed and began to contemplate the worth of a smile.

*

Palidin went up to his room, packed his bag, and with nothing else to do that he could think of, sat on the bed to wait. He figured he had about an hour to kill before Jucy picked him up at three o'clock.

"This is going to be an adventure and a half," he thought. "Maybe I should just get out of here. Either head for home and forget about this fiasco or go to that ranch and try to talk to that Burgess lady myself. Jucy has a car and she knows the country. That's something, anyway."

After a while, he grabbed his bag and left the room, boarded the elevator and headed for the lobby. The cage, which was what he called the elevator, stopped a good four feet above the lobby floor. Palidin had to duck down and climb out.

"It's a bugger," commented the elderly front desk clerk. "Sometimes it works great, other times . . . "

The woman behind the front desk was tall, grey-haired, wrinkled; wore a red satin dress, a pearl necklace and earrings, an identification pin on her lapel that read, "Glory." Palidin thought "Old Glory. She must have been very beautiful when she was younger."

"It's a good thing somebody wasn't getting on the thing," said Palidin.

"You checking out?" asked Glory.

"I guess so," said Palidin. "I might be back, though. I'm sorry that I'm past the checkout time."

"It doesn't matter much, dearie. We've got plenty of rooms, a lot more of them than guests. It gets downright lonesome here sometimes. Are you in a hurry, dearie?"

"Not really. Why?"

"Would you just stand there and keep an eye on the desk while I use the washroom. I don't like to leave it."

"Sure. Take your time. I've got the best part of an hour to kill."

"I'll just be a couple of minutes," said Glory and disappeared into a room that led off from behind the desk.

Palidin waited.

He suddenly got the feeling that somebody was staring at him. He checked the lobby, found it empty. Then he realized what had given him the feeling. Bob Hope was looking at him from the picture on the wall.

"Help!" Bob seemed to be saying. "Get me out of here! I've been in wilder places in Philadelphia!"

Palidin grinned to himself, reached up and removed the picture from the wall, stuffed it in his bag, not knowing that that one swift, unpremeditated movement, that little petty theft was the proverbial straw that broke the camel's back. Bob Hope's autographed picture was the keystone of the Vogue Hotel and Palidin had removed it.

Glory returned. "Thanks, dearie," she said.

"No problem."

"You owe for three nights. Sixty dollars."

Palidin gave her the sixty dollars.

"You say you might be back?"

"Maybe. I don't know for sure. If not, it's been nice knowing you."

"Come again any time, dearie."

"Thanks. See ya."

"Bye."

Palidin left the Vogue and went out in the hot Texas sun to wait for Jucy. He didn't have to wait long. Jucy showed up early. She drove up in a yellow Fairlane convertible.

"You been waitin' long, honey?" she asked.

"Just a few minutes. I figured you might be early."

"Now, ain't that somethin'! We're anxious little devils, aren't we? Get in here beside me! I could just eat you up! I'm takin' you home!"

seven

Brandy Burgess's eyelids hung from their veined, watery balls as if they were too big, had been slit with a razor and still hadn't healed. The blue irises, warmed and softened by their six years in the Texas wilderness and their previous seventy-four years of use, radiated like two tiny planets out over the long, proud nose, across a mile of pasture to alight on the hazy mesa.

Below the nose and the crooked little black mustache, two freckled, bluish lips parted to reveal five thousand dollars worth of teeth. Below that was the exaggerated chin, and below that were the sacs of his throat and neck.

Today, Brandy Burgess was dressed in black — black ten-gallon hat, black kerchief around his neck, black shirt, pants, boots, socks, belt, gun belt and holster. The only thing that Brandy had on that wasn't black was the handle of his Colt .45.

Brandy Burgess sat on a black gelding called Jonah.

"I don't know why," he whispered to himself. "But I smell trouble."

Jonah agreed, snorted and nodded.

"I reckon the marshal will be showin' up any minute. Crafty hombre, the marshal. Ah! There he is, Jonah. I'd know that white mare anywhere. Let's take cover, boy. I ain't hankerin' for a shoot-out just yet. Giddy up!"

Brandy rode Jonah over to a large boulder, dismounted and took cover in its shadow.

"I'm waitin' for ya, lawman!" he yelled. "Eh? Give myself up?" Brandy pulled his .45 from its holster. "Come and get me, you cowardly coyote. Take that."

POW! POW!

Zing!

"Ya missed!"

POW! POW! POW!

"I think I got 'im. Or he's trying to lead me to believe I did. He's played that game before. Can't trust a lawman. What to do, what to do? Prob'ly should try to hightail it out of here. I see his rifle's still on the saddle. Might not be able to reach me with that peashooter of his. And with any luck, he might be wounded, even dead. Well, if he's wounded, he'll rot there before I go get him."

Brandy climbed into the saddle and rode off toward the cottage, the hideout he called Merna's Butt. Jonah galloped for the first hundred yards or so, then slowed to a walk.

Brandy started to sing.

> *I'm as lonesome as a stray on a dark and windy day,*
> *So I'm headin' for Wyoming and it's there I'm gonna*
> *stay.*
> *Gonna ride across the prairie 'neath the western sky*
> *To me darlin' Mary Ellen, yippee ti yi yi.*

About a mile down the dusty trail, he came to a fence post. "Whoa," he said to Jonah.

Jonah stopped immediately and waited while Brandy uncoiled his rope, broadened the noose by twirling it over his head several times and lassoed the post.

"Got 'im!" said Brandy. "First throw. You wait here, boy. I'll brand 'im."

Brandy dismounted, and as he walked toward the post he neatly recoiled his rope. He removed the rope from the post, then, as quick as he possibly could, swung and drew his Colt .45.

"Hold it right there, Billy!" he drawled. "Hands up! You been followin' me, Billy? Train? I'm goin' straight, Billy. Hankerin' to git meself that little ranch outside o' Bella Rosa. Ride on, Billy, before I turn you into a waterin' can. I ain't robbin' no train, I tell you! See ya, Billy."

Brandy walked back to Jonah and climbed into his saddle.

"Let's go, boy. We gotta git this here steer back to the herd."

*

"I wonder if Palidin has that . . . that rich man's smile. Or that American smile? Prob'ly not, him bein' from Brennen Sidin'. Unless he learned it on his travels. Pal's in Texas this very minute, doin' God knows what. Pal's been everywhere — Toronto, Texas, God knows where else. I've never been anywhere. Newcastle's as far as I've been. No wonder a lad don't smile right. If a lad was walkin' down the street in Texas and didn't smile, everyone would prob'ly think him crazy, some kind a backwoods lad. Nutbeam's from Smyrna Mills, Maine, seen lots of stuff, too, no doubt, and look at the smile he has. Smiles enough in one grin to keep two or three people goin' all day.

"Lillian's smile was the best of all — made you tremble with excitement or somethin', love maybe, just to see it. She's prob'ly smilin' at somebody else right now, makin' him feel good. Somebody else will grab that girl sure as hell if I don't do somethin' about it. But what does a lad do? Walkin' around smilin' ain't gonna change things, ain't gonna bring us together. What I need to do is go right down there and get her. I've been settin' on me arse and that's no good. I need to go right down there to the States and ask her to marry me, get a job and make something of myself. Ain't ever gonna get ahead here in this woods. A lad's gotta try. No harm in tryin'."

Dryfly stood and started walking back toward the river. There was a germ of an idea in his young head that he thought might have possibilities.

At the shore, he whistled for Shadrack to come and fetch him, then waited. The picnic had now become a full-scale party with whooping and singing and loud talking all over the place. Dryfly had to whistle three times before Shad heard him and came to get him.

Back on the island, Dryfly approached David O'Hara, couldn't say what he wanted to say, went to the bar and poured himself a stiff drink of scotch, tossed it back, fixed a smile on his face, then approached David again. He took a deep breath, said, "Mr. O'Hara, I need to talk to you."

"Yes, Dryfly. What is it, my man?"

"Oh, ah, I, ah, you, ah . . . didn't I hear you say you lived not too far from Stockbridge?"

"Just up the highway. Nice town, Stockbridge. You know those Cornpoppers aren't too bad after you've had a few drinks."

"Oh, ah, like, do you have to go by it to get home?"

"Yes, right past it. It's just off the turnpike. You'd like Stockbridge. It's a nice little town in the mountains. Good fishing there, too. The Housatonic is right near there. They stock some nice trout in there."

"Well, I was thinkin' I might go."

"Well, you should, Dryfly. You'd like it. You have a girl-friend down there, don't you?"

"Yeah . . . Lillian Wallace. Could I get a ride with you?"

"To Stockbridge?"

"Yeah, tomorrow."

"Well! I ah, well, I, ah, don't know. I mean, I wasn't sure if I was heading straight back. I, ah, had thoughts of maybe doing some fishing in Maine. Ah, I hear Moosehead Lake has some good fishing in it. But well, I don't know, I suppose we could work something out. Does this girl know you're coming?"

"I'm gonna call her tonight."

"Well, I ah . . . "

"Like, if you aren't going straight there, I might be able to find another way, but I just thought . . . "

"No, no. You come with me, Dryfly. You'll enjoy it down there. It'll be good for you. Can you be packed and ready at eight in the morning?"

"Sure can."

"Well, you just got yourself a ride."

Dryfly smiled, this time genuinely.

"Thanks, Mr. O'Hara."

That evening, after the picnic was over, Dryfly hired Shad-rack to drive him into Blackville. Shad waited in the van while Dry entered the only phone booth in the village and dialed Lillian Wallace.

"Hello."

"Hi . . . is Lillian there?"

"Just a moment."

Dryfly waited for Lillian to come to the phone. He couldn't remember ever being more excited in his life.

"Hello." It was Lillian's soft, wonderful voice.

"Hello, Lillian?"

"Yes."

"It's Dryfly."

"Dryfly. How are you? What a surprise! What's the occasion?"

"I just thought I'd call ya. I'm in a phone booth in Blackville."

"How wonderful! How are you?"

"Good. Good. You?"

"Quite well, thanks. I was just about to answer your letter."

"Yeah?"

"My goodness, you did go on in that last one."

"Only because I love you so much."

"How sweet."

"I'm comin' down, Lillian."

"You are?"

"Yep. Tomorrow."

"Tomorrow!"

"Yeah . . . if it's all right."

"Well, I don't know. This is such a surprise."

"Yeah, well, it's a surprise for me, too."

"You know, of course, that I'm just home for the weekend, that I'm off to university again on Monday."

"Oh . . . well, I guess I forgot about that. Where's university?"

"New Haven. Could you come to New Haven?"

"Ah, I don't know. Where's New Haven?"

"Southern Connecticut . . . about a hundred and fifty miles from here. When do you expect to arrive in Stockbridge?"

"I don't know. I'm leavin' in the mornin'."

"Then, you'll be here tomorrow evening. I'm driving to New Haven tomorrow evening. How are you getting here?"

"A sport, David O'Hara."

"Hmm. I need to think things over, Dryfly. Could I call you back in, let's say, an hour?"

"Well, I guess so. I'll just wait here by the phone booth."

Dryfly gave Lillian the number of the phone booth and went back to wait in the van with Shad.

"What'd she say?" asked Shad.

"I don't like it. She's trying to figure somethin' out. I forgot that she was goin' to university. She's off to New Haven tomorrow night."

"Hmm. I think you're crazy, Dryfly."

"Why?"

"She don't want you around."

"Only one way to find out."

"I can't imagine why you'd want to spend all your money goin' to the States, especially with that old sport. How you gonna get around after he drops you off?"

"Don't know. Bus, maybe, whatever . . . "

"How much money you got?'

"Hundred and ten dollars after I give Nutbeam the money for the rifle."

"Hmm . . . I could prob'ly drive you down for that much money, and you'd have wheels while you were there. Maybe I could link up with some of them little hard-bellies down there."

"We wouldn't have much money for two lads."

"Enough for gas, a burger now and again. We could sleep in the van."

"What about school?"

"I need a break. We'll get a map and go, Dry. I always wanted to go somewhere. When she calls back, tell her we'll meet her wherever she wants us to."

"You sure?"

"Sure . . . why not?"

When he heard the telephone ring, Dryfly jumped from the van and ran to answer it.

"I'm here," he said.

"Boy! I've been a busy girl, but I think I have something worked out. I'm staying in an apartment with a friend of mine. I gave her a call and she said it would be okay if you stayed with us . . . on the sofa, of course. If you can get the guy to drop you off at the Red Lion Inn, I'll be waiting for you there. I'll have dinner there tomorrow evening and just hang around and wait."

"No need to . . . plans have changed. Shad's bringing me in his van. We'll meet you in New Haven."

"Shad? Oh . . . Dryfly, I don't know if I can put *two* guys up."

"You won't have to. Shad said he'd stay in the van."

"How long you plannin' on staying?"

"I don't know . . . a week maybe."

"Shad's gonna stay in the van for a week?"

"He has a mattress in the back."

"I love you, Dryfly."

"Oh, God!"

"What?"

"You just made me the happiest man in the whole world."

"Dryfly?"

"Yeah?"

"Shad can sleep on the sofa."

"Ha! The van's good enough for him. How do we get there?"

*

When Jucy unlocked her door and opened it to reveal her lush apartment, Palidin couldn't believe his eyes. There were white carpets and white furniture that Palidin thought it quite possible to get lost in; there were pink drapes that covered but a little of the massive windows that gave the apartment a magnificent view of the city; there were books and valuable paintings and prints, interesting lamps and vases. He could see the dining room with its ceiling-to-floor china cabinet, its big oval mahogany table that you could see yourself in and upon which sat a silver candelabra.

Palidin whistled as he stepped in and toed off his shoes.

"I didn't know they made apartments like this. This must cost you a fortune. You have this whole place to yourself?"

"Well, a poor girl can't be living in a little old dive, now, can she? Make yourself comfy, honey, and I'll pour us a nice drink."

"You have a bar, too!"

"Of course, doll. A girl can't entertain without a bar, can she? What would you like? You sit and I'll fix us a nice Remy Martin . . . or how about a nice martini? Yes, a martini would be perfect." Jucy kicked off her high-heeled shoes and headed for the bar.

Palidin romped about for a few moments before sitting. He looked in on a large bathroom that he figured was nearly as big as his whole apartment in Toronto; he glanced into the bedroom and noticed that there was a king-sized water bed and mirrors to no end. There was another bedroom, too, not quite so luxurious as the first one, yet as nice as anything Palidin had ever seen.

"I can't believe you stay here by yourself," he commented.

"Well, I have the occasional friend over, but mostly I stay alone. Do you like olives or a twist?"

"Olives, please."

Palidin sat on the big, soft, white sofa. In front of him sat a coffee table with a display of artifacts beneath its glass top.

"You into archeology?" he asked.

"Who, me? Not me. Those awful things belonged to . . . Tony, I believe. He left them here. You want them?"

"No, no, I was just curious."

"Darn! Now look what stupid little old me did. Over-poured. Oh, well, I guess I'll just have to use the bigger glasses. Y'all drink martinis in Canada?"

"Occasionally." Palidin could hear the ice tinkling as Jucy stirred the martinis.

"Why don't you put some music on, honey?"

Palidin went to the stereo and fingered through the albums. "What would you like to hear?" he asked.

"Oh . . . how about Bill Monroe?"

"Sure thing," said Palidin and grinned to himself. "No way she pays for this place," he thought.

In a minute, Bill Monroe was singing "I Saw Her Little Footprints in the Snow," and Jucy was placing a gigantic martini on the table in front of Palidin. She sat close beside him, put her hand on his leg, stared into his eyes and sipped her drink.

Palidin picked up his drink, gestured "cheers," sipped, sat his glass down and moved slightly away from her.

"So, how long have you been working for West Wind Sports?" he asked.

"Huh?"

"How long you been working for . . . "

"Oh, about nine years. You have the most incredible eyes . . . do you like me, Palidin?"

"Ah, yes . . . very much. You know, this is the nicest apartment I've ever been in."

"Would you like to see more of it? I could show you the bedroom. It has an incredible view. Tee hee hee . . . umm . . . I love martinis . . . did you see?"

"See what?"

"The mirrors in the bedroom? The ones on the ceiling? Tee hee! I call them my rear view mirrors. Don't you think that's silly?"

"Huh? Oh! Yeah! That's very good! Rear view mirrors . . . what time is it? We should plan what we're doing tonight."

"Plan? Why don't we just let it happen? You're a man, I'm a woman. I'm sure we'll manage to, shall we say, get into things."

Jucy moved closer to Palidin. She set her drink down and put her arms around him, blew into his ear.

"Ha!" Palidin shivered, stood.

"What's the matter?"

Palidin stared dreamily, curiously at Jucy. She could not tell from his expression whether he was about to laugh or cry.

"Why are you looking at me like that?" she asked.

"Like what?"

"I don't know . . . you just seem strange. Come and sit down, silly boy!"

"Jucy, have you ever . . . have you ever thought that there might be a star for every person? Have you ever thought that maybe everything — life, death, existence . . . have you ever thought that it might all be very simple?"

"I don't bother my head with that silly old stuff, honey."

"But you might know . . . you might know all there is to know right up there in your head, and it might be too simple for words, it might be beyond words. You might not even have to think about it, let alone discuss it. And if that's the case, a bee or a tree could have that same knowledge. The sperm, the fetus . . . I believe that we're all a part of the whole . . . that we all exist spiritually . . . either inside or outside material bodies; that when all spirits are within bodies, God will be alive and well and living on Earth, here with us; and so will you, and so will I and so will everyone who ever existed, for it is impossible not to exist. Do you believe that God will choose a beautiful body to occupy? — I'm sorry, Jucy. Let's drink to you, to this luxury, for we may not always have it. I mean, we didn't *always* have it. Cheers! What was it Khayyam said . . . 'Why fret if today be sweet?' Cheers!"

Jucy smiled, feeling very satisfied. She drank, to what she wasn't sure. "You don't want to make love to me, do you?"

"It doesn't matter if we make love. It matters only that we love."

*

Meanwhile, back at Merna's Butt, Brandy Burgess removed the saddle from Jonah's back, then put him in the stable next to Star, his white Arabian mare. He watered and fed both horses some oats, and because Jonah had performed exceptionally well throughout the afternoon Brandy rewarded him with a couple of carrots.

"A carrot a day keeps you keen, lean and mean," said Brandy, scratching and patting Jonah's neck. He grinned with a boyish innocence at the munching and crunching, the sound of Jonah eating carrots.

Satisfied the horses were well attended to, Brandy left the stable and crossed the yard to the water trough beside his little bent and unkempt shack. Here, he removed his hat, splashed some water on his face and hair, spit, sputtered, washed and drank, then entered through the squeaky, latchless door of the shack in search of a towel. He found one hanging over the rusty little barrel-like stove and dried himself off.

He was feeling a bit hungry, but his plans did not include eating so early in the evening. Brandy liked feeling a bit hungry. Feeling hungry, in his opinion, was a healthy feeling.

"I'll read for a while, have a snooze and then eat," he thought, then put on his wire-rimmed glasses, grabbed his ragged, dog-eared copy of *Riders of the Purple Sage* and went to his cot.

"Oh! My back," he grumbled as he sat and bent to remove his boots. "I'll not get these damned things off today. Not as young as I used to be. Maybe I'll not ride the range tomorrow, give my back a break. Either that or I'll have to cut these boots off with my Bowie."

He relaxed, opened his book, began to read, and for an hour the one room, the shack where multi-millionaire Brandy Burgess lived would have been as quiet as a tomb if it hadn't been for the fly that buzzed monotonously on the smoke-stained and smeared little window.

Then, Brandy spoke aloud.

"Yeah, ahuh. I'm having my nap, now, like a good buckaroo. Wouldn't mind getting tucked in. Getting tucked in is not easy to come by. Say your prayers, say your prayers. Oh God, I'm old. Burnin' the candle at both ends. Ya gotta. Ain't no other way. That way you die with your boots on. No doubt I'll die with my boots on. Couldn't get 'em off with a crowbar. I'm tired, God."

Brandy removed his glasses, turned over and went to sleep.

The little shack was filled with the sounds of the fly buzzing and Brandy snoring — the fly in desperation and panic, Brandy in child-like peace. For two hours he slept, then awoke, sat up, stretched, scratched and yawned. He stood, went to the window and noticed that the sun had already dipped behind the mesa, the western horizon ablaze with oranges and reds. He also saw the fly.

"Need to get out, do you, Mr. Fly? Well, permit me the honour. I have the key to your glass calaboose, hombre." He opened the window and set the fly free.

"Now," he said. "It's time to eat."

He stuffed a can of beans, a couple of biscuits, a table-spoon and a small frying pan into a canvas bag, grabbed his canteen, left the shack, filled the canteen at the water trough and headed out. He walked across the rolling landscape for an hour, came to a clump of trees and set his bag down beside the biggest one of all, the one he called the Hanging Tree.

For the next ten minutes he gathered dry sticks. Then, he lit a small fire. He opened the beans with his Bowie knife, dumped them into the frying pan and held the pan over the flames until they began to bubble. Then he spooned them into his mouth straight from the frying pan. When the beans were gone, he soaked up the remaining sauce with the biscuits and ate them as sort of a dessert.

Finished, he sat with his back against the Hanging Tree and sipped water from the canteen.

The sun had completely vanished, and a half-moon was sailing through a wisp of clouds in the north. If he had been facing southeast, he would have seen the yellow glow of San Antonio sixty or seventy miles away, but as long as he looked northward, there was only the moon and the stars and the dew-laden Texas plains.

With his tummy full, his thirst quenched, Brandy sighed contentedly.

"Let me see. They're probably watching their televisions. What's it called? Leave it to . . . Otter? Weasel? Beaver? Trying to hear Beaver's wisdom over the yak, yak, yak of their teen-age daughters on the telephone. Drinking beer, as much of it as they can before their brat sons drink it all, their feet up on the fat asses of their wives. Smelling their fingers, eating wienies, smoking Pall Malls. Polishing up their Chevies. Mowing down the few wild flowers they have left. Inventorying their assets . . . a house, a car, a paved driveway, a sit-on lawn mower, maybe even a sit-on vacuum cleaner, a fur coat, velvet artwork and a freezer full of french fries, fish sticks wrapped in aluminum foil and a twelve-year-old pound of elk-burger at the very bot-tom. Going to the movies? The shopping mall? Playing bingo? Shooting grouse, deer, and my brother, the Texas red wolf?"

Brandy Burgess wasn't sure whether he was listing all the things that money could buy, or wondering what the poor people were doing. It didn't matter, for every night he'd sit beneath the Hanging Tree, eat beans and think about things. It was a ritual. It didn't matter whether he started off his thoughts with television, as he had done this night, or girls, jet planes, going to the moon, or cowboy songs, it always ended in the same way. His thoughts always ended with "my brother, the Texas red wolf."

The Hanging Tree grew from a knoll from which you could see for miles and miles in every direction. If you faced north, you could see all the way to the stark, blue phantoms in the distance, the mesas. If you looked east, west or south, your eyes would behold a vast, sparsely-grassed plain, but in the distance, in the light of day, if you looked carefully, you would see the silos of the approaching civilization, and at night, the contaminated glow of San Antonio. Brandy Burgess knew that the only reason this land was not cultivated and turned into rich, green pastures for beef cattle was because he owned it. He had had it in mind to buy up all the ranches for miles around and give it back to nature, to give it back to his brother, the Texas red wolf. He purchased six of them, tore down the houses, barns, bunkhouses, corrals and silos, and cleaned up to look as if they had never existed. The six ranches had cost him six million dollars, and he had planned to spend his remaining millions doing the same thing.

"You must be crazy," said his wife and daughter. "If you continue to spend money like you're doing, investing with no return, the business will collapse."

"Screw the business!" said Brandy and bought another ranch, a big three-million-dollar one.

"Screw you!" said his wife and daughter and tried to have him declared old, senile, incapable, crazy.

Brandy took two of his horses and rode north to Merna's Butt, to the only place on Earth where he could hear his brother, the Texas red wolf. Every night, he'd go to the Hanging Tree and listen to him bay and howl and bark.

Brandy Burgess was listening now, but he was not hearing

his brother. Instead, a jet crossed the sky from west to east, making more noise than a thousand wolves, a chalk line through the stars. It spurred deep melancholy into the heart of Brandy Burgess.

Brandy Burgess hadn't heard his brother for over a year and knew deep in his heart that he would never hear him again.

eight

Dryfly showed up at the Cabbage Island Salmon Club at eight o'clock in the morning and told David O'Hara about the change in plans. David pretended to be disappointed, but Dryfly could tell that he was actually quite relieved.

"You're a good guide, Dryfly. Hope to see you next year."

"Yeah, I'll be around. Ever been to New Haven?"

"Yes. Many times."

"Big place?"

"Not so big, but you're getting close to the Big Apple when you're down there. It's not the safest city to wander around in at night. You'll be all right."

"Hope so. Well, I'll be seeing ya."

"Yeah. Oh, Dryfly, I guess I better give you a tip."

"You don't have to . . . "

"No, I insist! You're the best guide I ever had. This was the first year that I actually enjoyed myself up here. Here you go, buy your girl dinner in New Haven."

David O'Hara handed Dryfly an American twenty-dollar bill.

"Thanks," said Dryfly

"My pleasure. See you next year."

"Yeah. Take 'er easy."

Dryfly headed home to wait for Shad. When he got there, Nutbeam, Shirley and Sally were breakfasting in the kitchen.

"Better eat something before you go," said Nutbeam. "You got a long trail ahead of ya."

"I had a piece of molasses cake earlier, before you got up."

"Are you gonna be anywhere near Palidin?" asked Shirley.

"I don't think so."

"Well, if ya see him, bring 'im home with ya. Surely to God, he kin find something to do around here without hangin' around with a bunch o' cowboys in Texas."

"I don't think New Haven, Connecticut, is anywhere near Texas," said Dryfly.

"It's in the States, ain't it?"

"The States is a big place," said Nutbeam. "Big as Canada, almost." Nutbeam lifted his head as if he were listening for something. "Here comes Shad," he said.

Thirty seconds later, Shad knocked on the door.

It never ceased to amaze Dryfly how well Nutbeam could hear.

"Come in, Shad," said Nutbeam.

Shad entered.

"Ready, Dry?"

"Yeah. Where'd you leave the van, on the other side of the river?"

"Yeah. Should've made plans to meet over there, saved time. How's she goin', Nutbeam, old dog?"

"The choicest. You boys look after yourselves down there. You know, you'll be going right by Smyrna Mills. You could stay there with my friends, if ya needed to."

"You ain't got no friends in Smyrna Mills," said Shirley.

"Yeah, I know, but they could."

"That's all right, Nut. We'll be okay. Well, Dry, let's hit the road."

"Yeah. We're off."

"Ya got enough money?"

"I think so."

"Clean clothes?"

"Yeah."

"You'll only be a few days?"

"No more than a week."

"And ya won't drive too fast?"

"Just the limit."

"And don't get drunk and spend all your money foolish."

"We won't."

"God, I wish you lads would git yer hair cut."

"Mom, we gotta go."

"What are them people gonna think o' you, way down there with long hair?"

Dryfly kissed Shirley on the cheek. "See ya, Mom. We'll be back in less than a week."

"Well, you lads be good boys, and if ya see Palidin . . . "

"I know, we'll bring 'im home."

As Shadrack and Dryfly walked over the hill, down the shore and across the bridge to the van, everyone in Brennen Siding was either out front waving or peeking out their windows.

"That's the last we'll see of them lads," said Bert Todder to himself. "They'll see the city lights and that'll be it."

"Oh yeah, yeah, yeah. Headin' way down to the States," said Lindon Tucker. "Yes sir, takin' off, they are. Think I might go way over to Fredericton again this fall. Lay right back and take 'er easy, yeah."

"May God be their road map," said John Kaston.

"I could've been an American one time," said Stan Tuney. "All I had to do was go to Maine and pick potatoes."

"Bless us and save us, I never thought I'd see the day that Dryfly Ramsey would ever leave the river," said Helen MacDonald.

"They'll never be the same," said Bob Nash to Rita.

"Poor little Shad," said Rita.

Dan Brennen watched them going, but said nothing. Dan didn't like the fact that they were leaving. "When they come back," he thought, "they'll know something I don't."

So, down the road they went.

In the next ten hours they would see their first city, Fredericton; their first four-lane highway, Interstate 95; their first mountain, Mount Katahdin; their first glimpse of the Atlantic Ocean at Portland; their first skyscraper, shopping mall, mourning dove and green grass in April.

And Bob Nash was right. They would never be the same.

*

The next morning, Jucy maneuvered her yellow Fairlane convertible west on Interstate 10 toward the Burgess Ranch. Palidin sat beside her, his attention fixed on the massive ranches rolling by. He saw trees he'd never seen before, mountains in the distance, and here and there what he took to be oil wells.

And then there were fewer trees, fewer ranches, fewer everything. Then Jucy took an exit, drove up a dirt road for several miles until they came to a sign that read, "The Burgess Ranch." In the distance Palidin could see a large home and several other buildings. Jucy drove down the driveway and pulled up beside the house.

As they got out of the car, Palidin noticed an elderly black man watching them, leaning on his dung-fork handle, an unlit stub of a cigar protruding from his big lips.

Palidin nodded a greeting.

"Howdy, y'all," said the man. "Y'all lookin' fo' somethin'?"

"Yes," said Palidin. "I need to see Miss Linda Burgess."

"What yo wan' with Miss Linda?"

"Ah . . . business. Is she at home?"

"Ain' home. Done gone to Ne' Yawk. Won' be back till don' know when."

"Shit!"

"Well, that's that, honey!" said Jucy. "Let's you and me go somewhere quiet and have our picnic. I swear I could eat a foot-long salami!"

Palidin ignored her. "And you don't know when she'll be back?" he asked.

"Nobody knows dat, not even Miss Burgess herself."

"How about Mr. Burgess?"

"Ole Brandy? No ole Brandy here. Him livin' a day's ride from here at Merna's Butt. He don' wanna see no one, nuther. Who yo, anyway?"

"My name is Palidin Ramsey. It's very important that I talk to a Burgess. Merna's Butt. Can we drive there?"

"Not unless you's drivin' a hoss. That shiny car ain' gonna git ya thar, kin tell yo dat mech. Ole Brandy wouldn' talk to yo, anyway. Him talk to me sometimes, but he ain' likely to talk to no one else. Him don' like bein' disturbed."

Disappointed, Palidin sighed. "I'd sure like to try and talk to him, at least," he said.

"Well, I reckon you could ride on up thar and try, but I don't reckon y'all know what yer in fer."

"Aw, c'mon, Palidin, honey. I'm hungry."

"How could I ride to a . . . up there? I mean, where could I rent a horse?"

"Aw, honey. You don't want to ride no old pony for no reason at all other than to see a silly old man who's crazier than the birds. C'mon and have our picnic."

"Yo cain' ren' no hoss, but I reckon yo could have Bornice for a day or two," said the old man, smiling.

"Bernice?"

"Bornice, ma mule. She right thar in the barn. All ya'd have to do is saddle 'er up. That's if ya don't mind ridin' a mule."

"You say a day's ride from here?"

"'Bout that, s'long's Bornice don' git contrary."

"Could the mule carry both Jucy and myself?"

The black man chuckled at the name Jucy.

"I ain't ridin' no old mule!" said Jucy. "If you're gonna go ridin' 'cross the dusty old ranch, you're gonna do it alone."

"We could picnic out there . . . "

"We can picnic here, too. C'mon, honey. Don't ruin our nice plans."

"My plans are to see Brandy Burgess," said Palidin, softly.

Jucy got back in the car and slammed the door. "Then do it alone! I'm headin' back to town."

"I'll see you when I get back," said Palidin.

"Maybe you will and maybe you won't!" said Jucy haughtily and started the engine.

"Thanks," said Palidin.

"Yeah," said Jucy and drove off, tires spinning up the dust.

"So, where's that mule?" asked Palidin.

"Yo givin' up a mighty purdy gal fo' a mule," said the old man.

"What's your name?" asked Palidin.

"Name's Cav. Folly me. I'll ready Bornice."

Palidin followed Cav into the barn and up to a stall where stood a floppy-eared, grey-faced old mule. It was munching on some alfalfa and seemed hardly to notice that the two humans had entered her stall.

"She's older'n you, mos' likely, but she be the best."

Palidin noticed that there were no other animals in the barn.

"I thought a ranch like this would have a whole bunch of horses," he commented.

"Oh, we got 'em, thirty, forty o' dem, some bein' ridden, some in the corral. Ole Bornice here is ma own personal mule. She like to walk backward sometimes, but she the bes'. You ever ride a mule?"

"Never rode anything. Backward?"

"Jis' now and agin. Does as she's tol', mostly. Won' even have to tether 'er when ya bed down fer de night."

"Bed down?"

"Tol' ya t'was a day's ride. You ain' got a day, and you don' know the trail good 'nough to see by night. You'll be bedrollin' it, sho as ma name's Cav. There's a bedroll right on the saddle. Reckon you gonna be wantin' grub, too. You saddle ole Bornice, and I'll fetch you some grub from Beatrix in the kitchen."

"Ah, Cav?"

"Yes, suh?"

"I don't know how to saddle a mule."

"Hee, hee, hee, hee, hee! Now, ain' you a city slicker. Don' know how to saddle a mule!"

"I told you, I've never ridden a horse."

"Well, don' fret none. Cav'll lorn ya."

Ten minutes later when Palidin headed north down a dusty trail, he thought, "Now, there's Southern hospitality." He did not know that Cav was Brandy's only link to the outside world. This was Saturday, and every Saturday it was Cav's chore to ride to Merna's Butt with beans, whiskey, flour, clean clothes and any other things that Brandy might need. Palidin was carrying that parcel as he rode north. He was saving Cav a very long and tiring ride.

"You'll git thar, s'long's Bornice be good. Jes stay on that trail till ya come to a little shack and barn. That'll be Merna's Butt," Cav had told him. "If ole Brandy's dressed in white, you'll not git in no trouble. If him dressed in black, ya's best take cover fer a spell, yell at 'im, tell 'im yer Sundance, or Billy the Kid."

Palidin had no trouble following the trail. He followed it

all through the hot afternoon and evening, stopping only once to stretch his legs, have a snack and drink from the canteen Cav had provided. The water in the canteen was warm and smelled, the poorest water Palidin had ever sipped.

When the sun went down with a blazing farewell, Palidin dismounted and removed the saddle from Bornice. She immediately began to eat the sparse grass that grew seemingly everywhere.

"There's no trees around," he thought. "That means no firewood. It's hotter than hell, anyway. Won't need a fire."

The cook, Beatrix, had packed him a can of sardines, six hard-boiled eggs in a plastic jar, a small bottle of baby dill pickles and some biscuits. Palidin had eaten a third of it along the trail. He now ate another third of it and saved the rest for tomorrow. By the time he finished, the stars were beginning to reveal themselves, and it was beginning to cool down a bit, so he wrapped himself in his bedroll and lay down using Bornice's saddle for a pillow.

A coyote mournfully beckoned the moon.

"Just like in the movies," thought Palidin. "But I wish I had a fire. It's getting chilly out here. Hope old Bernice, or Bornice, don't run off. Ha! I bet a Texas Ranger slept right in this same spot. This is probably a waste of time and energy, but at least I'm seeing what I wanted to see in Texas." Palidin yawned and wrapped his blanket tighter about him, covered up his head.

"Smells like horse shit," he thought. "Ha! The romantic life of a cowboy . . . a cowboy without a campfire." Palidin uncovered his head again, gazed at the stars. "The Texas stars. They're the same old stars. The same stars that shine on the Dungarvon. The good old haunted Dungarvon. The same stars that shine on Mom and Sally. Sally . . . where will she go? She'll have to go one day. She'll have to pack up her childhood dreams and fantasies — the barren, the river, the wisdom, the history, the culture — everything. Pack them in a little chest of memories and walk away. And if she's wise, she'll carry them with her, for such a chest of valuables cannot be found anywhere else. Ha! Hello for authenticity, individuality! I hope Dryfly has the wisdom to hold onto his heritage.

Hold onto a heritage like that, and you can cross a river on a marble slab. Assume any other semblance and the world will smile, perhaps, but pass you by."

The coyote howled once again.

Paladin, Paladin, where do you roam?
Paladin, Paladin, far far from home.

Palidin's voice sounded so forlorn in the cold night that he could very well have been mistaken for a singing phantom by the roadside.

*

Four-fifty-seven Enfield street was a three-storey red brick townhouse. It had a lawn (rare in that part of New Haven), a back yard with a swimming pool, several ancient oaks and maples, a paved driveway and a parking space big enough for three cars. Charles and Noreen Du Pont lived on the ground floor with their cat Tootsy, Lillian Wallace and her friend Janice occupied the second floor, and Archibald Vincent Cole, the third.

When Shadrack and Dryfly pulled into the driveway of 457 Enfield Street, Dryfly was beside himself. It seemed unreal that he could be so close to Lillian Wallace, that he was actually going to see her in her own environment. Lillian Wallace's environment had been a mystery to him ever since he first met her.

Now he was here, and his heart pounded with excitement and anticipation.

Shad, too, was excited. Dryfly had told him that Lillian was sharing an apartment with a friend. "If she's anything like Lillian, she's a good looker," thought Shad. "This is gonna be one good little holiday. Dry and me way down here with two gorgeous chicks. S'pose we ain't gonna have none too good a time! Couldn't be better! Look out America!"

They grabbed their bags, climbed the stairs and knocked on Lillian's door. Shadrack stood behind Dryfly as they waited.

The door opened and there she was — golden hair, blue eyes and a smile to die for.

The word "Dryfly" escaped her pretty lips, and before Dryfly could say a word he was being hugged and hugged and hugged.

"Oh! I'm so glad you're here," she whispered.

A muffled, "You smell so good," came from Dryfly.

While they hugged, Lillian's friend Janice Lynch came to the door to meet the boys.

She was a tall girl, taller than Lillian, taller than Shadrack, taller than Dryfly, taller than most men — about six-six, Shad reckoned, if you included the orange Afro hair that bushed some twelve inches in all directions from her head. Shad had never seen such a tall woman or so much hair on one person. Shad noticed that her smile was pretty enough, but her skin had a middle-aged softness about it and was very white; she had a mole the size of a dime on her right cheek.

Shad was standing in the shadows of the outdoors and Janice had to squint past Lillian and Dryfly to get a better look at him.

"You must be Shadrack," she said. Her voice was deep and loud.

Lillian withdrew from Dryfly's embrace.

"Yes," she said, smiling. "Come in, Shadrack. Janice, this is my friend Dryfly and this is Shadrack, down here all the way from Canada."

"Hello, Shadrack," she droned and took Shad's hand in a mighty grasp that nearly put him to his knees. "I heard a lot about you. Lillian was right, you are red-haired and freckled. And Dryfly, I thought I'd never get to look at you. Well, just don't stand there all night, come in, come in!"

Shadrack and Dryfly were led into a living room with old but fairly comfortable-looking furniture — a large red sofa and chair, cushions strewn about on a worn Persian rug, a coffee table cluttered with textbooks, paper, pens, a couple of packs of Lucky Strikes, drinking glasses and a half-empty bottle of pink bubbly; there were end tables that were equally cluttered, an old grandfather clock and a bunch of monkey-tail artwork, a lava lamp and a stereo system that must have cost thousands of dollars. A stack of albums three feet high stood beside the stereo. But what dominated the room and what caught the eye of both Shadrack and Dryfly most of all was the beautiful and massive Steinway piano in the corner.

Dryfly sat on the sofa beside Lillian, Shad took the chair and Janice sat on a cushion on the floor.

"I expected you earlier," said Lillian.

"We got lost. Seven times," said Dryfly. "Mostly here in the city."

"So, what do you boys do?" asked Janice.

"Ah, I've been guiding," said Dryfly.

"Not too much lately," said Shad. "Still in school."

"I'm skipping classes tomorrow," said Lillian, looking at Dryfly. "We can spend the whole day together."

"Me, too," boomed Janice, looking at Shad.

Shad swallowed, grinned at Dryfly. "Good, good, good," he said.

"Oh, I'm so glad you came down," said Lillian, taking Dryfly's hand. "I missed you so much!"

"I missed you, too," said Dryfly.

"C'mon, Shadrack," said Janice, standing. "Let's pour some drinks. I have a bottle of bourbon that I'd like to see the bottom of."

Janice led Shad into a kitchen with a squeaky tiled floor, an ancient fridge that hummed loudly in B flat, pink cupboards, a chrome table and chairs and an aquarium with what Shad took to be a leech stuck to the inside of the glass.

The bottle of bourbon that Janice had referred to was gigantic, a hundred and thirty-three ounces.

"A Texas mickey," said Janice, picking it up. "Should do the trick. How long you down for?"

"It's very big," said Shad and thought, "Everything is very big."

"Ah, a few days, maybe. I'm not sure. It's up to Dryfly."

Janice got some glasses from the cupboard, ice from the fridge, and started pouring the drinks with a generosity that Shad could only grin at.

"You're in school," she said. "College? University?"

"Ah . . . Blackville High . . . grade eleven."

"Jesus! You're old enough to be teaching in the place."

"Ah . . . I quit one time, lost a few years."

"I like a man who knows what he's doing. Most of the scum around here quit and never go back. You're cute, you know that? Me? I'm an anesthesiologist. You want dope, I got it. Is it cold where you're from?"

"In the winter."

"I was in Canada once. Nova Scotia. Tin whistles and bag-pipes! Lillian tells me you're into music. You're not into tin whistles and bagpipes, are you?"

"Ah, no. I play the banjo."

Janice put the four tall drinks on a tray, then yelled to the living room. "Get decent, you two! You got all night for poontang! It's party time!"

When Shadrack and Janice entered the living room, Dryfly and Lillian were kissing. They parted reluctantly and accepted the drinks from Janice.

The party began.

They drank, got drunk, ate pizza, talked and raved. At three in the morning Janice played the piano. Shad was drunk and very tired from the long drive from Brennen Siding. He fell asleep listening to the beautiful music.

Dryfly, on the other hand, listened and held Lillian, his heart soaring and leaping with the goodness, joy and purity of the moment. When Janice played Chopin's Étude, Op. 10 No. 3, he had never heard anything so beautiful in all his life. The music entered his soul, carried him through his youth. He closed his eyes and envisioned Brennen Siding, the boys in the store, his mother, Nutbeam and Sally. He saw himself on the foot-bridge, the Dungarvon below, a great moon above, the same moon that shone on Lillian Wallace. He opened his eyes to see if it were really true that he was actually there beside her.

He was.

He wept openly.

Lillian held him and whispered, "It's all right, my love . . . it's all right."

But, kissing away his tears, she too began to cry.

Janice stopped abruptly and swung to gaze on the hopeless

lovers. She lit a cigarette, looked at the grandfather clock, thought of time, recognized the value of the moment and in a voice as soft as an angel's said, "Damn you, clock."

She went to her bedroom, returned momentarily, picked Shad up as if he were a little boy and carried him off to bed with her, leaving Lillian to do . . . whatever with Dryfly Ramsey.

Lillian and Dryfly watched Janice carry Shad off with awe. When the reality of what they were watching surfaced, they laughed for five minutes. They laughed until Janice called from the bedroom, "Shut up, you two! I'm a weightlifter, remember?"

"I don't know what come over me," said Dryfly, drying his tears. "The crying, I mean. The music . . . tired and drunk, I guess."

"It's the pain," said Lillian. "The pain of knowing."

"You know, I've never been so . . . somethin', I don't know."

"Your cup runneth over?"

"Yeah."

"Mine too."

"You know, some nights when I'm alone on the bridge, or sittin' by the river, I close my eyes and speak to you as if you were right there beside me. I carry on whole conversations with you."

"And what do we talk about?"

"Don't you know? I mean, am I not really talking to you?"

"Well, let's see. We say I love you a whole bunch."

"Yes . . . and we always hug, and you always kiss me with your cool lips . . . like this . . . "

" And then you rise and look tall and handsome, and you say that you don't give a damn about money and material things, that you don't know the meaning of the word security . . . "

"And you say you know no other way of living, that our love is hopelessly wrong. That you love me, but . . . there's always the but."

"Not hopelessly wrong. Hopelessly right and no but."

"I'm not sure if I know what that means."

"It means that we're in love while millions aren't and that we should treasure every moment, painful as they are. I've thought about calling it off, Dryfly, but there's only one thing more painful than loving you from afar, and that's not loving you at all. I don't know how I let this happen to me. I thought I'd grow out of it. I never dreamed that love was such a powerful emotion. I'll always love you, Dryfly Ramsey. Always. And no buts."

"Okay, I'm game. Let's love each other forever."

"We have no choice."

"It was meant to be."

"I have this little poem . . . "

"For me?"

"For you.

> *My field of timothy,*
> *Along the Housatonic,*
> *Is lady-bugged*
> *And buttercupped*
> *In June.*
> *Do red-wing blackbirds*
> *Frequent*
> *The field you know?*
> *Is it wild-strawberried in July?*
> *I'll show you mine . . .*
> *If you'll show me yours."*

"You once told me that you thought I should be a poet," said Dryfly. "Well, I did write one, just because you told me I should. Maybe I wrote it on the same night that you wrote that one. Want to hear it?"

Lillian smiled. "Let's hear it," she said.

> *"God made me what I am.*
> *I can only be me,*
> *A guide on the Miramichi.*
> *If I offend you with my acts,*
> *It's God who has to face the facts."*

"Want to go to bed?"

Dryfly nodded.

Lillian took his hand and led him to her room.

nine

Palidin Ramsey rode into Merna's Butt under a glaring sun. Bornice had been walking backward for an hour and was lathered and drooling, but she knew where she was going and that she would soon be there. Otherwise, she would have said, "You been takin' me fo' a ride! Git off ma back!" Bornice had picked up Cav's accent.

Brandy Burgess was watering Star at the trough when he saw the lone rider backing up the trail and because it was Sunday didn't pay the intrusion much attention, thought it was Cav coming. But as Palidin approached, Brandy soon realized that this was a white man on Cav's mule, and that was a most unusual occurrence. He left Star still drinking at the trough, slipped into the shadows of the stable and drew his gun. He watched Bornice back directly up beside the trough, nod a greeting to Star and begin to drink. He watched the slim man with the long brown hair and blond beard dismount.

"Hands up!" said Brandy Burgess, pulling back the hammer of his revolver.

"Huh?" said Palidin and turned to face the voice.

"Careful how you turn, hombre! Hands up, I say!"

Palidin saw the old man dressed in black, the gun, lifted his arms above his head.

"Now, remove that gun belt," drawled Brandy.

"Ah . . . I don't have a gun belt . . . I ah . . . "

"Shut up! Remove that gun belt, I say!"

"Are you blind? I mean, can't you see? I mean . . . "

"You suggestin' that I'm blind, hombre? I should make you eat those words. Maybe I should git you to do a little dance for me and the boys. What do ya think of that, boys? Should I get this hombre to dance fer us?"

Palidin's mysterious brown eyes scanned the area for the boys. Seeing no one, he thought, "They told me he was crazy, but I didn't think . . . "

Brandy pulled the trigger. BANG! Sand and dust slapped the leg of Palidin's jeans as the bullet hit but a few inches from his right sneaker.

Palidin had never feared anything in his life, but the report of the revolver startled him to such a degree that he nearly fainted.

"Dance, hombre!" shouted Brandy. "When I say dance, you dance!" Brandy fired again. POW!

Palidin jumped.

"Now, that's more like it," crooned Brandy. "I know'd this here dandy could dance, eh boys? What you wantin', dandy?"

Palidin breathed a great sigh, gathered his thoughts. "This has to be Brandy Burgess . . . and he's dressed in black. Cav told me something about saying I was Wyatt Earp or someone, if he was dressed in black.

"My name's Wyatt Earp," said Palidin. "Cav sent me."

"Earp, you say? Ya hear that, boys? It's the marshal. Keep him covered. I'll remove his sidearm." Brandy moved cautiously toward Palidin. When he was close enough, he removed an invisible pistol from an invisible holster at Palidin's side. He looked at the invisible gun, said "Buntline Special. You're Earp all right. Okay, Earp, you jist walk nice and slow toward the camp . . . and no tricks."

Palidin started to walk toward the shack, took but one step when Brandy said, "Hold it!"

Palidin stopped.

"How do I know you ain't carryin' a derringer in your boot?"

"I'm not wearing boots," said Palidin, somewhat amazed at the absurdity of it all.

"Kick off them boots, Earp! Now, I say!"

Palidin toed off his sneakers.

"Good. Now, march!"

Palidin crossed the yard and entered Brandy's shack.

"Now, you sit there by the stove and don't you move. Keep

an eye on him, Sundance, and I'll get the provisions from the mule." Brandy went back outside and untied the bag from Bornice's saddle. Then he led her to the stable, removed the saddle and put her in a stall with some hay and oats. "The bastard rode you too hard. Ha! Backwards!" he affectionately slapped Bornice's rump. "And you were thirsty as hell when you got here. He's a greenhorn, that's fer sure. Wonder what the asshole wants?" On his way back to the shack, he picked up Palidin's sneakers, wondered what he should do with them, decided, and threw them on the roof of the shack.

Shaken, in a state of disbelief and needing desperately to pee, Palidin waited in the shack. Fingering his short blond beard, he eyed the back door and the dirty little window, thinking that he should perhaps try to escape. "My sneakers are in the middle of the yard," he thought. "I'll need something on my feet."

"Keep your eyes peeled for a posse, boys!" Brandy shouted from just outside the door. "I'll question the hostage."

"Hostage?" thought Palidin. "He's holding me hostage?"

Brandy entered the shack, gun in one hand, the bag of provisions in the other. He sat at the table across from Palidin, removed a handkerchief from his pocket and began polishing the barrel, the sights, the pearl handle.

"Seems to me you're in a mess o' trouble, Earp," he said after what seemed like a very long time. "What brings you to Merna's Butt?"

"How do you deal with a crazy man?" Palidin asked himself. "What should I say? The truth? Lie? Play his game? I should've listened to Jucy."

"I . . . I came to take you in," said Palidin. "We're planning on having a hanging in San Antonio, and you're to be at centre stage."

Brandy smiled broadly, nearly chuckled. "This kid's not so stupid," he thought.

When Palidin saw Brandy's little black mustache turn up at the corners, the smile, he saw sanity there. This caused him to make a quick study of the eyes, and he saw sanity there, too. "This old jeezer's playing cowboy," he thought.

"You ain't man enough to take me in," said Brandy. "And I ain't done nothin' wrong that you can prove. Billy robbed that train, not me."

"Yeah, but you gunned down, ah . . . Joe . . . ah, Joe Smith. The whole town saw you do it."

Brandy chuckled. "He drew first," he said. "Help me off with these boots, would ya? I've been wearin' the damned things for three days. Can't get the suckers off." He held his leg up within reach of Palidin. "Take 'em off, but move slow. I still got the gun."

Palidin removed first one boot and then the other. The smell of Brandy's feet nearly made him gag, made his eyes run water. "You sure you only had these boots on for three days?" he asked.

"Ha! I didn't say anything about the socks. Ha! Thanks a million, hombre. How come you rode in here on Cav's mule?"

"I needed to talk to you. Cav loaned me the mule, gave me that stuff for you, and here I am."

"Cav hates that ride up here. Gettin' old, too, I reckon. You talk funny. Where you from?"

"Canada. New Brunswick, Canada."

"New Brunswick . . . I know somebody from New Brunswick . . . Now who was that . . . ?"

Palidin shrugged. "Anyway, I've been in Toronto for the last while."

"Toronto, eh? I used to have a store there."

"Used to?"

"Bah! A long story. What brings you all the way to Texas?"

"I came here to see you. I have something I thought you might be interested in selling in your stores."

Brandy sat back with a jolt, his watery old eyes spat fire; he gritted his teeth. "Selling? Are you talking about selling? You're just another one of them goddamned salesmen, aren't ya?" he growled, then shouted, "Well, you're shit out of luck, asshole!" Brandy Burgess was very disappointed in Palidin. At first, he had liked Palidin, had seen a sparkle in his eye. Not only that, but Palidin had shown that he was capable of playing, and anyone who was capable of playing, really playing, according to Brandy's way of thinking, was special, humane, not governed by society — a rare find. But a salesman? Bah! Out for the buck!

Palidin sensed by the anger and disappointment in Brandy's voice that he had taken the wrong approach, had revealed too much too soon. He decided to backtrack a bit.

"It doesn't matter," he sighed. "It was just an idea I had. You wouldn't have been interested, anyway. So I'll be off, I guess." Palidin stood, made as if to go.

"Go!" snapped Brandy. "Get to hell out of here! Who the hell do you think you are, barging in on a man's privacy! I put up with leeches like you for long enough! Make tracks!"

"I'll saddle up the mule," said Palidin and glanced down at Brandy's feet. "I could do with a breath of fresh air."

"You ain't ridin' that mule no more today! You got 'im all lathered up already! You can walk to wherever you're goin', for all I care, but you ain't ridin' no animal to death!" Brandy put his gun back in his holster and wiped his brow with his handkerchief.

Palidin threw up his hands in resignation. "One fiasco after another," he sighed.

"What?"

"I should have known. You don't care. You made your money."

"Money? What in tarnation do you know about money? What in tarnation do you *want* with money? Do you have it in mind to buy your little wifey a fur coat? Is that it? Maybe she needs another pair of shoes. How many pairs does she have already, fifty? A hundred? A hundred and fifty? It'll never end, you know. A room full of shoes here, half of them made of alligators; a room full of coats there, made from the hides of rodents. Thirty-six pairs of smoked glasses, eight cars, five houses, four dogs that cost more money to groom than most people pay for rent. And when you get all these possessions stored in your heart, you play tennis, golf, polo, hunt foxes and wolves to make more fur coats. Games, games, games. You can't buy your dreams with money."

"You can buy security!" said Palidin, raising his voice for the first time. He thought of Sally. "And an education!"

"Bullshit! How secure you gonna be when you're eighty? Get out of here!"

"You can have a warm house in the winter, food in your cupboard!"

"And sit back and wish you had done the things you wanted to do instead of making money until it was too late to do anything else. Don't you realize that everything's just a game? I can tell you that making money is one game that should be abolished. It's foul! It stinks of greed! When you were a child, what did you want to be?"

"What's that got to do with anything? Childish whims are childish whims!"

"We start as children and we end as children," said Brandy, softly. "Only the aged know that, of course. When I was a child, I wanted so little. . . and I had so much. I didn't know how valuable everything around me was at the time. Can you buy a mother? A father? An imagination capable of flying like a bird, of fighting lions? Bah! You wouldn't know about that. You were brought up with your ear against a radio and your eyes glued to a television! I've seen guys like you, city zombies! I dealt with them every day! A real man, a man with an imagination could wrap every one of you and your kind around his little finger! Fools, the lot of ya, to think that money makes a difference in the man! Money tarnishes the man, the heart, the soul, the imagination, everything — and that's the long and short of it. Now, leave!"

Palidin left the shack, slamming the door behind him. He stepped into the hot, glaring sunlight, zipped down his fly and urinated on the dry ground in front of the shack. He scanned the yard for his sneakers. "Damn!" he swore, zipped up, swung and without knocking opened the door and stepped back into the shack, confronted Brandy once again.

Brandy was changing his clothes, had already removed his black pants and was hauling on a white pair.

"Where's my sneakers?" asked Palidin.

"You back again? What do think this is, a soup kitchen?"

"Where's my sneakers?"

"Go to hell! Find them!" said Brandy and grabbed his gun.

"It might interest you to know that I am not a salesman."

"Ha!"

"I never sold anything more than a salmon in my life!"

"Brat!"

"I was brought up in the woods!" said Palidin. "The Dungarvon woods. A woods that makes your Texas playground look like a kindergarten!"

"Get out of my . . . "

"My playground was the river, the starlit night. The bees, the blackflies, the ants were my friends, that's if they survived the onslaught of DDT that millionaires like you sprayed on them every June!"

"Go to hell!"

"Hell, all right! I followed the trail of the devil, his tracks as real before me as the air I breathed. I could smell him! Don't tell me about hell, about . . . imagination! A child makes do with a great many fantasies, and yes, and even plays with the insects when he has nothing — no father, nothing!"

Palidin was tired, emotional, disappointed and frustrated. He'd been shot at. "I've no time for games!" he continued. "I'm aware of the so-called powerful people and their dreams of conquer and destroy, and I'm familiar with the bourgeoisie standing around in their black turtlenecks and berets, fantasizing greatness! If you're gonna be something, or if you are something — black, white, male, female, gay, a hunchback or blind as the proverbial bat — be it! Don't go through your life pretending you're something you're not! I'm getting out of here. Shoot me if you want, cowboy! But let a man die with his boots on! Now, where's my sneakers?"

"You find them," said Brandy, childishly.

"Oh, God," sighed Palidin.

"I'll give you just one clue."

Palidin shook his head, dismayed.

"They're not in this building."

"God Almighty! Ha! I can't believe this! Tell me you didn't hide my sneakers. No, no, don't tell me. You want me to search, right?"

"Bet ya can't find them."

"I'll find them," sighed Palidin.

"Bet ya can't."

Palidin left the shack, ran out into the yard. Brandy followed him to the door.

"You're gettin' colder! Ha, ha! Colder!"

*

When Shad awoke in Janice's bed, opened his eyes, scanned the room and the sleeping girl beside him, he thought that perhaps this was his dying moment. "I must've been roary-eyed drunk. Feel awful . . . ha! If I'd known I was gonna be this dry in the mornin', I'd have drank more last night . Prob'ly made a big fool of myself, God! I don't remember comin' to bed, takin' my clothes off. Let me see . . . she was playing the piano. That's the last thing I remember. Must have had an extra stiff drink about that time. Must've had quite a few. Still got me shorts on. She don't look too bad asleep like that. Kind of pretty in the face. She must've looked pretty last night, anyway. A tall girl. It's all that curly hair. Wouldn't look so tall without the hair. I don't think we did anything . . . I'd remember something like that, wouldn't I? Great piano player. Played that fancy stuff. I've seen worse . . . smells good . . . a doctor . . . anna-something-or-other . . . prob'ly got lotsa money . . . wonder how she was? Maybe I should get up, get dressed. She'll prob'ly be all over me when she wakes up. Then again . . . if she still looks that good, here in the morning . . . must've told her I own a farm right on the banks of the Miramichi River. That usually does the trick . . . back home, anyway . . . not bad at all, not bad at all, sleeping like that. Dry'll make fun of a lad all the way home, though. But I can handle Dry. And she ain't that bad, really . . . long eyelashes . . . soft-lookin' skin . . . nice and warm . . . wished I could remember. Might've been all right, you know. Maybe I should give her a little nudge, roll over or something . . . wake her up. Better think some more first. It might be just the hangover. Feel like this a lot when I'm hungover. I'll have to hang out with somebody while I'm down here, though. Dry'll want to be with Lillian a lot. I could do worse . . . wonder what time it is? She'd prob'ly not like it if ya woke her up too early. Course, it wouldn't be intentional. Rolling over, snoring really loud, coughing, scratching, stuff like that . . . maybe I just need to use the bathroom. That's prob'ly it. Course, not much fun in using the bathroom . . . and it might not be. Maybe she was really good and I *do* remember, way down deep in my subconscious. Ya never know, it might work that way . . . and what have I got to lose? I'm already here and Dryfly knows it, so does Lillian . . . and she's not that bad, kind of pretty, really . . . gettin' prettier all the time . . . what to do, what to do."

Janice stirred, opened her eyes.

"Good morning. How are you this morning?" Her voice sounded soft, sleepy.

"I'm not sure."

"You passed out."

"Sorry."

"That's okay. I get that a lot."

"Really?"

"I'm not that great anymore, don't practice enough, I guess. I used to be better. You're heavy, you know that?"

"Sorry . . . ah, you didn't think it was that good, eh?"

"I've done better. Did you like it?"

"Ah . . . oh, yeah! It was just great! Ah . . . I was just thinkin' that maybe, ah, you know, maybe we could do it again . . . "

"Sure. Tonight, maybe . . . " Janice stretched and yawned.

"Well, ah, I was sort of thinking about maybe . . . right now . . . "

"Now? It's kind of early, isn't it? What time is it?"

"I don't know. It's bright outside. I'd like it, if you would . . . I mean, ah, it's never too early for that stuff."

"Well . . . I don't know how well I can do it, hungover like this. I'll shower, brush my teeth, see how I feel, okay?"

"Sure . . . I'll wait here, keep the bed warm."

"Ah . . . sure. I'll just be ten minutes or so?"

"Great."

Janice swung out of bed, grabbed a robe and headed for the bedroom door. "Hope I don't wake everyone in the house," she said.

"We won't," said Shad. "We'll take it nice and easy."

"Pretty music again? The old soft pedal?"

"Whatever you say."

"Want to make us some coffee? There's instant in the cupboard."

"Sure . . . I'll have it ready for you by the time you're finished your shower."

Shad waited for a few minutes, then got up, pulled on his pants and went to the kitchen. There, he found the coffee, sugar, cream, filled and plugged in the kettle and waited for it to boil. When the steam spewed from the spout, he found two mugs and made the coffee, sat it on a tray along with the cream and sugar and carried it back to the bedroom. He cleared a place on a somewhat cluttered bureau for the coffee, then removed his pants and got back in bed.

When he heard Janice turn off the shower, his heart accelerated and his breath quickened. "I sure am ready, now," he thought. "I'll have to try and not be too heavy. She's a big girl. I wouldn't have thought she'd find me so heavy. Oh, well . . . "

Then he heard her brushing her teeth, gargling.

"This is gonna be the very best," he thought. "Got 'er made!"

A few minutes later, someone started playing the piano in the living room. Shad listened for a minute.

"That's Janice," he thought. "She'll wake up everyone in the house."

A minute later, he carried the coffee to the living room. He was extremely embarrassed, but he was grateful that his stupidity was his very own secret.

*

When Dryfly awakened to the sound of Janice playing the piano, Lillian Wallace, his princess, the girl of his dreams and fantasies, the love of his life, was in his arms, spooned against him. His heart was on the high end of the seesaw of love.

Cupid had nocked, aimed and spent his arrow with deadly accuracy, had flown about like a frenzied hummingbird placing perpetual moonlight over Dryfly's world, hearts in his eyes, angelic choirs singing "Love Me Tender" in his ears, doves about his head. Aphrodite had paid a visit to Dryfly during the night, too, and had given him dew-laden rose petals from her very own garden. Dryfly shared them with Lillian. Aphrodite had been around only briefly, but Dryfly could still smell her.

Dryfly snuggled up to Lillian and kissed her hair just to make sure he wasn't dreaming.

"I love you," he whispered.

"I love you, too," said Lillian and turned to face him, snuggling into his arms.

Dryfly held her even closer.

"There's something coming between us," she said.

"What?"

"That."

"Oh. Yeah."

The gods had blessed Lillian during the night, as well. Contradictory to her nature, perhaps to her better intentions, she took Dryfly's hand and led him up first one path and then another in search of Ecstasy — Ecstasy, that warm, lilac-scented, life-filled dale in Paradise. Eve stumbled upon it once, stole it from God and gave it to man. Lillian found it now. She recognized it immediately by the throbbing, rhythmical music that came from its depths. She declared it her own, then gave it to Dryfly with love from her heart and soul. They opened and entered, exited and re-entered every door there, explored it completely, left no leaf unturned. Lillian romped about boldly, taking no precautions, giving generously, an attitude transmitted to her by the gods. "Precaution turns Ecstasy into a dull place, reeks of selfishness, suggests greed," they told her. "There's no future in it . . . tonight you must give."

Now they were looking into each other's eyes, holding each other, feeling each other's warmth and passion, remembering their journey down Ecstasy Lane.

They kissed, went sailing off into an emotional cloud of stars and planets; a galaxy here, a quasar there, they transcended the whole universe. They could have been searching for God.

They had little need to search.

They were in love.

God was with them.

*

Brandy Burgess had hidden Palidin's only footwear, his sneakers, and looking for them in every nook and cranny in Merna's Butt after the bizarre and disappointing interview with the old fool was not what Palidin Ramsey considered to be a good time. Frustrated often to the verge of tears, tolerating the farce of Brandy gleefully shouting Palidin's hot or cold position, he searched for half an hour, looked up to the sky to pray to God that He might spare him any further lampoonery — and there they were, like two blue rubber dinghies on the green sea of Brandy's roof.

Palidin stood on a rain barrel and managed to pull himself up onto the roof, sat, donned his sneakers, then climbed back down.

While Brandy watched Palidin search and shouted his estimation of Palidin's position — "You're freezing! You're warmer! You're warm! You're cold!" et cetera — he finished changing his clothes. When Palidin first met him, he had been dressed completely in black. He was now dressed in white and had a star pinned to the chest pocket of his coat.

"Thanks for nothing," said Palidin and started walking in the direction of the Burgess ranch. He figured it would take him two days to get there, and he was determined to get at it and get it over with. He was ready to walk all the way to San Antonio if he had to. So long as there was a bus there that would take him away from Texas and anyone and everyone connected with West Wind Sports, walking seemed like a small price to pay.

"See ya, Sundance!" shouted Brandy. "Good luck. And try to go straight, will ya? I don't want to see you in my clink for a spell, ya hear?"

Palidin had limped along the dusty trail three or four hundred yards when it occurred to him that he didn't have any water with him. "I'll never make it without water," he thought. "I'll have to get my canteen back." Palidin's list of pleasant thoughts did not include the thought of going back and confronting Brandy Burgess for his canteen, but he had no alternative; the sun was very hot, he'd need water. "I'll just go back there, go in the stable, get the canteen off the saddle, fill it at the trough and head out again. If old Brandy wants to play games, I'll just ignore him."

As he walked back to Merna's Butt, Palidin realized just how sore, tired and hungry he was feeling. "This is awful," he thought. "The worst scrape I've ever gotten into. I'll keep the stable between the shack and myself and hopefully old Brandy is in the shack. If I can just sneak in and out without confronting him, that'll be the very best."

He approached the stable and eased his way along one end of it, made it to the corner and peeked around. There was no sign of Brandy anywhere. "So far so good," thought Palidin and made a dash for the stable door, stepped into the cooler shadows within. He breathed a sigh of relief at the fact that the only occupants of the stable that he could see were the two horses and Bornice.

He grabbed the canteen from the saddle, remembered that he still had a dill pickle or two, perhaps even a boiled egg left, and was reaching into the saddlebag to get it when he heard a movement behind him. Palidin froze.

"Now, ain't this a fine howdy-doody," growled Brandy. "Caught ya red-handed."

Palidin sighed and turned to face the sheriff of Merna's Butt.

Brandy, dressed in white, stood with his legs spread, his hand dangling close to his revolver as if he would draw and shoot if Palidin made the slightest move.

"I needed my canteen," said Palidin. "I couldn't walk all the way back to the ranch without my canteen. And see, I had a dill pickle left."

"How do I know you didn't have it in mind to steal my

horses, the saddles, the mule, everything. You ain't got the best of reputations in these parts, Sundance."

"I wasn't stealing anything. I got my pickle and my canteen. I'll just fill it at the trough and I'll be out of your hair. Okay?"

"Yep. You could've been stealing me blind, all right."

"I wasn't stealing!"

"Well, I guess that we'll just have to see what the judge thinks of that."

"Ha!" Palidin couldn't help but laugh.

Brandy drew his gun and pointed it at Palidin.

"What are you gonna do, take me to jail?"

"For a start. And if Judge Pea reckons you guilty of horse stealin', I reckon we'll have us a hangin'. Now, you just walk nice and slow out that door. And get those hands up!" Brandy cocked his revolver.

"Careful with that thing," cautioned Palidin. "I'll do whatever you say."

"You're darn tootin' you'll do as I say! Now, march!"

Brandy marched Palidin across the yard and around the shack. Behind the shack there was a knoll about five feet tall, a tomb-like protuberance with a door on the side of it.

Brandy lifted the heavy latch, opened the door and told Palidin to go in.

"You want me to go in there?" asked Palidin, amazed.

"I ain't whistling Dixie," said Brandy. "Git in!"

"No!" said Palidin. "It's dark in there! There's bugs, rattlesnakes, scorpions, rats, God-knows-what in there! You're crazy!"

"Now, now, Sundance, don't stall now. You'll git a fair trial. Judge Pea never hung a man who had a good alibi, which you ain't got, since I caught ya red-handed."

"I'm not getting in there!"

Brandy pulled the trigger. The bullet hit two inches from Palidin's toe. Palidin was so startled by this that he jumped into the darkness of the tomb. And before he knew it, Brandy had slammed the door shut and fixed the latch in place. Palidin was left standing in darkness — total, except for one tiny crack in the door through which he could see the light of day.

His concern about the snakes, scorpions, rats, et cetera was very real. He did not sit, did not move an inch, just stood there listening to his own heart beating, his own breath.

"There have to be some pretty weird creatures in here," he thought and closed his eyes. He began to think of warm things: summer nights, bees buzzing around on roses and daisies, trout swimming in Tuney brook, butterflies in the Dungarvon swamps. "Relax," he told himself. "My heart is warm, I'm smiling, I am the image of God . . . "

The scorpion that was but a few inches from his feet picked up his warmth, breathed a sigh of relief and continued its hunt; a mouse that had been eating a potato went back to its eating; a spider came out of its hiding place to continue weaving its web.

Palidin thought he could hear the activity. "Good," he thought and opened his eyes to watch the tiny light coming through the crack in the door. It became his friend. He stared at it continuously, watched it change from day yellow to evening red, then to moonlight blue.

It was perhaps ten or eleven o'clock at night before there was a sound, a movement outside the door.

"You in there, Sundance?" came a whisper.

Palidin did not answer.

"Sundance! I've come to break you out."

"Yes, I'm here."

"It's Billy! I've come to break ya out!"

Brandy's voice seemed miles and miles away. To Palidin, even his own voice seemed far off.

"I'm gonna have to pull the door down with my horse!"

"You'll disturb the goodness here."

"What?"

"Don't disturb everything . . . I . . . it's okay. I'm quite all right."

"I have your mule here. Get ready to mount up and ride fast!"

"I'm ready . . . I'm ready."

There were a few scratching sounds, a creak, and then KERTHRASH! The door came off its hinges, went flying.

Brandy had tied a rope to the door and had pulled it off with Jonah.

Palidin snapped out of his trance, dashed from the tomb, which was really the root cellar, climbed onto Bornice's saddle and headed in the direction of the Burgess ranch.

"No, no, you fool!" shouted Brandy, who was dressed in black once again. "Not that way! They'll have a posse waiting for you thataway! Follow me! I've got a plan! Hurry!"

Against his better judgment, Palidin swung the mule and followed Brandy, Billy, or whoever this was, in the direction of the moon.

They rode for a mile or two out across the plains. Then Brandy, who was a considerable distance ahead, pulled Jonah to a halt and waited for Palidin.

Palidin pulled up beside him. "What's the matter?" he asked.

"Here," said Brandy, handing him something. "You're gonna need this."

"What's this? A gun . . . I have no need for a gun."

"You will where we're going!"

"Where are we goin'?"

"I'll tell ya when we git to the Hangin' Tree," said Brandy and rode off.

Palidin strapped on the gun belt and followed.

They rode in a great arc for a while until they came to a knoll in the middle of what Palidin took to be the biggest field he had ever seen. There was a great oak tree on the knoll, and because Brandy pulled up beneath it and dismounted, Palidin assumed it must be the Hanging Tree.

"We'll be safe here for a while," said Brandy. "I'll git a fire started. You must be hungry, Sundance. I brought some grub."

"Food," breathed Palidin. "Yes, I am hungry."

There was a little pile of wood beneath the tree that Brandy had obviously gathered up earlier. He piled some of it in a neat little pyramid and set fire to it. Then he started hurrying around from saddlebag to saddlebag, removed a frying pan from one, a can of beans and biscuits from another; he removed a small bucket, a knife and a spoon from one of Bornice's saddlebags and a bottle from the other, then busied himself opening the can, dumping the beans into the pan and warming them up over the fire. As he waited for the beans to boil, he took a long swig from the bottle and handed it to Palidin.

All evening, Brandy had felt like the proverbial piece of shit. He had lingered behind his shack with every intention of freeing Palidin from the root cellar. All Palidin had to do was whimper, ask, show some sign of discomfort. Brandy couldn't believe Palidin's silence. "What manner of man is he?" Brandy asked himself. "Most men would scream and holler and pound. Hell, he could've kicked that old door down in a minute! But he just stayed there . . . as if . . . as if he enjoyed it in there. Strangest man I ever saw. Weird, peaceful, young. Maybe I went too far. Maybe I'm losing it. I'm tired and every bone in my body aches, but I thought my mind was clear. God, maybe I'm losing it!"

"Here, Sundance," he said. "Wet yer whistle."

Palidin sniffed the bottle. His hungry stomach growled and cringed at the odour of the whiskey. "Don't do this to me," said his stomach.

Palidin drank deeply because the whiskey was real and he was suddenly feeling cold and clammy.

When the beans were ready, Brandy loaded up a plate and handed it to Palidin along with a spoon and a couple of biscuits. Palidin ate like a savage. They were seated with their backs against the Hanging Tree, and it wasn't until they finished the last of the beans that Brandy spoke.

"So you need money," he said. "Money's never been a problem for you and me, Sundance. I'll git you money. Here, have another drink."

"You have a bucket. Aren't you gonna make some coffee?"

"Up to you, whiskey or coffee. Don't matter to me."

Palidin took a drink of the whiskey.

"That sheriff is gonna be madder than a pissed-on hornets' nest when he finds out I sprung ya, Sundance."

"Oh, God!" breathed Palidin. "I feel so sorry for you."

"Don't feel sorry. It's not the first time I've been in trouble with the law."

Palidin closed his eyes and shook his head with dismay.

"The way I reckon it, you need money and you need it bad," said Brandy. "I don't know what trouble you got yerself into besides horse rustlin' and I don't care, but you and me have been ridin' together for a long time, and I'm a man who sticks by his sidekick. Now, why don't you tell me what it is you're needin'."

"Is this just another game, or are you ready to talk business?" asked Palidin.

"Business *is* a game," said Brandy. "And it's clear to me you ain't much of a hand at playin' it. You go to Brandy Burgess for money, then you have to expect to play Brandy Burgess's game. What you sellin'?"

Palidin was so tired that he doubted he could gather up enough energy to talk, but what else had he to do out here under a hanging tree with a crazy man. He drank once more from the whiskey bottle and handed it to Brandy.

"No, Sundance, that's for you. You keep it. That stuff will kill ya."

"It'll give you energy. I need energy."

"Beans give ya energy. Whiskey will kill ya."

"Well, I have an idea for making money and that's about it," said Palidin.

"And you wanted to sell this idea to me?"

"Well, I thought maybe you might be interested."

"I'm not in business anymore. How come you didn't go to see my useless daughter?"

"I did. She's in New York or somewhere."

"She is, eh? She's not at the ranch?"

"So Cav told me."

"Hmm. What's this idea worth to you?"

"I don't know. I don't have a clue."

"You're gonna have to tell me what it is.

"I can't do that."

"Eh?"

"I can't do that."

"Why you speakin' like you're a ghost or somethin'? You're gonna have to tell me, buddy. Ya gotta trust yer sidekick."

"Why would you pay for it if you already know about it?"

"'Cause I ain't gonna buy it, anyway. I ain't got one red cent. Cav and Beatrix look after me. That daughter of mine wishes me dead, and that's about the long and short of it. You see, I made just one mistake. I signed everything over to her. I could have given it to anybody, but I gave it to her and she's a witch . . . just like her mother. Oh, I didn't care at the time. I didn't want anything except out, freedom, but I should have known better than to give it to her. I reckon I should've given it to you, Billy. Two, three hundred million dollars . . . just like that," he snapped his fingers. "Gone! I got something out of it, though. My old lady ate and drank herself to death. Ha! Course, she probably would have done that anyway. What's your plan, Billy?"

"Ah, my name's not Billy, sir."

"Oh, yeah, pardon me, Sundance. I'm Billy, I guess. You all right, Sundance? You ain't been hit, have you? Shh! Listen!"

"What? I didn't hear anything."

"Listen!"

Palidin did hear something now. A coyote yapped, then howled in the distance.

"A coyote," said Palidin.

"Yeah . . . guess you're right. Not long ago, it might have been my brother."

"Your brother howls at the moon?"

"My brother *really* knew how to howl. Haven't heard him for a long, long time. Maybe he's dead. Maybe the Texas red wolf is dead."

"The Texas red wolf?"

"The most beautiful, princely animal you ever laid your eyes on. Gone, I think. I spent millions trying to save him, but I think he's gone. Hope not. I come here every night, just to listen for him. Maybe, maybe, maybe . . . I don't know, I don't know . . . money can't buy back the Texas red wolf, young fella! This was his land once upon a time. It's still his land, goddamn it! They had no right to gun my brother down the way they did! They turned him into a villain, put a bounty on him and gunned him down for the sake of a few dollars, a cow here, a sheep there. He didn't ask for much."

Palidin sipped some more whiskey, its effects rushing over him all of a sudden. He was feeling warm, almost giddy.

"Do you think they're extinct?" he asked.

"Maybe, maybe not. There was one around a few years back, when I first took over this here country. Heard 'im myself many times. The last one, I think."

"This idea I have. Well, it's not really just an idea. I mean it was, but I experimented, and it works every time. It never fails! God, that's good whiskey! Anyway, Brandy . . . you want me to call you Brandy? Billy? I'll call you Billy, if ya want. Anyway, I made this flyhook, did something to the hook, I mean, and it worked every time. Every time! Do you believe that? Every time I threw it in the water a salmon grabbed it! You see, I have this little sister, and she sort of lives in the woods, if ya know what I mean, and she won't stand much of a chance of making it in the outside world unless she gets out . . . you sure you won't have another drink there, Brandy?"

Brandy declined.

"Anyway, what I had it in mind to do was to sell that idea I had for catching salmon, make a few bucks to help Mom and Nutbeam put Sally through school, maybe send her to UNB or somewhere, you know, get her educated. I know you don't think much of money 'cause you had so much of it. But, boys, I tell ya, I don't want to see Sally grow up to become a baby-maker and nothing else . . . know what I mean? You know when you put me in that dungeon or tomb or whatever it was? Well, I wasn't scared, you know that? I mean, I know that if you relax and not bully your way around in someone else's terrain, nothing will bother you. It's fear that makes bees sting you and snakes bite you and stuff like that . . . Brandy? You asleep or something, Brandy?"

"No, Sundance, I'm here. I was just thinkin' about who it is that I know from up your way. I know somebody, I'm sure of it."

"I'm sorry about your friend the wolf. I mean, I hope he's not gone . . . forever. Maybe I should just forget about that old flyhook thing I do."

"How much do you love the salmon?" asked Brandy.

"I love the salmon . . . I love the salmon more than . . . I love the salmon more than beans . . . ha! God, that's a gorgeous moon! Coyotes howling. *This* is the Texas I wanted to see! What do ya think of old Bornice, Brandy? You know what? I think old Bornice is the very best of a mule! She didn't walk backwards all the way here tonight. You know? I wish Dryfly was here right now. He'd love it!"

"Dryfly?"

"Dryfly's my brother. He howls sometimes, too. Do you believe in making things happen? I mean, if you want to *be* somebody, or *do* something, you sort of have to make it happen?"

"All I ever wanted to be is a cowboy. I made all the wrong things happen. I failed, Sundance. All my life, all I ever wanted to do was ride like the wind, a Colt .45 on my hip."

"You're doing that, aren't you? I mean, no way could I keep up with you riding out here. You're doing it!"

"I'm an old man. For an old man to pursue adventure, his dreams . . . they say I'm crazy."

"Ten thousand dollars! Ten thousand dollars would give Sally what she needs. I guess I can make that some other way, huh?"

"No doubt about it. There's the coyote again."

"Yeah."

"Sounds lonesome, don't he?"

"Sure does. What a wonderful world we live in!"

"Guess maybe another swig o' that whiskey wouldn't kill a man."

"There's still half a bottle there. Help yourself."

"Have to be careful of this stuff. A hundred and eighty proof."

"Ha! Too late!"

"Makes you feel like a kid again, don't it? Got a bit of the peyote in it, I reckon."

"Must be quite a change for you, living out here in a shack after being so rich. That ranch house back there must have fifty rooms in it."

"Thirty-eight. I was about to tear it down, set fire to it or something."

"For your brother the wolf?"

"They thought I was crazy. In that house, I had a bed to sleep on. I do yet."

"I'll put some more wood on the fire."

"No, you fool! Ya want to attract the Comanche?"

"The Comanche? Oh! Oh, yeah. Indians. I imagine there's about as many of them around here as there are Texas red wolves. O Canada! My true north strong and free! Li, li, li, li, I stand on guard for thee! God, that's good stuff! So, let's do something, Randy."

"Brandy."

"Yeah. Ha! Let's do something!"

"In that house, back at the ranch, there's a safe. Must be ten, twenty, thirty thousand dollars in it. Easy pickin', like takin' candy from a baby. I know the combination. Just ride in, shoot the dogs and clean up."

"Shoot the dogs?"

"There's a German Shepherd and a Doberman, trained to kill."

"Hey! Brandy! Dogs won't kill a pixie! Hey! I'll teach ya! I'm from Brennen Siding, two miles down the river from Gordon. More ugly dogs in Gordon than you can shake a stick at. All ya need to do is sort of a little ballet dance — pixie-like."

"How you know that?"

"I . . . wandered around at night. You stand on your tiptoes, see. It takes two to do it right. You put your fingers together kind of fruity-like and dance by the dogs . . . piece of cake."

"That's a queer power, if it works."

"Yeah . . ."

ten

Dan Brennen wasn't sure if it had been his grandfather or great-grandfather who first settled in Brennen Siding; he wasn't even sure if the pioneer of this little community was related to him at all. All he knew was that it had definitely been a Brennen — "The place was called Brennen Siding, wasn't it?" — and "I'm a Brennen, aren't I?" — and, therefore, it must have been some old relative of his who stormed the briny Atlantic to pole a leaky dugout all the way up the Miramichi and the Renous, possibly from Newcastle, to settle these banks of the Dungarvon.

Dan was very proud to be a Brennen; his pride leaned on the edge of arrogance; he'd even boast about it if he saw an opening.

All the land grants in this area were about the same size, somewhere around a hundred acres. "That's not good enough," thought Dan, somewhere back when he was a fledgeling. "A Brennen should own just a bit more. I'll declare that my property is a bit bigger . . . I'm a Brennen, after all. I'll say I own a hundred and ten acres. Nobody else will ever know. Who counts acres, anyway?"

So, one night at Bernie Hanley's store, Dan said, "Funny, ain't it, how the Brennens ended up with more land than everyone else. We have a hundred and ten acres back there!" He waved his arm as if gesturing at a gigantic spread, vast as the Dungarvon itself.

Dan Brennen's land grew every time he talked about it. It went from a hundred and ten to a hundred and forty, to a hundred and seventy-five, to two hundred, to three hundred.

What Dan didn't know was that right from the beginning everybody in the store, from Bob Nash to Lindon Tucker, knew exactly how much land he had, but because Dan was a good friend they would not contradict him. "Let him rave. Let him have his dreams. If he wants to be the mayor of Brennen Siding, it's all right with us."

Dan took great pride in being the owner of so much property, and nobody else cared. Dan's land grew until he forgot the original acreage. He started to *believe* he owned more land than everyone else. He sometimes walked around his field, or through the woods, with his shoulders back and chest stuck out like he was a great lord, or a Texas rancher. He even started to concern himself about it, feel responsible for his vast holdings, feel responsible for the whole community. He put a "No Fishing" sign up on Bert Todder's brook. "It'll keep the damned trout fishermen from going back there and burnin' the woods down," was how he got away with it.

Lately, however, his concerns took a bit of a nosedive. Dan stumbled upon the realization that Brennen Siding was not growing. Brennen Siding was, indeed, shrinking. It shrank in population every time one of its youth packed up and left.

"Shadrack and Dryfly left for the States. My world is growing smaller."

Dan Brennen tried to voice his concerns at Bernie Hanley's store to the men who didn't seem to care.

"You know, boys, things are lookin' pretty grim fer Brennen Siding," said Dan. "Never thought of it before, but you know, there ain't no young lads to speak of in Brennen Siding. Mine's all gone, so's yours, John. I was thinking about that the other day when I was considerin' makin' out my will, wonderin' if any of my lads would ever want to come back here and take over and look after my four hundred acres back there."

John Kaston nodded thoughtfully.

"My Shad just took off to the States yesterday mornin' with Dryfly Ramsey. God knows if they'll ever come back."

"I don't imagine me and you'll ever get around to havin' young lads, eh Stan?" put in Bert Todder.

"No, sir, ain't a single soul left in my family. I'm the last of the Tuneys in these parts."

"Course, Lindon here might have a few. Tee hee hee . . . "

"Might have a few, yeah, Bert. A lad never knows. A lad meets up with the right woman, might have a few."

"A man would have to go to work if he sired three or four young lads," said Stan Tuney and winked knowingly at Bernie Hanley, who was standing behind the counter sucking on a peppermint.

"Yeah," said Lindon. "A lad might have to go to work. Oh, I might not have any young lads. Could've had young lads. Too old, now. Almost had a young lad once. I did, yeah. A little blond lady in Fredericton. Drunk vodker, she did, yeah. Yeah, yes sir, almost had a young lad, I did. Come pretty close that time, I did. A man never knows."

"That young Sally o' Shirley Ramsey's looks a bit like you, Lindon," teased Bert.

"That's true, yeah," added Stan Tuney. "Her ears ain't a bit big like that Nutbeam's."

"It ain't no young lad o' mine, Shirley Ramsey's ain't!" said Lindon, reddening a bit.

"There's been just one young lad born in the last ten or fifteen years," said Dan Brennen. "And it don't look like there'll be another for God knows how long. Not one young lad! Not a baby! Not one!"

"I'm doin' everything I can do," grinned Bob Nash.

All the men except Dan grinned at this little joke.

"Sally's the only young lad around here," said Dan Brennen, a bit annoyed that the men were making light of his choice of conversation. "It seems pretty strange that a Ramsey should inherit a whole community!"

"What community?" said Bob Nash. "Fifty years from now there'll be nothing here but trees and caved-in basements. Look how quick Brattlebane grew up after Joe Black died. Ten years and there were popples twenty feet tall growing around his house. One day some lad'll paddle down the river and put up a sign saying this is where Brennen Siding used to be."

"Cains River used to be all settled one time," said Bernie Hanley. "Ain't many livin' up there now that I know of."

"Same with the Sabbies and the Bartholomew," added Dan Brennen. "There used to be mills all over the place, sawmills, shingle mills, gristmills. You know, I heard of a few lads out on the main river, the Miramichi, that's not only lettin' their fields grow up, but they're plantin' trees! Takin' the old fields that their fathers and grandfathers sweated and slaved over for a hundred years tryin' to keep them clear, and plantin' them full o' Christmas trees!"

"How d'ya plant a Christmas tree?" teased Bert Todder. "Put a bulb in the ground? Tee hee hee, sob, sob! I soon gotta go."

"No, but what d'ya s'pose is the reason everyone just packs right up and leaves when they get to be a certain age, though? That's what I'd like to know." Dan Brennen was trying his best to keep the conversation serious.

"That's just it," said Bob Nash. "All the young lads nowdays are gettin' educated. It's work, employment that takes them all away soon's they get big enough."

"Yeah, yeah, that's fer sure, yeah. Oh, yeah, yeah, yeah. Work'll drive a man off every time, yeah," said Lindon Tucker.

Everyone except Dan laughed.

"If some of you lads had've had the brains of a chub, you might have got yerself a woman and had some kids!" said Dan, looking directly at the lone tooth, the grinning.

"I had a girlfriend one time," put in Stan Tuney. "And I just figured out lately how come I never knocked her up."

"How come?" asked Bernie Hanley.

"I was too into fishin'," said Stan. "I kept wearin' me chest waders to bed. Ya ever try to make a young lad wit' a pair o' chest waders on?"

"Tee, hee, hee, sob, snort!"

"Ha, ha, ha!"

"Ho, ho, ho!"

"Yi, yi, yi, yi, yi! Oh yeah, yep! Chest waders . . . yi, yi, yi, yi, yi!"

Frustrated as Dan Brennen was, he couldn't help chuckling at this one. He sobered up quickly, however, and said, "T'aint no laughin' matter, though, boys."

"But it gives a whole new meaning to wearin' rubbers!" joked Bert Todder. "Tee, hee, hee, sob! Gettin' late. Gotta go. Oh, I don't know, though. Maybe a lad should've got married, settled down, had a few young lads . . . always liked young lads, and Dan's right, I don't really have anyone to leave me place to, or anything. I always wanted a son, you know . . . yes sir. Oh well!"

"Well, you're not too old, Bert. Get yourself a good woman, any woman, have a couple o' young lads. Ain't nothin' to it," said Dan.

"Oh, I don't know. Could've had, I suppose. Could've had . . . tee, hee, hee, sob, snort . . . "

Bernie Hanley was the only one in the store who knew that Bert was not laughing.

*

By the time Dryfly and Lillian reluctantly left their bedroom, finished their lengthy shower and dressed, Janice had coffee brewed and a breakfast of croissants and strawberry jam on the table.

Both Shadrack and Dryfly sipped the coffee, too polite to declare they'd never had it before and found it much too aromatic and sweet. With the exception of the kitchen in the Cabbage Island Salmon Club, you'd have a task and a half to find a jar of Maxwell House in Brennen Siding. King Cole, Salada, or Red Rose, on the other hand, could be found gracing the shelves of every kitchen from Shirley Ramsey's to Stan Tuney's.

"Why were you playing the piano so early, Janice?" asked Lillian.

"Shadrack and I decided to make beautiful music together. What's everyone doing today?"

Shadrack and Dryfly both shrugged.

"I thought we'd give them the grand tour," said Lillian. "The campus, the city, maybe have dinner later at Tony's. Do you guys like Italian?"

"Never had it," said Dryfly.

"Great, sure, the very best," said Shadrack.

"Okay," said Janice. "Then, I thought I'd take Shadrack to a few clubs or something. Give you two a chance to be alone for a while."

And so the day began. After breakfast, they drove about the

city from top to bottom, from one end to the other, in Janice's new red Mustang. Shadrack and Dryfly found most of the city beautiful, some of it coarse and drab, all of it exciting.

The highlight of the city, of course, was Yale University. The boys were in awe. Not even having visited the likes of UNB, they couldn't believe a school could be so massive.

They entered a bookstore at one point, and Lillian purchased a copy of Kahlil Gibran's *The Prophet* and gave it to Dryfly.

Dryfly leafed through the thin, black-covered book. "It reads like the Bible or something," he commented. "I should buy you a book, too. What would you like to read?"

"Oh, I don't know," said Lillian. "Let's shop around."

A few minutes later, Dryfly spied a copy of Stephen Leacock's *Arcadian Adventures with the Idle Rich*. "Stephen Leacock," he thought. "A Canadian. It costs more than I wanna pay, but . . . what the hell." He bought it for Lillian.

"Have you read it?" asked Lillian.

"No, but I know he's Canadian . And the title seems right."

Lillian smiled and accepted the gift.

Shadrack and Janice also shopped in the bookstore. Janice picked up a copy of *Herodotus: The Histories*. Shad, although he wanted just about every book he looked at, bought nothing. "I can't risk spending my few dollars on books," he thought.

The day moved along. They shopped, walked through parks, looked at monuments and buildings, stopped for a beer in a little bar whose bartender turned a blind eye to the legal age, held hands, sang, and went to Tony's.

At Tony's, Janice did the ordering and soon the table was laden with spaghetti and meatballs, lasagna, hot Italian sausage, garlic bread, Tuscany wine.

When the waiter came over and handed Dryfly the cheque, Dryfly shuddered. "Seventy-five dollars!" he thought. "That'll take up just about every cent I have!" But before he could reach for his wallet, Janice snapped the cheque from his hand.

"My treat," she said.

"But . . . ," Dryfly tried to protest.

"I'm a liberated woman," said Janice. "No arguments!"

Under the circumstances, Dryfly gave in with a shrug.

On the way back to 457 Enfield Street, Lillian asked, "So, Janice, where are you taking Shadrack?"

"The Big Apple," said Janice.

"New York!" said Lillian, as if she thought perhaps Janice was joking.

"New York!" exclaimed Shad. "How far is New York?"

"Ninety minutes," said Janice. "We're spending the night. I've already booked us a room at the Belmont Plaza."

"Good, good, the very best," said Shad, grinning back at Dry.

*

Dryfly and Lillian watched Shad and Janice pull away. Janice revved the Mustang, squealed and burned rubber for a hundred feet, rounded the corner and was gone. Dryfly and Lillian climbed the stairs, entered the apartment, lit a couple of candles, put an album on the stereo and sat beside each other on the sofa.

"You like Old Blue Eyes?" asked Lillian.

"Love them," said Dryfly.

Lillian laughed an easy little laugh. "I meant Sinatra, silly," she said. "I put Sinatra on the stereo."

Dryfly listened to "Stardust" for a few seconds. "It's beautiful," he said. "Everything is beautiful. I kind of feel like I died and went to Heaven. I feel . . . so good bein' here, and yet I feel kind of lonesome, too."

"You mean you're homesick?"

"No, not homesick. The opposite, maybe. It's the knowing that we'll be parting tomorrow or the next day that makes me lonesome. Do you think that we'll ever be together? I mean, really together?"

"I . . . I don't know. Maybe. I don't want to be with anyone else. I really don't want to think about it. I just want to let things happen."

"Will you marry me?" Dryfly had been thinking about marrying Lillian, but in no way had intended to ask that question. It sort of slipped out as if it *had* to be asked, as if it was meant to be. He'd thought of asking Lillian to marry him a million times, really, and had just as often pondered what her answer would be. Though often a dreamer, down deep inside Dryfly was a very practical person, a realist. In his dreams, Lillian always answered, "No." It was the only right answer — she was rich and beautiful, Dryfly was not. Lillian had places to go, people to meet, things to do. So did Dryfly, but somehow he thought that her needs and his needs were on a very different scale. He would struggle through life, guide, work in the woods, drive a truck, or perhaps, at the very best, be a poor Canadian artist; Lillian would sail through life, be a doctor, a lawyer, a businesswoman, inherit millions of dollars . . .

Lillian had dreamed of Dryfly asking that old, "will you marry me?" question a million times, too. In her dreams, she had always answered, "Yes! Yes, yes, yes, yes, yes!" She had a hundred thousand dollars in the bank. When she turned twenty-one, she'd get a million more. She could marry Dryfly Ramsey if she wanted. She could do whatever she damn well pleased. She knew that Dryfly was genuinely in love with her, that he was not courting her father's money, and that was the most important thing in the world to her. She loved Dryfly with all her heart and knew she would be happy with him — she had given up her virginity to him because she knew that she wanted to marry him. Dryfly didn't know it, but Lillian had already given him his engagement present.

But now he had popped the question and was waiting for an answer. She felt she needed to think.

She caressed Dryfly's long hair with her fingers. She moved closer to him, kissed his brow, eyes, nose and lips; she nibbled on his earlobe, sending a shiver all the way down to his toes. She unbuttoned his shirt, kissed his nipples. She unzipped his fly, exposed his penis . . .

"When I'm twenty-one," she said.

"What about when you're twenty-one?"

"I'll marry you."

"You will?"

"Uh huh."

*

The turnpikes and highways, the bridges and skyways, the reeking tunnels, the thousands of yellow taxis, the lights, the skyscrapers, the smog, the people and the filth. All that was the city of New York totally mesmerized Shad, held him in wonder, in a state of disbelief, even fear.

"Are you sure you can drive in this stuff?" were the only words he spoke from the time he entered the city until Janice pulled up in front of the Belmont Plaza. If you were to ask him what he was thinking during that period of time, he would probably tell you, "Why? Why did they build the pyramids? Why did they build the Great Wall? Why did they build New York?" A fish out of water, a polar bear in Kenya, a live eastern cougar in a Miramichi hunting camp, a lemon eater at a whistling contest. If Shad had had antennae and green skin, he would have been no more an alien.

They got out of the car. Janice passed the keys and a five-dollar bill to a black man in a uniform and said, "I'd like for it to be in one piece in the morning. New York! Love it! Tonight's on me, Shad! What do you want to do?"

They were still on the sidewalk, and Shad was trying to read the writing high above them on the building across the street. "The . . . Waldorf . . . Astoria . . . huh?"

"What do you want to do?"

"Dance, party, drink, eat, look up."

"Ha! My kind of guy! We'll check in, then see what this junkyard has to offer."

A true Miramichier, Shad whooped and turned a handspring on the sidewalk. Then, with some difficulty he composed himself, wiped the grin off his face and followed Janice inside and up to the front desk.

"Mr. and Mrs. Shadrack Nash from Brennen Siding!" announced Janice. "We'd like a room with a view!"

"The penthouse is vacant, madam." said the clerk. He was looking at Shad when he said that, and Janice detected a hint of sarcasm in his voice.

"Who do we look like, the Rockefellers? I just want a room! High up!"

Janice filled out a card, and the clerk handed her a key. "Room 2815," he said. "The bellman will show you up."

The front desk clerk rang a little bell, and almost immediately a tall, uniformed black bellman appeared at Shadrack's side.

"G'day!" said Shad. "How's she goin'? Lead the way, old dog!"

"Ha!" laughed Janice. "Lead the way!"

They followed the bellman across the lobby and into the elevator. As they zoomed up to the twenty-eighth floor, Shad asked, "You from around here?"

"Queens," said the bellman. "You?"

"We're from Brennen Siding!" said Janice. "We need a bell-hop like we need a hole in the head! Shad? Have you got a dollar on ya for this guy? It's their business to get tipped, you know!"

The elevator doors opened, and they started down the hall. Shad reached into his pocket and pulled out his every cent. Nineteen dollars.

The bellman stopped, unlocked a door, turned on the lights, showed them in and waited for his tip.

Shad handed him a Canadian dollar.

"What's this?" asked the bellman.

"A dollar bill," said Shadrack.

"This is a dollar?"

"Yes, sir, it is."

"Where you from, man, England?"

"We're from Brennen Siding!" said Janice.

The bellhop frowned, looked at the bill, shrugged and left.

"What an asshole!" said Janice.

"A jeezless hick!" said Shad.

While Janice peed, combed, and fixed her make up, Shad opened the curtains to check out the view.

It was ten o'clock in the evening, and he could see thousands of lighted windows on hundreds of buildings tapering into the sky. "I'm twenty-eight floors up, and I'm not halfway as high as most of those buildings go," he thought. "I'm not in the Dungarvon swamps now! Expect to see Batman swing from building to building any minute. The Waldorf Astoria — think I heard of that on TV or someplace. That one over there's got ITT on top of it . . . I Tell Tales? I Time Travel? Probably a theatre. Ha! Those people down there look no bigger than ants. Look out, old city, Shadrack Nash is on a tear! God, if the boys could only see me now! New York! Right this very minute, somebody out there is being murdered, prob'ly— murdered, mugged, being born, dying, screwing . . . speaking of which, I wonder what my tall little darlin' has in mind? She's a good lookin' woman, really. Nearly old enough to be my mother, but she looks not too bad. I'll show her the lad, if that's what she wants."

"So, what's on your mind, Mr. Nash?"

"I was just thinking we should go somewhere and have a little drink."

"You're a man after my own heart. Need to freshen up first?"

"Yeah. I'll just be a minute."

Shad went into the bathroom, combed his hair, washed his face, cleaned his teeth the best he could with his finger (he had forgotten his toothbrush), then stepped back out to join her whom he now referred to as his tall little darlin'.

"I hope we'll be able to get into places with jeans on," he said.

"This is America. You can court the President with jeans on if you have enough money."

"Yeah, well, I s'pose I should mention that . . . You see, I . . . "

"Shad! I told you that tonight was on me!"

"Well, I . . . "

"When I go to Brennen Siding, you can foot the bill. Now, I know a nice little place we can try for a starter. Like jazz?"

"The very best! Let's get at 'er!"

A minute later, they were on the street. Janice whistled down a cab. They climbed into the back seat and headed for Broadway.

Shad, elated, high on life, bold as a hungry porcupine, threw his arm across Janice's shoulders and said, "Boys, I don't s'pose we ain't gonna have none too good a time tonight!"

eleven

Bert Todder turned off the light, slid in under the sheet and the heavy grey blanket, yawned, scratched his massive belly and closed his eyes. Downstairs in the parlour the clock struck eleven. Then silence crept in.

He had just returned from his night of fun and frivolity at Bernie Hanley's store. The boys had all been there, and they had had a good laugh. Dan Brennen had tried like hell to talk seriously, which Bert knew was pretty much impossible in the spring of the year after the boys had already guided for a week and had money in their pockets, the miseries of winter a memory. Bert had walked home via the footbridge and had experienced something that he thought was very strange — he thought he had heard someone walking toward him on the bridge, but by the time he had reached the far end he still hadn't met anybody.

"I can't figure it out," he thought. "Loose boards maybe. Echoes. Must've been someone walkin' away from me, and in the night it must've just sounded like he was walkin' toward me. Strange thing, though. Everything's strange these days. I'm goin' crazy, I think. Oh, well, I'll check the boards in the mornin', anyway. A loose board could be a dangerous outfit on a bridge like that. Ya could trip, fall through and skin yerself all up on the wire beneath. God knows what."

Then, eerily, slowly, the old grey blanket started to slide toward the foot of the bed.

"Goddamn it!" thought Bert and pulled it back up. He opened his eyes, saw only the darkness of the room, turned over on his left side and scratched his butt. "Them gov'ment lads don't look after that bridge good 'nough. Don't look after the Gordon Road, either. It's gettin' so muddy ya kin hardly drive on it. Get a big rain and ya'll need a hellycopter to get to Brennen Siding. The whole bunch o' them are lazier than I don't know what. All they do is lean on their shovels. That bridge needs a whole new boardwalk. Someone should tell them, get it done before somebody gets hurt. And that road needs gravel. Goddamned Liberal gov'ment, that's what it is! I never voted Liberal in my life, and I'm not about to!"

The blanket started sliding down again, more quickly this time.

"Boys, wouldn't that make a man just . . . just . . . just wanna tear it all up! Oh!" He pulled the blanket back up.

"I'll bring that loose board racket up at the store tomorrow night. Maybe we can fix it up a bit ourselves. No sense waitin' for them gov'ment lads. They'll not fix it till 'lection time, ya kin bet on that!"

Snap, the blanket flew off the bed with such force that it landed on the dresser across the room, upsetting a glass that Bert had left there. This startled Bert so that he sat as if he were a jack-in-the-box.

"What the hell." He heard a movement in the room, then outside the room, then footsteps on the stairs. "Who's there?" he yelled.

The footsteps stopped. The house grew quiet again.

Bert turned on the light, went to the closet where he kept his rifle and shotgun. He didn't know what he might be confronting here in his very own house, and he had to give some thought to the matter. "The rifle? I shot thirty-six deer, eight moose, seventeen porcupines, a bobcat, two foxes, four rabbits, three dogs and a cow with that rifle. Or the shotgun? Hundreds of partridge, hundreds of woodcock, a few rabbits, a raven, an owl, a bunch of them friggin' mergansers, a crane." He grabbed the shotgun and some shells, loaded it and headed for the stairs. "Ya can't miss with a shotgun."

"I'm fifty-two years old, and this is the first time anyone ever come into this house," he thought. "What's the world comin' to?"

He went down the stairs, crossed the hall, turned on the lights and entered the parlour. Gazing at the floors, the walls, the ceiling, he knew there was something different, something wrong, but he couldn't figure out what. "The little rug is in its usual place in the center of the floor. The big armchair hasn't been touched. The table under the window hasn't been moved, so nobody came in through the window. Course, why would anybody come in through the window? I haven't locked a door for years. The old organ still looks the same —dusty, closed. No one's played it since Mom died; the old yeller pictures on top. The pictures. There's Mom and Dad. Uncle Lou in his new Model-T Ford. Cousin Dale's graduation picture, and Linda in her confirmation dress. There's Sydney with his big white horse that was always black . . . I thought . . . I'm sure that horse was a black horse. There's Clark with them pants on that was always too long in the legs, all piled up at the bottom . . . tee, hee, hee, sob, sob, snort . . . how come I always thought Sydney's horse was black? It *was* black! By the Lord liftin' . . . black with a white nose! He's white as the driven snow, now. And the clock's stopped. I heard it ring a few minutes ago. Must've just stopped. Why would that horse turn white like that?" Bert shrugged, made his way cautiously through the parlour and entered the kitchen, turned on the lights.

Everything seemed the same here, too. There was the plate where he had left it after his bed-lunch of baloney and Helen MacDonald's homemade bread, there on the table right where he'd left it. The cup beside it, still half full of tea, still steaming warm. "Now, what the hell . . . the fire's out. I had a fire on in that stove, but it's as cold as ice. What the . . . and it's like a barn in here!"

The flap of his one-piece Stanfield's underwear came undone. Bert felt a chill on his bum. "Damn it, I must be goin' crazy," he thought and swung to go back to the parlour.

The lights were off in the parlour.

"I . . . I'm sure I just turned them on. And there was nobody in there, anyway. I'm sure of that, unless he was behind the door, or behind the big chair. What's goin' on here . . . ?" Fear touched him. He felt the hair stand up on the back of his neck. He was not a man who scared easily, couldn't recall ever experiencing that sensation before. Once maybe, the time he had confronted and found himself between a bear and her cubs back on Tuney Brook. That time, he just turned and ran like hell. But this was different. He was feeling fear of the unknown. And perhaps it *wasn't* the unknown. Perhaps it was someone he knew very well playing a trick on him. Someone like Dryfly or Shadrack. "A dangerous trick," he thought. "Anybody who knows me knows better than to sneak around in my house at night with me in it. Shad and Dry are in the States, anyway, and even if they weren't, they'd not sneak around like that."

"When I was a young lad, me and Bernie used to go in old Fred Hanley's house and party. One night Fred woke up and came downstairs. Me and Bernie hid behind the door; Fred turned off all the lights, leavin' us there in the dark. Old Fred was deaf, hadn't heard us at all, just thought he'd left the lights on. But there's nobody around like Bernie and me anymore . . . 'cept Shad and Dry . . . and they're in the States. Bernie and me did a lotta things together . . . play, drift, drink, laugh. Christ! We used to pole all the way up the river to Gordon, bark at the dogs like two fools! Tee, hee, hee, sob, sob, sob . . . God, Bernie! You got married, ya bastard! Got religion! Started a store! I never married, so I didn't. Nobody'd have me . . . nobody'd have me. Not even Shirley Ramsey. Shirley was the nicest, prettiest little . . . and Mary Hardwood. Felt Mary Hardwood's tit one time . . . tee, hee, hee . . . there in the moonlight. Just the two of us on the footbridge. But not even she would have me. Nobody'd have me! And now they're all gone . . . sob, sob . . . a lotta good yer old store's doin' ya now, Bernie. Three or four of us lads standin' back drinkin' ginger ale. Yer wife dead now for nearly a year. Yer as alone as me. God, it's cold in here! Alone and cold and, haunted by a white horse that should be black. Here where Brennen Siding used to be . . . sob, sob, sob . . . "

He cocked the shotgun.

"If there's somebody in this house, you're about to git yer head blowed off!" he shouted. "I don't care if yer the goddamned Whooper!"

He moved toward the parlour.

His breath and heart accelerated.

When he stepped into the parlour, the light in the kitchen went out.

"I . . . this is no joke, whoever you are!" he said, his voice sounding like someone else's there in the dark.

He began to shiver and tremble. He wasn't sure if it was from fear or the cold. It might have had something to do with the fact that all he could see was the horse in the picture on the organ. His brother Sydney's horse, glowing, white as snow. "Sydney jumped to avoid a rolling log on Silas Landing . . . came down on a peevee handle . . . last of the Todders, 'cept for me. God, it's cold in here!"

"I got a shotgun here — a twelve-gauge! Double barrel! Buckshot! Better show yerself! I'm warnin' ya!" Bert's voice sounded adolescent, squeaked, held no threat in it. "Tee, hee, hee, sob, sob! I ain't foolin'," he rasped.

There were tears in his eyes. He closed them trying to block out the spectacle of the glowing white horse. He bit his lip with his one single incisor.

"Pull yourself together," he thought. "You're a grown man. There's always a reason for everything. Git a grip on yourself."

He opened his eyes, took a single step forward, stopped, listened. He thought he could hear something to his right, but his heart and lungs were making such a noise that he wasn't sure. He took a deep breath to compose himself. "I'll just take one big step over to the light switch and turn it on," he decided. "And if there's someone in this room, he'll be in big shit. I'll do it so quick that whoever it is that's here won't have time to hide." But down deep, Bert knew that when he flipped the switch, the light might not come on, and that if it did come on there would be nobody there. Nobody! For someone to be there, supposing it was a killer, a drunken maniac, a whole roomful of alien zombies, would be too much to ask. Things were happening, he could hear movement, there should be an explanation. But an explanation, too, would be too much to ask. He took a quick, long stride toward the light switch, hit his toe on something. He didn't know what, but it was enough to cause him to jump back in agony. He came down on the little braided rug, the rug his mother had made, the rug that had been there in the middle of the parlour floor for twenty-five years or more. The rug slid, Bert lost his balance and fell forward, full-length, smack on his big belly— and the shotgun.

BANG!

He didn't even hear the discharge.

The only tooth he had disappeared along with the rest of his face.

Bert Todder would not laugh "Tee, hee, hee," or cry . . . ever again.

*

As sure as bachelors visit, Lindon Tucker's claim to fame for the next two years would be the fact that he had heard the shot. He was out peeing up against the back wall of his outdoor toilet when he heard it. It startled him a bit, but it was not an unusual thing to hear a shot coming from Bert Todder's house this time of night — Bert quite frequently shot skunks and porcupines that were threatening to occupy his sheds. Lindon glanced down at Bert's house, saw that every light in the house was on, shrugged the shot off as being nothing more than Bert on pest control, zipped up his fly and went back into his house and then to bed.

Nutbeam was already in bed with his wife Shirley when he heard the shot.

"Hear that?" he asked.

"Hear what?"

"A shot."

"No."

"A twelve-gauge, I think. Sounded like it came from Bert Todder's. Sounded like it came from inside a building. Bert must be shooting a porcupine. Wouldn't shoot a skunk inside like that."

"Bert's always killin' somethin'."

"But this shot sounded different. I can't believe you didn't hear it."

"I ain't got your big floppy ears, remember?"

"Yeah . . . I suppose that's it. Did you hear Sally today?"

"Screaming and crying, you mean?"

"No, she talked."

"She can't talk. Too young to talk. What'd she say?"

"I called her poopy bum. She said 'I not poopy bum!' I swear it, as plain as day."

"Ha! She might've. Naggy talked young like that. So did Palidin. She'll be talkin' too much soon enough. Well, goodnight, love."

"Goodnight, Shirl."

"You leave the door unlocked?"

"Yeah, why?"

"Just in case Dryfly comes home in the night and wants to git in."

"It's unlocked."

"Poor little Dryfly."

"What d'ya mean, poor little Dryfly?"

"Went way down there to see that girl. Prob'ly make a fool of himself."

"Why? Do you think him a fool?"

"No, but she's a big, rich lady. He'll never get his hands on her."

"Dryfly's not as stupid as he looks."

"You think he looks stupid?"

"Well . . . "

"See ya in the mornin'."

"Yeah, goodnight."

*

Times Square's plethora of neon and glowworms leaped, crawled, poured, pierced, pitched, plunged, pooped, popped, soared, striped, danced, flashed, flickered, flitted, vibrated, quivered and boogied. It seemed New Yorkers had bottled the spectrum.

While Janice paid the cabby, Shad stood on the sidewalk and gawked, and when she turned to look at him, she could see some of the lights reflecting off his teeth, tongue and tonsils. Coming from a community where lights were as sparse as Eve's clothesline, this spectacle held Shad in a clinch with awe.

The sidewalks were crowded with everything from the breezy and glamorous highbrows to Greek widows, from leathered hookers to robed fanatics, from high-heeled fruits to hippie freaks, from pinstriped patricians to pimps in Panamas. Shad would never see so much skin in one place ever again.

Raising her voice above the cacophony of car horns, sirens, bar music and loudmouthed people, Janice said, "There's a bar! Let's check it out!"

They entered a bar big enough to house a Renous reunion and found a table. Janice waved over a waiter and ordered two Cutty Sarks.

"He old enough?" asked the waiter, gesturing Shad.

"He's my father," said Janice.

The waiter shrugged and went to the bar. When he returned with the drinks, Janice asked him if there was a band.

"Is the President white?" asked the waiter.

"Thanks," said Janice. "So, how do ya like New York?"

"Love it! You come down here a lot?"

"I lived down here for a while . . . Queens. Hated it, loved it, hated it again. Got into my own medicine, got kicked out of the state, had a nervous breakdown, moved home."

"You and Lillian old friends?"

"I'm a friend of the family. Do you know Bill?"

"Bill Wallace? Me and Bill are just like that!" Shad held up two fingers.

"Did you know he got married again?"

"He did, eh?"

"He's retiring, too, so he says. Wants to sail around the world."

"Takin' Lillian with him?"

"That's up to her, I guess. She's at Yale. I don't think so. Your friend Dryfly's getting himself quite a catch."

"Naw, he'll never get her."

"Of course he will. She's crazy about him. He makes her laugh. You'll never find a better man than the one who makes you laugh. When the laughter stops, the honeymoon's over. Got a girlfriend, Shad?"

"Naw. Not really."

They talked for a few minutes about things in general but were intruded upon by a rock 'n' roll band. It was a good band; Shad liked it a lot, but it was much too loud for Janice, so they downed their drinks and moved on to another bar, one with a folksinger in the corner who played Dylan stuff, harmonica and all. Here, they ordered a couple of beers. Shad didn't like the beer. It was cold and much too light for his tastes. Shad was used to drinking warm Moosehead, purchased fresh, or perhaps not so fresh, from a Blackville bootlegger.

The room was thick with cigarette and marijuana smoke, and everyone seemed very contented and happy, smiles all over the place. Philosophy seemed to be the general topic of conversation throughout the room, and although Shad hardly knew the meaning of the word, he and Janice moved, perhaps through the back door, into its realm as well.

"Do you have a pet?" she asked.

"Naw. The odd old tomcat hangs around the barn, that's about it. You?"

"I used to have a dog. A big blond half-shepherd, half-Lab called Earthling. I love dogs, cats, animals. Should have been a vet."

"I always wanted a dog. Mom would never allow one in the house."

"Abused child."

"Ha!"

"You're a hunter, I suppose."

"Me? Naw. Hunted squirrels when I was a kid. Used to sell their tails to Bert Todder for tyin' flies. Ten cents apiece."

"Ten cents. It's not putting much value on the life of an animal, is it?"

"Guess not. Never thought of it that way. Anyway, I don't hunt anymore. Sold my rifle."

"I've been reading Herodotus."

"Any good?"

Janice shrugged.

"Who wrote it?" asked Shad.

Janice smiled. "Herodotus," she said. "The father of history."

"Oh yeah, that lad." Shad nodded thoughtfully, turned his attention to the head-bobbing folksinger. "God! He's good," he thought. "And all he has is a guitar and a mouth organ. I could do that. I have a guitar and a mouth organ. You don't even have to be able to sing that good, if ya do Dylan stuff, folk songs. Must work on it when I get back home. "

"Did you hear about the mass murders that happened down here a few weeks ago?"

"No."

"Some maniac went berserk and killed eleven women."

"Did they catch the lad?"

Janice looked at Shad thoughtfully. "You knew it was a man, didn't you? You just knew."

"Yeah, I guess. Did they get him?"

"He shot the eleven women, then shot himself."

"Quite a racket, eh?"

"I've been thinking about it, you know? And there's a very dark and gloomy possibility out there. I'm a doctor, Shadrack. I might be pretty much of a failure, but I'm a doctor nevertheless. And all my life I've been concerned with two things — the welfare of women and the welfare of animals. Men have been nothing but a pain in the ass. They hurt you, break your heart, beat their wives, abuse their children, ignore you if you're too tall, or too short, or your tits are too big or too small. But lately I've come to the realization that if you're into the welfare of women and animals, you're into the welfare of mankind."

Shad wasn't sure where Janice was coming from, said nothing, waited. The folksinger was taking a break from the Dylan stuff, was singing a song that Shad had never heard before, whistling between the verses. "Whistlin's a good idea, too," thought Shad. "Whistlin's just like havin' another instrument. I can whistle."

"It has several angles," Janice was saying. "You can look

into zoology, anthropology, history, philosophy, archeology, even theology. It doesn't matter how you look at it, it all adds up. Man, animals . . . we're all earthlings. We're not gods! We are a part of, or somewhere on, nature's ladder. Maybe it's underestimating nature to think that we've forgotten our roots, that we ever *knew* our roots, that there ever were roots, but I think that we've forgotten that we're earthlings, animals! You don't give a shit, do you? Anyway, I called my dog Earthling."

"Do you believe in things just sort of happening over a long period of time?" asked Shad.

"Evolution, you mean?"

"Yeah."

"I'm not sure. I guess so. How do you know about evolution? You're still in high school."

"I lived with a lady. She taught me a lot of things."

"You lived with a woman? At your age?"

"It wasn't like that. She was an old woman. I sort of took care of her in her old age. She died, left me her farm. That's where I live."

"With your parents?"

"No, alone."

"I'm impressed. When I first met you, you seemed like such a shy little fellow."

"I was. I'm a Miramichier."

"Even your accent seems to have changed."

"Ha! We have accents all over the place, town to town, settlement to settlement, mile to mile. You learn to speak them all and fit in wherever you go."

"Would you ever consider moving down to New England, or somewhere else in the States?"

"I don't know. I'm in a rut, I think."

"You're not in a rut, if you know you're in a rut."

"Oh, I guess I know I'm in a rut. But it's a pretty good rut. We have clean air, clean water, great people, the most beautiful river in the world, the forest, the animals, the salmon."

"Have you travelled much?"

"No. This is my first real trip."

"So how do you know you live beside the most beautiful river in the world?"

"Just ask any American who's been there. But that's bullshit, too. Hilda Porter, the old lady I lived with, thought that man don't . . . doesn't belong. We were damned by God in the Garden of Eden, she used to say. Maybe the whole of Earth was Eden before Eve ate the apple."

"Eve, being a woman, carries the blame forever."

"Wantin' the apple was the first sign of greed. Man *and* woman have been sayin' I want, I want, I want ever since. I want a fig leaf, I want a fur coat, I want to own the land and the rivers, I want a car, I want to get to the stars. I want to get off of this godforsaken planet. We seem to need so much, eh?"

"The planet's not godforsaken, we are. It's all very depressing, isn't it?"

"Yeah."

"Maybe it's this bar. Let's try somewhere else. I know a place about a block from here."

"Great! Sure!"

twelve

Palidin slept beneath the Hanging Tree until the heat of the morning sun made it impossible for him to sleep any longer. He rose, stretched and gazed at the sprawling landscape. There was a very flat-topped hill or mountain in the distance, a few clumps of trees here and there, the sparkle of a stream, wild flowers and grass. A plane chalked the sky overhead, a smaller one buzzed on the horizon. Bornice grazed some two hundred yards away. Brandy Burgess and Jonah were gone.

"So, where the hell am I?" Palidin asked himself. "Which way did we come from last night? Well, I guess it doesn't matter much. I'll get Bornice, saddle her up and let her lead the way to wherever. With any luck, she'll take me back to the ranch."

Palidin walked down through the field toward Bornice. When he got to within twenty feet of her, she lifted her head, showed him the whites of her eyes, bolted and ran. She stopped about a hundred yards away and looked back at him.

"I guess I startled her," he thought and approached her once again.

Again, when he got close to her, she trotted off and stopped a hundred yards or so away. This time, she arched her back and peed.

Palidin had all the side effects that a hangover could offer and was in no mood for games. He felt he had little choice in the matter, however, so he followed her once again. This time when he started walking toward her, she began to walk away. When Palidin stopped, she stopped; when he ran, she ran. Once he tried walking away from her, and when he looked back to see her whereabouts she was following him, but still she kept her distance. He followed her and she followed him for what seemed to be an hour or so, and they were now back to where they started. It was a ridiculous game of cat and mouse that Palidin had little patience for, and he was about to give up when he heard the sound of approaching hooves.

Brandy Burgess rode up, dressed in black.

"Don't shoot, Billy!" he shouted. "It's me! Sundance!"

"Can you do something with this miserable mule?" pleaded Palidin.

"What's wrong with the mule?" asked Brandy as he reined Jonah to a halt beside Palidin.

"I can't get close to her! I've been chasing her all morning."

"Maybe she doesn't like the smell of ya, Billy. Ha, ha! Come here, Bornice! Git saddled! We have ridin' to do!"

Bornice bobbed her head and walked up to stand beside her saddle.

"They're sorta like a woman. Ya gotta let 'em know who's boss," said Brandy, who stiffly dismounted and helped Palidin saddle up.

"So, where we going?" asked Palidin, climbing into the saddle.

"We're ridin' on into the ranch and pullin' that job I told ya about, Billy. Reckon we should be there at just about the right time if we ride hard."

"My name's Palidin."

"Yeah, sure, whatever you say, partner. Ya got yer gun, I see. Good. You're sure gonna need it tonight. Giddyup!"

As they rode off into the morning, Brandy sang,

> *I can see the moon on high, I can hear the cattle low,*
> *As I bid my last good-bye to the herd that I love so.*
> *Headin' south across the prairie 'neath the western sky*
> *To me darlin' Mary Ellen, yippee ti yi yi.*
>
> *Yippee ti!*
> *Yippee ti yi yi!*
> *Yippee ti! Yippee ti yi yi!*
> *Headin' south across the prairie 'neath the western sky*
> *To me darlin' Mary Ellen, yippee ti yi yi.*

Palidin grinned, then laughed so hard that the tears rolled down his cheeks. When he sobered up, he thought, "I only regret one thing. I'll never be able to tell this to anybody. No one would ever believe it."

They rode all day and into the night, stopping only twice to drink from their canteens and eat from the bag of biscuits that Brandy brought along. Not once did Brandy forget his fantasy. Except for the long silences when he seemed either to be in deep thought or asleep in the saddle, he was Sundance, and he never called Palidin anything other than Billy. It must have been two or three o'clock in the morning before they saw the lights of the Burgess Ranch, a mere glow in the distance. When they finally dismounted in the deep shadows beside the barn that sat some two hundred yards from the huge, sprawling house, Palidin's butt felt as if it had been flogged, and his legs and back were so stiff that he nearly fell. He was nothing less than amazed at the perseverance and stamina of the old man.

"As soon as we step out from behind this barn, them dogs o' Linda's are gonna rush us like two bats outta hell," whispered Brandy. "Your trick for gettin' by dogs better work."

"It works for some people — it works for me," said Palidin. "Brandy, there's something you better get straight. I'm only helping you get this money because you say that it's your money and I believe you. I know you're not lying about that, and I don't think you've been properly cared for, or justly used. I'm gonna help you, perhaps for adventure's sake, but as soon as we get out of there, I'm taking off for San Antonio, hopping a plane and heading north to Canada."

"And by God, I'll head for the Canadian River country, Billy. Now, how do we handle those dogs?"

"Hold up your left hand like this. Yeah, that's right, like a fag." Palidin held his right arm up, extended his hand out and touched Brandy's fingertips with his own. "Now, we're going to tiptoe our way to the house."

"Now?"

"Whenever you're ready."

"This is all there is to it?"

"All there is."

"It'll never work!"

"It works. You just have to be . . . happy."

"You're crazy! You don't know those dogs! I tried comin' to this house before, and I was lucky to get away with my life!"

"Okay, it's finished! See ya later."

"Wait! You go first!"

"It won't work that way. I have the . . . power, but it takes two to pull it off."

"How does it work? Where did you learn it?"

"I learned it from a Micmac Indian. I don't know how it works, exactly . . . but you have to be happy, a pixie."

"Well, I must be crazy after all! But, okay. We'll be torn to shreds, but let's get at it. Here, tie this kerchief over your face. We don't want to be recognized."

Arms bent up from the elbow, hands and fingers extended, touching each other fingertips to fingertips like two masked fags in a tulip patch, they headed for the house. Brandy felt a bit afraid at first, but he immediately learned something. It was impossible to do this, to ballet dance in this way without feeling happy. He was grinning like a flattered idiot and so was Palidin.

Tippytoe, tippytoe, tippytoe all the way to the house.

The German shepherd and the Doberman pinscher eyed them suspiciously at first, then grinned too and wagged their tails, pleased as puppies with the show. When he got to the door of the house, Brandy was awed, speechless, overwhelmed. This was the best trick he'd ever seen. "Who *is* this man?" he asked himself.

Brandy's hand was trembling with excitement when he inserted the key into the lock. They entered a large drawing room, which was about all that Palidin could tell in the dark. The first step he took told him that the floor was marble, that he must proceed slowly, step gently.

"This way," whispered Brandy and led Palidin across the room to another smaller room, a parlour or a living room. They entered. The floor creaked. They stopped and waited.

When they were convinced that nobody had heard the creaking floor, they continued their way across this second room and entered a third, a den with a fireplace. Brandy headed straight for the fireplace.

"Careful of the sofa," he whispered.

To the left of the fireplace was a picture which Brandy opened like a window or a door. It was on hinges. Behind the picture was the safe.

"There's no windows in here," whispered Brandy. "Turn on the light."

"They'll see the light coming from under the door."

"Only if they're awake and romping around. Now, turn on the light. There's a lamp right beside you."

Palidin fumbled in the darkness, found the lamp and turned it on. The lamp immediately illuminated the most beautiful room that Palidin had ever seen. There was a large stone fireplace with Texas longhorns over the mantle; there was a large oak desk, expensive antique chairs, paintings everywhere, a blue plush carpet on the floor. There was something else, too, on the floor to the right of the fireplace. Palidin saw it, but Brandy did not. Brandy was busy opening the safe.

Clink, click, jingle, jiggle. Brandy opened the safe. "It's here," he whispered. "Nobody's been in here since I left. I'm the only one who knows the combination." He removed a stack of bills six inches thick, handed them to Palidin. Palidin fanned the bills, noticed that they were all hundreds, then stuffed them under his shirt.

Brandy closed the safe and swung the picture back in place. "Okay. Let's get out of here," he whispered and swung to go. It was then that he saw what Palidin had seen.

There on the floor to the right of the fireplace sat a taxidermist's masterpiece, Snoopy's idol, Bo Peep's dream come true and Brandy Burgess's worst nightmare — the mounted, glass-eyed, plastic-tongued and perpetually sneering Texas red wolf.

The first thing that Brandy did was gasp. Then he groaned as if he were in agony, threw his head back, removed his big black hat and crushed it in his hands, pulled on his long white hair, grit his teeth, sniffed, sneered and fell to his knees. In a matter of seconds, it seemed that he aged twenty years. He sighed deeply, swallowed. His already watery eyes flooded with tears. He crawled to the wolf and embraced it. He began to sob like a little boy, a very lonesome and tired little boy.

Palidin said nothing, waited.

Finally Brandy spoke.

He did not whisper.

"I'm tired. Old and very tired." It seemed he was talking to the wolf.

Palidin wanted to reach out and touch him, give him a shoulder to lean on, say something, but he gave Brandy time instead, time to say adios to his brother.

Brandy's sobbing subsided in a minute or so, and after but a few seconds of silence, during which time he seemed to be thinking, he grabbed the poker from the front of the fireplace and smashed the wolf in the teeth. He then came down on its nose; the third blow crushed its head; the fourth bent its back; the fifth gashed its side. He beat the wolf until there was nothing left but a bunch of tattered fur, wire and stuffing; he hammered at it until he nearly exhausted himself. Then as quick as a wink, he swung and drew his gun, aimed it at the door.

Cav and Beatrix were standing in the door. They both had their mouths open, and they both held baseball bats.

"What in the name of . . . who? What's going on here?" Beatrix, a tall, fat woman with grey hair, pugged at the back, was the first to speak.

"My God A'mighty, sweet Jesus Christ. It's mista . . . " said Cav.

"Shut up!" snapped Brandy. "I'll do the talkin' here!"

"Yes suh, Mista Burgess suh, I mean Mista Robber." Cav was actually grinning, seemed happy to see his old boss.

"Why, blow me down if it ain't Mr. Burgess!" said Beatrix.

"Dat ain' no Mista Burgess, Bea! Don't you know the Sundance Kid when ya see 'im?"

"I know who I'm lookin' at, Cav," said Beatrix. Then she swung and glared at Palidin. "But who might you be?"

"I'm . . . I . . ."

"This here's me partner, Ma'am, but never mind who he is! Who shot this here wolf?"

"Why, George brought him in. Nearly two years ago, now. Why'd you do that?"

"Never mind! George, you say? Who's George?"

"I tol' you 'bout George, suh. Him Miss Linda's man, mind?"

"Does anybody know what that son of a bitch has done? Didn't I spend millions trying to prevent this type of thing from happening? Why, I have a mind to hunt that worthless bastard down and blow his head off! Is Linda in the house?"

"No, sir. I believe she's in New York, or at least that's where she said she was going. She travels a lot, you know. You look near dead, Mr. Burgess. Why don't you let me make you a nice hot drink and get you some food. Stay all night in your nice comfortable bed. Nobody will ever know."

"I wouldn't sleep in this house if you could bring back that wolf's life! Now, me and my partner are ridin' on out of here! And if you see this here George creature, you tell him that I intend to gun 'im down! And I mean it."

"Yo rode all the way down hea to tar up dat wolf, suh?"

"None of your business why I rode in here. Now, get out of my way!"

"Yes, suh!"

"C'mon, partner!"

"Ah . . . maybe I'll just . . . "

"Maybe you'll just ride on out of here with me! C'mon, I say!"

"Look, I really have had enough. You can have all the . . . "

"Shut up!"

"I don't want anything other than to . . . "

"Shut up! At least meet me by the horses. Cav, call in those dogs!"

"How you git pass dem dogs, suh?"

"Best trick you ever saw. But I'll tell ya about it some other time. Right now, me and Billy are ridin' on outta here. C'mon, Billy!"

"I'll see you out to your horse, but I'm not riding a single mile tonight," said Palidin. "I couldn't ride a horse tonight if I tried."

Cav called in the dogs and he and Beatrix stood in the door and waved good-bye to Palidin and Brandy until they disappeared into the night.

When they got to where they left the horse and the mule, Brandy stopped and leaned against Jonah. "I've been hit!" he said. "Hit bad, Billy. You'll have to help me into the saddle."

"Hit! Nobody fired any shots!"

"I'm hurtin' bad, Billy. Please . . . "

"You all right, Brandy?"

"I think I'm seein' the end of the trail, Billy. Help me, will ya?" Brandy reached for Palidin, staggered weakly, almost fell.

"You can't ride tonight," said Palidin, holding him up. "You won't get anywhere in the shape you're in."

"I'm hit bad, Billy."

"C'mon, I'll help you back to the house."

"No! No! I wanna meet me maker out on the lone prairie, Billy. Just like me brother did. Please, Billy?"

"Tch! I'll have to tie you in the saddle or something . . . "

"No . . . no, I'll be all right. You just help me up and ride with me out there for a mile or so. Where it's peaceful, Billy."

"Well . . . here, give me your arm . . . now your foot . . . up you go! Hold on! Good. Now wait for me."

"They'll be after us come mornin', Billy."

Palidin mounted Bornice. "I doubt that," he said. "Did they even know the money was there?"

"There'll be a posse, Billy. Giddyup!"

"Giddyup!" said Palidin.

Bornice started backing up toward the barn.

"No! Ho! No! Go straight ahead, you stupid mule!"

Palidin managed to rein Bornice around, but she was tired; she was home, within a stone's throw of her cozy stable, and she did not want to leave any more than Palidin wanted to. She went backward, forward, around in circles, continually edging toward the stable, determined that there she would stay. Brandy had already ridden off and Palidin had no idea what to do about this occurrence. Five, ten, fifteen minutes might have passed before she finally gave in to Palidin's urgings and began walking backwards, out across the Texas plains. Palidin swung around in the saddle so he could see where he was going.

"Heigh O, Bornice." he grumbled. "I hope you got eyes in your ass."

Palidin rode this way for what could have been half a mile. Then Bornice gave in completely, swung and started following what Palidin hoped was Brandy's trail. He swung around in the saddle again and began searching the dim night for the old man and Jonah.

"Brandy!" he shouted, but got no answer.

He called out every hundred yards or so and was beginning to worry. He wasn't even sure if he and Bornice were travelling in the right direction. "Brandy might be in trouble," he thought. "He might have fallen off his horse. He seemed in pretty bad shape, the old fool! Here I am with all this money under my shirt. I could be in big trouble. The Texas police, troopers, rangers, whatever, would probably just love getting their hands on a guy like me. What I should do is ride back to the ranch, get out on the highway and hitch a ride back to San Antonio, get on the bus and never look back."

Palidin crested a little knoll, and there in the distance he saw the light of a campfire. Brandy had reined up beside a little stand of trees and had built a fire, and as Palidin rode up, the old man was removing the saddle from Jonah's back. Palidin dismounted.

"Let me help you with that," said Palidin.

"No, no, I'm all right. Put some water in the boiling pail. I could do with a hot drink."

"But I thought you were . . . "

"I'm all right. It took ya long enough to get here! I thought maybe you had skipped with the loot. What's your name again?"

"Palidin! I told ya a hundred times! Palidin!"

"We pulled it off, kid! God, I'm tired."

"You're tired! I'd give a million dollars for a bed right now. Won't your daughter or someone send the police after us when they find out that we took all that money?"

"Nobody knew it was there. It's my money, anyway. I stashed money all over the place. You don't think I left myself without a nest egg, do ya?"

"You said you were broke."

"Did I? Well, I didn't have any money at Merna's Butt, if that's what you mean. I'm still angry as a hornet, you know that? To think that some miserable fortune hunter went out and shot what could very well have been the very last wolf . . . Christ! What's the world coming to?"

"The water's getting hot. What've ya got? Coffee?"

"Yeah . . . here . . . and somewhere in here . . . " Brandy searched for something in his saddlebag. "Here it is. A little whiskey to spike it with."

"Oh God, not that stuff again! It seems I've been hung over for a week."

Brandy came over to the fire and kept an eye on the brewing coffee while Palidin removed the saddle from Bornice. When Palidin had finished this chore, Brandy poured the coffee into two tin cups, spiked it generously with whiskey and handed one to Palidin. With their backs against their saddles, they sat by the little fire. Palidin removed the money from his shirt and handed it to Brandy.

Brandy took it and stared at it thoughtfully.

"Any idea how much is there?" asked Palidin.

"Ten, twenty, thirty thousand. Maybe more. I'll split it with ya."

"Ah, you can't do that. I couldn't take your money."

"You earned it."

"I didn't do anything except give you a hard time. You're not playing games now, are you?"

"The game's over. Here." Brandy handed Palidin half the stack of bills. "Take this and tell me what your magic hook is all about. There's about fifteen thousand there. That should be enough for a magic hook."

"You mean, you're buying my idea?"

"That's what you wanted, wasn't it?"

"Yeah, but . . . "

"Is that not enough?"

"I . . . I don't know . . . I mean . . . "

"You don't know! Of course, you don't know! And you will never know, because once I buy it, it's mine. Of course, I'll need the idea written down on paper."

"Fifteen thousand dollars is a lot of money. But, I don't know . . . "

"Take it or leave it. Here's another thousand or so for your troubles. Call it expenses."

"Hell, Brandy, I don't know. How do you know the idea even works?"

"Ha! Do you think I care?"

"Well, you're buying it, aren't you?"

"Yes, I am. And then the idea will be mine. That's the way it works! If it's a bad idea, then I will have lost my investment, and I'll remember you as a fraud. Frauds don't get very far in the business world. You'll have however much money you have there and that's about it."

"What are you gonna do. I mean, after I leave?"

"I'm ridin' back to Merna's Butt where I'll play games till the day I die, which won't be too far down the road at the rate I'm burning the candle." Brandy climbed stiffly to his feet and went to where he'd left his saddlebags, searched through one and returned with a pen and a piece of crumpled paper.

"This will do," he said. "Write down whatever it is about your magic fishing hook, date it and sign it." He handed the paper and pen to Palidin.

Palidin sighed, unsure of what he should do.

"What's the matter, chickening out?"

"Well, it really does work. I mean, it never failed."

"And every fisherman in North America, maybe the world, will be using it, haulin' fish from the lakes and rivers like they were in a storage bin. That's what we're talkin' here, ain't it?"

Palidin sighed again.

"You're a Canadian. Newfoundland's a part of Canada, if I'm not mistaken."

"Yeah, since 1949."

"In 1911 the Newfoundland white wolf became extinct,

due primarily to a bounty. The Newfoundland white wolf, the *Canis Lupus beothucus*, so named for the Beothuk Indians. Best name in the world for an extinct wolf, couldn't be more fit!"

"The Beothuk Indians. They're extinct, too, right?"

"The Japanese wolf became extinct in 1905; in 1915 the Kenai wolf of Alaska disappeared; the last Florida black wolf was seen in 1917; in 1920, we saw the last New Mexican wolf and Texas grey wolf; in 1926, the great plains lobo wolf vanished from the face of the Earth. In 1940, the southern Rocky Mountain wolf bid us farewell. And in 1950, the brown wolf, the great Cascade Mountain brown wolf waved good-bye. I think that one breathed its last breath in Canada, too. And now, I'm afraid . . . "

"Your brother?"

"My brother."

"I'm sorry."

"The Mexican silver grizzly, the Atlas bear, the Bali tiger, the Arizona jaguar, the Barbary lion and the Cape lion with its black mane, the Oregon bison, the eastern elk, Dawson's caribou. The dodo, the passenger pigeon, the imperial woodpecker, the American ivory-billed woodpecker, the Labrador duck, the painted vulture, the great auk, the elephant bird . . . ha! That one was over ten feet tall and weighed over a thousand pounds, its eggs more than three feet in circumference. Grosbeaks, thrushes, fly-catchers, wrens — there's a list a mile long and gettin' longer. And there's reptiles and turtles and fish on that list."

"I'm not a hunter," said Palidin. "But I suppose I'm just as guilty. I've fished."

"Aw, I'm not attacking you, young fella. If anyone's to blame, it's grubs like me. I made more money than the good Lord ever meant for one person to have, sellin' rifles, ammunition, fishing rods, lures, nets, waders, traps, skinning knives. Clothes to kill in. Look good while you kill. God, I don't want to think about it! But that's why I . . . I . . ." Brandy whimpered, sighed. "The wolf . . . you understand where I'm coming from? Why I did . . ."

"Yeah, I understand." said Palidin and stared, amazed, at the old man.

Brandy was slumped. His watery eyes reflected the little fire, and so did the tear that coursed its way down his cheek. Palidin searched for the right words, thought that maybe it might be better to say nothing, to give Brandy a little time to reason things out. He waited, listened to the crackle of the little fire, the periodic sniff from Brandy.

"It was all a waste of time," muttered Brandy after a while.

"You didn't know. And if people hadn't purchased their guns from you, they'd have bought them somewhere else. It wouldn't have mattered. What matters is that you've learned . . ."

"I learned twenty years too late! Forty years too late! Sixty years too late! I was obsessed with money. Money replaced everything. Creatures all over the world sacrificed their simple lives just to keep me in martinis and Cadillacs."

"But you learned and you bought all this land in an effort to save the wolf. You tried."

"You see, I knew what was happening. All the time I knew. But I allowed it to continue, thinking that I could solve the problem later with money — that I could do anything with money. I ignored the writing on the wall. A woman married me for my money. I raised a daughter to think of nothing but money. 'I want, I want, I want,' they screamed and whined and pestered and . . . aw, what's the use?"

"And you did try to solve the problem with money by buying all this land. I assume it will become a park, that it hasn't been retaken in some way by your company or whatever?"

"I was allowed to keep it — as a playground for a childish old man, they said. They pushed me out, urged me to move to an island in the Pacific, hang up the spurs."

"You could still do things."

"Like what?"

"A man of your calibre could make people listen. You could make public speeches, tell the world about what you've learned, let them in on your wisdom."

"Do you realize what you're saying? Can't you see the contradiction in a man that's made millions selling knives for cutting throats trying to sincerely tell people not to go out and cut throats? They'd laugh me out of the arena as just another raving politician. And besides, they took away my power."

"You're just falling victim to your own fears, your own considered weakness. You knew how to make millions, but you were certainly no philosopher. When you saw them pushing you out, you should have gracefully allowed it to happen, you should have retired and manipulated from behind the scenes. But you didn't want to give up the power, the money! Money did it to you again."

Brandy sat quietly for a moment, then said, "I'm so tired."

"I'll get the blankets," said Palidin, rising and tossing the last of his spiked coffee into the fire. The fire gave a little puff as the alcohol exploded. The sleeping bags were on the ground ten feet away. Palidin fetched them and spread them out by the fire. Brandy wrapped himself in and turned on his side to watch the fire. Palidin, too, wrapped himself in and lay watching the fire.

"It's a magnetic hook," said Palidin.

"Huh?"

"I magnetize the hook. Fish can't resist it."

"Ha!"

"On the Dungarvon, every time I threw it in the water, a salmon grabbed it. Nobody else would be catching anything, and I was getting fish all over the place. It was almost scary."

"Does anyone else know about this?"

"Ah . . . I told my brother. Dryfly knows about it."

"Shit!"

"Oh, don't worry about Dryfly. He's not much of a fisherman and has probably forgotten it all, anyway. He's just one of those lads that will stay in Brennen Siding for the rest of his life, marry a girl from down the road. And I told him not to tell anybody."

"You're not lying to me, are you? The hook works?"

"Every time."

"Christ! It's worth millions!"

"Yeah, I know . . . ah, Brandy?"

"Yeah?"

"The eastern cougar still exists, I think. In New Brunswick, I mean."

"What do ya mean you think?"

"They're kind of like Big Foot or UFOs, ya know. There are sightings."

"The eastern cougar, eh?"

"It may or may not exist, sort of like your wolf."

There was a long period of silence, maybe five minutes passed before either spoke again.

"I wished I could remember who it was I knew. There was somebody in my life from New Brunswick. Gonna stick around for a spell, kid?"

"I reckon I might. Cav is gonna be wantin' his mule back."

"You could ride Star, if you want."

"Much obliged."

"Good night, Billy."

"Good night, Sundance."

There was another few moments of silence. Then, uncannily, at the very same moment they both began to sing,

Yippee ti!
Yippee ti yi yi!
Yippee ti!
Yippee ti yi yi!
Headin' south across the prairie 'neath the western sky
To me darlin' Mary Ellen, yippee ti yi yi!

thirteen

Shadrack and Dryfly stayed in the United States for four days, and with more than just a little reluctance, especially for Dryfly, they prepared themselves for the drive back to Brennen Siding. Then the moment came, and they found themselves standing beside Shad's van, saying goodbye to Lillian and Janice.

"Well, I guess this is it," said Dryfly to Lillian. "We're off!"

Lillian embraced him and kissed him gently, her lips cool as always. "You take care," she said. "And I'll see you in a couple of weeks."

Lillian would be finishing up her exams in a week or so, and she was planning to spend the summer at her father's cottage in Brennen Siding. She and Dryfly would be together for the whole summer.

"This was the best time I ever had," said Dryfly. "I love it here. I hate to leave."

"I'll see you in a couple of weeks. I love you."

"I love to hear you say that. I love you, too."

Shad shook Janice's hand.

"You gonna try and get up to stay with Lillian for a while?" he asked.

"You bet," said Janice. "You're quite a guy, Shadrack. I'm moving to Boston soon, I think. Back to work. Come and see me sometime."

"Yep! I'll be dropping in. Well, gimme a kiss, little darlin', and we'll hit the road."

Janice smiled down at Shad, her massive pumpkin-orange hairdo framed her face like a splash of rising sun. She leaned and kissed Shad. "You look after number one," she said.

Ten minutes later, the boys were heading north on Interstate 95.

"Boys, these American lads got 'er made!" said Shad. "So much to do! Look at this highway! Where in New Brunswick would you see a highway like this? This is where it's at, Dry!"

Dryfly was feeling very lonesome, remembering the smell, the touch, the warmth, the soft voice, the beauty and spirit of Lillian. "This is where Lillian is at," he muttered.

"You know what, Dry? Janice told me that Lillian likes you."

"Hmm."

"Do you have any idea just how rich she is?"

"I'm not sure, Shad."

"According to Janice, she's got a bundle and a half! You wanna hang onto her, I tell ya! Get her and you'll never have to work a day in your life. Do you think she'll have ya?"

"Maybe . . . "

"You'll be a big shot just like old Bill. Live down here somewhere, take a scoot up to Brennen Siding once, twice a year for a little fishin'. Damn! I can't wait to get back to tell the boys about New York! You should've seen it, Dry! Make any buildin' in New Haven look like a toy. I saw a rock 'n' roll band down there that . . . well, I can't tell ya how good it was! Awhoop!" Shad was feeling very good, sang "I got sunshine on a cloudy day! And when it's cold outside, I got the month of May!"

Dryfly was feeling what he thought was very good, too, but he wasn't completely sure about how he felt because he was feeling so much — excitement, love, loneliness, strength, weakness, fear, bewilderment. He had left home with so little, and now he had so much. He allowed a long sigh to escape, then closed his eyes to think about what Lillian had said to him the night before.

"I don't want you to change one little thing about you," she had told him. "You're perfect the way you are, my man of the river. I don't want to ever take you away from your river. It's you. Your accent is you, your wit is you, your smile is you, your childhood is you, and I love you. Promise me you won't change."

Dryfly promised.

"You all right?" asked Shad.

"Yeah, I'm all right. I was just thinking that I've changed," said Dryfly.

*

Shad and Dry crossed the Maine-New Brunswick border at Houlton, connected up with the Trans-Canada at Woodstock and followed the St. John River to Fredericton. It was on this stretch of road that they encountered yet another experience — the experience of coming home to New Brunswick. If they had known then what they would know twenty years later, they might have said what any worldly person says when they experience that drive down the St. John River — "New Brunswick is the most beautiful country in the world!" But instead, they feasted their eyes and said things like:

"Pretty."

"Bigger than the States."

"Yeah, lots of room, that's for sure."

"This road runs all the way to British Columbia."

"Look at that sunset on the water!"

"Let's you and me run the Dungarvon or the Cains this summer!"

"Sounds good to me. We could do something like that every weekend."

"Big cities smell, don't they?"

"Yeah, I feel sorry for people living in big cities."

"Ever thought about goin' to Quebec?"

"All French in Quebec."

"Montreal won the cup."

"A long ways to Quebec."

"A long ways to British Columbia. "

"A long ways to China."

"Close to the States, though."

"Three hours and just about anybody can be in the States."

"We should be more like the States."

"More money in the States."

"Money can't buy this, can it?"

"Money bought Cabbage Island and the Lindon Tucker pool . . . and a whole bunch more."

"Yeah," with a shrug.

"There's the old Maple Leaf!"

"Not so old."

"No blood on *that* flag."

"O Canada! Our home and native land!"

"Whoop! It's good to be back!"

It didn't matter who said what, they were one voice, the voice of Canadians.

*

When they arrived at Brennen Siding, the April sun had already taken its bows and had stepped behind its crimson curtain — end of show for the day. Shadrack dropped Dryfly off at the Cabbage Island Salmon Club and hurried on to Blackville to tell the boys about his adventures in Connecticut and especially about his night in New York City. He knew that having been to New York would for a while give him that edge of mystery, that little extra spice in the popularity recipe. He'd seen it happen before with other guys. It seemed that when Billy Bean first came back from Toronto he could get any girl he wanted. Gary Perkins also found himself in first place in the popularity contest when he returned from his two weeks of picking potatoes in Mars Hill, Maine. Nobody knew much about where Mars Hill, Maine, was, but it didn't matter; Gary had been there, had been *somewhere* outside of the province, and he could have been in Athens as far as the teenagers in the Blackville area were concerned.

Fifteen minutes from the time he dropped Dryfly off, Shad pulled up in front of Biff's Canteen in Blackville. He noticed that there were only seven or eight guys and girls around, but "It's enough," he thought and stepped out of his van, dusted off one of his props, the "I Heart New York" bumper sticker, gazed up at the canteen and said with just a hint of an American accent, "Christ, it's good to be back!"

"Where ya been, Shad?" asked Eldon Clark.

"Oh, around. New Haven, New York — around." Shad patted the van as if it were a pet. "Yes, sir, this old baby has seen a lotta road in the last while."

"You've been to New York?" asked Mary Wilson, one of the prettier, more adventuresome girls in the group.

"Oh, yeah," said Shad casually. Although he rarely smoked, at this point he lit up a Winston's. "You know, there was a time when I didn't like American cigarettes. But like anything else, I guess you get used to them."

"Tell us about New York," said Eldon.

"Oh, nothing much to tell. It's big, I can say that. Lots of tall buildings, lots of action, bars everywhere. Broadway was fun."

"Did you see the Statue of Liberty?" asked Randy King.

Shad hadn't seen the Statue of Liberty. He and Janice had checked out of the Belmont and had driven directly back to New Haven. "Oh, yeah," he lied.

"Was it big?"

"Is the President white?"

"Huh?"

"Oh yeah . . . big."

"Boy! I wouldn't mind seeing New York," said Mary Wilson.

Shad flipped his cigarette onto the sidewalk. He had just lit it and the butt was nearly full length, but this was a statement from Shad, too. This was his way of saying, "Money? Money means nothing to Shadrack Nash. Shadrack Nash has been to New York, and handling himself in this neck of the woods is going to be a piece of cake."

"I got some friends down there," said Shad. "Maybe I could take you along with me sometime."

"Yeah! I'd love to."

Shad smiled at the thought of it. Mary thought that he was just being cool. Shad's smile broadened into a grin. "The bullshit is working just fine," he thought.

"How come you went down to New York?" asked David.

"Ah, I needed to get away for a while. I took Dryfly with me as far as New Haven. This girlfriend of mine, Janice Lynch. She's a doctor, you know. We went on down to New York, stayed at the Plaza, had a ball."

David Carlyle came up the street with his dog, Bluff, saw the little gathering and stopped to chat. Bluff was a big, blond, very well-mannered dog, and no one could recall ever seeing David without her.

"Hey! How's she goin', Shad?"

"Not too bad, David. How ya been?" said Shad.

"Good, good, the very best! You?"

"Not too bad. Same old dog, I see."

"Ah, yeah."

Here, for effect, Shad reached down and scratched Bluff's head, said "Ah, the animal!"

*

With Dryfly, it was all about loneliness.

Winter and summer rallied for the last time, as indicated by the sun's hot, vermilion prophesies of warmer days to come. Robins sang "so long" to the day, starlings chatted in budding alders. The river, glazed with sunset, sang "Peace in the Valley," its audience captured, mesmerized and, like Nutbeam, all ears.

Dryfly made his way over the hill and up along the shore to the footbridge. He could hear someone hammering, driving nails, tap, tap, tap in the distance. It could have been coming from as near as the other side of the river, or it could have been two miles downstream at the Furlong Bridge, such was the stillness of the evening. At times, he was so close to the water's edge that he could see his reflection strolling there beside him. He stopped and gazed down at himself. He was two bodies crotched from the same sneakers. His reflection stared back at him with tired, lonesome eyes, handsome in a way. "If I had a beard, I'd look like Palidin, a bit," he thought. "Ha! I've made ends meet."

Dryfly lifted his gaze from his reflection, looked up at the sky, clear, deep. He looked upstream, downstream, scanned the little farms — Nutbeam's, John Kaston's, Helen MacDonald's, Bert Todder's, Lindon Tucker's — across the way. As he scanned, he noticed that someone was on the footbridge, kneeling, toward the far end.

"That's where the hammering's comin' from," he concluded. "Someone's fixin' the bridge."

Dryfly kept on walking, came to the bridge and mounted the abutment.

Although the light was growing dim, he could now see who it was there hammering.

Often, when crossing the bridge, it was Dryfly's practice to stop on the middle abutment, watch the river flow, think, discuss things with his alter ego. His alter ego took on different personalities on different nights — everyone from Romeo to Hank Snow to God. On Romeo nights he thought of Lillian. On Hank Snow nights, he sang. On God nights, he prayed. Tonight, after the eye-opening experience of his trip to New Haven, no longer the virgin, no longer the boy, he felt like doing all three. But these things were things you did alone; thus he was disappointed to be intruded upon by the lone carpenter — or anyone else.

Tap, tap, tap, tap, tap. The kneeling carpenter paid no attention to Dryfly's approaching footsteps whatsoever.

Intruded upon or not, Dryfly could not resist stopping on the middle abutment, in the middle of his river, to at least take a look around. From somewhere upstream, the sound of an outboard motor starting up came to his ear. "Someone givin' up the fishin' for the day," he thought. "About time, too. It'll be dark soon." He listened to the motor fading into the distance, heading for Gordon.

The tapping stopped.

Dryfly looked to investigate.

The carpenter was gone.

"Boy! Bert sure left in a hurry," he thought.

*

Nutbeam and Shirley were so glad to see their wandering boy come home that it seemed to Dryfly that he'd been away for years. After the initial hugs, handshakes and pats on the back, Shirley put the tea on and brought out a plate of molasses cookies. They sat at the kitchen table to talk.

"So, tell us all about it," began Nutbeam.

"Not much to tell," said Dryfly.

"New Haven a big place?"

"Real big."

"Big as Newcastle, big as Fredericton, how big?"

"Bigger than them both, I think."

"Did ya git to see Lillian?" asked Shirley.

"Yeah. She's doin' the very best."

"Was she good to you?"

"Of course, Mom! How've you guys been doin'?"

"Oh, nothin' goin' on around here," said Nutbeam. "How far away is it?"

"We drove about twelve hours to get there."

"Good God! That far! Did ya see any mountains?"

"One . . . in Maine. Just stickin' right up there in the middle of nowhere."

"I know that mountain!" said Nutbeam. "Mount Katahdin, right?"

"Yeah, I guess so."

"But that was the only one?"

"Far as I remember. I brought ya back something." Dryfly's bag was beside him. He unzipped it, removed a tube-like object wrapped in brown paper and handed it to Shirley.

"What is it, another calendar?" she asked. "Here, Nut, you'd better open it."

"It's not a calendar," said Dryfly. "It ain't very much. Didn't have much money to throw around. It's sort of for everyone, Sally, too, I guess."

Nutbeam unwrapped and unrolled the poster.

"Hmm . . . it's . . . it's very, very pretty, Dryfly. Thanks a million. What's it say, Shirley?"

Shirley read, "Desiderata . . . Go placidly amid the noise and haste, and remember what peace there may be in silence. As far as possible without surrender be on good terms with all persons . . . " Shirley read on, and Nutbeam listened intently, his big floppy ears sucking up every word. Shirley read, "Exercise caution in your business affairs; for the world is full of trickery," and Nutbeam nodded and affirmed his agreement with a "Hmm." He agreed again when she read, "Many fears are born of fatigue and loneliness," and he nodded thoughtfully when she covered, "You are a child of the universe no less than the trees and the stars." He sighed deeply when she wrapped it up with the "With all its sham, drudgery and broken dreams, it is still a beautiful world. Be careful. Strive to be happy."

"Isn't that wonderful!" said Shirley. "Where's it from, Dryfly, the Bible?"

"Dunno," shrugged Dryfly. "Just thought you'd like it."

"Like it! We'll frame it, Shirley," said Nutbeam. "We'll frame it and put it right . . . ah . . . right . . . " Nutbeam had so many calendars hanging in the kitchen that there was no space left for hanging anything else.

"We'll take down that old calendar with the dog on it and hang this up in its place. We don't need fourteen calendars," said Shirley.

"Well, well, I like that calendar, but I guess you're right. Maybe I'll hang it in the bedroom — the calendar, I mean. You'll have to teach me what it says, Shirl!"

"I already told you what it says."

"I know, I know, but I wanna learn to say it, myself."

"We'll both teach ya," said Dryfly.

"What's it called again?"

"'Desiderata.'"

"'Desiderata' . . . wonder what that means?"

Desiderata. Taken from the Latin, *desidero*, meaning desire, long for, miss? Or *desidiosus*, meaning lazy? Dryfly wasn't aware of a single Latin word, but his consideration of "Desiderata" was probably as comprehensive as most people's. "Some people consider, others desider. And then again, it might have something to do with baby sitter," he said.

"God only knows," said Shirley.

"How's Sally makin' out?" asked Dryfly.

"She's startin' to talk, Dryfly. Sayin' a new word every day! I never saw the like of it! And she can take a few steps, too! First thing ya know, she'll be goin' to school. First thing ya know, she be all growed up, a young lady. First thing ya know, she'll be gettin' married and havin' babies. First thing ya know, she'll . . . "

"She's doin' okay, dear," put in Shirley. "You've only been away for four days, and she hasn't become the Queen of England yet."

"Ha!" said Nutbeam. "Not yet."

fourteen

James Lowery stepped into the West Wind Sports building and beelined for the elevator. In the elevator he pushed the ten button and anxiously tapped his alligator shoes on the carpeted floor. He could have had a bee up his ass. He was so anxious, so beside himself, that he wasn't even smiling.

"Hurry, hurry, hurry!" he said to the elevator.

Ten seconds later he stormed past Jucy, greeted her with a "Follow me," and entered his office. Jucy heard the urgency in his voice, didn't quite know what to make of it.

"What's the matter?" she asked.

"Where's that Canadian kid?"

"Canadian kid?"

"Yes, yes! You know, the one with the flyhook! Where is he?"

"Oh, thank God! I thought maybe something was wrong."

"Nothing's wrong! Where is he?"

"He's . . . I'm not sure. I mean, I drove him out to the Burgess ranch. Must be two weeks ago, now. I imagine he's back in Canada by now."

"Damn it! Damn it, damn it, damn it! Do you have his address? His Canadian address?"

"Why, er . . . no . . . Toronto maybe. Why?"

"Never mind. Who'd he see at the ranch?"

"Just an old man. The last I saw of him he was talking about renting a mule, in a big huff to ride somewhere to see Mr. Burgess."

"He may still be up there?"

"Well, I . . . "

"Never mind. Get back to your phone. Get me Neil Billings! Hurry!"

"You mean the lab?"

"Yes! Hurry!"

Jucy hurried back to her desk, called the lab.

James Lowery waited, answered the phone before it finished its first ring.

"Neil?"

"Jim?"

"What did you find out?"

"We photographed and analyzed, took it apart, tested and tasted and smelled every hair and thread on it. Nothing."

"Nothing!"

"Nothing."

"There's got to be something!"

"Nothing."

"Well, do it all again!"

"There's nothing peculiar about it, I tell you!"

"Nothing peculiar about it! Don't tell me there's nothing peculiar about it! Didn't I tell you . . . ?"

"I know, I know, I know! You caught fish on it."

"Every cast! Nobody else bagged a thing, and I . . ."

"I know, I know, I know! Ya caught sixteen. But there's nothing peculiar about it."

"Go over it again, anyway!"

James Lowery hung up, scratched his brow, ran his fingers through his curly red hair. "There has to be something," he said to himself. "I have to find that kid." He picked up the phone again.

"Jucy! What was that kid's name?"

"Palidin you mean?"

"Palidin! Palidin what?"

"Ah . . . Rambut, Ramsey, Ram something-or-other. He left his bag at my apartment."

"He did? It's still there?"

"Yes. I guess that means he might still be around."

"Yes, yes, you're a doll. I'm taking the day off. Phone the Burgess ranch. Tell them I'm coming out and that I want a horse this time."

"A horse? You want a horse?"

"A horse! You don't think I'm gonna let him fill my Jeep full of holes again, do you? The old fool won't shoot a horse, that I'll bet on, and I'm not about to walk that distance again in my bare feet."

"But can you ride a horse?"

"Yes, yes! Get to it!"

"He stripped you naked and made you walk . . . "

"Shut up!"

"I'm sorry, I . . . "

"Listen, if Palidin comes back to your apartment while I'm out there looking for him, keep him there no matter what. Keep him there, supposing you have to tie him down, ya hear?"

"You *know* I can do that."

"Just keep him there!"

"Would you like a little something to tie you over while you're out there on that nasty old ranch? It would only take a minute."

"Now, stop that!"

"I'm sorry. You know what I mean."

"Ah . . . hell! Well, okay. Get in here."

*

Star, the white Arabian mare, was like a Corvette with heavy duty suspension, graceful to look at, lots of power and speed but lacking the smooth, quiet comfort of the Cadillac. Bornice was the Cadillac. Palidin had returned Bornice to Cav and had been riding Star for nearly a week. He wished he had Bornice back. Bornice had character, a personality, a mind of her own. Star was too broken, too willing to obey humans, had forgotten her strength and size, lacked dignity. Bornice would walk backwards, try and stomp on your feet while you saddled her, occasionally go where she felt like going even if her rider intended to go in the opposite direction. She rebelled in many subtle little ways, never let you forget that she was a mule, demanded your respect.

On Star and Jonah, Palidin and Brandy rode north until they came to the little town of Rocksprings. There they purchased some supplies — food, drink, fishing gear, a change of clothes, a new pair of boots for Palidin — then rode for another day until they came to the rocky headwaters of the Llano River.

At first sight of the Llano, Palidin said, "You know, we could've bought a couple of plane tickets. Could've been fishing the Dungarvon by now. What fish in its right mind would stay in water like this?"

"More snakes than fish," chuckled Brandy. "If your magnetic flyhook works here, it'll work anywhere."

"We've come all this way to fish for snakes, have we?"

"Relax, partner, there's fish here, whether ya believe it or not. Catfish mostly, the odd bluegill and a real winner called gar. Ever see a gar?"

"I'm not sure if I want to. Catfish are bottom feeders and won't take a fly, anyway, will they?"

"Does it matter what you throw at them? If ya kin magnetize a flyhook, why not a spoon?"

"Never thought of that," said Palidin. "But come to think of it, black salmon like lures so much that you're not even allowed to fish with them on the Miramichi system. Do you suppose that that has anything to do with them being magnetic?"

"Makes sense, they're made of metal."

"Hmm."

"I'll tether the horses over there in that meadow. You gather some wood, set up camp. It'll be chilly here tonight, believe it or not."

There weren't many trees in this area of the Llano — a few dogwoods, a couple of sick-looking old pines, some bushes that Palidin couldn't identify, and that was about it, but he gathered what he could find, and after an hour or so of lugging in the hot sun he had what he hoped was enough to last the night.

All the time Palidin lugged, he thought about fishing, his invention, the fact that he had never considered magnetizing a lure before. "If it's all about magnets," he thought, "all you really need is a hook. There's a possibility that fish don't actually see the hook at all, that they're drawn by the magnetic pull only. That would explain why you can catch a salmon on a copper-coloured fly in the Cains. The Cains has really swampy, copper-coloured water . . . a copper-coloured fly in the Cains would be pretty much invisible. And in the fall when the red maple leaves fall to add an even darker copper tint to the water, the Mickey Finn, the General Practitioner, red and yellow flies like that, are the most productive. When the water is crystal clear in the middle of the summer, on a day when there's a few white clouds in the sky, you generally use a Butterfly. A Butterfly has white wings. If the sun is very bright and is reflecting the fields, forest, grassy meadows, the greenery, a Green Machine is very productive. Maybe there's more than just the magnet. Maybe it has something to do with the ripples and waves. Maybe the secret has as much to do with magnifying as magnetizing. Water magnifies, doesn't it? Wished I had a real river to experiment in."

Palidin's brother Dryfly had run this basic theory past David O'Hara earlier as a joke, the stuff about the invisible food. A coincidence? Telepathy between brothers? Had they talked about it at some time or another? Do all Miramichiers reason in this way while they're fishing? Do Miramichiers realize that they have one of the few remaining *real* rivers left to fish in? To Dryfly, the invisible food theory was just a joke, of course. To Palidin, it was a dead serious study. Miramichiers know that they have the best river in the world, no jokes or studies required. All they have to do is look at the river for a minute, see its cleanliness, its pristine beauty, its depths so occupied with salmon, trout, smelts, shad, gaspereaux, chub, eels, lampreys, minnows, the occasional bass, yes, and even catfish, that its surface is constantly moving, animated.

When Brandy returned from tending the horses, Palidin asked, "You ever been to the Miramichi?"

"Nope. But I'm damn sure I know someone from up that way."

"That's where we should be fishing. The Miramichi!"

"What's the matter with this?"

"Oh, it's nice and all that, but I've been here for an hour and I haven't seen one fish move."

"So? What do you expect, the fish to be moving all over the place? A school a minute, for God's sake?"

Palidin gazed at the sun-baked hills, the boulders, the nearly treeless terrain, the murky, algae-infested water, and did not comment any further. He thought, however, that he'd be heading for the Miramichi, the Dungarvon, Brennen Siding, very, very soon.

That evening, they magnetized a lure and caught five catfish, two bluegills and a gar. When Palidin pulled in the gar, he wasn't sure whether it was a fish or a lizard.

"So, what do ya think?" asked Palidin.

"I think you should keep your mouth shut," said Brandy.

Palidin took this as sound advice.

Later that night, while Brandy snored peacefully and coyote calls glanced about from moon to Earth, Palidin sat in the dancing reflections of a little fire contemplating his future.

"Brandy's like the future . . . older. Everything will be older in the future. Here in the present, we are young, small, narrow, naive little children. All of our dreams are so . . . so childish, all based on possessions we can never really employ, but dreams nonetheless. Dreams, worthless, really. They'd be nothing if they weren't weighed against the future and the past. What is good today was evil in the past. What is evil today may be good tomorrow. The basic ingredients of a new religion maybe. A new religion based on one commandment: 'Thou shalt not do today what may be considered evil tomorrow.' If those before us had've thought that way, maybe Earth would be a better place. Teach your children. You really never possess anything but your own . . . self . . . your own body. To be satisfied is to . . . to desire little . . . and . . . and love all."

Palidin could have been compiling his very own "Desiderata."

He threw a stick on the fire and wrapped his blanket tighter about him, inched a little closer to the fire for warmth.

They were camped but a few yards from the river. He heard a disturbance at the water's edge, first the tinkle of water, then a sound that resembled someone eating a juicy peach. He looked to investigate.

The little fire lit up what looked like a catfish standing beside the water.

"A standing fish," thought Palidin. "I'm going crazy."

The catfish looked about, seemed to feel the air with its barbels, then wobbled? hobbled? waddled? . . . slithered toward the fire.

"Brandy?"

When the catfish got to within a few feet of the fire, it stopped, looked about again, didn't seem to like the feel of the fire, turned and began to make its way back to the river.

"Brandy!"

"Huh?"

The catfish jumped into the water.

"Ah . . . nothin'."

Palidin slept very little that night.

*

James stormed through the door, up to Jucy's desk and said, "Did that Palidin kid show up?"

"Ah, no . . . "

"Jucy, you're taking a few days off."

"I am?"

"You're going home to your apartment and staying there until that kid shows up."

"I can't do that!"

"Sure ya can! It's our only hope. I rode all the way up to Brandy's shack only to find that both he and the kid had left. The old man at the ranch told me that the kid returned his mule and rode back toward Brandy's shack on the old fool's horse not more than a few days ago. That means they're still out there. He'll be back, and he'll be dropping in to pick up the stuff he left at your place. I want you there when he comes." James Lowery smiled his usual scheming smile.

"But who'll look after things around here?"

"You can take your typewriter and fingernail file home with you. I'll drop in occasionally."

"Today?"

"Right now. For all we know, he might be knocking on your door at this very minute."

"But who'll answer the phone?"

"Don't worry about it. I'll get someone else. Now, take off!"

"Yes, sir. What's this all about, anyway? Why do y'all need to see little old Palidin so much?"

"Wouldn't you like to know!"

"Well, honey, I was just asking."

"You just mind your own business."

"Ah . . . honey?"

"Yes?"

"Should I call Mrs. Lowery and tell her where you'll be spending so much of your time during the next few days?"

"You . . . oh, I see. So, what is it now?"

"I saw the cutest little dress at Brenda's yesterday. It looked so sexy on me . . . "

"Now, that's blackmail!"

"Now, you want me to look sexy, don't you? If I don't look sexy, how else am I ever gonna keep little old Palidin around until you get there?"

Jucy was pouting. James Lowery sighed. "The slut *is* blackmailing me."

"How much?" he asked.

"Only slightly more than a hundred dollars, and it's low in the front just like you like. It's red and a slit up the . . ."

"Okay, okay! Buy it!"

"Really?"

"Yes, yes, buy it!"

"Ooh, you're the sweetest thang!"

"Get out of here. I'm beat! My ass is sore, my back aches. I hate horses with a passion!"

"Oh, poor baby! Let me give you a little back rub."

"Ah, you should go home, be there . . . "

"How's this?"

"Umm . . . "

"Now, doesn't that feel good?"

"Umm . . . come into my office."

*

When Brandy awakened, it was so early that a few stars were still shining. The eastern horizon was paling a bit, the only indication that dawn was approaching. He slapped and shook the sand and scorpions from his boots, pulled them on and stood. "My back," he groaned. "I'm getting way, way, way too old for this. The kid's still sleeping. Quite a kid, that. Never met anyone like him. He's sticking with me, even though he must think me crazier than all getout. Maybe I am crazy, maybe I am crazy. That was the slickest trick I ever saw in my life. How'd he do that? Just walked right through those killer dogs as if they were pigeons. And when I locked him in the root cellar, he came out all dreamy. It almost seemed as if he liked it in there. And this magnet stuff . . . usually I'd be lucky to catch a fish in three or four days of fishin', and last night we caught eight? Nine? Could've caught a lot more. Who'd have thought? A magnetic hook. A good-looking young feller. Makes sense whenever he talks. A Canadian. Canada. Now there's a place a man could still be himself. He's different than us. Wouldn't take the money. Didn't even want me to pay for his new boots. He's not your average American. I'll bet that he's not even your average Canadian. He's got some kind of glow about him. I can't figure it out. It seems he knows something, something that no one else knows. He's like . . . who? Ariel? Puck? Now in the twilight of dawn it wouldn't surprise me if he vanished. No one so ethereal should haunt beyond the cockcrow. And he does haunt. He haunts me, at least. Strangest man I ever knew. What was it he said to me? I followed the trail of the devil, his tracks as real before me as the air I breathed. What did he mean by that? He'll be leaving soon . . . and . . . and I'm glad I knew him."

Brandy stiffly made his way to the water's edge, sat on a boulder.

"He's a spirit," thought Brandy in reference to Palidin. "No different than the rest of us spirits inhabiting bodies so that we can be seen, so that we can play our games, impose our trickery. I'm so old, so very, very old. How close to death do you have to be to understand the meaning, the worth of life? The body gets old, the spirit is ageless. Why would a spirit, the very essence of freedom, wish to be imprisoned in an old body. The eyes blurry with veins and tears, a fluttering rumble in the ears, a nagging suspicion of every taste and smell, no music, no dancing — just abandonment, humility and pain. Hell! I've so little time! He's leaving, and I can't stay young another day."

"Wake up! Wake up, partner! Gonna sleep your life away?"

"It's not even daylight yet!"

"It's comin', it's comin'! Get up! Me and you has got us a sunrise date!"

"Huh? What're ya talkin' about? I'm cold." Palidin sat up, yawned. "We goin' fishin'?"

"Don't ya remember, Billy?"

"I don't think so." Palidin yawned again, thought. "He's callin' me Billy again. Must have a little adventure in mind. Oh, well, might as well play along. Anything's as much fun as fishing for those things, those catfish, those walking catfish. Should I tell him about that? Naw, he'd never believe it. Maybe I was stoned or something. Maybe the smoke from one of these shrubs around here has something in it that will make you hallucinate. Maybe that bush that I broke the dead branches from for the fire was a peyote bush or something. I'll not mention it."

"How soon we forget," said Brandy. "Last night in the saloon, you were all mouth. Big shot! 'Do it right,' ya said. 'I'll meet ya at sunrise,' ya said. You had no intention of meeting me at sunrise, had ya? You meant to skip just like the yellerbelly I always knew you were! Well, as ya kin see, it didn't work! I'm here and ready to slap leather, so get yer boots on and yer gun, prepare yerself to meet yer maker."

"C'mon, Brandy! Snap out of it! I'm cold and sleepy! It can't be more than five o'clock!" Palidin lay down again, wrapped his blanket tighter about him in an attempt to repel the dew and the chill.

Brandy sighed. "Well, sure, Billy, catch a few more winks. Have a quick dream about your useless life, about all the men you shot in the back. Think about how much of a snake-in-the-grass you are. Think about it! Then, think about how you're about to die at sunrise. Oh, I know what yer up to. You're thinkin' you might get a chance to shoot *me* in the back! But you ain't, Billy. I'm keepin' an eye on you! We're gonna do this face to face! Man to man! The best man, the fastest gun will walk away. I ain't sayin' I'll win this fight. And if I lose, I want you to bury me right here by the Llano. Not too deep, mind you, just a few inches, so that the critters can find me rottin' carcass, have a good snack on the old bones . . . if I win, I'll do the same for you, although I doubt if even a river rat would eat the likes of you! You've got about a half an hour, Billy. Then it's you and me, face to face, man to man."

"All right," mumbled Palidin. "But keep your mouth shut for the half hour, I'm trying to sleep."

"Ha!" Brandy stood, removed his gun from its holster, checked to see if it was loaded. It was. Then he went to the boulder where Palidin had left *his* gun. Brandy had insisted that Palidin wear a gun. Palidin hated it but wore it anyway to keep the old man happy. He'd never fired it, so it still had the same bullets in it that Brandy had put in it on the night of the root-cellar incident. Satisfied with the loaded gun situation, Brandy, in what was by now a very grey dawn, gathered some sticks and lit a small fire. He then filled the boiling pail with water from the river and sat it over the fire to boil. He'd boil it and boil it and boil it, taking no chances that Palidin might pick up and get sick on whatever undesirable bacteria that surely lived in the Llano. "The young fella will have a tough time of it . . . for a while," he thought. "Don't want him to get sick on top of everything else."

Sitting watching the fire blaze up around the blackened little boiling pail, his watery eyes even more watery with the sting of smoke, Brandy thought, "I can't believe how quickly I made up my mind! Just like that! It's his presence. I should have known all along that this was how it would be. That's his purpose. Why else would someone like him come along just when age is taking such an outrageous toll on me. He's not *real*. That's what it is about him! He's not *real*. A ghost in

Texas. Nobody knows who he is or where he's from. Perfect! That stupid religion that Linda raves on about. Hinduism. It's the kid's karma. Religions. Juxtapose it with Christianity and we're talkin' about predestination. Killing me is his cross to bear. But only he will bear it, and hopefully he won't have to bear it for long. Linda . . . should never underestimate Linda. Underneath all those sissy actions and frills, there's a Burgess. Maybe she's right. Maybe the individual soul and the universal soul are the same. The only thing I've not done in my life is kill a person. At least not intentionally, not knowing about it, not murder. And will this be murder? Who will be killing whom? He will pull the trigger, but I loaded the gun and gave it to him, told him where to aim. His chance to murder. My chance to commit suicide, all in one instant. He's a Canadian ghost in Texas; I'm a forgotten spirit. God! How many times in my life have I contradicted myself? Nonexisting existences — an oxymoron. Sell flyhooks and rifles to make money so you can save the animal. My whole life has been one great contradiction. The spirit exists and will continue to exist, as sure as the spirit of my brother the wolf exists. All extinct animals will exist forever in the heart, in the conscience of man. Man will steal, cheat, batter, destroy, torture and kill everything as sure as . . . as sure as sin. But if religions are right, and they're all basically the same, we pay severely. Every human being must do everything. Sow a seed, nurture and destroy. Judge and ye shall be judged. We all die; we all face extinction. If I had've died forty years ago, I would just be put back here to do what I've done anyway. Karma!"

"Palidin! Palidin! Get up!"

Palidin hadn't managed to get back to sleep. He sat up. "Brandy, I . . . "

"Are you familiar with Plato?"

"I . . . yes, I . . . "

"You are?"

"Of course. Everyone in my home settlement reads Plato every night before they go to bed." This was a joke, a bit of sarcasm.

"Ha! Well. Then you know."

"Know what?"

"Plato thought that the soul always was, and always will be, as indestructible as the . . . as the azure. It enters the body with just a smidgen of knowledge about its former self, which doesn't matter because knowledge doesn't seem to have much to do with it. If the souls that are in you and me have always existed, where were all the souls when there were but two people on Earth? Where were all the souls when there was nobody walking around here but Adam and Eve?"

"Ah, Brandy, it's early. I . . . "

"How many people do you think are living on this planet at this very moment?"

"Ah, I don't know. Five, six, seven billion."

"That's a lot of souls. I'll wager that there's quite a few souls *not* wandering round in bodies right now, too."

From a yawn, Palidin managed to ask, "Wha', wha', what's your point?"

"Well, maybe there's no point at all, if ya can believe that there's an infinite number of souls soarin' about the universe, but if the number *isn't* infinite, if there's a magic number of let's say ten billion. Don't you see? We're almost there! Every soul will be alive! All the good and all the evil that ever existed, everything that ever happened throughout history, all the pain and hunger, happiness and love and hate and wars and rape and murder and battering and caressing, everything will be happening on Earth all at the same time! Don't you see the potential?"

"The raising of the dead. Armageddon. God will be here. I know that."

"So it doesn't matter whether our bodies are dead. There will be a body for us, a vessel for us. It's our destiny to return, to exist at some point, all of us, for the great war! Palidin! Palidin, my boy, I'm not gonna have a gunfight with you at sunrise after all. You and me are on the same side, I think. It wouldn't be right if you killed me now, because, for all I know, I might have more things to do while this old body can still breathe a breath."

"Whew!" said Palidin. "I was itchin' to gun you down."

Brandy laughed heartily, "Ha, ha, ha! You were?"

"Just joking. I'm on the side of all the souls that ever laughed." Palidin looked into the bubbling water in the boiling pail. "You gonna put some coffee in that stuff?"

"Ha, ha, ha! Just as soon's the tadpoles break down, partner."

Brandy sat on the ground beside Palidin and for a minute they said nothing, watched the water boil. On the eastern horizon, a streak of crimson heralded the rising sun. Birds awakened each other with chirps and peeps and whistles. One of the horses snorted and stomped, spooked perhaps by a snake or a Gila monster.

"Ah, Brandy?"

"Yeah?"

"Nobody knows what the magic number is."

"I know."

Brandy spooned some instant coffee into the boiling water, poured the steaming brew into a couple of tin cups. They sipped quietly, thoughtfully.

"Ah, Brandy?"

"Yeah?"

"Have you ever heard of a walking catfish?"

"Not this far west. There's a few in Florida, I think. Never heard tell of any in Texas."

"From Florida to Texas . . . "

"A long way to walk."

"Especially for a catfish."

fifteen

Bert Todder was the newsman of Brennen Siding, the reporter. Bert Todder visited everybody in Brennen Siding at least once a week. Always happy, always witty, a comical one-tooth smile, a laugh (tee hee hee sob snort sniff) that often sounded very much like he was crying, and a store of gossip about everybody, dog, cat, pig, cow and horse, in the settlement made him a welcome guest every time he stepped into the house. The U. S. of A. had Walter Cronkite, Bob Hope and Ed Sullivan; Brennen Siding had Bert Todder.

As soon as he came off the river, or on his days off, which were many, he'd eat a tremendous amount of food, usually potatoes and salmon, pork, beef or baloney, then make his rounds. He'd go to every house, interview, entertain and gossip with the women and children. Then he'd go to Bernie Hanley's store and talk to the men. Seeing him so frequently meant that nobody ever felt it necessary to visit Bert Todder.

Bert was missed on the very next night after his fatal accident.

Helen MacDonald asked herself, "I wonder where Bert is?"

Elva Nash said, "Bert was supposed to drop in and pick up a bottle of chow-chow. Guess he must've forgot."

At the store, Lindon Tucker said, "I guess, oh, ah, I guess maybe Bert, Bert, Bert Todder must be courtin' tonight. Yeah. Yep. Oh yeah, yeah, yeah. Yes sir. Uh huh. Courtin', yeah."

Stan Tuney lied, "Bert's off to Chatham tonight. Gone down to pick up a net. There's a lad down there sellin' four-inch mesh nets. All ya want for two dollars. I think that's what he told me now. Remember that net we stole from the priest in Renous, Bob?"

"Ah, I . . . I seem to've forgot about that, Stan . . . I, ah . . . "

When a week lapsed and Bert still hadn't showed up, the comments changed somewhat.

"I never saw Bert Todder for a week," said Dan Brennen. "Guess he must be ugly at someone. I think I might've said he had the brains of a chub or something like that."

"Keeps his lights burnin' all night," said Bob Nash. "Wouldn't wanna be payin' his power bill."

"I was gonna drop in and see 'im the other night," said Bernie Hanley. "But I said, if Bert wants to be alone for a while, no sense pushin' 'im. He ain't bought as much as a package of tobacco here for a week."

"Strange lad. Mind the time I sold me shore to Bill Wallace? Bert got ugly and never spoke to me for six months. Bert wanted to sell *his* shore to Bill, see. Thought I jumped in ahead of 'im."

"Oh, yeah. Bert kin git ugly, yeah. Yeah, he kin be strange, that's for sure, yeah. Yeah. Yeah. Yes sir. Di, di, di, di, di; di, di, di, di; for tomorrow never comes. Yes, sir. Yeah."

A month went by.

"Do you suppose that Bert's sick or somethin'?" asked Bernie Hanley.

"No, he ain't sick," said Stan Tuney. "Don't know what's wrong with him."

"How ya know he ain't sick?" asked Dan Brennen.

"I see 'im just about every night out on the bridge," said Stan.

"That's true, yeah," put in Bob Nash. "Saw 'im meself. Hammerin' and sawin' out on the bridge. Checked it out tonight when I was comin' over here. Couldn't see where he'd done a tap."

"Met 'im, met 'im, met 'im on the road yistiddy," said Lindon Tucker. "Oh, down there by the crooked birch, yeah. Yes sir. Met 'im down there by the crooked birch, I did, just before ya git to where ya kin see the river. Along there, yeah. Bert was way down there for some reason, yeah. Oh yeah."

"And?"

"Oh, nothin'."

"So, what did he have to say?"

"Nothin'. Jist walked into the woods. Never spoke a word, no. Ya know, but ya know, though, there ain't no amount o' shad runnin' yet. Thought there'd be more shad."

"Ya know what I think? I think Bert's courtin' Helen MacDonald. I think that's why ya never see 'im," said Stan Tuney. "I think he's either over at Helen's, or Helen's over at Bert's. That's why his light's on all the time."

"See what they're doin', yeah. Yi, yi, yi, yi, yi! The light right on so he kin get a better look at it, yeah. Yi, yi, yi, yi, yi!"

"He ain't spendin' his time with Helen," commented John Kaston. "Helen's a good Christian woman. Speakin' of which, that Dryfly Ramsey and that daughter of Bill Wallace's are shackin' up in Bill's camp! Did you lads know that?"

"Frank Layton dropped in the other night and asked me if I'd guide old Doctor Madison," said Bob Nash.

"Doctor Madison! Bert always guided Madison, didn't he?"

"Yeah, that's what I told Frank. Anyway, Frank said that he went over to Bert's, knocked on the door and got no answer. Bert wouldn't come to the door. The lights were all on, but Bert just let him knock."

"Yeah, yeah, yeah, yeah. Same thing happened to me, yeah," said Lindon Tucker. "I, I, I, I, I went over there the other night after I left here, yeah. Knocked, but no Bert. Me, yeah. And, and, and, and, and, and I, and I, I, I just hadda turn and keep on home. Bert should bury the porcupine."

"What porcupine?"

"Oh, oh, oh, Bert shot a porcupine one night a while back. Shot 'im in the shed, yeah. Must be underneath the floorboards, I think, yeah, by the smell of it, yeah. Gimme another bottle of ginger ale there, Bernie old dog."

*

It was the middle of May, and warm, gentle showers rained green on Brennen Siding. The grass grew, trees budded and seeds germinated so vigorously that you couldn't sleep at night for the sound of it. So many fish were entering the sweet waters of the Miramichi that you had to get behind a tree to tie your hook on. *Finally* it was done snowing! *Finally* those days of bitter cold temperatures were gone! *Finally* it was spring!

It was a Saturday afternoon, and Lillian Wallace and Dryfly Ramsey sat on the veranda of Bill Wallace's cottage, sipping from mugs of hot chocolate. Dryfly was gazing out at the rain-pecked river; Lillian was watching Dryfly.

"We'll enjoy about a week of this, and then the flies will take over," said Dryfly. "You know, every time I think of little Bonzie getting lost in the woods back of the barren, of all places. The flies must have been the worst. Did I ever tell you about Palidin not minding the flies, that they don't seem to bother him?"

"You told me once that they don't bother *you.*"

"That was a lot of, I don't know, just young lad's talking, bullshitting. The flies will eat ya up if you're exposed to them. Except Palidin. What d'ya think of that?"

"Of the flies not biting Palidin? Oh, I don't know. Some people can walk on red-hot embers, lay on beds of nails, bend spoons with their minds. Some kind of power, I suppose."

"Palidin was always alone. Even when he was with some-body, he was all alone. You just knew it. I saw him free a bee from a window, and it didn't sting him! He just picked it up and carried it out in the palm of his hand, kind of a smile on his face. Ha! I tried it once. It stung me the second I touched it."

"I should go shopping," said Lillian.

"We could take a drive in to Blackville," suggested Dryfly.

"Newcastle, or maybe even Fredericton is where I need to go."

"Why? What d'ya need?"

"Oh, a few things. I should be able to get what I need in Newcastle. When's your birthday, Dry?"

"January the fourth."

"Oh."

"Why?"

"Just wondering."

"When's yours?"

"October . . . October thirtieth, a Libra."

"Can't remember my birthday. I guess I must've been right out of 'er."

Lillian nodded thoughtfully, didn't get the joke.

Dryfly shifted his gaze from the river, eyed Lillian. He restrained a sudden urge to grab her, pull up her purple sweater and pink blouse, plant hundreds of tickling kisses on her belly.

"Want to?" he asked.

"Want to what?"

"Go to Newcastle?"

"I guess it might be a good day for it, but would you mind if I went alone?"

"Well, it doesn't matter to me. How come?"

"Well . . . there's something I have to do. I want to surprise you."

"You know the way?"

"Oh, I think I can find it."

"Well, maybe you could drop me off at Shad's place. I'll visit with him while you're gone. You can pick me up on your way back."

"Great."

A half-hour later, Lillian dropped Dryfly off at Shad's place across the river from Blackville and headed onward to Newcastle in her new yellow Chevy convertible.

Shad was in the kitchen playing his guitar and singing "Blowing in the Wind" to his new girlfriend, Mary Wilson, when Dryfly knocked on the door.

"How's she goin', Dry?"

"Hi, Dry."

"Shad. Mary. Good. What're you lads up to?"

"Not too much. How'd you come down? Lillian?"

"Yeah. She's gone to Newcastle. Where'd ya get the mouth organ?" asked Dry.

"Bought it the other day, went out and splurged, spent me last bucks on it."

"Can ya play it?"

"I'm learnin'. Not much to it. I'm tryin' to get that Dylan sound."

"Like that guy in New York you told me about?"

"Yeah. Good stuff, that. I like it."

"Not gonna play the banjo anymore?"

"Once in a while, maybe. You know, for the act. But I thought maybe I'd work on a little somethin' of my own, do the odd single, do some Dylan and Lightfoot stuff. I've been practising my whistlin', too."

"Well, I hope ya do better at it than we did with the act."

"Yeah. That shouldn't be too hard. What're ya doin' tonight? Anything?"

"Don't know. No plans. What's goin' on?"

"Dance."

"Lyman MacFee?"

"Yeah."

"You goin'?"

"Can't afford it."

"Ain't got another rifle to sell?"

"Ha! Take a look at that!" Shad passed a piece of paper to Dry.

Dry scanned it.

"A tax bill. Three hundred and sixty dollars! Where ya gonna get that kind of money, Shad?"

"Don't know. I never thought of taxes." Shad sighed deeply. "I can't afford this place, Dry."

"Sure ya can."

"I don't know how."

"You'll have to cut some of the lumber, that's all."

"I ain't out of school for another month or more."

"You'll have to get somebody to cut it for ya. Give them so much a cord."

"Who? Everyone I know would walk in there and cut every tree they see, clear-cut it. I don't want it one big brush pile back there!"

"Get your father to cut it," put in Mary.

"Dad?"

"Yeah. He'd cut it right," said Dry.

"Yeah. Never thought of Dad. You could help him, Dry."

"Me? I never worked in the woods."

"Be good money in it. There's a real good chance back there. Big, tall spruce with hardly a limb on them. Lillian's here, you must need money."

"Yeah, I could do with a few bucks. I don't know . . . "

"Dad's gettin' kind of old for runnin' a chain saw. You could run Dad's saw, and he could yard."

"I don't know. Lillian's here . . ."

"Ya can't be with her day and night, Dry!"

Dry wanted to say, "Why not?" but thought better of it.

"I don't know how she'd like it up there by herself. I don't know. I'll talk it over with her."

"Soon's school's over, I'll go to work with ya. We could work back there all summer, Dry. Have a pile o' money by fall. Maybe by fall we'd have enough money to go to Toronto or somewhere."

"Why would I wanna go to Toronto?"

"Why not? Ya can't stay around here for the rest of your life!"

"You not goin' back to school in the fall?"

"Naw. Can't afford it. It's time a lad got out of here. No money, have to work in the woods to make any, get maybe ten gigs a year in a band if you're lucky. We'll go to the woods, make some money and get the hell out of here!"

"Yeah . . . "

"Think it over, Dry. Wanna have a game of forty-five?"

"The three of us?"

"Nothin' else to do."

*

Two hours later Lillian came, and she and Dry drove back to Brennen Siding in the rain. They left the car at the Cabbage Island Salmon Club and walked across the bridge to the cottage, both carrying armloads of groceries. By the time they got there, they were soaking wet.

"Whew! I'm getting out of these clothes and jumping into the shower!" said Lillian.

"Me, too," said Dryfly.

They showered, made love under the heat lamp, pulled on their bathrobes and went to the living room. Dryfly poured them drinks.

"I'll start dinner," said Lillian, and with drink in hand headed for the kitchen.

"I'll start a fire in the fireplace," said Dry.

Dryfly started a fire, then put on an album, *Sweet Baby James*, by James Taylor, sat on the huge, comfortable sofa, sang along. "There was a young cowboy who lived on the range . . . " He could hear the rain on the roof sixteen feet above him, Lillian banging around in the kitchen. He sipped his Chivas Regal, lit a Rothmans.

"So, how'd ya like Newcastle?" he called to her.

"Nice little town!" she called back. "Can't buy much there, though. Couldn't find fresh mushrooms anywhere. Had to buy a can. I got us a couple of nice porterhouse steaks, though. Got you a carton of cigarettes, too. There on the mantel."

"Thanks."

Dryfly sat back, adjusted his robe, the beautiful white bathrobe Lillian had brought him from Connecticut as a gift. He gazed into the fire, then followed the massive stone fireplace all the way up to the roof. "Got 'er made?" he asked himself. "Got 'er made."

Lillian returned from the kitchen, said, "You look cozy," and sat beside him. She gestured a toast. "Cheers, my love," she said.

"Mud in your eye," said Dry.

Lillian smiled that beautiful smile that Dryfly had dreamed so much about, that smile that always sent little thrills running through his entire body.

"I phoned Dad from Newcastle," she said.

"Yeah? How's Bill?"

"Well, I've seen him happier. But he's fine."

"What's he unhappy about?"

"You." And there was the smile again.

"Does he know I'm staying here with you?"

"He does now."

"And?"

"He said 'Get that hick to hell out of there and come home!'"

"And?"

"I said, 'Dad, I'm in love with him. I'm very, very happy.'"

"And?"

"And he said 'I'm sorry I never made you happy.' I said 'You can make me happy, now.' He paused for a minute, then said, 'Tell that Dryfly to get a name!'"

"Ha!"

"I told him I loved him; he told me that he loved me and that was it. 'Have fun playing house,' he said. He thinks we're playing house. And you know what? He's right. We *are* playing house, and I love it. Isn't that what all young people do?"

"So what's he want you to call me?"

"I don't know. I guess he doesn't like 'Dryfly' — for a name, that is."

"I'll change my name for you."

"Don't change your name, Dryfly. I like your name. Oops, I almost forgot. I have to chill the wine." Lillian pecked Dryfly on the cheek and went back to the kitchen.

Dryfly tossed back his drink, stood, went to the bar and poured himself another. There was a mirror behind the bar. Dryfly lit another cigarette and sized himself up in the mirror — the straight brown hair still slick from his shower, the thin face, the eyes, the white bathrobe, the drink in hand, the long cigarette. "Who are you?" he asked himself. "You don't look much like a lumberjack. What name should I call you? Ralph? Fred? Harry? John? Peter? Keith? David? Dryfly. Bill's right, old dog. You can't be Dryfly." And suddenly Dryfly felt very, very sad.

The fire that he'd started was pretty basic: paper and kindling. He went to it and added a couple of logs. He turned over the album. He went to the big window, gazed out at a grey evening, the river, the spooky-looking forest across the way. The pane in front of him reflected the room behind him — the warm, crackling fire, the paintings of waterfowl, the hardwood floors, the luxurious furniture, the bar. "This living room is as big as our whole house, and this is just their cottage. That leather sofa cost more than we probably paid for our whole house."

Lillian returned.

"You know what I was thinking?" she asked as she came to stand beside him. "I was thinking we should get into salmon fishing."

"Fishing?"

"Sure. I was looking at some beautiful rods and gear in Newcastle. That's what the Miramichi is all about. We should be doing it. You could teach me how to fish, couldn't you?"

"Yeah . . . "

"Is there something wrong, Dryfly?"

"No, I'm all right."

"Tonight, we're eating by candlelight."

"Like last night and the night before?"

"Of course. In the dining room. I have a surprise for you."

"Yeah? What?"

"You'll have to wait and see. Give me a kiss."

Dryfly took her in his arms, kissed her, held her close, nuzzled her hair, nipped her earlobe.

"I've never been happier in my life," she whispered.

"Oh, Lillian. I love you so much . . . I . . . "

"Now let me go. I need to finish dinner. Want to set the table?"

"Sure."

Lillian went back to the kitchen, and Dryfly crossed the living room and entered the dining room. He put place mats and linen napkins on the big oak table, put out the silver cutlery, lit candles.

Lillian started bringing the meal from the kitchen. She had prepared porterhouse steaks, a salad, warmed-up bread, green peppers, onions, mushrooms, rice. She set a bottle of Châteauneuf-du-Pape on the table, a bottle of Mumm's champagne in an ice bucket beside the table. Before sitting, she went to the living room and replaced James Taylor with Joni Mitchell's *Ladies of the Canyon.*

They sat to eat.

"Like?"

"Umm!"

Dryfly was Shirley Ramsey's son. Like everyone else in Brennen Siding, when Shirley Ramsey cooked a steak, she kept it in the pan for a good hour, maybe more, cooked it so much that it was actually dried out, as well-done as it could possibly be without being burned. When Dryfly cut into the porterhouse, it was rare, browned on the outside, bloody in the middle. Lillian's was rare, too. He watched her cut off a piece, eat it. She seemed to be enjoying it. Dryfly shrugged and tried his. "It's . . . good," he thought, surprised.

Dryfly was a fast eater, forced himself to slow down so that he wouldn't finish fifteen minutes before Lillian, as he did the first night they'd dined here together. He chewed, sipped wine, chewed some more.

Every night when they ate at this table Dryfly spent considerable time looking at one particular painting. It was of the back of a balding man in a grey suit. The man was looking at a very ugly painting, the kind that a monkey could paint with his tail, a bunch of colours dripped and splattered everywhere. The man was holding his hands behind his back, one white glove on and one off. He held a hat, an umbrella and something that Dryfly thought might be a book; he wasn't sure. Even though he couldn't see the man's face, Dryfly could tell that he was somehow fascinated with the blotches and drips on the canvas, perhaps asking himself why anyone would paint such a thing, what manner of person could do that and call himself an artist. And who on Earth would purchase such a thing?

"Norman Rockwell," said Lillian.

"Huh?"

"That's a Norman Rockwell. It's not an original, but it's signed. He spends a lot of time in Stockbridge. Like it?"

"I like the painting, but not the painting in the painting."

"More wine?"

"Yeah. Sure."

"Dad has a couple of originals at home."

"Yeah?"

"See the one with the ducks?"

"Yeah."

"An Atherton."

"Ha! He from down your way?"

"Atherton? Vermont, maybe. I'm not sure."

"I'd like to be an artist one day. Couldn't paint anything that good."

"Why not?"

"I don't know. I guess I could learn, maybe."

"You should start."

"Yeah. Ah, Shad wants me to go to work for him."

"Shad? What doing?"

"Cuttin' logs, pulp, whatever."

"As a lumberjack, you mean?"

"Yeah, with Bob, back on Shad's land."

"Oh, Dry!"

"What's the matter?"

"You don't want to do that!"

"Why not? I need the money."

"Yes, but a lumberjack?"

"Why not? Everyone I know works in the woods."

Lillian put down her fork, sipped her wine. "When would you start?"

"I'm not sure. Shad needs the money. Real soon, I think."

"You mean, like Monday or something?"

"Well, maybe not that soon, but soon."

"So what am I supposed to do all the time you're in the woods?"

Dryfly thought for a moment. "Fish?"

Lillian laughed pleasantly.

"Lindon Tucker can guide you," said Dryfly, grinning at the thought. "Yep, yeah, oh yeah, yeah, yeah, yep. Guiding a little darlin', I am!"

Lillian laughed and laughed.

"I love you!" said Dryfly, also laughing.

"Could you do that kind of work?" asked Lillian.

Dryfly shrugged. "Workin' in the woods? I'm not sure. I guess I could. I'd have to get used to it."

"Why don't you become an artist? You just told me that you always wanted to be one."

Dryfly sighed. "I don't know. We'll see. But for now, I need money."

"You don't, you know."

"Yes I do. I . . . I don't like it — living off of you."

"It doesn't bother me a bit."

All Dryfly could do was sigh.

"Dryfly?"

"Yeah?"

"I think Dryfly would be a perfect name to write on the corner of a painting."

"Yeah."

They finished their dinner. Outside, the wind blew, the rain came down. Joni Mitchell sang "Big Yellow Taxi." They carried the champagne to the living room, got a couple of glasses from the bar, popped the cork and sat on the sofa in front of the fire.

"I'm getting kind of tipsy, you know?" said Lillian.

"A couple of scotches, a bottle of wine, now this . . . "

"Please don't go to work."

"I need money."

"I have enough money to do us the summer and lots, lots more. I want you here with me every minute. We owe it to ourselves. Let's not worry about money, not yet. Let's just . . . play house."

"Well, I suppose I'll have to not go to work in the woods, then. Anything to keep you happy."

"Thank you, my love. Thank you."

"Oh, it was a tough decision, but, well, it's all right. I'll stay here with you."

"I love you."

"I love you, too."

"Here."

"What's this?"

"Your surprise."

"What is it?"

"Open it and find out."

Dryfly started opening the neatly wrapped little package tied with ribbon.

"I hope this is not a bad time to give it to you," said Lillian. "I hope so much that you will like it."

Inside the paper was a little blue velvet box. Inside the box was a gold ring mounted with a pale blue stone and tiny diamonds on either side.

"It's beautiful," said Dryfly. "It's the most beautiful ring I've ever seen!"

"It's for you. Our engagement ring."

Dryfly's eyes clouded with tears.

"I hope it fits. Try it on."

Dryfly could not speak. He slipped the ring on his finger. Too small. He tried it on his little finger. Just right.

"I like men to wear rings on their little finger, anyway," said Lillian.

"I . . . I . . . "

"Shh. Let me hold you."

"I . . . I . . . "

"Shh . . . don't say anything. I'm so glad you like it, my love. I've thought about you so much. From that very first summer. Just being here with you is a dream come true."

"Sob, sob, sob . . . I'm sorry I . . . sniff . . . ," Dryfly wiped the tears from his eyes. "It's the most beautiful thing anyone's ever given me . . . sniff . . . I don't deserve it . . . it must've cost a fortune."

"Don't . . . please . . . just promise me you'll always wear it."

"I'll *always* wear it! *Always!* Forever and ever!"

"Mud in your eye?"

"Mud in your eye."

They drank. Dry sat his glass down.

"There's something I've been wanting to do all day," he said.

"Really? And what might that be?"

"This!"

He untied her robe, opened it. "Belly!" he said. "Belly, belly, belly!" and planted about a . . . well, a hundred kisses there . . . maybe more. "Belly, belly, belly, belly, belly!"

*

Bob Nash, Dan Brennen, Lindon Tucker, John Kaston and Stan Tuney were at Bernie Hanley's store, eating potato chips and drinking ginger ale. For some reason, perhaps the full moon, and much to the delight of Bernie Hanley, they were lingering a bit later than usual. "They've been grumbling all evening," thought Bernie. "But sales are great."

Bob Nash was so pissed off at Dryfly Ramsey that he was actually gritting his teeth.

"Boys oh boys oh boys oh boys oh boys, that Wallace girl must be hard up for a man! And, and, and to see him settin' right back there in front o' the fireplace, smokin' them great big long tailor-made cigarettes, and his feet right up, and him all washed with his hair slicked right back, ya'd think he was old Bill Wallace himself!"

"Shackin' up!" commented John Kaston.

"And he wouldn't go to work with ya."

"Well, I jist tell ya now, I went in and there he was. So I said, 'Shad wants us to cut some lumber off his land.' I knowed he already knowed about it, 'cause Shad told me, but I thought I'd mention it anyway. Anyway, he said, get Nutbeam to help ya. He needs the money more than I do! Him with not a red cent!"

"No, no, no, no, no, Dryfly ain't gotta red cent, that's fer sure, Bob old buddy, buddy, pal. Butty butty butty butty butty, but he ain't gonna go to work all the same, is he, Bob?"

"No, the son of a whore ain't gonna do a tap!"

"I met 'im on the road the other day drivin' that big shiny car o' hers, head right back. Christ! I thought it was the Rawleigh man comin'!"

"Ha!"

"So, did ya go to Nutbeam?" asked Stan Tuney.

"Well, not at first. And, and, and, and that's another racket I got into! When I left Dryfly, I went up to Bert's. That was about nine, ten o'clock at night. I knocked. The lights were all on, and I had a feelin' Bert was in there, but do you think he'd come to the door? No, sir! I must've knocked ten times, and, and, and no Bert."

"What d'ya s'pose is wrong with the stupid jeezer?" asked Bernie Hanley.

"Ah, he's crazier than arsehole, jist like all the rest of the Todders! He got somethin' in his head now, somethin' somebody said or somethin', and he thinks he's gittin' even by stayin' away and hidin'. And you just watch! He'll show up one o' these days jist like nothin' ever happened."

"You wouldn't think Bert would be the one to let a little thing like whatever it was that whatever one of us said bother 'im. He never cared what he said to anyone else! Made fun of everybody that ever walked, Bert Todder did," said Stan Tuney.

"Ya could never tell whether he was laughin' at ya or cryin', anyway," said Bob Nash.

"Must be two months since he stepped foot in here," said Bernie Hanley. "Must be buyin' his groceries in Blackville, or Renous. Course, I don't care if he ever comes back. He never bought all that much from me, anyway. Want another bottle o' ginger ale there, Lindon?"

"Oh ah, oh ah, oh ah, sure, sure, the very best, sure thing," said Lindon, then sang, "Di di di di di, di di di di di, for tomorrow never comes."

"Well, I'll tell ya why Bert ain't buyin' from you, Bernie. He's too goddamned scared he might be helpin' ya out!" said Stan Tuney.

"Well, like I said, I don't care if he ever comes back. He kin lay over there and rot, for all I care!"

"So is Nutbeam gonna help ya with Shad's land?" asked John Kaston.

"Yep, we're goin' at 'er the first thing Monday mornin'."

"Have ya cruised it yet?"

"Shad took me back yesterday, and ya never saw the like of it! The prettiest chance ya ever saw in all your life! The big, tall princess pine and black spruce, white pine as big as that furnacette at the butt, hardly a limb on them; logs, veneer — I can't wait to get at 'er."

sixteen

When Palidin and Brandy rode up to the Burgess ranch house, Cav came running out with his hands up and trying not to smile when he said, "Don' shoot, gen'lemen! Don' shoot, it's jis' me, Cav!"

"Mawnin', Cav," said Brandy, dismounting. "That useless daughter o' mine and her plastic fortune-seeker back yet?"

"No, suh, they not back. Miz Burgess in Chicargo as far as I know, suh. You home fer a while?"

"No, but if ya don't mind, Cav, me man, I'd like for y'all to do us a favour."

"Anything ole Cav kin do, he'll do, suh."

"Give us a drive to San Antonio, would ya?"

"Yes, suh, no problem, suh. Right now?"

"Right now, if ya don't mind, Cav."

"I'll get the limousine, suh."

They unsaddled the horses and put them in the stable. Palidin bid a quick farewell to Bornice the mule, and they were off. Cav drove. Palidin and Brandy sat in the back seat of the Rolls Royce.

"Drink?" asked Brandy.

"I guess I could stand a tad," grinned Palidin.

Brandy opened the bar. "Scotch? Rye? Bourbon? What would ya like, son?"

"Ah, scotch."

Brandy poured.

"Thanks," said Palidin, accepting the half-full tumbler from Brandy, no ice, no mix, just straight scotch.

They sipped for a moment before either spoke.

"I wish you'd come with me, Brandy," said Palidin.

"Oh, you know how it is. Maybe in September. You said the fishing's the best in September."

"Yeah . . . ya know, I never thought I'd say this, but I'm going to miss you, you know that?"

"Yeah, well . . . you sure you don't want some money?"

"No, the plane ticket's great."

"I know it, but . . ."

"Well, I've learned a lot from you these last few weeks. Sally might not get to Harvard, but she'll get educated, and that's what counts. So you're moving out of Merna's Butt?"

"Just for the summer. It's gettin' too hot. Think I might go wolf-searchin' in Alaska, for the summer, that is. Head east and fish with you in the fall. Without your magic hooks, we'll do it right, then head back to Merna's Butt for the winter. Ya could come down in the fall. I'd like that."

"Well, maybe. Who knows. Might. I'll spend the summer in Brennen Siding, anyway, see what happens."

When they pulled up in front of the West Wind Sports building, Palidin was struck by the old leaving-a-friend blues, an emotion that brought the tears to his eyes.

They shook hands, hugged.

"You look after yourself, now, ya hear?"

"You, too, ya hear?"

"See ya in September."

"I'll be there . . . and I know the salmon will be."

"See ya, Billy."

"Ha! See ya, Sundance, you old hombre. And thanks very much."

"I wish you'd take some money, kid."

"Yeah, well, see ya later, Brandy," said Palidin, then yelled to Cav who was still in the car. "See ya, Cav! Thanks!"

"Y'all come back, now!" said Cav.

Palidin entered the West Wind Sports building, crossed the lobby and went up to the tenth floor. When he got off the elevator, there was Jucy in all her lipstick-and-polish glory. When she looked up to see Palidin, she almost gasped. "It's you!" she said.

"Yep, it's me. I need to get into your apartment."

"Where have you been, honey?"

"I was a-ridin' the range," said Palidin grinning.

"Well, I sure am glad you ain't back in Canader already! Mr. Lowery's been pacin' the floor, lookin' for you."

"Well, you just tell him to relax. I don't have to see him anymore. I'm going home. I just wanted to pick up my gear, change my clothes and have a bath."

"You sure are tanned! And your beard is all bushy. I swear you look like a prospector! Ha! Poor baby! I'll tell Mr. Lowery you're here." Jucy picked up the phone, punched a button. "He's here, Mr. Lowery . . . yes, Palidin."

Lowery rushed out of his office smiling as if he were greeting a long-lost friend.

"Palidin! Palidin, my boy! God, it's good to see you! Come into my office! Jucy, we don't want to be disturbed."

"Yes, sir."

James Lowery led Palidin into his office and closed the door. "Have a seat," he said.

Palidin sat.

"So how did you do it? I mean, I tried your fly."

"And?"

"Remarkable! Absolutely incredible! Every cast!"

"Ha!"

"We want to make you a deal."

"Too late," said Palidin. "I already sold the idea."

"No, no, you can't do that! You came to me, remember?" Lowery's smile fell like a partridge. One minute it had been flying high through a bright autumn day; the next second, dead, tumbling to the ground, shot by a hunter.

"I came to West Wind Sports."

"Yes, and you talked to me!"

"I sold the idea to West Wind Sports."

"To whom?"

"Brandy Burgess."

"You what?"

"I sold the idea to Brandy Burgess."

"You can't sell anything to him! He's insane! How much did he pay you?"

"He . . . he gave me a pair of boots."

"You fool! A pair of boots?"

Palidin held out one foot. "What do you think?" he asked.

Lowery breathed a long, deep sigh.

"Why?" he asked.

"Ah, simply because I like the way Brandy Burgess, Sundance to his friends, plays."

Lowery ignored Palidin's humor.

"I'd be willing to bet that this company would give you as much as fifty thousand dollars for your little secret."

"Not enough."

"You mean you have a figure in mind?" Lowery's smile, returned from the dead, took flight.

"I suppose I do, sort of."

"Palidin, my boy, I went fishing a few weeks ago and tried that fly of yours. I never saw anything like it in all my life. I caught a fish every cast . . . others were there fishing right in the same water and never got as much as a nibble. I brought the fly back to the lab and had the boys dissect it. They found nothing unusual. What's your secret? What's your price?"

Palidin grinned. A new, and what he considered a very amusing, idea suddenly crossed his mind. "You see, Mr. Lowery, that's the thing right there. The fact that you can find nothing unusual about the fly is in itself the reason why the fly, the idea, is worth so much. So long as it remains a secret within your company, no one else will ever be able to copy it."

"Hmm. You're sure about that?"

"Absolutely. I've been thinking it over and have decided that I should get a million dollars up front, and let's say ten percent of the retail cost of every fly that's sold. You pay about an average of one dollar for an ordinary fly. I figure an angler would pay ten times that amount for one that I've kissed."

"Kissed?"

"That's it."

"You mean, you kiss the fly? That's all?"

"That's about it."

"Do you expect me to believe that?"

"It doesn't matter to me if you believe me or not. I really don't care anymore if I get any money for the idea or not."

"But a kiss?"

"I have magic lips. I've been calling it the old fish-lips kiss. What's more, whoever I kiss is blessed with the same power. To get the secret from me, you simply have to kiss me."

"Kiss you!"

"Well, as much as I'd enjoy kissing you, Mr. Lowery, I've sold the idea already. Mr. Burgess gave me these nice boots for a kiss, and, well, I'm afraid you'll have to kiss Mr. Burgess." Palidin stood and went to the door, opened it. "Good day, Mr. Lowery," he said and headed for the elevator. "I'm going home to Canada, Jucy. I just want to pick up my things from your apartment. Could I borrow a key, leave it somewhere for you?"

"I have a spare." Jucy reached for her purse. "You can just leave this one on the big table, lock the door behind you."

"But Palidin, you don't expect me to believe . . ."

"Believe whatever you want, Mr. Lowery," said Palidin.

Jucy searched her purse, found the key, handed it to Palidin.

Palidin leaned toward her, gave her a little kiss. "Be a good girl," he said.

The elevator doors opened and Palidin stepped in.

"But wait!" called Lowery.

"See ya," said Palidin. The doors closed, and he was gone.

"He was such a handsome man!" said Jucy.

"Yeah . . . Jucy, c'mon into my office."

*

Bob and Elva Nash arrived at Shad's place at three o'clock Saturday afternoon. Shad had been watching for Bob's red pick-up and met them in the driveway. Shad's house was a disaster, and Elva would bitch and nag if she were to enter an unkempt house. If Shad could help it, he would not give her the chance.

"Hi Mom! Hi Dad! What's up?"

"Shoppin', shoppin', shoppin'! God, I hate shoppin'!" said Bob.

"Well, how else ya gonna get your socks and your boots and your fertilizer?" said Elva.

"And the groceries and the wallpaper and the bloomers and the cushion covers. The goddamned cushion covers! We must've looked in every store in Newcastle for cushion covers!"

"Well, maybe we should've bought a new sofa!"

"Red! Red cushion covers! There was blue and orange and pink and yellow and green and purple and every colour under the sun! But no, we had to have red! Red cushion covers! Shad, yer gonna have to paint this house one o' these days. See up there under the eaves?"

"Yeah . . . let's sit over here in the sun. Nice day, eh?"

"Nice day for gettin' more done than shoppin'!" said Bob.

"Well, the next time, I'm gonna go by myself! What d'ya want me to do, put green cushion covers on a red sofa? You should mow the grass, Shad!"

"I know, Mom. I know."

"We got our first scale, Shad. I think you'll be happy with this." Bob handed Shad a cheque.

"Great! A hundred and eighty dollars! Great!"

"Well, ya don't want to spend it foolish! Go out and buy yourself some good clothes! Get rid of them old, patched jeans and that old robe and, for God sakes, get your hair cut!" advised Elva.

"You should put in a garden," said Bob.

"Yeah . . . might," said Shad. "Pretty good chance back there, eh?"

"Back there by the broken-down popple there's a stand that you wouldn't believe! Forty cord right there, I figure. That Nutbeam's a son of a whore to work, too, Shad. He never stops! Best man to work I ever seen."

"Well, that's good. Maybe I won't have to go back with yas."

"Oh, you'll have to come back with us. Take that money and buy yourself a new chain saw, Shad."

Shad didn't want to spend the summer working in the woods and had been wondering how he was going to get out of it.

"Yeah, well, I only have the summer. Gotta put in a garden, paint the house . . ."

"You kin do that stuff in the evenin's. There's enough lumber back there to keep us goin' for a year, I'd say. You're gonna have to tear that old shed down, Shad . . . there's a run o' salmon on."

"Is there?"

"Lindon Tucker got a twelve-pounder last night. Prettiest fish ya ever saw! That thick through the belly and just as silver and bright. When will ya be gettin' outta school?"

"The twenty-fifth. Another three weeks."

"Boys, that's too bad. You should be back there with us, now. I could be givin' you a cheque twice that big if you had a chain saw and were back there with us."

"Yeah, well, I got an awful lotta work to do around here."

"And, and, and ya wouldn't wanna have to go to work!" put in Elva. "Ya just wanna set right back and drink that dirty old wine like, like, like old, old, old I don't know who! Like, like, like Dryfly Ramsey. I'm surprised you're not shackin' up with some, some, some tramp! And ya wouldn't wanna do a tap o' work!"

"Now, he'll come back with us! Leave 'im alone! You'll come back with Nutbeam and me, won't ya, Shad?"

"Ah . . . yes, of course. Can't wait."

"Well, we gotta get goin'. I got a million things to do, and I'd kinda like to wet a line before dark. I'd put me garden right over there, Shad, if I were you. Right over there by the barn."

"Yeah . . . that's kind of where I had in mind. Well, thanks, Dad, for dropping off the cheque."

"No trouble, no trouble. There'll be another one next week and one the week after. We're gonna do good back there."

"Well, you just look after your money, that's all I can say!" said Elva.

"I will, Mom. I will."

Shad walked his parents over to the pickup.

"You been sayin' your prayers and goin' to church?" asked Elva, getting into the truck.

"Ah . . . haven't been to church lately. Need a new suit."

"Well, that's what you should do with that money. Get

yourself a new suit and go to church. You should drive up and hear John speak. You haven't stepped foot inside . . ."

"Close the door, Elva. Shad'll go to whatever church he wants to. C'mon up and go fishin' some night, Shad!"

"Yeah . . . Wednesday, maybe . . ."

"See ya, Shad!"

"Get that hair cut!"

"Bye."

Shad watched until the red pickup disappeared in the distance, then jumped into his VW minibus and headed over the river to the village.

"Gotta get this cheque cashed before the credit union closes," he thought.

He made it, cashed the cheque, went to the bootlegger's, bought two pints of Five-Thirty Rye, then went to Biff's Canteen. It was early; he found he was the only customer in the place. Sylvy Dunn worked behind the counter.

"Gimme a wiener 'n' chips," ordered Shad. "Three extra wieners."

"You're around early," said Sylvy.

"Yeah. Didn't feel like cookin'."

"Still goin' out with Mary Wilson?"

"Off and on."

"Goin' in the talent contest?"

"Never heard nothin' about it."

"Two weeks from tonight. There's the poster right behind ya."

Shad swung on his stool, read the poster.

TALENT CONTEST
JUNE 21, 8:00 PM.
THE HIGH SCHOOL AUDITORIUM.
FIRST PRIZE $25.00
SECOND PRIZE $15.00
THIRD PRIZE $10.00
Come one, come all!
SPONSORED BY THE BLACKVILLE ORANGEMEN.

Shad had been practicing finger picking on his guitar. His harmonica playing was coming along nicely, too.

"I just might," he said. "I just might give it a try."

"Billy Bean's goin' in it."

"Is he? Anyone from the Rapids?"

"Don't know. Why?"

"Lotta good singers down there."

Through the big window in the front of the canteen, Shad watched the SMT bus pull up and a tall, slim, fair-skinned man get off. The man had long brown hair and a bushy blond beard.

"Who in the name of God is that?" asked Sylvy.

"I'm not sure. Looks like Palidin Ramsey. I thought he was in Texas or someplace."

"Maybe he was. He's wearin' cowboy boots."

*

Palidin Ramsey's flight from San Antonio to Fredericton was more like that of a grasshopper than a bird, San Antonio to Houston, Houston to Chicago, Chicago to Toronto, Toronto to Montreal, Montreal to Fredericton. Hop, hop, hop, hop, hop.

Exhausted from flying and waiting around in airports between flights, Palidin took a bus from the Fredericton airport downtown to the Lord Beaverbrook Hotel. Here, from a bellman, he learned that the SMT bus terminal was less than a hundred yards up Queen Street on the left. At the SMT terminal it surprised him not at all to learn that he had another two-and-a-half-hour wait for the bus departure that would take him to Blackville. Palidin put his bag in a locker and spent the two and a half hours exploring Fredericton.

Fredericton, the elm-shaded streets, the greenery, the beautiful old townhouses, the gentle flow of the St. John River, the easy, relaxed gait of its Maritime people . . . "It's like a giant oasis," thought Palidin. "Mecca. The jewel of Canada, of North America, of the world, probably." At the time, Palidin was not exaggerating or being pretentious in any way. At the time, Palidin still hadn't been to Florence.

And then he was on the bus, winding along the swift little Nashwaak with its forested hills and rich, green valleys, and then the Miramichi greeted him with wide-open arms, Boiestown, Doaktown, Blackville; mothers, peaceful, kind, welcoming their wayworn son. Fredericton, the Nashwaak, the Miramichi, by the time Palidin stepped down from the bus in front of Biff's Canteen, he actually felt relaxed, revived, rested.

"Blackville," he thought. "Now what? Brennen Siding? A twelve-mile walk. It's a perfect day, but . . ." He sighed, not feeling *that* rested. "Maybe I could hire somebody to drive me home. Brandy gave me a thousand dollars to get me here. I still have more than half that left . . . Brandy. God, I miss him."

"Hey, Pal!" somebody called from the open door of the canteen.

It was Shadrack Nash.

"Shad?"

"Yeah! Need a ride home?"

"Yeah."

"C'mon in, have a Pepsi! I'll run ya back soon's I eat!"

Shad went back to his stool. Palidin entered and sat beside him.

"How've ya been, Shad?"

"Good, good. You?"

"Great."

"Heard you were way down to Texas."

"Just got back."

"What were you doin' down there?"

"Ah . . . nothing much."

"I was to New York a few weeks ago."

"Yeah? Big city."

"Ever been there?"

"No."

"You wouldn't believe how big! Makes . . . makes Blackville look like fly shit."

"Were you planning on going to Brennen Siding?"

"No. But I'll run ya back. Won't be nothin' goin' on around here for a while."

"Great."

Sylvy served Shad a big plate of french fries and deep-fried wieners. Shad smothered the meal with salt and catsup, began to eat.

Palidin ordered a Pepsi and sipped on it while Shad ate. It seemed they had very little to talk about. Shad and Palidin *never* had much to talk about. Shad was Dryfly's friend. Palidin was only a little older than Shad and Dry, but he was worlds apart. Shad would never hang around with somebody like Palidin, was feeling self-conscious just sitting there beside him. Shad didn't think for a second that Palidin would ever put the make on him or anything like that. "It's his eyes — those brown eyes. As John Kaston would say, those lambent eyes, that make me feel . . . inferior? Like I'm made out of glass? Weird," thought Shad.

After a number of minutes went by, Shad said, "You gonna be sticking around here for a while?"

"I'm not sure. I'd like to for the summer."

"Nothin' goin' on around here. I'm apt to end up workin' in the woods."

"Better than doing nothing."

"Want the job? Nutbeam's back there."

"Back where?"

"Dad and Nutbeam are cutting my ground."

"I don't know. Maybe."

Palidin was feeling hungry, but he had no intention of having canteen food. He was looking forward to having something of Shirley's, supposing if she had nothing more to offer than bread and molasses. He swung on his stool so that he wasn't watching Shad eat, gazed through the big window at the graveyard across the street.

"Lumbering," he thought. "The cutting down of trees. An honorable profession? In moderation, I suppose. I don't know if it's for me."

This line of thinking took on a whole new dimension fifteen minutes later as Shad manoeuvred the VW minibus over the potholes and bumps of the Gordon Road.

The Gordon Road branched off the Dungarvon Road near

Blackville and ran fourteen miles through a vast forest of black spruce, white pine, red pine, green fir and yellow birch — a colourful piece of real estate, to say the least — to the settlement of Gordon.

The last time Palidin Ramsey had travelled the Gordon Road, that beautiful, lush forest was still there, giving the road the appearance of a winding, shadowy lane. This day, however, through the window of Shadrack's VW minibus, Palidin's eyes encountered a somewhat different scene. Fifty-two lumberjacks had entered the forest that lined the Gordon Road and with chain saws and heavier equipment had transformed a silk purse into a sow's ear, had given a baby's bottom the appearance of a toad's back, had devastated five thousand acres of wilderness by cutting down every tree that was big enough for a canoe pole and tramping down the rest. This day, for a good three miles of the Gordon Road, through the window of Shad's minibus, Palidin's eyes encountered a network of machine tracks, mud holes and brush piles.

"What have they done to my forest?" asked Palidin.

"What's that?"

"They've destroyed the forest!"

"Yeah."

"Who did this?"

"A bunch a guys. The mill owns it, I think."

"Why?"

"Work, lumber. A man's gotta eat."

Palidin sighed, said no more, sat thinking.

"The work of Earth's keeper," he thought. "What was it that Brandy asked? From an old poem. Yeah. Why should the spirits of mortals be proud? . . . or something like that. Why, indeed. Men and their demanding wives could eat very well on a lot less devastation! Man's gotta eat, at what expense? Are we blind? Can't we see what we're doing here? This is just one little example! My mother's gravel pit is another. And the Mactaquac damn is right up there, too. Oh, Brandy, Brandy, Brandy! You tried so hard, did so little. Your brother's gone. Will all our earthling brothers go? In the newspaper someone referred to the hunting of animals, deer and whatnot, as the harvesting of animals. Bullshit! Bullshit? No, a much fouler excrement fertilizes that tasteless weed. There's nothing animal about it. It's the stuff of human greed. God! Where's a pen when ya need it?"

"I guess there's a big run of fish on," commented Shad.

"Yeah, great!" muttered Palidin.

"God, he's strange!" thought Shad.

So Palidin was in a state of anger and frustration when he stepped through the door of his mother's and Nutbeam's house.

Shirley didn't recognize him at first. The cowboy boots made him look taller, the beard made him look like a prospector, and he was tanned and thin.

"Palidin?" asked Shirley.

"Palidin!" exclaimed Nutbeam.

"Up! Up!" said Sally, who was hanging upside down. Nutbeam was holding her by the feet.

"You're home," said Shirley, rushing to Palidin with wide-open arms.

"You're not home, are ya?" said Nutbeam, uprighting Sally, who ran under the table to hide. "Ya can't be!"

"I'm here," said Palidin.

Palidin hugged Shirley, shook hands with Nutbeam and sat with a sigh at the table. He suddenly felt very, very tired.

"Where have ya been? What have ya been doin'?" asked Nutbeam.

"What in the name of God took ya to Texas?" asked Shirley.

"Who dat?" asked Sally. She fluttered her bottom lip with her fingers and hummed. She could have been a strange little engine beneath the table.

"I just wanted to see the country," said Palidin. "And it's good to be back."

"Big place, Texas?" asked Nutbeam.

"Yeah."

"What's it like?"

For some reason, Palidin thought of Jucy. "Rolling," he said.

"Well, well, well, well! You're home!"

"You must be hungry," said Shirley. "Want some beans?"

"Sure. What's all the news around here?"

"Well, I'm workin' in the woods with Bob Nash," said Nutbeam. "We're cuttin' Shad's property. Makin' good money."

"A good thing, too," said Shirley. "We were down to our last cent."

"And how's Dryfly?"

"Couldn't be better," said Nutbeam.

"He got the diamond," said Shirley.

seventeen

Shad practiced his guitar-playing every evening, played until his fingers got too sore to play any more. He sang, too. The same two songs, over and over again. Gordon Lightfoot's "Ribbon of Darkness," in which Shad whistled at the beginning and at the end, and Bob Dylan's "Blowing in the Wind." In "Blowing in the Wind," Shad, of course, played the harmonica. "Ribbon of Darkness" and "Blowing in the Wind" were the two songs that Shad planned to sing in the talent contest. He didn't think he sang well enough to seriously compete for first prize. There were too many good singers in the area, and they'd surely be there, but he thought he might have a chance of winning second or third prize because he was doing something different. He would wear bell-bottom jeans, a slouch hat, an afghan; he would finger-pick his guitar (a style he figured nobody else would employ), play the harmonica, whistle, and last and perhaps most importantly, he planned to throw in a bit of comedy. A good, solid, wellrehearsed, all-around act.

Shad had a theory. Shad figured that the most important thing in life was knowing oneself. You cannot rise above something if you aren't aware of that something. Only when you are aware of your own mediocrity can you rise above being ordinary. Ordinary people do not cut the mustard. Ordinary stars fall, a streak through space and nothing more, gone, forgotten. Shad was aware that he wasn't that great an entertainer and therefore felt himself in a position to do something about it. What he lacked in voice and musicianship he planned to supplement with authenticity, heart, the smile, personality, the stuff of stars that continue to shine.

"And it all," he thought, "must have an element of surprise. And that's where Dryfly comes in."

Saturday, June twenty-first rolled around, and Shad found himself backstage at the school auditorium, pacing the floor in nervous anticipation. There were about twenty-five other people backstage with him, everyone from eighty-three-year-old Clark Holmes to four-year-old Kelly Ann Shaw, Lester McTavish from the Rapids, who had a voice that old Hank Snow himself would die for, and Lorna Munn, who was said to be a trained singer. Billy Bean was there, too, and Shad knew that Billy would be tough to beat if for no other reason than that he looked so much like Elvis Presley, Elvis Presley in a Beatle haircut. Lyman MacFee was also there, going from one person to another, interviewing and writing down their names, what songs they planned to sing, if it was their first time on stage, et cetera. Lyman MacFee, the manager of Brigham's Store, the lead singer of the Cornpoppers, a twenty-five or thirty-year veteran of every stage from Juniper to Chatham, was the emcee.

"Thank God, Lyman MacFee's not competing," thought Shad.

The show was to begin at eight o'clock, but everybody in the cast as well as the audience knew that in Blackville, and perhaps all the Miramichi area, eight o'clock meant eightish, eight-thirty, or even nine. Even if the audience *did* show up in time, which they never did, for some reason the entertainment would not start until at least a half-hour later. Thus, when Shad peeped through the curtain at eight o'clock, there were but ten or fifteen people seated out front, and most of these were little old women, children and short people who wanted a front seat so that they could better see the show. The younger and taller people would wander in later. The very last people to show up for the show would be the men who really gathered here to talk and the teenagers who came here to hustle and drink rum, all standing at the back of the hall. These standees would pay attention to what was happening on the stage only if, one, the entertainer was extraordinarily good, at which point they'd whoop and tramp their feet in time to the music and holler things like, "Drive 'er! Walk back on 'er!" and "Play 'er close to the floor!"; and two, if the entertainer left a lot to be desired, in which case there'd be mumbles and chuckles, "Look at the belly on that!" "Boys, poor old Hank Williams must be turning over in his grave, don't ya think?" "Who ever told that lad he could sing?", stuff like that.

To say the least, for an entertainer this virtual party at the back of the hall made it a very difficult gig. The people who were closer to the party than the stage soon found, with all the conversation, feet-shuffling, rum-drinking and laughter, that they couldn't tell if the act on the stage was good, bad or indifferent, so they, too, began to party. At which point the people in front of these people would find themselves in the same predicament, not being able to hear. This would some- times snowball to the point where everybody in the hall would be partying in an atmosphere more like a dance than a con- cert. An actor's nightmare.

The audience would hush for certain acts, however. This would come from respect and/or pity for the entertainer on the stage. There was nothing that would hush a Miramichi audience more quickly than eighty-three-year-old Clark Holmes singing "The Scow at Cowden's Shore" or "Peelhead He's the Boy." Kelly Ann Shaw could bring them to a hush, too, be- cause she was four years old, tiny, beautiful and talented. Shad knew this, asked Lyman MacFee if he could go on right after either Clark or Kelly Ann.

Lyman MacFee checked his schedule, scratched and wrote. "Kelly's on right after Ben Brown, then you," he said.

"Good, great, the very best. I'm nervous as hell," said Shad.

"Don't be nervous. They're all friends, just ordinary lads from around here."

"That's what makes me nervous," said Shad.

At eight-thirty the show began. The curtain went up, and Lyman MacFee stepped to the microphone to address a full house, many of whom were eating fudge from little brown paper bags and drinking pop. "There's the usual murmuring, whispering, sniffing and coughing, the rattling of brown pa- per bags. In a few minutes those pop bottles will be rolling beneath their feet," thought Lyman. A baby cried.

"Good evening, ladies and gentlemen, and welcome to the

show! My name is Lyman MacFee and I'm your emcee." The microphone squeaked and hummed and squeaked again. Lyman walked back to the amplifier, adjusted a few buttons, then returned to the mike.

"How's she goin', Lyman old dog?" somebody yelled from the audience.

The audience rumbled with laughter.

"Tonight we have a great show lined up for you, some of the best singers and musicians this side of the Nashwaak, and because there's such a big turnout I'm gonna get this show rolling. Our first contestant is a young fellow who needs no introduction, for I know you all know him and have heard him sing before. Nevertheless, let's put our hands together and give a big, warm welcome to Mr. Charles McDuff, who's here tonight all the way from Black River Bridge!"

Clap, clap, clap, clap, clap.

"What'd he say?"

"Turn 'er up a bit!"

Charles MacDuff, being the first contestant up, managed to hold the audience all the way through "Your Cheating Heart" and "The Leaves Mustn't Fall."

"He's not that good," thought Shad. "But the fact that he held the audience makes him a strong contender for a prize."

Then, Lyman MacFee introduced Bob, Ralph and Herman, the Holden brothers from Red Bank. Bob played "Maple Sugar" on the fiddle, Ralph played the guitar and Herman stepdanced.

"Yahoo!"

"Whoop!"

"Walk back on 'er!"

This was a tough act to follow. Maxine Hartt, the next up, sang "Little Arrows" and "D-i-v-o-r-c-e" to a partying audience. Few could hear her.

Dora Smith from Blissfield had a tough time being heard, too. Dora Smith sang "Honky Tonk Angels" and "D-i-v-o-r-c-e."

Billy Bean sang "There's a Singing Water Falls" and "Your Cheating Heart." Carrie LeBlanc from Rogersville sang "The French Song" and "Wooden Heart." Ben Brown played the mouth organ and stepdanced.

Then Lyman MacFee introduced Kelly Ann Shaw, the prettiest little girl you ever laid your eyes on. Four years old, little blond curls, big blue eyes, a voice like an angel. To a hushed audience, with her father backing her up on the guitar, she sang "Let the Sun Shine In." She received a big round of applause, then sang "D-i-v-o-r-c-e."

"She'll win, sure as hell," thought Shad. Butterflies bobbed and flipped and flopped in his stomach, his palms perspired, he took a deep breath to calm himself down.

"Wasn't that wonderful? Just four years old!" shouted Lyman MacFee over the din of applause. "And next we have a lad you might have seen playin' the banjo at the odd dance in the area. He's also part of the comedy team, Shadrack and Dryfly."

A few chuckles came from the audience.

"Let's hear it for Shadrack Nash!"

Shad stepped up to the microphone. With his long red hair and beard, in his afghan, bellbottom jeans and big slouch hat, he could have been a refugee from a flower-child commune in California. The very sight of him captured the attention of the audience.

Shad took his time, looked the audience over, made eye contact with a number of people before he spoke. He could see his mother and father halfway back, Nutbeam, Shirley, Palidin and little Sally closer to the front, and in the very front seat, sitting with the children, short people and old ladies, were Dryfly Ramsey and Lillian Wallace. Shad nodded at Dryfly, Dryfly nodded back, the signal that he was ready to do his thing when the time came.

Shad strummed a G chord.

"I'd have been here sooner, but I was out back there signing autographs," said Shad. "I have fifteen or twenty of them here, if anyone would like one after the show."

To Shad's surprise and delight, everyone laughed.

"I just got back from South America," he continued. "I didn't like it much. It was too chilly, spent half the night urgin' Tina."

Nothing, not a chuckle. Shad shrugged, moved along.

"On my way back, I stopped off to play a little golf by the golf of Mexico." Nobody laughed at this either.

"I met a very beautiful woman down there. She had the friendliest eyes . . . kept looking at each other. She wore a Biblical gown, low and be-hole."

Shad continued, not getting the volume of laughter he wanted but holding the attention of the audience. He was happy with that.

"And now I'd like to sing you a little Bob Dylan song." Shad snapped his harmonica into its holder, blew into it, adjusted the capo on the fifth fret of his guitar, strummed a C chord. He sang "Blowing in the Wind," sounding for all the world like Bob Dylan. Between two of the verses, he took a break on the harmonica, played it well, didn't make a mistake. When he finished the song, he was rewarded with rich, warm applause.

"Thank you! Thanks a lot!" said Shad. "And now I'd like to do a Gordon Lightfoot song. I have to pucker up here. I start it off and end it whistling, you see."

Shad strummed a D chord and started whistling the melody of "Ribbon of Darkness." He was about halfway into the verse when he wrinkled up his nose, then screwed up his face, had to stop whistling.

"Ahem!" he said, gathering himself. "I'm sorry. I'll have to try that again." He pointed his finger at somebody in the front row, as if he were very unhappy with what that person was doing. He started whistling again. This time, he whistled for no more than five seconds before the same thing happened, the wrinkled nose, the screwed-up face.

"Dryfly, stop that!" he yelled, pointed his accusing finger at the front row.

"What's wrong with you?" yelled Dryfly.

"How can you ask me that, doin' what you're doin'?" snapped Shad, screwing up his face more than ever.

"I'm not doing anything!"

"You are so!"

"What?"

"You're . . . you're . . . ooh! You're eating a lemon!"

The whole concept of Dryfly Ramsey eating a lemon while

Shadrack Nash tried to whistle on the stage hit the audience as being extremely funny. They laughed and laughed and laughed, then applauded.

Shad smiled and bowed. He felt like a star and didn't want to relinquish the moment. "I'm allowed two songs. I didn't really sing 'Ribbon of Darkness,' that was just comedy. Have to think of another song quick . . ."

The laughter and applause subsided.

"Thank you very much," said Shad. "And now I'd like to sing a little song that's one of my favourites in the whole world. It's a little song that Dryfly Ramsey wrote for someone I guess he loved very much. Nobody's ever heard this song except me, as far as I know. I think everyone deserves to hear it, and because he won't ever get around to doin' it for ya . . ." Shad looked at Dryfly. "I hope you don't mind if I sing it for everyone, Dry."

Dryfly blushed, felt like crawling into a hole somewhere, but he nodded. What else could he do?

Shad strummed a D chord. "It's called 'Sandy Hill,'" he said, and began to sing.

> The full moon was rising o'er Sandy Hill
> Where the old school house used to be.
> Through the meadow I strolled
> Till I came to the bridge,
> The river ran peaceful and free.
> I stopped for your smile
> And you showed me your wallpapered room,
> Then we sat in the light of the moon
> By your window.
> You laughed when I told you my reason for paying a call
> And I felt myself falling
> In love with you.

Shad wasn't the greatest singer in the whole world, but he was doing a fair job, and the three to four hundred people watching him, listening to his every word, gave him . . . confidence? power? charisma?

He sang on.

You wanted to talk,
So we walked by the river,
You sang me a song about kindness.
The night and I listened to the warm melody
That put all our troubles behind us.
You talked about people,
And places where I'd never been
And you called me your very best friend
As I held you.
You said all the things that I wanted to hear most of all
And I felt myself falling
In love with you.

When the show was over, Lyman MacFee approached the three judges, discussed matters for a minute or so, then announced the winners.

"Third prize goes to Clark Holmes!"

Clap, clap, clap, clap, clap!

"Second prize to little Kelly Ann Shaw."

Clap, clap, clap, clap, clap!

"And our first prize winners . . ."

Shad's heart sank. "Winners? Well, so much for that. There was only one of me."

"Let's hear it for Shadrack and Dryfly!"

Dryfly nudged Lillian. "We won," he said.

Lillian squeezed his hand, kissed him on the cheek.

"Nothin' to it," said Shad, grinning to himself. "I'll collect my winnings and find a little lady for the night."

*

"That's a beautiful song, Dryfly," said Lillian, later, back at the cottage. "How come you never sang it for me?"

"I don't know. Never got around to it, I guess. Shad did a good job on it. Didn't know he was such a good singer."

"He's not. It's heart that makes him good. Did you write that song for me?"

"I wrote you a lot of songs. Let's have a drink, shall we?"

Dryfly went to the bar, poured them a couple of scotches, returned to the sofa where Lillian waited.

"But that one," persisted Lillian. "Was that one for me?"

"That one. It was Nutbeam and Mom who . . . what's the word? Inspired? They inspired that song. I wrote it for them. But I sang it a thousand times . . . for you."

"I love you, Dryfly."

"I love you, too. You know, when Shad sang that song tonight, I cried."

"I know."

"All my life I dreamed of this." He gestured at the room. "I dreamed and dreamed and dreamed of being here with you — walking the fields, crossing the bridge, sailing down the river. I'd sing to you, talk to you. I'd lie in bed in the darkness of my room. Remember the old house? In that old house I'd lie in the dark and feel like a . . . a million dollars, because I could see your pretty smile. God! I'm crazy. I feel like crying again! Ha!

"And now I'm here. Dreams *do* come true. One time when I was sitting on the balcony thinking of you, I looked up and saw a heart-shaped cloud. I knew then that there was something more to my love for you than just puppy love. That heart-shaped cloud was a symbol, an omen. Omens, symbols . . . they're everywhere. You just have to recognize them.

"But you have to really want it . . . here . . . in your heart. And to love as deeply as I do, you have to be a romantic fool. Do you think you can love someone to death?"

"I don't know. Why?"

"I don't know. I fear for your life, I guess."

"Dryfly?"

"Yes?"

"Pole me up the river?"

"Tonight?"

"Yes! In the moonlight."

"Now?"

"Right now! I want to see you — out there, in your world, your kingdom."

"It's not my world."

"Yes it is. You see, my father acquired a fishing pool, but he really has nothing at all. When I fell in love with you, I acquired a whole river."

"But we don't have a canoe."

"Tonight we borrow from the club. Tomorrow I'm buying us one."

"Tomorrow's Sunday."

"Well, Monday, then."

"You shouldn't be spending your money like that."

"Why not? It's an investment. You're an investment! The returns will be astronomical! You can't tell me that you aren't itching to be out there! You'd rather be on that river than anywhere else in the world! And I want to be out there with you. It's summer, we're here, we're in love! Let's go!"

A few minutes later, they were walking through the dew-laden meadow toward the footbridge, the moon like a huge inflated condom high above the river.

Two hours later, after Dryfly had poled them all the way to Gordon and they had sailed back down, Dryfly undressed and got into bed. Lillian went to the kitchen. Dryfly waited. He heard something pop, wondered what she was doing. In a minute or so, Lillian came into the room, sat on the foot of the bed. She had an open bottle of champagne in her hand. She smiled naughtily at Dryfly.

"Champagne, no glasses. What's up?" asked Dryfly.

"All my life I've had a fantasy about sipping champagne from the navels of Brazilian boys. You don't happen to speak Spanish, do you?"

"Ah! Si, señorita! Si!"

eighteen

A few days later, Palidin paid Lillian and Dryfly a visit.
Knock, knock, knock.
Dryfly opened the door.
"I'm looking for a bagpipe player, a piper," said Palidin.
"I'm your man," said Dryfly, grinning. "And Lillian here is pretty hot on the accordion."
"You must make beautiful music together. I want to book you for the town-crier contest I'm holding. Available?"
"Wouldn't wanna miss *that* one," laughed Dryfly. "Come in."
"And this must be Palidin," said Lillian.
"Oh, I'm sorry," said Dryfly. "I . . . this . . ."
"Yes. I'm Palidin," said Palidin. "And you're Lillian Wallace."
"Why, you two don't look at all alike," said Lillian.
Palidin was six feet tall, had light brown hair, blond beard, dark eyes — his mother's — and the fine features of his father, Buck Ramsey. Dryfly was slightly shorter, had Buck's blue eyes, but the dark hair and more prominent features of Shirley. He wasn't as handsome as Palidin, but attractive all the same. Lillian was right; no one would ever take them for brothers.
They sat in the living room.
"You have a nice place here," commented Palidin, grinning again. It seemed strange to see Dryfly lounging around in such a luxurious place.
"It'll do," said Dryfly, grinning, sensing Palidin's observation. "What's going on?"
"Pretty quiet. I wanted to talk to you about something."
"Sure."
"Can we go for a walk?" Palidin looked at Lillian. "I have something I'd like to run across Dryfly privately. Hope you don't mind."

"Oh, don't mind me," said Lillian. "I've got things to do in the kitchen. You guys stay right here and talk. I'll make us some lemonade."

"Great. Thanks, Lillian. I'll only keep Dry from you for a couple of minutes."

Lillian smiled her pretty smile, winked at Dryfly and went to the kitchen.

"So, what's on your mind?" asked Dryfly.

"Well, I wanted to talk to you about the flyhook."

"Flyhook? You mean . . ."

"The magnetic flyhook."

"Okay, shoot."

"Ever try it?"

"No, I don't think I have. Can't remember, anyway."

"Did you ever tell anyone about it?"

"I . . . I don't think so. Why?"

Palidin sighed. "I hope you haven't. It's a killer."

"It really works?"

"Like a charm. It works too well."

"How can a flyhook work too well?"

"It catches fish every time. You might as well go fishing with a net. You have to get behind a tree to tie your hook on."

"Old joke."

"Yeah, well, in this case, it's very nearly true. With a magnetized hook you might as well go to the river with a net, and that's the problem."

"That's a problem?"

"Well, what do you think would happen if some of the guys around here found out about it?"

"They'd all be using it, that's for sure."

"Yes, and they'd kill every fish in the river."

"And not just the guys from around here."

"Exactly. And I've learned that it works on other fish as well."

"Ha!"

"I had a walking catfish follow me all the way from Florida to Texas just because I had some change in my pocket."

"Huh?"

"Just joking."

"Well, quite the little item you've discovered there. So what do we do?"

"Tell nobody! Not a soul! Ever! Not even your children, or your grandchildren!"

"Seems kind of selfish, in a way."

"Not at all. Keeping this to ourselves is the most generous thing we could possibly do."

"Yeah, well . . . sure. It's your discovery. Sure. I don't fish much, anyway. Okay, the secret is ours."

"Great! That's what I wanted to hear. I feel a whole lot better. We'll use it occasionally, if and when we really need a fish. I don't see any harm in that. Shake on it."

They shook hands, looked into each other's eyes. It was the first time in years that they actually touched each other. Dryfly couldn't figure out why he felt so uncomfortable looking into his brother's eyes. It wasn't the handshake; it was the eyes. And Palidin thought that he was very, very unfamiliar with Dryfly, like strangers. "How can that be?" he asked himself. "We're brothers; we grew up in the same little, breezy shack, slept under the same rags, ate our mother's bread and molasses, drank from the same pickle bottles."

"So . . . ah, when's Lillian going back?" asked Palidin.

"September. I'm going back with her. I'm gonna get into landscaping."

"Ha! Good! Know anything about it?"

"No, but I'll learn. I want to learn everything there is to know about it, from design to planting to pruning, everything. Lillian tells me that in Cape Cod, in an area between Truro and Provincetown, they're having a problem with erosion. The wind and the rain and the sea is threatening to wash that part of the Cape away, I guess. The right kind of planting could save it. And, of course, there's always lawns."

"Maybe you should take Nutbeam with you. He could get rich making lawn ornaments for ya."

"Ha! Pornographic lawn ornaments!"

"Wind driven!"

They laughed heartily.

"And what are *you* doing this fall?" asked Dryfly.

"I'm thinking about going to Fredericton."

"Not so far away this time."

"Well, I don't know how long I'll stay there. I'll try it for a while."

"Shad's moving to Fredericton, too."

"He is? He's closing up the house?"

"Nope. Bob and Elva are staying there for the winter. Closer to Blackville and all that. It'll be good for them. They've made a lot of money off that lumber of Shad's."

"I know! Nutbeam's doing great! He's talking about buying a car!"

"Good! Good! They need a car. Who's gonna drive it?"

"That's what I was wondering. Nutbeam can't read or write, won't be able to get a licence."

"And I doubt if you could ever get Mom to drive." Dryfly stood, went to the window, looked down on the river. A lone angler stood waist-deep in it, casting. Dry thought it looked like Bert Todder.

"You never know about Mom. She'll surprise you sometimes," said Palidin.

Dryfly looked at Palidin, then back at the river. The angler was gone.

"He disappeared!" said Dryfly.

"Who?"

"Bert was there, and then he wasn't. All in a second . . ." Dryfly looked wide-eyed at Palidin, seeking an explanation.

Palidin stood, joined Dryfly at the window. "Bert?"

"Yes. He was right there. Could he have fallen and drowned?"

"Not enough water there"

"Then . . ."

"The Whooper . . ."

"Ha."

"He's god of these woods."

"He has hooves."

"He won't hurt you . . . intentionally . . . if you love his place."

"Ready for some lemonade?" called Lillian from the kitchen.

"We're ready!" called Dryfly.

Lillian came from the kitchen carrying a tray laden with three tall glasses of iced lemonade.

"I'm glad you dropped in," said Lillian to Palidin. "It's time we got to know each other better."

"Yes!" said Palidin. "It's time we *all* got to know each other better."

"I'll get the gin," said Dryfly.

*

For several years before Shirley Ramsey met the big-eared, big-mouthed, long-this, long-that and very tall Matthew Nutbeam, she thought that he was either a wicked criminal taking refuge in the Brennen Siding area, or the devil, the latter more often than not. However, the Fates had already played their parts, and a few short years was all it took to flip the fear and loneliness coin to its lovely happy-face side. Eros, Aphrodite, and Priapus were not behind the door either, for the beautiful and healthy Sally Nutbeam slipped into the world just as soon as an opening could be found. Only they who know the history and beauty of the Miramichi, and specifically the Dungarvon, can fathom and acccept the fact that not just one, but *all* the gods eventually retire there. Retired they are, perhaps, but not completely idle.

"It's Sunday. It's such a nice day. You and me and Sally should do something, Shirley. Go for a walk, visit Dryfly and Lillian, go on a picnic or something."

"Haven't been on a picnic for years, not since . . ."

"Not since Bonzie. I know, love."

"The woods scares me."

"You're living in the wrong country, then."

"It always scared me, ever since I was a little girl. You kin git lost so easy in the woods. Poor little Bonzie."

"I've been lost and I know how bad it kin be, but you have to learn to mark your path. The woods kin be a beautiful place, and it kin be a scary place, but it's never a boring place. I lived in the woods for years and years, all alone, if you call havin' no people around bein' alone, and I know what it's like. You know how you sometimes feel you're bein' watched? Well, in the woods you're *always* bein' watched. But the eyes of the forest aren't always black. They kin be jist as warm and welcoming as a mother's. I should take you and Sally back and show you my camp. You've never been back there, have you?"

"It's back on Todder Brook, ain't it? How far back is it?"

"That's the strange thing about bein' in the woods. You never quite know about distance. I'm not sure if my old camp is a half a mile or a mile and a half from here. It's not far, back there beside the brook. Wanna go back?"

"No, Nut, dear, you go back if ya want, but I'm just as happy to stay right here. Maybe I'll weed the garden or somethin'."

"You don't wanna let John Kaston see ya weedin' on Sunday."

"Give 'im somethin' to preach about."

"Ha! Well, maybe I'll take a walk back to the camp, meself. I'll take Sally with me."

"An awful long walk for Sally."

"I kin carry 'er if she gets tired. We'll take a few cookies and have a little picnic back there, her and me. If she starts to cry or don't wanna be back there for some reason, I'll bring her home."

"What if she poops herself?"

Nutbeam shrugged. "No odds," he said, and somehow Shirley knew what he meant.

Sally and Nutbeam headed back to Nutbeam's camp, but they hadn't walked for much more than a few hundred yards before Nutbeam realized that Sally was walking much too slowly, that it would take them all day to get to the camp at the rate they were going. So he picked her up and carried her all the way back, stopping frequently to show her a bird, a tree, a berry, a flower, anything and everything he thought she might fancy.

"This little thing is a blueberry, Sally."

"Booberry, booberry, booberry."

"Now, this here's what you might call yer pine tree and . . . look! That's a moose bird on it."

"Moose . . . Dada. Dat not a moose!"

"And this bush. Why, it's named after you, Sally! This is a sallybush!"

"Sally. I Sally, you Dada!"

When they got to the camp, Nutbeam set Sally on a tree stump and went inside. The camp had been built half in and half out of the ground and was windowless. Nutbeam wanted to check things out first before taking Sally inside. "It's dark as a dungeon in there," he thought. "And there'll be cobwebs. The roof might be starting to rot."

"You wait right here, Sally, darlin', I'll just check things out, make sure it's safe for you to go in."

He stepped inside and lit a match, spotted the lantern on the table, lit it.

"Yep, there's plenty of cobwebs," he thought, waving his long arms about, clearing them. "And she's startin' to rot, but not too bad . . . yet. God! It seems so small, now. I can't believe I lived here for so long. All alone until Shad and Dry found me. Who'd have thought I'd ever be where I am today? A house, a nice wife, a beautiful little girl. A good job workin' in the woods. Makin' enough money to put grub on the table. Maybe even gonna git a car. Can't wait to see Shirley drivin' a car! The good Lord has favoured me, for sure." He went back outside to get Sally.

She was not on the stump where he'd left her.

She was gone.

Nutbeam's heart leaped right into his throat, and he was grasped by the sharp steel claws of panic.

He swung in a complete circle, his eyes searching frantically for the little girl. She had been dressed in pink. He saw nothing pink.

"Sally!" he shouted.

No answer.

"Sally!" he shouted again.

In the Dungarvon woods his voice seemed very tiny, seemed to drop from his big mouth to land at his big feet, seemed small even to his own big floppy ears.

He heard himself whimper.

"SALLY!" he screamed. "Oh, God! Sally! Answer me! SALLY!

Where could she be? Where could she have gone so quickly? Where do I begin to look? Fool! Nothin' would do but you'd bring that little girl back here in the fly-infested woods! And, and, and you left her alone! Oh, God, what do I do? What will Shirley say? Oh, oh, oh, oh, oh! SALLY! SALLY! SALLY! SALLEEEE!"

"I'll make a big circle. I'll make a big circle. That's all I can do. She walks slow, she can't be far. The hill. She prob'ly wouldn't go up the hill. The brook. The water might draw 'er . . ." The fear, the panic, their ensuing flow of adrenalin, rained insanity, irrationality upon Nutbeam. He was as lost as Sally. If he had stopped to reason, he would have listened, for his ears were big and floppy. He could hear things that no other person could hear. He would have heard Sally saying, "Moose! Moose!" not more than a hundred feet away. He did not look for tracks either. He just struck out in an easterly direction. He was hoping for the best.

At about the same moment that Nutbeam was lighting the match inside the camp, Sally spotted a beautiful blue bird. She was onto her feet and heading for it in an instant. She fell over an old tree root, thought about crying, but there was the bird hopping from branch to branch, shrub to shrub. She quickly forgot whatever injuries she may have acquired from the fall and continued her pursuit of the bird. This time she disappeared into the foliage to the west of Nutbeam's camp, and although she didn't know it, she was lost in a matter of seconds. "Moose! Moose!" was first and foremost on her mind.

It wasn't long, however, before she realized that she was in a strange place and that Dada was not with her. All she could see was alder bushes, the mossy ground and old shoreline fir trees, the green beards hanging from their dead limbs. She could hear the brook and the occasional rustle in the leaves as the moose (the blue jay) moved about. The little blue-eyed girl in the pink dress amid all this scenery appeared as an Emily Carr or an A.Y. Jackson dream . . . or nightmare.

And then there was the little boy with the big blue eyes and blond hair very much like her own, and the funny fat man with one tooth.

"Hello, Sally," said the little boy.

"Tee, hee, hee, sob, snort, sniff," laughed, or cried, the man.

*

Dear Billy,

I'm not much for writing letters. Don't know where to start.

I've been thinking about a lot of the things we talked about on the trail and I'm going back to Texas, to Merna's Butt. It will be hot and I'll have to keep an eye open for twisters, but what the hell! Maybe I'll die there and do as much good as a rebellious ghost as I did as a sorry tycoon.

Recently, I went into a store here in Nome. They had this booth set up, selling tickets, raising money for the conservation of animals. The prize was a fifteen-hundred-dollar rifle with telescopic sights. Well, I suppose it might be the mentality of hunters to call it a wise conservational move, but I think a camera would have been more appropriate.

You know, I thought that Nome would be different, but man is here in all his glory, carries rifles, eats Hershey chocolate bars, dentists are doing well, there's talk of a TV station. I expect it's the same in Canada where you are.

By the way, I remembered who it was I knew from New Brunswick. The reason I couldn't remember before was because I really didn't know the fellow. I just knew of him. It was a singer, a fellow by the name of Henry Burr. One of the greatest singers ever lived, in my opinion. "In the Shade of the Old Apple Tree," "When You and I Were Young, Maggie." "Goodnight, Little Girl, Goodnight" sold close to three and a half million copies way back then. In the forties! And it seems to me that he hung around with Thomas Edison, pioneered in the experimental stages of the phonograph or something. He made the first transcontinental broadcast, too. Quite the fellow! Dead for quite some time, but was the Bing Crosby of his day. I listened to him many times, live and on the radio.

Anyway, I don't know if I'll get to visit you in September. Depends on how I feel. I've been well and all that, but you never know at my age.

Look after yourself, buddy. I'll be at Merna's Butt.

Sundance

*

When Nutbeam had completed his first circle and had returned to the camp with no Sally and a lot less hope of finding her, he sat on the stump where he had last seen her and cried and cried and cried. "What have I done? What have I done? I've lost my little girl!" He tried desperately to gather his thoughts. "What to do! Go for help? Get a bunch of men in here? She *can't* have gone far! No animal would hurt her, would it? Naw! I just have to find her, that's all. But where? She's so small! And . . . and . . . so pretty. SALLY! SALLEEE!"

"Dada . . . Dada!"

"What? Where? Sally! Oh, Sally!"

Sally Nutbeam ran to her father's arms, smiling.

"Where were you, Sally, my love, my love, my love? You found your way back! How did you ever find your way back, you smart, smart girl?"

Sally pointed to the direction from which she had come.

"What, Sally?"

"Dat boy and dat man brung me. Where da boy go, Dada?"

"What boy? What man, Sally?"

Sally was already becoming familiar with mysteries. She shrugged.

*

It was August before John Kaston went to visit Bert Todder and found him in somewhat of a mature state of decomposition. John was a preacher, a Christian, prayed all the way to the nearest phone. He phoned a doctor, an undertaker and the RCMP, then went back to Brennen Siding and spread the news. Bert Todder, always good for a joke, always kind, forever everybody's friend, the settlement's reporter, was dead. From John's description, everyone naturally assumed that he committed suicide. All were shocked and horrified. Brennen Siding would never be the same.

Helen MacDonald wept bitter tears, blamed herself, Bert

Todder had tried to seduce her for years. "He'd prob'ly be alive today if I had've come across," she said to herself.

"Every time I think o' Bert, I see that tooth, that one tooth, fair in the middle of his mouth," said Stan Tuney. "I'm gonna miss that tooth."

"The last of the Todders," said Dan Brennen.

"Bert, oh Bert, Bert Todder sure et a lotta potatoes, Bert did. Poor old buddy Bert, Tater Todder, I used to call 'im, so I did, yeah. Poor old Bert. Tater Todder, yeah."

"Bert tied the best fly in this country," commented Bob Nash. "No one could tie a fly like Bert Todder. He could tie the prettiest little Oriole in the dear wide world. The feathers just sorta like a little roof over the hook. Sell me a few o' them, will ya, Bernie? Just fer keepsakes."

"Why d'ya suppose he done it?" pondered Bernie. "With a shotgun, yet!"

"No tail," said Stan Tuney. "That's what old Sigmond Fried claimed, anyway."

"Who?"

"Sigmond Fried. You must've heard o' him. Lad from over Fredericton way there, I think. Claimed that no tail was bad fer ya."

"It's a, it's a, it's a wonder me and you ain't dead, Stan, partner, pal, buddy," said Lindon.

This kind of conversation went on in Brennen Siding for a good many days, but it was a long, long time before anyone mentioned fish farts. It was just too painful.

*

Palidin Ramsey sat so quiet that he could have been a stone. Mosquitoes hummed around him, seeking blood. Nighthawks croaking frog-like swooped through the air seeking mosquitoes. The river ran peacefully by, a million fireflies flickering and glimmering against its forested walls, giving it the appearance of an airport runway. Jewels like the Dungarvon are as rare as walking catfish. Little wonder that one such as Palidin, there beside it in its trance, could think

789

of nothing but pleasure. "It's a pleasure to be alive. It's a pleasure to be here, naked, beneath the stars and the moon, watching the fire-flies, the natural lights of the world. This — all of this is a highlight, a beauty mark on the face of God. How many times in Toronto, in Texas, did I think of you, old river? As children, growing up here, we had so little, and yet so much because you were here — like a brother . . . ha! Like Brandy's wolf! I came back, just like everyone comes back, you're a magnet. People return here year after year to fish the salmon; the salmon themselves return here year after year as if drawn by some invisible force, your magnetism. They appear like ghosts and haunt the pools and eddies. And the lads around here? It's like you flow in their veins. You're their sustenance, their entertainment, their theatre. Look at the forest, the great haunting forest. It actually seems to drink from you, from your smooth, sweet waters. You flow on and on and on. It's all so . . . so fitting, so relevant. The salmon return, the fishermen return, tales are repeated. If you scream, you get an echo. When you leave, you return. Lost men walk in circles. Are we all lost? Or are we never lost? I am here! I am *never* there! Only another can be there! I am always here. I am never lost! Ha! Do we just keep moving around and around like lost men? Are we nothing more than spirits haunting the forest? Have not the flowers and the insects as much presence as I?"

Palidin was sitting on a rock. He stood and walked to the water's edge, bent down and washed his face in the Dungarvon. As he washed, the water fell from his beard, trickled down his skin. He flicked it from his fingers, watched it drop like rain on the river.

"Like rain," he thought. "I'm making it rain! Rain. A truly holy experience. It dances on the water, maps grey window-panes with tiny streams, rises, falls, flows in wells and springs, sometimes whispering, sometimes murmuring. I suppose it fell on the hair of Jesus, ran down his face to rise again until it falls to touch me. To touch us all, here and now — a blessing."

"The Dungarvon. The Dungarvon River! Pure, clean, untouched, unspoiled. Please, please never desert us!"

Palidin waded waist-deep into the water, then submerged the rest of himself with a splash. He began to swim against the current, stroke after stroke after stroke, the current holding him stationary, though not in battle, perhaps in union, everything flowing: blood, water, molecules, thoughts, condensation, spirits. A mutual respect, river and man, buddies like dew and rain, the universe and God. The fish gathered just to see.